CHARLIE

LOVE SEQUENCE BOOK ONE

DAPHNE LEIGH

MARBLE CITY PRESS, LLC

1

Rob told me our marriage was over on my twenty-sixth birthday while I was wiping his cum from the inside of my thighs. The day I moved out and into my parents' pool house was the same day my best friend moved in with him. I can't stop thinking about them fucking in the bed I picked out.

Bethany has been there for me since I was twelve, through all the times I thought Rob was cheating on me but couldn't prove it. All the times he showed his narcissistic asshole side. It hurt more when I found out she was having an affair with him than when he told me I had to leave. She has my old life, and I have a one-room pool house and no job prospects. Fuck me for thinking it was a good idea to work for Rob's family. I put all my eggs in one basket and look where it fucking got me: a one-way ticket to the worst year of my life.

Arty MacLeod bursts into my life a couple of months into my pity party for one. At eighty-five, his body is shrunken and wrinkled, but his brain is as sharp as a tack. He has an endless list of small jobs for me to do and follows me from room to room, regaling me with stories while I work, his hands moving a mile a minute while he talks.

After helping him for a few weeks, we have our routine down pat. That's why I know today is different the second I walk in his door. He's perched on a chair at his dining table, tea for two spread out on the shiny mahogany.

"What's this?" I ask, slipping off my jacket and draping it across the back of a chair. Arty's dressed in a brown tweed suit, matching bowtie, and a pocket square that bring out the green in the jacket. Harris tweed, he proudly told me last week.

"I have a proposal," Arty says, carefully pouring tea into our cups. I plop a sugar cube in each one as he pours in some milk.

"Do tell, Arty." I sip my tea, pinky up like a good girl.

"Your mother and I were talking—"

I groan inwardly, already knowing this is going to be a disaster.

"She told me you have a small business?" One thick eyebrow rises above the rim of his glasses.

"I do?" The only thing I've been doing since I met Rob is working in his family's landscaping business. Then it dawns on me. "Well, I *did*," I say slowly, nervous about where this is leading. "Back before Rob hired me on, I made genealogy charts."

Arty takes a long sip of his tea, waiting for me to elaborate.

"They weren't anything special," I say, shrugging.

"This is not just a genealogy chart, Charlie," Arty says, retrieving a rolled-up piece of parchment from the buffet. It's almost as wide as he is tall. Pushing a couple of chairs aside, he spreads it out all the way to the far end of the table.

I run my fingers along the edge, the paper bumpy under my fingertips. It brings back memories of happier times.

"I forgot about this," I whisper, memories flooding back. It's a months-long labor of love that I had gifted my mother years and years ago. I had practiced my calligraphy for weeks before I felt confident enough to start on the chart, not to mention the hours I had put into each watercolor vignette that accompanied the most interesting ancestors. Rob and I were only engaged at that point. He had still been trying. Kind of.

I found my passion while making that chart and created a

successful business – until Rob convinced me to close up shop and work for him. Biggest mistake of my pitiful life.

"This is a work of art," Arty says as he sits back down, motioning for me to do the same. "Now tell me how you did it."

"Like how I actually made the chart?" I ask, trying to understand what he means.

"No, how did you find all of your ancestors? You have eighteen generations on that piece of paper."

I smile. "Well, that comes from being a bit obsessive. My mom was always curious about her genealogy, and I was determined to give her the best gift possible. I researched as much as possible online and then headed to Europe for a couple of months."

"And you made this into a business? You did this for other people?"

"I didn't travel for anyone else. I would research back as far as I could online, which on average seemed to be eight to ten generations."

"Do you have a passport?" Arty asks, nibbling on a scone.

"I do." In fact, I just received a new one in the mail a few months ago. Rob and I were supposed to go on a Mediterranean tour to celebrate our fifth anniversary. He's probably getting ready to go with Bethany. I feel my soul folding in on itself, trying to make itself small enough to escape the pain, when Arty interrupts my thoughts.

"It's settled, then."

I take a deep breath, blinking back tears. "What's settled?"

"I'm sending you to Scotland to research my genealogy and make me one of these." He taps the chart for emphasis.

"To Scotland?" *Scotland? Holy shit.*

"I want something like this to pass down to my grandkids. I only have a few years left, so there's no time to waste. I'll see what flights are leaving next week."

"Wait a minute, Arty," I protest, "First off, I don't have any money—"

"I'm paying for it," he says, cutting me off. "You have three months." He starts rolling up the parchment. "And I want it framed. What was number two?"

"Number two?"

"The second reason you can't go."

I wrack my brain for a reason – any reason – why this is completely nuts.

Arty smirks when I don't say anything else. "That's what I thought. Finish your tea and then go home and start packing. I'll email you once I figure out the flights."

"Yes, sir." I peck his weathered cheek before gulping down the last of my tea, my mind spinning.

I get an email from Arty later that night requesting my bank account information so he can wire the money. I almost fall over when I read the flight details attached to the email. I spend the next four hours chucking piles of dirty clothes into the washing machine and trying to get my mess of a life in order. My flight leaves in two days.

Single in Scotland. Fuck. Yes.

2

———————

I jump when the taxi driver clears his throat, my thoughts snapping back to reality. I step out of the cab and take my bags from him, murmuring my thanks as I press a couple of bills into his hand. As he drives away, I spin slowly, taking in my surroundings. My heartbeat ratchets up a few notches. Salty spray crashes over the seawall turning everything slick.

It's wild and beautiful, and I love it.

I wrap my jacket tight against the wind and take a deep breath of salty air. Behind me, a row of 17th-century houses stand shoulder to shoulder. Old sentries guarding the harbor, each one painted a different color. Pink, sky blue, sage, yellow, white, red. I'm standing outside a cute little bookstore; the stone walls are painted white, the door a deep scarlet. A few doors down, a cafe sign creaks in the wind. I grin. How the hell did I get so lucky?

I pull my suitcases over the curb and check my phone for the address of the flat I'm renting. It's the same as the bookstore. Weird. A tiny bell tinkles above my head as I pull open the door, the wood rough against my fingers.

"Can I help you, dear?" A woman in her sixties stands at a sturdy desk, studying me from over the top of her reading glasses.

"I hope so," I say, dragging my suitcases over the threshold awkwardly. "I'm leasing a flat at 655 Scorrybreck Rd, but I'm not sure I'm in the right place."

"You must be Charlie!" she exclaims, smiling. Her eyes crinkle in the most adorable way. "I'm Millie. It's so nice to meet you." She wraps me in a shortbread-scented hug, her arms around my middle. "Come now, I'll show you upstairs!" We wind our way through stacks of books until we reach a door at the back of the shop. She opens it, revealing a steep staircase. She looks doubtfully between me, my suitcases, and the stairs. "Should I find Richard to help us?"

"No, I can manage," I assure her. I hike both suitcases up as high as possible and take the stairs sideways.

"Well, that was impressive," she laughs, "you're such a little thing; I wasn't sure if you could manage that."

"I worked at my husband's landscape company for years," I say, then amend, "ex-husband."

"I see," she says, her smile sympathetic. She pulls a black iron key from her pocket, unlocks the door at the top of the stairs, and pushes it open.

"Jesus," I blurt, stunned. The entire left wall of the flat consists of a large window overlooking the harbor. The start of the sunset reflects pinks and purples on the water. It's stunning. "This is beautiful." I lower my voice to a whisper, trying to preserve the magic. Floor-to-ceiling bookcases snag my attention. Every nook and cranny is filled with books and trinkets that make me itch to explore. Two overstuffed couches flank a carved coffee table, a small two-person dining set behind it. The living room opens up to a postage-stamp kitchen. The appliances look a bit dated, but nothing I hadn't expected.

"Your bedroom is back through here." Millie turns from the window and walks down the short hallway to the right of the kitchen, her sensible pumps echoing off the walls. She opens the door to show me a simple double bed. "The bathroom and a small office are right across the hall." She opens each door, waiting for me to nod my approval before moving on.

"Looks absolutely perfect," I murmur, making my way back to the main room, drawn by the view.

"Good." Millie smiles, then heads to the door. "Dinner is at six, dear."

"Dinner?"

"Did you think we'd let you eat alone in a strange country? It'll be on the table every Sunday night at six." Millie's smile warms her face.

A weight I didn't realize I was carrying lifts from my shoulders, "Thank you, Millie. It's nice to have a friend already."

I WANDER down the stairs and into the bookstore around 5:30, figuring I could poke around until it was time for dinner; the stacks of books lying haphazardly around the shop are calling to me like a siren's song.

"May I help you with something?" someone asks, the timbre of his voice doing something funny to my insides.

I spin on my heel and bump into a wall of lean muscle, bracing myself against his chest.

"Oh—" he stammers, taking a step back. A long, elegant finger pushes his glasses up his nose, blue eyes staring back at me owlishly.

"I'm so sorry," I laugh, my hand over my racing heart, "It seems like we may have startled each other." Dark hair curls around his face and over his ears, almost making him seem boyish, but that first impression fades quickly as I take in his bedroom eyes and chiseled jawline. God, he's beautiful.

"I just wasn't expecting..." He motions from my head to my toes, flustered. A blush creeps up his throat and into his cheeks.

He straightens, pulling on the lapels of his tweed jacket and clearing his throat. "Let's try that again. Is there anything I can help you with?"

His frank stare and deep brogue have my own cheeks flushing. "I'm Charlie; I'm renting the flat upstairs."

"*You're* Charlie. Of course you are." He slaps his hand to his forehead. "You've come down for dinner?"

"Yes, I'm early, though. I thought maybe I could look around the store?" I check my watch. "It's barely past 5:30, so I have a little time."

"Of course! You're more than welcome to look around any time." He rocks on his heels for a couple of seconds. "I'm going to get back to work. Let me know if you need anything."

I nod and move toward the books, watching him out of the corner of my eye as he rifles through a stack of papers. After a few minutes, he shrugs out of his jacket, rolling up his shirtsleeves to reveal muscled forearms. Fucking hell. I definitely hadn't expected that. He runs his hands through his hair, which explains its disheveled appearance. When I realize the book I'm holding is upside down, I snap it close and walk over to him.

"What are you working on?" I ask, keeping my voice soft so I don't startle him again.

"Ah, nothing fun, unfortunately." He shows me a page filled with columns and figures. "I come to help my mum every Sunday. She refuses to succumb to technology, so manual accounting it is."

"You're Millie's son!" I exclaim, the dots finally connecting.

"God, I should have introduced myself," he mutters. "Cameron." He reaches his hand over the desk.

His grasp is cool and firm.

"So, what do you do the rest of the week when you're not here?" I ask, curiosity getting the best of me.

"I'm an archeologist," he said, pushing his glasses back into place. "God, that sounds pompous." He laughs. "Everyone here knows everyone else's business. I haven't been asked that question in a very long time."

"Do you teach, or do you get to do all the cool stuff they show on TV?"

He chuckles. "I teach *and* I get to do the cool stuff."

I drag a chair over and sit on it backward, pushing my jacket sleeves up a bit. "Tell me what it's like," I say, checking my watch. "But hurry, we only have fifteen minutes till dinner."

"I can do better than just telling you. I'm heading to the Fairy

Pools next week if you want to come along?" He pauses, shyness creeping in a little. "If you're not busy, I mean."

"Seriously?" I squeal, my bracelets jangling as I jump up.

Cameron grins, a dimple winking at me from his left cheek. "It's settled then. Meet me out front at eight Friday morning. But first, dinner." He walks to the back of the shop and holds the door open for me.

3

———

I can't keep my eyes off Cameron as we eat dinner. I'm enamored with his easy demeanor and how he looks at his mom as she's telling stories about his surprisingly rakish university days. He doesn't stop her, only interjects his side of things every once in a while, sometimes both of them falling into fits of laughter so great they can barely finish the story.

"Now, Charlie," Millie says, standing up to start clearing the table, "make sure you're dressed for the weather Friday. It may be June, but that doesn't mean Mother Nature will cooperate."

"Yes, ma'am. Thank you so much for dinner, Millie. Can I help clean up before I go upstairs?"

"Goodness, no. That's Richard's job. I cook; he does dishes," she says with an exaggerated wink. "Go on and enjoy your evening!" She shoos Cameron and I out the door and back into the bookshop.

Cameron pauses amid the piles of twilight-lit books, looking at me with a fire in the depths of his midnight gaze. "You don't happen to have the next couple of hours free, by chance?" he asks, running his long fingers through his hair.

"I do," I respond, a smile tugging at my lips. "What do you have in mind?"

"Honestly? Nothing beyond spending more time with you." He grabs his jacket from behind the desk and grabs my hand, pulling me outside.

We walk out of the bookstore and step into a fairytale. Arcs of neon clouds paint the sky over our heads as soft music drifts down the street, the sound of bagpipes riding on the wind. Waves crash against the seawall, sending tiny droplets of salty water floating through the air.

My breath hitches as Cameron turns toward me, the streetlight gilding the planes of his face, reflecting in his eyes.

"There's nothing quite like the golden hour in the Highlands," he murmurs, pushing his glasses back into place. He holds his hand up, and I press my palm to his, my heartbeat thudding in my ears as the mist swirls in lazy circles around us. His touch lights me up, sparks of lust racing over my skin and lodging deep in my core.

A door slams and we jerk our hands apart, the moment shattered.

"Would you like to grab a drink?" he asks, looking at me through his eyelashes, his pinky caressing my hand like he wants to hold it, but he's too shy to ask.

"Over there?" I ask, pointing down the street.

Cameron nods, dark curls falling over his forehead.

"Yes, I would love to," I say, threading my fingers through his. I may barely know this man, but one thing I do know is I never want this night to end.

The music comes to an abrupt halt as we walk through the door of the pub. A strong breeze rushes ahead of us, whipping my hair around my head as I cross the threshold. I push it out of my face and freeze as a sea of curious eyeballs turn our way.

"Everyone," Cameron calls out, "this is Charlie." He winks at me, giving me the courage to stay put instead of running back outside. "Charlie, this is everyone." A loud cheer goes up, and the music starts again – fiddles, guitars, and piano all fighting for attention.

Cameron pulls me to a booth against the wall, making sure I'm settled before heading to the bar. By the time he comes back with a massive beer in each hand, my toes are tapping along to the music. I take a big gulp of the beer and lick the mustache from my top lip, looking up at Cameron just in time to see him watching me, his gaze following my tongue as it moves over my lips. He mutters something under his breath and raises his glass to his mouth, taking a couple of long drags. I watch as his Adam's apple bobs, the line of his throat long and elegant. My fingers itch to unbutton the top buttons of his shirt. Fuck if this man doesn't belong in a renaissance painting.

"What do you think?" he asks, raising his voice above the music.

"I love it!" I yell back, grinning. There's a wild cheer as bagpipes join in, the entire pub melting into absolute chaos. I'm obsessed. Chairs and tables are pushed against the walls as three couples make their way to the dance floor, their feet racing across the planks in a complicated jig.

Another cheer goes up as the music screeches to a halt, everyone standing and moving to the center of the room.

"What's going on?" I ask Cameron, leaning toward him so he can hear me.

He palms my jaw, angling my head to talk into my ear. "You'll see," he chuckles, his breath warm against the shell of my ear, heat pooling in my belly.

Before I can react, the woman beside me links her arm with mine, and half a second later, we're stomping around the pub, chanting in time with the music. Everyone is arm-in-arm, rotating in one giant circle, pulsing in and out with the music, grinning and sweaty, whatever cares they had brought with them long forgotten. When I feel I can't possibly take another step, the music grinds to a halt and everyone breaks apart, heading back to their seats.

Cameron pulls me close, our gazes locking, hunger replacing the shyness. We're both breathing hard, goofy grins plastered to our faces.

"You want to cool down outside?" he asks, brushing at a strand of hair stuck to my cheek.

I nod and he pulls me outside, cool air sliding over my skin like that first drink of ice-cold water. We lean against the side of the building, breathing hard. He catches me looking at him, and a smile tugs at his lips.

"You looked like a fire sprite in there," he murmurs, "I don't think I've ever seen anything so beautiful." He glances at his watch and pushes off the wall. "Fuck, I wish this night could last forever," he groans, taking my hands in his. "I have an eight o'clock class tomorrow morning, so I can't miss the last ferry." He stands in front of me, uncertainty playing over his features. "I had a lot of fun tonight, Charlie. Will I see you Friday?"

"I'll be here." Disappointment settles over my shoulders as he turns and walks away. He takes several steps and then pauses, turning back toward me. I crash into his embrace, burying my face in his chest and breathing deeply. He kisses my forehead before we step away from each other. "Goodnight, Charlie."

"Goodnight, Cameron," I murmur.

As I try to get comfortable in my tiny bed that night, it occurs to me that I feel Cameron's absence more acutely after just one night than I had ever felt with Rob. I wasted years on someone that didn't give a shit about me.

This is my chance. Go big or go home, right? Or in my case – go big, and then I'd *have* to go home. I vow to myself right then and there to make up for lost time.

The perfect Scottish summer is coming right up.

4

The days fly by once I get into a routine. The library is the most accessible place for me to work for now. I have access to several sources of online records through their computer system, which allows me to cross-check the information Arty had given me. By the end of the week, I've traced back several generations and have copious notes on every possible tidbit of information, not sure what I would need further down the road when I painted the scenes. By Thursday evening, I'm pretty happy with my progress, and I'm looking forward to a day not spent hunched over my laptop and notebook.

I rush down the stairs Friday morning, right at eight. I'm dressed in so many layers I've lost count: camisole, long johns, jeans, two pairs of socks, short-sleeved shirt, long-sleeved shirt, sweater, jacket. I feel like the marshmallow man. Cameron's waiting outside the bookstore, leaning against an old army green Defender. He's dressed in fewer layers than I am: weatherproof pants, flannel shirt, jacket, and ball cap. The sun is just starting to peek over the hills, the golden light highlighting his face.

"Well, aren't you the rugged outdoorsman," I tease, dropping my backpack into the back of his truck.

"Just wait," he wiggles his eyebrows, making his glasses slide down his nose. "We'll have to pick up several of my students on the way to the pools. This is just a scouting trip – getting the lay of the land, mapping the terrain, things like that." He opens the car door for me and ensures I'm all the way in before closing it carefully.

'Several' students turned out to be enough to pack into the back of the vehicle like sardines. I have to move over to the middle of the front bench seat to fit one more; not that I mind being pressed against Cameron, or the fact that he has to reach between my knees to shift gears. They're boisterous and make it impossible to hold a conversation, but I love it. It's exactly what I need. I haven't been around a group of young people in a while. They help to remind me of the carefree person I was before, of the pre-Rob Charlie. She was a great girl. I miss her.

We drive on winding single-track roads, mountains crowding us on both sides, music blasting out into the ether. After about ten minutes, he glances over at me and then down at my hands resting on my lap. I smile and grab his hand off the shifter, linking my fingers with his. He winks at me, a flash of his dimple, and then he's turning his attention back to the road. I trace the veins on the back of his hand with my fingertips. He squeezes my hand and motions for me to look up. All at once, the peaks open into a wide swath of valley bathed in greens and golds. The beauty is surreal. Cameron takes his hand back to downshift, and then we're pulling into a small parking area.

"Ready?"

I nod, meeting him at the back of the truck, carefully tucking my camera into my backpack. His students mill around, waiting for instructions. "Pick a partner. Each pair takes one section of the valley. Your job is to find any anomalies and map them," he says, holding up a clipboard with a gridded map of the area. "The more meticulous you are now, the easier our work will be later."

He turns to me as they squabble over who is going where and with whom. "Since you've never been here before, I thought we could hike to the top of the pools. We aren't usually blessed with weather like this. It would be a miserable hike most other days," he says, squinting against the sunlight.

"Sounds good," I say, shouldering my bag.

I can't take my eyes off him as he double-checks his pack and slings it over his shoulders. I'm struggling to fit this version of Cameron with the one from Sunday night. I had put him in such a neat box, and today he came along and demolished it. I try to ignore how his jacket pulls across his back as I follow him across the road and onto the trail. I force myself to look away when I notice the fit of his pants. Lord, these layers were a bad idea. I pull at the neck of my sweater, fanning it out several times, desperate for some cool air.

The pools stair-step down the valley, the water bubbling over several small waterfalls. It's the most beautiful place I have ever seen. We traverse the well-worn path to the highest pool in about forty-five minutes. The sun is beating down on our backs, the air filled with the heady musk of blooming heather.

"Do you want to take a break before going back down?" Cameron asks, holding his pack up to give his shoulders a reprieve.

"I'd love to snap some pictures," I say, setting my backpack on a rock and fishing out my camera and lens.

"Are you hungry?"

"Famished," I admit. The stale scone I had eaten this morning wore off a while ago.

"Good." His dimple flashes. "Go take your pictures, and we can eat when you're finished." He sets his bag down and sits on a rock, propping himself up with his elbows. God, he's cute.

I walk down to the pool directly below us and take some pictures uphill, hoping that I can somehow capture the beauty and magic of this place. The sun illuminates the grass, bright greens popping against the glittering blue water. It's mesmerizing. I return to Cameron and find he has laid out a small feast.

"This is amazing!" I sit cross-legged opposite him, and he hands me a steaming cup of coffee. There's some creamy soup with crusty bread and butter. It smells amazing. "Do you always bring meals like this on your excursions?" I ask, ripping into the bread.

"Fancier," he jokes, the corner of his mouth curling up. "I usually just bring a protein bar," he admits. I watch as he bites off a piece of bread, the muscles in his jaw working.

"Thank you," I blush, "I appreciate the thought."

"I know," he says as he smiles, "that's why I did it."

I can't manage to tear my gaze away as he licks a crumb from his lower lip.

5

———————

The bread is perfect – fresh and pillowy on the inside, crunchy on the outside.

"This is so good." I lick a bit of butter off my finger.

Cameron's gaze freezes on my mouth, his cheeks pink. "Tell me about yourself, Charlie," he says finally, taking a bite.

"There's not much to tell, if I'm being honest. My given name is Charlotte. I graduated with a bachelor's degree in business administration at nineteen and started my own small business. Quit when my ex needed help with his family business. Poured my life into that and then..." I pause, unsure what to say. "Then I came here."

"Graduated at nineteen? That's impressive. How long were you married?" he asks; his gaze holds no judgment, only curiosity.

"Five years."

"*Five years*? How old were you when you got married?"

"Barely twenty." I grimace and hold up my hands. "I know, I know. I should have listened to everyone that told me to wait."

"You're only twenty-six?" His eyes searched mine, waiting for my response.

I nod. "And I feel like I haven't even had a chance to live yet. How old are you?"

"Thirty-four. An old man compared to you."

"Experience is a good thing," I muse, immediately realizing how it sounds the second the words come out of my mouth. "I did *not* mean it like that," I stammer, the heat in his eyes lighting me on fire.

I'm boiling alive in these layers. I peel my jacket off, eyeing the water. "Does anyone ever swim?" I ask, fanning my shirt, wondering if he'd be scandalized if I stripped and jumped in.

"Yes, usually only the locals, though. It's freezing – a lot colder than it looks." His gaze slides from the water to my eyes. "Local legend says these pools are what made the fairies immortal."

"Well, in that case..." I shed my flannel and jeans, desperate to make contact with the cool air. Silk whispers over my stomach as I pull off my camisole, gooseflesh taking its place, my heart pounding as I stand there in only my bra and underwear. "Are you coming?" I flip my hair forward and pull it into a high bun, watching Cameron from the corner of my eye. He's stretched out, his hands behind his head, the brim of his hat pushed up, his full attention on me.

"Aye, I was just taking a moment to admire the view." He winks, pulling at his laces, loosening one boot and then the other. His gaze roots me in place as he stands and peels off his socks. Despite the cold, I can feel the crackle of heat between us. I slide his jacket down his arms, tossing it to the rocks. He grasps the bottom of his shirt, ignoring the buttons, and pulls it over his head. I watch his muscles flex as he pulls his pants off, revealing sculpted thighs and boxer briefs that don't leave much to the imagination.

He links his fingers with mine and guides me toward the pool, supporting me as we pick our way over the rocks.

"Ready?" he asks, pulling me to his side at the pool's edge. I pluck his hat off his head, sling back toward our clothes, then carefully lift his glasses from his face, setting them on a rock where they won't get crushed. We stare at each other for a second, the tension thick.

"Ready," I breathe, floating in this moment like a bubble in a glass of champagne.

"One, two, three... go!" We plunge into the water and come back up spluttering and laughing, our gazes locked and hands intertwined.

He pulls me closer, his hands sliding along my skin, coming to rest on my hips. His hair is slicked back, the elegant sweep of his jaw on display. The dark spikes of his eyelashes frame eyes the color of the sky. His gaze drops to my lips. My stomach tightens.

Caressing my cheek with one hand, he uses the other to pull me tight against his body. He bends down to me, his nose brushing mine gently before his lips melt into mine. I cling to him, my buoyancy making it hard to keep my footing. His hands sweep down over my backside and hook on my thighs as he backs up to the pool's edge, setting me on a rock just under the water. He sprinkles tiny kisses on my ear, my neck, and the swell of my chest. My nipples harden, begging for his touch. He pulses between my legs, setting my entire body on fire. I whimper, pulling his mouth back to mine. He deepens the kiss, his tongue dipping in to taste me. Sliding his hand up, his thumb caresses the side of my breast. I arch into him, desperate for his touch.

"Dr. MacDonald?"

He nips my bottom lips, his eyes hooded. "Fuck."

"Here!" he calls, angling his head so his voice will carry over the sound of the waterfall.

One of the students pokes her head over the lip of the pool. "Are you able to help Tanner and I?"

"Of course. Give me a minute." Once she disappears again, he presses a gentle kiss to my lips. He brushes his thumb over my cheek, his gaze intense. "I'll never forget this, Charlie." He sighs. "Time to activate teacher mode." We climb out of the pool together, our teeth chattering after thirty seconds. He scoops me into a hug, nestling his face into my neck. "Thank you for coming today," he murmurs into my hair.

"Thank you for bringing me; I loved it." Today will be burned into my memory forever.

He presses his forehead to mine, and I drown in the endless pools of his eyes. "I'll be in the field this weekend, so I won't be able to make it to dinner Sunday. Can I see you the weekend after?"

"Yes. Please," I say, not even trying to play it coy. I like him—a lot.

He smiles, cupping my jaw, catching my lips with his. The kiss is filled with inevitability. We're at a tipping point and there is no going back.

6
______

I daydream about Cameron at the most inconvenient times, like when I'm supposed to be working. I've caught myself staring into space several times over the last half an hour.

It's a problem.

I sigh, frustrated with my lack of progress. *Get with it, Charlie.* If I don't get further in my research soon, it will jeopardize my finish date. I can't do that to Arty – especially with him footing the bill for this trip. I need to get shit done now, so I don't feel guilty spending time with Cameron on Sunday. I scrub my hands over my face and gulp down the rest of my coffee. I can do this.

The following week passes the same way; only my daydreams are getting more explicit by the day. This wasn't the first time I've found myself squeezing my thighs together while looking up Arty's ancestors in the tiny registry office. I slam my laptop closed and walk back to the flat. Cameron will be here tomorrow. I don't know what to expect. As far as I know, he doesn't ever stay overnight, and there's no way we can disappear to my room for a couple of hours – the walls are thin, and I refuse to put Cameron or his parents in that position.

My phone dings, startling me. It's Cameron. My heart hammers in my chest.

Looking forward to seeing you tomorrow.

Me, too.

MY MOM WANTS me to help with inventory. I would love to see you after.

I can help with inventory, too. It will go faster that way.

YOU HAVE no idea how happy that makes me. This may be too soon to say this, but I couldn't stop thinking about you this week. I didn't get anything done at work.

I COVER my smile with my hand and do a little dance. God, he makes me happy.

Same. :)

What are you doing?

I'm sprawled across my bed.
I just got back from getting absolutely nothing done at the records office.

...because you were thinking about me?

...maybe.

:D

I jump when a video call comes through. Holy shit.

"Hey," he rasps. He's leaning against his headboard, glasses pushed up on top of his head. An open white button-down shirt is the only thing I can see other than the huge, cheesy grin pointed my way.

"Hi."

We stare at each other for a couple of seconds before we both start laughing.

"Why didn't we do this sooner?" he asks, "It's so good to see your face."

"I've missed you." The words slip out.

His face softens. "I wish I was with you right now."

This is unbearable. "What are you wearing?" I ask, giggling – *giggling!* Oh my God. Mortification heats my cheeks.

He coughs, surprised. "I have to admit, I had high hopes when I called, but I never thought you'd be the one saying those words."

"You have no idea what's been going through my head the last six days. This is tame in comparison."

"*Fuck, Charlie.*" He flips his camera. Black boxers cover his bottom half, his erection straining against them. God.

I lick my lips, imagining running my tongue down his length. He flips the camera back around, his eyes hooded.

"Your turn."

"Hang on." I jump up, strip out of my jeans and t-shirt then lay back on the bed. "Okay, ready now." I flip the camera, angling the phone so most of my body from the neck down was in the frame. I look at him looking at me, and I almost come undone.

He groans, the muscle in his jaw ticking. His hand moves down his body and out of the frame.

"Flip your camera," I order, desperate to see.

He does, then pulls the waistband of his boxers down, his cock springing up. I watch as he grasps it, running a hand from base to tip. I open the front clasp of my bra and palm my breast, pinching my nipple. He moans, his hand keeping a steady rhythm. I slide my hand down my stomach and underneath my underwear, pressing my fingers to either side of my clit. Seeing him fucking his hand is almost too much to handle.

"I need to see your face, Charlie," he says, groaning as he slides his hand down his shaft. I arch against my hand, my breathing unsteady.

We flip our cameras at the same time. His gaze meets mine, his eyelids dropping lower every time he strokes his cock. I moan as I feel the beginnings of my orgasm start.

"Oh, God," he whispers, fumbling with his phone. The screen flips again, and I see his hips bucking up, his hand slamming down. I groan, deep and primal. His abs contract right before he starts to come. His cock jerks, and I explode against my fingers. Cameron flips his camera mid-orgasm, and we finish while staring into each other's eyes. He tilts his head back, the strong column of his neck on display. I desperately want to lick it.

"Fuck," he chuckles in disbelief. "I'm going to go wash up. I'll be right back." The screen goes dark as he drops the phone onto the bed.

Holy shit. Had little ol' me just masturbated over video with my crush?

That is the hottest thing I have ever experienced. I prop my phone up against the bedside lamp and pad to the bathroom. I can't believe I just did that. As I wash up, I think about how I would have never done something like this before. I'm proud of myself for pushing my boundaries. I smile as I dry my hands. I'm happy for the first time in a long time. I walk back into the bedroom to see Cameron watching me, his lip caught in his teeth.

"You're fucking sexy, Charlie."

Instead of brushing off the compliment, I thank him.

"I want to stay on with you all night—"

"But you have an early drive tomorrow, so you're going to do the smart thing and hang up now and then go to bed," I finish for him. He looks like he might argue for a second, but he smiles instead. The kind of smile that allows you to see their soul. And all at once, I know this man is different.

7

Cameron explodes into my flat the following morning. He flings his jacket and briefcase on the couch and folds me into his body, his hands warm and sure on my back. His touch is gentle. Tender. He pulls my face to his, worshipping me with his lips.

"Cameron, was that you?" Millie's sing-song voice floats up the stairs. He holds a finger to his mouth and winks at me, his dimple making an appearance. I stand silently, Cameron's pelvis pinning me to the wall.

"Charlie?" I hear Millie's steps on the stairs.

Sorry, I mouth as I duck away from him and scurry for the door. "Hi, Millie!" I plaster a smile on my face.

"Hi, dear," she stops only a couple of steps from the bottom. "Is Cameron up there? I thought I heard him come in."

"Hullo, Mum." Cameron squeezes my ass as he brushes past me.

"There you are! Ready to get started?"

"Is there anything I can help with?" I ask.

Cameron says, "Yes" at the same time his mother says, "No". She looks at him with reproach. "Don't rope her in, Cameron; she's our guest."

He smirks. "Why don't we let her make that decision?" He turns to me, "We're working on inventory today. Would you like to help?"

"Yes," I say quickly, too quickly. Millie narrows her eyes and looks between Cameron and me like she's trying to figure out a puzzle.

Cameron shoots her a quick smile. "See, Mother? Plus, what's that phrase you always used to say when I was younger? Many hands make light work?"

"Naughty boy. She's our *guest*."

"You're right, I am a naughty boy." Cameron wiggles his eyebrows at me, grinning.

"Cameron!" I hiss, mortified.

His laugh echoes off the walls, his eyes like sapphires sparkling in the sun.

"Well, come on then," Millie huffs, heading back down to the bookshop.

"Yes, follow the naughty boy downstairs," Cameron whispers. I roll my eyes but follow him anyway.

Five hours fly by, and Cameron's company is the perfect remedy for tedious work.

"Come on!" Cameron whispers to me the second Millie breaks for tea. His hand envelopes mine as he pulls me out of the bookshop. He holds his finger over his lips, motioning for me to be quiet. The door snicks closed behind us; he grins at me – a broad, joyful smile that makes me melt.

"Do you know how many books I counted today?" he asks, his smile turning into a goofy smirk.

"No clue."

"Me neither. That's the problem. I was paying more attention to you than I was to the books. I couldn't stand to be holed up in there for one more second."

I honestly hadn't minded doing inventory. There was something relaxing about such a mundane, methodical task. My mind could empty and focus – almost like I was meditating. Plus... books.

"So, what are we going to do?"

"I haven't gotten that far yet. But I know what I want to do first."

He closes the distance between us, gripping my waist and pulling me tight against him. He brushes his lips across mine, soft as a feather. He pulls away before I can deepen the kiss, his thumb caressing my cheek. "Do you want to go see the Fairy Glen?"

"Yes, I've been wanting to go!"

"Come on, then." He grins, pulling me with him down the sidewalk. We stop at the cafe and grab some sandwiches before taking off in his Defender.

An emotion I can't place swells in me as we drive through the emerald hills – like an animal waking up after a long hibernation. My heart pounds in my ears, giddiness bubbling up until I have to slap a hand over my grin to keep it in. This place makes me happy. I had forgotten what that felt like.

I crank open the window, the wind turning my hair into a tornado, the air cool between my fingers. I lean back and close my eyes, the wind and music cocooning my senses. This summer was turning into a series of moments I will never forget.

I don't open my eyes until Cameron pulls off the road to park the car. He's looking at me, his expression soft.

"You're beautiful."

"So are you," I say, pushing a lock of dark hair off his forehead. I brush my fingers over the blush creeping up his cheeks, his skin soft against my fingertips. His eyes are impossibly blue, his eyelashes so dark they look like shadows. He smiles, his dimple flashing. I push my feelings down as we get out of the car. I know this isn't going anywhere. That it *can't* go anywhere. It's just for fun. He likes me. I want him—end of story.

The clouds take on an ominous hue as we start the hike. We both remain optimistic, especially as we near the Glen. Fat raindrops start coming down just as we descend into what looks like the birthplace of fairies. Whorls of rock are scattered over velvety grass. A worn path leads up to what looks like it could have been a rock spire at one time. Perhaps even a tower. We explore for about ten minutes before we're both soaked and shivering. Cameron wraps his arm around me as we run back down the path, trying to shield my body from the rain.

"Now what?" I ask when we get back to his car, my teeth chattering. "I don't want to get the seat wet!"

"Get in the back, I'll turn on the heat." He turns the truck on, cranks the heat, and hops in the back with me.

I fold in on myself, desperate for some warmth, my teeth chattering uncontrollably.

"You're going to have to strip, Charlie. Your lips are purple."

"Only if you strip with me," I say, trying to sound cheeky, but it gets lost in the chattering.

"Good thinking." He winks, but it's outshone by the massive shiver that shakes his shoulders.

We peel off our layers and drape them as best we can over the front vents. He pulls me onto his lap, squeezing me in his arms, one hand sweeping up and down my back. I rest my cheek against his shoulder. Slowly my shivering subsides, replaced by uneven breathing.

"Better? Your teeth aren't chattering anymore."

"Better," I say, trying to ignore the fire igniting in the places we're pressed together. I can't stop looking at his lips, licking mine like I want to lick his. My thoughts must be written on my face because his pupils blow wide a second later. He groans my name and I lose control.

I crush my mouth to his. His lips are so soft, molding to mine like they belong there. He cups my jaw, angling my head. His tongue slicks over my lips, pushing past them. He moans and repositions me so I'm straddling his waist. I gasp as his hard length presses against me, rocking against him, shuddering.

"You're sure you want this?" he asks, pressing his forehead to mine.

"Yes, Cameron. I want this. I want you."

His hand slides up my ribs and over my breast, rolling my nipple between his fingers. I pull his boxers down just enough for his cock to spring out, wrapping my hand around the base and squeezing lightly.

He groans and fucks my hand for a couple of strokes. "Charlotte, it's been a while..."

"It's okay," I smile, touched by his admission.

"No, it's not," he rasps, his voice strained. "Are you able to reach the condoms in the glove box?"

"I think so?" I disentangle myself from him and twist around, leaning forward toward the glove box. He runs his hands over my ass, kneading and spreading. He slides a finger through my arousal, moaning as he pushes it in.

"You're so wet," he groans, reaching up and rolling my clit underneath his fingers. My breath shudders out of me as he takes the condom from me, deftly rolling it over his shaft.

"Do you want me to turn around?" I ask, looking over my shoulder at him. He's breathing hard, his dark curls falling over his forehead.

He shakes his head, gripping my hips and guiding me back until the head of his cock is nestled at my entrance. I push back and impale myself, whimpering as he fills me. He moans as I squeeze around him. He has open access to my clit and uses it, circling the bundle of nerves until I'm panting his name. I grind against his fingers as I ride him, his head pushing against my g-spot with every thrust. He pushes and pulls with his fingers, stretching places he was already stretching with his cock, and fuck, it feels good.

"Please, for the love of God, don't stop," I sob.

Cameron bites my shoulder in reply. I explode around him, pinpricks of light swimming in my vision.

"God, Charlie," he moans, pounding up into me, holding me still with an arm around my middle. I move against him until the aftershocks are over and he stops twitching inside me.

I lean back, turning to bury my face in his neck. "I'm warm now."

His chuckle skitters through my bones. It's the sexiest fucking sound I've ever heard.

$$8$$

____

The following week goes by slow as molasses. By Saturday evening, I am cross-eyed from scanning through microfiche after microfiche. I still haven't attempted to start on the maternal side of Arty's family – some of the information has to be wrong, but I can't figure it out. It's pissing me off. Instead, I spend my time mapping out Arty's paternal side. I have a great start so far – five generations and counting. I'm hopeful I'll be able to trace at least one side back to a king or queen; that's where all the good stories are. One of my favorite parts is finding those little tidbits of goodness so I can bring someone's ancestry to life.

A knock on my door wakes me out of a dead sleep. I fumble around for my phone. Seven A.M. Fuck. I groan and drag myself from the bed, pulling on my robe. Cameron is standing there with a pastry bag and two coffees, a slight grimace on his face when he realizes he woke me up.

"I'm sorry, Charlie. I did bring coffee, though." He pushes it into my hands, a sacrifice to the sleep gods.

"I forgive you," I mumble, taking a careful sip.

"I wish we could do something today, but Mom wants me to stock the shelves, plus I still need to do the regular bookkeeping." He makes a face.

"I'll help."

"I can't ask you to do that, Charlie."

"You didn't ask me, I offered. I need a break from my research, anyway. Plus, I'd rather spend time with you working than not seeing you at all." I peck his cheek, his skin warm under my lips.

I'M in the middle of stocking some paperbacks when I hear Cameron cuss under his breath. He's standing at the desk, staring at the computer screen. He has the strangest look on his face.

"What's wrong?" I ask, walking over to him.

He shakes his head, his lips pressed into a tight line. He runs his hands through his hair before grabbing his jacket from the desk, his movements jerky.

"I need a break. Do you want to come to the cafe with me?" He won't look me in the eye. Alarm bells clang in my head. Fucking hell.

"Sure, let's go." I keep my voice under control despite my jackhammering heart.

He slides his hand into mine and pulls me outside, flipping the sign before locking the door behind us. We walk to the cafe in silence, fingers intertwined. I wish he would blurt out whatever it is, but at the same time, I don't want to hear it. Cameron pulls a chair out at one of the outside tables, the cold of the metal biting through my jeans as I sit down. He goes inside to get tea. I watch the waves batter the seawall. My stomach churns.

"Thank you," I murmur as he hands me tea and a croissant. I wrap my hands around the mug just as much for warmth as for comfort.

He sits down opposite me, his gaze on his croissant as he pulls off a bite. I take those few moments to study him. Memorize him. The slight curl of his hair as it falls over his forehead, the sharp cut of his jaw against the green of his scarf, the thick eyelashes shielding his eyes.

"Cameron, come on," I say, struggling to keep my breathing regular.

"God, I'm sorry." He pushes his glasses up his nose, his eyes finally meeting mine. "I just got an email offering me a spot on an African archeological team." The words tumble from his lips.

"Oh my God!" *Oh my God.* I'm going to be sick. I force a smile. "That's amazing news!"

"Is it, though?" he says, searching my face for the words I'm holding back, his eyes desperate.

"Of course it is! This is what you've been working for!" He's quiet. Too quiet. "We can still call each other—" I continue, but my voice doesn't sound convincing, so I stop.

"I'm not sure if we can." He groans in frustration. "The assignment is in a remote area. I have no idea how often I would have cell service." He squares his shoulders and meets my gaze, "I'm thinking about not taking it, Charlie."

"Cameron, no. You have to take it." It hurts like hell, but I mean it. There's no way I'll let him give up this opportunity for whatever this is between us.

His eyes shutter, "You don't understand the spell you have me under, do you?" He shakes his head, his eyes on the horizon.

"You can't turn down this job because of me! This is your *dream.* I'll still be here." I pause. "Well, maybe not *here*, but you know what I mean."

"Will you, though?" He takes my hand in his, tracing the sensitive skin inside my fingers. He sighs. "I'm not going to ask you to wait for me. There's no telling how long the project will last. You'll be long gone, back to your life in America."

He's right, of course, but hell if I'm going to tell him that.

He tells his family at dinner that night. He leaves in eight days. When I see how ecstatic his mom and dad are for him, I know I made the right decision. I walk with him to his car after dinner, doing my best to be happy for him. I stop next to his car, and he draws my body to him, cupping my face between his hands. He presses his forehead to mine, his eyes shining.

"Fuck." He inhales sharply. He starts to say something but then stops, blowing out a breath. "I'll see you Sunday for dinner." He kisses me quickly and drives off without looking back.

I want to scream after him to stay and see what this could become, that this was something special. But I don't. I wipe under my eyes, watching as his car disappears. I have a week to get my shit together.

9

———

Cameron brings me to a swanky farm-to-table restaurant the following Sunday. Millie and Richard are out of town at a baby shower, so we get this one dinner alone. One night alone. The meal is the best I've had in Scotland so far. I eat slowly, savoring the food and the company. His eyes are dark as the shadows from the candlelight caress his face.

He reaches across the table and pushes my hair back from my face, stroking my cheek with his thumb. "I don't know how to leave you."

I rest my cheek against his palm and smile even though my heart feels like it's breaking. "Yes, you do. First, you go home and pack. Then you get on that plane tomorrow morning. Then you live your dream."

He studies my face, his gaze catching on my lips. "Spend the night with me?" he asks, not waiting for my answer before leaning across the table and crushing his mouth to mine.

Desire rushes through my veins. I frame his face with my hands and pull him up with me as I stand. I sigh against his lips as our bodies fit together. He sucks my lower lip into his mouth and bites, soothing it with a swipe of his tongue. He rests his forehead against mine, "Yes or no, Charlie?"

"Yes. Definitely yes," I whisper, struggling to catch my breath.

He throws several bills on the table and wraps his arm around me, stroking the sensitive skin below my breast. He side-steps around me, his erection pressing into my side. I push back, barely able to stop myself from rubbing against him like a cat.

"Fuck, Charlie," he whispers, his hand sliding around my throat, the touch gentle. Possessive.

I turn to face him, running my hand from his shoulder to his fingertips. I tug lightly. "Come on." I pull him out of the restaurant, and we make it several steps before he crushes me against a wall in the alleyway. His lips move over mine hungrily, no sign of the tentativeness from last week. His thumb caresses the side of my breast, and I growl in frustration, pulling his hand up to cover my nipple. I push my fingers through his hair and tug. He groans, his hands sliding down to my hips and pressing me close.

His cock pushes against the seam of my jeans, the ridge against my clit. I cling to him, pushing my hips down. As his lips move to my ear, I drop my head back against the wall. I clutch the waistband of his pants and pull him closer, riding him.

He presses his forehead to the wall. "Fuck ... me," he groans, thrusting back once before holding my hips in a vice grip. He pierces my soul with his hooded gaze before backing up a couple of steps. He looks around to make sure no one is watching before reaching down and adjusting his cock. I can see the tip peeking out of his waistband before he pulls his shirt back down. I close the space between us in one stride, pushing him against the opposite wall. I cup him and stroke his length several times, pushing his shirt up with my other hand so I can see it. I pull his waistband out slightly and circle my tongue over him, following the ridge.

Cameron sucks a breath through his teeth and pulls me up to meet his mouth, cradling my face with his hands. He angles his lips over mine, fucking my mouth with his tongue. His hand drops to my ass, pulling me tight against his cock. I groan into his mouth, desperate. He turns me to the wall, pinning me with his chest as he grinds against me.

"I can't stop fucking thinking about doing this," he says, his breath hot on my ear as he slips his hand down the front of my pants. He cups me over my underwear. I push against him, wanting – *needing* – more. He palms my throat with his other hand, pulling me against him and angling my head back so he can look me in the eyes. I whimper as his finger inches closer to my center. He gazes at me, watching my reaction as he pulls the fabric aside. My eyes roll back as his fingertip slowly slides over my clit to where I'm wet and ready.

"God, Charlie," he groans, pushing into me. I moan and grind against his palm.

"Fuck me, Cameron – *please,*" I whisper, my lips a hairsbreadth from his.

"Soon." He pulls his hand away, his gaze holding mine as he licks his fingers clean. Stepping out of the alley, he stops every few feet to burn me alive with his kisses. He drops his keys twice before success-fully unlocking the door to the bookstore. We slam against the inside of the door, his lips crushing mine. I squirm against him, seeking out friction. Strong hands grip the back of my thighs as he lifts me, hoisting me onto the high library-style desk. I start to protest about how far away his cock is, but he ignores me.

"Unbutton," he growls, pulling my shoes off. I obey. He jerks my jeans from my legs as I pull my shirt over my head. He grabs scissors from the desk, and cuts both sides of my panties, pulling them away from my body with a groan.

He looks up at me, his eyes dark. Hungry.

God, he's beautiful.

He palms my thighs, squeezing. He runs his hands to my knees before pushing them open against the desk, exposing me to the cool air.

His eyes drink me in as if he's memorizing every freckle, every fold.

He holds my gaze as he lowers himself. Starting at my belly button, he traces a path with his lips. He pauses, letting the anticipation build before he swirls his tongue over my clit. I twist my fingers into his hair with a groan, holding him close. He pulls my hips up, hooking my knees over his shoulders, licking from bottom to top. I buck against his mouth as he dips his tongue inside me. I pull at him, needing more.

"Come for me," he growls, his lips slick against me.

"I've never—"I protest, but then I forget how to speak as he flattens his tongue over my clit, rolling it over and over. I squeeze my knees around his head as the pressure starts building, riding his face toward the light. I explode on his tongue, spasming as he continues his assault.

He pulls away when I relax my legs, wiping his face on his shoulder. He looks down at me, breathing hard, his dark curls falling over his forehead like a crown.

"Please," I beg. I feel vulnerable spread over the desk, but the way he looks at me gives me the confidence I never knew I had.

"Please, what, Charlie? Say it." His voice reverberates over me, goosebumps racing across my skin.

"Fuck me, Cameron. Please." I push myself into a sitting position so I can get my hands on him. He takes advantage of my height and captures a nipple in his mouth, sucking hard. My back bows, a garbled moan spilling from my mouth.

"Fucking hell, Charlie." His expression is pained as he adjusts himself.

I fold my arms around his neck and wiggle myself off the desk, wrapping my legs around his torso as I drop down. He grunts as I land against his cock. "Fuck me, Cameron," I breathe against his ear, rubbing myself against his hard length.

"If you don't stop, I won't be able to control myself, Charlie," he rasps, his voice strangled.

"I don't want control," I pant, my fingers digging into his shoulders as I pull myself up, grinding my clit up and down over the ridge of his head.

He walks toward the stairs, reaching underneath me to unbuckle his belt. His cock springs free, his skin searing mine.

"No," I mumble into his neck, "I can't make it up there. Now."

He growls his agreement, pressing my back into the nearest set of bookshelves. "Look at me."

I do. Hooded eyes burn me alive, a fire roaring in the deep abyss of ocean blue. He slides his hands below my butt, lifting me to free his cock from between us. Holding my gaze, he lowers me until his tip is nudging at my entrance. I try to impale myself, but his grip is relentless. He drags his cock through my slick folds, back and forth, dipping in a quarter inch more every time he passes my core. I'm trembling from anticipation, convulsing whenever he comes close. He pulls me away from the shelves and pivots to the window, setting me on the wide sill. He pushes his hair out of his face and brushes his lips over mine.

I look over my shoulder, eyes wide. This side of the building faces the alley. The streetlight shining directly into the window will give someone a show if they happened to be out at this hour. "Cameron, someone will see us."

"I want them to," he says darkly, his eyes glinting in the light. He looks down between us, a dark curl falling over his forehead.

I watch as he grips his cock, one stroke has him pulling his lower lip into his mouth. He drags it over me, sliding it back and forth over my clit until I'm shaking with need. He positions it at my entrance but stops and looks up at me, smoothing the hair from my face with a tender touch. "I want to see your face when I sink my cock into you, Charlie."

I nod incoherently, a breath shuddering out of me. I'm almost there, and he's barely touching me. He pushes into me. Only an inch, but I'm squeezing around him, desperate.

"Fuck, Charlie," he chokes, pulling out. A needy whine breaks free from my throat, but I strangle on it as he pushes a finger into me, crooking it up and rubbing until I'm on the edge. He pauses, looking at me through his lashes, "You're perfect. So fucking perfect." He keeps his finger inside me as he pushes his cock in below it.

I choke on a scream, bucking against him. He keeps his finger moving as he slowly pulls his cock back out, then in again. "Does it feel good?" he asks, his entire body shaking with restraint.

I nod, barely able to keep my eyes from rolling back in my head.

"I'm going to try something. If you don't like it, I'll stop. Just tell me." He stills when I don't answer, forcing me to answer him before he'll start moving again.

"I will. Promise," I rasp, my voice low and husky.

He looks where we're joined, his jaw flexing. He pulls his cock almost all the way out and then slides his free hand over my stomach, stopping just below my belly button. He presses down firmly, keeping the pressure there as he looks up at me. "Good?"

I moan my affirmation.

His gaze stays on my face as he pushes back in, his finger rubbing that spot again.

Holy fuck. Stars bloom behind my eyes. I can feel every ridge, every vein. I can feel the universe.

I sob his name, needing something I can't name. It's never felt like this before.

The sensation is too much and not enough. It's everything and nothing. I'm floating in the ether between worlds when he moves his hands, one gripping my hip. He reaches behind me with his other, swirling a finger where we're joined before sliding it over my back entrance. He jerks me forward, fully seating me on his cock as he pushes his finger in.

Oh my fucking God. My back feels like it's breaking. He sets a hard pace, his hand bruising as he pulls and pushes me to meet him. My body convulses around him, a sob clawing its way out of me as everything turns black.

Never could I have imagined it could be like this.

My vision returns just as he starts to come. His head is thrown back, his bottom lip held tightly in his teeth. He snaps his head down suddenly, our gazes locking. One more jilted thrust, and he's exploding in me, his hand leaving my hip to cradle the back of my head, his mouth crashing to mine.

We stay pressed together for a couple of minutes, harsh breaths puffing against tender skin. "You know what you're doing, don't you?" I mumble into his shoulder.

He eyes me. "And you took it like a fucking champ, Charlie."

I groan, his words making my pussy clench around him. He chuckles, but it doesn't quite reach his eyes as reality crashes around us.

10

The days drag by. It's been three weeks since Cameron left, but it feels more like three months. I spend mornings at the cafe, the tiny tables limiting me to my laptop. Every day around eleven, I grab a coffee and head to the pub where I can spread out a little. I'm trying not to dwell on the fact that I haven't heard from Cameron yet. It hurts more than I want to admit. Funny how hopes can rise to ridiculous heights without even realizing it. However, I find the more time I spend out in nature, pouring myself into my work – living – the more my perspective shifts. I begin to recognize my relationship with Cameron for what it was: the perfect person, the fucking wrong time. It was the best summer fling I could have ever hoped for.

I roll my shoulders, my muscles aching from the hours I've spent in this stupid booth. Frustration is beginning to set in. I'm still not making any progress on Arty's maternal side. My stomach grumbles at me, and I acknowledge it with a long sigh. I slide off the bench, careful not to disturb my papers, knowing one errant draft could send them flying. I lift my arms above my head and stretch, my back thankful for the respite.

One more day gone with almost nothing to show. *Hmph.*

As I hoist myself onto the stool at the bar, I realize that the energy is a little different tonight – a little darker. A lot edgier. Then I spot the reason why. Someone who is definitely not the normal wrinkly bartender is at the other end of the bar, his back to me as he pours a beer. He's not like anyone I've seen my entire time here. For one, he isn't over sixty. Secondly, his clothes are not typical – or maybe it's the body under them; gray jeans hug thick thighs, the bottoms shoved into beat-up leather boots. Tattoos shift over his muscles as he eases the tap closed.

"Charlie!" A regular raises his glass to me from across the bar, a wide smirk on his face.

I jump in my seat and grimace sheepishly, knowing I was caught.

The bartender glances over his shoulder at me, his eyebrow cocked with curiosity. He sets the beer down and wipes his hands, flipping the towel over his shoulder as he turns toward me.

My heart stutters in my chest. *Holy God.* I forget how to breathe.

Perfect white teeth flash from the depths of a dark beard. He pulls his hair into a bun as he stalks my way, his shirt riding up just enough to make the saliva evaporate from my mouth.

"What can I get you?" he asks, leaning against the bar, ducking, so his face is level with mine. Whisky eyes pull me into their depths without warning. I'm drowning.

"Lass?"

"Uh—um—" I stammer, heat rising in my cheeks. I break eye contact, desperately trying to get my mouth to work.

He lowers his head even more, looking me in the eye. "I won't bite ye, lass." His brogue skitters over my skin.

His gaze drops to my lips as I lick them. I take a deep breath, but it's filled with him. I can't escape. I push back, the stool cracking against the floor like a gunshot. He plants one hand on the bar, swings his legs over, and lands beside me.

"Easy," he whispers, righting the stool. I sway a bit, and he grasps my upper arms gently, either to hold me upright or to stop me from running – they both seem equally likely.

I must look positively feral looking up at him, my heart galloping in my chest.

I needed to get a fucking grip.

I blow out the breath I hadn't meant to hold and force myself to take deep, controlled breaths.

"Sorry about that." I pray to God he can't see my stained cheeks in the low light. "May I have the fish and chips, please?" I force a smile.

"Aye. Are you feeling well?" He looks me up and down, worried.

"I'm fine, thank you." I jerk from his grasp and turn back to my table, my senses jumbled. I don't dare look back as I slide into the booth. A thousand bees buzz under my skin. *Breathe in. Breathe out.* Is this what a panic attack feels like? I massage my temples, forcing myself to focus on the notes in front of me. Tracing Arty's lineage helps to center me, my breathing slowly returning to normal.

"Do you want to eat at the bar?"

I jump, startled. The bartender holds a plate piled high with steaming crispy fish and golden fries. "Oh! Give me one second." I shuffle my papers around, attempting to stack them in some semblance of order. He sets the plate down on the spot I cleared, grabs my empty glass, and heads back to the bar. I sigh in relief. That wasn't so bad. I break a fry in half, blowing on it before taking a tiny bite. A frosty glass of beer plunks on the table from over my shoulder. His shadow looms over me from behind the bench, his hair tickling my collarbone. I shiver.

If he's going to be here regularly, I'll have to break tradition and start sitting on the other side of the booth so he can't surprise me. Hell, who am I kidding? If he's here every day, I'll have to find a different spot to work; there is no way I will be able to concentrate with him around.

"Thank you," I say, my voice husky. I clear my throat, embarrassed.

"My pleasure." He slides into the bench across from me and reaches out his hand. "I'm Jack."

"Charlotte," I say, my hand impossibly small inside his. "My friends call me Charlie." A Celtic tattoo wraps around his left forearm, smaller tattoos scattered over his knuckles.

"It's nice to meet you, Charlotte." His fingers pass over the sensitive skin of my wrist before he releases my hand. "What is all this?" he asks, flipping the paper closest to him so he can read it.

"Careful!"

He chuckles. "Don't worry, I'll be gentle." He winks, his gaze dipping to my lips before returning to reading the paper.

"I'm not so sure," I say under my breath, studying the rough callouses that cover his broad hands.

"Mmm," he hums, the sound so throaty it's almost a moan. I press my thighs together, mortified that one innocent sound could make me react that way.

"I didn't mean it like that," I mutter, covering my cheeks with my hands.

I have to crane my neck as he pushes himself up from the table. He studies me for a second before one side of his mouth quirks up. "I did." He slides the paper toward me with one thick finger. "This is wrong."

I snatch the page from him, examining it.

"Jack, you lazy ass, I need a refill!" someone shouts from the bar. He glances over, scowling at the interruption.

"Stay?" he asks, turning his molten gaze back to me.

"What?"

He squats down, looking up at me through thick eyelashes. "Stay." He sweeps a strand of hair out of my face, tucking it behind my ear. "We close at midnight. I'll tell you what I know about the family you have on this paper if you stay."

I fight the urge to push my cheek into his palm, my scrambled brain failing to send a warning signal.

"Please?" He gives me puppy eyes, a lopsided grin tugging at his lips.

Fuckkk. "Maybe."

He studies me for a second longer, then nods, only turning back to the bar when someone yells his name. "Shut up, you old geezer," he shouts, laughing.

I watch him go, unable to tear my gaze away. I swallow heavily. This feels dangerous.

11

———————

By the time I drink the last of my beer, my laptop is close to dying. I usually don't use it in the pub, but if Jack was right, I have a ton of new research ahead of me. I lean over to look for an outlet under the table. Nothing. Hmph. I scan the wall until I get to the only visible outlet, nothing except for one in the hallway leading to the kitchen. Then I spot one on a support post by the bar. Of fucking course. I debate in my head for thirty seconds, ultimately deciding that it's safer not to put myself anywhere near that specimen of a man.

Jack pulls the laptop from my hands. "You didn't believe me?" He walks over to the bar and plugs it in.

"Believe what?" I ask, trailing behind him.

"When I told you I wouldn't bite."

"No, I don't believe that at all."

"Good girl." He winks, his eyes sparkling.

This is bad. *Really bad.*

I settle myself on the stool and open the laptop, ignoring him. *Trying* to ignore him.

"Beer?" he asks, his hand poised over an empty glass behind the bar.

"Please," I drop my gaze, determined to keep working.

I'm finally starting to make some headway when the music turns down and the lights on the far side of the pub turn off. I look up to see Jack flipping chairs over the tables and sweeping under them. I check my watch – it's past midnight. I hop down and slide the laptop into my bag, startled by how much time had slipped past.

"I meant it when I said I would help you," Jack says, walking over to me, "Just give me a few more minutes to finish cleaning up."

"Let me at least help." I hold my hand out for the broom.

He hesitates before gently placing it in my hand. "Thank you, lass." He pulls the towel from his shoulder and starts wiping down the bar. I watch his muscles move under his skin, the broom forgotten. He freezes, evidently feeling my gaze, but he doesn't turn. I pick up sweeping where he left off, trying desperately to keep my eyes on the floor. I hear him push through the kitchen doors, and I take a deep breath, shaking the tension out of my body. I'm finishing up as he shoulders back through the kitchen door, holding two steaming plates of pasta.

"I'm starving and figure you might be, too? It's been a while since you ate."

"Thank you." I can't help the grin as I hand him the broom, sliding into the seat he's holding for me. I twirl the pasta around my fork, ultra-aware of how close he's sitting to me. "You know, I think this may be the first meal a man has made for me, " I blurt, wincing as I realize how pathetic it sounds.

"I'm glad I'm your first," he winks, raising his loaded fork in salute. "I take that back," he says, his expression darkening. "I can see the indent from a wedding ring. He never cooked for you? Not once? In how many years?"

"We were married five years," I whisper, mortified.

"Fuck him." He twirls the pasta around his fork and holds it out to me.

My stomach flutters as I take the bite, his warm honey gaze sliding over me.

The pasta is delicious, a velvety cream sauce enrobes each strand, bits of prosciutto and peas dotting my plate. Jack finishes his plate first, nursing a beer while he waits for me to finish. I watch with fascination as he drinks. His Adam's apple bobbing, the slow wipe of his hand across his lips. The small sigh of satisfaction after each gulp. I want those lips on me. I want to hear him sigh with my mouth around his cock. I squirm in my seat. Fucking hell.

He clears our plates once I finish and then asks me to spread my papers out on the bar. It isn't wide enough for all generations, so I only show him the maternal grandparents and great-grandparents. He studies them for a minute before turning back to me. "What's this for, exactly?"

"A family tree for a good friend. We're both doing each other a favor, I think."

"Is this what you do for your job?" He runs his finger over some of the rough sketches I doodled in the margins.

"Yeah. Well, I mean, it's what I used to do. This is my first one in years."

"Why?"

I grimace. "That's a long story."

"Let me guess. Your ex made you stop?" His eyes flash with something I can't quite place.

I start to protest, taken aback by the anger in his words, but I bite my tongue instead. I'm not going to make excuses anymore. "You're right," I admit, fighting the shame that washes through me.

"Hey." He pushes my chin up with his fingers. "I'm glad you're here doing something you love. That's all anyone can ask for." He smiles, his hand lingering, his gaze dipping to my lips.

I break the tension, looking through the pages to find the one he had singled out. "Here." I slide it over to him. "This is where you said I made a mistake. I spent the last few hours reviewing the connections, but I'm having difficulty locating records. Any ideas?"

"You would need to go to Harris for that."

"Harris? Why? And how do you know that?"

He laughed, "I grew up there. These are the last names of all my mates, so I can only imagine they must be their great-great grandparents, although, as you've probably noticed, there aren't many surnames in Scotland, so I could be wrong."

I scribble *Harris* down on the page, hoping he's right. "Any other tips?" I ask, hopeful.

"That's all I have. I suppose I could have told you that and not made you stay, but I'm glad I did." He gathers the papers, careful to collect them in order. I place them in their folder and slide them carefully next to my laptop in my bag.

The song playing over the speakers changes to something slow and sweet.

"Dance with me," he says, holding out his hand, letting me decide if I want to take it or not.

"I can't dance," I protest, flashbacks from junior high filling my head. I reach out anyway, and he pulls me in, tucking me against his chest. One hand holds mine, the other spans the entire width of my waist. I can feel him through my sweater – he burns my skin like a sip of whisky. I melt into him, following his lead. He spins me out, his hand grazing the side of my breast as he pulls me back in. My heart races as he folds me into his chest, his hand pressing against my lower back, tilting my pelvis. He moves his leg between mine, not missing a single beat. A couple more steps and the pressure from his leg sets me on fire. He dips me back, his body arching over me, his breath hot against my ear. He swings me into an upright position, his face inches from mine.

I jump at the loud clapping coming from the kitchen area and take a large step away from Jack. "I'm finished, boss. Just wanted to let you know before I left." I look over Jack's shoulder to see a middle-aged man with a twinkle in his eye. He winks at me as he pulls his apron off and heads back into the kitchen.

"He would do that, the jerk." Jack smiles ruefully. He flips our stools, sets them on the bar, and then props the broom in the corner. "As much as I would love to do this all night, I have to catch the early ferry. Can I give you a ride?" He takes my bag from me, slinging it over his shoulder.

"You don't *have* to do that," I protest, "I'm right up the road."

"Do you really think I would be okay with you walking home alone at two in the morning? I would be up all night worrying about you." His hand is warm on my back as he guides me out the door, turning to lock up. I look around the lot for his car, but the only thing in it is a vintage motorcycle.

"Oh no," I say, shaking my head as he tosses me a helmet.

"Oh, yes." He grins, holding out his jacket, encouraging me to slip my arms in. The smell of leather and rain envelope me. I never want to take it off.

He throws one leg over the bike, pushing down a pedal with his foot. He's entirely at ease and it's easily one of the hottest things I've ever seen. Barring the last night I had with Cameron, of course. I push the memory into a box and slam the lid closed before it can escape again. The engine roars to life. "Get on!" he yells, motioning to the tiny space behind him.

Not thrilled with the idea of walking home alone either, I straddle the bike, trying my best to keep some distance between us. He looks over his shoulder and laughs, wrapping his hands around each of my legs and pulling me snugly against his back. "Don't want you falling off, now do we?" I grab his middle and squeeze my eyes shut as he pulls out of the parking spot.

"Where to, Sassenach?"

"The bookstore," I choke out. This is turning into some Jamie Fraser-type shit and I am fucking here for it.

"Of course, where else could you possibly be staying," he yells, pulling to an elegant stop and cutting the engine.

I pull off the helmet and flip my head upside down to gather my hair into an unruly bun. He watches me, leaning against the bike, one boot resting on the curb. His arms are crossed over his chest, his muscles on full display. I shrug off his jacket and drape it over the bike, scared to meet his gaze. This man is trouble. I can feel it in my bones. I stand there for a second, unsure of what to say.

"Thank you for the ride, Jack." I stick out my hand, realizing how stupid I look a second too late. He grabs my fingers and pulls me into a gentle embrace. I close my eyes and melt into him, allowing myself to live in the moment. He rests his chin on my head for a couple of seconds before burying his face in my neck, hugging me tightly. He inhales, squeezing me between his expanding chest and vice-like arms.

"Are you smelling me?" I tease, pulling back to look at him.

His answering growl lodges low in my belly. Heat floods to my center making me squeeze my thighs together. His pupils blow out wide. My knees wobble. I watch emotion war over his face until one wins and he disentangles himself from me and deposits me back onto the sidewalk.

"It was very nice to meet you, Charlotte." He raises my palm to his mouth, his facial hair a delicious contrast to the softness of his lips.

"Call me Charlie," I correct softly, squeezing my hand tight when he releases it.

"You told me your friends call you Charlie." He cups my face, brushing his thumb over my bottom lip. "I have no intention of being your friend, Charlotte."

Oh fuck.

He slips the helmet over his head, flipping up the visor to wink at me before peeling out.

I gaze at the stars, wishing he hadn't left, wishing I had pulled him off his bike and up to my flat. I don't know what this is, but it feels wild and out of control – feelings I had always guarded myself against. My nerve endings are firing a mile a minute: danger, lust, excitement, a bit of panic. Maybe *this* is what life is supposed to be like.

It wasn't until the next morning that I realize he didn't ask me for my number.

12

I spend the next few days figuring out my plans for Harris, simultaneously trying not to obsess over Jack and keeping Cameron stuffed in a box. I'm not successful.

Harris is a tiny island off the western coast of Scotland in a chain of islands called the Outer Hebrides. I can only find one house available for a few weeks. It looks cute online but I'm worried it's going to turn out to be a complete shit hole. I plan to rent a car on the day of the ferry departure. The thought of having to drive on the left side of the road terrifies me, but I don't see what choice I have with how remote Harris is. Plus, I am starting to feel brave enough to explore.

The night before my departure, I head back to the pub one last time. There's a woman bartending who has no clue who Jack is. I leave my number anyway, my heart heavy as I push through the door one last time.

The ferry is enormous, closer to the size of a small cruise ship. The workers direct me to my parking spot, only inches from the car in front of me. Instead of fighting everyone else for a seat inside, I head directly to the top deck and position myself at the front of the boat. The wind is wild and unrelenting. I love it. I don't go inside until I'm so cold I can barely feel my fingers. I order a coffee from the little cafe on board and find an empty seat, using the downtime to read the book I've been hanging on to since my flight from home. Before I know it, there's an announcement for everyone to head back to their cars and listen for further instructions. I let the rush die for a couple of minutes before heading to the stairs. At the bottom of the stairwell, in a crush of people, there's a man that stands over the rest – tawny hair, a rugged beard, a beat-up jacket covering broad shoulders. My heart flies to my throat.

"Jack!" I shout, desperately trying to push past people. The final announcement sounds over the speakers, and lights flash a warning. He looks up at me, but I know there's not anything either of us can do. Tears prick at my eyes as I watch him get carried away by the crowd. I make my way back to my car, angry at myself. Angry at the universe. I drive off the ferry when it's my turn, my foot light on the pedal, trying to give myself extra time to spot him. I park in a spot where I have a clear view of the rest of the vehicles coming off the ferry. My heart is filled with the most dangerous thing known to humankind: hope. There's no sign of him or his motorcycle.

God fucking damn it. I slam my hands against the steering wheel. Then I take a deep breath, put my big girl panties on and punch in the Airbnb address.

These islands are a type of wild I haven't ever experienced before. The drive over from the neighboring island is terrifying, but I can't help be in total awe of the beauty surrounding me. I pull into every scenic pull-off to take pictures, my bones permanently chilled by the time I turn onto the road of the rental address. As a gorgeous stone manor house comes into view, my foot eases off the gas. I pull into the circular drive and cut the engine, stepping out of the car in awe. The house itself is beautiful, but beyond it is a charming storybook cottage that looks just like the pictures online. Past that lies the true stunner: a castle perched on the edge of a loch, towers like fingers reaching up to the sun's warmth. I wrap my arms around myself, freezing cold but unable to tear my gaze from the view.

Gravel crunches under my feet as I walk to the front door, making me thankful I wore my chucks. I knock lightly on the door, then use the bell when no one answers. I'm just starting to walk back to the car to grab my phone when the door swings open, and a black and white speed demon shoots out, knocking me on my butt.

"Milo! Down boy!" his owner yells, clapping to get his dog's attention.

"Oh no, he's fine," I laugh, scratching Milo's ears, the cold forgotten. He is the most beautiful dog I've ever seen – silky patches of black and white hair, eyes the color of milk chocolate.

"Are you a good boy, Milo?" I coo, enjoying his slobbery kisses.

"Milo, come now. Leave the lady alone."

A strong hand extends toward me. I grasp it, letting him help me up. His fingers brushed over my palm sending sparks shooting through me. I take a step back. "I don't think I realized how much I missed having a dog around," I say, brushing off the seat of my pants.

"I'm Lachlan, and you must be Charlotte?" He asks, reaching toward me for a handshake.

The sparks fizz through me again as his hand closes around mine. "Please, call me Charlie." I had expected Lachlan to be much, much older than he is. He's at least six inches taller than me, sandy hair ruffling in the wind. Freckled hazel eyes gaze back at me, openly curious. He's cute. Really cute. He doesn't have an accent, and it's almost startling after hearing nothing but Scottish accents for the past few weeks.

"You'll have to forgive me. It seems like you caught me in the middle of a nap," he chuckles, running his fingers through his disheveled hair. "Give me one second, and I'll grab the keys to the cottage?"

"Of course." I smile. "Take your time. I'll just play with Milo here."

Lachlan nods, then goes back inside, leaving the door ajar.

He comes back out in less than a minute, looking slightly more put together, a pair of keys dangling from his hand. "Unfortunately, the lane is not wide enough to drive the car down to the cottage, but you picked the perfect time to come. The walk should be pleasant most days."

"That's fine with me," I say as I open the trunk of my car. Lachlan whisks the suitcases out before I can protest. "You don't have to do that!"

Lachlan turns and smiles, dimples flashing. "You're right, but I want to."

"Well, thank you."

"You're welcome. So, tell me what brings you here to this forsaken corner of Scotland."

"I'm working on a family tree," I say, following him down the rocky path.

"Ahhh, that's what brought me back here years ago."

"Oh? Where are you from?"

"I'm from here – I grew up just down the road – but I went to a boarding school in England, then university in America before coming back."

"That sounds amazing. I would have given anything to be able to get away from home for high school and college," I say wistfully.

"It's not all it's cracked up to be." Lachlan grimaces. "Trust me." Grief flashes in his eyes briefly before he locks it down.

I study his face for a second. The smattering of freckles over his nose stand out in stark relief against his porcelain skin. His eyes are an amazing blue-green-hazel color... and they're looking back at me. Shit.

"Oh my God. Sorry." My cheeks burn. "I must be a little tired from the drive."

Lachlan raised his eyebrow, his lips twisting suspiciously. "After you." He gestures for me to open the cottage door. I push against the worn wood of the door, painted the prettiest sky-blue color. The interior white-washed tongue-and-groove butting against the thick beams that supported the vaulted ceiling. The wall facing the loch is made of windows that stretch from floor to ceiling. The castle rises straight from the water like a fairytale haunt. I could already envision coffee on the deck in the mornings, watching the mist rise from the water. As much as I adored Millie's flat, I knew I would never want to leave this place.

"Charlie?" Lachlan says, bringing me out of my daydream.

I smile sheepishly "It's so beautiful here."

"Isn't it though?" He joins me at the window, gazing out over the water. He looks at the view a few seconds longer, then turns to me. "Before I go, I wanted to show you how to work the stove; it can be a bit temperamental."

"Lead the way!" He spends the next ten minutes showing me the house's quirks, making sure I have the gist of everything before he heads back toward the door.

"If you have questions about anything, I left my phone number on the pad of paper on the counter." He hesitates, his hand poised above the doorknob. "Join me at the local pub tonight for supper?"

"That sounds great. Pretty sure I'm not running back to get groceries tonight anyway."

"Perfect. Meet me up at the house at six." He grins, dimples flashing. My breath catches in my throat. I take back what I said about him being cute earlier. He's not. He's fucking hot.

13

I take my time unpacking and spend way too long in the shower. By the time I'm swiping on some lip gloss, it's close to six. I pull on a pair of distressed jeans, a soft brown leather jacket, and boots and head up to the house. Lachlan is waiting for me beside a sexy forest green Jaguar. A woman around my age stands beside him, bouncing on the balls of her feet.

"Charlie, this is Isla."

Isla rushes in for a hug. "It's so good to have another girl around! Usually, it's just me and the guys unless I go into Stornoway," She beams, golden eyes sparkling.

"It's nice to meet you." I return her smile, loving her already. Her ruby red hair is piled on top of her head in a messy knot, pieces escaping to frame her peaches and cream complexion. She wears what looks like several layers under her jacket and ripped overalls. Duck boots round out her look. She's freaking adorable.

I turn toward Lachlan's steady gaze. He looks posh in his gray sweater, dark jeans, and loafers.

"Ready?" He opens the door for me while Isla scrambles into the back seat on the driver's side.

It only takes about five minutes to reach the pub. It's in the castle's shadow, the towers rising so high they made me dizzy.

"Is Jay not coming?" Isla asked Lachlan, her gaze scanning the cars in the parking lot.

"No, he's chasing after his new woman and doesn't have time for us anymore." He makes a face, but his eyes are dancing.

"Who's Jay?" I ask, confused.

"Her older—"

"—and uglier," Isla chimes in.

"—brother," Lachlan finishes, laughing. "I've known both of them since we were mates in grade school."

"You two aren't together?" I ask, sitting in the chair Lachlan pulls out for me.

"Hell, no." Isla shudders.

Lachlan laughs. "I live in the manor house because I work with Jay on the farm. Isla lives there because she prefers it over living with her brother."

"I prefer it over him knowing everything about my sex life," she amends.

"Understandable," I laugh.

"Are you single?" she asks, glancing up from the menu.

I hesitate, then nod. I wish I wasn't. I've been doing pretty well except at night when I would give up almost anything to see his face. Run my hands through his hair. Fuck.

"Oh God, did I stick my foot in my mouth?" Isla asks, her eyes round.

"No, I was dating a guy, but he had to leave the country for work. It wasn't ever anything official."

"Good. You and I can go on the hunt together. I need some action." She wiggles her eyebrows comically. Lachlan pretends to gag next to her, plugging his ears in case she says anything else. She snorts and rolls her eyes.

The waiter sets the check on the table. Before I can react, Lachlan places his card on it and hands it back. "Let me pay my part!" I protest, placing some bills on the table.

Lachlan's hand covers mine, pushing it away. "Just think of it as a 'Welcome to Harris' meal. I have a feeling we're going to be doing this a lot – you can pay another time." He pulls his hand away slowly, his fingertips tracing my fingers. Butterflies attack my stomach as I meet his eyes. Lord have mercy.

"Deal," I rasp, clearing my throat. I try to act normal, but it's hard when his gaze is pure heat.

"Let's go!" Isla says, pushing Lachlan out of the booth, oblivious to the tension.

My mind is in a whirlwind on the five-minute drive back. I feel horribly guilty that I've met two guys that I find insanely attractive since Cameron left. My brain knows we ended things cleanly, but my heart tells me I'm cheating. Lachlan's voice pulls me out of my personal hell.

"Beach?" He asks Isla, pulling into the driveway of the manor house.

"I can't. I have work to do before the party starts. You should show Charlie, though." She looks at me. "You'll love it."

"Sure." I shrug. "It's not like I have anything else planned."

"Let's go then." Lachlan swings his keys over his finger. "You can change if you want to. Although what you're wearing is perfectly fine to walk on the beach."

"What do you usually wear?" I ask, wondering if he usually goes swimming.

"Usually, a group of us play rugby or football, so I wear my gym clothes."

"Is the rugby ball like an American football?"

"A little bigger. I do have a football, though – someone's kid left it. Want me to bring it?"

I nod. "I'll meet you back out here in five?"

He grins. "Perfect."

I jog back to the cottage, careful not to twist an ankle on the rocks. I root through my suitcase until I find a loose t-shirt, sports bra, and joggers. I pair it with a pair of athletic sandals.

Lachlan is already waiting by the time I make my way back up. He grins at me, his eyes sparkling. He's in a well-loved t-shirt and basketball shorts, a football in his arm.

"Ready?"

I nod and hop in the car. I've heard great things about the beaches here and can't wait to finally see one in person. We drive about ten minutes on a single-track road before Lachlan turns off, bumping across a small parking area. Bright green hills fill up the entire windshield.

"We have to walk over the dunes to get to the beach," he explains when he sees my confusion.

"Those are dunes?" I look at them in wonder. They're huge – at least a few stories high.

"Hard to believe, isn't it? Especially with all that grass. It's much more obvious from the beach side." He opens my door and pulls me out of the car, his fingers linking with mine. My heart gallops in my chest as we walk along the path. There are fences on either side; big, hairy cows munching on the greenest grass I have ever seen. The path takes us over the top of the dune and then winds down to the beach.

"Holy shit," I breathe as I get the first glimpse of the beach. The tide is out, and the beach goes on for what has to be a mile. Dark mountains frame the turquoise water.

"I love when people see the beauty of our island for the first time," he murmurs, his gaze heavy on my skin.

"You don't take it for granted, do you?" I ask.

"Never. Someday people will find what we have here and want it for themselves. Until then, I will treasure every peaceful day I have on these deserted beaches." He tosses me the football.

"I like that," I say, palming the football and walking backward a few steps. He holds his hands up, but I'm still way too close. I raise my eyebrow and jog back a dozen or so more steps. I get ready to throw the ball, but he doesn't change positions, still standing there with both hands out. "This is *football,* Lachlan. Get ready to run."

He readjusts half-heartedly. I step back and throw the ball, aiming for a few yards past him to his left. I watch his eyes follow the ball, his jaw dropping slightly. He reaches his arm out a second too late.

"Fucking hell, Charlie!" he yells as he jogs to retrieve the ball.

"I warned you!" I laugh, positioning myself as he draws his arm back. The ball sails toward me, his throw hard and straight. I push myself across the sand, my calves screaming. The slap of the ball against my arms makes me grin. I love when people don't take it easy on me just because I'm a girl. I throw it back. He's ready this time. I watch him jump into the air, the trajectory of the ball throwing him back into the sand. A couple more throws, and he's peeling off his shirt, sweat glistening on tan skin. I'm distracted by his abs the next time he throws the ball, and I miss catching it by a couple of inches. I throw it back at him. Hard. His fingertips barely snag the ball. He throws it down to the sand, doing a little victory dance. The evening light gilds every single muscle. My mouth is like the Sahara in a drought. My heart stutters. Holy fuck. I swallow, licking my lips. I need to get control of myself.

"You okay?" he laughs.

"I'm good," I mumble, unable to keep a grin from spreading over my face.

He jogs toward me, all hot and sweaty and gorgeous. I do the first thing that pops into my head – turn toward the water and run. I pump my arms, pushing my legs as hard as they'll go. He splashes into the water a second after me, twisting under me as he tackles me to the sand. We freeze, our gazes locked. A wave crashes into us, arcing over our bodies.

"Fuck, this is hot," Lachlan breathes. He pushes my hair away from my face and cradles my head in his hands. Another wave crashes over us, the force knocking us apart, shattering the moment.

It's pitch black when we pull back into the curved driveway at the house. His hand is warm in mine as he pulls me out of the car. I hold on for a second longer than I should, and his thumb swipes over my palm, leaving my skin tingling.

"I'll walk you down to the cottage. Can't have you breaking an ankle on your first night here." He says, rummaging in his trunk and pulling out a flashlight. He grabs my hand again, almost as if by reflex, then drops it abruptly.

"Sorry," he mutters, continuing on the path. I slam into him when he stops suddenly. His hands wrap around my waist, steadying me. With the flashlight pointing at the ground, I can only see the glitter of his eyes. "If I'm being completely honest, I'm not sorry." He stares down at me, emotions warring in his eyes. Finally, he turns, linking his fingers with mine, not letting go this time. "Why do I feel like I've known you for years?" he rasps, leading me toward the cottage.

I clear my heart out of my throat. "I've always thought it means we were connected in a past life. Nothing else makes sense."

He nods as if it makes perfect sense. We stop at the cottage's front door, the light haloing his head. He clicks off his flashlight and pockets it, grabbing my other hand in his. "I don't want to say goodnight." Pulling our linked hands up, he traces my fingers with his other hand.

"Then don't," I blurt. I take a deep breath. "Is there anything to drink in there?"

"Of course. What kind of a host do you think I am?"

"Come on, then." I pull him inside, closing the door against the blustery wind.

"Charlie." He pauses, hanging his coat on the hook. "I didn't come in because I expect anything. Just want to get that out in the open."

"I know." I smile. He pushes a broad hand through his hair, his watch glinting in the dim light. "How 'bout I make a fire, and you pour us something to drink?"

"Deal."

I put my rusty girl scout skills to work and have the fire going by the time Lachlan returns with two glasses of amber liquid.

"Impressive." He nods toward the fire.

"To my barely adequate fire-making skills." I raise my glass, and we clink them together, our gazes locked as we take a sip. "Oh my God," I groan, "this is amazing."

His chin drops, his eyes darkening. He clears his throat. "It's a family recipe. My grandfather taught me how to make an Old Fashioned. It's been my go-to drink ever since."

"I can see why." I take another sip, the slow burn lighting me up like a live wire. Lachlan drops into a chair, crossing his ankle over his knee, his shoulders relaxed. He looks elegant despite wearing a t-shirt and shorts. "You don't look like you work on a farm," I observe, sitting on the sofa, folding my legs under me.

He laughs, his eyes softening. "You're right. I oversee the financial side." He takes a sip of his drink, catching a drop from the side of the glass with his tongue. I inhale sharply as his gaze locks with mine. "Don't look at me like that, Charlie."

"Like what?" I ask, trying to keep my breathing even.

"Like *that*," he growls, setting his glass on a coaster.

I drop my gaze, but it lands squarely on his crotch.

Fuck.

I close my eyes, but all I see is his hard length straining against his zipper. I plunk the glass down and stand, walking to the window. The lights flick off, then strong arms wrap around my waist. His chest to my back, the smell of citrus and wood enveloping me. I'm about to question the lights, but my eyes start to adjust, and I see the waves crashing far below, moonlight reflecting off the water. My heartbeat is a steady anthem in my ears. I relax my muscles and drop my head back, resting it against his shoulder.

"You smell so good," he murmurs, his lips pressed to my hair. He sweeps it off my neck, pressing his lips to the sensitive skin below my ear. He pulls back slightly, nuzzling my hair. He presses a kiss on my head. "I'm going to say goodnight, Charlie. I want to stay, but the second I touched you my willpower went out the window. If this is going somewhere, I don't want to get there fast. I want to enjoy it." He turns me around, nudging my chin up. "Is that okay?"

"Yes," I whisper, pretty sure that was one of the hottest things anyone had ever said to me. He studies me for a second, making sure

I understand, then brushes his lips over mine, his touch light and fast. He takes a step back, his hands dropping away from me slowly.

He grabs his jacket and pauses at the front door. "Goodnight, Charlie."

"Goodnight, Lach," I manage. The second he closes the door, I strip and step into a freezing cold shower. But even that doesn't wipe the huge grin off my face.

14

———

I open my eyes a fraction, my vision foggy with sleep, trying to figure out what had woken me up.

Thump, thump, thump.

I rub my eyes and stumble to the front door, cracking it just enough to see who's outside.

"Morning, Charlie!" Isla's smile is way too bright for this early in the morning.

"Morning," I mumble, hoping she'll be quick so I can go back to bed.

"Breakfast is ready," she says. "I tried to text, but you didn't answer—"

"Breakfast?"

"Did you think I would let you sit by yourself in this tiny cold cottage?" She fists her hands on her hips.

"Yes?"

She scoffs, reaching through the door to grab my jacket off the peg. "Arms in." She holds it out so I can slip my arms in.

I follow her to the house, unsure how I feel about the situation. I'm not used to this type of friendship.

I decide I'm one hundred percent okay with it the second I walk through their front door and smell the coffee. The house is big, but it's decorated in a way that makes it feel cozy. Shelves filled with books and trinkets cover the walls. Rugs are strewn across the scarred wood floor. Milo bounds up to me, spinning in circles before sitting at my feet. I croon to him and scratch his ears before following Isla into the kitchen. Lachlan is there, clad in only an apron and boxers.

"Morning, love." He winks at me. "Sorry for the lack of dress; *someone* didn't tell me she was going to fetch you."

"Don't lie," Isla pouted. "You just wanted her to see your muscles."

"I don't mind," I smile, biting my lip.

He clears his throat when he sees me ogling his ass.

I laugh, "You do have nice muscles, Lachlan." I shrug like it isn't a big deal.

"Oh, stop it! His ego is already big enough." Isla flops into a chair, motioning for me to sit. "Lachlan, will you get us coffee, please?"

"Anything for you, Princess." He rolls his eyes at the back of her head.

"Do you have plans today?" Isla asks me, taking a mug from Lachlan.

"Not really. I was planning to start on my research, but that's flexible."

"Good, it's settled then."

"What's settled?" I ask as Lachlan sets a platter of eggs, salmon, and potatoes on the table. It smells heavenly.

"We're going shopping."

"Shopping?" My empty pockets cry.

"Jay's throwing a party in a couple of days; we need to get all the stuff for it. It will be boring with just Lachlan, so please come with us." She looked at me with big doe eyes, blinking several times slowly.

"Okay," I laugh, spearing a potato and blowing on it before popping it in my mouth. Isla grins, bouncing in her seat, her gigantic bun flopping around her head. "What kind of party is it?"

"It's a masquerade ball!" Isla breathes, practically swooning. "It's the best night of the year, you'll see."

"That's a big claim when I'm usually not the type of person that likes parties."

Isla looks personally affronted, but before she can say anything, Lachlan butts in, "So tell us, then, Charlie," Lachlan begins, taking off his apron. "Who are you?" I make sure to keep my eyes above his chin this time.

"Ummm..." I take another bite, thinking. "I'm a girl that's sick of letting shit happen to her, so instead, I'm learning how to make shit happen." Fuck, that sounded prophetic.

"I like you, Charlie," Isla says, eyes sparkling over a wide grin.

"I like you, too," I laugh, "So what's on the agenda?"

Isla pulls a folded piece of paper out of her back pocket and reads off the list, ticking each one off on her fingers. "Grocery, florist, hardware store, party supply. I know that's a lot, but we can go out and have some fun afterward. Maybe it'll make up for it."

Lachlan pushes away from the table. "Meet you both back here in twenty minutes."

"Thanks for breakfast!" I call as I head for the front door.

The day flashes by in a whirlwind. Store after store, shopping bag after shopping bag until they're crowded around Isla in the back of the car.

"I need to buy a truck," Isla grumbles as she squeezes herself into the back, declining, yet again, to sit in the front.

"What kind of car do you have?"

"I have a mustang and a motorcycle."

I twist in my seat to face her. "Damn! Seriously?" It's hard to imagine her tiny body on a motorcycle.

"Seriously." She beams. "They're my pride and joy. I'll show you next time we have a chance."

"Are we still going to do the 'fun' part I was promised this morning?" Lachlan asks as we get in the car after the last store.

"Let's go skating! It's right there!" Isla begs, pointing out the skating center.

"Don't you have to work tomorrow?" Lachlan asks.

"And?"

"Fine. Are you good with that, Charlie?" He glances over at me, his eyes glowing in the evening light.

"I haven't been skating since elementary school, but I'm willing to try."

"I'll help you," Lachlan says, cocking his eyebrow when I blush. I get out of the car before my body can give anything else away.

It's dark inside; black lights and smoke machines are everywhere. Lachlan pays again, completely ignoring my protestations. The three of us sit side-by-side on a bench lacing up our skates. Lachlan is next to me, his thigh pressed to mine, his arm brushing against mine every time he pulls at his laces. Every touch sends sparks shooting through me, each one lodging in my core until I'm on fire. Lachlan finishes before me and crouches down, helping me with my other skate.

"I've enjoyed spending time with you today," he whispers after Isla pushes away from the bench. He ties the bow and rests his hands on my knees, starting to push himself up. Before he can stand, I pull his face to mine, pressing my lips to his. He cradles my head with his hand, his fingers threading through my hair. His tongue swipes over my bottom lip before he bites it softly. Every nerve ending in my body comes alive. He pushes off me smoothly, skating backward with his hands held out to me. I stand up slowly, shuffling my feet toward him.

"Take my hands."

"How will you skate if I'm holding your hands?" I ask, envious of the people flying around the rink.

"Trust me, Charlie." He beckons with his fingers; I grab onto him and immediately lose control. My feet start to slip out from under me, but Lach grabs me around my waist, steadying me. He moves back as soon as I have my balance, taking my hands in his once more. He helps me step down onto the rink, and we skate a slow lap. I cling to the wall when we get close to our starting point, waving at Lach to keep going. He skates away – still backward – holding my gaze. He grins before flipping around. My mouth hangs open as I watch him skate. His movements are fluid, weaving in and out, turning forward and back.

"Get ready!" he says on his second pass.

"Ready for what?" I ask, but he's already halfway around the rink. I shriek as he skates up behind me, barely slowing. He scoops me up in his arms, one hand gripping under my knees and the other around my back. I wrap my arms around him in a vice grip.

"Trust me," he whispers, his breath hot on my ear.

I force myself to relax my muscles as we zoom around the rink. Two laps in, the mood in the rink changes as a sweet, slow song comes on. Lach skates to the center of the rink and sets me down gently, running one hand down my calf to my foot, angling it forward so the toe stop is pressed to the floor.

"That will help you keep your balance," he murmurs, pulling my arms up around his neck and then wrapping his around my waist. I look around and spot Isla among a sea of couples swaying back and forth in time to the music.

"Are you enjoying yourself?"

"Other than feeling like I may break my neck any second, yes," I chuckle, my gaze fixed on the freckle on the edge of his lip.

He cups my chin, running his thumb along my jawline. "I like you," he whispers, a tentative smile pulling at his lips.

My heart jumps to my throat. "No," I rasp, " I have to leave in a couple of months."

"Too late, Charlie." His thumb pulls at my bottom lip, and I groan as heat pools in my center. "We may as well see where it goes," he whispers, his lips a hairsbreadth from mine.

He was right. It was too late. I liked him from the first moment I saw him. I sink into his lips, pushing my fingers into the hair at the nape of his neck, groaning as he devours me. The song ends far too soon, replaced by an electronic dance beat. We break the kiss, staring at each other, wide-eyed.

Isla grabs my hand a second later and drags me away from him. She commandeers me for the rest of the night, even shooing Lach off to bed when we get home so we can have some girl time. I'm disappointed, but thankful for the time to cool down and get my head on straight.

15

———————

Isla comes barging through my door on the day of the party at an ungodly hour, shooing me into her car, barely giving me time to pull on a pair of jeans and a hoodie.

"How in God's name do you have so much energy this early in the morning?" I grumble, taking the cup of coffee she's pressing into my hands.

Isla grins, shifting gears as we round a curve, "Aren't you excited?" she asks, glancing over at me, her eyes sparkling.

"Not particularly," I say, deadpan.

"Charlie!"

"It's a costume party, Isla. I don't have a costume. And in case you haven't noticed, I'm not one to dress up."

"Oh, come on, live a little." She nudges me with her elbow. "You don't even need to worry about the costume. I have something perfect at home. Just relax today, okay? When's the last time you've had a girls' day?"

"Never."

"Well, there ya go. It's not going to hurt you to have your hair, makeup, and nails done... with as much bubbly as we want."

"That sounds marginally better," I say, pretty sure alcohol will be the only thing that gets me through the day. I don't have anything against the girly stuff, it just doesn't come naturally.

Isla and I sit side by side through our appointments, and I take the opportunity to get to know her better. I learn that she's my age, hasn't ever had a serious boyfriend, and bartends at the local pub. She has so many facets – super sweet and bubbly on the surface, but bubbly people don't usually ride motorcycles and bartend. She's fascinating.

We arrive back home hours later, my hair piled on top of my head, tiny ringlets escaping in just the right places. My makeup initially startled me, but every time I glance in a mirror, I fall in love with it a little more. It makes me appear to be half-woman and half-fawn. Shadows and highlights work together to transform my face into something animalistic and ethereal. Butterflies are already fluttering in my stomach. I take a deep breath, mentally making the decision that I'll enjoy myself tonight; this is the first (and probably last) time I'll be going to a costume party. Especially a costume party in a castle. In Scotland. A shiver races down my spine, the suspense thick.

Isla pulls me into her house, insisting we get ready together. The front hall is dark and cozy, a set of imposing walnut stairs to one side and a hallway on the other. I follow her up the stairs, admiring the chandelier that is easily the size of my bedroom in the cottage. "Come on!" Isla urges, ushering me through the door she's holding open. "Wait there." She pushes me down onto a huge four-poster monster of a bed and disappears through a door, coming out a second later with a frothy cream dress in her arms.

"This is gorgeous," I whisper, running my fingers over the folds of fabric.

"Wait until you see it on!" She lays it across the bed and returns to the closet, rummaging around some more, coming comes back with gold slippers, an assortment of gold jewelry, and a hairpiece. "Strip!" she commands, removing the dress from the hanger with gentle hands.

I slip off my jeans and hoodie, tossing them into the chair in the corner of the room.

"Arms up."

I do what she says, the cool silk gliding over my skin and giving me goosebumps. The fabric is gathered on one shoulder, adorned with an intricate gold brooch. The material fits tight to my breasts, then falls in a swirling waterfall to my feet. Isla fastens a gold chain around my waist, the end disappearing into the fabric around my legs.

She slides a carved gold cuff up my arm to encircle my bicep, then several gold bangles onto my opposite wrist. "One last thing," she whispers, her eyes lighting up. She carefully places a band with gold antlers on my head, fiddling with my hair until only the antlers are visible, high and regal on my head. The effect is mesmerizing.

"You're a magician." I'm in awe as I twist and turn in front of a full-length mirror. The dress floats around my ankles, my nude flats disappearing so I look like a barefoot summertime woodland fairy.

"That's all you, baby. Now go downstairs. Lach should be waiting. I'm sure he's already making a drink and grumbling that we're running late. I'll be down in a sec."

I do what she says, freezing mid-step when I see Lachlan in the kitchen. A high-collared black jacket fits perfectly over his broad shoulders, gold swirling over the lapels and around the collar. A matching mask covers his eyes and one side of his face. He looks like he stepped out of a 19th-century novel.

"Fuck, Charlie," Lachlan breathes, his gaze sliding from my antlers to my slippers, stunned.

"Isla is a miracle worker," I laugh, spinning to give him the full effect.

"Isla has nothing to do with it," he growls, "you're stunning in everything you wear. And I bet even more stunning in what you don't." His teeth sink into his bottom lip, his eyes dark. "Drink?" he asks, snapping an orange peel over a glass of amber liquid.

"Please." Now seems like the perfect time for a little liquid courage.

"You look amazing," I blurt as he hands me the glass.

He ducks his head and murmurs his thanks. I smile as a blush stains his cheeks pink.

"I'll meet you there!" Isla calls from the front door, "Jay came to pick me up – I forgot part of my costume there."

I wonder if I'll get to meet Jay tonight. The elusive older brother. I have to admit I'm a bit intrigued.

The second Isla closes the door, Lach is at my side, pulling me to him. He's careful with my makeup, pushing my chin up with the slightest touch, his lips whisper soft against mine.

He kisses my jaw. "Are you ready to go?" he asks, his breath hot against my skin. I shiver, goosebumps cascading down my arms.

I nod and follow him outside. "So, do I finally get to meet Jay?"

"You might not be so eager once you meet him. He was in an awful mood this morning." Lachlan grimaces. "Your chariot awaits, milady." He opens the car door and sweeps his arm out in a grand gesture.

"Thank you." I smile, carefully folding myself into the tiny seat.

We're pulling into the castle drive after a few minutes, intimidating wrought iron gates and stone pillars marking the entrance. Dark hills lit from behind by the rosy glow of the sunset create a moody background. Fog hovers over the grass, tendrils reaching out to caress the car.

"This has to be the most beautiful thing I've ever seen," I whisper, staring at the castle in awe. Four rounded towers anchor each corner, the expanse between a solid wall of stacked rock. Arched windows spill golden light over the landscaping and frame a beautiful marble staircase that leads to the massive front door.

"Isn't it? It still takes my breath away, and I've been around it my entire life," Lachlan says before he steps out and hands his keys to the valet. He opens my door, helps me out, and then extends his arm to me as we walk to the steps.

Halfway up, the heavy front doors swing open, and Isla bounds out a moment later. "Finally!" She punches Lachlan on the shoulder. "Lookin' good, jerk-face."

Lachlan snorts, "Not so bad yourself, short stuff."

Isla huffs and turns to me, squeezing me into a tight hug. "I'm so glad you're here."

"Me too," I murmur, "You look amazing." Her red hair is braided loosely, tiny tendrils sneaking out to float around her face. She's not wearing a mask. Instead, every exposed inch of her skin has been painted with fish scales in blues, purples, and silvers. She's wearing a purple satin corset and a shimmering green skirt that hugs her body down to her calves, flaring out in a pouf of deep blue iridescent fabric.

"You should have seen what I wore last year," she says, wiggling her eyebrows. Grabbing my hand, she pulls me away from Lach and through the door. "I have to introduce you to Jay." I hold on tight as she leads me through a maze of halls, throngs of people milling around in ridiculously gorgeous costumes. Where did all these people come from? It's more people than I've seen in one place since I left the States. The crowd disappears as we walk further into the interior of the house.

"Jay?" Isla knocks lightly on the frame of a heavy wood door. The door is ajar, firelight reflecting on its surface. She pushes the door open and pulls me into the room. The walls curve around us, and I realize we must be in one of the towers. Stairs wind their way up the wall, the spaces in between filled with thousands of books. Two heavy leather chairs sit in front of the most enormous fireplace I have ever seen. Jay is sitting facing the fire, his back to us. He has an ankle crossed over his knee, gold-ringed fingers drum on the arm of the chair—awareness flares inside me as my gaze trails over the veins on the back of his hand.

"Jay, this is Charlie." I feel frozen in place, but Isla jerks me forward, oblivious.

He's wearing a mask that covers everything but his lips – a lion's face surrounded by a wild mane of hair. Whisky eyes pin me in place, my cheeks heating as he lazily peruses my body. Mortification rips through me as my nipples harden. His gaze narrows on them, his eyes darkening. My heart feels like it's going to explode as I suck in a ragged gasp of air, my vision going black around the edges. I have to get out of this room. I do the only thing I'm good at.

I run.

16

———

"Dance with me, Charlotte."

My heart tumbles in my chest. Jay takes a step closer and leans against the doorframe, far too close to where I'm attempting to disappear into the wall. The neck of his billowing white shirt is open, revealing a fine dusting of hair. Tan riding pants hug his legs – and other things – making it difficult to pull my gaze away. He exudes feline grace, reminding me of a lion stalking his prey.

"I can't dance," I whisper, adrenaline roaring through my veins as I force my gaze back to the dance floor.

"It wasn't a question," he growls. The heat of his hand burns through my dress as he guides me toward the dance floor. He spins me so I'm facing him, placing one hand on my waist.

I grip his muscled shoulder, trying to keep up with his steps and failing miserably.

"Let me lead, Charlotte."

I bristle. "I'm fucking trying." His lips twist, but I can't tell if he's pissed or holding back a smile.

"Close your eyes."

"You have a death wish, don't you?" I mutter under my breath, stumbling over his foot again.

He chuckles, the sound crackling over my skin. "Trust me. Close your eyes."

My body responds to his command before I can retort, and my senses take over. The brush of his wild hair on my bare shoulder. The heat of his fingers caressing my lower back. I shiver as he runs a finger along my spine, goosebumps racing over my skin. He hums deep in his throat, the sound registering in my core. I hate to admit it, but he was right; it was much easier to keep up with his steps this way. I open my eyes again, my attention snagging on his rings. They're intricate skulls, one carved from bone, the other from wood, both inlaid with gold.

I clear my throat, pushing past my nerves. "I like your rings."

His eyes flash dangerously. "They'd look better around your neck."

I stare up at him in shock, a breathless, "Fuck," passing my lips before I clamp them together.

"May I?" Lachlan appears at our sides, his hand grazing my hip. Jay growls his displeasure before handing me over, leaving me with a light brush of his lips over my cheek, the scent of whisky and leather mixing with Lachlan's citrus and wood. I'm pressed between them for a split second, Jay to my front, Lachlan to my back. Desire spikes through me. I bite back a moan, my teeth lodging in my lower lip. Jay exchanges a look with Lachlan, but I can't read it with his mask covering most of his face. Lachlan spins me toward him, my aching nipples brushing against his jacket. I clench my jaw, desperately trying to regain control. Lachlan presses his fingers into my back, melting the tension away.

"You okay, Barley?"

"Barley?"

"Trying out some nicknames. Everyone uses Charlie – I want something different." We sway to the music, Lach studying my face. "What was that back there?"

"What was what?" I play dumb.

"When you were between Jay and me... I felt that little spark—"

"Little?" I blurt. "It was a goddamn explosion" I slap my hand over my mouth and turn away from him. I make it one step before his hand is on my elbow, spinning me back to him and pulling me close.

"It's okay, Harlot."

I squeak in indignation.

"Sorry!" He ducks his head, failing to hide his smile. "It's the only nickname I could think of that rhymed with Charlotte. I'll keep working on it."

"You better," I mutter.

"So that explosion..."

"Bring it up one more time, and I'm going to find something sharp to stab you with."

"God, you're magnificent." His eyes sparkle as he leads me around the dance floor.

LACHLAN COMMANDEERS me for the rest of the evening until I finally manage to escape to the terrace for some air, but I quickly realize I'm not alone. I smell him before I see him —expensive cologne, summer thunderstorms, and leather. As my eyes slowly adjust to the dark, I can make out his silhouette leaning against the outside wall of the castle. Waiting.

Jay's gaze captures mine, solid and steady. "Stay."

"Why?"

"You know why," he growls. Desire pools in my stomach, heavy and warm. My heart works double-time, each beat higher and higher in my throat. He pushes off the wall and stalks toward me. I mirror his movements, stepping back into the grass.

God, he's beautiful – like a beast prowling the castle grounds.

"Run," he breathes. I'm sure I didn't hear him right until I see the look in his eyes, like he's an apex predator and I'm the prey. My fight or flight kicks in, a strangled sound ripping from my throat as I hike up my dress and run. Every cell of my body is vibrating with adrenaline and need. My slippers are slick with dew, my feet so cold I can barely feel them. A laugh bubbles up as I look behind me; he's gaining fast.

"Jay!" Isla yells from the terrace, "Have you seen Charlie? We're about to leave!"

He ignores her, hot on my heels.

I reach a tall boulder and collapse against the far side, struggling to catch my breath.

"Charlie!" Isla calls out, seemingly giving up on Jay answering her. I draw in a breath to shout, but Jay materializes out of the dark, placing a warm finger against my lips.

"Shhh." He settles himself in front of me, his hooded gaze shattering my resistance.

I reach up to slide his mask off, but his fingers circle my wrists, stopping me. "Don't ruin the magic, mo chridhe."

My heart hammers against my ribs so loudly I'm sure he can hear it. I drop my gaze. His hand dwarfs my chin as he cups it and gently pushes it up so I'm looking him in the eyes. "Good girl," he murmurs. He traces his fingers across my chin, over my cheek, and into my hair, cupping the base of my skull. "May I?" he asks, wiggling one of the pins in my hair.

I nod, unable to find words. He carefully pulls the pins from my hair one by one, shaking my hair loose so it falls around my shoulders. "You shouldna wear your hair up," he says, his fingertip following a strand from behind my ear, over my shoulder, and across the upper swell of my chest. I draw in a sharp breath, his finger pressing into the top of my breast for a split second. His gaze drops to my mouth, his touch not far behind. He traces my lower lip, pulling on it gently.

"Why?" I whisper, warring against the lust pulsing through my body.

He grasps a handful of hair at the base of my skull, pulling gently to expose my neck. I moan, melting against him. "That's why," he groans, his lips against my neck.

"Jay!" Isla bellows from a few yards away. He bends and scoops me up without warning, annoyance flashing over his face.

"Look whom I found trying to get to Lallybroch!" Jay says, rounding the stone and heading toward Isla's voice.

Lallybroch? I look over his shoulder, barely able to make out the rock I had been leaning against. It was one of a dozen stones rising like giants from the earth. Goosebumps race down my arms. "If I had realized those were standing stones, I would have been paying more attention to them and less to you," I say under my breath.

"I doubt that, lass," he rumbles, his eyes twinkling behind his mask.

He sets me down on the path, his hand lingering on my back. I catch it in mine and squeeze lightly. "It was nice meeting you, Jay."

"Charlotte," he purrs, pressing a warm kiss to my palm.

Isla grabs my arm and drags me toward the door, but I can't bear to break our eye contact. His face stays in shadow as he removes his mask. I am desperate not to leave. For once in my life, I feel like I *belong*.

"What the heck were you doing by the stones?" Isla asks, startling me out of my fantasy as we head toward the front drive.

"I just wanted to see them," I hedge, not sure I want to talk about what has happened yet.

She looks at me askance. "Well, you're soaked. Lachlan's waiting to take you home."

"What about you?" I look at her closely, noticing the color high on her cheeks.

"A girl never tells her secrets," she laughs.

"You better tell me tomorrow," I grumble.

"You know I will. Goodnight, Charlie." She wraps her arm around my neck and gives me a quick peck on the cheek.

She hands me over to Lachlan at the front of the house. I fold myself into his car, pulling my skirts in so they don't get caught in the door. He drops into the driver's seat, wood and citrus invading my senses.

"Did you have fun?"

"Yes." I grin. "I had an amazing time."

"I hope Jay didn't scare you. He can be... intense."

"He didn't," I say quickly. Too quickly.

Lachlan cocks his eyebrow and chuckles. "He has that effect on most women." His fingers skim over my thigh as he picks up my hand, the touch sends a spark to my core, joining the blaze already there. "You're beautiful." He traces each of my fingers, his eyes on mine.

"Thank you," I whisper, the fire burning hotter.

I arch against the seat when he pushes his thumb into the center of my palm, a low moan teasing its way out of my throat.

"God, Charlie," he rasps, his eyes dark.

"Let's go," I beg, "Please."

"Going." He cranks the wheel, spins us around, and peels out of the parking area. I shriek, uncontrollable giggles tumbling from my mouth. "I like when you laugh," he says, smiling. The planes of his face glow in the light of the dashboard. He lifts my hand to the shifter knob, his hand covering mine as he downshifts.

"I really like you," I blurt.

He pulls into the driveway and puts the car in park. We sit in the dark for a second before he jerks the keys from the ignition. He gets out and slams the door.

My heartbeat is pounding in my ears, mortification creeping up my neck. I start to open my door, but he wrenches it open and pulls me out. His lips are on my throat, his body molding to mine, pressing me against the car.

"I like you, too," he growls, his tongue swiping over my pulse. "God, I've wanted to do this all night. But there were too many people. And then Jay stole you away." He bites the area between my neck and shoulder, and I melt against him. We lose ourselves in each other's eyes for two beats before our lips collide. I'm desperate for his touch, but his fingers are cupped around my jaw, holding my mouth to his. I whimper in protest, arching into him, biting and pulling at his lower lip. His hands slide down my neck, over my shoulders, and down my arms, not stopping until his fingers are linked with mine. I try to pull away, needing to touch him.

He pulls his head back, groaning, "You can't touch me unless we're taking this back to your bed, Charlie." His pupils are blown out, his cheeks flushed.

"Come on, then." I pull him toward the cottage. The wind blows off the sea, rough and wild. Blood thrums through my veins. I haven't felt this alive since – a pang shoots through me – since Cameron. I look up at the moon as Lach wraps his arms around me, wondering if Cam is looking up at it, too. Lach's face blocks my view, so I close my eyes and live for this moment.

17

———

I reach behind me and fumble with the doorknob as I sink into Lach's lips. We stumble through the door, kicking it closed behind us. He pushes me against it, cradling my face in his hands. I unfasten his jacket and push it over his shoulders; he pulls his hands away long enough to let it drop to the floor, then slides his fingers up my legs, hooking my thighs. I groan into his mouth as he pulls my legs around his waist, his hands on my ass supporting my weight. He moves away from the door, but we only make it two feet before he presses me into the bookshelves, his pelvis pinning me in place.

The second I feel those shelves on my back, my mind races back to that night in the bookstore. Dark curls. Midnight eyes. My heart throbs with pain and I break the kiss with a gasp. "I'm sorry. I'm not ready to do this."

He gently sets me on the floor, wrapping his arm around me and pulling my head to his chest. "There's nothing to be sorry for." He kisses my hair, rubbing comforting circles on my back. "Do you want me to leave?" He pulls back and nudges my chin so I'm looking at him.

"No—" I blurt, involuntarily squeezing him tighter.

"Why don't I go grab some food and we can just hang out?"

I nod, unable to find the words to tell him what I'm feeling.

He kisses my forehead. "Get changed into something comfortable while I'm gone, okay?"

I nod again and watch as he leaves, my mind racing. The fact that he's going to get me food after I turned him down makes tears well in my eyes. The last twenty-four hours have been so overwhelming.

The door opens and Lach pops his head in, "I forgot to give you this earlier; it was delivered today." He sets a package just inside the door and leaves again.

I change into shorts and a t-shirt, then scrub the makeup from my face before my curiosity gets the best of me. The package is wrapped in brown paper. I flip it over to find African stamps covering most of the other side. Cameron. My hands shake as I ease the paper open and slide out a book. It's an old copy of Pride and Prejudice. A note flutters to the floor when I open the cover.

My Dearest Charlie,

I can't stop thinking about how much of a mistake this was. I miss you. I desperately hope you are not as miserable as I.

Yours Always,

Cam.

Regret shoots through me. I never should have told him to go. I wish I had been selfish and insisted he stay. I thumb through the pages, reading the passages that he had underlined in pencil.

"Till this moment I never knew myself."

"You are too generous to trifle with me. If your feelings are still what they were last April, tell me at once. My affections and wishes are unchanged, but one word from you will silence me on the subject forever."

"Charlie?"

I slam the book closed, my heart in my throat.

"Feeling better?" Lach asks, pushing through the door. He sits on the couch and starts pulling foil containers from a brown paper bag.

I blush, nodding my head. He must see something in my face because he raises an eyebrow, waiting for me to elaborate. I sigh. "The guy I was dating before I came to Harris sent that package to me." His gaze drops from mine.

"I see."

I sit next to him. "I'm a mess, Lachlan. I don't know if it's the divorce, or if it's being here or what." I scrub my hands over my face and gulp down the glass of wine he hands me.

"What do you mean?" He pulls the lids off a multitude of containers. The smell of butter chicken fills the room, making my mouth water.

"This guy I dated. I like him. A lot. I feel like it could have gone somewhere if circumstances were different."

"Right person, wrong time?" he asks, handing me a piece of naan.

I nod. "And then I met you." Heat creeps up my cheeks, but I'm determined to get this out, the alcohol in my veins fueling my courage. I twist toward him and nudge his chin with my knuckle so he's looking at me. "I really like you. I've had an amazing time the last few days."

"I'm not seeing the problem yet," he says, dipping his chin and pressing his lips to my fingers before I drop my hand.

I tear off a piece of bread with my teeth, giving myself a few precious seconds to admit something to him I hadn't fully admitted to myself yet. Fuck it. "And then tonight, when I met Jay..." I trail off, not sure how to finish the sentence.

"You liked him, too." Lach finishes, his lips twisting into a smile.

"You think it's funny?"

"It's okay to have feelings for multiple people, Charlie. That's just how it works sometimes."

"So you've liked more than one woman before?"

He shakes his head. "I've never had the desire to date more than one person at a time."

"See!" I groan. "Life just doesn't work that way."

"Why not? I knew a woman who dated three guys. They were all happy."

"For how long?" I ask, dumbfounded.

"Years."

I gape at him. "What happened?"

"That's a story for another time, Charlie. Eat." He holds a piece of chicken to my lips and I open obediently.

He grabs the remote and turns on the TV, flipping through some movies. We decide on a new release and I cuddle up to his side, completely content. My eyes start getting heavy twenty minutes in and the next thing I know, Lach is carrying me to the bed and cocooning me with his warmth.

Heavy pounding wakes me from a dead sleep. I slip out from under Lach's arm and pull on my robe before opening the door. Isla jerks when it swings open under her fist, startled.

"Good morning?" I croak, pushing my knotted hair out of my face.

"Come up to the house with me. Now."

"Why?" I groan, just wanting to go back to sleep.

"Because." She pushes past me and pulls me into the bathroom, ignoring my protests. "Brush your teeth," she commands. She brushes my hair while I take care of my teeth. I'm too groggy to question her. I put my hair in a ponytail and swipe some Chapstick over my lips. Lach is waiting by the front door for us, I tense, waiting to see Isla's reaction, but she only rolls her eyes.

"You better have coffee," I grumble, shivering as we step out into the cold. I stumble up the path to the house, the wind ripping my hair from the elastic. Isla holds the door to the manor house open for me, pushing me through when I hesitate a little too long. I turn to ask her what's happening, but she mumbles something I don't quite catch and disappears upstairs. I head toward the kitchen, desperate for some caffeine. I'm only a few feet from the coffee pot before I realize this is a setup. Jack is sitting on a stool at the island, a piece of toast halfway to his mouth. He's barefoot, his leg crossed at the knee over worn corduroy pants. An earth-colored sweater hugs his torso. One gorgeous eyebrow cocked up.

It takes my brain a few seconds to catch up.

"Oh my God. *Oh my God!*"

This can't be happening.

I pivot and hightail it past Lach to the front door, wrenching it open. Jack catches the door before I can slam it closed, cornering me in the front entrance.

The wind howls around us, my hair lashing out at him. He traps it with his hands, cupping my face.

"How are you even here?" I whisper, horrified. "I'm in my robe and slippers, for fuck's sake." And I just slept with Lachlan. Well, not *slept* with him, but still. Oh. My. God.

He growls, "How am *I* here? How are *you* here? How do you know my sister? How do you know Lachlan?" He brushes his thumb over my cheek, his gaze clinging to my lips.

"*Isla's* your sister?" Suddenly everything is crystal clear. "You're Jay," I whisper, groaning into my hands.

Isla bursts outside. "Will one of you please explain what's going on?"

"Charlie's the girl," Lachlan says from behind her.

"The girl?" She looks confused for a second. "*The* girl." She gapes. "The one you've been looking for?" Her eyes narrow. "Wait, you knew who she was last night, didn't you?" She turns to me. "But you..." She spins toward Lachlan. "And you! Oh, this is going to be messy." She grins.

I turn to Lachlan, "Did you know about this last night?"

He shrugs. "He wanted to tell you himself."

"Of fucking course," I mutter.

"Some privacy, please." Jack grinds out, his patience evaporating.

"You better tell me the whole story later," Isla pouts. Lach slips out the door before Isla goes back inside. I watch as he walks down the path toward the cottage.

"I feel like such an idiot," I groan once they're out of earshot. Embarrassment doesn't sit well with me, and I'm absolutely mortified.

"Stop," Jack says gruffly, his hands pressed to the wall on either side of my head, trapping me between his arms. His hair tangles with mine in the wind, strands of red, brown, and copper melding into one. His eyes are pools of molten gold – lion's eyes. Alarm bells clang through me.

"Don't even think about it," he growls.

Danger.

I duck under his arm and run down the path to the cottage. I don't know how to do this. My heart will shatter into so many pieces and I'll never be able to find them all.

"Charlotte." He grasps my wrist and spins me toward him. He looks wounded and more than a little pissed off.

"I'm sorry," I pant, trying to come up with the right words to tell him how I feel. To tell him about Cameron and Lach. To tell him I'm still healing from Rob.

"I'm not him, Charlotte. Whoever you're thinking of, I'm not him."

I laugh, "No, you're so much worse."

He glowers at me.

"This," I say, pointing between us, "is dangerous. I know you can feel it. It's like a tempest that will destroy everything in its path. I have a life back in the states." I gesture toward the castle across the loch. "And you, *you* have a fucking *castle*, Jack."

He exhales sharply through his nose. "None of that matters," he insists, "You *belong*, Charlotte. I can feel it in here." He taps his hand to his chest.

I know. God, I know.

This wild and untamed man is like the missing piece of my soul that I've been looking for my entire life. A piece I knew would fit perfectly if I could manage to rearrange all the others. I rub my breastbone to relieve the ache.

"Give me a reason, Charlotte. Just give me one reason and I'll never talk to you again."

I can't stand the thought of never talking to him again, but I'm not ready for this.

"Jack, I don't need you to go away; I just need time."

"Time," he repeats.

I nod.

"Done." He extends his hand to me, "Friends?"

"Friends." I grasp his hand, unprepared for the energy that erupts between us the second our skin touches. I jerk away from his touch.

"For now," he mutters, his eyes narrowing at my reaction. "Just promise me one thing, Sassenach."

"What?" I ask, rubbing my palm.

"Stop running."

I roll my eyes. "Why?"

"Because it makes me want to catch you and fuck you until you lose your voice from screaming my name."

"Oh," I breathe, turning away slowly, my heart beating like hummingbird wings in my chest. It takes everything in me not to look back.

Lach is waiting for me, leaning against the doorframe, a light in his eyes that wasn't there yesterday. "I'm not staying, but I wanted to let you know that I meant what I said last night."

"Remind me," I say, stalling. I don't want him to leave. The gray sweatpants slung low on his hips leave absolutely nothing to the imagination. I swallow hard, dragging my gaze back up to his face.

"You don't have to settle for one person, Charlie." He cups my face with both of his hands, staring into my soul. "*You are worth it.* I bet I could find ten guys that would fall over themselves to be able to have a single taste of you."

My core spasms. "*You* may be fine with that, but I'm sure Jack—Jay... hell, I don't even know what to call him now. But I'm sure *he* wouldn't be okay with it."

"Are you sure about that?" He asks, an emotion I can't place flashing in his eyes. He presses a kiss to my forehead and leaves, closing the door gently behind him.

Fuck.

18

I bury myself back in bed, hoping the feathers of the duvet will somehow lull me back into sleep. Jack's face dominates my thoughts. The tiny freckle below his left eye. The way he bites his lip. His wild hair.

God, that hair.

I press a pillow over my face and scream. I throw it to the other side of the room and fling the covers aside. *Why.* Why now? Why here? I shove two pieces of bread into the toaster, jamming the lever down. *What the fuck, universe?* I hold the toast in my teeth as I pull on my jacket, slamming the door behind me. Instead of risking heading up toward my car – and possibly running into *him* – I take the tiny path behind the cottage that looks like it has been out of use for years. The weather today is good by Scottish standards – not rainy, not sunny. I bury my hands in my pockets as I walk, safe from the biting wind, enjoying the mystery of where the path will take me.

It ends up bringing me down almost to sea level before curving around and heading in the opposite direction from the house. I take my time, collecting a small bouquet of heather and thistle as I go, enjoying the peace that comes with being in wide-open spaces. After thirty minutes or so, the path turns to sand, and I find myself at the top of a small dune, looking down at a huge expanse of pristine beach, violent turquoise water roiling against a backdrop of stormy mountains. I can feel my consciousness expand, the beauty too much for it to hold on to, the connection too great for me to fully understand.

"Carebear!"

I turn to see Lach walking down the path toward me. "I like that one better," I say, laughing at the nickname. He's wearing charcoal athletic shorts and a deep green t-shirt that match the color of his eyes. He links his fingers with mine, taking in the view together.

"So you're the girl?" he asks, his gaze glued to the horizon.

"I guess? I didn't realize..."

"He wouldn't shut up about you."

I shrug awkwardly.

He clears his throat. "Did you think about our talk any more?"

I don't say anything, not willing to admit it's the only thing I've been able to think about.

"Be with both of us, Charlie." The words tumble out of his mouth.

"I can't."

"Why not?"

"What would people think?"

"Who gives a flying fuck what people think? I sure as hell don't. And Isla is used to it, so you don't have to worry about her."

I gape at him. "What do you mean she's *used* to it?"

"This isn't the first time Jack and I—" he trails off, ending his sentence with a shrug, his cheeks pink.

"Not the first time you've done what, exactly?" I ask. I need details. Now.

"Shared." He clears his throat, slowly raising his head to look at me.

"You shared a woman before? Like you both dated her at the same time?"

He nods. "And more."

"More? What does that mean?" I clamp my thighs together as that moment at the masquerade flashes through my mind.

"More than dating, Charlie. We were fucking her." He licks his lips, and suddenly, all I can think about is how his tongue would feel between my legs.

"At the same time?" I blurt, mortified the second the question tumbled from my lips.

"No, not at the same time. That wasn't something she was comfortable with."

"But you guys would have been if she was?"

"Yes, Charlie." The words come out in a low rumble.

I think for a second. "But what would you get out of it? Seems like you both would be getting the short end of the stick."

"We'd be getting you, Carebear. You are definitely not the short end of the stick." He rolls his shoulders, easing the tension.

"How many times have you done this?"

"Only once. Jay, our university roommate and I all fell for the same girl."

"All three of you?" He nods. "And it worked?"

"It did for a long time. Our roommate moved away first, then I went to study for my MBA. She and Jack got their own place." Lachlan presses his lips to the back of my hand. "No pressure. Just think about it."

'Just think about it.' Ha. Like I wasn't going to have to rearrange all of my pre-existing ideas about relationships. Like society would accept it. Like it was the most normal thing in the world.

"Give me some time to figure out how I feel about it?"

"Of course. What does that look like to you? Do you want me to stay scarce?" He pulls away from me, and I feel the loss in my soul.

"NO. No. I want to go slow. I want to get to know you...be friends first."

"Thank fuck. That I can deal with. I may get carpal tunnel, but I'll manage."

I laugh. Really laugh. He stops walking, staring at me like I grew a third eye.

"Motherfucker you're beautiful," he breathes, his eyes luminous. He shakes his head to clear it. "Despite what it seems, I wasn't stalking you. I came down here to jog." He peels off his shirt and tucks it into his waistband. "See ya later, Carebear." He winks and jogs away toward the water. Thirty seconds later, he smacks his ass with his hand like he knows I'm still watching. I spin on my heel and walk the other way before he can look back and catch me staring.

I breathe deep, the cool air helping to clear my mind. I have to admit that the idea of exploring a relationship with both of them is enticing. But that doesn't leave any room for Cam. He didn't sign up to share me with two strangers and I could never in a million years ask him. So that leaves me with three options: Cam, who wasn't even here; Lach and Jack, who are here and willing; or not being in a relationship at all. The third option was by far the easiest and the only option that guaranteed I wouldn't leave Scotland with a broken heart. I pick up a smooth rock and skip it over the water, watching as it bounces five, six, seven times. But the third option was also the most boring.

After walking for an hour, I finally decide that I'm not going to make any decision at all. If something is going to happen, I'll let it happen naturally.

The conversation plays over and over in my head as I make my way back to the cottage. Despite myself, I can't help but imagine what it would be like to be with both of them. After failing to distract myself with work, I give up and head into the bedroom, pulling my trusty vibrator from the nightstand. I shuck off my leggings and sprawl on the bed, running the smooth silicone through the moisture that has been building since I talked with Lach. I imagine myself in Jay's lap, Lach's head between my legs, his tongue doing unimaginable things. *Oh God, Lach,* I moan, the pressure already building.

"Are you praying to me, Carebear?" Lach's voice drifts through my open window.

"Fuck," I whimper, his voice sending me over the edge. I press the toy to my clit, clenching my jaw to keep in my scream as I splinter into a million pieces. As I come down, I expect mortification to settle in, but it doesn't. If anything, I'm more turned on than I was before.

"Charlie."

I walk to the window on shaky legs, the toy held out of sight. Lach is standing there, color high in his cheeks.

"Next time, let me help. You are my god. I want to worship you with my hands and praise you with my tongue until you beg me to stop without asking for anything in return. Do you understand?"

I nod, swallowing around the knot in my throat.

His gaze burns into mine. "I will get you off and leave if that's what you want, just let me take care of you." He nods as if we just agreed on something and then continues up the path.

I stand there, dazed. Nobody has ever said anything like that to me before.

19

I struggle to regulate my breathing as terror races through my veins, my hands shaking as I grip the steering wheel. Isla's in the passenger seat, trying not to laugh. This is my second try driving to Stornoway. I gave up the first time and then waited until Isla had a day off work to try again. These sheer cliffs, slick roads, and single-lane highways will be the death of me, but I don't have a choice. I need to make up for lost time. I feel like this trip has been a failure so far, and I can't bear the thought of facing Arty with nothing to show.

The records office is located in the back room of the local library, which suits me fine. I use Jack's tip to find the error in my research and can work off that to add more generations to the tree. Once I have that part finished, I can start on the real work: the calligraphy and paintings. My favorite part, though admittedly, it's way more complicated than the research.

Isla gossips about people I don't know the entire time I do my research. Every time I look at her, she's in a different position: straddling the chair, sitting on the back of it with her feet on the seat, lying on the floor with her legs propped up on the wall. Normally this would be infuriating, but with Isla, I can't help but find it endearing.

After her hundredth position change, I ask her if she wants to grab lunch.

"Really?"

I laugh at her expression. She looks so relieved I'm afraid she might cry. "Really. Let's go."

We only have to walk several doors down to find a cute little cafe that seems promising.

"Can I ask you a favor?" Isla blows on a steaming spoonful of stew.

"Sure?" I rip off a chunk of bread and dip it into the thick sauce.

"I have to run to Glasgow for a few days; will you take care of Sorcha for me?"

"Who's Sorcha?"

"My pony," she laughs.

I raise an eyebrow at her.

"God, sometimes I forget we haven't known each other for very long. I've had Sorcha since I was a little girl. I couldn't bear the thought of getting rid of her, so I've kept her all these years."

"That's sweet," I say. Imagining Isla as a tiny sassy brat makes me smile. "What exactly do you need me to do?"

"Just brush her and let her out to pasture in the morning, then feed her grain and hay in her stall in the evenings. It'll take ten or fifteen minutes tops."

"It's been a while since I've had to take care of a horse, but I'm sure I can manage that. Where do you keep her?"

"There's a stable over at Jay's."

I groan.

"Oh, stop it. He's never at the barn anyway. The chance of you seeing him is practically zero."

"Fine," I grumble, "When do you leave?"

"Tomorrow." She grimaces, wincing a little as she waits for my reaction.

"You fucking owe me."

"Deal." She holds out her spoon and cheers me with it.

The following morning, I take the bike Isla loaned me and ride it over to the castle. I go past the main entrance, turning into the second drive, hoping to eliminate any chance of seeing Jack. Slept-in mascara and a messy bun is not exactly the impression I want to give. Again. I lean the bike against the side of the barn and push open the heavy double doors. There are eight stalls, and only three of them are occupied.

Sorcha is in the first stall – small speckled pony with a gray mane. The second horse is a beautiful flaxen chestnut, her coat the perfect backdrop for her gorgeous mane. I stop in my tracks as I approach the third horse. He stands much taller than the other two, curious brown eyes staring me down. I sweep his forelock out of his eyes and rub his velvety nose.

"Well, aren't you a gorgeous boy," I murmur. He nuzzles into me gently as I press a kiss to his muzzle. He's the most beautiful horse I have ever seen. His mane is so long that I can't see the end of it unless I stand on my tiptoes and peer over the stall door. He's black as pitch, not a speck of white anywhere. He nibbles at my fleece, making soft whinnying noises.

"Looks like he has good taste in women."

I jump.

"What are you doing here?" I ask, spinning to face Jack.

He chuckles. "I think I'm the one that should be asking *you* that. But since you asked, I'm feeding Lucius."

I'm going to kill Isla.

"Your turn," he prods, smirking.

"I'm feeding Sorcha for Isla."

He nods but doesn't say anything.

I slide Sorch's bridle over her head and walk her out of her stall, clipping her to the lead ropes attached to the barn posts. I find the brushes in a caddy hanging on the wall, so I get to work with the curry comb first, ignoring Jack as he leads Lucius into the paddock.

"What are you up to today?"

My heart jumps to my throat at his nearness, and I whirl toward him. "Stop doing that!"

He leans against a stall door, shrugging an apology.

"I'm going back to Lewis to do some research." I wince as I say it, dreading the drive.

"Why the face?"

"The drive is awful," I admit.

"I'll drive you. I have to stock up on a few things anyway." I mull it over for a second. "It's not a big deal, Charlotte. I can drop you off, do what I need, and pick you up on the way home."

"You're sure?"

"I wouldn't have offered if I wasn't."

"Okay." I chew my lip. This feels dangerous. I give Sorcha a final brush before looking up at him. "Thank you," I whisper, the words getting stuck in my throat.

"I'll pick you up in an hour." Gravel crunches under his heel as he turns and walks out of the barn.

God. That man could melt the polar ice caps with one look. I lead Sorcha out to the pasture, realizing Jack has already thrown out hay for her. Damn it. I don't need another thing to the growing list of Jack's pros. The con list is pitiful; the only thing on it is 'Scotland,' and 'Scotland' is under pros, too. I'm fucked.

I pedal back to the house as fast as I can. I shiver through an ice-cold shower and pick out the ugliest clothes I own: a pair of boyfriend jeans and an oversized t-shirt. A swipe of mascara, Chapstick and my trusty combat boots complete the look. I smirk at myself in the mirror. I don't feel sexy at all. Success.

I'm waiting outside, sipping on a mug of coffee, when Jack pulls up.

He laughs when he sees what I'm wearing. "I know what you're trying to do. It won't work, Sassenach. Besides, you look fucking adorable." His grin sucks the oxygen from the air. "Here." He pushes a foil packet into my hands as I get into the truck.

"What's this?"

"Just in case you haven't eaten."

"I haven't. Thank you." I peel it open to find a bacon, egg, and cheese sandwich. My mouth immediately starts watering. I take a huge bite, my eyes rolling back. "This is so good."

Jack is frozen with his hand on the back of my headrest. He had started to turn to back up, but he hadn't made it past my face.

"God, Charlotte."

"What?"

"Don't fucking do that."

I want to pretend like I don't know what he was talking about, but I'm in the middle of slowly licking a drop of egg yolk from my finger, my eyes on him. I swallow hard. "Yes, sir."

His eyes darken. "Good girl."

20

―――――

I admire his effortless driving over hills and hairpin turns, loving the fact that I'm able to enjoy the scenery. And by the scenery, I mean the veins riding over the back of his hands and up his forearms.

"What brings you to Stornoway?" Jack asks, breaking the silence that has settled over us like a warm blanket.

"More research," I say, making a face. If I'm not able to wrap it up today, I'm going to scream. Now that my artistic side has a chance to create again, it's raring to go. As great as it is to feel that part of me come alive after so long, it makes it feel like the research is dragging on forever.

"Not quite the same as the pub, is it?" His lips twist into a tiny smirk, and I know he's thinking about that night. I can still feel his hand spanning my back, his thigh anchored between my legs. I clench my thighs against the visceral response the memory invokes and try to concentrate on the view outside my window.

"Not quite. They could at least serve beer if I have to spend all day in that cramped space."

Jack laughs. "Why don't I help you? We can go there first, get twice the work done, and then we can run my errands."

My heart rate ticks up. "Really? It'll be boring," I warn.

"Being in the same room as you – breathing the same air – will never be boring."

My face heats under his gaze. I know he's right. There's no possible way it'll be boring when we're elbow to elbow in that tiny room.

"Deal," I say just as we pull into the parking lot.

I smile at the woman at the front desk as we pass. Her face is pinched in disapproval; she's probably still hung up on Isla's non-stop chatter the day before.

"Now what?" Jack asks as he shrugs his broad shoulders out of his jacket, draping it over the back of the chair.

"Now I find the microfiche for the dates in question, and we look through it until our eyes bleed."

"Sounds like fun," he deadpans, sitting at one of the machines.

The microfiche is filed by date; each year consists of scanned pages of births, baptisms, marriages, and deaths. It's an enormous amount of information to sift through, but I've narrowed down the dates through online research, so now I just have to confirm everything and go back a couple more generations if I can. I pull out six different years and place them between our machines, setting down my list in front of them.

"These are the names we're looking for and the approximate dates," I explain, pointing to the information I had jotted down in my notebook. "We need to confirm the years and then try to find the full month, day, and year if possible. If you see any records that show the parents let me know; I'd love to add a couple more generations to the tree even though I probably don't need them. I'd love to give Arty the best tree possible."

"He sounds like a great man," Jack says as he loads the first film into the machine.

"He is." I smile. "I don't deserve him."

"I guarantee you that's not true." Jack scribbles something down on the paper. I reach for the pen, my hand brushing his. Sparks race over my skin, my pulse skyrocketing. I stare at him.

"Sassenach?" Jack's voice is soft, like I'm a horse he's trying not to spook.

"Do you feel that, too?" I ask, my voice barely a whisper. I grab his hand and turn it so his palm is facing up. I run my finger over his palm and up each finger, pressing my nail into his skin.

Jack licks his lips, his gaze on our hands. "If you feel like you're on the most terrifying rollercoaster you've ever been on, then yes."

I swallow. "Do you like rollercoasters?"

He laughs. "Aye, Charlotte, I do."

WE WRAP UP AN HOUR LATER. Jack surprises me by finding way more information than I could have ever found on my own, including two more generations of Arty's family members. I'm thrilled. The worst part of the project is finally finished.

"Thank you so much for helping," I say as we slide into a booth at a pub that looks like it's been around for fifteen hundred years.

"My pleasure, Charlotte. I enjoyed it."

"You did not," I laugh, toying with the paper ring I pulled off the utensils.

"I was spending time with you. Of course I enjoyed it."

I try to hold in my grin and fail miserably.

"There she is," Jack murmurs, his eyes going soft.

My heart flutters in my chest, and I bury my face in the beer menu to hide the smile I just can't shake.

When I can't decide on a beer, Jack orders an entire flight, finishing the ones I don't like.

"Tell me about yourself," Jack says, breaking open the crust of his meat pie to let out the steam.

"You already know most of it," I say, popping a piece of crust into my mouth.

"Not what's happened to you – I want to know *you*." His gaze is intense. "What are your hopes and dreams? What did you want to be when you were little? What's your favorite book? Your favorite movie?

I want to know the stuff that's independent of the things you can't control."

"I'll put you to sleep," I laugh.

"You could never put me to sleep, Charlotte." He blows on a piece of meat, his eyes on me. "Trust me."

"Okay," I say, ignoring the heat pooling in my center. "I wanted to be a marine biologist when I was little."

"What about now? Is that something you still want to do?"

"No, I don't think so. I would be content to run my little business now. It checks all the boxes for me, and it used to bring in enough to live on."

"The calling of a simple life, eh, Sassenach?"

"You could say that."

"I know how you feel. I ran hard for years. I had my fingers in way too many things. It wore me down to the point that I didn't want to leave the farm. I learned my lesson."

"But what about that night in the pub?" I ask.

"My friend called in a favor. And now I'll never be able to return it because that's the night I met you. I could help him out a thousand times, and it still wouldn't be payment enough."

Fuck. I gulp down my beer. When I set my glass down, he traps my hand under his.

"No matter what happens between us, I'll always be thankful for that night."

"I'm thankful I met you, too," I say, my heart in my throat. "I don't think I'll ever forget that evening. It was magical, wasn't it?"

"To many more magical nights," he teases, raising his glass.

I groan, but I still lift my glass to his.

"Hey, I know you need time. I'm not pushing for anything past friendship."

My heart drops. "Don't get all dramatic on me, now. I'm fine with the teasing. And the flirting. I'll let you know if you ever go too far."

He laughs, "I have absolutely no doubt about that."

"What about you – what did you want to be when you were little?"

"Exactly what I'm doing now. I knew from the time I was toddling around the estate that I wanted to spend my life there. I know it sounds cliche to say it's in my blood, but I don't know how else to describe it. That's why all of us eventually came back." He smiles. "There's just something about that place. I hope you get to experience it before—" he stops abruptly, frustration marring his features.

"Before I leave?" I finish, voicing what he doesn't want to say.

"Yes, that."

"Me, too." The food sits heavy in my stomach. I *will* have to leave eventually. "Can we promise not to bring that up unless we absolutely have to?"

"Good idea." He spears a carrot and pops it into his mouth, not meeting my gaze.

"Well, that was a mood killer." I chuckle. "What are the errands you need to do?"

"I have to go to the feed store and make a quick grocery run. Shouldn't take too long." He pulls out his wallet and motions the waiter over.

"Jack, let me at least pay for my meal," I protest. "You drove me all the way here and then helped me for hours. I owe you."

"I offered, Charlotte. You owe me nothing."

We spend the next couple of hours ticking items off his list, and I find that in addition to being sexually attracted to him, I really like who he is as a person. I can hear the love and respect he carries for his family and friends in his words. It's when we're driving back to Harris, his arm over the back of my seat, that I realize I'm royally fucked.

21

I've been avoiding the guys for the last few days, and it's starting to wear on me. Despite being at my favorite part of the process, I haven't made any progress on Arty's tree. I've become an irritable recluse who only gets out to sneak around the barn taking care of Sorcha. I finally concede that I need a day off to clear my head, and I'm determined to get outside despite the horrible weather. I bundle up in the same clothes I wore on my hike with Cameron – which doesn't help my frame of mind one bit. I pack some snacks, water, and my camera and head down the path to the beach. The wind is so strong that I can barely place one foot in front of the other. Despite that, wild water and cliffs lure me further down the path. The cold air against my skin is invigorating, blowing away the cobwebs of confusion that have been there since that night in the pub.

Mist starts coming down as I drop my backpack in a small cave, looping my camera around my neck. I walk the beach until my toes are numb, taking a lifetime's worth of pictures. I'm not thinking about any of the guys for the first time in weeks. I jog close to the surf, blood working to warm my extremities. I turn back toward the cave as the rain picks up, but it isn't nearly soon enough. Lightning flashes overhead, a giant thunderclap seconds behind. *Fuck.* I debate trying to scurry back up the path, but I'm not in the mood to risk my life today. Waiting it out seems like a decent second option. I get to the cave just before the downpour starts. I carry my bag further into the cave and find a little alcove that provides enough of a wind break to be comfortable. The forlorn sound of the wind blowing over the mouth of the cave makes me shudder, and my mood plummets.

"Charlotte!" a disembodied voice floats into the cave on a gust of wind. I run to the entrance, scanning the beach. Jack is riding the gorgeous black stallion I met in the barn the other day.

"Jack!" I wave my arms, smiling like a fool when he spots me. He prods the horse into a gallop, coming to a stop and dismounting in one smooth motion. He loops the reins over the animal's neck before turning to me, lines of worry etched between his brows.

Beads of water cling to his face, his eyelashes sticking together in dark points. "God, I was worried about you, Charlotte. Why did you go out in this weather?" He doesn't come any closer, but I'm unsure if it's because he's respecting my boundaries or because he's pissed off.

"I didn't realize," I say, ashamed that I put him in danger. "Do you think he can get us back to the house?" I ask, gesturing toward the horse.

"I don't think so," he sighs, "the path was treacherous on the way down and I don't want to risk it again. I shouldn't have even come down, but I had a feeling you were here." He shakes the water from his hair. "Come on then." He strides into the cave, grabbing my wrist as he brushes past me.

"What about the horse?"

"Trust me, he's not going anywhere, and neither will you if you don't get in here and warm up."

Jack makes a small fire out of driftwood, the light flickering over his face in a silent caress. His eyes reflect the flames, reminding me of molten lava – mesmerizing and deadly. I clear my throat, uncomfortable with how my body responds to him.

His mouth twists. "You don't have to keep doing that, you know," he says, shredding a twig and watching each piece shrivel in the fire.

"Doing what?"

"Building that damn wall." He meets my gaze. "I won't hurt you, Charlotte."

"It's not you—" I start.

"It's me?" Jack finishes my sentence, his words sarcastic. "Bullshit. It's *not* you – it's that bastard you wasted all those years on."

"That's part of it," I admit.

"And the other part?" he asks, one eyebrow lifting toward his hairline.

"I don't know how to do this."

"Do what, Charlotte?"

My cheeks flame just thinking about having to explain what I mean. That probably means I shouldn't, right? "Lachlan told me about the two of you."

He doesn't say anything, just waits for me to continue.

"I don't know how to do something like that. I don't know if I even can."

"And that's perfectly fine, Charlotte. No one is pressuring you to do anything. We just want you to be happy. *But* if you want that – or think you might – the first step is talking about it."

Can I talk about it? Talking about it doesn't mean I have to do anything. God. How am I even considering this? I peel off my jacket and fan my shirt away from my body. Why is it so fucking hot in here?

"I have an idea," he says, pushing himself up, "wait here."

Like I have anywhere else to go. He walks further into the cave and comes back with a dusty bottle. He wipes it on his pants and turns the label toward me. "I hid this back here when I was fifteen years old," he laughs. "I can't believe it's still here." He removes the wax seal with his pocketknife and then pops the cork using the attachment. He takes a swig, testing it before handing it to me.

Dubious, I peer through the opening at the golden liquid. "You're sure it's okay?" I ask, wondering how it can still be good after twenty-five years

"Better than okay, Good whisky only gets better with age."

I take a swig, spluttering as the smooth heat spreads through my body. "You're right; that's glorious," I agree, taking another sip before handing it back to him.

"It better be; that bottle is probably worth three thousand pounds now."

I choke. "Three *thousand*? Why the hell are we drinking it?"

"We're stuck in a cave during one of the worst storms I've ever seen, Sassenach. *That* is why we're drinking it." He shakes his head, chuckling, "Couldn't have planned it better if I tried."

We pass the bottle several more times, and sure enough, I can feel myself loosening up. "Now what?" I ask him.

"Now you talk."

"Alcohol was your plan?" I laugh, taking the bottle from his outstretched hand. Our fingers brush, the heat spreading through me utterly unrelated to the whisky this time.

"A damn good one," he says, throwing one of his twigs at me with a smirk.

"Fine." I pout. "Ask me something."

"Tell me about your last relationship, that way I know how bad I have to beat the bastard if I ever see him."

I sigh. This is going to suck. "Rob and I met the first year in college and married a couple of months after graduating. He was my first real boyfriend." I wince at how lame that sounds. "He went to work for his dad in the family landscape business and I went on to graduate school. I did the ancestry stuff on the side, eventually growing it enough to pay for school entirely. Rob's parents died a couple of years after that and he was really struggling with the responsibility of the business. I stepped in before he could bankrupt it. Eventually, our marriage turned into a job, too." I look at Jack, unsure if he wants to keep hearing about my failures.

"Go on," he says, passing me the bottle again.

I take a long swig. "Rob started getting nasty a couple of years ago. We both worked long hours so we didn't have to see each other." I laugh, "Actually, it was me working long hours. Rob was, well, Rob."

"What does that mean?" he asks, the muscle in his jaw twitching.

"Not working. Fucking random chicks. Fucking not so random

chicks." My mind flashes back to finding them in bed together, and a stabbing pain shoots through my chest. I don't miss Rob, but I sure as hell miss my friend. "I found him in bed with my best friend."

Jack's at my side before I can blink, his hands engulfing mine as he pulls me into his embrace. He envelops me in warm whisky and leather. He presses his lips to my hair, one hand moving in comforting circles over my back.

"God, I'm sorry."

I squeeze my arms around his neck, my body melting against his. He smooths my hair away from my face as I blink back tears.

"Have you talked to anyone about this yet?" he asks, pulling back a little so he can look me in the face.

I shake my head. "I would have talked to *her*," I sniff.

He cups my face, his thumbs wiping the tears away.

"I'm honored you shared with me, Charlotte."

"Thank you for letting me cry on you. I think that was another first."

He turns toward the fire, one arm hugging me against his side. "You've been strong your entire life, haven't you?"

"Strong? I wouldn't call it that." I laugh. Embarrassment creeps up my neck. Vulnerability is not my forte.

"Your douche canoe ex cheated on you with your ex-best friend, and instead of wallowing, you come to Scotland on a new adventure, make new friends, and you're living your truth. If that's not strong, I'm not sure what that is."

"Impulsive?"

Jack laughs. "Maybe some of that, too. Whatever it is, I'm glad you're here."

"I am, too." I twirl a twig between my fingers, watching the flames eat away at a log.

"That was one huge fucking first step, Charlotte."

I grin.

He turns toward me, his gaze soft. "You should be proud of yourself."

I lean my head against his shoulder. "Thank you for listening."

"Always," he murmurs, pressing a kiss to the crown of my head. "Is there anything else you'd like to talk about?"

I consider for a moment. "Yes. I want you to tell me about...well, what Lachlan told me about." I don't even know how to put it into words.

He nods, taking a second to organize his thoughts. "We were in university. There was a girl on the floor below us who was fun to be around. Her name was Emily. She would hang out in our suite all the time. The four of us would go to movies, go to dinner... we pretty much did everything together. Over time all three of us fell for her. It took her a long time to admit it, but she fell in love with us, too." He pauses to sip from the bottle, passing it to me. "Eventually, life caught up with us. Lachlan and our other roommate moved away to different schools."

"What happened after that?"

"I married her."

Fuck. He *married* her?

"Someday, I'll tell you about what happened after that, but not tonight. Go on, ask another question."

I took a long drag from the bottle, my pulse thrumming in my throat. "How did it work exactly? The logistics of it all?"

"The sex, you mean?"

I choke on the fire sliding down my throat.

"I'll take that as a yes," he laughs. He squeezes my knee, his fingers strong and sexy as fuck. My stomach flutters. "I'm sure every relationship is different, especially when it comes to poly relationships. But Em's comfort, protection, and pleasure were always our top priority. We kept our communication wide open."

"So... did you take turns?" I'm having a hard time wrapping my head around it all.

Jack nods. "Yes, she rotated nights."

I feel a twinge of disappointment. "Looking back, is there anything you would have done differently regarding that part of the relationship?"

"It was never an option she would consider, but the guys were gunning for a huge bed at the beginning. It was so easy when all of us were together. We didn't want to separate it." He runs his hand through his hair. "I'm not explaining this well. We were fine with her having separate relationships with each of us, I just wish she had let us..." He trails off, his cheeks heating.

"What, Jack?"

"I don't know how to put this so it won't scare you off."

"You haven't scared me yet," I say. If the throbbing between my legs is any indication, it's completely the opposite.

"I wish she had let us worship her. Together. There's something about being able to watch your woman being ravished that is a fucking turn-on."

"Fuck—" I breathe, biting my lip to keep in a groan.

Jack's gaze snaps to mine, taking in my flushed cheeks and glassy eyes. I cover my face with my hands, focusing on breathing. This has to be the worst thing to consider after coming out of a five-year marriage, but God, my body wants it.

Jack's fingers grip my chin, forcing me to look at him. He sees my dilated pupils and curses. "So much fucking trouble," he murmurs, his grip softening into a caress, this thumb pulling at my bottom lip.

"Friends, remember?" I stammer, barely able to get the words out of my throat.

"Right." Jack stands up, cold air taking his place. "It sounds like the storm is over, so we may as well make a break for it."

I regret saying those two words the entire hike back.

Jack pauses at the path leading to the cottage, the fire in his eyes banked. "Have a good evening, Sassenach." He continues walking toward the main house.

"Jack," I call. He stops but doesn't look back. "I don't think I can do this much longer."

He turns. "Do what?"

"Pretend," I whisper, my heart jackhammering in my throat.

"Pretend *what,* Charlotte."

"That I want to be friends."

The fire in his eyes roars back to life. "When you give your consent Charlotte, I'll lick every square inch of your body until you're sobbing my name, and then I'll fuck you until you can't walk for a week. That's the only warning I'm going to give you."

"Yes, sir." I squeeze my thighs, desperate to relieve the ache. Then he's behind me, pulling me against his front, his cock pressing into my back.

"Can I touch you, Charlotte?" he rasps, his breath hot against the shell of my ear.

I nod, but he holds still, waiting. "Yes," I sob, grinding back against him. He slides his hand beneath my waistband, his fingers coming to rest on either side of my clit. He clamps an arm underneath my breasts, holding me up as my knees buckle. "You have no idea how many times I've thought about doing this," he growls, pushing one thick finger into me, rocking the heel of his palm against my clit. I explode around him, grinding against him as the orgasm batters my senses. He leaves his hand in place as I come down, pulling away slowly after the tremors stop. I stare up at him as he licks me from his fingers, his gaze never leaving mine. He palms my throat and kisses the spot right next to my lips.

"Have a good evening, Charlotte," he says before turning and walking up the path as if nothing happened. Like he hadn't just shattered my world into a million pieces.

22

"Come to the gym with me," Isla whines, bouncing her leg up and down underneath my tiny kitchen table.

"Isla," I groan, "The gym is the last place I want to go."

"Look – I know you're in shape now, but that's because you had that horrible job. What will happen now that you're not working outside all the time? You're going to feel like shit, that's what," she says, answering her question.

She has a good point. "Fine."

I throw on some cut-off leggings, a sports bra, and an oversized t-shirt. I sit down at the table to pull on my socks and shoes, down the rest of my coffee, and then Isla drags me out the door.

She drives like a bat out of hell, jerking to a stop in front of a warehouse a few miles away.

"This doesn't look shady at all," I chide, not seeing a sign anywhere. "How do people even know it's a gym?"

"Kind of a long story, but it was too far to drive to Stornoway every day, so we all chipped in, bought the warehouse, outfitted it, and then told everyone in Harris about it. Anyone with the keycode can come and use it whenever they want."

"Do you charge them?" I ask, getting a distinct impression that they don't.

"Nope, we were gonna do it anyway." She keyed in the code and held the door open for me.

"Who is we, exactly?"

"Me and the guys."

I gape as I take in three rows of cardio equipment, a large area for free weights, and a huge space filled with weight machines. "Isla, this is not just equipment for the three of you."

"Four of us," she corrects. "It's grown a little since we started."

"Wait, four of you?"

"Yeah, me, Lach, Jay, and their old university roommate."

A cheer goes up as we make our way inside, a handful of people calling out to Isla, greeting her with smiles and waves. She ducks her head and smiles back. "Where do you want to start?" she asks me.

I stare at her blankly. "I haven't been to a gym in my entire life."

"You have a body like that and you've never been to a gym? Fuck off."

I laugh. "Teach me, coach?"

"Sure, but you have to call me coach."

"Yes, coach." We both dissolve into a fit of giggles.

Isla peels off her sweatshirt and I catch myself gaping at the muscle hugging her curves in all the right places. She's fucking sexy.

"Holy hell, Isla. Where has all that been hiding?"

"Just wait till it gets warmer." She wiggles her eyebrows at me. "You always want to warm up first," she says, serious now. "*Always.*" She motions for me to get on the treadmill next to hers. She leans over and increases the incline to as high as it goes. "Now you adjust the speed to whatever is comfortable."

Two minutes later, I'm a soggy dripping mess. I pull my hair up high on my head, wrapping it around my hand and securing it into a messy bun. My face feels like it's on fire, and I'm positive I look like a tomato. I don't make a peep, though, determined to at least try to keep up with Isla. All those years in that fucking job have to be good for something, right?

After ten minutes, Isla slams the stop button on her control panel. "That's enough of that. Now we get to do the really fun stuff."

Really fun? Did that imply the treadmill was supposed to be *fun*? I'm screwed. I follow her over to the free weights, admiring her leg muscles. She's all lithe muscles and sexy curves. I want that. I know I'm not awful to look at, but if I'm being honest with myself, I haven't taken care of myself. I've neglected nourishing my body, especially on the days I worked twelve-plus hours. It made me scrawny. I've gained a bit of weight since stopping, enough that I had to go up a couple of pants sizes, and I feel somewhat out of my element. A little disappointed in myself, if I'm being honest. At least working toward being healthy will give me some focus outside of work – something I can keep doing when I get home.

Home. That one word has my stomach dropping to the floor.

"You good?" Isla asks, interrupting my spiraling thoughts.

"Yes, coach!" I plaster a smile on my face.

She studies me for a second, clearly not believing me. "We're going to start with basics, okay? First, we'll go over squats and lunges." She spends the next five minutes showing me the moves, where my weight should be, and where my knees shouldn't be. I follow her lead, using weights considerably lighter than hers.

"Jay!" Isla breaks into a grin.

I whip around, coming face to face with him. I gasp like a fish out of water as all the oxygen is sucked from the room.

"Charlotte." Surprise flits over his face, but he hides it quickly. He's wearing gym shorts that are on the shorter side, showing off *very* developed leg muscles. A white tank top hangs from his frame, his bulging muscles on full display.

"I was lonely, so I brought her along," Isla says, dropping down into another squat.

"Do you guys have family workout sessions or something?" I ask, smirking at the thought.

"Yes, actually." Lachlan walks up from behind Jack, slapping him on the shoulder in greeting.

"We don't always get to see each other as much as we'd like, but this helps." Jack shrugs.

"You guys are lucky to have each other," I say, envious of their bond.

"We really are," Isla says, the other two nodding. "I don't know where any of us would be if we didn't have each other." Emotion wells as I watch the three of them share sappy smiles. She claps her hands, "Okay, enough of the sappy stuff – time to get to work!"

The guys settle in the free-weight area with us, Lachlan at the barbells, and Jack on a bench. I do my best to focus on Isla and follow her instructions: sit back farther, weight on your heels, don't rotate your leg, but my eyes keep wandering over to the guys. I watch as Jack's torso arches above the bench with each press. I wonder if his back bows like that when he comes. I bite my lip as a vision of my head bobbing over his cock flashes through my mind. Fuck.

My eyes meet his as he cradles the bar. He holds my gaze as he stands up, lifting the hem of his shirt to wipe his forehead. His abs are hard and tight, covered in a dusting of dark hair. I get a peek at one pec jutting out from his chest before his shirt drops back into place. I knew he had a good body, but never in my wildest imagination had I thought he would look like *this*.

"Just go over there!" Isla says, laughing. "You two are hardly getting anything done because you're mooning at each other. Plus, he can teach you how to bench correctly."

"That seems like a horrible idea," I say, my voice cracking.

"Don't be ridiculous." She hands me my water bottle and pushes me toward him. "Jack, teach her how to bench and do some leg stuff, okay? I'm going over to the machines."

"Sure," Jack says, looking utterly unsure despite the heat in his eyes. He motions for me to lie on the bench as he pulls the plates off the end of the bar. "The bar is heavy on its own, so we'll start empty and go from there, okay?" I nod. He walks behind the bench and looks down at me. An image of him stretching over me flashes across my eyes, and my stomach clenches. I squeeze my eyes closed and take a couple of deep breaths.

"You okay?"

"I'm fine." That's a lie. I open my eyes again, only to look directly at his crotch. I jerk my gaze up to his face, mortification flooding my cheeks. He doesn't say anything, to my immense relief, only motions for me to grip the bar.

"This is a simple movement. You lower and raise the bar keeping your elbows perpendicular to your body. I'll hold on for the first couple of reps in case the bar is too heavy, okay?"

I nod, keeping my eyes glued to the bar. He raises it out of its cradle and then lets me take most of the weight as I lower it toward my body. It's heavy, but the weight doesn't even register as he bends over me, my eyes directly in line with his torso. This is way too close to 69ing. His gaze locks with mine as I run through the movements. He grabs the bar from me when my arms start trembling, and I jump up, putting some distance between us. His steady gaze stays on me. Dark. Heated.

"Ready for squats?"

I'm ready for more than just squats.

"This is called a Smith machine," he says, stopping at what can only be a torture device. "You load the plates here, then twist the bar to unlock it so you can do your lifts." I force myself to keep my eyes above his shoulders as he demonstrates a squat. "Your turn."

I step under the bar and settle it over my shoulders.

"Feet apart," Jack says from behind me, tapping the inside of my right foot with his toe. I widen my stance and lower myself. My knees pop and crack like Rice Krispies.

"You need to sit back more to take the pressure off your knees."

I try, but it doesn't feel any different.

"Pretend you're going to sit on my knee," he says, kneeling behind me.

I follow his instructions, feeling the strain in my thighs this time.

"Good. Now ten more." He doesn't move.

I touch down on his leg a little harder each time, my muscles shaking more and more with each rep. By the last one, the heat between my legs is nestled snugly against his knee. I should be mortified, but I'm too fucking turned on to care. I rack the bar and turn toward him, surprised to see he's sitting on a bench ten feet away, his gaze everywhere but on me.

"You good?"

"I'm fine," he mutters.

He's not fine, but I let it go. "What's next, deadlifts?" I ask, trying to fill up the awkward silence.

"There's no way in hell I would survive teaching you deadlifts, Charlotte," he grinds out, finally looking up at me, his expression tight.

"Was I really that bad?" My face heats with embarrassment.

"Bad? No." He cocks his eyebrow, and I realize I must be missing something.

"Then what?"

He looks around to make sure no one is watching, then palms his crotch. "I have the biggest fucking hard-on right now, Charlotte!" he hisses, keeping his voice low.

Oh. *Oh.* I can't tear my eyes away from his hand and the way it's wrapped around his cock. I clear my throat. "I guess telling me to sit on your knee wasn't the best idea, huh?"

"The best idea I've ever had," he growls. "Go tell Lachlan he needs to show you how to do deadlifts."

"That's not a good idea," I protest. All I want to do is go home and take an ice-cold shower.

"Lachlan!" Jack bellows, waving him down.

I watch Lach as he runs over, his shorts not hiding a damn thing. I stare at the mat. Hard.

"Do you want to help Charlotte with deadlifts?"

"Abso-fucking-lutely," he grins. His cock twitches, and I suck in a sharp breath, my gaze bouncing between them. I wonder if this is how it will work if I decide to go further with them. One taps out, and the other steps in to finish the job. As appealing as that sounds, I would much rather both of them finish the job at once.

"Charlotte." My name slides out of Jack's lips, a whispered warning.

Lachlan licks his lips, color high in his cheeks. "You're thinking about fucking us, aren't you?"

I splutter, "No."

"Don't lie, Sassenach," Jack says, standing up and taking a step toward me.

Lachlan steps between us. "Maybe we'll go with hip thrusts and get some of this sexual tension worked out?"

I nod mutely. Anything to get them separated. Anything to stop thinking about ripping down their shorts and taking what I want.

23

I wake up bright and early with a text from Isla asking me to check on Sorcha. I have a mini panic attack wondering if Jack will be at the barn again. Do I want to avoid him, or am I hoping for the perfect meet cute? Does he even wake up this early?

I rub my eyes. Hell, if I know. I don't even know what he does all day long. I don't know anything about him other than the fact that he hits all the right buttons. Fuck-me hair. Whisky eyes. Muscles for days. Lips that I can't stop thinking about.

Fuck. I have to get control of myself. Jack and Lachlan are a hard no. Really hard... *sigh.* I already know they're not the kind of guys you have a fling with and leave. They're the kind of men that get under your skin. The kind you never get over. The kind that can break your heart. They're the last thing I need when this summer ends with me going home. I'm starting to hate that word.

I throw on leggings and a hoodie, pulling the hood over yesterday's messy bun. I opt for rain boots, realizing too late that they're impossible to wear while riding a bike. After a few minutes of awkward pedaling, I jerk them off, throw them in the basket and pedal barefoot.

I move over to the shoulder when I hear a vehicle behind me, slowing down but not stopping because I loathe the idea of having to put my bare feet on the nasty wet road. An old farm truck blows past me, the gust of wind making the front tire of the bike wobble. After it passes, I sigh in relief, moving back into the road again. I round a bend, my attention on the loch, fog rising from the water, the castle a misty enigma in the background. I turn forward, and my heart skips a beat. The truck is right in front of me, stopped in the middle of the road. I squeeze on the break with my free hand.

"Fuck, fuck, fuck!" The front wheel locks up, pitching me over the handlebars.

Strong arms catch me, easily tossing the bike aside before it does any damage. I sink to the ground, my hand on my chest. "What the hell, Lach?"

He crouches down, his eyes scanning my limbs for damage. "I'm sorry, Carebear. I stopped to see if you wanted a ride. I didn't mean for you to run into me."

I take the hand he extends to me, jumping from one foot to the other as I pull on my boots, holding a hand up before he even asks me why I wasn't wearing them in the first place.

"I'll take the ride. Put the tailgate down and I'll sit on it," I say, throwing pride to the wind. He raises his eyebrow at me. "I'm muddy, Lach. I'm not getting in your truck like this."

"Fine," he says, annoyed. He places the bike in the truck bed and then lowers the tailgate, helping me up.

Thirty seconds later, we're pulling into the barn. I hop down, and a ball of black and white fur promptly knocks me on my ass. Mud soaks through my leggings in under a second. I don't even try to get up. I'm totally defeated, and it's not even nine a.m. Milo apologizes with long, hot licks up the side of my face. I pull him into a hug, blinking back tears.

"Easy," Lach chuckles, holding out his hand to help me up. Again.

I show him my scraped-up, mud-covered hands.

"A little mud never hurt anyone; come on." He reaches out and pulls me up smoothly. "There we go." His smile gives me butterflies. He drags his thumbs over my cheeks, painting a line with the mud.

"War paint for my little warrior." His hands dwarf my face. I grab one and turn it over, tracing the veins with my muddy fingertips.

Lach clears his throat. "I have an idea," he says, his gaze intense. "You've missed out on doing normal things the last five years, right?"

I nod.

"Let's fix that. Tell me what you feel you missed, and we'll do it."

"I can't – I have to finish Arty's tree." Disappointment sours in my stomach, followed by guilt for being ungrateful for the job.

"Yes, you can. We can stay in the highlands. That way, you'll still have time to work."

I mull it over for a minute. I'm only worried about finishing the tree; I can handle that by setting goals for the time I have left. As long as I stick to them, I can make it work. "It's a deal." I grin, my cheeks stretching wide.

Lach takes a deep breath, the material of his shirt stretching over his shoulders and arms. "You're beautiful when you smile, Charlie." He runs his thumb over my cheek in a light caress. "I can't wait to see how you look when..." His voice fades out, his gaze unfocused. He groans, deep and low. It travels straight to my core. I release a breath that's dangerously close to a moan and his eyes snap to mine. I back away from him slowly, desperately needing some space to clear the lust from my brain.

Lach clears his throat. "What do you want to do first?" he asks; only two steps and he's beside me again, the tension suffocating.

"Take a shower," I say truthfully.

Lach stills, his jaw working. "Then what," he grinds out, his gaze heavy.

"I want a tour of the farm." I've been dying to see what Lach and Jay spend so much of their lives on, and this is the perfect excuse.

"Done. When?"

I look at my wrist, then back up at him. "Now?" Lachlan grabs my arm and pulls me into the barn, up a set of stairs I hadn't noticed before. "Where are we going?"

"You said you wanted a shower, so we're going to shower."

"Together?" I balk, stopping in my tracks.

He turns toward me, confusion swirling in his eyes. "Are you scared of me, Charlie?"

I scrunch my forehead. "No. Not at all."

"Then why are you scared to take a shower with me? I would never hurt you. We can shower in our underwear, for all I care." He pulls me toward him, caressing my cheek with his thumb. "It's my fault you're in the state you're in. Just let me take care of you. Please."

"That sounds nice," I admit.

Lach nudges my chin up until I'm looking at him. "Nobody has ever taken care of you, have they?"

I shake my head, feeling pathetic.

He bends down, his lips whisper-light on mine. "I will take care of you forever if you let me, Carebear."

I laugh. "Is that a marriage proposal?"

He licks his lips, his pupils dilating. "Would you say yes?"

My breath whooshes out of my body. Would I?

A smile tugs at the corner of his lips. "Come on." He pulls me into a mostly bare bedroom except for a bed and a dresser pushed against the wall.

"Whose room is this?"

"Back in the day, it was for the stable master. Now, it's only used when we want to wash up before returning to the house."

I nod, my nerves ramping up with every step we take. He motions for me to sit on the bed before making his way into the attached bathroom to turn on the shower. He pauses in the doorway, studying me, tendrils of tension reaching out to snatch the breath from my lungs. I tear my gaze from him, trying to steady my breathing as I wrestle with my boots. I hiss when the heel scrapes against my hand. Lach drops to his knees in front of me, gently pulling the boots from my feet and placing them beside the bed.

"Arms up," he murmurs, grasping the hem of my sweatshirt and dragging it over my head. He stalls, my arms tangled over my head, his face a hairsbreadth from mine. His gaze drops to my lips, groaning before jerking the sweatshirt off the rest of the way and backing away from me.

My heart is in my throat, sex crackling through the air, coating my skin. "Tell me what you were just thinking about." He shakes his head, taking another step back. I walk to him, my body thrumming with need. "Tell me."

He runs a hand over his face, his chest rising and falling rapidly. "I want to tie you up and make you come in every position possible."

"Yes, please."

He clears his throat. "Not yet. You said you needed time; let me give you time. I didn't bring you up here to ravish you, Charlie." He rolls his shoulders, getting himself under control. Closing the distance between us, he hooks his fingers into my waistband, pulling my leggings down. I clutch his shoulders as I step out of them, vulnerable in my sports bra and underwear. He unbuttons his shirt, sliding it off his shoulders. My gaze follows his hands as he unbuckles his belt, unbuttons his pants, and slides the zipper down.

"For fuck's sake, Charlie!" My gaze swings back up to his face. "I'm holding on by a thread. If you keep looking at me like that, I'm going to—" he stops, his jaw clenching, struggling for control.

"You're going to what?" I push, wanting him to do everything he's been thinking of. I want to be used.

"Just get in the fucking shower, Charlie."

I'm throbbing with need and as I pull off my sports bra, our gazes locked. I hook my thumbs in my underwear and let them fall to my ankles, stepping out of them before turning and walking into the bathroom, my heart in my throat.

I step under the water, moaning as the heat melts away my shitty morning. I close my eyes, dipping my head back into the stream. Silent as a snake, Lach slips in behind me, hugging me to his chest, his arms tight around my abdomen. His cock presses into me, the fabric of his boxers a disappointing barrier.

"Shampoo," he says, holding out a cupped hand. I squeeze some into his hand. My mewl of protest as he steps back, turns into a guttural moan, his strong fingers pressing into my scalp, massaging the shampoo through my hair. He tips my head back into the spray, rinsing it out. My eyes flutter open as he turns me around, my gaze colliding with his.

"Let me touch you," I plead.

He swallows, his gaze volleying between my eyes and my lips. He spins me around suddenly, my back to his front. "You don't get to touch me until I've explored every square inch of your body," he rasps, his breath hot on my ear. I bend with him as he reaches for the body wash. He slides one hand over my stomach, his other has a vice grip on my hip, keeping us glued together. He brings his hand to my collarbone, soaping up my neck, upper chest, and between my breasts. I groan, arching against him, my eyes fluttering closed as the water sluices over me.

"Tell me what you want, Charlotte. " His hand skates under my breasts, sliding against sensitive skin. I gasp, grinding against him.

"Touch me," I moan, "Please, Lach."

He brings his hand up my stomach to gently cup one breast, his thumb flicking over my nipple. "Here?" he growls, kneading, pulling, twisting. I squeeze my thighs together as the need becomes unbearable, snaking my hand down my body to the apex of my thighs, sliding a finger over my clit before sinking it inside.

"Ah, ah, ah, Carebear," Lach scolds, pulling my hand up to his mouth and licking it clean. "That pussy is mine." He locks my hands behind me in a tight grip, pressing me flat to the glass. Our gazes collide in the mirror, the feral, animalistic need in his eyes shooting arrows of lust straight to my core.

"Please," I whisper, writhing against the glass, desperate for the friction it refuses to give. He holds my gaze as he slides a hand over my waist, down my stomach, and between my thighs, one thick finger circling my clit. I groan, going limp in his arms as my body tremors.

He moans into my ear, grinding his cock against my ass. "Let me taste you, Carebear." He sucks my earlobe into his mouth, and I arch against him, desperate for more.

"Yes, anything," I sob.

He releases my wrists, putting pressure on my back. "Bend over for me. There you go. That's a good girl," he purrs as he helps me widen my stance.

I press my face to the glass as he runs his hand along my spine, between my cheeks, his thumb sliding into me as his fingers work my clit. I push back into him, his name ripping from me in a low moan. I feel him drop to his knees behind me, a flash of self-consciousness before everything but his tongue fades into the background. He buries his face, his tongue lapping at the bundle of nerves before pushing up inside.

He flips me around and latches on to my clit, sucking me into his mouth. I buck against him, following as he lowers himself to the shower floor, pulling me down with him, my knees straddling his head. I hold myself over him as the water falls around us, trying not to suffocate him.

"Sit on my fucking face, Charlie," he barks, pulling me down roughly, his tongue lashing out.

Oh fuck.

I moan, sliding my hands into his hair, pulling him to me, riding him with everything I have. He slides a finger inside me, rubbing a spot that has me screaming his name as my body shatters into a million pieces.

24

Lach wraps me up in a big fluffy towel and drives me back to the cottage before leaving to find a change of clothes. I throw on a tank top with a cropped hoodie and joggers, still following Millie's advice to layer. I abandon the galoshes and opt for my trusty hiking boots. I go back to that day at the fairy pools as I lace them up. The feel of Cam's arms under my fingers as I helped him undress. The feel of his body between my legs as the frigid water lapped over our skin. Most of all, though, I miss our conversations.

There's a knock at the door as I swipe one last coat of mascara over my lashes. I open the door to Jay's large frame leaning against the side of the cottage. Canvas pants obscenely hug his legs, his arms crossed over his chest. I have trouble tearing my gaze away from the way his flannel shirt is pulling over his biceps.

"Hey, you," I say, sliding my gaze up his torso one last time and up to his mouth.

"Charlotte." He dips his head in greeting. "Lach sent me. He said you wanted a tour of the farm?"

I take a second to process the change of plans, deciding that I could definitely use some time away from Lach to get my head on straight. Plus, who better to take me on a tour than the man himself?

"That would be amazing." I grin, brushing past him and heading for his truck, ignoring the urge to rub against him like a cat.

Jack corners me against the locked truck, one hand hot on my hip, his lips close to my ear. "We're living in the moment today, Charlotte. I don't want to hear you talking about the end of the summer a single time. Do you understand?"

"Yes, sir," I whisper, intending my words to sound snide, but they are breathy and filled with desire.

Jack swears. "Get in," he growls, unlocking the door and wrenching it open.

I can't hide my grin as I climb in. Hot and bothered Jack is my favorite side of his personality by far.

"Hey, Carebear!" Lachlan ducks under Jack's arm, pressing a kiss to my cheek. "What'd I miss?"

"Hurry up and get in," Jack grumbles. Lach gets in on my right, and Jack slams his door a little too hard on my left. I smother a smile at being sandwiched between them. I like it—a lot.

We sit there for a minute, nobody moving a muscle. "Penny for your thoughts," I blurt when the silence gets too loud.

Jack clears his throat. "Honestly? I still can't believe you're here. The day after we met in the pub, I wasn't sure I would ever see you again. I went back and asked around town to see if anyone knew where you went, but nobody did. And then the ferry." His voice caught. "I waited for you."

"I waited for you, too," I whisper, my heart aching over the hurt in his eyes.

He smiles softly. "I had to trust that the gods would bring us together eventually."

"And they did." I reach over and lace my fingers through his.

He stares at me, his gaze roaming over my face, memorizing this moment. He pulls my hand toward his making me lean toward him and kisses me softly on the forehead. He presses his lips to each of my fingers before letting go of my hand to start the truck. Lachlan stretches his arm behind me, tracing lazy circles on my shoulder.

Is this how it will be if I decide to take the leap with them? I imagined something messy and awkward. Not this.

"Ready?" Jack asks, putting the truck in drive.

"I think so," I whisper, answering the question swirling nonstop through my mind. Can I really do this? Especially so soon after Rob? I look over at Jack, his hair blowing wild in the wind, totally in his element as we lurch and bump over the farm roads. I turn my gaze to Lachlan, his ever-present smirk twisting his lips. "What?" I ask when he stares back at me.

"Did you see the cows?" He points to the pasture to the right, to the enormous orange hairy cows that are impossible to miss.

"Those tiny things?"

"Do you know why they have hooves and not feet?" His eyes twinkle, his smirk turning into a barely controlled grin.

"Why Lachlan?"

"Because they lactose." I glance at Jack, get one look at the grimace on his face, and fall into a fit of giggles. The wind roars through the cab as we drive through a wide-open valley, my hair twisting around my head like a tornado. Lachlan catches it in a fist and pulls lightly, grinning when I scowl at him. I sneak a glance over at Jack, his ruggedness stealing the breath from my lungs. One large hand palms the steering wheel, and his other arm is out the window, pointing as he tells me about where he grew up. I can hear the passion in his voice as he explains the farm's history. How he's working to keep it the same as it has been for generations – honoring the ancestors that worked the land before him. His smile is loose and easy, his eyes sparkling; this is an entirely different side of him. I'm intrigued.

"Your turn," he says gruffly, breaking a comfortable silence.

"For what?"

"To share your thoughts."

I protest. He cocks his eyebrow at me. Pulling the truck to a stop, he twists in his seat to face me. His gaze is unrelenting. Heat races up my neck, settling into my cheeks. I duck my head and cover my face with my hands.

"Don't," he says, gently pulling my hands away. "Come on. Out with it."

Lachlan pulls my hand into his lap, twining his fingers through mine, squeezing them to bolster my courage. I take a deep breath. "I'm happy. I'm still not sure about everything, but right now, this feels right." I look between them, my heart in my throat.

Lachlan grins. "Finally."

I hold up my hand. "We need to go slow. I know myself, and I'll regret it if I run from this."

"We'll take it day by day... minute by minute if we have to, lass," Jack says gruffly. His wink sets my heart racing, nipples aching, heat pooling in places it shouldn't. His gaze drops to my lips and then further south, darkening when he sees my nipples pebbled against my shirt.

He swears under his breath. "Get out."

"What? Why?" I ask, but he's already slamming his door and heading to the bed of the truck. Lachlan pulls me to the edge of the seat, engulfing my waist in his hands, and lifts me from the truck. He covers my lips with his, sweeping his tongue against mine before sliding me down his body until my feet touch the ground.

He presses his forehead to mine, his gaze hot and hungry. "I need to taste you again, Charlie."

"It's been an hour, Lach," I say, laughing him off.

He pulls me flush against him, his erection hard against my hip. "I don't care if it was seconds ago, I'd still crave you. If I could live off your orgasms alone, I would, Charlie, I swear to God."

My core throbs at the picture his words create.

He spins me around, and we walk down a wide path, gravel crunching under our feet. Jack reaches out and grabs my hand, his fingers engulfing mine, shivering as his callouses scrape over sensitive skin. Lachlan slides a hand into my back pocket, giving my butt a firm squeeze. The three of us walk together, pulses thrumming from the simplest of touches. Jack brings my hand to his mouth, pressing his full lips to my skin, his teeth grazing my knuckles, and my body tightens into a ball of desire. His whisky eyes lock on mine as he nips at me, soothing the bites with a swipe of his tongue. He brushes his fingers over my cheek, tucking a strand of hair behind my ear. Lachlan pushes my hair off my neck and presses a kiss to the skin under my ear, goosebumps racing over my skin.

"Where are we going?" I ask Jack as we walk into a copse of trees.

"Craigh na Dun," he says, winking.

25

Jack motions for me to follow him into a clearing in the trees, and there, on top of a hill, sits a stone circle. It's magical. Magnificent pine trees soar high above our heads, their needles forming a thick carpet under our feet. Moss and lichen clamber for purchase over the stones, swirling carvings peeking out from the few bare spots.

Jack sets his pack against a tree and moves toward me. My stomach somersaults as I stand my ground. He grips my hips and pushes me back until I'm flush against a stone.

"Does this remind you of anything, Sassenach?" His chin is almost to his chest as he looks down at me, need swirling through his amber eyes.

The night of the masquerade party flashes through my mind.

"I can see your face this time," I murmur, trying to memorize every detail. The tiny freckle below his left eye. The scar that cuts through his right eyebrow. The dimples mostly hidden by his beard.

He pushes his thumb against my lower lip, dragging it to the side, his gaze locked on my mouth. "God, Charlotte." His hand drops to my neck, cupping sensitive skin, my blood thrumming under his fingers. His gaze follows his hand as it slips further down my collarbone, stopping over my hammering heart. "You feel it, too," he says, a statement, not a question.

How can I not? Our souls have been orbiting each other at a dizzying pace since the day we met. His gaze is heavy, his lips so close I can feel their heat.

"I can smell him on you," he growls, rocking his hips into me.

I groan, closing the distance between us, pressing my lips to his and inviting the rough sweep of his tongue. We're two stars colliding, exploding, creating a black hole of insatiable need. He slides his palm over the small of my back, pulling me into his body, his hard length pressed to my stomach.

A low groan from behind Jack has my eyes flying open.

Lach.

Every nerve comes alive, energy vibrating through my body, gathering in my core. I moan as Jack lodges his thigh between my legs. He grips my ass, lifting my toes off the ground as he turns me around. Lach steps forward, running his hands over my shoulders and down my arms, his lips hot on my ear. I break the kiss, gasping for air. Jack fists his hand in my hair, pulling to expose my neck. Turning my face to the side, Lach captures my mouth in a fierce kiss, moaning against my lips like a man possessed.

"I feel like I've been waiting ten years to do that again," he murmurs. Jack grips my jaw, turning my face back to him, his gaze dark. Possessive.

"This was the biggest fucking mistake of my life," he whispers, tracing my bottom lip. "You're going to break my heart, aren't you, Sassenach?" He angles his head, holding my gaze, his lips brushing against mine. "It doesn't fucking matter now. It's done."

I open for him, our tongues clashing in an epic battle. There's an inevitability to this kiss, like the three of us are standing on the edge of a precipice, ready to jump. Jack pulls away and turns me so I'm facing Lach, sliding his hands over my stomach and up to cup my breasts, his thumbs flicking over my nipples. Lach presses into me, his hands diving into my hair, pulling my face to his, devouring me.

Jack rocks his hips against my ass, his breath hot on my ear. He groans as he snakes his hand inside the front of my leggings. I gasp as he slides a finger over me. "God, you're so wet." He presses a finger inside me, forcing me to arch back against him, breaking my kiss with Lachlan. Instead of complaining, he switches his attention to my nipple, biting and kissing it through my shirt. I moan, grinding against the heel of Jack's hand. "Can we take off your pants?" Jack asks, his mouth pressed to my ear.

I nod, desperate for more. He pulls his hand away, licking me off his fingers before grasping my jaw and pulling my lips to his. Lach pushes my leggings down, helping me step out of them. Jack grasps the back of my thighs with both hands, lifting me off the ground and pulling my knees to my chest, my legs spread wide. I struggle in his grip, but Lach cradles my face, stroking my cheek with his thumb. "Give me one minute, Carebear. If you don't like it, we'll stop. I promise."

"Okay," I whisper, my heart galloping, turned on and terrified at the same time.

He steps forward, his gaze dropping between my thighs.

"You're so fucking pretty," he groans, kneeling before me and breathing me in. I buck against his mouth as he slides his tongue over me, my entire world narrowing to our connection. He rolls his tongue over my clit, pulling the nub into his mouth as he pushes two fingers into me, sinking them in until his pinky knuckle is nudging my asshole. A guttural sound tears its way from my throat, part protest, part ecstasy.

"You're doing so good, Charlotte," Jack groans against my ear. Lach twists his hand, fingers curling into my g-spot, working it over and over as he drags his tongue over my clit. I reach up and wrap my hand around Jack's neck, pulling his face down as I stretch toward him, our lips meeting in a clash of tongues and teeth. I gasp against his mouth as the first tremors start. He groans against my lips. "Come for us, baby." I try to hang on for a second longer, but Lach is relentless. I explode, spasming around his fingers as he licks me into oblivion.

"You're so fucking perfect," Lach rasps, his chest heaving with each breath. Jack sets me down gently, gripping my hips to keep me upright as Lach helps me with my leggings. He turns me around in his arms and sweeps a strand of hair out of my face, his fingers lingering on my cheek. "Are you hungry?"

"Yes, but not for food." I palm his erection, the moan that slips from his lips chasing a shiver down my spine. I need more. So much more. I grasp the front of Lach's shirt and pull him toward me, sliding my hand under his shirt and over his stomach.

He circles my wrist, pulling it up to his mouth and kissing my palm. He raises an eyebrow when my stomach grumbles. "Come on, let's eat."

The sun is slanting through the trees, a magical golden haze settling over us as we eat from the spread of meat and cheese Jack pulls from his backpack. I tuck my knees to my chest, watching them as I sip crisp white wine from a plastic cup. They're telling the worst stories they have about each other, cussing each other out one second, wiping away tears of laughter the next. I know without a shadow of a doubt that this will be the moment I remember falling in love with them.

26

"Charlotte."

I spin around, the hay in my arms forgotten. Jack is standing in the shadows, a shaft of sunlight gilding one side of his face. "Yes?" I ask when I realize he's waiting for me to say something. It's been two days since he and Lach decimated the last of my crumbling walls. Two days of closing myself up in the cabin, feeling vulnerable. Terrified of the feelings I can't seem to ignore any longer.

"Why are you here?" he asks, focusing on the piece of hay he's twisting between his fingers.

"Isla asked me to take care of Sorcha."

"No, why are you *here?*" His whisky eyes meet mine, emotions warring in their depths. He takes the hay from me, tossing it into the hay rack in Sorcha's stall. He walks back to me slowly, his gaze heated, studying me. I flinch when he reaches out, but he only pulls a piece of straw from my hair. "Are you scared of me, lass?"

"No. I'm scared of this." I motion between us, the hurt in his eyes drawing an honest answer from me.

"What is 'this,' exactly? Aren't we just friends?" He raises an eyebrow, his gaze moving to my lips, then away. He boosts himself onto the stack of bales against the wall, his legs hanging over the side.

"This is scary as fuck," I whisper. We're on the same level now, and I'm having a hard time not looking at his lips, remembering how they felt moving over mine.

"This is life, Charlotte. It's wild and amazing and the scary parts are the best parts."

"That's what I used to think." My voice cracks. "but I know better now." I drop my gaze, the humiliation of the last five years washing over me in waves.

"Come here," he whispers. I walk toward him, stopping just shy of his knees. "Look at me," he demands, his voice doing sinful things to my body.

I look at him.

"Charlotte. He never deserved you." He leans forward and pulls me in, wrapping his arms around my back and tucking my head under his chin. I clutch him, burying my face in his neck.

"I want to forget, Jack," I say, my lips moving against his neck, "I just don't know how." I lick my lips, the tip of my tongue touching his skin, the burst of salt turning my insides to liquid.

Everything but the pulse under my lips freezes.

I suck in a jagged breath, leaning back so I can look at him. His beard tickles my palm as I cup his face. I run a fingertip over his eyebrow, over the tiny dip of a scar, over the bridge of his nose. He's still as stone, barely breathing. I drop my hand. "I don't know how to let it go," I whisper, the words barely audible.

"One step at a time, Charlotte," he says, pushing my hair away from my face with a gentle hand. I nuzzle my face into his palm, desperate for his touch. His eyes darken. He licks his lips, his gaze dipping to my mouth. Cupping my face in both hands, he presses a gentle kiss to my eyes, to my nose, next to my mouth. I turn my head to catch his lips with mine, sinking into him with a groan. He tenta-tively traces his tongue over my bottom lip. I angle my head, allowing him full access. He pushes into me over and over, hard and insistent.

When he comes up for air, I slide my tongue over his bottom lip, sucking and biting.

"Charlotte," he whispers, breathing hard. He rests his forehead against mine, his eyes closed.

I laugh, my insides fizzing like champagne bubbles.

He pulls me in, nestling me between his legs. I stare at him, half in wonder, half in absolute terror. This man... "This doesn't change the fact that I have to go back home," I blurt, refusing to let myself forget that I don't live here. I expect him to pull away, expect him to be hurt.

"I know," he murmurs, tracing his finger over my eyebrows. "And that's okay, Charlotte. I'm here for whatever you need. Whether that's friendship or something more."

I feel a huge burden fall from my shoulders. We may kiss, but that doesn't mean it has to go further. And if it does, that doesn't have to mean anything profound, either. He runs his finger down my nose and over the bow of my lips, pulling at my lower lip, his gaze narrowing to my mouth. He slicks his tongue over his bottom lip, and that's the final straw. I crush my mouth to his, my body coming alive with the drag of his teeth over tender flesh, the swipe of his tongue over mine.

It's not enough.

I whimper and he moans in response. My toes curl and my back arches, the tips of my breasts seeking friction. He splays his hand over my back, holding me in place as he lazily draws circles over my ribcage, purposely avoiding the places I want him to touch. I groan in frustration and arch further, pushing my chest against him. He sucks my lip into his mouth just as his hand closes over my breast, rolling my nipple between his fingers. I gasp and pull my mouth from his, raining kisses over his cheeks and down his neck as he kneads and plucks at me. His breaths are heavy against my ear, ratcheting my drive even higher.

"Charlotte." He pulls away from me, the air between us dousing the fire. His hand trembles as he runs it through his hair.

"What's wrong?"

"Nothing's wrong, lass." He tips my head up to meet his gaze. "I want to cherish this." His throat bobs. "Even if we're just friends, it doesn't mean we have to race to the finish line. I want to savor you like you're my last meal."

I would have dropped my panties for him right then and there if he was willing. I nod and take a couple of deep breaths, my gaze catching on the thick length straining against his zipper. He caresses my cheeks with his thumbs, his hands cradling my face. We stare at each other, not saying anything.

He grins suddenly. "I—" he stops short, pressing a kiss to my forehead.

"You what?" I ask, stepping back so he can stand.

"Everything seems different since the day we met, Charlotte. You're invading my senses. The air I breathe like you, for fuck's sake." He catches my hand in his, peppering kisses over my knuckles. "I hope you know how amazing you are."

My cheeks warm as I hold his gaze. "You're not so bad yourself," I say, giving him an exaggerated wink.

"Hey." He pulls me back to him, his face only inches from mine. "I mean it."

"Yes, sir," I say, my voice husky.

His nostrils flare and he grabs my ass, pulling me against his cock, rolling his hips against mine. "I can't wait to fucking destroy you." He spins us around, pinning me to the bales, and shoves his thigh between my legs, rocking it back and forth. He dips his head until his mouth is against my ear, "Let me hear how much you like it." I drop my head back against the hay, clamping my mouth closed to keep in the moan, self-consciousness breaking through the haze.

"Let go, Charlotte," Jack rumbles, eyes so dark I can only see a sliver of whisky around his pupils. He fists my shirt in his hands, ripping it open, buttons popping. He pushes his thumbs into my bra, pulling my breasts from the cups, kneading and pinching until I'm dizzy with need. I sob his name when he stops moving his leg, pleading for him to keep going. He holds my gaze as he lowers his mouth, swirling his tongue around my nipple, drawing it deep into his mouth, his groan vibrating all the way to my core. I cry out as he drags his teeth over my nipple, rocking my pelvis against his thigh, desperate for release.

"That's my fucking girl," he groans as he moves to my other breast, flicking my nipple with his tongue. "Take what you need," he rasps against me, pressing his thigh in tighter. I roll my hips against his leg twice and I'm there, falling apart in his hands. He palms my throat, pulling my face to his, plundering my mouth. He thrusts against me slowly, his cock an iron rod against my hip.

"Fuck, Charlotte," he groans, gathering me in his arms and pulling me into his body.

"Let me get you there, Jack," I practically beg, running my hand over him. All I can think about is how he'll feel, how he'll taste.

"God." He bites his lip and covers my hand with his, thrusting against my fingers. He grits his teeth and pulls my hand away, linking his fingers with mine. "Not until I know you're not going anywhere."

"But—"

He shushes me, wrapping his arms around my waist. "Can we stay like this forever?" he mumbles into my hair, squeezing me against him.

"If I could unzip your skin and climb inside you, I would."

"Oh fuck," he laughs, his chest shaking under my cheek. "How about we go take care of the horses and save climbing into each other's skin for tomorrow?"

"Deal," I say, grinning. God, I love him.

27

Isla shoves open the door to the cottage, scaring the ever-loving shit out of me.

"Hey! You wanna come with us to Jack's?"

"I'm in the middle of something," I say, gesturing to the papers spread over the kitchen table. I've been organizing my notes for the last three days, and I finally have a good idea of the vignettes that will bring out the personality of Arty's ancestry.

"You've been in the middle of something for days. Time for a break."

I sigh. "I don't even know the last time I showered, Isla."

"Perfect timing then! We leave in an hour." She grins at me, her eyes sparkling.

"Fine," I grumble, closing my laptop and shoving back from the table.

"Bring your bathing suit!" she yells as she slams the door.

Seriously? I know she did that on purpose. If she had told me that from the beginning, I never would have agreed to go.

An hour later, I'm walking up the hill to the house in loose linen pants and a white t-shirt, my barely-there swimsuit hidden underneath. I have a towel and a change of clothes in the bag over my shoulder. Isla is already in the coupe's backseat, and Lach is leaning against the passenger door, waiting on me. He's in swim trunks and flip-flops, a beach towel draped over his shoulders, leaving his arms and abs on full display. The sun gilds the light dusting of golden hair over his chest, and I barely restrain myself from running my fingers through it.

"Ready, Carebear?" His smile is brighter than the sun itself. I nod and grin back at him as flashes from the other day race through my mind, tightening my nipples and flushing my cheeks. I hug my bag to my chest as I get in the car, mortified that I can't go be around him for ten seconds without wanting to jump him.

"Whose car is that?" I ask as we pull up to Jack's, pointing to the expensive-looking sedan parked in the drive.

"Lorna's," Lachlan says, slamming his door, then coming around to open mine.

Who the hell is Lorna?

I follow them around the back, my steps faltering when my gaze lands on Jack. He's hugging a woman, pressing a long kiss to her cheek. He steps around her and drops to his knees, his face cracking into the biggest smile I have ever seen. Two little kids tumble into his arms, shrieking as he hauls them up and swings them around.

"Lorna!" Isla calls, waving her over.

She's beautiful. Long wavy hair, hazel eyes, and a smattering of freckles over pink cheeks.

"Lorna, this is—"

"Charlie, I've heard so much about you." She smiles wide and pulls me into a hug.

Isla laughs. "Charlie, this Lorna, Jack's sister."

I let out the breath I've been holding. "Nice to meet you, Lorna," I smile, "These are your kids?"

"Yes! Daniel, Lorelei, come meet Charlie!"

They're around three years old, their hair so blonde it's almost white. They're dirty, sticky, and absolutely adorable.

I drop to my knees and hold out my hands to them. "I'm Charlie, it's nice to meet you both," I say, shaking their hands.

They giggle and take off running.

"Drink?" Lorna asks, moving toward a table set up near the stairs leading up to a terrace.

"Yes, please," the three of us answer simultaneously.

Lorna and I sit on a blanket, sipping on glasses of chilled white wine while Jack tumbles with the kids. Lach is halfway to dreamland on a lounger, and Isla is dipping her toes in the loch.

"Tell me about yourself, Charlie," Lorna says, her expression open and curious.

"There's honestly not much to tell. I'm from the U.S. and here on a job for three months."

"Isla told me a little about your work – something about a family tree?"

"Yes, it's the family tree for an old friend. I'm here researching his ancestors, and then I'll draw up a tree for him that can be framed and handed down to his grandkids."

"That's fascinating. Only until you're finished with the job?"

"Unfortunately, yes. "

She pouts her lip a bit, looking over at Jack. "You're going to break his heart, aren't you?" she asks, her voice sad.

I choke out a startled laugh. "Definitely not. I am not the heart-breaking type, Lorna. Look at me."

"I am looking at you." Her pout turns into a frown. She breaks our gaze and turns to watch Jack and her kids, her expression softening.

"Isn't he great?"

I watch as Jack swings Daniel up in the air until he's shrieking with giggles.

"He is," I murmur, finding it hard to swallow. "This is the first time I've seen him with kids – he seems like a natural."

"Right? I can't wait until little Jacks are running around every-where. He's going to be such a great father."

Jack looks over at me and grins, his face glowing with joy. I swallow around a lump in my throat, blinking back the sudden mois-ture in my eyes.

Lach sits down next to me, cradling my face in his hands as he plants a kiss on my lips. "She's amazing, isn't she, Lorna?"

"I've only just met her, Lachlan," she scolds, rolling her eyes.

"It doesn't matter. I knew the second Milo tackled her that she was special." He kisses me again, softer this time. "Let me know if you need anything, okay?" I nod, and he stands back up, heading toward the water.

"Oh, Charlie," Lorna whispers, her eyes sad.

My heart thumps painfully.

"I've seen this before, and it didn't end well."

I open my mouth, immediately on the defensive, but I stop and take a second to organize my thoughts before speaking. "Tell me about it," I say instead.

"The four of them had a great relationship for a while. It seemed to bring out the best in all of them. Then Emily decided she wanted to settle down but couldn't see herself doing it with all of them. So she picked the most established one and proceeded to make him miserable."

"I settled down in college and felt like I was dying the entire time. I want life, chaos... I want to be happy. And I want *them* to be happy," I tell her, my words sincere.

"Well, you've succeeded there. I haven't seen them this carefree in years. Just be careful. They've been through a lot."

"I will," I murmur.

"Guard your heart, Charlie. I worry about the guys, but we women need to stick together, too."

Isla comes back with a wine bottle, filling our cups.

Lorna lays back on the blanket, releasing a gigantic sigh. "I almost forgot what it feels like not to have a tiny human attached to my hip," she says, smiling blissfully.

"Do you want me to put them down for their nap?" Isla asks, lying beside her, stretching out like a cat in the sun.

"Jack already offered. I told him he should be out here enjoying himself, but he insisted."

"I wish you'd let us take them overnight, " Isla props herself up to look at Lorna. "You could sleep... or go on a date and *not* sleep." She winks at Lorna.

I smile. I love their family's teasing banter. It makes me feel warm and comforted – so bizarre, but it's probably one of my favorite things about this trip. It was a privilege to be around them.

"I will one of these days. I promise."

"I'm going to hold you to that." Isla lays back down, turning her face to the sun, taking advantage of the unseasonable warm weather.

"So, what are your plans for the rest of your time here, Charlie?" Lorna asks.

My heart sinks like it does every time I think about how fast the time is passing. "My number one goal is to finish my commission, but that goes without saying. On top of that? I plan on making the most out of every single second I have left. I've never felt quite like I do here. I don't know how to describe it, but it feels like I've come home."

"Maybe you have," Lorna says, smiling.

"I wish," I whisper wistfully. "Arty gave me enough to live on for a few months, but after that, I'll have to be an adult again and get a real job."

"Why?" Isla sits up and stares at me, her voice tinged with frustration.

"Because I'm poor. I'll be okay once the divorce goes through. But who knows how long that will take. The only money I have is what Arty gave me."

Lorna sits up beside Isla, furious. "That's not right, Charlie. You helped your ex build that business, didn't you?" She and Jack must have had an in-depth conversation about me at one point. I'll have to decide how I feel about that later.

"I guess?"

"Were you there from the beginning? Did you help bring in clients?"

I nod.

"And I know you worked harder than that douchebag," Isla hisses, her tone venomous.

I laugh. "God, I love you guys."

"I'm serious, Charlie – did you?" Lorna asks.

I think about all the days I was out on jobs while he was playing golf. All the days he had 'meetings' while I worked my ass off out in the heat, my literal blood, sweat, and tears sinking into the soil day after day.

"Yes. I honestly can't even remember the last time he came home with dirt under his nails."

"Fuck him," Isla grinds out, looking murderous.

"I'm going to make some calls Monday. We need to find you a good lawyer, Charlie."

"You don't need to do that," I protest.

"No, I don't, but I want to. We're in your corner, Charlie. I barely know you, and I can tell you're not used to relying on anyone – that you've had zero support. Whatever happens between you, Jack, and Lach, Isla and I are here for you. Always."

"Thank you. Truly."

"Well, you don't need to worry about that anymore, now do you? Come on, let's go swimming." Isla grabs my hand and pulls me up. "You coming, Lorna?"

"In a little bit, I'm going to make sure Jack didn't have trouble putting the twins down first." She stands and heads for the house, leaving me with an inpatient Isla. I wave her on, assuring her I'll only be a second.

If I'm being honest, I was hoping I would never get to the point where I had to wear my swimsuit in front of anybody. It's the only one I packed when I grabbed my clothes the night I caught Rob cheating. I bought it for the trip to Europe that never happened – and it would have been perfect for that – but here it seems scandalous. I look up at the house, wondering if I can rip my clothes off and get into the water before anyone sees me, but Jack is on the deck, deep in conversation with Lorna. I turn away from him and pull my shirt off, adjusting my suit before looking back at him to make sure he's not paying attention.

My heart jumps into my throat when I see his eyes trained on me. I turn back toward the water, struggling between being embarrassed and wanting to give him a show at the same time. I untie the drawstring of my pants and look back over my shoulder at him. He's leaning on the railing now, focused only on me. I watch him as I shimmy my pants off, slowly letting the fabric fall away from my ass, revealing a scrap of fabric I have the audacity to call a bikini bottom. Jack vaults himself over the railing, his long strides eating up the ground between us.

"I'll give you a ten-second head start," he growls. "Run."

Fuck.

28

———————

My mind takes a second to process his command. Did he really tell me to run? And why the fuck does that turn me on? I shriek when he starts counting down and I bolt toward the water, grabbing Isla's hand as I pass her. We crash into the water together in a tangle of limbs. I come up choking and spluttering, but Isla rises out of the water like a mermaid, flinging her hair over her head in a wide arc.

"How are you so damn hot?" I protest, splashing her.

"Gross!" Jack yells right before he tackles me. He cradles my head, spinning us under the water so he winds up underneath me. He pulls my mouth against his as he stands up, I cling to him, wrapping my leg around his hips.

"Ewww!" Isla screeches, sending a sheet of water our way.

Jack sets me down and disappears under the water, popping up fifty yards away.

"Does he usually do that?" I gape.

Isla laughs, shaking her head. "I think he needs to work off some steam. Did you see the way he was looking at you?" She wiggles her eyebrows, grinning.

"He was not," I laugh, sending a wave of water toward her.

Jack pushes out of the water right in front of me, water streaming down his torso. "Yes, I was, Sassenach. You're a fucking snack."

Heat pools in my stomach. If I'm a snack, I want him to be my last meal.

He shakes his hair out of his face. I stand there frozen, watching the rivulets of water running over the ridges of his stomach. Holy hell.

"My eyes are up here, Charlotte."

Mortification rolls over me, heat rushing to my cheeks. I meet his gaze, ready for the cheeky smirk, but it's all heat. He pulls his bottom lip into his mouth and lust spikes through me, a lightning bolt straight between my thighs. I sink into the cold water but realize too late that I'm now eye-level with his crotch. Wet swim trunks don't hide a damn thing. He's massive, and I can't tear my eyes away. I groan and submerge myself until the water closes over my head. Aiming toward a floating platform, I swim underwater until my breath runs out. I pull myself up onto the ancient wooden planks and lie on my back, taking deep breaths. I'm panting over a big dick like a hussy. I grin to myself.

Jack bursts from the water, boosting himself onto the platform. "That's an awfully big smile you have there," he says, his voice smoke and whisky.

"That's an awfully big—" I slap my hand over my mouth, my eyes wide. Why the fuck can't I control myself when I'm around him?

He turns toward me, cocking an eyebrow. "An awfully big what?"

I roll away from him until I plop off into the water. Escape is the only answer. I open my eyes under the water to try to see where the platform is with the sole plan of getting back to shore and hi-tailing it back to the cottage. I push up for a breath, but Jack is already there, grabbing my arms so I can't go back under.

He slides his hands over my waist, the rough scrape of his callouses setting my nerves on fire. "A big what, Charlotte?" he asks roughly.

I press my forehead to his chest, my gaze traveling down his body, the dusting of hair on his lower stomach snagging my attention before I look further down, his swim trunks almost obscene the way they're tented. My heart rate picks up, throbbing in forbidden places. I moan, squeezing my hands into fists. I want him so bad I can barely think straight. I look up at him through my lashes, letting him see everything.

"Fuck...me." His gaze anchors on my lips as he traces them with his thumb. "I wish we were alone," he murmurs.

I hum my agreement, watching as he slides his tongue over his lips. God. I want his tongue on me. In me.

"Jack! Come help with the burgers?" Lorna calls from the deck, sounding frazzled.

"I better go help." He brushes his lips over the corner of my mouth and wades out of the water, grabbing a towel to wrap around his waist.

I watch Jack pause by Lach's chair and say something to him. Lach raises his head to look at me, then sits up, motioning for me to join him. I walk to him and sit down between his legs; he pulls me against his chest, his warm sun-kissed skin making me shiver. He nuzzles my neck, rubbing my arms with his hands to warm me up.

"Are you having a good time?" he asks, his voice husky with sleep.

"Yes, maybe too much."

"How can you have too much of a good time, Carebear?" He pulls my hair over one shoulder, pressing his lips to the sensitive skin behind my ear.

I take a second to think of a less scary way to spin how I'm feeling, but I give up. "I feel like I belong here, and I don't understand it. If I'm being honest, it's terrifying. I have to leave eventually."

"Do you, though?"

I twist to look at him. "Yes! I don't have any money. I have to go back and figure out the rest of my life."

Lach extricates himself from the chair and stands in front of me, his fingers tracing my jaw. He squats down, bringing his eyes to the same level as mine. "I want you to listen to me, okay? I don't want you to respond. Just think about it."

"Okay." I bite my lip, suddenly nervous.

"If you want to stay, we'll figure it out. This may feel like home to you, but you feel like home to us."

I pull in a breath, starting to protest, but he presses a finger to my lips. "Listen. If you want to stay, you should stay. There's no obligation, nothing to pay back. Just you staying with your people, ok?"

"You're only one-third of this equation, how do you know Jack feels the same way?"

"You have no clue, do you?" He shakes his head, not hiding his frustration. "Jack was ready to propose to you the second you showed up here. He's been holding back. A lot."

I groan. This was supposed to be a simple working holiday, for fuck's sake.

"It's not that deep, Charlie. I know you have trauma in the past that makes it hard to trust us, but we're not him. I'm not trying to guilt you into staying – I'm letting you know there are options so that you can make the best decision for you. We both like spending time with you– whether or not it turns into something more – and we'll take you for as long as we can get you. No strings."

He stands up and massages my shoulders with strong fingers. My heart hammers with awareness, the smooth skin of his stomach only inches from my face. I lean forward and swipe my tongue along the ridge of muscle on his right side. Encouraged by his groan, I do the same to the other side, then trail kisses from his navel to his waistband.

"Speaking of strings," I murmur, looking around to make sure everyone's inside. I pull on the tie of his swim trunks, pulling them down just enough to see the base of his cock. My mouth is watering with how badly I want to taste him. "Please?" I whisper, looking up at him with fuck-me eyes.

"God, Charlie. I don't know how I can say no when you look at me like you're starved for it."

"I am," I rasp. He's heavy in my hand as I pull him out, his skin like silk against my palm. I lick one long stroke from his balls to the tip, swirling my tongue over the glistening drop of pre-cum. He shudders as I draw him into my mouth, hissing as I hollow my cheeks and bob my head.

"Charlie," he groans, "This wasn't supposed to happen yet."

I hum my disagreement. He swears and bucks his hips, sinking into me. He jerks back when I gag. "Fuck, I'm sorry, Charlie." He tries to pull me up, but I don't budge. He grabs my ponytail and pulls my head back.

"Harder," I gasp, the bite of pain fueling the fire in my veins. He clenches his jaw, looking at me look up at him, my hair still tight in his fist.

"I won't be able to control myself if we keep going. I want to fuck your face like it's the last fuck of my life, and there won't be anything gentle or sweet about that."

"I don't want gentle and sweet. I want you. In my mouth. Now." I pump my hand over him, waiting for him to release me so I can devour him. I'm not sure I've ever wanted something this bad in my entire life. I can see it in his eyes when he gives in.

"If you want me to stop, tap twice on my leg, okay?"

I nod, my eyes on the prize. I'm on him the second he lets go, sliding my hand over him as I suck and lick his head. I tease his frenulum until he buries his hands in my hair, but he still doesn't take control. I grab his ass and pull him toward me, burying his cock in my throat. He moans, gripping the sides of my face and holding me still as he fucks my mouth. I feel it when he starts to tense.

"I'm so close, Charlie." He pulls away, jerking out of my hands and backing up a couple of steps.

"Please, Lach." I crawl to him.

"I can't be gentle with you, Charlie. I want it too much. You deserve better than that."

"It's not about what I deserve, Lach. I want to make you feel good."

He closes the distance between us, cupping my face in his hands as I look up at him.

"Please."

"Fuck, Charlie." He grits his teeth as I take him back into my mouth. I've never felt like this before. I feel free. I am free to be who I am and tell him what I want – what I need. I sneak a hand down between my legs as he chases his release, staring up at him, our gazes locked, tears leaking from the corners of my eyes. He groans, his entire body arching as he pulls my head forward to take one last thrust. I swallow him down and then lick him clean.

"Get the fuck up here," he growls, pulling up his trunks, lifting me, and wrapping my legs around his torso. He rests his forehead against mine, still breathing heavily. "You are a mother-fucking goddess, Charlie. You could eat me alive, and I would figure out a way to say thank you after. And fuck if you didn't look like you wanted it."

I laugh, low and husky. "I want way more than that, but that's a good start."

He slides his hand into my hair and pulls my lips to his, kissing me like he didn't just fuck my mouth. A shiver of need races down my spine, and I move against him, desperate for some friction.

"Dinner's ready," Jack says from behind us, his deep brogue raising the tiny hairs on my arms. Lach kisses me one last time and then sets me down.

Jack slaps my ass as Lach pulls on his shorts and walks toward the house, running his hand over the globe of my ass cheek and straight to my center, sliding a finger inside before I realize what he's doing.

"Fuck, Charlotte. Did he get you ready for me?" He pulls his finger out and licks it off slowly. "Come on, let's eat."

29

———

Watching Jack build a bonfire for the last thirty minutes has been a true test of self-control. His wild hair is pulled back into a bun, shirt long-forgotten, tattoos on full display. His skin is velvety in the evening light, and I desperately want to run my hands over him to find out if it's as soft as it looks.

I pull my towel tighter around my arms, tucking my legs up against my torso. The air has a bite to it, but I can't bear to stray from his orbit. I'm tracing his back muscles with my eyes when he stands and turns, my eyes once again level with his crotch. I look for a second longer than I should before raising my head, our gazes colliding. He bites his lip, his eyes dark as they slowly coast over my body.

"Are you cold?" he asks, arching his eyebrow.

"A little." I cover my breasts to hide the evidence. He smirks and tosses me his discarded hoodie before turning back to the fire. His scent invades all my senses as I pull it on over my bikini top. I close my eyes and breathe in, the image of him stretched out over me flashes in my mind, a spike of lust lodging in my core.

I open my eyes and take several deep breaths, wrestling for self-control. I try thinking of everything except him, but my body has a mind of its own, the heartbeat between my legs growing stronger every second. I squeeze my thighs together, desperate. Jack's gaze flies to mine, taking in my hooded eyes and flushed cheeks. I straighten, a stubborn tilt to my chin.

"Can I help you with something?"

His brogue sets every tiny hair on my body at attention. I shiver, swallowing a groan as I shift in my seat.

"Touch yourself, Charlotte," he whispers. The firelight flickers around him, he looks like a Greek fire god here to avenge my tragic sex life.

"What? No!" I hiss, "Someone will see us!" I can hear Isla and Lorna laughing up on the deck, and even though I know they can't see us, they only need to come down the stairs and look to the right to have a direct view.

His eyes are pinned to the apex of my thighs, to the moisture gathering there. "Fuck, Charlotte." He palms his cock, rubbing himself through his swim trunks. I watch, breathless, as the veins on his arm pop out more with each stroke of his hand. His gaze brands me, and I know without a doubt that I'll never be the same after this.

"Touch yourself," he commands, erasing any willpower I have left.

Oh, God. This is really happening.

My heartbeat thunders in my ears as I run my hand over my breast, arching my back as I roll my nipple between my fingers. Jack's stilted groan gives me the confidence to keep going. I slide my hand over my stomach, then lower, opening my legs. Jack steps closer, dropping to his knees just out of reach.

"Keep going." His voice is ragged, his hand keeping a steady pace on his cock.

I push my fingers under the fabric of my swimsuit, slowly sliding one finger over my slit. I'm soaking wet.

"I need to see you," he whispers as he unties the sides of my swim-suit and pulls the fabric away. "You're so fucking perfect."

"Your turn," I rasp, feeling like I'll die if I don't see all of him.

Jack jerks down his swim trunks and then sits back on his heels, his hand stroking from base to tip.

I sink a finger inside me as the head of his cock disappears in his hand, a whimper escaping my lips. The fire outlines his muscled body, every square inch of him bathed in flickering light. Toes digging into the earth, thick thighs spread wide, broad shoulders tapering down to washboard abs. I watch as he moves his hand over himself, mirroring his movements with my fingers.

"Can I?" Jack asks, sliding a hand up my leg and kneading my thigh.

I don't know what he's asking, but the answer is yes. Always yes. I nod. He pushes a thick finger into me, and I arch against his hand, my hips bucking in the air.

"Fuck," he mutters, frustration and lust warring over his features as he watches me come undone. He pulls his finger from me and spreads my arousal over his cock.

"Jack, please," I whimper, bereft without him inside me.

He closes the distance between us and pushes my legs wide, his hands rough. His eyes are barely open as he plunges two fingers into me. I roll my hips against him, my ass sliding to the edge of the chair. He pulls out and licks his fingers, his gaze never leaving mine. He rests his head on my inner thigh, heavy breaths puffing against my sex. He breathes in, a deep groan vibrating through him and into me. I contort, trying to get his mouth on me, but he only pushes his fingers into me again.

He chuckles. "Not until we're somewhere no one can hear you scream, mo maighdeann-mhara."

I moan, cradling my clit between my fingers, pushing and pulling in time with his thrusts, his other hand pumping furiously.

It's too much. I drop my head back against the chair.

"Look at me, damn it." His voice is deeper, darker. An edgy side he hasn't shown me yet. I meet his gaze.

"Good girl." He moans my name as our hands pick up speed. We come together, our gasps and groans melding into an obscene symphony. He waits for the tremors to stop before pulling his fingers away, licks them clean, then cups my face, bringing my mouth to his in a mind-melting kiss. We break apart to breathe, and he presses his forehead to mine, chest heaving.

"What did that mean?" I ask, wrapping my arms around his neck, the warmth of his skin keeping the cold at bay.

"Maighdeann-mhara?" he asks. "It means selkie."

"The women that turn into seals?"

He nods. "You remind me of the old folk stories. You're beautiful as you are, but when I touch you, mo chridhe, you shed your insecurities and become the most magnificent creature I have ever seen." He caresses my cheek with the back of one finger and kisses me tenderly.

"Oh." My heart pounds in my chest. "And 'mo chridhe'?" I ask, the syllables unfamiliar on my lips.

He presses one last kiss to my lips before standing and adjusting himself. "That," he chuckles, "means I fucking belong to you."

30

———————

The guys and I are still sitting around the fire as it burns down to embers, empty beer bottles littering the ground between us. We sit in separate chairs, watching the flames flit in and out of the charred logs.

"Let's play truth or dare, " Lach says, a seductive smile on his face.

"Yes, let's!" I agree; my inhibitions are just low enough that I want to play, even though some logical part of the back of my brains whispers it's dangerous.

"Pick one." Lach brings his bottle to his lips, the strong column of his throat glowing in the firelight as he tips his head back.

"Dare." I trust him enough to know he won't dare me to do something I'm uncomfortable with. That's a good feeling. Really good.

"I dare you to kiss me."

"I don't need a dare for that," I laugh as I slide onto his lap and press my mouth to his. He caresses my jaw, curling his other hand into my hair.

"Your go," I grin, turning toward Jack.

"Truth."

My heart thunders in my ears. Do I dare?

"Just ask it, Charlotte." He reaches over and tugs at the end of my ponytail.

I take a deep breath. "Tell me how you feel about me... about this?" I motion between the three of us.

He leans forward, his hands cupping my face. His gaze holds mine. "You are the first thing I think of when I wake up. The last thing I think of when I go to sleep. The only thing I think of when my hand is around my cock."

Heat rushes between my legs. Fuck.

"Is that clear enough for you, Charlotte?"

"Crystal," I murmur, trying to breathe.

His thumbs stroke over my heated cheeks. "Truth or dare?"

"Truth." I can't drag my gaze away as he sweeps his tongue over his lips.

"Have you ever been with more than one guy before?"

Heat races through my veins at the thought. I shake my head. "Rob was the only person I've ever slept with until I was in Portree."

"Wait, what happened in Portree?" Lach asks, his hand rubbing slow lazy circles over my back.

"I dated someone while I was there. He had to leave around the same time I did, so it worked out perfectly."

"So what you're saying is we get most of your firsts," Jack rasps, pulling me into his lap and wrapping his arms around me, nuzzling his face into my hair.

"I wish I could give both of you all of my firsts," I murmur, snuggling into him, my eyes heavy.

MY SENSES WAKE UP SLOWLY—FIRST golden light on my eyelids, then the warmth of skin under my cheek. I crack open one eye to find myself nestled into Jack, his arm a band across my hips pulling me tightly to his chest.

I close my eyes again, burrowing into the safety of Jack's body. It feels so *good*. I breathe deep, inhaling his scent and blowing out the demons that have plagued me for so long. My heart flutters at the possibility that I have found what I've yearned for my entire life.

Guilt twinges, reminding me that someone's missing. The person I can talk with forever about all the mundane things only we find interesting. The one that will sit and read with me, not caring if that's all we did the entire day. The one with floppy hair and cute nerdy glasses. I let myself wallow in memories before pushing them back into the box I had put him in.

"Morning, sunshine," Lach says, coming into the room with a tray in his hands.

I look up at him, at his tender smile. My heart flutters against my ribs.

"Good morning." I try to wipe the grin off my face but fail miserably.

"I hope you don't mind that we brought you up here when you passed out last night, it seemed easier than taking you to the cottage." He sets the tray down at the foot of the bed. "I scrounged up some stuff in the kitchen; I wasn't sure what you'd be in the mood for."

My mouth is watering at the smells coming from the tray: scones, eggs, bacon, croissants, and a luscious bowl of strawberries. Lach pours steaming coffee into the three mugs and hands me one. Jack groans as I sit up, stretching his full length, then sitting up next to me, pulling his hair back before pressing a kiss to my cheek. I squeeze my hands into fists to prevent myself from manhandling the miles of velvety skin so blatantly on display.

"Thank you, Lach, this is amazing." My voice comes out rusty, and I cough, trying to clear my throat. "Sorry," I laugh.

"Don't apologize. You sound fucking sexy."

I smile into my coffee.

"I think it's time," Jack says, popping a strawberry into his mouth. Lach climbs onto the bed, propping himself up on an elbow.

I raise my eyebrows. "Time for what?"

"The Talk."

"The skeletons in the closet talk?" I ask, chuckling.

Jack nods, sipping his coffee. "Are you up for it?"

"Sure." Not like there was much about me they didn't know already.

"Do you want me to start first?" Jack asks, pushing a lock of hair behind my ear.

I nod.

"I'm just going to rip off the bandaid," he begins.

My heart drops like a stone. This was it. This was the other shoe.

He leans back against the headboard and just looks at me for a couple of seconds, like he's trying to figure out how to say it.

"We need to tell you about Emily."

"Okay," I croak, taking a deep breath, trying to calm my heart

"She died eleven years ago." He looks out the window, his expression hard to read.

"I'm so sorry," I whisper, my heart breaking for him.

"She was six months pregnant when she died."

"God. I can't even imagine."

"It was a long time ago." He gives me a small smile. "It's mostly good memories left with only a little bit of sadness."

"Thank you for telling me," I murmur, sliding my hand over his.

"That's not all." He clears his throat, glancing at Lach. "Emily is..."

"She's the girl I was telling you about – the one we both had a relationship with," Lach interjects.

"So you both lost her." I can't even begin to imagine a loss like that. My heart hurts for them. "Will you tell me about her?"

Jack looks at Lach, but he motions for Jack to tell me. He flops back against the pillows, his eyes closed, a small smile on his full lips. "We met her in our first year of uni. We were inseparable. She and I did everything together – same major, same graduation date. She wanted to settle down after graduation. Lach and our roommate moved to different schools, so she stayed with me – probably more for convenience, honestly. She didn't want to live all the way out here, so we leased a flat in Glasgow and lived there."

"I can't see you living the city life."

"I didn't love it, Sassenach." He looks over at me, the morning light making his eyes glow. "We lived there until the accident. I had grown to hate the place so much that I only grabbed a couple of things after she died. I had an estate manager sell the rest. I came back here the day after the funeral." He scrubs his hands over his face. "We weren't a perfect couple – if I'm being honest, we weren't compatible in many ways – but I did love her, and I would have loved that baby with my entire being."

He rolls onto his side, his gaze connecting with mine. "I don't want you to think she's a ghost that haunts me, Charlotte. It was a long time ago. I'm at peace now."

"Thank you for telling me." I cup his jaw and kiss him gently.

"Your turn," he says gruffly.

"I have nothing to tell you," I shrug, "Rob and Portree Guy are the only two people I've ever been involved with. Since you mentioned kids, one thing I need to say – even though this is ridiculously premature – is that I've been told the probability of me having kids is pretty slim. An inhospitable environment, or something like that."

"Well, fuck," Lach says.

My heart jumps to my throat.

"That's all you've got?" He crawls toward me, knocking my elbow from underneath me, so I'm flat on the bed. He traps my legs between his and reaches over me to pin my hands above my head. "Let's spice things up a little bit."

31

I stare at Lach as he stretches above me, all hard muscle and tanned, freckled skin. He groans and rolls his hips against me. I try to pull my hands out of his grip, but he holds on even tighter until I stop struggling. "Do you trust us?" he asks, tonguing the shell of my ear, his voice raising goosebumps on my arms.

I nod, arching my body against his, my nipples desperate for friction.

"Good." He releases me suddenly and climbs off the bed, walking to an antique armoire, and pulling out a plain cardboard box.

"What's that?" I ask, looking between them for an answer.

"We ordered a few things after our picnic the other day," Jack says, taking the box from Lach and setting it in front of me. I sit with one leg tucked underneath me as I open it and peer inside, pulling out the first thing I see. "A butt plug?" I raise an eyebrow, stifling an uncomfortable giggle.

Jack sits beside me, taking the package from me and opening it. "If – and I do mean if – you want to have sex with both of us, we need to get you ready first. If we don't take the time to stretch you, it'll hurt. I want you begging for more the first time I sink my cock into your luscious ass."

Heat throbs between my legs as I pull out the next thing. "Another one?"

"We got a few different sizes so that you can work up to the bigger one," Jack explains, pulling a third from the box and setting it on the bed.

"Hey, I thought one was for me," Lach protests, pulling the box across the bed so he can look inside.

"For you?" I squeak, a flood of desire drenching my bikini bottoms. I adjust my foot underneath me and push against my heel, desperate for relief.

Lach blushes. "We used to—" He stops short. "I'm bisexual, Charlie." The words tumble from his mouth.

My gaze flies to Jack. Did they...?

"I'm straight as a fucking arrow, Sassenach," Jack says, lifting his hands in the air like he wants nothing to do with this conversation.

"Before – when we were with Emily – our roommate and I sometimes..." He clears his throat. "I think you get the picture."

I can't breathe as my imagination takes over. Lach stretched over me, thrusting away as a shadowed mystery man rails him from behind. I rock my hips, rolling my clit over my heel. Fucking hell. I don't think I've been this turned on in my entire life.

"That doesn't mean—" Lach stammers, his cheeks paling a bit, misunderstanding my reaction.

"Shut up, you idiot," Jack says gruffly. "She likes it."

Lach studies me. "Oh fuck, you do, don't you?"

I nod, releasing a shaky breath. "I'm learning all sorts of new things about myself."

"Are you now?" Jack breathes, his gaze locked on my lips. "Why don't we find out if you like this, too." He grabs the smallest box and takes out a slim black silicone toy with a rounded base. "Do you think you're ready?"

I take it from him, testing the weight and size in my hand. It doesn't seem like it would do much, but the idea of having anything in me right now sounds fucking marvelous.

"Yes," I whisper.

He turns to Lach, "Do you have time?"

"All the time in the world for this," he rasps, his eyes dark. "Where do you want me?"

"Lay down across the bed. She can straddle you, and I'll come from behind."

My gaze volleys between them as they decide how they're going to manhandle me. I stand up, pull the sweatshirt off over my head, and then untie both pieces of my bikini, letting them drop to the floor. Lach grabs my waist and pulls me to him, cupping my jaw as he devours my lips. I hear Jack opening boxes, and then the water running in the bathroom. When he returns, he steps up behind me, pulling my body against his, palming my throat. He slides his other hand down my stomach and into my folds, sinking a finger deep.

"You're so fucking wet, Charlotte," he groans, bringing my arousal up to my clit and sliding his finger over it with the lightest touch. I bear my hips down, needing more friction, but he squeezes his hand around my throat enough to stop me from moving. Lach dips his head and catches my nipple in his mouth, sucking it deep. I arch against his mouth, needing just a little more to finally feel some relief.

I sob when he pushes himself back onto the bed, and I pop out of his mouth. Jack releases me, and I follow Lach, letting his hands guide me into a straddle position over his torso. "Come on, you know the drill, knees by my ears, Carebear," he urges. When I hesitate, he grabs me and lifts me into place. Jack pushes down on my lower back until I collapse my torso to the bed, my ass in the air, clit positioned right above Lach's mouth.

"Fuck, Charlotte," Jack breathes, kneading my cheeks.

I jerk as Lach slides his tongue over me. He continues with light strokes while Jack caresses me, his fingers skirting closer to my sensitive flesh until I push back into his hands, pliant and ready. I hear the squirt of lube just as Lach angles his head and sucks my nub into his mouth. I shudder as Jack places his thumb at my tailbone and slowly slides it down my crack. I arch into his touch as he circles me, a low guttural moan tearing its way out of my throat as he pushes in. I look back at him, my muscles clenching around him when I see the way he's looking at me. Lach rolls his tongue over my clit, and I drop my forehead to the bed, moaning for more.

Jack pulls his finger out, something cold pressing to me a second later. "Relax, Charlotte."

I nod, breathing slowly, concentrating on relaxing my muscles.

"Good girl," he breathes, working the toy past the tight ring of muscle, holding it there to give me time to adjust. I groan as Lach grabs my thighs and pulls me tightly against his mouth. Jack steadily pushes in the toy little by little as I ride Lach's face. I feel a slight release of pressure as the toy sinks all the way in. I sit back on Lach's chest to check on him – worried he's suffocating underneath me – but the plug moves, and I'm overwhelmed by an incredible fullness. I whimper, the sensation on the cusp between pain and pleasure.

"Get back here," Lach says, pulling me back toward his face.

"I'm going to suffocate you," I groan, unable to keep myself from rolling my hips against him.

"I want my last breath to be with my face buried in your pussy, Charlie." He lifts me into position and pulls my clit into his mouth. Jack pushes me back down, so my face is pressed into the bed, then smacks my ass, smoothing his palm over the sting.

"Please fuck me," I pant, the torture of feeling empty and full at the same time more than I can bear.

"Not yet, mo chridhe. Not until we can take you together. Not until I know you're ours. But I do have this."

I look back to see him holding a vibrator in his hand.

"In me. Now," I beg, arching my back to make it easier for him. He nudges it at my entrance, swirling it through my arousal. I push back, desperate, and he sinks it into me with one thrust.

"Oh, God," I sob, clenching the sheets in my hands, undulating my body over Lach's tongue, and pushing back as Jach thrusts into me.

"You're taking it so well, Charlotte," Jack says roughly.

I groan in response, moving against them faster and faster as my world narrows to one tiny pinprick, ecstasy taking over my senses. I hear a click, and my whole body convulses as he turns the vibrator on. One more click and the butt plug is shattering everything I thought I knew. I shudder, sobs turning into screams as my entire body convulses.

"My turn," Jack growls, flipping me over and covering me with his body. He adjusts himself in his pants so his cock is riding over me, sucking on my bottom lip before pushing his tongue into my mouth. He thrusts his hips, rolling my clit in between us, and I cry out as my entire world explodes around me.

My ears are ringing as I come back down. Jack is breathing hard into my neck, his cock an iron rod pressed into my stomach. Lach pulls the toys from me slowly and sets them on the nightstand. "Fuck," I groan as I gasp for breath. "Let me get you both there," I beg, looking over at Lach, his cock tenting his pajama pants.

Jack rolls off of me and scrubs his hands over his face. "The second my cock is in you, you're mine, Sassenach. I won't let you go. Do you understand?" He meets my gaze, the flames in his eyes threatening to burn me alive.

"I have two hands," I remind him, wiggling my eyebrows suggestively.

"Fine," he says gruffly. "Let's go shower."

32

Jack leaves me on the bed, utterly boneless in the aftermath of the hottest thing I've experienced in my entire life. I hear him murmur something to Lachlan as he starts the shower, and the next thing I know, Lach is scooping me up and carrying me into the bathroom.

The shower is a thing of dreams – easily the size of my room back in the pool house. There are more showerheads in this single shower than I've seen in my entire life. He sets me down carefully, ensuring my feet are under me before letting go while Jack starts soaping up his arms. I'm mesmerized by his hands sliding over muscle, by the bubbles sticking to his skin. I take the soap from him and move around to his back, lathering up the massive expanse of muscle, then move down to his waist. I slip my hands around the front, pressing my breasts to his back. The ridges of his abs are hard under my hands as I explore his torso. He groans as I roam lower, my fingers brushing the base of his cock. I wrap my hands around him, pumping twice before moving over to Lach and doing the same thing to him.

"Teasing isn't nice, Sassenach," Jack growls into my ear. He grabs my shoulders, pushes me to the middle of the shower, and holds me there while he fiddles with a knob. A waist-high shower head turns on, and he adjusts it to hit square between my legs. He turns a dial, and it becomes a massager, shooting jets of water right onto my clit. My knees start to shake, and I step out of the stream, but Jack pushes me back into it. "Don't move."

They close in on me, soapy hands slipping over my skin. I blow out a shaky breath and anchor myself with a hand on each of their cocks. My breath stutters as their heads disappear into my hands, then I slowly push back toward their bodies, twisting my hands as I repeat the motion. My legs start trembling so much that I have to sink to my knees. The guys drop with me, Lach pushing my legs open wide as Jack detaches the showerhead and aims the spray. I jerk when it hits me, swearing as their low chuckles lodge into my core.

They're on either side of me, knees spread, sitting on their heels, cocks begging to be touched. Licked.

"Don't even think about it," Jack growls, taking my hand and wrapping it around his cock. He covers my hand with his, squeezing and pumping. I take Lach in my other hand, mirroring the movement. The shower fills with heaving breathing, grunts, and moans as all three of us tip closer to the edge.

"Come for me," I rasp, my gaze volleying between their cocks as I stroke them, rocking my hips against the onslaught of water. They grunt simultaneously, bucking into my hands as ropes of cum swirl down the drain. As soon as Jack releases my hand, I slip it between my legs.

"No, you don't. This one belongs to me." He stands and pulls me up with him, pressing me to the glass. He cups my cheek and angles my face before crushing his lips to mine. He slides his fingers through my folds, pushing two of them in. My mewl of protest as he pulls his hand away turns into a moan as he puts them in his mouth, his eyes rolling back as he tastes me. "I can't fucking wait any longer," he grinds out, the fire in his eyes burning me alive. He picks me up by the waist, and I wrap my legs around him as he carries me out of the shower straight to the bedroom. I catch a glimpse of Lach pulling on dress pants right before Jack tosses me onto the bed, crawling up after me. He pushes my thighs open wide, dipping his head to breathe me in. His groan has me shaking with need.

"Have fun, Carebear. I have a meeting in town. I'll be back in a few hours," Lach presses a kiss to my temple and winks before leaving the room.

"Now there's no one to hear you scream, Charlotte," Jack says before running his tongue over me, his moan skittering over my body. I clamp my legs around his head, bucking against his mouth, already on the brink.

He stops and forces my knees to the bed, holding them there until I stop struggling. I'm breathing hard, desire pooling as his gaze slides from my heaving breasts, over my stomach, to the apex of my thighs. "Put your back against the headboard. I want you to watch while I destroy you."

My heart thunders in my ears as I push myself back.

"Good girl." He tucks a towel under me and then leans across to pull at something attached to the corner of the bed. "What's your safe word, Charlotte?"

My breath stutters and I can only shake my head.

"Pick one." He sets my wrist on the bed, loops a silky rope around it, and then presses my thigh open, running the rope over it and back to my wrist, securing both tightly to the bed.

Fuck. A flood of heat rushes through me, and I worry for a split second that he's going to see me dripping on his bed, but the thought is gone as fast as it came, replaced by the primal need to relinquish control.

"Give me a safe word, Charlotte," he growls, his words sound like a warning. A promise.

My brain isn't working, so I say the first thing that comes to mind. "Kelly Clarkson?"

He stops in the middle of tying my other leg, staring at me for a second before barking out a laugh. "God, I fucking love you," he chuckles as he ties the last knot.

I don't have time to process his words before he kneels in front of me, his pupils blown wide as he looks at me spread open for him.

"Fucking hell," he groans, his gaze pinned between my thighs as he drags his thumb through my arousal and then down to circle my ass.

"Please, Jack," I whisper.

"Please, what?" he purrs, lightly running the tip of his finger over my clit.

"Lick me, bite me, fuck me. I don't care what you do," I sob, "I need to come."

"Like this?" He runs his tongue along the crease of my thigh. I struggle against the ropes, desperate to hold his head where I want it. His gaze locks with mine as he runs his tongue through my center, dipping inside, lapping me up like I'm the best thing he's ever tasted.

Fuck.

I whimper as he pushes his tongue against my clit. I jerk against him as he sucks me into his mouth, his eyes never leaving mine. I moan, so close to tipping over the edge. He pulls away but doesn't give me time to protest before pushing two fingers into me, curling them, and massaging that spot until I can barely breathe.

"I feel like I'm going to pee," I say, the pressure building.

"You won't," he promises, continuing the onslaught.

The visual of his fingers in me is so fucking hot that I can't bear to pull my eyes away. "Oh God," I roll my pelvis against him, on the verge of wetting his bed or having the best orgasm of my life. "I—"

"You're not going to fucking pee, Charlotte. Stop thinking and feel." He seals his mouth over my clit, alternating between sucking and licking.

I explode underneath him, the pressure finally too much to hold in. I feel liquid gush from me as I rock against his mouth, screaming his name. He reaches over and pulls at one of the ropes, untying it. I pull his head to me, grinding against him until the last tremor fades. He's grinning when he pulls away from me, wiping his face on the towel and then throwing it into the basket next to the bed. "You're fucking magnificent," he says as he unties me, pulling me to him, curling his body around mine as he pulls the fluffy duvet over us.

"Your mouth is what's fucking magnificent," I mumble as I snuggle into his warmth and promptly fall asleep.

33

———

I hole myself up in the cottage for three days following the day at the lake. I pour myself into my work, sketching ideas while out on the deck every morning and practicing my rusty calligraphy in front of the fire, sipping hot cocoa every night. On the third day, I finally feel confident enough to roll out the thick, expensive parchment and begin laying out Arty's tree.

I let my mind wander while I work, mainly to the other morning and my conversation with Lorna – to the irrefutable fact that Jack wants kids. He probably doesn't think it's a big deal now, but a couple of years down the road? Regret. Resentment. Heartbreak. I blink quickly, and a tear drops to the parchment; I watch as it sucks ink into its center. I bang my palm on the table, frustrated with myself.

Who says this is even going anywhere? I take a deep breath. It's okay to live in the moment. To enjoy my time in Scotland and then go home like I've been planning from the start. No harm, no foul. Yes, I may leave with a broken heart, but isn't that part of life?

The questions turn round and round in my head until I feel like I'm losing my mind. I put away my art supplies and crank the music, dancing around the cottage, forcing my body to release the stress. My heart nearly leaves my body when someone bangs on the door. I scramble to turn the music down, poking my head out the door to find Jack loaded down with dishes.

"Are ye ignoring us, lass?" He pushes past me, pressing a heated kiss to my lips.

"Just trying to get some work done," I say, praying my smile is convincing.

"I hope you're ready for some company. We've missed you."

"We—?"

"Charlie!" Isla barges through the door, a pitcher of something pink and fruity in her hands, Lachlan right behind her.

"Isla was worried you died, so here we are," he laughs, his eyes sparkling.

I smile, my mood instantly lifting. "I'm glad you're all here. I don't think I could eat another sandwich if my life depended on it."

"Ew. Why didn't you tell me? Sandwiches are the worst. " Isla makes a face as she grabs glasses from the kitchen while Jack sets out plates and Lachlan places the utensils.

The three of them move together like a well-oiled machine. It makes me yearn for the tight-knit family I never had. I love my parents, but it wasn't ever easy like this. Jack pulls out a chair for me at the head of the table, and we all sit down. Isla passes around the pitcher of white peach sangria while the guys dish out the food.

Tears well in my eyes. This feels so *right*. It feels like home. I blow out a shaky breath and take a couple of gulps of wine.

"So why are you ignoring us?" Isla asks, popping a bite of fried fish into her mouth.

"I promise I'm not," I laugh, "I turned my phone off because I needed to get some work done."

Isla raises her eyebrow at me.

I shrug. I'm not exactly going to tell her I've been daydreaming about fucking her brother and childhood friend for the last seventy-two hours. Or that I've been giving myself pep talks about leaving.

Lach squeezes my knee under the table, making me jerk. He chuckles, "A little jumpy, lass?"

I give him a dirty look and shove a chip into my mouth, avoiding his question.

The night flies by as we talk, every story we tell reminding one of us of another. I haven't laughed this much in years. I feel so relaxed, my social anxiety completely gone – which I tell myself is the wine even though I know damn well it's the people.

After dinner, Lach and I clean up while Jack works on getting a fire started, and Isla runs back to the house to grab another pitcher of sangria.

"Is everything okay?" Lachlan asks, cornering me in the hallway on my way to the bathroom. He nudges my chin up, forcing me to meet his gaze. "We didn't do anything the other morning that made you uncomfortable, did we?"

His words startle me out of my selfish pity fest. "God, no. You were both amazing."

"What then, Charlie? Don't tell me it's nothing. I know you better than that."

"It was just something Lorna said the other day. About how good Jack is with kids... how she can't wait to see a bunch of little Jacks running around."

"I'm not following."

I sigh. "I know this is completely premature, and I shouldn't even be thinking about it, let alone worrying about it, but what if the doctors are right and I can't have kids?"

"Carebear," he whispers, a tender smile pulling at his lips. "Does this mean you're thinking about staying?" He cups my jaw, caressing my cheek with his thumb.

"That is *not* what I said."

"Oh, but it is," he laughs, scooping me up and spinning me around.

"Lach!" I protest, struggling in his arms. He ignores me, capturing my mouth with his, trapping me in a slow, sensual kiss that soothes the deepest depths of my soul.

"You two just need to fuck already," Isla calls as she barges through the door with a full pitcher in her hands

"How do you know we haven't?" Lach asks, linking his fingers with mine.

"Lachlan, I have known you my entire life. I have never seen you like this. The tension is bloody unbearable."

He laughs. "Well, you'll have to bear it a little longer. It's not happening until we know she's staying."

Isla looks at me, studying my face, then says to Lach, "That's stupid."

"It was your brother's decision," Lach murmurs, pulling my hand to his lips.

"Ah. Well, that I understand. Good fucking luck," she chuckles. We follow her onto the deck and settle in the big wooden chairs.

After another glass of sangria, my thoughts start slipping out of my mouth. "Why does it feel like we've been doing this for years? Like I've known the three of you forever?" I rub my hands over my face. "I just don't understand it."

"You don't have to understand, Sassenach. This is your dachaigh – your home," Jack says, his gaze blanketing me.

"It can't be. I can only stay for six months out of the year on my visa. I don't have the qualifications to get a different one."

"Marry one of us," Lach says, not a hint of humor in his tone.

Panic bubbles up my throat. "Funny."

"I'm not fucking kidding," he says, leaning forward, resting his elbows on his knees, the fire gilding his face with a fierce glow. "Marry one of us legally and you'll be allowed stay. We don't have to have every last detail nailed down. We'll figure it out."

"While I appreciate the sentiment, there are two problems. One, I'm still married to Rob. And two, we haven't known each other long enough. You may like me now and want to keep me around for some fun, but what if you change your mind in a month? In a year?"

Jack jerks in his seat like I slapped him. "We aren't fucking changing our minds, Charlotte."

The truth is, I don't have enough confidence in myself to believe they won't tire of me. "We can talk about this once I'm divorced.

There's no point in going round in circles when it changes nothing." I get up and refill my glass.

"Take a break and come camping with me tomorrow," Jack says as I sit back down, taking my hand in his.

I clear the negativity from my mind and focus on him. Stray wisps of hair frame his face, copper in the firelight. His gaze holds mine, hopeful and determined.

"Okay," I say softly, my heart pounding.

He turns to Lach. "Are you free?"

"No, I'll be entertaining clients on the boat tomorrow." He turns toward me, "I think it'll be good for you to get away for a night. You've been working hard and you deserve a break."

"Wait, what boat?" I ask.

"You'll see soon enough. I've been saving it for a special date night. Just the two of us."

I bite my lip, thinking of what we could do on a boat with nobody around. My gaze lowers to his full lips, then to his throat as he swallows.

"Charlie," he says, his voice a warning. A siren's song.

"Okay, that's my cue to get the hell out of here." Isla jumps up and gives me a quick hug. "Don't be a stranger," she whispers as she squeezes me.

Both of the guys get up as she heads back inside. Jack bends down, brushing his lips over mine. "Get your sleep tonight. I'll see you in the morning."

I nod, wishing he'd stay, but too unsure of myself to ask.

"I'll see you when you get back from camping," Lach says, pressing a kiss to my hair.

"Why are you leaving?" I rasp, immediately regretting asking.

"You've had about a pitcher of sangria tonight. You need your sleep."

"I have not!" I protest, pushing to my feet. I grip his arm to keep me upright, my head spinning like a top. "I take that back," I groan.

He chuckles, "Go wash up. I'll tuck you in before I leave."

"Really?"

"Yes, really. Go on." I squeal when he smacks my ass as I walk past him.

I put on my skimpiest nightie, my body buzzing from the alcohol. Lach is sitting at the foot of my bed when I come in.

"Fuck, Charlie," he whispers, his gaze roaming over me.

"Yes, that's exactly what I want you to do," I purr, sitting next to him.

"You know I can't do that." He stands, pulling me to my feet and turning down the sheets. "Go on, get in."

"Touch me," I beg, climbing onto the bed, giving him my best fuck-me eyes.

"You've had too much to drink, Charlie."

"Then I'll touch me," I pout, sliding my hand over my stomach and underneath the lace of my panties.

"Charlie," he croaks, his gaze glued to my hand.

I moan, circling my fingers over my clit. He pulls my panties off and presses my knees to the bed, his eyes drinking me in.

"You, too," I demand.

He takes his time unbuckling his belt and unzipping his pants. It seems like it takes him an hour to push his hand inside his boxers and pull out his cock. Two pumps and I can see the precum glistening.

"Are you clean?" I pant, unable to tear my gaze away from his hand as he slides it over his cock.

"Yes," he grinds out.

"Cum on me. Please," I beg, seeing the hesitation in his eyes.

He pulls my hand away from between my legs, his jaw muscle jumping as he leans over me, sliding the head of his cock back and forth over my clit. "Fuck, Charlie." He moans, thrusting into his hand as he comes.

I try to pull my hand away from his hold, desperate to touch myself, but he swats it away. "Let me look at you for a second. You look so fucking hot with my cum dripping down your pussy."

"Fuck," I groan, his words stoking the flames higher. "Lachlan, please."

He gathers his cum with his thumb and uses it as lubrication, slowly rolling the bundle of nerves and forth. "Does that feel good?" He places two fingers on either side of my clit, squeezing them together as he rocks his fingers over me. "I can't fucking wait to bury my cock in you, Charlie. You know why?" he rasps, concentrating on his hand between my legs.

"Why?" I moan, bucking my hips.

"Because it will feel like coming home." He lowers his face between my legs and sucks me into his mouth. I gasp, biting my hand to stifle my scream. He lets go of my wrist to keep my thighs pressed to the bed, and I immediately thread my fingers through his hair, pulling him closer. His low chuckle vibrates against my skin, sending me over the edge.

34

From the moment I wake up, my heart beats like a drum. Camping with Jack. Alone. Goosebumps race down my arms as I pull on a t-shirt and leggings, skipping underwear for reasons I absolutely will not acknowledge.

I turn on the kettle and make tea, too wound up to risk coffee. Jack knocks softly on the door as I plop in the tea bags. The butterflies in my stomach go haywire. I take a deep breath and open the door, pushing a mug into his hands.

"You ready?" he asks gruffly, nodding his head in thanks.

"Yep." I swing my backpack over one shoulder and grab my tea.

He raises an eyebrow. "No coffee this morning?"

"Nope!" I say, acting like it's completely normal.

His eyes narrow, but he doesn't say anything as he follows me outside. He takes my bag and opens the door for me. He throws my bag in the back on his way around the truck and hops in, hissing as the tea spills over the rim and onto his hand.

"Let me hold it." I say, setting my mug on the dash, my hand covering his as he works his fingers out of the handle. I swear my skin sparks when we touch. I inhale sharply, my senses narrowing to that small touch. I look up at him when he doesn't let go. He's focused on my lips, his pupils dilated. He slides his seat all the way back and I move without fully meaning to, keeping my hand over his, the mug between us as I straddle him.

"Let go," he says gruffly, pulling the mug out of my hand before tossing it out the window.

"Hey!"

"I need both of my hands right now," he says, caressing my face, his whisky eyes capturing my soul.

"Good morning," I whisper, suddenly feeling shy.

"Good morning, Sassenach." His gaze tracks his fingers as they explore my face like he's memorizing this moment – memorizing me. My heart swells, physically hurting. I blink back tears. His fingers tremble against my lips. He catches a tear with his thumb. "I feel it, too," he says softly, taking a deep, shuddering breath.

"This—" I start, determined to remind him why this won't work. Can't work.

"Don't," he interrupts. "I can see the wheels turning in your head, Charlotte. Stop overthinking everything. Just live in this moment. Be present."

I link my arms behind his head and brush my lips against his, the kiss slow and sweet. His fingers sweep over my ribs, and I arch into him, needing more. He chuckles against my mouth, moving his hands in lazy circles higher and higher on my sides. He slides the back of one finger over the side of my breast; I bite back a moan. He pulls back, looking me in the eyes.

"I want to hear how I make you feel, Charlotte."

"Yes, sir," I say, trying to be sarcastic, but the words are breathless and heavy with need. Gaze darkening, his hands coast across the sides of my breasts, then cover them, kneading. I push into him, desperate for his touch. He pulses against my center as he rolls my nipples between his fingers. My eyes roll back, my body rocking against him. I don't hold back my moan this time. My body is strung tight, so close.

"Good girl," he whispers against my ear, his voice vibrating over my skin.

Oh, God. I whimper, and he answers with a moan, his mouth slamming down on mine.

"Get a room!" Isla yells at us as she stomps past us on the way to grab something from her car.

"We'll have to finish this later," Jack growls, lifting me and depositing me back in my seat. "Buckle up."

I'm still throbbing forty-five minutes later when we pull into the ferry parking lot.

"What do you want to do while we wait?" he asks, giving me a ridiculously sexy wink.

"NOT that," I say, looking at the cars surrounding us. I think for a second. "How about another game of truth or dare?"

He raises an eyebrow. "Okay."

"You first. Truth or dare?"

"Truth."

I start small. "What is the number one thing you want to accomplish in the next ten years?"

He doesn't even think before answering. "I want to have kids."

His words are a knife to my heart. Fuck, that hurts. I suck in a breath and blink rapidly to clear my vision. I turn my face away from him, not wanting to have to explain my reaction.

"Truth or dare?"

"Truth," I whisper.

"Tell me about when you've been the happiest."

"Honestly?"

"Yes, Charlotte." His gaze is intense.

"Probably the last month or so." My laugh borders on hysteria. "How lame does that sound?"

"Not lame," he says, his voice gruff.

"Truth or dare?" I volley back, desperate to get the attention away from myself.

"Dare." There's a challenge in his eyes.

"I dare you to tell me how you feel about me." The words fall from my lips before I can think, my heart beating a loud staccato against my ribs.

He turns in his seat, holding my gaze. "I don't need a dare to tell you, Charlotte. From the second we met, my soul has been orbiting yours. I can't take a breath without wanting it to be filled with you. You're the first thing on my mind when I wake up in the morning and the thing on my mind when I go to sleep." He cups my face, running his thumb over my bottom lip. "I've lost count of the number of times I've fucked my hand, imagining it's your lips wrapped around my cock.

"How's that for lame?" he asks, flashing a crooked smile.

"Not lame," I croak, fanning myself.

"Oh, just wait, Sassenach," he warns as he puts the car in drive and follows the vehicle in front of us onto the ferry.

"So, where exactly are we going?" I ask as I unbuckle, my eyes glued to the way his pants are pulling over his ass as we wind our way through cars to the stairs. Jack turns suddenly, grabbing my shoulders and pushing me against the wall in the stairwell. My breath whooshes out of me as he palms my throat, forcing my chin up to meet his gaze. "What are you doing?" I rasp, resisting the urge to climb him like a tree.

"Replacing a horrible memory." His lips move against mine in a slow, sensual dance. I moan and open for him, sucking his bottom lip into my mouth. He groans against me, sliding his hand into my hair and grasping it tightly. I gasp into his mouth, and he growls in response, raining kisses over my jaw and down my neck. My eyelashes flutter open when I hear a giggle; a little boy with big brown eyes is staring at me over his mom's shoulder, waving at me with a sticky hand.

"Memory replaced," I whisper, gently extricating myself from his grasp. I link my fingers with his and pull him up the stairs. He prowls after me, his beast barely caged, each puff of breath against my neck sending tremors to my core.

I pick seats in a dark corner, sit against the wall, and turn to him. "You never told me where we're going."

He chuckles, "The Quirang. It's a hilly region in Skye. You're going to love it."

"I'll love anywhere if I get to go there with you," I say as I dig for my book in my backpack.

"Really?" He grins, his amber eyes sparkling as he tugs the book out of my hands.

I laugh. "Really."

He looks at the book's cover, then back up at me, his eyebrow raised. "What is this?"

I try to snatch the book from his hand, realizing too late that the cover has three barely clothed men on it, but he pulls it out of my reach. He opens it, flipping through pages, color slowly rising to his cheeks.

Mortification stains my face scarlet.

"How long have you been reading books like this, mo chridhe?"

"Why does that matter?" I ask, intimidated by the look in his eyes.

"Because I want to know how long your heart has been yearning for us. I want to know how long your body has been begging to be worshipped by more than two hands and one tongue."

I lick my lips, feeling extraordinarily vulnerable. I meet his golden gaze, "Years. Since I was sixteen."

His deep chuckle skitters over my skin, lodging in my core. "And I was worried we were dragging you to the dark side without you fully understanding what you were getting into." He tips my chin up, studying me. "But you want it, don't you?"

"More than anything," I confess, the words tumbling from my lips.

"Such a dirty girl." The baritone of his voice slides through my veins, fire and ice colliding between my legs. My eyes flutter closed as the throbbing intensifies. "I can't wait to see you on your knees begging for it like a good girl." A shiver courses through me, his breath hot against my ear.

"Not until I make you beg first," I rasp, gasping as he pushes a finger between my legs, my clit rolling under his fingertip.

"We'll see about that," he growls, his body blocking me from anyone passing by as his hand works between my legs. He pulls away suddenly, tweaking my nipple before pulling out his phone.

"Jack," I whimper, " Please."

"Who's begging now, mo chridhe?" He cups my face, pulling at my bottom lip, his gaze slightly unfocused. I lick his thumb, sucking it into my mouth, swirling my tongue over him.

"Fuck," he mutters, then pushes it in farther. I hollow my cheeks, and he pulls away abruptly. "You're fucking dangerous." He eyes me, something primal in the set of his jaw, in the lines bracketing his mouth.

A spark ignites in response, lighting up a wild, insatiable part of me that I've kept buried all these years, and that's the moment I realize I can finally let my freak flag fly.

35

As we pull into the campsite, the hills open into a wide valley draped in green velvet. The beauty has my heart pounding in my chest, like something inside me is screaming, '*This is home! This is where you belong!*'.

"This is incredible," I murmur as Jack opens my door.

"It is, isn't it, lass? Do you want to hike it first?" I nod, my hand disappearing inside his as he helps me from the truck. Instead of releasing me, he tucks both of our hands in the front pocket of his jacket as we turn and gaze at the view. "My grandad used to bring me here every summer. Those are some of the best memories of my childhood."

"Will you tell me more about how you grew up?" I ask, the sudden urge to know everything about him gripping me by the throat. He pulls my bag and his pack from the back of the truck and straps it on, grabbing my hand again as we head toward the trail.

"What do you want to know?"

"Everything."

He chuckles. "The three of us lived in the manor house with our parents until they died when I was thirteen."

My stomach drops. "Jack, I had no idea. You don't have to tell me about it if you don't want to."

"It's okay, lass. It was a long time ago." He smiles, his eyes sad. "They were on an anniversary trip and had taken a private plane to the Orkneys. The wind was terrible that day. The pilot lost control."

"God, I'm so sorry."

"They died together, Sassenach. That's all anyone could ask for. After that, we moved onto the estate with our grandad. It must have been a huge burden for him, but he never let on. He was an amazing man. I wish you could have met him – you would have loved him."

"I'm sure I would have," I murmur, wistful.

"All three of us went to university, but we couldn't stay away long, and came right back right after graduation. Harris is home. It just doesn't feel the same anywhere else."

I'm envious of that. My home never felt like anything other than a house. I've never had a special connection with a place. At least not until I came to Scotland. I push that thought to the back of my mind to examine later.

"So you took over the estate once your grandad died?"

Jack nods. "I'm the only one that actually wanted the responsibility, so I took it on. It's a challenge almost every day, but I love it."

"What's your favorite part about managing it?" I ask, curious about what makes him so passionate.

"Probably when this little auburn-haired lass shows up to feed my sister's pony," he teases, winking.

"Jack," I groan, "Seriously!"

He stops walking and faces me. "I'm being completely serious."

I blush and push up on my tiptoes to kiss him, balancing myself with a hand on his chest.

The entire hike is an experience I'll never forget. I've never been anywhere that's so wide open. So wild. So free. It makes my heart sing. We hold hands the whole way, neither of us wanting to let go after finally taking that step. When we return to the vehicle, Jack starts setting up camp, transforming his truck into something I didn't even know was possible. There's a sleeping area on top of the bed cover, a makeshift kitchen, and a small firepit that he can pack out.

"This is homey," I grin, butterflies beating against my stomach.

"I'm glad you think so, lass. I know this isn't for everyone."

"I spent the last five years doing hard labor outside. This is a vacation."

His lips twist into a grimace, but he doesn't say anything, just rolls his shoulders back and shifts into dinner mode. He has me trim the ends of the asparagus as he heats oil in a pan. I watch as he washes rice and puts it on the burner, then he pulls smoked salmon and butter from the cooler. He sheds his jacket and sweater, leaving him in only joggers and a tee. The evening light highlights the veins in his arms, but that's not the only thing it's accentuating, and I can't stop my gaze from bouncing down until I finally give up trying to be good and close my eyes.

This is torture. My brain tells me to run. It tells me to spare both of our feelings and get the fuck out. Jack wants kids. I can't have kids. He lives in Scotland. I don't. End of Story. Besides the fact that I'm still fucking married. But my heart sings a different tune. Especially when he looks at me the way he's looking at me right now.

"What?" I ask, trying to hold in my smile and failing miserably.

"I'm just thinking about how perfect today was. And about how hot you are." He grins, abandoning the stove and wrapping me in a bear hug, lifting my feet off the ground. I wind my arms around his neck and hug him back. Tears prick my eyes as the realization hits that I have someone solid in my life I can lean on – several someones, actually. It feels so goddamn good.

"Why does it seem like we've known each other forever?" Jack mumbles against my neck.

"I have no fucking clue," I whisper, pressing a kiss to his cheek, suddenly feeling shy. There are stars in his eyes, his gaze reverent. He smiles at me as he sets me back on the ground, my heart fluttering in my chest.

"God, ignore me," he laughs.

"Never." I grab his face and bring it to mine, kissing him hard before pushing him toward the pan.

He pulls the asparagus out of the pan, sears the salmon, and then starts on a sauce. After whisking for a couple of minutes, he calls me over.

"Something's off about the sauce. Will you try it and tell me what you think?" He dips his finger in and holds it out to me, his eyebrow cocked, a challenge in his eyes.

It takes me less than a second to let lust take over, and then I'm swirling my tongue around his finger, sucking him in to his third knuckle. The sauce is divine, creamy with a tang of lemon. Perfectly seasoned. I release his finger with a pop and lick my lips. "It's perfect." I give him an exaggerated wink as he stands there, his lip caught in his teeth, nostrils flared.

"Fucking hell, Charlotte." He grabs the back of my neck and pulls me to him, crushing his lips to mine. I tug on his beard, pulling him even closer. He breaks the kiss, picking me up and placing me in one of the camping chairs. "If we don't stop, dinner will burn."

Several minutes later, Jack hands me a plate and a mug and sits in the chair beside me. "You feel it too, don't you?"

"Yes," I whisper, terrified to admit it.

He nods and takes a bite of his food. "Eat," he commands.

Yes, sir. Hmph. He watches as I lift the fork to my mouth, his gaze darkening when my lips close around the tines.

He takes a few more bites before talking again. "Have you decided to stop running yet?"

I swallow, gulping down some water to wash it down. "I don't want to leave," I say honestly.

"Really?"

"Yes—but that doesn't mean I won't have to. There's the divorce. The visa. There are a lot of things out of my control."

"We'll deal with that when they come. Just promise me you won't run, Charlotte."

"I promise." I take a deep breath. "Just promise me you'll take it slow. Rob was the only guy I had ever been with until recently. So I am very, *very* out of practice."

"Tell me more about the guy in Portree," Jack says, "I kept meaning to ask, but it seems like there's not much time to talk when we're together." He smirks before biting down on a piece of asparagus.

"We dated for a few weeks before I came here. He had to leave the country for work."

"Lucky fucker," he laughs. "Who was it? I know almost everyone there." He pulls a beer from the cooler, pops the top, and takes a long pull.

I clear my throat, a little uncomfortable with that possibility. "You know Millie that owns the bookstore?"

Jack freezes, his eyes wide.

"Her son," I finish.

Jack splutters, his eyes watering. He stares at me, a strange expression on his face. "You broke his heart, didn't you?" he asks.

"I hope not. Maybe?" I bury my face in my hands, feelings rushing back. I miss Cam—a lot.

"Even if you did, he's still a lucky fucker." He chuckles. "You probably made his entire life, Sassenach."

"I did not; if anything, it was the other way around." I think back to the night in the bookstore and bite my lip.

"Trust me." He takes the plate from my hands and pulls me into his lap. I lean back against him, and he rests his chin on my shoulder.

"I have to tell you something, but I don't want you to get upset."

My heart drops.

"Cameron was our university roommate."

"Oh my God! Really? Why would that upset me?"

He raises an eyebrow, waiting for me to connect the dots.

Oh fuck.

Their *roommate.* The roommate Lach said he sometimes ... *fuck.* My stomach tightens as heat pools between my legs.

"Please tell me you're joking. That I didn't manage to sleep with all of you within a month and a half." Mortification seeps into my bones.

Jack clears his throat. "Let me remind you that we haven't technically fucked yet."

"God, what are the chances?" I giggle, the absurdity of the situation sinking in. An unladylike snort leads to full-on belly laughs.

"Seems like it was meant to be, doesn't it?" Jack says, wiping a tear from my cheek. "I think we have a call to make when we get home?"

"We do?" I sober up immediately. Telling Cameron I'm in a relationship with his two best friends is not something I have any desire to do.

"Don't you think he deserves to know?"

"What if he hates me?" I whisper.

"Why would he hate you?"

"Even *I* hate myself for moving on so quickly."

"So, you're completely over him, are you? You don't think about him anymore? You don't miss him?"

"How can someone not miss Cameron?" I sigh, snuggling into his chest.

"Exactly. I have a feeling things are about to get a little more interesting, Sassenach."

I don't know what that means, but I like the sound of it.

36

I squirm in his lap, trying to get comfortable. His fingers press into my hips, keeping me still.

"Stop. Moving."

I look at him out of the corner, raising my eyebrow. "You're a bossy motherfucker, aren't you?"

"The correct answer is 'Yes, Sir.'"

He pulses under me. A warning? A promise? Desire blazes through me, setting my skin on fire.

"Understood?"

I want to fight against his controlling tone, but lust grips me by the throat, and I can only nod.

"Good girl. Do you want dessert?"

Only if it's you. "Yes, please," I whisper, the words strangled.

I help him clean out the pan and heat the crepes. He plates them and cuts up the strawberries while I drizzle the Nutella. I swipe my thumb over the spoon and smear it over his bottom lip.

"Let me help you with that." I stand on my tiptoes and run my tongue over his lip. I suck the Nutella off his lip, sweeping my tongue into his mouth to get the last traces of it. He groans and bands his arms around my back, biting my lip before pushing his tongue into my mouth.

The smell of something burning breaks through the haze.

"Shit," Jack murmurs against my lips. Without breaking our kiss, he reaches behind me and turns the burner off. He angles my head, his hands engulfing both sides of my face. I moan as he pushes his fingers into my hair and tugs. His hands trail down my back, his pace maddeningly slow. He reaches my waistband, and I arch, begging him with my body to move his hands lower. He stops, breaking our kiss, trailing his lips over my jaw, down my neck, and over my collarbone. My nipples ache for his touch. He swirls his tongue over the hollow of my throat, chuckling against my skin when I mewl and squirm against him.

He pulls back a little to look at me. "Let's eat."

"Only if it's me."

"We have all night, Charlotte. You'll need your energy."

"Fine," I say, taking the plate from him.

"It doesn't bother you that I'm moving faster with Lach?" I blurt, the thought suddenly occurring to me, the words tumbling from my lips before I can reel them back in.

"It's not a contest, Sassenach. Your relationship with him is between the two of you. Our relationship is between us."

"God, you're perfect. Where have you been my whole life?"

"I've been here. Waiting for you, mo chridhe." He cups my chin, pulling my lips to his. "Now eat," he says gruffly, motioning for me to sit by the fire.

After popping the last bite into my mouth, I lick my fingers, staring into the fire.

"Penny for your thoughts," Jack says, his golden eyes studying my face.

I laugh. "I think there has to be a mischievous divine being that planned out every chaotic step that has led me here. I still can't quite believe how much has changed in a couple of months."

"You're fucking telling me," he chuckles, leaning forward to put his elbows on his knees. "I feel like every piece of my soul – no matter how minuscule – is repositioning itself to make a home for you at the very center of my being."

"Jack—"

"Don't," he says, cutting me off. "I don't need you to say anything back. I just want you to know." He pulls his phone out of his pocket and fiddles with it for a second before the song 'Turning Page' comes on. I take the hand he holds out to me, melting into him as he pulls me close. We sway together for several seconds before he spins me away from him, drawing me back into his arms.

"I think it's time for bed," he murmurs against my lips as the song ends, breaking away from me to extinguish the fire. I help him tidy up, my heart in my throat the entire time. Effervescent anticipation sparks through me, snuffing out everything except the feel of his hands, the smell of his skin, the timbre of his voice.

"Go," he says, smacking my ass and motioning for me to climb up into the tent.

I scramble up the ladder, twisting to face Jack as he prowls after me. He looks feral, his eyes glowing in the lantern light, the rest of his face cast in shadow. I yelp when he doesn't stop, pushing me back until I'm against the side of the tent. He sits on his heels and pulls me onto his lap, nesting my heat over his hard length.

"Fuck. You are going to be the death of me," he grinds out, restraint etched in the lines of his face.

The tension from today – from *every* day – is compressed like a spring inside of me, just waiting to be released. I rock against him, desperate for relief. I moan as stars explode behind my eyelids.

He grips my jaw, forcing me to look at him. "There you are, my beautiful selkie," he murmurs, rolling his hips against me. He flips me around and lays on his back, straddling my legs over his hips. I moan as he pulls me down slowly, the head of his cock pressing against my clit.

There are way too many layers of clothes between us.

I want him inside me. Now.

I lean forward and clutch his shoulders, his muscles bunching under my fingers as I ride him. I look down to where we're pressed together. The tie on his shorts is barely hanging on, creating a gap between his abdomen and waistband. His cock is right there. I slide down, taking his shorts with me, the head of his cock peeking out. Wide and smooth and perfect.

God. I don't think I've ever wanted something so badly.

I push his shirt up his chest. If I'm getting there – and I am – he is too. I have a score to even up. I look at him through my eyelashes, trying to control my breathing.

"Charlotte," he groans, protesting. I tilt my pelvis, dragging my clit over him, shuddering as it catches on the ridge. "Fuck," his voice trembles.

"Don't you dare tell me to stop."

"Don't. Fucking. Stop," he grinds out, arching underneath me as I rock back.

He grips my hips, pulling me forward and pushing me back the entire length of his shaft.

"Oh God," I moan, looking between us, at the drop of pre-cum just begging to be tasted.

"Look at me. Now." He grips my jaw, forcing me to meet his gaze.

My heartbeat ratchets up even higher, the command in his voice calling to something deep inside me. His gaze is hooded, smoky whisky eyes ensnaring me. He groans in frustration, jerking his hips against mine. "These need to go." He reaches between us and rips open the entire crotch seam of my leggings. He holds my hips still, breathing hard, a fraction of an inch between us.

"We are not fucking tonight, Sassenach. Don't even try. I just need to feel you on me." He settles me over his length, steel sliding against silk. I swear, moaning his name as I undulate my hips, rolling my clit back and forth over him.

Just another half an inch and he'll be in me. I clench around nothing. I close my eyes and whimper, struggling for restraint, wanting nothing more than to impale myself on him.

"Open your eyes."

I do.

"What do you need?" He asks, his arms shaking with each push and pull, his control close to snapping.

"I need to feel you in me." I arch my back as his head catches on my entrance, then slides past, leaving me desperate to be filled. He reaches around my thighs and pushes two fingers inside me as I slide back. My body bows, a low-keening moan coming from deep in my chest. His thumb circles the sensitive skin of my back entrance and I lose it. I push upright and hold his hand against me, riding his fingers and the length of his cock, angling my hips so my clit stays under constant pressure.

Fuck. Yes.

He pushes up to a sitting position as I start to come, gripping my ass cheeks and pumping himself through my folds. "You're so pretty when you come for me," he groans into my neck, punctuating each word with a thrust. We shudder against each other, the flames of ecstasy consuming us until we're nothing but ashes.

37

———————

Light filters through the tent, bathing the interior in a golden glow. Jack had thrown his arm over my waist in the night, my back snug against his chest, one leg nudged between mine. I bask in the effervescent euphoria bubbling under my skin, taking a moment to appreciate the peace blanketing my heart. I carefully extricate myself from his limbs and climb down the ladder, the chilly air making me extra thankful for the emergency pair of joggers I packed yesterday. I rummage around in the cooler and pull out bread, eggs, bacon, and cheese.

Having the chance to cook him a meal gives me the warm fuzzies – he's taken such good care of me and has never given me a chance to reciprocate. I'm just finishing cooking the bacon and eggs when I hear Jack waking up. He yawns and then pokes his head out of the tent.

"Good morning, mo chridhe," he murmurs, his voice thick with sleep. He's adorably rumpled, and I can't help but melt into him the second his feet are on solid ground. I breathe him in, my cheek pressed to his chest. He kisses my head, not letting go until I'm the one that pulls away to check on the toast.

"What do you need help with?" he asks as I slide the eggs onto the toast, topping them with cheese and bacon.

"Absolutely nothing," I smile, handing a plate to him. "I'm happy to be able to do something for you finally." I press the coffee and pour it into mugs, motioning for him to sit before I hand it to him.

"I appreciate the sentiment, but I'm not keeping score. Being near you is enough."

"Stop," I protest, sitting next to him, setting my mug on the ground where I'm less likely to spill it all over myself.

"I'm not going to stop, Charlotte. You center my soul. I feel as if I've barely been living for a long time now – just going through the motions to get through every day. That night in the pub... God, I wish you could have felt what I was feeling. What I still feel." He takes a massive bite of his sandwich, licking the yolk dripping down his finger with one long swipe of his tongue. My stomach tightens. I take a bite, barely tasting it, emotions crowding out my senses.

"I felt it too. Still feel it," I say softly, picking up my mug and taking a careful sip. "It's like fate manipulated every part of my life to bring me to that one singular moment." I meet his gaze, my heart in my throat, vulnerability threatening to strangle the breath from my lungs. I swallow around the lump in my throat. "I think I—"

"Love you." Jack finishes, one side of his mouth tilting up in a sheepish smile.

"You do?" I blow out a shuddering breath, hope clawing its way up from the deepest pits of hell.

"Yes, Charlotte. I love you more than I thought I could ever love someone. It's infiltrated every single molecule in my body, pierced the core of every atom until I'm positive I wouldn't exist without you."

"How?" I ask, exasperated. "I fucked one of your best friends, and I've done everything but with the other. How can you still want me?" I blurt it out, finally voicing the niggling doubt that has been inside me this whole time.

He stands up and leans over me, palming my throat, his thumb pushing my chin, forcing me to meet his gaze. "Nothing you do could ever make me love you less. Do you understand me?" I don't answer right away, and his eyes darken with frustration. He lowers his mouth to mine, pushing his tongue past my lips in a fiery kiss that steals my breath away. "Do you understand?" he asks again.

"Yes! Fuck!" I croak, the enormity of the situation crashing over me. "This is going to be so messy. The visa, the divorce, I'll have to find a job and somewhere to stay."

"You won't be doing it alone, Charlotte, we'll be right there by your side the entire time," he assures me. "We'll sit down with Lach when we get back and get in touch with Cam. Then we'll take it day by day, okay?" He cups my jaw, caressing my cheek with his thumb.

I nod. Can I really do this? Move thousands of miles for two – maybe three – guys that have changed my entire world? My other option is to go back to the meager existence I had before I came here. Returning to shades of gray when I've been living in technicolor for the last two months. I can't imagine going back to that life any more than I can imagine going back to Rob.

Jack pulls me into his arms, tipping my chin to capture my lips with his. I open for him, finally surrendering to the inevitability of this. Of him. Of them.

"What do you say we pack up and head back? I'm anxious to tell Lach about Cam and figure out a game plan," Jack says, his lips trailing along my jaw as he speaks.

"He's not going to be mad, is he?" I ask.

"God, no. He'll be ecstatic. He and Cam had a thing going for years but stopped after Emily broke things off. The feelings are still there, though, as far as I'm aware." He folds the chairs and throws them into the truck. "You have no idea how good it will feel for all of us to be together again."

"If Cam agrees to go along with it," I remind him. "How are we going to get in touch with him?"

"Is he still in Africa?"

"I think so. I haven't heard from him in a couple of weeks."

"Lach has a satellite phone on his boat. We'll try that first," Jack says as he begins breaking down the camp.

"How do you know who to call?" I ask as I help him fold the bedding.

"I don't, but I'm hoping the university does."

"Where exactly does he teach? Like what part of Scotland?" I ask, imagining some creepy old school in a remote part of the highlands.

"Lewis."

I gape at him. I never dreamed it would be so close. "Wait,where does he live?"

"Did the two of you skip the whole getting to know each other part?" he asks, chuckling as he closes up the back of the truck.

I shrug. "Kind of? I know *him* but not *about* him, if that makes sense."

"I'm just teasing you, Sassenach. He lives in the east wing."

"Of the *castle*?" Every new tidbit of information is a goddamn revelation.

He nods. "It would just be sitting there empty otherwise. I tried to get Lach and Isla to move in, too, but they prefer having their own space."

He opens the door for me, and I climb in, protesting as he pulls the belt across me and buckles me in. "I can do that myself, you know."

"I know." He smiles, planting a warm kiss on my cheek before carefully closing the door.

"So, don't people with castles usually have titles?" I ask once he's behind the wheel, my curiosity piqued.

"It depends. The title will always pass down through the generations regardless of whether they keep their ancestral lands."

"Oh." I think about it for a second. "The castle is your ancestral home, right?"

He nods.

"Do you have a title?"

"Duke of Dunmore," he says nonchalantly, like he's telling me the grass is green or the sky is blue.

"You're joking."

He laughs, his eyes sparkling, "I wish you could see your face right now."

"It's like you live in a fucking fairytale. So that makes Isla...?"

"Lady Isla MacLeod."

"Not Duchess?"

"No, that's reserved for you."

Fucking hell.

38

———

W e're sitting in the driveway waiting on Lach, and I cannot stop fidgeting. Jack is pacing outside the truck, trying to get a phone number to reach Cam, leaving me all alone in here with my thoughts.

Duchess.

I'm sure most girls would be ecstatic. Me? Not so much. It just feels like one more worry piled on top of all the others.

What If I'm not enough?

Fuck that. Those are Rob's words coming back to haunt me. I scrub my hands over my face as I try to push the feelings away. *I can do this. I deserve this.* I chant the words over and over, desperate to believe them.

"Good news," Jack says as he climbs back in the truck, "They gave me a number to call."

"Carebear!" Lach grins as he slides in next to me; his sandy hair is messy and completely adorable.

"I missed you," I murmur, cupping his face and bringing his lips to mine. I sink into his warmth, basking in the safety and peace I feel being sandwiched between them.

"I missed you, too. Now, will one of you tell me what the heck is going on?"

"I'll tell you on the way," I murmur, heat already creeping up my cheeks.

"On the way to what?" Lach asks, closing his door.

"To the boat?" I say, looking to Jack for confirmation.

"For the love of God, will one of you please tell me what's going on?"

"Cameron," I croak, my heart in my throat, my nerves getting the best of me.

"What about him?" He raises his eyebrows, waiting. Confusion hits, his forehead scrunching. "Wait. How do you know about Cameron?"

I open my mouth to explain, but nothing comes out.

"She fucked him," Jack informs him with a huge grin.

"That is not helping," I hiss.

"I don't understand," Lach says, evidently completely lost.

"The guy in Portree—" I start to say.

"Was Cameron," he finishes, understanding dawning. "Well, fuck. We're going to the boat to call him?"

I nod, studying his face for a clue as to what he's thinking.

He laces his fingers through mine, pulling my hand to his lips. "How do you feel about it?"

"Me? How do *you* feel about it? I was worried you'd be disappointed."

"Why would I be disappointed?"

"Because I slept with him. Because I'm complicating everything."

"Life is messy, Charlie. That's part of the fun. Either it will work out with him, or it won't. We'll figure it out."

He puts his arm around me, and I melt into him. Jack palms my thigh and squeezes lightly, giving me the reassurance I need.

"If you already slept with him, you know what that means?" Lach muses, tossing a glance at Jack.

"What?" I ask, my gaze bouncing between them both.

"It means that to make it fair, we each get our first time alone with you," Jack says, his hand inching higher on my thigh.

My mouth goes dry. "That makes sense." I like the idea of being intimate with each of them alone before we... God. Goosebumps race over my entire body as a vision of tangled limbs flashes through my mind. I lick my lips. "So, are there rules to this?"

"Assuming Cameron is on board, the four of us will have to sit down and hash it out," Jack says, moving his hand until his pinkie is wedged in the crease of my thigh. I swallow a gasp as he slides it toward my center, my heart beating in my throat.

We turn into a gravel drive, following it around a bend before a cute little marina comes into view. There are a few dozen boats, most of them tattered fishing vessels that look like they've spent the last hundred years on the water.

"There's something I have to tell you," Lach says, extending his hand to help me out of the truck.

My heart sinks, but I don't have time to respond before Jack butts in.

"Surprise her," he says, "trust me, you'll want to see the look on her face."

"Hey!" I swat at his arm. "I think finding out that you're a duke is enough of a surprise for one day." I follow them onto a long dock, gaping at the boat floating perpendicularly to it. It's the biggest boat I've ever seen. I wonder if it belongs to someone who summers on the island. Although, Harris seems like an odd place for that. I bump into Lach when he stops short, and he grabs me by the shoulders to stop me from tumbling into the water. I swivel my head around, my gaze snagging on a pretty sailboat. Larger than I thought Lach could afford, but maybe he got a deal on it. "Is that her?" I ask, pointing to it. "The *Nauti Buoy*?" I raise an eyebrow, pressing my lips together to keep my laugh in.

"Do you really think I would name my boat that?" He asks incredulously.

"No?" I grimace. "What's the name of your boat then?"

He turns my body toward the yacht. "Meet *Whisky Business*." My gaze travels to the bow and I read the name as the words fall from his lips, but my brain still can't comprehend it.

"I don't—" I stop, looking between them. "That's almost the size of a fucking cruise ship. You're joking, right?"

"Told you I should have told her first," Lach grumbles to Jack. He turns to the boat and calls up to someone on deck. A ramp is lowered and I follow Lach up, my knees like jelly. He jumps off the ramp and turns toward me, catching me in his arms and carrying me onto the boat. Everything is white and chrome and blindingly sparkling.

"This is yours?" I breathe, unable to make this boat and Lachlan fit together. He has never struck me as the ostentatious type, and this is lightyears beyond that.

"It is."

"Please tell me why someone needs a boat this big."

"And there it is," Jack laughs, "I *told* you."

"God, I love you," Lach whispers, pulling me into a hug and swinging me around. "Give me thirty seconds to explain," he says, setting my feet firmly on the ground, "then you can ask questions and judge all you want."

I nod, not letting on how uneasy this makes me feel – like maybe he's not the person I thought he was.

"I've been lucky," he begins, "Very lucky. I invested in some businesses that have done better than I could have ever imagined. I used some of the money to buy *Whisky Business*. Most of the year she's used by people with terminal illnesses to take one last dream vacation. Many of them have caregivers, nurses, and family that they would have to take with them to go on a trip. The size of the boat allows for that. I get to use the boat for pleasure and business, and I also get the satisfaction of knowing that I'm helping people fulfill their dreams before they die. Win-win."

I'm completely dazed as he takes my elbow and guides me to a gorgeous semi-circle white sofa, pressing a glass of wine into my hands.

"So..." I try to gather my thoughts and fail miserably. "You're a millionaire?" I blurt, my cheeks flushing scarlet the second the words leave my mouth. "Oh God, don't answer that. I'm sorry."

"Billionaire, Carebear," Lach says without preamble. "Not many people know anything about what I do or what I'm worth, but if we're going to make this work, we need to be open with each other." He runs his hand through his hair. "I can't tell you that without also telling you that my goal is to donate all of my money before I die."

A duke and a billionaire. This life was meant for someone that doesn't wear jeans and sneakers ninety-nine percent of the time. For someone with more than a couple thousand dollars in her bank account. Not someone barely out of a failed marriage with no job and no prospects. Fucking hell.

"Hey." Jack takes my hand in his. "None of this changes anything."

"If you say so," I whisper, finding those words incredibly hard to believe.

His jaw ticks. "It doesn't. Money and titles mean nothing."

I clamp my mouth shut as Lach returns with a phone in his hand. He pulls the antenna out and hands it to Jack. "Do you want to do the honors?"

The look Jack gives me tells me our conversation isn't over. He takes the phone from Lach, looks at a note on his cell, and punches in a number. I can hear it ringing faintly before Jack greets someone and asks for Cameron. An expression of annoyance crosses his face before thanking the other person at the end of the line and hanging up.

"He's not there."

"What do you mean he's not there?" Lach demands.

Jack shrugs. "They said he left two days ago."

"Fuck." Lach runs his hand through his hair.

"What about his cell phone? Maybe he's back in range?"

"Go ahead," Jack says, motioning for me to call. I click the call button, my heart in my throat. It rings several times before going to an automated voicemail.

"I'll get back in touch with the university first thing in the morning and we'll go from there," Jack says, frustration radiating off his skin.

"Well, that was fucking anticlimactic. Come on, let's go home. I'll cook dinner," Lach grumbles, his shoulders slumped.

Disappointment sours in my stomach as we traipse off the boat. The ride back is utterly silent, all of us lost in our thoughts.

As we pull into the manor house drive, a cab is parked along the street. Jack slams on the brakes, all three of us lurching forward, holding our breath as we watch for a glimpse of dark curls and cerulean eyes.

39

———

I whimper as dark curls become visible over the top of the car. I'm climbing over Lach and throwing open the door before either of the guys has time to react. I swear it all happens in slow motion. Gravel crunches under my chucks as I run toward him. He turns. Our gazes collide, stormy seas taking me under. My name is on his lips as he closes the distance between us, his arms collapsing around me as I plow into him.

"Charlie," he whispers, his voice cracking, "God, I missed you." We squeeze each other tight, but it's impossible to feel close enough when there's clothing between us.

I lean back, taking him in. "Why are you here?"

"I was miserable," he chuckles, shaking his head. "I asked a colleague to take my place – I left as soon as they arrived."

"Why were you miserable?" I ask, desperate to hear the words confirming the maelstrom of emotions swirling through me.

He cups my face, the corner of his mouth quirking, "Because the world is dull without you by my side, my little witch. The spell you have me under only grew with the distance. All I could think about was the feel of your skin under my hands, the smell of your hair, the way you taste." He burrows his face against my neck, "The sounds you make when you cum." He lifts his head, tilting my chin with one long finger, "Your turn. How are *you* here?"

"We'll discuss that inside," Jack says gruffly, coming up behind us. Cameron spins around, keeping one hand on my hip, "Jay!" He reaches out and they complete a complicated handshake before Jack pulls him into a hug. "It's good to see you, man."

"Cam." Lach greets him and pulls him into a fierce embrace, winking at me over his shoulder. Cameron looks between me, Jack, and Lach, trying to puzzle out the mystery of the century.

"I'm going to need a drink, aren't I?" He asks, taking his bag from the cab driver and slipping a bill into his hand.

"Several," I confirm, my heart in my throat. What if he doesn't want this? What if it's too much? We follow the guys toward the house, but I pull him back before entering. "Wait, aren't you exhausted? Do you want to get some sleep first?"

"I won't be sleeping for a while, Charlie," he whispers, catching my bottom lip between his teeth. The doorbell digs into my back as he presses me against the front of the house, one hand pulling me flush against him, the other fisted in my hair. My body ignites as he slides his tongue against mine, deepening the kiss. He tilts my hips, pressing his cock against me. I moan into his mouth as he slowly rolls his hips, lighting my world on fire. He breaks the kiss, pressing his forehead to mine, our breaths mingling. "I need you, Charlie. Can this wait? I want to take you home."

I shake my head, "It can't wait, I'm sorry," I whisper, my breath catching in my throat, shuddering out of me on a stifled sob.

"Okay." He breathes in deeply, steadying himself. "Let's go inside and get this over with." He brushes his lips over mine one last time before stepping away and tidying himself.

I follow him inside, my gaze roaming over him, barely believing he's here. And now I have to tell him what I did–what I'm doing. What I want to do. Fuck.

We find them in the kitchen, Jack is sitting at the counter with a cup of coffee and Lach is pulling ingredients out of the fridge.

"I spiked it with Bailey's," Jack says, pushing two more mugs toward Cam and me, motioning for us to sit.

Cam takes a long sip and groans. "I've missed your coffee." He eyes all of us, taking in Jack's bouncing knee, Lach's concentration on the fridge, and my teeth lodged in my bottom lip. "Rip off the bandaid," he says, squeezing my knee.

"It's not her fault," Jack mutters, but I hold up my hand to stop him.

"It *is* my fault. I should be the one to tell him." I take a sip of my coffee, collecting my thoughts. I look up at Cam, memorizing the way his curls fall over his forehead, how his glasses frame oceans of expression, the sharp cut of his jaw, his dimples barely peeking out. I take a deep breath and begin. "After you left, I started working on the tree in the pub in the afternoons. Jack was bartending one night and offered to help me... so, I stayed. He made me dinner, helped me with my work, danced with me, and drove me back to the flat on his bike."

"Well, fuck. I never had a chance, did I?" he says, looking over at Jack, his chuckle devoid of humor.

"Just wait 'till I'm done, okay?" I take his hand in mine, tracing his fingers. "We didn't get each other's numbers before I left Portree and came here."

"Here?"

I nod. "I rented the cottage."

"What are the fucking chances?" He shakes his head in disbelief.

"Exactly. I met Lach when I checked in and, well.."

"*I* didn't have a chance," Lach says, his gaze leaving the potato in his hand and landing on me.

"Can you feel it?" I rasp, looking back at Cam.

"Feel what?" he asks, licking his lips.

"The inevitability of this. Of us," I circle my hand, encompassing the four of us. "I feel like I'm going to suffocate in it."

"The inevitability of what, Charlie? I want you to say exactly what you mean so there's no misunderstanding."

I clear my throat and straighten, squaring my shoulders. "You. Me. Jack. Lach. All of us. Together."

"Fucking, you mean?"

"Not just fucking. Living. Loving."

He scrubs his hands over his face. "I don't know if I'm strong enough to do that again," he says, his gaze lingering on Lach.

"It won't be the same," Jack insists, downing the rest of his coffee in one gulp, re-filling his mug with a healthy pour of Bailey's.

"You don't know that."

"Yes, we do," Lach says, meeting Cam's gaze. "For one, we're not in college anymore. We've all matured since then. We're much better at communicating now. Second, she's nothing like Em. Third, she doesn't want sex to be separate. She wants us together."

"You do?" he asks me, hope in his words. "What about us?" he whispers, turning to Lach, his voice so low I can barely hear him.

Lach's lips twist into a smile, "She already knows."

Cam pales a little. "You do?" he asks again.

I nod, trying to hide a smile. "It's fucking hot."

He blows out a heavy breath and throws back his drink, holding his mug out to Jack. "This is not at all how I was expecting today to go. I came here hoping to get advice from Isla."

"Did I hear my name?" Isla croaks from the hallway. She shuffles into the kitchen, rubbing her eyes and yawning.

"Late night last night?" Jack chuckles, pouring her some coffee.

"Very. I kicked him out at four this morning."

"When will you start giving them a chance, Isla?" Lach asks, a hint of worry in his voice.

"I've been burned too many times to fall for that. Sex is all I need." She sips her coffee, her eyes swiveling around the room. "Cameron!" she kisses him on his cheek. "You're back early." She glances down at our intertwined hands. "It is way too early to try to figure this out." Seh raises an eyebrow at me. "Charlotte, spill."

"Cameron is the guy I dated in Portree."

"No he fucking isn't," she splutters, choking on her coffee. "You can't tell me there wasn't some sort of divine intervention here. Absolutely sickening." She throws a wink over her shoulder before stomping out of the room.

"We're not doing this only for you to leave in a month, are we?" Cam asks, chewing on his bottom lip.

I shake my head. "I'll have to go back to the states for the divorce and figure out a job and visa, but I want to stay." We stop talking as Lach drops sausages into the skillet, the sizzling too loud to hold a conversation.

"We have something else to talk about," Lach says as he plates the food on a large platter.

"What's that?" Cam asks, watching him with a look in his eyes that makes heat pool in my stomach.

"You're the only one that's fucked her," he says, setting the dish in front of us. There are three large sausages with scoops of mashed potatoes placed to look like testicles and two links forming a vulva, a tiny pearl onion where the clit should be. I giggle, snort, and then giggle even more.

"You goddamn son of a bitch," Jack laughs.

"It's a masterpiece," Cam says, his eyes sparkling with laughter, "but can we get back to what you just said?"

"That you're the only one that's fucked her?" Lach asks, pulling a stool to the other side of the counter.

"Yes, that."

"We've talked about it briefly, and I think the only thing to do would be to even up the score."

Cameron nods thoughtfully. "You're good with that?" he asks me, putting food on my plate before filling his own.

"I think it's the only way to start this off on fair footing. Then I think sex should only be when we're all there."

"What about other stuff?" Lach asks, biting into his sausage.

My cheeks heat as my imagination takes over. "I'm okay with other stuff being separate as long as the actual sex is all of us together. What do you guys think?"

"What about Cameron and I?" Lach asks. "If we decide to explore that again?" he elaborates, his words tentative.

"I think it should be the same rules."

"I agree," Cam says, his cheeks flushed scarlet.

"It's settled then? No group sex until we even up the playing field and then only group sex from then on?" Jack confirms.

"Agreed," Cam and Lach, and I say in unison.

"How long might that be?" Cam asks, looking at me and then down at his lap, where his cock is pressed against his thigh.

I lick my lips, remembering that one tiny taste I had in the alley, "Not long. In the meantime, I have a mouth capable of taking care of that for you."

"Fuck," he breathes, his jaw flexing.

"I think that's our cue to leave," Jack says, pushing his stool back as he stands.

"You, maybe," Lach laughs, "this is where I live." He turns to Cam and me, "Why don't the two of you go to the cottage or back to your apartment and catch up with each other?"

"Are you guys sure?" I ask, suddenly uncertain in this new territory.

"Yes, Sassenach. Go." Jack gently pushes both of us toward the door. I turn back toward him to argue but only catch a glimpse of a huge grin and an eyebrow waggle as he closes the door.

40

———

My hair whips at my face as I look up at Cam, suddenly shy. "Do you want to go to the cottage or back to your place?"

"Is there room for me to do what I'm going to do to you in the cottage?" he asks, tipping up my chin. I shiver as the deep timbre of his voice rumbles over me.

"No," I croak, licking my parched lips. He guides me over to Jack's truck and opens the door, motioning for me to hop in.

"Lach can drive him back," he reassures me when he sees my hesitation. We're pulling into the castle drive a couple of minutes later, a comfortable silence cocooning us – like we both know there's no point in talking until we do everything possible. Except fuck. This will be an exercise in restraint, although I suppose it's good practice for later.

Cam doesn't wait until we're inside. The second he opens my door to the car, he pushes his hands into my hair and pulls my mouth to his. He slicks his tongue across my lips and I open, inviting him in. He slides one hand down my back, around my waist, and up to cup my breast.

"God, I forgot how perfect they are," he mumbles against my lips. I moan as his fingers close over my nipple, arching into his touch. "Fuck, Charlie. I have to get you inside. I need to feel your skin against mine." He links his fingers with mine and pulls me to a side entrance, lifting and carrying me over the threshold. Our gazes collide, both of us caught in a torrent of emotion so poignant it brings tears to my eyes.

"I missed you so fucking much," he rasps, setting me down so he can kiss me properly. I press my body to him, but I know that even when our clothes are gone, it still won't be close enough. I lean back so I can see his face, tracing the bow of his lips, the divot in his chin, the sharp sweep of his jaw, memorizing the tiny flaws that make him imperfectly perfect.

"I think I love you," I blurt, the words tumbling from my mouth before I can give them the thought they deserve.

"You think?" His dimples flash. "I think I've loved you since you turned that chair around and sat there listening to me like I was the most fascinating person you've ever met. I think I've loved you since we stood outside the bookshop and the mist coated your eyelashes like fairy dust." He presses his forehead to mine. "I *knew* I loved you the second I stepped foot on that airplane to leave and I felt like my life was ending."

I sniffle, then laugh at the irony of it all. "Why did we ever think it was a good idea for you to go?"

"I haven't the faintest idea. But maybe you wouldn't have met the guys, and things would be completely different right now."

"You're sure you're okay with all of this?" I ask, needing reassurance.

"I'm positive, Charlie." He runs one fingertip over my eyebrows, down my nose, lingering on my lower lip. "You're a goddamn supernova. You pulled us into orbit and now we're all fucked. In the best kind of way."

"You have a way with words that I'll never get enough of," my whisper is deep and throaty and tells him exactly what I'm thinking about.

"Come on." He pulls me through a maze of hallways, through a beautiful art gallery with twenty-foot ceilings, into a large open hall-way, and then stops in front of an intricately carved door. He twists the doorknob but pauses before opening the door, looking at me with a mixture of wonder and disbelief. "I never thought I would see you standing in front of my door, looking at me like that."

"Like what?"

"Like you want me to drop to my knees right here in the hallway and make you come until you beg me to stop."

"Yes, please."

He grins and scoops me up before walking into the room and tossing me onto a gigantic four-poster bed. He crawls up after me, sliding his body over mine. "You better fuck them quick, Charlie."

I moan, his words sending tremors through my body. I frame his face with my hands and pull him to me, nipping at his bottom lip before kissing him deeply.

"What magic is in your kisses that I would willingly drown in them, little witch?" He asks, pulling away with a groan. He rubs his nose against mine before rolling off of me. "I have to shower before we take this any further. Give me twenty minutes?"

I nod, wanting to ask to join him but also respecting how he must feel after a full day of traveling. "Let me know if you need help," I say, giving him an exaggerated wink.

"Trust me, we'll be in the shower together by morning. Why don't you relax while you wait? There's a small bar by the terrace – make us a couple of drinks?"

"Okay." I smile as he starts unbuttoning his shirt. My breath is ripped from my lungs as I'm reminded of what he looks like under his button-downs and chinos. I've never had the time or light to appreciate him properly, but today – with the opulence of his room as a backdrop – is the perfect opportunity. He finishes with the last button and slides the shirt off his shoulders, lithe muscles flexing as he pulls it off and lays it over a chair. The veins riding over his biceps and forearms are blue smudges under almost translucent skin.

"Don't look at me like that," he breathes, his nostrils flaring as he pulls his belt from the loops in one fluid motion.

"Like what?" Like I need him like I need the air I breathe? Like he's the last morsel of food on this island? Like he's a piece of my heart that I just realized has been missing my entire life?

"Like you'd rather lick every part of me if it meant I didn't have to leave you to shower." He grabs my ankles and pulls me to the end of the bed.

I wrap my legs around him as he hovers over me, making me want things I can't have. "I'll do way more than lick you," I say, my voice husky with need.

He chuckles. "I'm sure you will, my beautiful girl." He peppers kisses over my cheek and down my neck, one hand sliding under my shirt and closing over my breast. I arch into him, urging him on. He pulls my bra to the side and rolls my nipple between his fingers until I'm writhing under him.

"Cam, please," I moan.

He groans, breathing me in before sucking my nipple into his mouth, pulling until my toes curl. Until I'm rocking against him, my body begging him for more.

"You're so pretty when you beg," he growls, his gaze roaming over my body, branding me. "Do it again."

Fuck. I clamp my jaw shut, but he only has to roll his hips against me one more time for me to crack. "Please."

"Tell me what you want."

He moves to my other breast, sucking my nipple into his mouth with one long, hard pull.

"Fuck!" I sob, squirming under him.

"Tell me," he demands.

"I—" I groan and grind against him as he pulls me back into his mouth. "I want your mouth—" He slides his hands down my waist, licking a line down the center of my abdomen. I whimper when he reaches my waistband, groaning when he stops.

"I'm waiting, little witch."

"I want you to fuck me with your tongue," I say, the last words coming out on a sob as he rips off my pants and underwear and fastens his mouth to my clit. My mouth opens on a silent scream as he pushes two fingers into me, and I come apart, my world fracturing into a million facets, his face reflecting from every single one of them.

41

I'm staring up at the angels on the ceiling, boneless and breathless. I wonder if they're judging me. I study them. Bare breasts. Rosy cheeks. Hell, maybe they like watching. I chuckle to myself and sit up as I hear Cam start the shower. I have to hunt for my underwear but leave my pants on the floor – there's no point in putting them on when he's just going to be taking them off later. I would never admit it to the guys, but I wish I had one more time alone with Cam. Every time I think back to the night in the bookstore I come undone.

I walk to his dresser on shaky legs and pick up a family picture framed in gold. Cam is front and center – maybe a year old – his parents looking down at him with absolute adoration in their eyes. A faded polaroid is propped up next to it. Much younger versions of Jack, Lach, and Cam smile at the camera, their arms around each other – that kind of easy camaraderie that only comes from knowing someone your entire life. Judging by how young and carefree they look, the picture must have been taken in their first year of university. I wish I had known them back then. My life would have been so different.

I make my way over to the bar cabinet, pausing at the terrace doors to admire the view of the expansive grounds. Hundred-year-old trees pepper the manicured lawn, birds flitting in and out of their branches. I open the doors and breathe in the bite of the air. Cam may call me a witch, but the real magic is in the walls of this place. I can feel the history waiting to be discovered, the vignettes begging to be painted.

A heather-scented breeze ruffles the sheer curtains covering the windows as I poke around in the liquor cabinet. I keep it simple and pull out bottles of whisky, simple syrup, and lemon juice. It won't be as good as freshly made and pressed, but I have a feeling that we won't be paying attention to what the drink tastes like anyway. I'm stirring the cocktails with my finger – after an unfruitful search for a utensil – when Cam comes out of the bathroom with a towel wrapped around his waist. He leans against the doorframe, watching me.

I freeze mid-stir. "What?"

He stalks toward me, his gaze burning me alive. He slides his palm from my shoulder to my hand and pulls it to his mouth, swirling his tongue over my finger. "Whisky sour?" he murmurs, nipping my skin.

"Mmhmm." My gaze narrows to the tip of his tongue as he swipes it over my skin, soothing the sting of his bite. All I can think of is how badly I want him to do that between my legs.

"Let's drink them out on the terrace."

"Like this?" I ask, looking down at my bare legs.

"Who's going to see?"

"Good point." I follow him out the door, dark gray flagstone cold against my bare feet. "This is beautiful," I breathe, slowly turning to take it all in. I prop my hip on the intricate balustrade and take a sip of my drink.

"Yes, it is," he rasps, his eyes on me. He sits at an iron garden table, his legs spread wide, the towel barely covering him.

"Cam," I groan. I set my drink down and drop to my knees between his legs.

"Charlie, you don't need to do that."

I chuckle. "Yes, I do." I slide my palm up his thigh, slowly pushing the towel away. "I need to do this like I need to breathe." I lick my lips and look up at him through my eyelashes. His eyes darken as I bend to press a kiss to the inside of his knee. When he doesn't stop me, I lick, kiss, and bite my way up his muscled thigh. I snake my hand under the towel and pull it from where he has it tucked, letting it fall to the sides of the chair.

Fuck. Me.

I didn't have the chance to appreciate this the last two times, and God, do I regret that. A breath shudders past my lips as I lift him from his thigh and slide my hand over smooth velvet and hard steel. His balls are high and tight and fucking perfect.

"You were made by the gods, Cameron. There's no other explanation."

He only groans in response as I run my tongue over his head and then blow lightly, getting perverse satisfaction from the chill that tremors through his body. He pushes my hair away from my face as I lick him from the base to the tip, rolling my tongue over that bit of sensitive skin at the end. His hand spasms around my neck, his careful restraint close to snapping.

I want him out of control. I want him begging.

I alternate licking and sucking the smooth skin of his scrotum, heat pooling between my legs at the guttural curse he utters as I pass my tongue over his perineum. "You like that?" I murmur, massaging him with the tip of my tongue. He thrusts his hips into the air, groaning. His breaths come hard and fast as he looks down at me, his dark ringlets dripping from the shower.

"Tell me what you want," I say, my voice husky with need as I struggle to control my breathing.

Cam leans forward, one finger tilting my chin up to him. There's a set to his jaw I haven't seen before, a primal gleam in his eyes. "I want you to fucking eat me alive, little witch," he growls, his nostrils flaring. "I want to scream your name until my throat is raw. I want to feel like you're sucking my soul out of my body through my cock. I want to see tears coursing down your cheeks as I fuck your throat, and then I want to taste what's weeping down your thighs after I cum. I want to drown in you and for you to suffocate on me. Is that clear enough for you?"

"Crystal," I croak, my body thrumming like a live wire.

Loud clapping startles me; I press a hand to my chest as I turn to see Jack and Lachlan standing about twenty feet away, shit-eating grins plastered on their faces. I tense and start to move away from Cam, but his hand on my shoulder keeps me in place.

"Very eloquent," Lach chuckles, biting his lip and waggling his eyebrows at us.

"What are you two doing here?" I ask, vulnerability and lust ping-ponging through me.

"We talked and decided it wasn't fair to ask you to abstain when you haven't seen each other for weeks," Jack says. He holds out a paper bag for me to take. "The only thing we ask is that you use these. In fact, we all need to be using them, or our first time together won't be what any of us are hoping for."

I take the bag from him and peek inside, not surprised to see the butt plugs and lube.

"We'll leave now," Lach rasps, his gaze volleying between Cam's cock and my mouth. "We'll be out here this evening in case you want observers." He winks, but the erection pressing against his pants makes it abundantly clear that he's not joking. The idea of them watching Cam destroy me lights me up like a damn Christmas tree.

I look up at Cam, raising an eyebrow in a silent question. A slow grin spreads across his face as he catches my meaning.

"I think our little witch wants you to watch," Cam chuckles, caressing my cheek with his thumb.

A sharp intake of breath has me glancing up at Jack, his whisky gaze drawing me in. "Is that what you want, Sassenach?"

Absofuckinglutely I do.

Lust has my vocal cords in a chokehold, so I can only nod.

"You two finish here, and Lach and I will prepare a space that's a little more comfortable. Why don't we meet for dinner at seven?" Jack asks, not quite able to keep the smile off his face.

"Perfect," Cam murmurs, his attention on my hand as it creeps up his thigh.

Jack and Lach turn and head back inside, and I turn back to Cam, determined to give him the best blowjob of his goddamned life.

42

Cameron watches me, waiting, one dark curl falling over his brow. His looks are paralyzing. If you told me he was chiseled from marble and brought to life by the gods, I would have believed it. I shuffle between his legs and cup his face between my hands, tracing his lower lip with my thumb. He pushes his hands into my hair and returns my gaze, something profound and indescribable traveling between us. I only pull away when I can no longer ignore the hard cock pressed into my ribs or the throbbing at the juncture of my thighs.

"May I?" Cameron asks, grasping the hem of my shirt and tugs like he wants to pull it over my head.

I nod and reach behind me to unclasp my bra, then lift my hands over my head as he pulls it away from my body.

"Fuck," he groans, palming my tits. I look down at his hands, then further down to his cock, and sit down on my heels so he's nestled against the underside of my cleavage. Cam bites his lip as he thrusts up, squeezing my breasts together to hug his shaft. The visual of the head of his cock plowing through soft mounds of flesh has me rocking against my foot, desperate to relieve the ache.

"Don't you fucking dare. That orgasm is mine," he growls,

releasing my breasts to wind a hand in the length of my hair. He pulls me up on my knees and stands up, his cock only millimeters from my lips.

I look at him through my eyelashes, my heart in my throat. I used to think giving blowjobs was one of those chores that you do because it has to be done, but fuck if my mouth isn't watering. I hold his gaze as I slick my tongue over the drop of pre-cum, groaning as I truly taste him for the first time. His hand trembles in my hair as I wrap my lips around him, swirling my tongue over the ridge of his head.

"Charlie, I won't—" his words turn into a moan as I grab his ass and pull him to me. I hold still as he rocks his hips against me gently. I don't want gentle. I want him to lose himself in me. I take in more of him until I gag, pull away, and repeat. I concentrate on my breathing as he slides in, opening my throat and praying to the gods that I can do this for him. I swallow around him and feel him tense, his hands moving to frame my face, trembling with restraint. Our gazes collide as I draw back, and I let him see everything I'm feeling. Everything I want. Everything I need.

A strangled sound leaves his throat as his grasp on me tightens. He thrusts into me, and I greedily accept, moaning around him.

"You're so fucking pretty with your lips around my cock, little witch," he grinds out, thrusting again.

It's still not enough. He has the control of a fucking saint. On his next thrust, I slide my hand over his ass and find the spot behind his balls. I press on it with my thumb, massaging him, and finally, his head falls back as his back bows, pleasure overriding his system. He holds my face in a fierce grip and slams into my mouth. More. I need more. I want it all. I slide my finger over his cock between thrusts, coating it in saliva. As he pulls back, I slip my finger between his cheeks and tease the sensitive skin of his entrance.

"Fuck, Charlie!" he drops his chin to his chest, his gaze ensnaring me. My avenging angel laying claim to what belongs to him.

I carefully push my finger against the tight ring of muscle, slowly working my way in until I can feel his prostate. He roars, the animal inside him taking control as he fucks my mouth with hard, punishing thrusts.

I watch him with streaming eyes as he takes what's his. As I give him everything I am. His moan skitters over my skin as he pulls my face against him on one last thrust, his cum hitting the back of my throat in hot spurts. His grip slowly eases as he comes back down, and then he's wiping away my tears with his thumbs. He pulls me up, his grip softening to a caress as he plunders my mouth. He peels off my underwear and walks me back until my thighs hit the balustrade and I'm forced to sit. The rough stone scrapes against my skin as he presses my thighs open and drops between them.

"Did sucking my cock make you wet, Charlie?" He asks before catching the desire dripping down the insides of my thighs with his tongue, his lips vibrating against me as he moans. He slides his tongue along my slit before sucking my clit into his mouth. My back bows and I hang on to his head, trying to ride him and not fall simultaneously. "Stand up," he says gruffly, realizing my predicament. I stand and he moves so his back is against the balustrade and then turns me to face him. "One knee on the railing, your hands wherever you need them to stay steady."

I nod and close the distance between us, my pussy fitting to his mouth as I place my knee on the balustrade. My knees almost buckle when he immediately sucks me in, and I grasp onto his hair as I ride his face.

A warm hand slides over my hip, I groan as Lach's scent drifts over me.

"May I?" He asks, holding up the paper bag with one finger, his hazel eyes hopeful and hungry.

I look down at Cameron, angling my pelvis away so he can talk.

"It's up to you, Charlie. It'll always be up to you," he mumbles as he pulls me back to his mouth, pulsing his tongue against me.

Can I do this? Can I be with all three of them like this? "Yes, " I answer Lach, my voice trembling as I swivel my head in search of Jack.

"Jay!" Lach calls out, not taking his eyes off me for a second. "You're needed!"

Jack comes out onto the terrace midway through rolling up his sleeves, looking sexy as fuck. He stops short, his eyes darkening as he takes in the scene. "Is that so?" he asks, a smile pulling at his lips. He hops over the balustrade, strides toward me, and slides his hand over my throat. "I knew they'd look better around your neck, Sassenach," he breathes, squeezing the slightest bit before capturing my mouth with his and taking me under.

43

I shudder as Cam drags his tongue over me. One of Jack's hands is around my throat, the other grasping my chin, holding me steady as he ravages my mouth. Lach is behind me, running his hands over my body, palming my tits, sucking and kissing and licking. They're completely overwhelming my system and I can't fucking get enough.

Lach drops to his knees behind me and kneads my ass, his thumbs getting closer and closer to that forbidden place until I squirm in his grip and push back toward him. He teases me with his tongue, swirling it over me until I'm moaning into Jack's mouth. I wrap my arms around Jack's neck just as my legs start to turn to jelly, and he wraps an arm around my waist, supporting my weight.

Lach steps away for a second, then comes back, his hands spreading my ass and squirting lube between my cheeks. Cam pushes a finger into me, rubbing that place inside that feels so damn good. My back arches as I ride his mouth, giving Lach the opening he needs to massage my ass, ever so slowly convincing that muscle to give in. A garbled groan tears out of my throat as he pushes his finger in, sliding in and out of me so gently it makes me want to scream.

"Are you ready, Carebear?" Lach whispers, pressing cold silicone against me.

I nod and relax my body, going boneless in Jack's arms, dropping my head and watching Cam as he laps me up like I'm honey from the promised land. He pulses the flat of his tongue against my clit as Lach slowly pushes the butt plug into me. I whimper as it slides home, the feeling so strange but so *good* at the same time. I hear Lach unzip his pants, and then he grips my hip, his other hand working his cock.

God, I want him so deep in me I can feel him in my throat.

Shifting my weight so I can unbuckle Jack's pants, I push them down to pool around his ankles and pull him out, the weight of him heavy and warm in my hand.

"Sassenach—" he starts to protest, but I spit on my palm and slide it down his shaft in one long stroke. He thrusts up to meet me, greedy for the touch.

"That's what I thought," I murmur, smirking up at him.

Lach grunts and then half moans, half whimpers. Goosebumps race over every inch of me as I look back and see Cam's hand wrapped around Lach's cock.

Fuck. I've never been this turned on in my entire life.

I moan as my world narrows to the feel of Jack in my hands, Cam's steady suctioning on my clit, and the sound of Lach falling apart behind me, his fingers spasming against my hip with each stroke of Cam's hand. The guys echo me, Cam's hum vibrating over me, bringing me to the precipice of something I can't comprehend.

I look up at Jack. "Please let me taste you. Please."

"Charlotte, I can't be gentle when it's like this. I lose control. We can't."

"I don't want you controlled. I want the real you," I rasp, my mouth starting to water just thinking about him.

"Get out of your head, man. She can take it. She was made for us," Lach says from between clenched teeth, his eyes glued to Cam's elegant fingers sliding over his cock.

"You don't fucking understand," Jack growls, his hand sliding back to my neck. "I want to lay you on the bed and fuck your throat until you can't breathe. I want to squeeze your throat until I can feel my cock sliding inside of you underneath my palm."

I stand up and step away from Cam. Jack closes the distance until we're chest to chest, the balustrade the only thing between us. "And what if I tell you that's what I want? Will you give it to me, Jack?"

His jaw clenches, his nostrils flaring as he breathes me in, his gaze traveling down my body. He's about to answer when the sound of Cam gagging has us looking over. Lach has Cam's hair fisted in his hands and is ramming into him in measured strokes.

"Fuck," I whimper, my pussy clenching on air.

"Get the fuck over here," Jack grinds out, stepping out of his pants before lifting me over the balustrade. He lies down in the grass and tries to pull me down to his mouth, but I turn before lowering myself onto him. He moans under me, sliding his tongue through me and massaging the sensitive skin stretched around the butt plug with his thumb. A sound I don't recognize tears its way out of my mouth from somewhere deep in my body. I focus on Jack's cock, taking him in both of my hands, one over the other, squeezing and twisting. He palms my thighs and buries his face in me, his tongue lapping at my g-spot.

I can hear Lach slamming into Cameron's mouth as I press my clit to Jack's chin and ride him like a fucking horse. Sliding my tongue over his head, I give him a gentle warning before licking the precum from his slit. His abs contract as he angles his hips toward my mouth, but I don't do what I know he wants. Instead, I press him to his stomach, licking and nibbling the sensitive skin on the underside of his cock until he's shouting at me to stop teasing him, goddamnit! He kneads my ass cheeks with both hands and then lifts me off his mouth, moving me down his body.

"I have to feel you on my cock for just a second, Sassenach," he says, his voice coarse with need. I hover over him, desperately wanting to sink down onto him, but I also want to respect his boundaries. He slides himself through my folds, rolling my clit under the ridge of his head. I whimper, rocking my hips against him. He positions the head of his shaft at my entrance and pulses against me, his arms trembling with restraint. I lower my weight the tiniest bit until he's spreading me, his head on the verge of entering me completely.

"Not fucking yet," he breathes, wrenching my hips back up to his mouth.

When he pulls my clit into his mouth, alternating suction with licks, I know it's time to stop playing. I want us to get there together, and I'm fucking close. I glance at Lach as I lift Jack's cock, his gaze is volleying between where Jack's mouth is sealed to my pussy and the way Cameron's lips are stretched over his cock.

Oh, God. This is too much. I don't waste any time dropping my mouth onto Jack's cock, bottoming out on his pubic bone. He roars under me, his mouth wide open against me as his back bows. He grabs my waist and pulls it down until my back is arched, my clit the only thing in contact with his mouth, and then he slides two fingers into me, hooking them and rubbing until I feel like I'm going to explode.

I whimper around his cock, meeting him thrust for thrust, barely able to breathe, the lack of oxygen heightening all of my senses. I rock back and forth over him, the outside world disappearing as I chase my orgasm. He slides one hand down my back and into my hair, his touch tentative and questioning. I moan around his shaft, encouraging him. He must understand because a second later he's pushing my head down to meet every thrust, sucking my clit into his mouth in one long pull and pulsing his fingers inside me.

I scream around his cock and he thrusts harder, pushing into my throat, his hips pumping as my body draws tight as a bow. Cum slides down my throat in hot pulses as my entire existence shatters into a million pieces. It's in that moment, floating among the shards of my broken body, that I realize the guys are the only ones who have ever been able to make me feel whole again.

44

———

"How are you feeling?" Jack whispers to me, his golden gaze reaching into the depths of my soul. I grasp his arm as he places me on the edge of the bed, not ready to break the contact. I don't answer right away. Of course, on the surface, I feel good. I just had two mind-melting orgasms within the last couple of hours.

"I'm scared," I say, my heart jumping to my throat as I admit it.

"About what?" Lach asks, coming back inside from the terrace, his clothes bundled in his arms. Cam follows him through the door, and all of us begin to pull on our clothes like this is an everyday occurrence.

"I'm scared this won't last. I'm scared I'm going to move here and something will change. I'm scared I'll lose myself again." My voice cracks and I press my lips tightly together, doing my best not to break down in front of them. Why am I even telling them this? It's my own insecurities. My own problems.

"Do you think we're not terrified that *you'll* change your mind, Charlie?" There's a bite to Lach's voice that isn't usually there. "Every morning when I wake up, I wonder if today will be the day you tell us you're going back." He drags his fingers through his hair as he paces the room. "I know you'll eventually have to leave to take care of things, but will you come back? Or will you decide this was some crazy fling you had while on holiday?"

"Okay, we obviously have some things to talk about," Jack says, rolling his shoulders like he's getting ready for a fight. "But let's do it in the kitchen? I'm starving." He links his fingers with mine and pulls me out the door, leaving the other two to follow.

"What do you mean that you're scared you'll lose yourself again?" Cam asks, wrapping an arm around my waist as we walk down the hallway.

"My entire existence was intertwined with Rob's. So much so that I lost everything when he cheated on me. I lost all of my friends, my house, my money, my fucking life. I liked what Rob liked. Rob's hobbies became my hobbies. I can't do that again."

"Good. We don't want that, either," Lach interjects. "We want you the way you are now. And we'll still want you in ten years when you've grown into yourself even more. And in fifty years, when you're an old biddy sitting outside hunched in front of a canvas, we'll still fucking want you, Charlie. Don't you get it? We've been waiting for you our entire fucking lives."

A tear slips down my cheek before I can stop it.

Cam steps in front of me, stopping me in my tracks. "We'll spend every day for the rest of our lives showing you how precious you are to us. You can be whomever you want to be, Charlie. We'll be by your side supporting you the entire way."

"Charlotte." The intensity of Jack's voice has me spinning around. I crash into his chest and he pulls me close, pressing a kiss to my forehead. "I know it's scary, but I promise we'll always be here for you." He pulls a ring off his finger and pushes it onto the ring finger of my left hand. I run my fingers over the thick, worn band. "We are yours and you are ours. Finding each other was the hard part. Now we need to figure out how to make it work." He kisses me gently, his touch reverent. "Let's make food, and then we can sit down and figure everything out while we eat. I think it'll make us feel better to have a solid plan in place."

The guys sit me at the u-shaped bench seat in the kitchen while they cook dinner, their easy banter making me smile. The small touches and glances between Cam and Lach make me feel a warm giddiness I've never experienced before. Jack pushes through the back door, a platter of steaks in his hand, and sets it on the table, followed by four beers. He rummages around in several drawers while the other two finish up, finally pulling out a notebook and pen. He slides in next to me just as the other two set down a salad and a bowl of roasted potatoes.

"I could get used to this," I murmur, the side of my mouth quirking despite trying to hold back my smile.

"That's the fucking plan, Sassenach," Jack mutters, handing me a beer.

I snort. "You guys are just going to wait on me hand and foot for the rest of my life?"

"Yes, goddamnit! Why is that so hard for you to believe?" Lach holds my gaze, frustration blazing in his eyes.

"I'm sorry, I—" Fuck.

"You what, Charlie? Can we please get to the truth of what this really is so we can move past it?"

My heart clenches. "I don't feel like I deserve this. All three of you are so interesting and complicated and good-looking. And then there's little ole me who's never done anything interesting in her entire life. I'm a blank canvas with no depth."

"No. You're looking at it all wrong. We want you to paint us into the fabric of your life, Charlie, and a blank canvas is a perfect place to start. A midnight sky that reminds you of Cam's eyes. Deep caramel that brings back the memories of the warmth of Jack's embrace." He pauses, then barks out a laugh. "Hell, I don't know what color I would be."

I finish for him. "You'll be the luminescence in every grain of sand, the shimmering in every ripple of water. You'll be what makes it come alive." I grab the notebook from Jack and scribble down everything Lach just said. "I'm going to frame this and hang it next to my bed."

Cam clears his throat, his eyes suspiciously bright as he takes a pull of his beer.

Jack tips up my chin and studies me. "Better now?"

I nod, chuckling. "Go ahead and eat, I know you're hungry."

"Thank God."

The guys dive in, serving me before they serve themselves.

"How's the family tree going?" Cam asks before popping a piece of his steak in his mouth.

"Good! I need to find somewhere to buy paint, though. I only have some of the colors I need to paint the vignettes. I probably need a few nibs and ink for my pen, too."

"Fucking finally!" Lach shouts, high-giving Jack.

"What was that about?" I glance at Cam, but he looks just as perplexed as I feel.

"We've wanted a reason to take you into the city for a while now, but we knew that if we suggested it, you would say that you had to work on the family tree."

"Why do you want to take me into the city? And what city are we talking about exactly?"

"Any city will do, lass. We want to wine and dine you properly," Jack grins.

Oh. That sounds nice.

"How quickly do you need the paints?"

"I'd love to have them by the start of next week."

"This coming weekend it is, then."

As we finish our food, Jack pulls the notebook back over to his side and has me rattle off everything that's been worrying me – every loose end, every logistical nightmare down to the nitty-gritty details. Then we all methodically discuss them one by one and devise a plan for how we'll tackle them. For once in my life, I feel like I have people in my corner rooting for me. They make me feel safe and cared for. They make me feel loved.

Jack pulls me aside as we're leaving the kitchen, his hand circling my wrist and pulling me close. "This is completely your decision, but if you want your first time with all three of us to be in a swanky hotel with room service, this weekend will be perfect. But that also means—"

"That I have to sleep with all three of you before this weekend."

"Exactly." His voice is husky and sexy as hell.

"Have you been thinking about our first time, Jack?"

He chuckles. "I haven't stopped thinking about it since the day I met you. I'm going to fuck you in every single room of this castle, Sassenach."

45

———

Cam grips my hip and pushes me against the smooth wood paneling of the hallway, his lips melting me into a puddle of hormones. We have free rein tonight – the guys insisted they had encroached enough and that we deserved time to ourselves. I am *really* looking forward to time alone with Cam. I run my palms over the light stubble on his jaw, pulling his face to mine. He pushes my hair away from my face as he angles his head to deepen the kiss, then breaks away to yawn into his elbow.

"God, I'm sorry, Charlie. The jetlag is starting to catch up with me." Big, blue, sleepy eyes gaze down at me, his lashes a dark smudge against his porcelain skin.

I stand on my tiptoes and press a chaste kiss to his lips. "Why don't you take a nap while I shower?" I pull him down the hallway, our fingers intertwined.

He captures me with his body, pressing me back against the wall with his hips. I can't look away as he swipes his tongue over his full bottom lip. "I don't want a nap, Charlie." I groan as he rolls his hips against me, his cock making direct contact with my clit. "What I want," he says, his gaze narrowing to my lips, "is to sink my cock into your pussy and fuck away the memory of the last six weeks." He drags his thumb over my bottom lip, his hunger seeping into me, twisting through my veins. He palms my thighs and pulls me up, wrapping my legs around his waist. I bounce against him with every step he takes toward his room, velvet heat against molten steel. By the time we make it to his door, all I want to do is tear off his clothes and impale myself.

"I should shower," I say again as he lays me down on the bed, but it comes out as a question instead of a statement.

"Later," he says, his voice muted as he pulls his shirt over his head. "I want to smell him on you while I claim you, little witch. You're fucking mine tonight." I whimper as he drops his pants and palms his cock. He grabs the waistband of my leggings and pulls them off in one smooth movement.

"Touch yourself," he says roughly, pushing my knees toward my chest and opening them wide. I slide my hand down my stomach and push my fingers into the moisture gathered between my thighs. His jaw flexes as I push two fingers inside, then bring them back up to cradle my clit. "Is that what you like, Charlie?" He brings my hand to his mouth, groaning as he licks my fingers clean. He slides two fingers into me, filling me, teasing that spot until my back bows off the bed. "Like this?" he breathes, our gazes locked together. "Or like this?" He slides his fingers to my clit, trapping it between his digits as he rocks his hand back and forth.

"Fuck," I whimper, my eyes fluttering closed.

"Or maybe this," he mumbles, sucking the nub into his mouth while his fingers work back and forth. My mouth opens in a silent scream, my fingers spasming in his hair. Just as I start to tense, he pulls away.

"No, Cam. Please."

"Not yet." He climbs on top of me, the tip of his cock resting between my thighs. He positions himself at my entrance, tips my chin so I'm looking him in the eyes, and then slams home.

Oh my God. My eyes roll back as my body adjusts to his size. This feels so incredibly right. Like he's been a part of me all along.

"Let me hear how much you like it, Charlie." He pulls out and slides back in slowly, bending down to suck a nipple into his mouth. I moan as he drives into me again, raising my hips to meet him. "Good fucking girl," he breathes into my ear, punctuating each word with a hard thrust. "I've been dreaming about how you look when you cum with my cock buried inside you." He shifts above me, fitting his pelvis against mine. He slides into me with his hips tilted, his pubic bone grinding on my clit.

"Oh fuck," I whimper, stars exploding across the inside of my eyelids. I never realized it could be like this. Rob used to cum and then told me it was my fault I didn't get there with him.

"Open your eyes, Charlie."

I empty my mind and look up at him, our souls connecting as he thrusts again. The storminess of his eyes takes me under, waves pummeling me from all sides. My body tenses around him as he drives into me, my breath stuttering as I reach for the summit.

"Cum for me, little witch," he rasps.

I dig my nails into his ass, pulling him against me as I meet his thrusts. He slows and pulses in and out, the head of his cock rocking back and forth over my g-spot while he rolls my clit between our bodies. He reaches underneath me and slides along my crack, a garbled groan tearing its way out of my throat as he pushes in. He chuckles. "That's what you wanted, isn't it? It's like you were made for us."

He braces his forearms on either side of my head as my walls clench around him, each thrust causing another tremor to race through me. I claw at his back, moaning as my body convulses, pleasure edged with pain racing through my nerve endings. It explodes from me in a primal scream, echoed by Cam's roar as we ride the wave together.

My ears ring as my body slowly comes back into itself, my breaths coming in short, jerky gasps.

"Holy fuck," he whispers, grinning like a maniac before catching my lips with his. He rolls off of me and lays on his side, pulling me to him. "Has it ever been like this for you before, Charlie? Because my brain can't even comprehend what just happened."

I snuggle against him as he pulls the fluffy duvet over us. "I don't have much experience, but I've never experienced what I have with the three of you before."

"I'm glad you found us, Charlie," he mumbles, his lips pressed to my hair.

Not a minute later, I feel his body relax as he falls asleep. I carefully sneak out from under his arm and wash up in the bathroom. By the time I finish, he's rolled to his back, his disheveled hair a dark halo against the stark white of his pillowcase. I slide under the covers and mold my body to his. I could get used to this.

46

The guys and I are sitting around the kitchen table shoveling cereal into our mouths when Jack brings up what we talked about yesterday.

"Do we need to figure out dates so this goes smoothly?" Jack asks, lifting the bowl to his mouth to drink the milk.

"Are we planning sex now? That's kinda sad," I snort, shoving another bite into my mouth. I'm famished after yesterday's fuck fest.

"If we want it done by the weekend, then yes, I suggest we schedule it," Jack grumbles. He looks scary when he's grumpy. I like it.

"Why am I the one planning this?" I ask, peeved about having to plan anything, let alone sex.

"Yeah, good question," Lach chimes in, exacerbating the situation.

"I don't want her to plan it, you idiot, I just want the dates confirmed."

"Fine. Tuesday and Thursday. That will give me a day to rest and downtime before the weekend. Plus, I need a couple of days to finish up some stuff on the family tree before I'm ready to start on the vignettes and calligraphy, anyway."

"Who's first?" Lach asks, wiggling his eyebrows at me.

"Nope. Do not involve me in this. For all I care, you two can duke it out like cowboys."

They start talking over each other, arguing about why they should get to go first and why the other should go second.

"The two of you are ridiculous," Cam yells over them, exasperated. "Pick a number between one and a hundred. Whoever is the closest gets Tuesday. The other one gets Thursday."

"That doesn't even make sense—it should be the other way around," Lach protests.

"Are you serious right now?" I ask them, "Maybe we should just do away with this whole thing and keep to the group since that seems to create fewer argum–"

"Sixty-nine!" Lach yells before the words are even out of my mouth.

"Eleven," Jack grumbles

"Forty-two," Cam says, his lips twisting into a smirk as he watches them try to figure out who won. "Lach, you're Tuesday. Jack, you get Thursday."

"Fucking hell," Jack moans, scrubbing his hands over his face.

Lach jumps up, pumping his arm in the air. "You and me! Tuesday, baby! You better get plenty of sleep the next couple of nights." His enthusiasm is infectious and I smile despite myself. Jack stands up, stacks our cereal bowls and takes them to the sink.

Lach moves to sit next to me. "Sooo... have you thought about it at all?"

"No, I haven't thought about how your cock will feel stretching me. Or how it will feel to come around it. Why do you ask?"

He chokes. "God, Charlie. Stop saying stuff like that, or we won't make it to Tuesday."

"Make me," I smirk, my laugh dying as his eyes darken. I shriek and leap out of my seat, running outside before he can grab me. I look back, stumbling as I see him running toward me, the muscles of his torso gilded by the morning sun.

I dodge him, yelling at Jack to save me instead of standing there watching. He steps out of the doorframe but doesn't move to help me.

"I won't be saving you if I catch you, Sassenach," he says, his words a dark promise.

Goosebumps race over every inch of my skin. I loop around and run by him, making sure I'm just out of reach, and flip him off as I run away. "Thanks for nothing, asshole," I call at him over my shoulder, laughing as I dance out of Lach's reach.

"You've fucking done it now, Carebear," Lach says, his eyes on Jack instead of me.

I follow his gaze to see Jack sliding off his slippers and pulling his hair into a bun.

What...? Fuck.

I run backward for a couple of steps, unable to force myself to take my eyes off the glorious specimen of a man barreling toward me. My mind catches up with my hormones, and I whip around, dodging a fence before I dash into the orchard. I dart in and out of the trees, hiding to give myself a chance to catch my breath. The edge of the woods is only about fifty feet away. I have no idea where Jack is, but if I can make it there, I'll be golden. Do I even want to escape him? I don't really understand the rules of this game, but fuck it's fun. I scan the area for any signs of him before I run to the next tree, then to the next. Almost there.

"Sassenach," Jack breathes, only a few feet behind me.

I scream and bolt into the trees, not feeling the branches whipping across my arms or the rough roots under my feet. Survival was the only thing on my mind. How's that for a psychological mind fuck? I see an old ruin ahead and adjust my course, darting inside and pressing myself to the wall. The light filters through the trees, casting a golden-green glow over everything. Tiny white petals flutter down like snowflakes with breeze. Vines tumble over the ground, climbing the walls haphazardly, only allowing small glimpses of what lies underneath. It's breathtakingly beautiful.

I squeak when Jack rushes through the opening, his body pressing to mine before I can even blink. He traps my wrists in his hand, locking them above my head. "Do you know what I would do to you if it were Thursday?"

"What would you do to me, Jack?" I ask, my voice husky.

"First, I would pin your hands behind your back..." He spins me around, pulling my hands down to hold them between our bodies. "And then I would bend you over this rock." He uses one hand to push my leggings down, his grip staying strong on my hands as he squats down and pulls them off. Heat pools in my stomach when he can't resist touching his tongue to my clit before standing back up. His hand is warm on my shoulder, pushing me down until I drop to my knees. He presses me flat against the rock, the cold surface heightening the feeling in my already hyper-sensitive nipples.

"Then what?" I ask, my heart beating like hummingbird wings in my chest.

"I would watch as I slowly sink every inch of my cock into your tight little pussy." He drags his thumb over me, getting it wet before pushing it in. I arch my back as he feathers the pad of his finger over my g-spot. I gasp and push back against his hand, his fingers sliding over me, coming to rest on my clit. "Fuck," he breathes, his voice pained. He releases my hands and grips my hips, pulling me back so I'm fully exposed. He bends down and buries his face in my heat, dragging his tongue on my clit before thrusting inside. His groan vibrates against me, my entire body clenching, begging for more.

"God, Charlotte, I'm not fucking strong enough for this." I hear him unbuckling his belt and then his moan as he fists his cock.

I trust him enough to know that he won't put us in a situation that will compromise everything we've built, but fuck do I want him in me. He slides his cock through the moisture between my thighs, his head catching on my clit. I pulse my body over him, so fucking close I want to cry. He palms my ass, spreading my cheeks and guiding his cock between them. He pushes my cheeks tight against his cock and thrusts, the ridge of his shaft sliding over my back entrance, making me squirm. I move my hand between my legs and rub my clit, pushing back against him, my body desperate for him to lose control and slam into me.

He stops suddenly, guiding my knees together. "Don't fucking move," he rasps, sliding his cock against in the V of my legs. He reaches around, batting my hand away and replacing it with his. He slides his other hand along my crack, teasing me with light touches until I'm moaning into my arm, arching my ass to make it easier for him.

"Relax, mo chridhe."

I force the tension out of my muscles and his finger slips in without resistance.

"Fuck, Charlotte."

I squeeze around his finger, rocking my hips.

"This fucking ass is mine this weekend," he rasps, sliding his finger in and out before adding a second.

"Oh God," I moan. My body seizes, my mind emptying of everything but how he's making me feel.

He thrusts, his pelvis pushing his fingers in a little more each time. "This is what you crave, isn't it, Sassenach? You want to feel so fucking good that you're forced to surrender to it." He drops his head to my back, his breathing ragged. "You want this to be the one place you can give up your control and feel vulnerable. I want you to be able to do that with me. I'll give that to you for the rest of my life if you'll let me, Charlotte."

How is he in my head? How can he see into the depths of my soul to the real me? I bite down on a sob as the first tremors grip me. His thrusts become less controlled the closer he gets. I push my hips back too much, his cock nudges my entrance and I cry out, desperately needing him to fill me, but he readjusts and thrusts again, toppling us both over the edge at a maddening pace.

"You drive me fucking crazy, Charlotte," he pants, his breath hot on my neck. He stands and helps me to my feet, helping me pull on my clothes before he attends to his. He cups my face, his whisky eyes making my nerve endings buzz. "I hope you know how much you mean to me." He presses his lips to mine and then wraps his arms around me, burying his face in my neck. "Thank you for saving me, Charlie."

I pull out of his embrace to look him in the face. "Charlie? I thought you said you didn't want to be friends with me."

He grabs my hands and draws me back to him. "I take it back. I want everything you have to give me."

I laugh. "I gave you everything the night we met, Jack."

"Thank fuck."

47

———

"Isla?" I call as I poke my head in the pub.

"In here!"

Warm wood tones envelop me as I follow her voice to a small office beside the bar.

"Thank you so much for coming to help, Charlotte. I was really in a bind."

Isla had called me a few hours ago, absolutely frantic. Her boss had a health emergency which left her and the chef on their own. She stands up and gives me a tight hug. I hold her at arm's length and whistle at her. The woman is absolutely gorgeous. Her hair is half up, soft curls framing her face, the rest tumbling down her back in a fiery waterfall. Her boobs are perfectly showcased in a leather corset top. Jeans that look like they were painted on and combat boots complete the ensemble. Utter perfection.

"You're going to have to take me shopping sometime," I say, looking down at my pitiful t-shirt and jeans.

"I would love to. I always keep an extra outfit here, just in case. Do you want to see it?"

"Seriously? That would be amazing."

"You'll get better tips, too," she says, grabbing a garment bag from the back corner of the office and handing it to me.

"You're a godsend. I could use some extra tip money right now." I lay the bag on the bar and unzip it to find gorgeous black leather moto leggings and a slinky silver top. "I only have my chucks," I moan.

"What size are you?"

"Eight."

"Are you comfortable with heels?"

"Not really." I grimace.

"You take my boots and I'll wear the heels. They may be a little big on you, but they should be fine."

I protest, but Isla plops herself on a barstool and unlaces them. "I think it'll be pretty easy tonight. There will be a mad rush around dinnertime, but we'll probably end up closing early." She hands me the first boot and starts on the second. "You'll just need to take food and drink orders from customers sitting at the tables and bring their food to them once it's ready." She hands me the other boot and then slides off the stool, padding to the office to retrieve her heels.

"Sounds easy enough," I say, shucking off my jeans and pulling on the leggings. I shed my shirt and carefully pull on the top, the fabric like cool water sliding over my skin. I step into the boots and immediately feel like a badass.

"We have about fifteen minutes until the chef gets here," Isla says as she comes out of the office again, fastening large hoops to her ears. "Holy fuck, Charlie. I'm going to call the guys and tell them they need to eat here tonight."

"God, don't do that," I groan, "The tension is already unbearable."

"Oh, I'm going to do it. It'll be the one thing that brings me joy while I'm busting my ass behind the bar." She snickers. "Plus, we're going to have live music tonight. Have you ever danced with them?"

"I've danced with all of them, actually." I smirk.

"Together?"

I sigh. "No, not together. That sounds like torture."

"Someday, someone will waltz in here, and I'll get to experience a third of what you have."

"All of what I have," I correct her.

"I don't think so. Your relationship with the guys has really opened my eyes. They each satisfy something different, don't they?"

I think about it for a second. Jack with his rough, all-consuming heat. Lach, with his humor and protectiveness. Cam and his sweet nothings. I nod. "They do."

"See. It's been hard enough to find one man that's willing to stick around. Not that I make it easy. I'm not going to change to make someone more comfortable."

"Nor should you. Someone is out there waiting, Isla. Someone that will meet you where you're at and love you for who you are."

She shrugs. "Maybe, maybe not. I'm okay with being spinster Auntie Isla, too."

"You don't look like a spinster to me," I laugh.

"Fine. *Hot* spinster." She shimmies her shoulders and we both dissolve into a fit of giggles. We hear the chef banging around in the kitchen and Isla shifts into work mode. "You take the tables, I'll take the bar. We clean at night, but I always give everything a quick wipe-down the next day. When you're done, I'll go over the menus with you."

I get to work pulling the chairs off the tables, spraying everything down with disinfectant, and wiping it clean. Isla is slicing up lemons and limes when I boost myself onto one of the barstools. She motions to a pile of menus with her chin.

"There should be a food menu and a bar menu in there. Why don't you look over them quickly and make sure you don't have any questions? Greer will write any specials up on the board behind me."

"Greer's the chef?"

Isla nods, scooping up the fruit and dumping it into tubs.

I scan the menus. Everything seems pretty straightforward.

"Now we need to make you a signature drink." She laughs at the face I make. "Everyone here has one. What's your favorite drink?"

I don't drink all that much, but I think back over the years, and it comes to me. "Gin and tonic with a ton of limes."

Isla turns to the board, a chalk marker in hand, and writes out

THE CHARLIE – HARRIS GIN, TONIC, LIME. "There, now it's official." She grins. She pulls her phone out of her back pocket and glances at the time. "Twenty minutes. Are you ready?"

"You're freaking me out a little. You said it won't be busy, but you're acting like a stampede is about it run through that door."

"We're never so busy that we run out of tables. Does that make you feel better?"

I glance around, counting about twenty-five tables. "I guess? Actually, no, not really. Fuck."

Isla plunks two shot glasses onto the bar and fills them with an amber liquid. "Time for a little liquid courage, Charlie." She hands one to me and holds hers in the air. "To you, for saving my ass."

"I'll drink to that," I laugh, tapping the bottom of the glass on the bar before throwing it back. Fire roars down my throat and settles in my stomach. "Fuck, Isla," I cough, wiping my eyes.

An amazon of a woman crashes through the door to the kitchen, grabs the chalk pen, and writes SCALLOPS AND LANGOUSTINE WITH SUMMER VEGETABLES - 18

My jaw drops. "Eighteen pounds? That would be fifty easy back home."

The woman turns toward me, her thick braid swinging over her shoulder. "That's one of the perks of living here. I just pulled them out of the water this morning." She sticks out her hand for me to shake. "Greer. You must be Charlie."

"Nice to meet you, Greer."

"I'd love to stick around and chat, but it's time to warm up the ovens. Good luck tonight."

"Why do I need luck?" I ask Isla, still feeling like there's something she's not telling me.

"When we have live music it tends to get a bit rowdy. It's nothing to worry about, though. You'll have a blast. You'll see."

SHE WAS RIGHT. We have a rush of old folks coming in for the early bird discount. It takes me about thirty minutes to feel comfortable answering questions and taking orders, but it comes naturally enough once I get the hang of it.

"Come get a drink," Isla calls during a lull, motioning for me to sit at the bar. "We'll have a small break before the younger crowd comes in. Do you want anything to eat?"

"Yes! Those burgers looked amazing. I'm famished."

"Greer! Two burgers, please!" she yells, angling her head toward the kitchen door. The color is high in her cheeks, her eyes sparkling. I can tell how much she loves it here and it makes me happy knowing she's happy. It's not a feeling I'm used to. The door to the pub bangs open as the band jostles through, making an incredible racket. "Guys, this is Charlie. She's helping out tonight."

All four look up at me with interest; the one closest sets his instrument down and walks over to me. The cocky grin on his face takes me aback, an immediate flush heating my skin.

"She's taken, you doofus." Isla laughs.

"And?" He takes my hand and opens his mouth to introduce himself.

"By my brother," Isla presses, raising an eyebrow at him as she plunks my drink onto the bar in front of me.

He immediately drops my hand. "Fuck. No disrespect meant. I'm Ewan. Nice to meet you."

"Nice to meet you too, Ewan," I laugh. I introduce myself to the other band members and turn back toward Isla and the burgers Greer sets in front of us. "They seem nice," I say, "have you dated any of them?"

"All of them." She grimaces.

I choke on my drink. "Seriously?"

"Yes, seriously! This is a tiny island. I'm pretty sure I've dated everyone in my age range that lives here. So, at this point, I'm either out of luck, or I have to wait until some god somewhere decides to drop one in my lap." She drowns her feelings in her burger, taking an enormous bite.

The door opens again and I look over my shoulder, fully expecting it to be the guys. "Or three...?"

Isla's jaw drops as three men amble in. The first is dark and brooding and looks ready for a fight. The second has a more slender build, sparkling caramel eyes and an easy grin. The third... oh my. Dark hair curls around his ears, the perfect backdrop for mischievous blue eyes. Full lips and a cleft in his chin perfectly round out his features. He's stacked. The kind of muscles that don't just come from the gym.

"Isla!" I hiss. "Chew your food!" When she doesn't move, I put my finger under her chin and close her mouth, then shove a napkin into her hand. I watch her features change: shock morphs into interest, and then her eyelids droop the tiniest bit as lust slides home.

I take another bite of my burger to hide my grin. This is going to be fun.

48

______

Isla sets down her burger and wipes her mouth, her gaze tracking the trio as they make their way up to the bar. One of them slides onto a barstool, the other two following suit.

"What can I get you," Isla asks, her voice husky and low. I cover my smile with my napkin and glance around to make sure there aren't any customers at my tables. When I see that I'm in the clear, I turn back to watch them. Isla is setting down pints of beer in front of them, leaning over the bar to hear them over the music. She points to the specials board and all three of them nod.

"Dylan," the guy closest to me extends his hand over the empty seat between us.

His easy smile teases out one of my own. "Charlie. Is that an American accent I hear?"

He laughs sheepishly. "It is. My brothers and I are over here on vacation. What about you?"

"Work," I say, immediately feeling guilty that I've condensed my time here into that one word. "What do you think so far?"

"Honestly? I wasn't so sure at first. Glasgow wasn't my cup of tea. Skye was much better."

"And how does Harris stack up?" I ask, popping my last fry into my mouth, following it with the last gulp of my drink.

"Harris is..." He pauses, searching for the right words. "Wild. Invigorating." He shrugs. "That doesn't do it justice. I feel alive here."

I nod. "I feel the same way. It's a special place, that's for sure." I stand, collecting my plate and glass. "I hope you enjoy the rest of your time here."

"You're leaving?"

"I'm helping Isla out tonight. Some folks just came in – I need to go take their orders."

"Her name's Isla?" He glances over to where she's slinging bottles like she's in the Cirque du Soleil.

"Just be careful, she's spicy," I warn him with a grin.

THE CROWD PICKS up as we near seven o'clock. True to her word, there is always at least one table free, most people seeming to prefer to stay on their feet either around the bar or dancing in the open area by the entrance. The guys still have their butts planted on their stools, all three watching Isla with rapt attention. She's doing a great job of ignoring them. I stop for a drink just as Greer brings out their food: three plates piled high with gigantic shrimp-like creatures. All three of them look at Greer with panic in their eyes.

She yells for Isla to help them, then heads back to the kitchen, chuckling.

Isla stands in front of the grumpy brother and picks up one of the langoustines. "First, you twist off their heads." The shell snaps, causing Dylan to jerk in his seat. I'm barely able to stifle a snort. "Then you suck out the juices. Do you mind if I eat this one?" she asks the grumpy one, her lips twisting as she holds in her laughter.

"Fine," he grumbles.

She closes her lips around the shell and tips her head back, sucking out all the good stuff. My gaze swings to the beefy brother and I watch his Adam's apple bob, his teeth lodged in his bottom lip. I look back at Isla, her gaze locked with his as she licks her lips.

I cough to hide my laugh and turn back to my tables before I ruin it for her.

The pub starts emptying around eight-thirty and I'm just about to sit back down next to Dylan when the door swings open, everyone's heads swiveling to see who it is. Cameron comes in first, his eyes lighting up when they land on me.

"Little witch," he murmurs, cradling my face and kissing me until my knees are jelly. "I've missed you." He sits at the far end of the bar, draping his coat over the back of the stool.

I'm about to ask if the other two are coming when Lach breezes in, shedding his suit jacket before pulling me close.

"You're so fucking hot," he breathes against my ear, pressing a kiss to my cheek.

Before I can respond, Jack steals me from his embrace, burying his face in my hair.

"God, I've missed you."

"It's been one day, Jack."

"I know." He cups my cheek and draws me in, the fire roaring in his eyes burning me alive. He breaks the kiss and leaves me to join Isla behind the bar. I come out of the haze with one hand clenched to the back of Dylan's stool to keep myself upright.

Dylan clears his throat, his eyes wide. And then it dawns on me. This is the first time the four of us have been in public together. Where people can see. Judge.

"Sorry about that," I whisper, my cheeks heating.

"You and the three of them?" he asks, his gaze swiveling between the guys and me.

"Yep." I don't know what to say.

"Huh." There is no judgment in his eyes, only curiosity. "And it works?"

I laugh. "You could say that."

"Good for you. Are you done working now?" he asks, changing the subject.

I look around me, making sure a customer hadn't snuck in while I was distracted. "Looks like it."

"Isla! A Charlie for Charlie, please!" he calls, motioning for me to sit.

"I'll get that," Jack growls, his eyes pinning me in place as he makes my drink.

"Thank you," I breathe, sliding my hand over his as he sets the drink in front of me.

"Does this remind you of anything, Sassenach?" He holds my gaze as he rounds the bar and walks toward me, folding me into his arms, dancing me back to the open floor. I press my cheek to his chest, breathing in whisky and leather, thinking about how much has changed since that night.

I lean back to look at him. "All we need is your motorcycle." My chuckle turns into a gasp as he dips me low.

"You're in luck. Come away with me?" he breathes against my ear as he pulls me back up, goosebumps to erupting over my entire body.

"Sharing is caring," Lach says as he sidles up to us, wrapping his arm around my waist. I'm pinned between them, barely breathing, memories crashing over me.

Jack presses his palm to my chest and watches as he slowly slides his hand around my neck. "Was I right?" he asks, looking back up at me, his eye dark.

"About what?" I ask, my voice strangled.

"Do they look better around your neck?" He turns me suddenly, so we're looking at our reflection in the mirrored wall behind the bar.

"Yes," I whisper, barely able to breathe.

"Get a room!" Isla yells at us, giving me an exaggerated wink.

"Come dance!" I beg, shrugging off the guys and holding my hands out to her. She looks down the bar, making sure everyone is topped off, and then comes over to me, wrapping her arms around my shoulders as we slow dance.

"Did I detect a little bit of spark?" I ask, wiggling my eyebrows at her suggestively.

"Maybe," she laughs, "but they're leaving tomorrow."

"And?"

"And tonight, you and I are going to watch a movie and have some much-needed girl time. I feel like I've hardly seen you recently."

"That will be really nice." I squeeze her tight, thankful for her friendship. The next song starts up, and there's a loud whoop from almost everyone left in the pub. I look around with wide eyes, letting Lach pull me to the edges of the dance floor.

Cameron comes to stand by me, grasping my hand in his. "You should recognize this song," he yells over the noise. And I do, from that night at the pub in Portree. It's strange to re-live so many memories in one night. It's giving me a strong sense of déjà vu. Lach grabs my other hand and we're all thrown into a chaotic dance of clapping and stomping. I look across the circle, giggling as the brothers jostle for a place next to Isla. Her hair is falling around her face, her eyes sparkling, and cheeks rosy.

"Last song of the night," Ewan announces as the band picks back up with something slow.

My attention is forced from Isla as the guys surround me. "We can't all dance together," I laugh, trying not to step on their toes.

"If we can all fuck together, then I'm pretty sure we can figure out how to dance together, Sassenach," Jack rumbles. My nipples pebble, heat pooling between my thighs as his words hit home. I sway with them, their hands roaming over me to the point of distraction. A slight sweep of fingers over my ribs, a palm squeezing my hip, a thumb dragging over my bottom lip. Fuck. The guys shift slightly and I get a glimpse of Isla in a similar position, the brothers taking turns dancing with her. I head to the bar for my drink when the music stops, fanning myself. I lean against the scarred wood as I sip, watching Isla kiss the brothers on their cheeks and then shoo them out the door.

"Isla, that could have been something spectacular," I say as she walks toward me.

She shrugs. "I'm sick of one-night stands. I'm ready for something real."

"Fair enough."

The guys sit Isla and me down at the bar, insisting we relax as they clean up.

"I could get used to this," Isla laughs as she flips off the lights, throwing the sparkling pub into darkness. "Ready for some girl time?"

"Yes," I groan, "my feet are killing me."

Jack opens the Mustang door for me and then wishes me goodnight, leaving me with a kiss on the cheek.

"Have you fucked them yet?" Isla asks as she gets in next to me, her grin bright in the dim car.

"If I had known this was going to be twenty questions, I would have left with one of the guys," I tease.

"Oh, stop. You've got to talk about it with someone, right? We'll change into comfy clothes, open a bottle of wine, and you'll be spilling all your secrets before you know it."

"Mmm. We'll see," I laugh. She opens up the throttle once we're on the main road, my shriek of surprise turning into uncontrollable giggles as we roar into the night.

49

———

Isla meets me in matching sweats and bunny slippers at the cottage. She has a gigantic bag slung over her shoulder that she proceeds to empty like Mary Poppins pulling things out of her carpet bag. Two bottles of wine, various charcuterie accoutrements, enough chocolate to last us a year, a variety of face masks and scrubs, a bottle of hair mask and a makeup bag filled with nail polish. My jaw drops further with every item she takes out.

"I told you, we're going to have a proper girls' night. Starting with the wine." She grabs two glasses from the kitchen and pours a healthy amount into each one. "To friendship!"

"To the best girlfriend anyone could ever ask for," I return, touching my glass to hers.

We gossip while we arrange a charcuterie board, taking it back to the couch so we can put on a movie.

"First, you have to tell me what's going on with you and the guys. I know it's weird, but all of you are my friends, and I don't like being left out of the loop."

My heart sinks. "Oh, God. I hadn't even thought about it like that."

"It's fine. We'll all have growing pains, I'm sure. We just need to keep communication open."

I gulp my wine, trying to organize my thoughts. "Since Cameron came back, we pivoted and decided that they should each have one-on-one time with me. Cam and I spent the night together after he came back."

"And?" she asks when I pause a little too long.

I clear my throat. "It was good. Really good."

"Who's next?"

"Lach on Tuesday, Jack on Thursday."

"Damn, girl." She whistles, her eyebrows almost to her hairline. "Then what?" she asks, snatching some chocolate-covered almonds from the board.

"Then we only have sex together."

A line forms between her eyebrows. "What about other stuff?"

"Other stuff is fine, just no sex." My face heats under her scrutiny.

"Good fucking luck," she murmurs, then downs the rest of the wine in her glass. "That sounds like a recipe for disaster."

"What? Why?"

"What happens when things get hot and heavy? You know how it is when you're in the moment. Do you really think there's not going to be a mistake or two or ten? Or what about when Lach or Cam leaves for work? You're going to abstain the entire time they're gone?"

I groan. Why hadn't that ever occurred to me? "So what do you think we should do?"

"I think there should only be two rules: respect and communication."

"How are you single?" I laugh, impressed that she had broken down something that seemed so complicated into two words.

"Honestly? I haven't given anyone a chance. I'm working on it." She claps. "Okay! That's enough guy talk." She pulls out the nail polish and I choose a color.

"So, what are your plans at the pub?" I ask, knowing there has to be something behind her working there, especially since it seems like she's practically running the place.

"I'm going to buy it from the guy that owns it once he's ready to retire." She grins, her whole face lighting up. "I have so many plans for it. I can't wait."

"I bet it'll be amazing."

"What about you? What will the next six months look like?"

I pull out my phone and open my notes app. "I have a list," I chuckle, "First, obviously, is finishing the family tree. I'll go home to deliver it, settle the divorce and apply for a work visa while I'm there."

"You realize how hard it is to get a work visa here, right?"

Lead settles in my stomach at the reminder. "Yeah, I did hear that. I guess I just have to hope it'll work out."

She carefully sets my right hand down and picks up my left, painting my thumb ballet pink. "Why don't you marry one of them, Charlie? It would be so much easier."

"Do you want the honest answer or the easy answer?"

"Honest."

"Because I've been relying on men my entire life, and look where that got me."

"Where are you now?" she asks, looking up at me.

"No man's land."

Isla shakes her head and continues painting my nails. "You're just being stubborn. Your way or the highway. It doesn't work like that in relationships."

I blink hard, pushing back the tears. "I know it sounds ridiculous, but I need to prove to myself that I can do it on my own, Isla. It may seem like I'm just being stubborn, but it's way more than that."

"Fine." She caps the bottle and puts it back in the bag. "Would you be okay with Jack hiring you? He could sponsor you."

I think about it for a second. "As long as it's for a legitimate job."

"Oh my God, I have the best idea! What if you paint the people that come to visit?"

"What people that come to visit?" I ask, confused.

"Jack is planning on opening up tours of the castle next spring. It's becoming increasingly expensive to keep it up, so he wants to get it to the point where it pays for itself. You could sell paintings of the castle in the gift shop and also offer portraits. It would be perfect."

"That does sound pretty idyllic," I agree, imagining myself painting with my toes in the grass, my shoulders warmed by the midday sun.

"Think about it," she says, her last words garbled as she yawns. "I think it's time for bed."

"Me, too," I yawn, grabbing the food and bringing it to the kitchen. We wash up, and I get her settled on the couch after she refuses to take my bed. I fall asleep quickly, my last thought being how nice it is to have a friend.

I wake up to the smell of frying bacon and fresh coffee the following day.

"Morning," I mumble, pushing the hair out of my face as I shuffle to the coffee maker.

"Morning, sleepyhead," Isla sings, plating bacon, eggs, and pancakes for both of us.

"Can I marry *you*?" I ask as I take the plate from her hands.

She laughs. "I thought it would do you good to start your day off strong. You have a big week this week."

"Shhh!" I hold up my hand, "Don't remind me yet. I need to drink my coffee first."

"Got it." She pretends to zip her lips. "What's on the agenda today?"

"Getting the tree completely done to the point that it only needs paint and calligraphy, which I'll do when the guys and I get back from the city," I say between bites.

"The city?" She raises an eyebrow.

"They're taking me to get supplies this weekend," I explain, popping the last bite of bacon into my mouth.

"Charlie! I swear to God, it's like pulling teeth to get information out of you."

"Sorry!" I grimace, gulping down some coffee, praying to the gods it'll do its magic quickly. "They're taking me to Edinburgh on Saturday."

"And you're staying overnight?" she prods.

I nod as I go back to the coffee maker to fill my mug.

"How are you so calm about it? I would be buzzing out of my shoes."

"Because I'm not awake yet, Isla," I deadpan.

"Oh." She gives me an apologetic smile. "I'll get out of your hair. I'm going to wash the car and bike today. If you need a break, you can come up and sit outside and read or something."

"Okay. I'll work on the tree for a while and come up when I need a break."

She leans down and squeezes me tight, her hair pooling around my shoulders. "Thank you, Charlie."

"For what?"

"For helping me last night. For being a good friend."

"I'm trying," I chuckle, "It doesn't come easily. I appreciate that you're patient with me, Isla."

She grins as she clinks her mug against mine. "Friends for life."

50

———

I took Isla up on her offer and joined her in the driveway late afternoon. Isla hauled a lawn chair from the garage and set it in the sun, motioning for me to lie down. I protest, but she waves me off and slips her headphones back on. I must've fallen asleep at some point because I wake to a warm hand sliding over my cheek and soft lips pressing against mine.

"Hey, sleepyhead," Lach croons, dragging his thumb over my bottom lip. "I couldn't reach you on your phone, so I had to hunt you down. I'm planning the last details for tomorrow – I need to know some of your favorite foods."

I rub my eyes, squinting against the sun. Lach is leaning over me, his eyes the same color as the sky. "What kind of food? Breakfast food, lunch food, dinner food? Snack food?"

His eyebrow goes up a little more with each type of food I mention. He chuckles. "Well, I guess that depends on how early you want to start tomorrow."

I push myself into a sitting position, making room for him to sit next to me, his broad hand massaging the large amount of thigh exposed by my lounge shorts. It's hard to think when he's touching me like this. I clear my throat. "Maybe we should start early after-noon? What exactly do you have planned?"

"Wouldn't you like to know?" he says, grinning.

"I hate surprises," I grumble, twisting the hem of my shirt in my fingers.

"Do you? Or do you hate that all of your previous surprises ended in disappointment?"

Fuck. I breathe out a long sigh. "My favorite thing is probably a good cheeseboard – the kind with the fruit, the chocolate, and all the little snacky things. If I'm thinking particularly of dinner food, my favorite dinner is probably a good steak and loaded baked potato. Is that even a thing here?"

"We'll make it a thing. But you'll have to call it by its proper name first – a jacket potato."

I laugh. "Is that really what it's called here?"

He nods, the corner of his mouth quirking. "Legend has it that men used to put the hot potatoes in their jacket pockets for warmth during the cold months."

"Is that true?"

"No fucking clue," he says, laughing. "You know that store that's on the road to Lewis?"

"The big one on the left?" I ask, trying to get my directionally chal-lenged brain to cooperate.

"That's the one. They used to have a bear that they kept in a cage. Growing up, we would buy Irn-Bru and biscuits to feed him."

I wrinkle my nose. "That doesn't sound healthy."

He shrugs. "It wasn't, not that we understood that when we were kids. By the time I got to secondary school, he was huge. One day a tourist poured petrol into an Irn-Bru can and gave it to him. The bear flipped out, broke out of his cage, and ran all the way to Harris until he fell over just down the road from here."

"Oh my God! Did he die?"

"No, he ran out of petrol."

My consternation for the bear turns into a surprisingly loud snort. I slap my hand over my mouth, but I can't stop laughing.

"Where the heck did you hear that one?" I ask, wiping the tears from my cheeks.

"Good ol' Dolly Parton," he says in a southern drawl which makes me laugh even more. "Okay, back to the matter at hand. What about dessert?"

My gaze drops to his lips.

"Me? Noted," he teases, pretending to write it down in a fake note-book. The side of his mouth quirks up, but his expression changes – eyelids drooping, pupils dilating. "Make sure you rest up tonight, Carebear," he says, his voice husky. He brushes his lips over mine. "I'll see you in the morning."

"Wait!" I stop him with a hand on his forearm. "What time tomorrow?"

"You tell me."

"Ten o'clock?" I think of all the things I need to do in the morning – shave, exfoliate, moisturize.

"Ten is perfect. I'll see you then. Sleep sweet, Charlie."

Isla walks over to me, sliding her headphone off one ear. "I have to say, it's fascinating watching you with each of them. When you're with Jack, you let him be in control – like there's a part of you that completely trusts that he'll take care of everything. You're confident and outgoing with Cam, encouraging him to take risks with you that he wouldn't normally take. And Lach balances them both out and keeps you grounded, doesn't he?"

I think about her words for a second, nodding. "I feel different with all three of them. When we're all together, I feel whole somehow."

"Have you thought any more about our conversation last night?"

"About the rules?" She nods. "A little bit. I want to say something to them, but I'm worried they'll be offended. Especially Jack – I feel like he's the one that's keeping us in a straight line and doing his best to start us off on solid ground."

"Jack isn't perfect, Charlie. You should talk to them. I don't want to see your relationship go south over some silly rule that wasn't thought out ahead of time."

"You're right," I say with a heavy sigh. "We have two long car rides this weekend; I can either tell them on the way to Edinburgh or on the way back home."

"Oh God, definitely not on the way there. Wait till after."

"Good thinking."

Isla walks back to her car and picks up a couple of towels, throwing me one. "Do you want to help me dry the car off? We can make dinner when we're done."

"Yes, please. I'm starving," I say, my stomach rumbling, "I think I only have apples and honey in the cottage, anyway."

Dinner is a fantastic seafood pasta with homemade garlic bread and a Caesar salad with the best dressing I've ever tasted. I'm not sure if it's because Lach showed up just in time to make it, but I would eat it for every meal if I could. We finish eating around seven o'clock, and Lach shoos me out of the kitchen with a kiss on my lips and a pat on my butt, telling me to get down to the cottage and sleep. Maybe it's the seriousness of what tomorrow represents or perhaps my developing feelings, but I really don't want to leave.

"Tell me a bedtime story?" I ask hopefully.

"Even I know that's a horrible idea," Isla says, rolling her eyes.

"We'll keep our clothes on. I promise."

"How can I resist a promise like that," he laughs, linking his fingers through mine. He calls out to Isla that he'll be back to help clean up in a little bit.

I thank him once we're on the path to the cottage, swinging our joined hands as we pick our way over the rocks, Milo joining us, weaving in and out of our legs. "I think I must be feeling a little sentimental today. Tomorrow and Thursday will change a lot, you know?"

"And how does that make you feel?" he asks, his thumb tracing circles over the sensitive skin between my thumb and forefinger.

"Excited. Nervous. A little scared." I say, honestly, bending down to scratch Milo's ears.

"I feel the same way, if that makes you feel any better. Having to rely on four people to keep a relationship intact is fucking scary."

I use my hip to jar open the cottage door and pull Lach inside with me. He sits and waits on the bed as I wash up, meticulously going through the steps of my routine: washing my face, washing it again. Serum. Moisturizer. I throw my hair up into a messy bun, change into my pajamas and return to the bedroom.

"God, you're sexy," he groans, grasping my waist and pulling me to him, his hands a little rougher than usual as he slides them down over my ass to my thighs. "I knew this was a bad idea," he rasps, his voice thick with need.

"I didn't bring you down here to seduce me," I say firmly, stepping out of his reach. "I just want to spend more time with you. Come on, think of your best bedtime story. Let's hear it."

He smacks my ass as he walks to the bed, pulls down the covers for me to slip under, tucks me in, then lays down on top of the comforter, pulling me against him.

"I don't have many stories that would put you to sleep. Would a lullaby do the trick?"

"You'll sing for me? Really?" I turn to face him, raking my fingers through his silky hair.

"Any time you ask, my love," he murmurs, pressing a soft kiss to my forehead.

I drift off to the dulcet tones of 'The Skye Boat Song', dreaming of a certain sandy-haired man and his dog Milo.

51

I thought I would have a hard time sleeping, but Lach's lullaby did the trick, and I was out cold until my alarm went off at seven-thirty. I blow on my coffee while waiting for the shower to warm up, dancing from foot to foot, anticipation crackling under my skin. I take my time getting ready, making sure my skin is smooth and silky, spritzing on my favorite perfume, and swiping on an extra coat of mascara and lip gloss instead of my usual Chapstick.

I make myself a couple of pieces of toast as I wait for Lach to text me back about what clothes to bring. As I'm drizzling honey over the melted butter, he texts me back: *comfortable layers*. Easy enough. I check the weather before throwing on a pair of shorts, a t-shirt, and a pullover, packing a bag with an extra change of clothes and some warmer layers. I toss in my toiletry bag and a few extra hairbands. I've never been a lingerie girl, but I find myself wishing I had something sexier to bring.

True to his word, there's a light knock on my door promptly at ten o'clock. My hands shake as I smooth them over my shirt. This is it.

I walk to the door, my heart in my throat, energy thrumming through my veins. But when I open the door, it's not Lach, it's Jack.

He's in loose lounge pants, a tank top, and flip-flops, his hair a wild, sexy mess.

"Where's Lach?" I ask, standing on my tiptoes to look over his shoulder.

"Nice to see you too, Sassenach," he grumbles, tugging at his beard.

"Sorry, I'm a little on edge," I apologize, gathering my things.

"Lach asked me to pick you up; he wasn't quite finished with the preparations."

"Preparations?"

He only smirks and gestures toward the door. "Your chariot awaits, milady." Once in the driveway, I look between Jack and his motorcycle dubiously. "Would you rather we borrow Isla's car?" he asks. "I thought it would be fun to take the bike, but I want you to be comfortable.

"This will be fine. I supposed I'll have to get used to riding on it eventually."

"I hope so," he says softly, stowing my bag away. I grimace as I pull the helmet over my perfectly coiffed hair, but my annoyance evaporates as I climb on and wrap my arms around him.

We pull to a stop in the marina parking lot several minutes later. Jack gives me a hand as I swing my leg over the bike, then unsnaps my helmet, gently sliding it off. He hands me my bag, and I stand there looking at him awkwardly – wondering how you say goodbye in a situation like this – when he cradles my face in his hands and presses a tender kiss to my lips.

"Have fun, mo chridhe; I'll see you on Thursday." He climbs back on the bike as I shoulder my bag, my heart in my throat.

The butterflies in my stomach melt into a molten ball of need as I look toward the marina and see Lach wiping down the side of the boat, shirtless, his skin glowing golden in the morning sun. As I walk toward him, my fingers itch to trace the freckles on his back like the dot-to-dot puzzles I loved as a child.

I open my mouth to say his name, but nothing comes out. I clear my throat and try again.

"Lach," I say, my voice low and husky as I slide my hand around his waist and press myself to his sun-warmed skin. He turns in my arms, caresses my face, and pulls me in for a kiss that goes from zero to sixty in half a second. He pushes his hand into the hair at the base of my skull and pulls, trailing kisses over my jaw and neck, then he captures my lips again, his hands framing my face.

"I was beginning to think this day would never come," he breathes when we finally manage to pull away from each other.

"I like this side of you," I murmur, the tenderness in his eyes doing something funny to my insides.

"I like every side of you," he says, one side of his mouth quirking up. "I like this side," he runs his hands over my waist. "And this side," he slides his hands over my ass. "And I really, really like this side," he groans, sliding his hands to my front and dragging them up my stomach and over my breasts. I moan and lean into his touch, watching his pupils dilate as he flicks his thumbs back and forth over my nipples.

"Is this all you brought?" he asks, taking my bag from me.

"I didn't think I would need very much; I kinda thought I'd be naked most of the time."

"Good fucking point, Carebear. Ready to go?"

I nod and he grabs his shirt from the railing, slipping it on before swinging me into his arms and walking up the gangway.

"First choice of the day: cave or ruins?"

I take a second to think before responding. "Cave," I say, confident in my choice. I love ruins, but many of them look the same after a while. The only cave I've been to is the one on the beach with Jack, so that option is an easy winner.

Lach motions up to one of the windows, and a flurry of activity takes over the deck. The anchor is hauled up, the ropes are removed, the horn blows, and then we're off, motoring toward deeper water. I'm a little nervous at first. The thought of being out at sea gives me anxiety, but Lach's easy manner and knowledge of the vessel ease my mind. He leads me to the rounded couch at the back of the ship and sits me down, bringing a bottle of champagne and two glasses from inside the cabin. He pops the cork and gives a generous pour, handing me one and raising his in the air.

"To a night of complete debauchery," he toasts. I grin and raise my glass, then take a sip and close my eyes as the bubbles coast over my tongue. The champagne is crisp with a hint of sweetness, perfect for a day like today.

"Debauchery?" I tease, raising my eyebrow.

"God, I hope so," he chuckles, reaching out and dragging his thumb over my bottom lip. I give into the temptation and swirl my tongue around the tip of his finger, sucking it into my mouth.

"I can't wait to have those pretty lips wrapped around my cock again," he breathes, sliding the saliva on his thumb around my lips and then pulling me to my feet, crushing his mouth to mine. His thick length presses against my stomach, my whole world narrowing to the desperate need to have him inside me.

I startle as the yacht rolls under us, and he steadies me.

"You okay?" He asks, concerned.

"I'll be fine. Just need to find my sea legs."

"I know the perfect distraction to tide us over until then," he murmurs, grabbing the champagne bottle with one hand and holding onto me with the other.

I follow him to the front of the boat, where he motions for me to sit on a wide cushion underneath the gigantic control room window.

"Give me your glass," he says, holding out his hand. I drink the last sip of champagne and hand it to him, watching as he sets it on a small side table. "Do you know why this is my favorite spot on the boat?" he asks, taking several steps away from me and turning his face to the breeze.

"Why?"

He faces me again, a lock of sandy hair falling over his forehead, his gaze locked with mine. "Because it's a blind spot. Nobody inside can see us."

"What if they come outside? I ask, swiveling my head and quickly realizing that he's right – I can't see any windows from this position.

"They won't. They're under strict instructions not to bother us unless we ask."

He licks his lips and my core clenches in response, my breathing stilted.

"Do you know what my second favorite thing is?" He asks, dropping to his knees in front of me.

"What?" I ask, squeezing my thighs together to relieve the ache between my legs.

He crawls toward me, his gaze lowering to the apex of my thighs. He pushes my knees apart.

"I can do this—" He slides his hand up my thigh and into my shorts, pushing my underwear to the side and running his fingertip over me, teasing me until my back bows off the cushion. He slowly sinks one finger in, then two, massaging my clit with his thumb until I'm panting and begging him to let me come. "—and nobody will hear you but me."

52

"Eyes on me."

I open my eyes, my gaze tracing Lach's full lower lip, his freckled cheeks, his blond eyelashes. I gasp as our eyes lock, arching against him as his thumb circles my clit.

"That's it," he breathes, coaxing me higher. "I want you right on the fucking edge." He slides his fingers out of me and up to cradle my clit.

"Oh, God," I moan as the first spasms start. He pulls his hand away, his eyes dark. Dangerous. "Why?" I half sob, lust threatening to drown me as I watch him lick off his fingers.

"Because this is going to be the best fuck of your entire life. I don't want you to ever be able to forget it."

"By not allowing me to get there?"

"By edging."

I look at him with my eyebrow raised, waiting for an answer, my pussy throbbing.

"It's when you delay climax. It's worth it. I promise."

"So, you're allowed to torture me, but I don't get to torture you?"

"By all means, Charlie, do your worst," he says, smirking, raising his hands in surrender.

I throw myself at him, twisting him under me as we fall to the cushions. I settle myself on top of his thighs. If he wants torture, then I'll give him torture. I lean over him, careful not to touch him with my torso, and suck his lower lip into my mouth. He opens to me immediately, our tongues mimicking what we're desperate for our bodies to be doing.

He groans as I pull my mouth away, moving to his ear, and biting his earlobe. His hand spasms on my hips as my breath teases across his skin.

"Do you prefer your torture by mouth or pussy?" I whisper, raining tiny kisses down his neck.

"Why not both?" he asks, all traces of humor gone.

"Fair enough," I laugh, "pick one for now."

He pulls my hips forward until I'm squarely settled over him. "Definitely pussy," he says, rocking my hips back and forth.

I stand up, staying out of sight of the control room windows, and step out of my shorts and panties. His jaw drops, his nostrils flaring as I shed my shirt and bra. Even though I'm exposed, I feel completely safe with him. I feel so alive. So free.

"Fuck, Charlie," he rasps, starting to sit up, but I push him back with a hand on his chest, settling myself on his thighs again. I ruck up his shirt, running my hands over his torso. I take my time unbuckling his belt; his breathing hitches, color creeping into his cheeks. I snap the belt away from his hips and unbutton his pants, motioning for him to lift his hips.

I pull his shorts down and then inch down his boxers until the base of his cock is exposed.

Fuck me.

I wasn't going to use my mouth yet, but I can't resist. I bend down, licking him, and he flexes his hips toward my mouth, demanding more.

"Oh God, Charlie," he moans, his hands clenching my thighs.

My laugh is wicked as I pull his boxers down until only the tip of his cock is covered, running my tongue up one side and down the other. I'm fighting it just as much as he is – my body is screaming at me to rip off his clothes and impale myself, but I keep myself on a tight rein, determined not to screw this up.

I stop breathing as I hook my fingers in the waistband of his boxers and pull them down. He springs out, and my core clenches painfully in response. He's so goddamn beautiful. I swirl my tongue around his head, paying particular attention to the spot underneath. He smells like soap and man and citrus, and I won't ever fucking get enough.

He flexes his hip and sinks into my mouth with a grunt, pushing until my lips are against his pubic bone. I control my gag reflex and take him deeper. His fingers tangle in my hair as he drops his head back. I hollow my cheeks, moaning around him as my pussy clenches around nothing, desperate for his fingers or his tongue or his cock.

"Charlie," he says raggedly, "turn around."

"No," I insist, even though I would do just about anything to get his mouth on me. "It's my turn to torture you, and I'm going to do a fucking good job." I walk my knees up his body, my clit dragging on the underside of his cock as I position myself, settling over him, his length nestled against me. He grabs my hips and pulls me down as he flexes up, grinding against me, the tip of his cock riding back and forth over my clit until I can barely breathe.

His jaw flexes as I take over, sliding myself along him, angling my hips to get the most friction. He sits up and pulls my lips to his, his hands shaking as he cradles my face. He palms my breasts and lowers his mouth to one nipple, then the other, sucking until I can feel the pull in my core.

I raise myself on my knees until the tip of his cock is nudging my entrance. Our gazes lock, our breathing erratic.

"Fuck, Charlie," he grinds out, flexing against me. I whimper, my body shaking with need. "One thrust," he whispers, his eyes pleading with me.

"Yes," I sob, "Please, Lach."

"Look at me."

I do. I would do anything he tells me to right now.

"Good fucking girl," he breathes, the smoky gray swirling in the depths of his eyes, taking me hostage as he holds me still. He pulls his hips away from mine and then thrusts into me, filling me. Completing me. I struggle against his grip, desperate to take what my body wants.

"You fit me like a fucking glove," he rasps through clenched teeth as he pulls back one more time and rams into me, my pussy clenching around him, a mix of pleasure and pain like I haven't experienced before.

"Fuck, Charlie," he says, his voice shaking. He pulls out and pushes my hips back so I'm sitting on his thighs. "You feel too fucking good." He hooks his leg around mine and flips me under him in one smooth motion. "Time to even up the score," he says, kissing the hollow of my throat, between my breasts, my navel, my pubic bone. My back arches as his breath feathers over my clit.

He lowers his face between my legs, our gazes locked. He drags his tongue up my slit, stopping before he reaches my clit. I squirm, trying to get his mouth to where I need it.

"Tell me what you want, Charlie." He drags the flat of his tongue over my clit and I swear my soul leaves my body. "This?" he asks, pushing a finger into me, chuckling as my back bows. He curls his finger, massaging my g-spot. "Or maybe this?" He fits his mouth over my clit, pulsing the suction until I'm screaming for him to let me cum. Just as my orgasm starts building, he pulls away, walking himself up my body with his elbows until his cock nudges at my entrance. He pulls my hips up and puts a pillow underneath me. "Or is this what you want?" he breathes, sliding his entire length into me. He lowers his weight, his pubic bone rocking back and forth over my clit.

"Oh, God, Lach."

"I like when you pray to me," he chuckles, pulling back and thrusting into me again.

"Please," I gasp, digging my nails into his ass.

He obeys. Three hard thrusts, and I'm on the precipice of something I know will change me forever.

"And now you can curse me like the devil I am," he says, rolling off me, his breaths coming hard and fast.

"Fuck," I sob. I circle my fingers over my clit as I give in and let need take control.

"Greedy little thing, aren't you?" Lach asks, watching as I push myself closer.

A giant horn blares from high above, startling us.

"Right on time," Lach grins, lifting my fingers to his mouth and licking them clean. "Ready for some adventure, Carebear?"

I reach up and push a lock of hair from his forehead, sweeping my thumb over his freckles before bringing his mouth down to meet mine. The kiss is tender and filled with promise. "I'm ready for anything as long as I'm with you," I murmur against his lips.

53

———

I can still feel my heart beating between my thighs as we prepare to disembark. We're anchored several hundred feet offshore, a small tender boat bobbing in the water below, waiting to ferry us to the island just off the bow. In true Scottish fashion, gale-force winds claw at us, each gust churning the water until it looks like we're caught in a washing machine.

"Is this safe?" I ask, looking up at Lach, my heart lodging in my throat as the boat rises over a swell.

"The captain has years of experience; he wouldn't put us at risk. We have lifejackets and a GPS beacon just in case," he says, tucking a stray strand of hair behind my ear.

"Okay," I whisper, steeling myself. I can do this.

"Hey," he whispers, tilting my face toward his, "We don't have to do this. We can motor to calmer water or head back toward the marina and do something on land instead."

"No," I insist, shaking my head. "This boat is an important part of who you are – I want to do this with you. You and I haven't had as much time together as I've had with Jack and Cam." I chew on my lip, meeting his gaze. "There's a hole in here that's been waiting to be filled by you." I flatten his hand over my heart, holding it there.

He wraps his arms around me and kisses the top of my head, his hand moving in comforting circles over my back. "I feel the same way, Charlie." He releases me and disappears into the cabin for a minute, coming back with a gigantic pack on his back.

"What's that for?" I ask. "I thought this was just a quick trip to see the cave."

He laughs sheepishly. "I'm making sure we were ready for anything. I packed flashlights and helmets in case you want to explore in the cave; I have firewood in case we want a fire... lunch, a blanket in case you get cold..." he says, ticking the items off on his fingers.

"And if you get cold?" I tease.

"I have one blanket in case *we* get cold," he says, biting his lip and wiggling his eyebrows up and down suggestively. I laugh and follow him down a set of stairs and over a walkway to the tender. He throws his pack to the captain, hops in, then grabs my waist and lifts me on board.

He looks at my face and immediately grabs a life jacket and fastens it around me, then does the same for himself, motioning for the captain to put his on as well. I lean against Lach and close my eyes, turning my face to the wind as we make our way toward shore. We hit the sand after a couple of minutes, and the captain hops out, steadying the boat. Lach hands him the pack, rolls up his linen pants and jumps out, holding his hands out to me. I brace myself on his shoulders, and he swings me away from the boat, sliding me down his body until my toes touch the sand.

"Is he going to stay there the whole time?" I ask, surreptitiously looking over my shoulder at the captain, making sure he isn't leaving. I can't help thinking that our odds of survival aren't great if we end up stranded here – the entire island is one giant rocky cliff face.

"He'll stay there the whole time," Lach promises. "We'll be on the other side of the island, so we won't be able to see him, but he'll be there waiting."

"Good." I force myself to take deep, calming breaths. "I think I need to get out a little bit more – expand my horizons, so I don't panic over tiny things," I murmur, more to myself than to Lach. "You probably think I'm ridiculous, don't you?"

"No, I absolutely do not think you're ridiculous. Having anxiety when you're doing something new is completely normal. Expected, even." He presses a firm kiss to my forehead, holding me there until I wrap my arms around him. "Are you ready?" he asks, threading his fingers through mine.

"Ready," I confirm, walking with him along the beach, the boat slowly disappearing from sight. "So, tell me about this cave," I say, carefully picking my way over the rocks.

"It's called Fingal's Cave. It's pretty popular due to the rock formations, but I'd be surprised if anybody is there today due to the wind."

"What makes it so special?"

"You'll have to wait and see, Carebear," he says, grinning, "I don't want to ruin it for you."

We round the bend, and there she is in all her glory. Rocky hexagonal spires of rock stretch toward the sky like giant stairs leading to the mouth of the largest cave I've ever seen.

"Oh my God," I breathe, my eyes wide as I take everything in. "I can't believe the rock forms like this naturally," I say, walking to the nearest stone and placing my palms flat on top of it, marveling at the shape.

"Isn't it amazing?" Lach asks, coming up behind me and wrapping an arm around my waist. "It's like something out of a fairytale. I wouldn't be surprised to find out a dragon used to live here. Or a family of giants."

I study the cave, the sheer magnitude of it making my heart beat faster. It stretches high above us, the wind whistling across the opening.

"So, what do you want to do first?" he asks, propping his pack against a rock to give his shoulders a break.

"What do *you* want to do first?" I echo, but he's shaking his head before I even get the last word out of my mouth.

"This is your day, Carebear."

"This is *our* day," I say, shuffling between his legs and wrapping my arms around his waist. I look at him. "Tell me what you want to do."

He takes his time answering, the heat in his gaze burning me alive. "You," he says finally, his voice husky. He tilts his head and presses his lips to mine, his tongue demanding entrance as he slides his hands over my ass, gripping me firmly.

"I thought we were drawing this out as long as possible," I murmur against his lips, groaning as he pulls me against him, our hips fitting together like we were made for each other.

"We are, but I can't manage to keep my hands off of you, Charlie," he rasps, lifting me until I'm balanced on my toes, then dragging my body down his, lighting me up like a goddamn firework. "You're the sweetest fucking torture," he breathes against my cheek, pushing his fingers into the hair at the base of my skull and pulling to expose my neck. "I'm going to spend the rest of my life learning how to draw every last drop of pleasure from your body," he says, kissing, licking, and biting his way down my neck.

"I'd like that," I whisper, my eyes fluttering closed, butterflies going haywire in my stomach.

"Would you now," he chuckles, cupping my breast and flicking his thumb over my nipple.

"Yes." I lean into his touch, a moan catching in my throat. He palms my thighs and lifts me, wrapping my legs around his waist.

"Go on then; tell me what you want, Charlie."

54

———

"What I want," I say, moaning as Lach rolls my nipple between his fingers, "is to find my voice."

He freezes, my response taking him by surprise. "What do you mean?" he asks, lifting me to sit on the rock, his hands gripping mine.

I look up at him, opening myself, letting him see me, then drop my gaze to our intertwined fingers. "Before I came here, I had only ever been with Rob. To him, I was just a body he could fuck when he needed a release. He didn't give a shit that I never got there, and he never made any effort to figure out what makes me tick."

Lach's hands clench. "I swear to God, I'll kill him if I ever see him, Charlie. You deserved so much better."

I bring one of his hands to my lips, kissing his knuckles, then press his palm to my cheek. "Don't worry, the lawyer Lorna recommended will take him to the goddamn cleaners. What I meant when I said I want to find my voice is I want to be able to tell the three of you what I like and what I want. I've never done that before, so it doesn't come naturally. You guys have opened up this incredible world to me, and I don't want to be a bystander. I want the words to come easily. I want a voice."

"I want that for you, too, my beautiful, courageous girl." He caresses my cheek with his thumb. "What does that look like to you? How can I help you?"

"I've been thinking about it for the last couple of weeks, and I think encouraging me to repeat the things you say will be the easiest way for me to get used to it."

The corner of his mouth pulls up. "So if I'm eating your pussy and I say, 'Do you like how my tongue feels on your clit?', you want me to encourage you to answer me using similar language?"

I nod, heat rising to my cheeks.

He chuckles, the low rasp scraping over my skin and making me shiver. "My dirty girl." He pushes his hand under my shirt and palms my breast, his scruff scraping my temple as he puts his lips to my ear. "I love your tits. They are a perfect handful." He squeezes them, tracing his finger around my areola. "Do you like it when I tease you?" he breathes.

"Yes," I moan, pushing into his hand. He pulls my shirt over my head, tossing it on the pack.

"Do you want my fingers or tongue?" he asks, a rough, desperate edge to his voice.

"Tongue." I cry out as he fastens his mouth over my nipple and pulls it into his mouth, my core spasming.

He moves to my other breast and then puts his forehead to mine, breathing hard. "Tell me what you want, Charlie."

I relax my mind and say what I'm feeling. "I want you to fuck me. Hard. I want to feel you pulsing inside me when I cum."

"Fuck, Charlie." His expression is pained. "You're not making this easy."

I start unbuckling his belt, relieved when he doesn't stop me. I wrench his pants open and then push his boxers down, humming as his thick length springs out. I run my hand down and back, a drop of precum glistening in the sun. "If I fuck you right now, I won't be able to stop," he says, bucking his hips as I squeeze him, groaning, "And I'm not ready for this to end,"

I shriek when he grabs my hips and flips me around, my torso pressed against the rock, only the tips of my toes touching the ground. He jerks my shorts and underwear down around my knees and positions his cock at my entrance.

Voices drift through the air, making both of us freeze.

I look back at him, my eyes wide, and God – the image of him with his nostrils flared, his jaw set – will stay with me forever. "Just one," he mouths, ramming into me. I bite my hand as my pussy clenches around him. He pulls out and I feel the loss in my soul.

"She's crying for me, Charlie," he says, his gaze locked between my legs. "Soon. I promise." He pulls up my underwear and shorts, then zips himself up. He helps me stand, pushing me against the rock and devouring my mouth. He pushes his thigh between my legs and I drop my weight, rocking against him. "Charlie, there are people coming," he mumbles against my lips, but his body betrays him, his hands sneaking up to my breasts. "No," he rasps, stepping away from me as he feels my thighs starting to clench. "Don't you dare," he breathes, his chest heaving as he watches me run my hand down my stomach on the way to my clit. "That orgasm belongs to me, Charlie. I'm going to fuck you with my tongue until I feel those first tremors, and then I'm going to bury my cock inside you and fuck you until we get there together." He frames my face with his hands, forcing me to look at him. "Do you understand?"

I nod, my pulse pounding in my ears. I've never felt like this. I never imagined myself being one of those people that doesn't care that someone could see us. I've never wanted anyone so much that I would risk everything. We step away from each other as a group of three people comes around the bend. They smile at us politely and continue toward the cave.

"Do you want to eat lunch now?" Lach asks, giving the intruders a dirty look.

"We may as well. Maybe they'll be gone by the time we're done and we can explore the cave alone."

"And what will we do in the cave alone?" he asks, raising one eyebrow.

"Stuff," I say, taking the containers he hands me.

"Stuff?"

"Mmhmm."

"This is the perfect time to work on your voice, Carebear."

"While we're eating?"

"Eating is innately sexual, don't you think?"

I look at his mouth, his tongue peeking out as he pushes a strawberry past his lips. I want that tongue doing dirty, nasty things to me. I bite my lip, keeping the words in.

"Tell me about one of your fantasies," he demands as he tears apart a crusty baguette.

My cheeks flush immediately, the one thing I can't seem to get out of my head rushing to the forefront of my mind.

"Tell me," he insists, spreading cheese on a piece of bread and handing it to me.

"I can't," I say, my heart pounding in my throat, butterflies going crazy in my stomach.

"Yes, you can," he coaxes.

I shake my head. How could I ever tell him what goes on in my mind? How dirty I really am?

"Nothing you say would ever change my opinion of you, Charlie," he says, reading my mind.

I shove the bread in my mouth to give myself time to think and he laughs – a deep, soulful belly laugh that instantly relaxes me. Fuck I love this man.

"If you want a voice, you need to practice using it, Charlie."

I nod and take a deep breath. "It involves all four of us."

"Thank God," he says, his eyes crinkling. "Your reaction made me a little nervous, if I'm being honest."

"All four of us at once," I say, letting the words tumble from my mouth before I can think about them.

"Now we're getting somewhere. What else?"

Oh God. I can't believe I'm even considering saying this out loud. Lach hands me another piece of bread and gives me an encouraging smile. I nibble on the edges, trying to figure out how to say it.

"Close your eyes and imagine it – it'll help the words flow."

I close my eyes and imagine it. The scene in my head is so vivid that I almost moan. "Jack is laying on the bed, propped up with pillows. He pulls me on top of him, but my back is to his front." I blow out an unsteady breath, keeping my eyes scrunched closed.

"Keep going," Lach says, his voice husky.

"Um," I lick my lips, "he..." I panic and open my eyes.

"He's fucking your ass?" Lach guesses, holding a strawberry to my lips.

"Yes," I breathe, biting down on the strawberry and covering my face with my hands.

"That can't be what's making this so hard. We knew that was going to happen the second he claimed your ass virginity."

I laugh, a bit of the tension easing from my shoulders. I hold his gaze as I keep talking, "You climb on top of me, eat me out, and then fuck me."

"While Jack is fucking you?"

I nod, clenching my thighs together to ease the ache.

"That's called double penetration," he says matter-of-factly. "Now you know what to call it next time. And where is Cam in all of this?"

You can do this, Charlie, I say to myself, talking myself up. I take a deep breath. "Fucking you."

"Fuck," he chokes out, gulping down some water. "Your fantasy is my cock buried in your pussy and Cam's cock buried in my ass?

"Or vice versa. I've imagined it both ways."

His pupils blow wide and he runs his hands through his hair, making it stick up. He studies me. "It's like you were made for us. Or maybe we were made for you?" he asks, thinking it over. "Can I ask you something kind of personal about Jack?"

I nod.

"If he were bi, would you share him?"

"Absolutely not. He's mine," I say, surprising myself.

"Charlie—" My name is a plea on his lips. A prayer. "Marry us. *Please.*"

"Last time I checked there are two more of you that would need to ask."

"Tell me what it'll take, Charlie."

"I don't want a proposal that is an afterthought to a conversation or sex. I want it to be planned. I want you all to be sure that's what you want."

"Do—" he starts, but I cut him off.

"And I want you and Cameron to propose to each other if that's what you want." He sniffs loudly. "Are you crying?"

"No. Maybe." Lach laughs, pulling me into a hug. "You make me so fucking happy, Charlie."

I squeeze him back, tears pricking my eyes when I realize what this feeling is. He feels like home.

55

Gravel crunches under our feet as we walk into the cave. Lach stops and throws his head back in a wild howl, the sound bouncing off the walls, surrounding us until that feral part of me claws its way to the surface and joins in. Lach grins, grabbing me and spinning us around until we're both dizzy and out of breath. Adrenaline bubbles under my skin – I feel alive and ready to take on the entire fucking world.

"You don't know how good it feels to be myself around you, Charlie," he murmurs, tucking a strand of hair behind my ear.

"Yes, I do." I run my fingers over his stubbled jaw, push up on my tiptoes and kiss him.

The sea sweeps through the mouth of the cave, collecting in pools before being sucked back into the open ocean. We walk hand-in-hand down a rocky path along the left side of the cave – the only precarious access to the cavern at the back. Lach pulls an electric lantern out of his bag and holds it in front of us, illuminating our surroundings.

"Close your eyes," he says, raising his voice above the roar of the water.

"I can barely see it as it is," I protest.

"Close your eyes, Charlie. Please."

I shuffle back until I feel the cave wall behind my back before I close my eyes, resisting the urge to peek as I hear him walking around, then the flare of a match and water splashing. I startle when the warmth of his hands cradles my face.

"Okay," he whispers, brushing his lips over mine.

A small gasp slips between my lips as I open my eyes. There are candles everywhere – lining the edges of the pools, floating in the water – light bouncing off the cave walls, casting everything in a dazzling watery golden glow.

Now I know why the pack was so heavy. "It's beautiful," I whisper, wishing I had my paints or a sketchbook. I pull out my phone and settle for a picture instead.

"Shall we?" he asks, raising an eyebrow, and sweeping his hand toward the pools.

I look between him and the water. "Shall we what?" I ask.

"Swim," he clarifies, stripping off his T-shirt.

Dark water typically terrifies me, but the fear diminishes with every inch of skin he exposes. I want to be next to him. On him. Impaled by him.

I blow out a shaky breath as he peels off his boxers, my body immediately reacting to his. Heat floods my veins as I pull off my clothing piece by piece. He groans as he wraps his arms around me, our naked bodies fitting together like two pieces of a puzzle. He walks me back until I'm flat against the cave wall, frames my face with his hands, thumbs on either side of my mouth, and just looks at me. I look back at him, emotion swirling through me, bubbling just under the surface

"I've never felt like this before," I whisper, my words tumbling over each other.

A line forms between his eyebrows. "You don't feel the same with Jack and Cameron?"

I shake my head, biting my lip as I try to find the words to explain how I feel. "I feel safe and cherished with Jack, needed and worshipped with Cam." I slide my hands down Lach's shoulders, moving to his waist, then his ass, pulling him against me.

"And with me?" he breathes, his lips against my ear.

"Free," I say simply.

I feel him smile. "Free is good. Let's finish this conversation later – maybe on the boat after we've finally fucked," he says, a hint of desperation behind his chuckle. I shiver as desire courses through me. He crushes his body to mine, our lips and tongues warring against each other until we're both gasping for air.

"Fuck," he mutters, pressing his forehead to mine, our chests heaving. "It's so difficult for me to stay in control when I'm with you."

"I don't want you controlled," I say, wondering how many times I'll have to tell them that before any of them will actually believe me. "I want you unrestrained. Wild. Raw." I cup his face, forcing him to look at me. "I want *you*. All of you."

In one smooth motion, he pulls my legs around his waist and sinks his cock into me, the rocks of the cave wall biting into my skin. My back bows in ecstasy as my body greedily takes everything he's willing to give.

"Are you sure?" he asks through clenched teeth, his hands trembling on my thighs. I moan my affirmation as he pulls back and thrusts again.

"You feel so fucking good," he groans, pulling out and sliding his cock up my slit until the head is resting on my clit, pulsing against me until my breaths become sobs and I'm straining against him, seconds away from coming.

"Not yet," he says, holding still until I back off the edge.

I slam my fist against his shoulder. "You can't keep doing this," I sob, desperately moving my hips against him. "I don't think I can take any more."

"That's a lie and you know it." He hikes my legs up higher and carries me to the nearest pool. I brace myself, expecting ice-cold water, but it's closer to room temperature – still cold enough to draw out the goosebumps. He releases me, making sure I'm steady on my feet before disappearing under the water. I shriek when I feel his head between my thighs, his tongue seeking out my clit.

Oh God. He's going to fucking drown and I'm not going to do one goddamn thing about it. His mouth feels so good. He explodes out of the water and spins me around, pushing me against the smooth rocks at the pool's edge and slamming into me from behind. I only get two punishing thrusts before he pulls out, his breathing ragged in my ear.

"Fuck Charlie, you feel so goddamn fucking good."

I'm so close, it doesn't matter that only his chest is touching me. A moan tears out of me as the first spasm hits.

"Don't you fucking dare," Lach growls. He presses his mouth to the back of my arm and bites me. Hard. My orgasm rips out from under me, the pain shocking my system.

"God. That was an asshole move," I snap, rubbing my arm.

"You'll thank me later," he says, fire dancing in his eyes as he presses an apology kiss to my arm.

"Why can't we have sex now and have it again later?" I argue, crossing my arms over my chest.

"Because it has to be perfect, Charlie. We get one day. One day for us to remember for the rest of our lives."

"Well that puts it in perspective, doesn't it?" I mumble, a sense of loss strangling me, dragging me down.

"Hey," he tips my chin, "Tell me what you're thinking."

I try to hold it in, but emotion gets the best of me. "One time? For the rest of our lives? That sounds miserable. And highly unrealistic, if I'm being honest." I sink into the water, his concerned gaze disappearing as I go under.

He pulls me back up. "You don't get to say that and disappear. Tell me what you're thinking, Charlie."

"Can we get dressed first?" I ask, rubbing at the goosebumps covering my arms.

He climbs out without a word and pulls two towels from the pack. We dress and gather the candles under a blanket of silence. Did I just screw this all up? I let out a shaky sigh as I follow him from the cave, blinking rapidly to push back the tears. Lach drops the pack when we reach the entrance and turns toward me, taking my hands in his.

"Did I just ruin our day?" I ask him, regretting opening my mouth in the worst way. Why didn't I just wait till after this weekend?

"Because you're communicating what you feel? Never." He tugs on my hands, pulling me down the beach. We lay down side by side, the sun warming our faces. "I'm ready when you are," he murmurs, squinting at me.

"Can I ask you a question first?"

"Of course."

"Do *you* only want one time?"

He barks out a laugh. "Fuck, no."

"Do you think Jack or Cam only want one time?"

"I don't think so."

"Then how did that become a rule?"

"It just feels like that's the easiest way for nobody to get hurt."

I turn to my side so I can look at him, tucking my arm under my head. "I don't want easy."

He turns toward me, propping himself up on his elbow. "What *do* you want, Charlie?"

"I want it to be real. I don't want any of us holding back because of what happened in the past."

"With Emily, you mean."

I nod. "I'm not her, Lach."

"You most definitely fucking aren't," he chuckles, rolling on top of me, and caressing my face with sandy fingers.

"Then why do we need rules?" I ask, tracing the freckles on his cheek with my thumb.

"You need to talk to Jack about that. I don't think he'll ever forgive himself for what happened. The last thing he wants is for the three of us to be ripped apart again."

"I would never—" I begin, but Lach cuts me off.

"It's not you he's worried about, Carebear. I don't think he trusts himself."

"That's stupid," I huff.

He murmurs his agreement, his pupils dilating as his gaze latches onto my lips. "Can we talk about Jack another time?" he asks, his voice hoarse.

"Yes," I laugh, wrapping my legs around him and pulling his face to mine. This kiss is different. The red-hot lust is still there, simmering under the surface, but beneath that, there's a current of fierce, undeniable love running fast and deep.

"Are you ready?" he asks when we both come up for air.

"Ready for what? Torture or sex?" I ask, raking my hands through his hair.

"Yes to both," he chuckles against my lips.

"I'm ready," I whisper.

56

———

Lach insists on giving me a tour once we're back on the boat. It quickly becomes evident the yacht was designed for the people Lach is passionate about helping. There are two kitchens, both equipped to make specialized meals for patients, complete with secure cold storage for medications. We pass several rooms dedicated to a clinic and a helipad in case of emergencies.

We stop in front of a glossy wood-paneled door toward the back of the boat. "This is my bedroom – our bedroom," Lach says. "Please note that this is the room farthest away from the control room and kitchens." He gives me an exaggerated wink.

"Noted," I laugh, remembering how he told me he would fuck me where no one could hear me scream.

Oh God. Is this finally happening? Butterflies go haywire in my stomach as he pushes open the door.

"Welcome home, Carebear." He swings me into his arms and carries me over the threshold. The room is dark and earthy – all greens and wood tones – and it even smells like him. A large bank of windows, mostly covered by velvet curtains, leads out to a balcony that runs the entire length of the room.

"Home?" I echo, running my fingers through the hair at the nape of his neck.

He carries me to the windows, setting me down so we're both looking out over the ocean. "I want you to consider this your home, too. Nobody will use this room but us, so you can bring some clothes and toiletries to leave here next time."

"Are you asking me to move in with you?" I tease, looking over my shoulder at him and batting my eyelashes.

He slides his hands around my waist, pulling me against him. "Move in with me, marry me, have babies with me. I want everything you'll give me, Charlie."

I turn in his arms, emotion crawling up my throat. "Really?"

He cups my face with his hands, his grip matching the urgency of his words. "Yes, Charlie. I love you more than I ever thought I could love someone. My dreams are filled with the four of us teaching our kids to swim at the beach. Little Charlies running around with wild hair and freckles."

My smile trembles as I run my fingers over the golden stubble on his jaw, letting myself believe in his dream for just a second. "I can see you now – in front of a computer with a kid on each knee, teaching them how to navigate the stock market."

He snorts. "Not quite the romantic picture I had envisioned, but yes, that too. Everything we want is right at our fingertips, we just have to reach out and grab it." He tilts my face up, his gaze holding mine. "Say yes, Charlie."

My heart squeezes painfully. "Lach—"

"Wait – I'll be right back!" he interrupts, running from the room. I turn back to the windows, gazing out over the horizon as I mull over his words. He wants kids with me.

With us.

Can I really do this? Be with all three of them for the rest of my life? I'm so far gone I can't imagine life any other way.

Lach grunts as he slams into the doorframe on his way back into the room, then collapses on the bed, gasping for air and clutching his arm.

"Not the entrance I wanted to make," he wheezes, rubbing his shoulder as he tries to catch his breath. I climb up next to him and pull the comforter over me, sighing in contentment. I'm pretty sure I could have the best nap ever in this bed: the rocking of the boat, the minimal light, a plethora of cozy blankets.

"Naptime?" Lach asks, the corner of his mouth pulling up as he watches my attempt to cover a gigantic yawn.

"Absolutely not. Not until I have that orgasm you promised me. *Then* I'll have the best sleep of my life."

"I'll get right on that," he laughs, "but first, there's a question I need to ask you. Do you want to stay rolled up like a burrito or should we go out on the balcony?"

My heart jumps to my throat as I scramble off the bed and follow him outside on shaky legs.

He turns to me, running his fingers through his hair nervously. "I was going to wait," he says, "but after our talk today, I'm having a hard time thinking about anything else." He caresses the swell of my cheek, then tilts my chin and covers my lips with his. His tongue sweeps over mine tentatively before he pulls back to study my face.

"Lach, you're making me nervous. Why are you staring at me like that?" I ask, my nerves bubbling over.

"Because I want this moment etched into my memory," he responds, sinking down onto one knee.

Oh fuck.

"Charlie, for the love of God, tell me you'll marry me. Tell me you can't live without me." His eyes search mine, desperation swirling through their depths. "Tell me I'm branded onto your heart like you are on mine." He squeezes my hands in his. "Tell me you'll stay forever," he says, his voice wavering.

I blink back tears as he reaches into his pocket and pulls out a small box. He sniffs, then laughs as I wipe at my eyes.

"I scoured the internet for days looking for a ring that would reflect how I feel for you. Nothing seemed right until I remembered I had this." He flips the clasp with his thumb and opens the box. A gorgeous diamond winks up at me, a halo of tiny diamonds surrounding it. "This was my grandmother's. She was feisty and independent. She would have loved you." He pulls the ring out of the box, holding it carefully between his thumb and forefinger, looking up at me with naked adoration. "Marry me, Charlie."

I frame his face with my hands, wiping a tear from his cheek with my thumb. "Will you finally fuck me if I say yes?" I ask, grinning. I wrap my arms around his neck and kiss him hard.

"Yes," he laughs, blinking back tears.

I hold his gaze as I pull him to his feet, our future spreading before us with endless possibilities, all of them infinitely better because we have each other. "Lachlan, I would be absolutely honored to be your wife."

"Really?" he whispers, "You mean it?"

"Yes. I can't imagine a life where you're not in it."

His fingers shake as he slides the ring onto my finger, then he kisses my hand before he wraps me in a tight hug. "I never let myself believe that you would actually say yes," he whispers against my ear. "I thought you would leave and forget about us."

"Impossible," I murmur, brushing my lips over his. I remember thinking I could go back to my same old boring life like nothing had changed. When I believed my love for them held no value. When I sent Cam off to a different country because I thought he'd be better off without me.

These men have changed the very essence of my being in the best ways possible. How could I ever turn my back on that?

"Lachlan, will you please make love to me now?"

"I thought you'd never fucking ask," he says roughly, pulling me inside and drawing the curtains.

57

I don't even get a chance to admire the ring on my finger before Lach has me caged in, my back pressed to the glass doors.

"This is it, Carebear," he warns, caressing my nose with his. "There's no going back after this."

I slide my hands over his shoulders and around his neck. "Good," I murmur. "Do you think I would chicken out right before we get to what I've been waiting for? It's been the longest two months of my life."

"Has it only been two months? It feels like a goddamn lifetime," he says roughly, pressing his mouth to mine in a tender kiss. "Was that a yes?" he asks when we finally pull away from each other, breathing heavily.

"Look at me," I demand, framing his face with my hands, forcing him to look at me. "Yes, I will marry you. Yes, I want to fuck you. Yes, I want you and everything that comes with you, including your two best friends. My answer is yes, Lachlan." I raise an eyebrow at him when he pulls out a phone and shoots off a text, a smile playing on his lips.

"I had to tell the captain our dinner plans," he explains.

"What do you mean our dinner plans? I thought we'd be having sex for the next few hours *at least*," I grumble, starting to get royally pissed off.

"I want to take you to this amazing little pub on North Uist. The food is to die for."

"I don't want food, Lach," I snap, ducking under his arm to go inside.

He follows me in, trapping me in a hug. "Hey, if you don't want to go to dinner with me, we don't have to go. I just thought it would be nice to have an actual date, just the two of us.

I immediately feel horrible for being such a brat.

"Plus, I was going to ask you to wear this." He walks to the bed, pulls a box out of the nightstand, and hands it to me.

I look down at the box, my cheeks heating as I read what it is. "A remote-control vibrator? You want me to wear this to dinner?" I imagine some sort of flat vibe that will sit in my underwear, but when he takes the box from me and opens it, I realize I'm completely wrong.

"I don't know how I could even walk with that in," I protest, studying the u-shaped contraption, my core feeling more like molten lava by the second.

"Oh, you'll be able to. It's the best-rated remote vibe on the market."

"Lach—"

He turns me around and pulls me against him, one arm banded around my waist. "Hold this," he says, handing me the vibe. "We're going to do a quick demonstration."

I take the vibe from him, begrudgingly noting the velvety feel of it, the slight hook at the end that I know will hit my g-spot perfectly. The little nubby end at the other side of the u-shape must go against my clit. My pussy clenches in anticipation as Lach slides his hands down my waist, pushing my shorts and underwear to the ground. I drop my head against his shoulder as he moves one hand between my legs, sliding easily in the moisture gathered there.

"Is this all for me, Carebear?" he asks, his breath ragged.

I moan in response as he pushes his middle finger inside me, rocking the heel of his palm against my clit with each thrust.

"Fuck, Charlie. Remind me why I'm not just throwing you across the bed and fucking you until you can't remember your name?"

"Dinner," I croak, instantly regretting saying it the second the word leaves my mouth. "Forget I said that," I beg, "Please lay me on the bed and fuck me until I can't remember my name. That sounds amazing."

"I will," he promises, taking the vibrator from me, "Later."

I don't get a chance to protest before he's pressing the vibe to my entrance, circling it there, and then slowly pushing it in. He holds me up with one arm as my knees give out, adjusting the vibe until the nubby part is nested against my clit.

He turns me to face him. "How does that feel?" he asks, kneading my butt cheeks, his nostrils flared, pupils dilated.

"Too fucking good," I breathe, squeezing my thighs together to relieve the pressure.

"Perfect. Let's go up on deck for some champagne, and you can decide if you want to go to dinner." He bends and pulls up my underwear, then my shorts, smacking my butt before motioning for me to follow him from the room.

"Yes, Coach." As I take a step, my smirk fades, the silicone delivering the most delicious pressure to my g-spot. "Oh Lord," I breathe, my voice just as shaky as my knees.

"If it's too much – if you can't take it—"

That motherfucker. "I can take it," I snap, concentrating on my breathing as I follow him out into the hallway.

"I'll make you a bet," he says, grinning. "I bet you can't stop yourself from cumming on the vibe."

"Fine. What do I get if I win?"

"Whatever you want."

"And if you win?"

"Whatever *I* want."

Oh fuck.

"Deal," I say before I can chicken out. "You're not going to turn this thing on when I'm in the middle of talking to someone, are you?" I ask, belatedly realizing the implications of accepting his challenge.

His eyes widen. "Who me? I would never do that."

"I swear to God, Lach. You better not."

"I thought you said you could take it."

"I can, dammit." I clench my jaw as he motions for me to climb the stairs.

He cups my ass halfway up, and I barely resist pushing back into his hands. "You have the perfect ass," he breathes. As I take the last step, he bends down and bites the swell of one cheek. I squeal and twist away from his grip but only make it a few feet before the pressure on my clit has me stumbling into the wall.

"Fucking hell," I mutter, giving Lach a dirty look.

"Just give yourself a little time to get used to it." He wraps me in his arms.

"I don't think I'll ever get used to this," I gasp, dropping my head against the wall as he grinds against me. I can feel his lips curl against my neck when he smiles, his tongue tracing the delicate line of my throat.

"How about that champagne," I rasp, desperate to numb the steady ache that's becoming impossible to ignore.

Lach leads me to a cozy seating area with a view of the setting sun and motions to someone behind us.

"Normally, I wouldn't have someone serving us, but I'm not too keen on leaving you here on your own at the moment."

"Why?"

"Because the second I'm not watching you, you're going to get the idea in your head that you can just get there without me knowing."

"I highly doubt—," I clamp my mouth closed to keep in a moan as I sit down and the vibe pushes into my g-spot and clit at the same tie. "Fuck," I whimper, holding myself perfectly still.

"All you have to do is rock back and forth a couple of times," he taunts, his gaze glued between my legs. He palms my thigh and pushes me back a fraction of an inch.

Pleasure courses through me, my eyes rolling back before I can wrestle myself back under control. *Get it together, Charlie.*

"Your champagne, Miss."

I open my eyes to a friendly smile and reach up to take the glass from him, gulping it down. His smile drops as he watches me, his gaze flying to Lach. "Is she okay?"

He bites his cheek to keep from smiling, but I can see the corners of his mouth twitch as he ensures him I'm fine, just a bit parched.

"Sit up straight, Charlie," he says after the man sets the bottle down and leaves, "It'll help even out the pressure. Better?" he asks, watching me like a hawk as I change positions.

"Barely," I mutter, pouring myself another glass of champagne.

"We can go back down to the room—"

"No!" I cut him off. "I'm going to win this bet if it kills me."

He chuckles, twisting the stem of his glass between his fingers, "Death by not cumming – is that even possible?" He reaches into his pocket and pulls out the remote. "Why don't we find out?"

58

"Do you want to change before dinner?" Lach asks, noticing the goosebumps racing over my body as the breeze from the open door caresses my skin. My shoulders shake as a shiver takes hold of my body.

"Yes, but I didn't think we'd be leaving the boat. I didn't bring anything appropriate for dinner."

"It's a pub, Charlie. You don't need to dress up. Although, this does give me an excuse to give you the present I brought you."

My heart jumps to my throat. "You got me a present?"

"Don't get too excited," he chuckles. He opens the closet, pulls out a box wrapped in newspaper, and hands it to me. I carefully pick at the tape, scanning over the article headings and pictures on the paper. I freeze, tilting the box so the paper is right-side up. It's filled with photos of the four of us, some of me alone, or me with one or all of the guys. I scan the words, realizing the 'articles' are all poems and song lyrics.

"Did you do this?" I ask, blinking back tears.

"I hope you like it because I'll be wrapping everything in that for at least the next twenty-five years."

I drop the box on the bed and throw my arms around his neck. "I love it," I whisper in his ear. "Thank you for such a thoughtful gift."

"You haven't even opened it yet," he laughs.

"I promise the paper is better than what's inside."

He chuckles, handing me the box again, and I carefully peel off the paper, saving it to frame when we get home. I lift the lid to find a dusty blue colored sweat suit, soft and silky beneath my fingertips.

"This is gorgeous," I murmur, pulling it out, and admiring the tailoring. It looks expensive and comfy as hell.

"It reminded me of the color of your eyes, and I know how much you like comfortable clothes..." he trails off, shrugging his shoulders.

"Thank you, Lach." I press a kiss to his cheek and strip right in the middle of the room, using his shoulder to balance as I pull on the sweatpants, studiously ignoring what the vibe is doing to me. "It's perfect!" I turn in a circle in front of him. "What do you think?"

"Stunning," he says, wrapping his arms around me and pulling me in for another kiss. When we finally break away from each other, we make our way to the deck. The boat is tied to an impressively large dock just outside a weathered, wood-planked building. Lach keeps me steady with a tight grip on my elbow as we walk down the gangway. I'm thankful for the support when my knees start wobbling with every step, my clit throbbing in time to my heartbeat. Every single time I move, the vibe press against my clit or my g-spot – even if I stay perfectly still, I can still feel it keeping me right on the cusp of a violent orgasm.

"How many people come here on boats this size that need a dock that big?" I ask.

"Me."

I gape at him. "You? You had this dock built?" He nods. "You like this place so much that you had a dock built so you could come whenever you wanted?" I ask incredulously, letting that information sink in, and finding I don't quite like the feeling of it.

"It's my sister's pub, Charlie."

"Are you fucking kidding me?" I screech, too mortified about the situation to care that I sound like a banshee. "Your sister? I'm meeting your sister with a remote-control vibe shoved up my pussy?" I shove my palms against his chest, blood pulsing in my temples, my blood pressure sky high. "We're turning around right now and taking this out." I spin on my heel, dragging him with me.

Someone calls out his name and I turn to see a blonde woman striding down the dock toward us. Lach holds his arms out to her, pulling her into a tight hug, his features softening.

"Pen, this is my fiancée, Charlie. Charlie, this is my sister, Pen," Lach introduces us, beaming.

I reach out to shake her hand, but she grabs my left hand instead, "You did it, Lachie! I'm so proud of you!" She pulls me into a hug, squeezing me tight around the neck. "I can't believe I'm going to have a sister!"

"Nice to meet you, Pen," I laugh. She's beautiful: delicate pixie features and blonde hair that waterfalls in thick waves over her shoulders. She's wearing a fitted army green coverall, but she pulled the top half off and tied the arms around her waist, revealing a white tank top underneath.

"It's Penelope, but Jack started calling me Pen as a joke, and it stuck."

"What do you prefer?" I ask, struggling to keep pace as she pulls me by the hand toward to pub.

"Pen is fine. I'm used to it now. Is Charlie a nickname?"

"My given name is Charlotte, but my friends call me Charlie."

"Charlie it is," she says, winking. "Are you hungry? I put together a tasting menu when Lach told me you were on the way."

"You're the chef here?"

"Sometimes the chef, sometimes the bartender, sometimes a waitress. It just depends on the day."

"Jack of all trades?" I ask as we approach the building.

"You could say that," she says proudly. "I took out a loan from Lach several years ago and finished paying it off a couple of months ago. I could never have done it without his help."

"Anything to get you off that godforsaken boat," Lach mutters.

"I used to dive for scallops," she explains, "I still go out in the crew now and then – that's why I thought the pub was a good idea. We had to ferry the scallops over to the mainland every day. Now we serve them here. Plus a lot of other local seafood. Even lamb that's raised here on the island."

"That's amazing, Pen. What an incredible accomplishment."

"Thank you," she grins, her blue eyes lighting up. "Come on." She holds the door open and then motions for us to sit in a large corner booth. "I'll be back with the food," she says before disappearing through the door that I assume leads to the kitchen.

"She's amazing, Lach."

"Isn't she? I'm so proud of everything she has accomplished so far. She's really carved a spot for herself here." He reaches across the table and grabs my hands, the callouses on his palms sending a thrill of lust zinging straight to my core.

"Now I understand why you had the dock built," I say begrudgingly. I start to cross my legs but quickly realize I can't do that without putting myself in an impossible situation. Fuck.

"How are you feeling?" Lach asks, his lips pursed, trying to hold in a laugh.

"Fine, thank you." I take a giant gulp of the beer in front of me. "What kind of beer is this? I don't usually find ones I like, but this one's amazing!"

"Pen has a brewery in the back. She started it last year."

"She made this? Holy shit."

"I know, right? I told her she needs to enter it into some competitions."

"She should! I don't know anything about beer, but this is the best I've ever tasted."

"Tell her that before we leave. Maybe she'll listen if it's coming from you."

I nod and take another gulp, setting my glass down to find Lach staring at me, a weird look on his face.

"What?" I ask, wiping at my mouth, wondering if I have something on my face. I jerk in my seat as the vibe starts moving inside me, the hooked part circling my g-spot. I clutch the table, lifting my weight off the bench.

"Lach – fuck," I gasp, barely stopping myself from rocking my hips on the bench seat. "Turn it off," I beg, my voice strangled as I attempt to keep myself together.

Lach fumbles under the table and the silicone nestled against my clit starts vibrating. A startled moan forces its way out of my lips before I can stop it. "Lach, please," I groan.

"I hope you two are hungry!" Pen says, her arms laden with plates. I shoot a glare at Lach before smiling up at her. Lach jerks and I hear something fall on the floor under the table.

Oh my fucking God.

Lach widens his eyes, an apology in his gaze before turning to Pen. "This looks amazing, Pen. You really outdid yourself." He helps her find space on the table for all the plates while I desperately try to hang on to my sanity and not orgasm in front of his little sister.

"Let me know if you two need anything," Pen says, glancing at the table and making sure everything is perfect before she leaves us.

I slide my hand between my legs, pressing the vibe tighter to my body, well past the point of rational thought. Lach dives under the table, scrambling for the remote.

"God, I'm sorry, Charlie." He clicks it off just as the first spasm starts.

"Oh fuck," I whimper.

"No, you don't." Lach grabs ice from his glass of water and shoves it down the front of my shirt before I can block him.

The cold switches my brain into survival mode. "It's stuck in my bra!" I hiss, reaching down the front of my shirt to dislodge it. I sag against the back of the booth, panting. "I almost lost the bet," I say, licking my lips.

"Maybe I should have left it on?" His finger hovers over the button, contemplating.

"Don't you fucking dare," I hiss. "Unless you want me to cum – loudly – in the middle of the pub."

"That's a horrible argument, Charlie. I would love to see that," he says, his voice dropping an octave.

My jaw drops. "You're a dirty, dirty man, Lachlan."

"I never pretended to be anything different."

"True," I laugh, remembering how he encouraged my relationship with Jack. "You know, if it weren't for you, all of this would have turned out very differently."

"I think about that almost every day," he admits, "I was so scared you'd think I was a perv."

"As it turns out, I'm a perv, too," I laugh. "Who knew."

59

____

I serve myself from the plates Pen set before us on the table.

"This is easily enough food for ten people," I grumble, wondering what's going to happen to it if we don't finish it.

"It won't go to waste, don't worry. Pen will take the leftovers to her neighbors."

"Her neighbors?" I ask, cutting the scallop with a fork before popping a piece in my mouth.

"She lives in an old folks' home."

"She what?" I ask, thinking I must have misunderstood him.

"It's a long story, but she rents an apartment in a retirement facility. Whenever she has extra food, she sneaks it in for her neighbors."

"I'm going to have to hear that story sometime," I chuckle. I imagine her sneaking down hallways and leaving trays of food on doormats.

"I'll leave that story to her. She's a fantastic storyteller."

I cut a piece of lamb, rolling my eyes in ecstasy as it melts in my mouth. Every dish is excellent – something you would expect from a Michelin restaurant, not a pub on a forgotten Scottish island.

"Why did she choose to open the pub here?" I ask. "She would have made a killing in pretty much any big city."

"This acted as her home base when she was fishing. She saw a need in the community and decided to fill it. There are places like this throughout the highlands – exceptional culinary talent that has been kept secret for years – and that's how they like it," he says, shrugging.

"Fulfillment, not recognition?"

"Exactly."

"That's kind of romantic."

Lach laughs. "I don't think she'd see it that way, but I agree. There's something special about it, isn't there?"

"It's how all the Hallmark movies start," I tell him, "Small town, cute little business..."

"I sure hope it works out like that. She's only met a few people her age here. I'm worried she won't ever meet that special person."

"You never know – meeting somebody wasn't even on the radar when I came to Scotland. And now I have three somebodies."

"Two somebodies and one fiancé," Lach corrects, grinning.

His smile startles me. He's so fucking gorgeous. My *fiancé*. Suddenly I don't care so much about the bet. All I care about is getting back to the boat and getting lost in each other.

"Lach—"

"I know. Me too. I'm about to bust through the zipper of my pants. I have no idea how I'll walk out of here with my dignity intact."

"Let's hurry," I plead, shoveling another bite of food into my mouth.

"'Hurry' isn't a word in Pen's vocabulary. She probably has a five-course dessert planned and a brewery tour after." He pulls me to his side and kisses my cheek. "I promise we'll survive this." He spoons some mussels onto his plate, snags one with his fork, and feeds it to me.

White wine, butter, and garlic explode over my tongue. "Damn. She can really cook, can't she?"

"Pen's amazing. She's good at so many different things." The adoration in his words is adorable.

After another ten minutes, I'm in absolute agony. "If you want me to be able to enjoy myself, I need to get this thing out of me. You've edged me to the point where I'm questioning my sanity."

"What about the bet?" he asks, sliding a piece of bread through the white wine sauce and holding it to my lips.

"You win," I say simply, taking the bread from him with my teeth and licking a drop of butter from my lips.

His gaze follows my tongue. "Only if I can take it out of you."

"What?" I balk, "People will see us go into the restroom together."

"So?"

It's hard to hold my resolve when he's looking at me like that – like he would strip me bare and fuck me right here on the bench seat if I told him it was okay.

He pulls the remote out of his pocket and turns it on high. I whimper, barely holding myself together. I notice several people looking over at us and mortification takes hold. "Fine!" I hiss, "You can do it. Just get this fucking thing out of me!"

"How are you two doing?" Pen asks, startling both of us. "Ready for dessert?"

"Always," Lach says easily, his finger hovering over the off button on the remote. I give him a death stare, and he finally presses it, giving me back my ability to form coherent words.

"Everything was amazing, Pen," I say, my voice high and breathy.

"Good," she smiles. "Dessert is made to order. It will be about twenty-five minutes. Feel free to take a walk – there's a path along the water to the right of the building. You'll have a gorgeous view of the sunset."

"That sounds lovely. Thank you, Pen."

I pull Lach from the booth once she's back in the kitchen. Once we're outside, I push Lach away from the front door, my grip on his arm startling him. "If you don't figure out a way to get this thing out of me in the next thirty seconds, I'm going to cum, and then all of your hard fucking work will be for nothing. Got it?"

"Don't you fucking dare." He picks me up, throws me over his shoulder, and starts jogging down the path.

"Where are we going?" I ask, my words ending on a huff as his shoulder digs into my stomach with every step.

"There's an old, abandoned fishing shack down this way – at least it used to be abandoned. We'll find out in a second." A handful of steps later, he's setting me down in front of a wood-planked door barely hanging onto its hinges. He peers through the window next to the door before trying the handle. The door creaks open, the sounds echoing off the stone walls. "All clear," he says, pulling me in after him. "Bed or bathroom?" He asks.

I look at the mildewed bed against the far wall and wrinkle my nose. The bathroom has to be better, right?

"Bathroom?" I answer, swinging my haze back to him. He's staring at me, his eyes hooded. "Lachlan?"

"I don't know if I can take that out of you, Carebear." The muscle in his jaw works as he tries to reel himself in. His restraint is holding on by a gossamer thread, and fuck if I don't want to break right through it.

"Yes, you can." I pull him toward the open door at the back corner, hoping it's the bathroom.

"Not unless you want our first time to be in an old fisherman's shack, I can't," he says, making a half-hearted attempt to pull away from me.

Once we're both in, I slam the door behind us and take a cursory look around – a small stand-up shower, a toilet, and a pedestal sink. It'll do. I stand on my tiptoes, framing his face with my hands, and slide my tongue along his bottom lip. I suck it into my mouth, his moan raising goosebumps over every inch of my skin, his arms finally wrapping around me, pulling me against his body. I slide my tongue over his, mimicking what our bodies should be doing.

"Fucking hell, Charlie," he rasps, pulling away and resting his forehead against mine. I push down my sweatpants, wiggling out of them, then push my underwear down. I have my hands braced on the sink behind me, ready to boost myself up, when I hear the click of a button. The vibe comes to life inside me, bringing me to the edge in less than a second. He pockets the remote and grabs my knees, hoisting me up onto the sink, my legs spread wide.

"Goddamnit, Charlie. You're too fucking sexy." He pulls my shirt off over my head and pushes the cups of my bra down, sucking one nipple into his mouth, then the other.

My world starts to narrow, and I fight it with everything I have. "Lach—" I try to warn him, but the words won't come out.

"You're so fucking perfect," he breathes, his gaze locked between my legs as he kneads my breasts.

"Lach!" I'm toeing the edge, ready to tumble over. Fuck the bet.

He pulls the vibe out of me without warning, and in those few seconds, before the tide consumes me, I jerk open his pants, push down his boxers and pull him out. He twitches in my hand, the drop of precum serving as a warning I absolutely will not heed. I position myself at the edge of the sink and pull him closer, nestling the head of his cock against my entrance.

He looks up at me. "Charlie—" he protests, but it's too late. He grasps my hips and rams into me. I'm spasming before he even bottoms out, squeezing him greedily. "Fuck," he groans into my neck, "this was not the plan, Charlie."

"I don't care what the plan was. I need you. Now." He picks me up from the sink and turns, pressing my back against the wall, his cock buried deep, his pubic bone riding over my clit with each thrust.

"Look at me, Charlie."

His gaze tips me over the edge, my entire world condensing to where our bodies are joined, then exploding outward in a violent burst of scorching heat that consumes me from the inside out.

60

Lach's breath shudders in my ear as he slides in, stretching me, milking his orgasm for all its worth. My pussy squeezes each time he pulls back, desperate to keep him inside.

"Fucking hell, Charlie," he pants, meeting my gaze, his eyes bright. "I think the world just tilted on its axis. Nothing will ever be the same."

"My pussy's that good?" I tease, cradling his face and pulling his mouth to mine, nipping and biting at his lips. He moans, his cock twitching back to life. I squeeze my legs around his hips, forcing him deeper.

"Charlie—"

"Shhh." I press my finger to his lips, never wanting this moment to end. "Can we stay like this forever?"

"If I could go about life with my cock buried inside you twenty-four seven, it would make me the happiest man alive. Unfortunately for us, Pen expects us back at the pub in five minutes."

"Shit!" I unlock my legs, and he lowers me, ensuring I'm steady before releasing me. We wash up at the sink together, laughing as we shake ourselves dry before dressing. As I wobble on one leg, attempting to keep my balance as I dress, I realize he never even took his pants off. I want to feel his skin under my hands, explore the ridges of his muscles, taste the salt on his skin. My knees give out as an aftershock grips me.

Lach grabs me around the waist. "You okay?"

"Just thinking about finally getting my hands on you once we're back on the boat."

"Mmmm," he groans, capturing my mouth with his. "Maybe I'll ask Pen for some whipped cream and hot fudge to go."

I smile against his lips, my body thrumming and ready for round two. "Yes, please. Speaking of Pen..."

"Fuck! I swear to God, everything disappears when I'm with you. No obligations, no stress. Just you and me in our own little bubble."

A knock on the door brings us down to earth. "Are you two finished in there? I have to take a piss."

Lach and I stare at each other wide-eyed. I crack first, the giggles sneaking up on me. By the time we open the door, both of us are wiping at our eyes, gasping for breath.

Lach takes my hand and pulls me out of the bathroom. Four burly dudes look at me, their cheeks stained varying shades of pink.

"Sorry about that," Lach apologizes, stalling in the doorway, "we didn't realize we had company." Dead silence. "Well," Lach says, the silence becoming awkward, "If you need a great place to eat, the pub just up the way is excellent. We're headed that way now if you want to join us. First beer is on me."

"Lach!" I hiss, absolutely mortified. I don't ever want to see these people again, and I especially don't want to drink a beer across a table from him.

"Gentlemen," I greet them, keeping my head high, "Hope your evening is as enjoyable as mine."

One of them snorts. "I highly doubt that, lass."

I grin and salute them as I follow Lach outside, slamming into his back when he stops short in the doorway, his eyes wide. "We forgot something in the bathroom!" he whispers, glancing over his shoulder when we hear the bathroom door close.

The vibrator. Fuck.

We're frozen in the doorway, trying to figure out what to do, when the door swings open, and one of the guys comes out with a wad of paper towel cradled in his palm, the vibe nestled inside.

"I think you forgot something," he says, walking toward us like it's an offering. "I debated not saying anything, but it looks expensive," he smiles, a dimple flashing through his beard.

I cover my cheeks with my hands as Lach takes it from him, slipping it into his pocket. "I know this just became infinitely more awkward, but you now know something that no one else knows, so we may as well get that beer together," Lach says with a self-deprecating laugh. "I'm Lach," he introduces himself, then steps to the side so they can see me. "This is my fiancée, Charlie. We just got engaged today," he beams. I wave awkwardly.

"Well, that explains a lot," a guy that looks like Paul Bunyan says.

"If only you knew how little that actually explains," I mutter.

"Oh, I do want to know," Paul Bunyon says, grabbing a bag by his feet and hoisting it onto his shoulder. "Lead the way."

"And your friends?" Lach asks, looking around the group.

"I don't know them," Paul Buyon says, shrugging. "We're the new crew for one of the boats. We met up at the docks, and then the captain pointed us back here to use the bathroom before figuring out where to get some food."

"What boat?" Lach asks, his shoulders stiffening.

"The *Master Baiter*," they say in unison.

I snort. "If you tell me the *Master Baiter* is Pen's boat, it will make my entire year."

"Did you say Pen? She was supposed to meet us, but I guess something came up," the quietest of the guys pipes in.

"Yeah, it did!" I laugh, elbowing Lach.

"Come on," Lach says, guiding me to the path. "I have to go tell Pen she needs to find a new crew."

"What? Why?" I look back at the shack to see the guys gathering their gear and filing out of the house, following us.

"Did you *see* them?"

"Yes, they are four handsome men that seem extremely competent. Didn't you *want* her to meet new people?" I ask, trying to keep up with him.

"Not *four* of them, Charlie."

"Don't be a hypocrite."

The only response I get is an unintelligible grumble before he opens the door for the guys and me. Seconds after all six of us get settled in the booth, Pen comes out with a large porcelain dish holding a towering chocolate souffle. Her steps falter when she sees the full table, but the need to get the souffle to the table before it falls takes precedence. She carefully sets the souffle on the table's edge and pushes it into the center, blowing out a breath of relief when it doesn't fall.

"Who are your friends?" She asks, studying the guys with interest.

I keep my mouth closed, waiting for someone to answer her, but there's only dead silence. I glance at Lach to find him openly contemplating each of them. They aren't paying him any attention. Instead, they're staring up at Pen with varying degrees of reverence and a strong underlying current of sexual tension. Color creeps up Pen's cheeks as the silence drags on.

"Pen, meet your new crew. Guys, this is Pen," I say in a rush, unable to take the silence any longer.

"Fuck," Paul Bunyan mutters.

"My crew?" Pen asks, panic flashing in her eyes. "I'm so confused."

"After orientation, the captain pointed us up to the old fishing shack," Paul explains, "When we got there, the bathroom was otherwise, um—" he clears his throat, "—occupied. Anyway, Lach invited us to come for a beer. And here we are."

"Here you are," Pen murmurs, her gaze roaming over the guys, then snapping back to Lach and I. "You did not," she says incredulously.

"Oh they did," says the guy who gave Lach the vibe back. "Loudly."

Oh my God. I start to slide under the table, but Lach hauls me back up. "We're in this together, Carebear. Don't you dare abandon me at a time like this."

Pen digs a spoon into the souffle rather violently, spooning portions onto dessert plates and passing them around. She spins on her heel and heads to the bar, returning with a tray filled with beer glasses. She motions for us to help ourselves, then takes the last one for herself.

"To love," she toasts, lifting her glass toward Lach and I, her movements stiff, "And to a killer scallop season," she finishes, clinking her glasses to each of the guys. She downs her entire beer in one go, slams the glass back on the tray and wipes her lips with the back of her hand.

"A *killer* scallop season?" Lach asks.

Pen leans over the table, her head between Lach and I so no one else can hear. "It seems like I may have girl-bossed a little too close to the sun this time. Pretty sure this crew will be the death of me," she mutters. "Okay! Who's ready for another?" she asks, straightening.

"I think it's time for Lach and I to go," I say, pulling Lach out of the booth. "Nice to meet you guys. Hopefully we'll see you around sometime," I call over my shoulder. I pull Pen into a tight hug, both of us making promises to get together soon, and then I'm pulling Lach away from the guys I'm pretty sure he's ready to murder.

"Give me one second," he says, disappearing into the kitchen. He returns thirty seconds later with a to-go bag hanging from his fingers.

We barely reach the boat before Lach wraps his arms around me. We're stumbling into walls as we rip at each other's clothes. We're both in our underwear by the time we make it to the bedroom. I notice the to-go bag still hanging from Lach's arm, looking at it suspiciously.

"You did not—"

"Oh, I did." He grins, reaching in and pulling out an entire canister of whipped cream and a full bottle of chocolate sauce.

I reach for the chocolate sauce, but he pulls it out of reach. "I get to do what I want, remember?"

"You just railed me in a public bathroom with four men listening. I think it's my turn."

"Fuck. You have a point." He hands me the bottle, and we face off, waiting to see what the other will do. I rush him, tackling him to the bed before he can brace himself. I jerk down his boxers, lust blazing through me as I pull out his cock. I hold the bottle above him, but he grabs my wrist to stop me.

"Wait." He pushes himself up to the head of the bed, propping himself up with several pillows. "I want to watch," he says, holding my gaze, "I want to see your lips stretch around my cock... see the tears in your eyes when you struggle to take all of me... see my cum glistening on your lips."

Fuck.

61

Lach looks like a golden god against the deep charcoal of the bedsheets. His breath hitches as I trace my fingertips from freckle to freckle, zigzagging over the ridges of his chest, his abs, stopping just shy of the base of his cock. He circles my wrist with his fingers, pulling my palm against his length, thrusting against me.

"Naughty boy," I whisper, pulling out of his grasp, determined to torture him as much as he tortured me over the last twelve hours.

"When I agreed to let you do what you want, I didn't realize you would punish me."

"Don't act so surprised when you're the one who started this." I smirk. I climb off the bed and walk to the dresser, rifling through the drawers until I find what I want.

I hold up the ties and his eyes burn with the fire of a thousand suns.

"Do naughty boys get tied up?" he asks, the corner of his mouth pulling up.

"Today they do," I say as I drop my bra and underwear on the floor. I straddle his legs and pull his left wrist to the headboard, leaning forward to loop the tie through the slat and around his wrist.

He turns his head and nips at my nipple, then opens his mouth wide and sucks me in. The pull of his mouth shoots a bolt of lust to my core, I thread my fingers through his hair and pull his mouth back to my breast, my body thrumming. He slides his free hand over the curve of my ass, then lower, sinking a finger into me with a low groan.

I clench around him, strung tight enough to cum from one touch. I grind against his hand, whimpering as his fingers brush against my ass.

"Who's in charge here?" he whispers, catching my lips with his and pulling me into a scorching kiss.

I pull away, panting. "I am, damn it. Give me your other hand." I bite my tongue to keep from groaning in disappointment as he pulls out of me. He licks me off his finger, his eyes rolling back as he tastes me.

"You have no fucking idea how good you taste, Charlie," he rasps, offering me his hand.

I loop the tie around his wrist, tying another slip knot. I steady my breathing and push myself back so I'm sitting on his thighs. The bottle of chocolate sauce is still warm as I grab it from the nightstand and carefully drizzle it around his head, catching the drips with my tongue before they run down his shaft and make a mess. I take only his tip into my mouth, swirling my tongue over him. He pushes his hips off the bed, desperate for me to take all of him.

I give him what he wants, sinking down until my lips press against taut skin. I breathe through my nose, swallowing around him, hollowing my cheeks as I slide back up. I meet his gaze as I run my tongue along the underside of his cock, sucking on his frenulum.

His composure cracks, naked lust evident in every tortured line on his face. The broken moan that escapes his lips echoes through me, urging me higher. I take him in my mouth again, taking him as deep as he'll go, worshipping him.

"God, Charlie," he grunts, flexing his hips and making me gag. He struggles at his restraints as I take him in again, lightly scraping my teeth over him. One jerk and his wrists are free and he's wrapping my hair in his fists, pulling my head back. There's a feral look in his eyes, nostrils flared, chest heaving in and out. Fuck yes.

"My fucking turn," he growls, lifting me so my pussy is level with his mouth. He holds my gaze while dragging his tongue through my folds and over my clit. My body trembles, a whimper escaping my lips as he traces his fingers down my crack, slipping in to caress the sensitive skin there. I buck against his mouth, but he holds me still, pulling me in tighter, pulsing his tongue against my clit, alternating pressure with soft licks. Bringing me right to the edge and backing off until I'm begging him not to stop. He lowers me down his body until we're face-to-face, his gaze locked with mine. I cradle his face, pressing my lips to his. He smells like sex and lust and *me.* I moan as he pushes his tongue into my mouth, fucking me with it. I wiggle in his grip until he loosens his hold, then lower myself so his cock slides between my legs, the head nestled against my clit. I roll my hips over him, lifting up on my knees and positioning him at my entrance. We stay like that, frozen in time, both of us shaking with need. Then I sink down, impaling myself.

"God," he groans, his fingers digging into my hips. He slams into me once, twice, then hooks his leg through mine and flips me over onto my back. I lock my legs around him, trying to keep him inside me, but he pulls out, sucking first one nipple, then the other into his mouth. I arch against him, never wanting him to stop.

"You're so fucking sexy," he groans, running his hand along my waist and over my hips. He slams into me again, looking down at where we're joined. "Your pussy stretches so pretty for me," he rasps, running his thumbs along my pussy lips, then up to my clit, rolling it between his fingers. My back bows, my fingers scrambling for purchase on the bed. He pulls out, hooking his hands under my thighs and lifts my ass off the bed.

"Do you know what we forgot?" he breathes, grabbing the base of his cock and positioning it at the top of my ass crack.

"What?" I moan, trying to wiggle out of his grip and regain some control.

He bears down with his pelvis, his cock sliding up through my crack, catching against my puckered skin.

"The butt plug." He does a complicated maneuver, and suddenly, I'm face down on the bed, my knees under me, my ass in the air.

"I like you like this," he chuckles, his voice low and gravelly. "Willing and pliant and ready to do whatever the fuck I want as long as I allow you to cum."

The feminist in me wants to scream in protest, but he's right.

He straddles my legs, putting pressure on my lower back, tilting my pelvis to give him better access. He drags the head of his cock over me, back and forth, back and forth, until I'm trembling with need.

"Please," I whisper, so quiet I'm afraid he won't hear me.

He does.

He pushes into me slowly, a quarter inch at a time, until he bottoms out. I circle my hips, reaching between my legs and sliding my fingers over my clit as he pulls out and slams back in. When he pulls back again, I try to follow him with my body, but he pushes me to the bed, pulling my knees out from under me, so I'm lying flat on my stomach.

"So fucking needy," he groans, "I like it." He palms my ass, kneading and squeezing, his thumbs passing closer and closer to my core, and I can't help but angle my hips, opening myself to him.

"I wish you could see yourself, Charlie. Your sweet pussy is dripping for me, begging me to bury myself inside. Your perfect little asshole winks at me every time I get close." He grazes it with his thumbs and my insides seize, anticipation paralyzing me.

"You like that, don't you?" he breathes.

I moan, barely noticing when he leans over to grab something from the nightstand drawer.

"This will be cold for just a second," he murmurs. I flinch as his thumb slides down my crack, the lube easing the path. He circles and then slowly pushes against the ring of muscle. He grabs something from off the bed and I hear a low vibration. He lifts me slightly, positioning it against my clit.

I bite my lip, the vibe bringing me way too close to the edge. "Lach—"

He pushes his thumb against me again, breaching the muscle, and my focus shifts to relaxing my muscles to let him in.

"Does this feel okay?"

I nod, and he pushes in further, stopping to let me adjust. He pulls his thumb out, then pushes back in, my ass following his movements, my body begging for more. I rock against the vibe, toeing the line again. Lach pulls out and I hear a box opening, then a squirt of lube. "This one's a little bigger than last time. If it's too much we can stop."

I mumble my understanding, ready to say yes to anything if it means I get to cum. My squeak of surprise at the cold lube quickly turns into a low moan as he pushes the toy into me. He goes slow – in, out, in a little more, then out. After several times, the uncomfortable feeling dissipates and I push back against his hand, insisting on more.

"On your knees."

I pull my knees under me and he slips the toy in all the way to the base.

Fuckkk.

He massages my ass, his fingers trembling.

"Charlie—" Lach pleads, his voice ragged.

"Yes, Lach. Please," I beg for him to do something. Anything. I just need to cum.

He palms his cock, sliding it up my slit, nudging at my entrance. One hand flexes on my hip like he's trying to stop himself from taking what he wants.

"Goddamnit, Charlie," he rasps, his control snapping under the pressure. He rams into me, a low groan escaping my lips as my entire body goes limp. He lowers himself over me, each thrust stoking the fire impossibly higher.

"I'm too fucking close, Charlie," he mumbles into my hair as he pushes into me in one long, smooth stroke. He grabs the vibe and slides his hand underneath my body, holding it against my clit.

Oh fuck.

I push back as he thrusts into me, then tilt my pelvis as he pulls back, sliding my clit along the vibe. The sensation of fullness quickly goes from feeling strange to feeling really fucking good. He moans in my ear, that desperate sound of surrender shoving me violently over the edge.

62

I sink into the bed, not caring that my hair will leave a wet patch on the comforter. The fan blades turn slowly over my head, clicking quietly with each rotation. Lach dropped me off at the cottage early this morning and then left me with only a chaste kiss and a pat on my butt out of respect for Jack. I immediately stripped my clothes off and stepped into a scalding hot shower, my mind replaying last night on repeat.

"Charlie!" Isla yells through the front door, banging her boot against it.

I sit up, wrapping my towel tightly around me, and pull open the door. Isla, the godsend she is, stands there with a bottle of wine in one hand and a bag of to-go boxes in the other.

"You're a goddamn angel," I say, taking the wine from her and grabbing two glasses from the kitchen.

"So how'd it go?" she asks, pouring the wine.

"Good," I say, a grin stretching across my face. "*Really* good."

"Details, Charlie! I need details!" she squeals, dragging me to the couch. She pops the lids off two containers, giving me a choice between bangers and mash and chips. I choose the fish after she assures me that she has no preference.

"He took me out on the boat," I begin, popping a piece of fish into my mouth, trying to figure out how much to tell her. "We went to a cave first, and then we stopped at Pen's pub for dinner."

"You got to see Pen?" she asks, pouting her lips. "I miss her so much. She's been so busy with the pub she never has time to get together anymore."

"She's quite the character, isn't she?" I ask, chuckling as I take a sip of my wine.

"She really is," Isla says, laughing. "Did you get to see the *Master Baiter*?"

"No, but I about died laughing when I heard the name. Speaking of which, I have to tell you about Pen and dessert."

"Oooh, juicy gossip?" she asks hopefully, rubbing her hands together.

"Maybe? Lach and I met her new crew members and brought them to the pub with us for a beer—"

"Wait," Isla interrupts, "where did you meet them?" she asks, confused.

My cheeks flush as I think back to that knock on the bathroom door. "Well," I clear my throat uncomfortably, "Lach and I were – using the facilities – and one of the crewmembers *also* needed to use the facilities."

"Ah," Isla says, her brow wrinkled. "Wait, what?"

I blow out a long breath through pursed lips, trying to decide how to say this delicately. Why not just go for it, right? "Lach and I were fucking in the bathroom of the abandoned fish shack near the pub. The guys came in to use the bathroom," I blurt, the words tumbling from my mouth.

Her jaw drops. "Please don't tell me your first time with the Lach was in the bathroom of that fucking shack," she grimaces.

"I know! I know! It sounds gross, but God, it was perfect," I say, dreamily. "I might still have a couple splinters in my back."

"You're so weird."

"There was a remote-control vibrator involved, so I can't be held accountable for the decisions I made during that period of time," I say, holding up my hands.

"Well, that makes a whole lot more sense. I'm surprised you didn't do it in the middle of the pub," she says, laughing, "Go on with your story."

"We brought the crew with us for a beer – an apology of sorts – and I saw the moment Pen laid eyes on them. And you should have seen how they were looking at her! I thought Lach was going to leap over the table and strangle them."

"She has a new crew every season," Isla says, confused, "Is there something different about this season?"

"Judging by the way she acted, I'm guessing so."

"So, I'm guessing they're not grizzly guys in their fifties and sixties?"

I laugh at that. "No, absolutely not. Every single one of them looks like they belong in the pages of an Eddie Bauer catalog. They're rough, rugged, and really fucking good-looking".

"Lord have mercy," Isla says, fanning herself, "Maybe she'll leave one for me."

"What about those guys that came into the pub the other night?"

Isla shrugs. "What's the point when they have to return to the US?"

"It could've been fun for a little while at least," I say, refilling our wine glasses.

She wrinkles her nose. "I get attached too easily. Last thing I need is to be wrapped up in a long-distance relationship when I'm trying to run a pub. Has Jack told you his plans for tomorrow?" she asks, changing the subject.

I shake my head. "I haven't talked to him since he dropped me off at the marina yesterday morning."

"Hey!" she shrieks, making me jump. "What's on your finger?" She pulls my hand close to her face. "Did he propose to you?" she asks, looking at me and then back down at the ring. "He fucking proposed to you!" She pulls me into a hug, her arms cutting off my air supply.

"Oh my God, Charlie! I'm so happy for you! Do Cam and Jack know yet?"

"I have no idea. I haven't had a chance to talk to them yet, and Lach didn't tell me if he had discussed it with them beforehand."

"This will be interesting," she says, laughing like an evil villain at the prospect of drama.

"I'm more worried about Cam feeling left out, but I'm thinking of proposing to him this weekend. Is that crazy?"

"Not crazy!" she gushes, bouncing up and down in her seat, "It's perfect! That way, he knows he's special to you and won't feel like he's the third wheel—well, the fourth wheel in your case."

I scrub my hands over my face, trying to stave off the sleepiness that comes from a full stomach and sleepless night. "I'll have to try to find a ring on Friday. Do you know where I can get something he'd like for cheap? I don't have a ton of money to spend."

"I have off tomorrow – why don't you let me find it for you?"

"Really? You'd do that for me?" Tears well in my eyes, exhaustion heightening my emotions.

"Of course! Just tell me what you want. I can send pictures, so you're picking it, not me."

I give it some thought, trying to imagine what he'd like. "It has to be old and have some cool history behind it, something that would mean a lot to him."

"Old. Check." She makes a checkmark on an imaginary list. "What else?"

"Something he can wear when he's out in the field – I don't want him to worry that it'll get ruined."

"Got it," she says, grinning. "This is the most excitement I've had in years." She slaps her knees and stands up. "Okay, I hate to run, but I have to head to work soon. Make sure you get some sleep."

"I'll try," I promise.

"Oh, I almost forgot, I brought you some beef stew for dinner. You just need to heat it on the stove." She hands me one last to-go box.

"How will I ever thank you, Isla?" I ask, my chin wobbling. "You have no idea how much your friendship means to me."

"As long as you're there for me when I finally find my man, we'll call it even," she says, pulling me into a tight hug.

"Only one man?" I tease, sniffling.

"I can barely handle one – I don't know how I would ever manage more," she says, making a face at the thought of it. She stands up and throws her food container in the trash. "Gotta run. I hope tomorrow goes exactly how you've always hoped... and that's all I'm gonna say because he's my brother, and it's gross."

"Thank you. Have a good night at work." Nerves set in as I close the door after her. I think about Jack, his muscled arms, his sexy tattoos. Heat blooms through my body, forcing me to shut down that line of thinking. Instead, I pull the curtains in my bedroom closed, falling asleep quickly only to dream about sweaty bodies and tangled limbs.

I wake several hours later to a text message from Jack:

Make sure you rest up tonight, mo chridhe. You'll need your energy for tomorrow. Sweet dreams.

Butterflies fill my stomach. I wonder what he has planned. Fucking me in every room in the castle like he told me before? God, I hope so.

63

I wake to Jack sliding into bed with me, wrapping the covers around us like a cocoon to keep in the heat.

"Fuck, you're warm," he murmurs, his lips moving against my neck. He wraps his arms around my waist and pulls me flush against his body, the heady scents of whisky and leather taking over my senses.

"Why do you smell so *good*?" I ask sleepily, burrowing my face into his shoulder and breathing deeply.

"Probably the beard oil Lorna makes for me."

"Don't ever change it," I whisper, pressing my lips to his skin. I blink, my eyelids heavy, and begin to drowse off when the reality of today slams into me like a freight train. Adrenaline floods my veins, making my heart race. His callouses leave a delicious trail of fire as he flattens his palm over my stomach, fingers spanning from my rib cage to the crease of my thigh. I suck in a breath when his thumb grazes the underside of my breast, my nipples greedy for his touch.

"Your heart's beating like a hummingbird," he murmurs, pressing a kiss to my pulse, sucking the delicate skin into his mouth. Groaning, I drop my head to the side to give him better access. He flexes his hips against my backside, and I push back, grinding against him.

"Charlotte," he groans, his voice rough, "If we don't get out of bed now, I'll keep you here for the next twenty-four hours. Longer if you'll let me."

"And how is that a bad thing?" I ask, turning in his arms. Golden eyes search mine, drinking me in, a smile pulling at his lips. There's a roughness about him – a raw sensuality – that has me curling my toes, desire engulfing me like an uncontrollable wildfire.

"It's not," he chuckles, tucking a strand of hair behind my ear, then running the back of his fingers over my cheek in a soft caress. "Except for the fact that I'll have some calls to make to cancel our plans."

"What kind of plans?" I ask, doubtful that anything could rank higher than staying in bed with him for the entire day.

"First, I'm making you breakfast. After that, I thought we could finally take that tour of the farm I promised you since we were interrupted the last time we tried," he says, his eyes losing focus as he thinks back to that day at the stone circle. "God, that was so fucking hot. Feeling your body move like that—" he groans.

He licks his lips, and that's all it takes for me to imagine them pressed against me. I squeeze my thighs together, attempting to stifle the insistent heartbeat that's taken residence between my legs.

"And after that?" I ask, my voice unsteady.

"I have a chef scheduled to give us a cooking lesson – then we'll eat what we make for dinner."

"That sounds fun," I concede, "What are we cooking?" My stomach rumbles right on cue.

"We'll have to talk about it and decide on something so he can go grocery shopping. Any ideas?" Jack asks, running his hand along the dip of my waist and then over the swell of my hip, my breath hitching as he slides it back up, grazing the side of my breast.

"I'll have to think about it," I muse when an idea doesn't come to me right away. "Anything after that?" I ask, lightly running my fingertip over the tattoo on his bicep, keeping my hand busy so I don't reach down and grab his cock.

"And then I fuck you in every room until you cum," he says,

palming one of my ass cheeks and pulling me roughly against him. "Oh, and there's a surprise waiting for you somewhere in the castle."

"Like a scavenger hunt?" I ask, wondering what the surprise is. "Is it—"

"You'll never guess," he says, cutting me off, "Don't even try."

"I honestly think that's the only thing you could have said that would have been able to get me out of this bed," I laugh, sitting up and stretching. His gaze slides down my body eagerly, snagging on my pebbled nipples and exposed midriff. He cups my breast and rolls my nipple between his fingers.

"Fucking hell, Charlotte," he says hoarsely, propping himself on his elbow before lifting my shirt and taking my nipple into his mouth. I arch against him, pushing my fingers into the hair at the nape of his neck and pulling him against me. He cups my throat with his fingers and pushes me down to the pillows, covering my body with his. He catches my lower lip between his teeth before dragging me into a scorching open-mouthed kiss. I twine my legs around his hips, rocking my hips against him, whimpering as desire engulfs me.

"I want to rip those goddamn shorts off your body and fuck you until you're screaming," he rasps, swiveling his hips against me. "I want to lick your pussy, and make you cum until my name is the only word you can remember. I want to squeeze these perfect tits together and fuck them until I'm begging you to let me cum in your mouth." He trails kisses from my neck to my nipple, sucking it deep into his mouth until my back bows off the bed, then he does the same to the other one. "But for right now, what I really want to do, is make you breakfast," he chuckles, rolling off of me, holding out his hand to help me up.

"God, you're such a tease," I grumble, climbing off the bed.

"You like it," he chuckles, sliding a hand down the back of my shorts to cup my ass. He can't resist reaching lower, his finger gliding over my pussy without resistance. He groans, sinking his finger inside me before sliding it up to circle my clit.

I jerk against his hand, sinking my nails into his shoulder when my knees start to give out.

"I have to fucking taste you," he growls, desperation in his voice.

I'll spend my whole life thinking about what Jack does next. He wrenches my shorts apart with impatient hands, ripping until the only thing left intact is the elastic waistband. He reaches between my legs with both arms, planting a hand on each butt cheek before lifting me, bringing my legs over his shoulders. He presses me to the wall, holding me there, my pussy right at mouth-level.

I look down at him as he breathes me in, his mouth open and nostrils flared. "Is this all for me, mo chridhe?" he asks, running his tongue along my slit to catch the moisture gathered there, lapping me up like ice cream. I squirm against him, trying to angle my hips so his mouth is on my clit, but he only presses me against the wall harder.

"Stay still," he growls before covering me with his mouth, fucking me with his tongue. I choke out a sob when he focuses his attention higher, sealing his lips around my clit and sucking.

I buck against him when he doesn't let up. "It's too much," I gasp, trying to twist away from him.

"No, it's fucking not, but it's about to be," he says gruffly, a wicked smile pulling at his lips. He shifts some of my weight to his left side and brings his right hand between us, sinking his thumb into me. His golden eyes trap me in their depths as he circles my asshole with his pointer finger. He holds my gaze as he seals his lips around me again, creating suction with his mouth that has me sobbing his name. I'm already on the edge when he pushes his finger past that tight ring of muscle, the added sensation shoving me over. I fist my hands in his hair, squeezing his head between my thighs, and ride his face, screaming his name as I cum.

64

———

Jack waits for the tremors to stop before lowering me down his body. I wrap my legs around his waist, his beard scratchy against my fingers as I pull him in for a heated taste. His taste melds with mine, stirring a possessiveness I didn't know existed inside me.

"Where are you taking me?" I squeak as he hoists me up and walks out of the bedroom, my bare backside exposed to the chilly morning air.

"I'm making you breakfast," he says with determination.

"Clothes would be nice," I suggest, chill bumps already racing their way over my body.

"Clothes are for pussies." He sets me down, bare-assed, on the counter.

"Exactly. My pussy would like some clothing, please. Plus," I say, "This is super unhygienic."

"There's this stuff called soap," he says, squirting some into his palm, "and hot water." He scrubs his hands and rinses them off under the steaming tap. "I promise I'll wash the counter after breakfast," he says, winking. "But right now, I want you naked."

I can't think of a retort, so I clamp my mouth shut, stiffening my body against the shiver that wraps around my torso.

Jack narrows his eyes at me, walks to the family room, and comes back with a fluffy blanket. He wraps it tightly around my shoulders, holding the ends at my neck.

"Your eyes remind me of the ocean," he murmurs, tracing my eyebrows with his thumb. I smile up at him, my heart in my throat. He splays his hand over my throat, the tips of his fingers on my jaw, and pushes my chin up, holding my gaze as he lowers his lips to mine. The kiss is tentative at first, leisurely exploring my lips before sliding his tongue over the seam of my mouth, asking me to open for him. He groans when I let him in, angling my head so he can deepen the kiss. We don't come up until we're both gasping for air, desperate for each other.

"Fuck," Jack breathes, pressing his forehead to mine. "I'm starting to think I planned all that for nothing. I don't know how we'll ever make it out of here when all I can think about is how your pussy will look when it's stretched by my cock."

"Ah, ah ah!" I scold, pushing him away with a light touch on his shoulder, pretending his words didn't just release a flood between my legs. "You can't get out of that surprise now that you've told me about it."

"Are you sure?" he asks, sliding his hand up my thigh, stopping just short of my weeping pussy. He squeezes my leg, massaging me, waiting for my answer. I'm not capable of a coherent response. I want him to take me to the bedroom and fuck my brains out, but we've been waiting a long time for this, and I want it to be perfect.

"I'm sure," I say finally, prying his hand away from my thigh. As he moves, his arm brushes against his cock, making it bob, the outline clear as day in those sinful gray joggers. All of my previous conviction flies out the window. I wrap my fingers around him, sliding my hand down his length.

"Charlie," Jack hisses, the warning in his voice unmistakable.

"Let me take care of that for you," I say, biting my lip and giving him my best puppy dog eyes.

"In you?" he asks, pulling my hand away and pressing his swollen cock between my thighs.

"In me," I say, pointing to my mouth, gasping as he rolls over my clit.

He nods once, and that's all the permission I need. I hop off the counter and drag a chair in from the family room. I push him onto it, feeling powerful as I stand over him, his gaze roaming over my body. I motion for him to lift his arms and pull off his shirt, moaning at the expanse of warm muscle that comes into view. He lunges forward, wrapping his arms around my hips and sucking one of my nipples into his mouth. He palms the back of my thighs and pulls me over him as he leans back, my legs hanging on either side of him, his cock nestled against my pussy. I swivel my hips with a groan, my heartbeat taking up residence in my clit.

"Jack," I protest, his name coming out more like a prayer than a protest.

"Say it again," he groans, grasping my hips and sliding me along his length. I jerk as his head rides over my clit, and he pauses there, pulsing against me until I have to climb off him before I cum again. I grab the jar of coconut oil from the cabinet by the oven and set it next to the chair. Kneeling between his spread legs, I hold his gaze as I lean down and nibble at the ridge of his cock through his pants.

"Charlotte," he warns, his hips jerking against my mouth.

"Yes?" I tease, hooking my fingers into his waistband. Folding his arms behind his head, he watches me with dark eyes. I pull down the front of his joggers inch by inch, the anticipation building until the only sound in the room is our labored breathing. My mouth is practically watering as I reveal the last of his thick shaft, the elastic of the waistband stretching over his head. He springs out, a deep groan tearing out of both of us as his length comes to rest against his thigh. I forgot how big he is. I want him so fucking badly. I want to feel him stretch me, use me, fuck me. I blow out a controlled breath through pursed lips, trying to get myself under control.

"You want me inside you, don't you?" he rasps, palming his cock and holding it in position. All I have to do is stand up and straddle him. He must see the indecision in my eyes because he starts stroking himself, flexing his hips each time his hand slides down his shaft. I whimper, fighting against my body's instincts.

I steel my shoulders. "My turn," I say, batting his hand away.

"Yes, ma'am," he chuckles, the sound sliding down my spine and stoking the fire in my core. I warm the oil in my hands, rubbing them together before sliding down his length in one firm stroke.

His head falls back, the sound that leaves his lips barely sounding human. He pulls his hips back and thrusts back up into my fist.

"You gave me an idea earlier," I whisper, smearing the oil from my other hand over my chest and breasts. Jack bites his lower lip as I shuffle as close as possible, settling him between my tits before enveloping him with slippery softness.

"Charlotte, I—"

"Can't be gentle?" I finish, bending to give him a playful lick. "I've heard that somewhere before, and I'm pretty sure I told you I don't want you to be gentle." I slide my body down, keeping pressure on him, then slide back up until the head of his cock disappears between my breasts. He doesn't move other than the slightest rocking of his hips. I hold his gaze as I sink down again, biting my lip in concentration, trying to live up to his fantasy. He still holds back.

"For fuck's sake," I mutter, grabbing his hands and smashing them against my breasts, hoping it will be enough to breach his control.

"I won't fucking break, Jack."

He looks at me, vulnerable. "Are you sure you won't run when you see the real me, Sassenach?"

"I already know the real you. You're a teddy bear with a control fetish."

"Teddy bear, hm?" Jack says, his eyes darkening even more, his gaze dropping to his imprisoned cock. He thrusts hard, his jaw clenched, desperate need finally showing in his eyes. Another thrust and his hips stutter against me, his breathing ragged.

"Stand up," I say, the need to taste him gripping me around the throat.

"Charlotte—"

"Stand up," I insist.

He stands, his cock bobbing against my cheek.

"Look at me," I command and he dips his chin, meeting my gaze. "I want to give you pleasure just as much as you want to give me pleasure, Jack. Let me." I take him in my hand, reveling in the sheer size of him, pumping him once before swirling my tongue over his head and taking him in my mouth.

He groans, a broken, defeated sound, his fingers caressing my face before finding their place in my hair. I keep my hand on him, focusing on his head until his hands tremble against me. I move one hand to his balls, gently massaging them as I bury his cock in my throat, taking him in until I can't breathe.

"Fuck, Charlotte," he rasps, on the cusp of surrendering. His fingers tense, tightening over my head, guiding me. The only warning I get is his hips jerking back before he sinks into me, bottoming out. I hum my approval, my eyes watering. I take a deep breath as he pulls out, swallowing around him as he thrusts again.

"Get up," he says roughly, grabbing my hands and pulling me up despite my protests. He steps out of his joggers and pulls me to the bedroom, stopping in front of the full-length mirror. His lips crash against mine, his tongue insistent in its exploration. "Turn," he says raggedly, grasping my hips and turning me, then walking me toward the mirror. "Cross your legs and push your ass back toward me," he demands.

"What?" I ask, confused.

"For the love of God, Charlie. I want us to get there together, but I am not fucking you yet. Cross your damn legs."

I cross my legs, looking at him in the mirror for reassurance. He's sliding his hand up and down his cock, tattoos rippling in the morning sunlight streaming through the window. His hair is falling around his face, golden brown waves framing whisky eyes that will haunt my dreams for the rest of my life. My stomach clenches with desire as he steps closer, positioning his cock between my legs.

"God, I can already feel how wet you are," he groans, gripping my hips and angling them how he wants. "Don't fucking move," he growls, moving his left arm to my chest, his hand at my throat. He's looking at me in the mirror, and I see the exact moment his control snaps. He thrusts, sliding along my slit until I can see the head of his cock between my legs. Then he pulls back, the ridge catching on my clit.

"Oh fuck," I sob, my hips jerking at the overstimulation.

He growls, thrusting again, this time pulsing his head over my clit until I'm, writhing in his arms.

"Push your hips back a little more," he murmurs, guiding me, reducing the chance of accidental penetration.

Two more thrusts and I'm jerking against him uncontrollably, watching his cum hit the glass as my orgasm rips through me like a tsunami.

65

"That was not part of my fucking plan," Jack grumbles, squatting in front of the mirror while he wipes it down, holding my gaze in the reflection.

"Oh yeah?" I smirk. "You have a *fucking* plan?"

He stands and turns toward me, a lion stalking its prey. "I *planned* to seduce you for the entire day until we couldn't stand it anymore."

"Well, to be fair, I don't think we could have lasted much longer. At least we made it an hour," I say, grinning as he cups my cheek, a smile playing over his lips.

"Come on, let's go get breakfast." He scoops me up and walks me to the counter, placing me back where we had started. He grabs the blanket that's now puddled on the floor and tucks it around me.

The light from the fridge highlights his features as he rifles through the groceries he brought with him that morning. "We have options," he says, looking over at me, "Pancakes or French toast?"

"French toast," I say without hesitation.

"Good choice. Bacon or sausage?"

"Bacon, but it has to be crispy."

"Noted. How do you like your eggs? Scrambled with cheese, over easy, sunny side up?"

"I like them all the ways." I shrug. "You choose." Jack thinks for a second, then starts piling food in his arms and carries it to the counter.

"Don't worry, I didn't forget about the coffee," he says, giving me an adorable wink as he starts the coffee maker.

I could get used to this. A super hot (almost) naked guy making me breakfast in the morning? Yes, please. And someone that gives me two orgasms before said breakfast? *Fuck yes.*

"Is there something else you'd rather do other than touring the farm today?" Jack asks, his muscles flexing as he whisks the batter for the French toast.

"No. I *want* to see the farm. I want to see what you do all day, every day. I want to hear all the stories about your parents and grandparents. Stories about little Jack growing up here." His cheeks flush, but instead of turning to hide it from me, he sets down his bowl and wraps his arms around me.

"I fucking love the way you love me," he says, his voice raw. "I hope I'm doing a good job of loving you back." I pull back slightly, startled by his words, cupping his face between my hands, and making him meet my gaze.

"You love me in a way nobody ever has before," I tell him, "You just have to promise me it will always stay like this. That we'll communicate and work through our problems."

"I promise," he whispers, brushing his lips over mine, the touch tender and poignant. "Fuck." He presses his forehead to mine, golden eyes pinning me in place. "I don't think I've ever felt this way before. Like I wrenched my heart out of my chest and placed it in your hands. It's terrifying."

"How do you think I feel? I have three chances to get my heart broken instead of just one." Just the thought of it starts the panic rising.

"You have zero chances of getting your heart broken, Sassenach. We were lost without you." My stomach chooses that second to rumble loudly. Jack chuckles, patting it gently, "Food is coming soon," he promises. I can't help but smack his ass as he turns back toward the stove, his joggers leaving absolutely nothing to the imagination.

I swear to God, this is the best breakfast I've ever eaten. The French toast is perfect, the bacon is crispy, and the eggs are cheesy and delicious. When we finish, he tells me to get dressed while he cleans up, refusing my offer of help. I spend a good ten minutes trying to decide what to wear before I finally land on jeans and an off-the-shoulder sweater – casual enough for a farm tour but still allows me to feel cute. I swipe on some mascara and lip gloss and then attempt to make my hair look nice, but I give up and throw it into the usual messy bun. Jack's sitting on the couch, a flannel over his t-shirt, hair pulled back, tapping away on his phone when I come out of the bedroom.

"Before we go, we need to confirm our plans for tonight with the chef. Is there anything, in particular, you're in the mood for or something you'd like to learn how to cook?"

I think about it for a second, racking my brain for an idea, but come up empty.

"Same," he says when I shake my head. "I'll stick with my original idea. It was the sexiest thing I could think of for a romantic evening—"

"Okay, okay!" I say, cutting him off and covering my ears. "Don't tell me anymore, I want it to be a surprise!"

He zips his mouth closed, his eyes sparkling, and shoots off one last text before pocketing his phone. "Ready?"

"Let's go," I say, excited to get the rest of the day started. I grab my jacket from the back of the couch and put all my weight into pulling open the front door.

"I'll get that fixed for you," he says, "although I *do* enjoy watching you try to open and close it. Especially the way it makes your tits jiggle."

"You jerk!" I fold my arms over my breasts, making a face at him, trying to keep the grin off my face. I fail miserably. He puts his hand in the back pocket of my jeans as we walk up the path, like he can't stand the thought of not touching me. I would have thought that was incredibly annoying just a few months ago. But *now*? Now I can't stand the thought of not touching him either. He hands me the motorcycle helmet when we reach the driveway, kicks up the kickstand, and gets on, motioning for me to sit behind him. I don't hesitate this time.

The ride to the castle is way too short. I'm finally comfortable enough to enjoy his warmth against the front of my body and the spectacular views as we make our way around the shore of the loch. He pulls in by the main entrance and cuts the engine, kicking down the stand, sliding off the motorcycle, and getting back on facing me. He flips up my visor, and suddenly, I feel like I'm in a fucking movie: a castle behind me, a motorcycle underneath me, and one of the hottest guys I've ever seen looking at me like I hung the moon.

"God, you look so fucking cute with the helmet," he grins. "We have one more decision to make; there are several ways of doing the farm tour. We can take the motorcycle and stick to the roads, take the truck and go off-road a little, or I have a utility vehicle that will allow us to go wherever we want; it's a bumpy ride, though."

"The utility vehicle," I respond. "I want to see everything."

"Good choice." He pulls the helmet from my head, and helps me fix my hair, tucking it behind my ears. "I'm looking forward to growing old with you, mo chridhe."

My heart clenches, the tenderness in his words chipping away at the last bit of wall still standing around my heart.

"You'll still love me when I'm old and wrinkled?" I ask. "When age spots pepper my skin and my boobs are down to my belly button?"

"I'll love you even more," he rasps, sliding his hand around my neck and pulling my mouth to his. He groans, pulling away and adjusting himself. "Let's go before I drag you inside and never let you leave."

"That sounds nice," I murmur, taking his hand as he helps me off the bike.

"Does it now?" he says, laughing.

I lean against him, pushing up on my tip toes to kiss him. "*Really* nice," I say against his lips, palming his cock and squeezing lightly.

"Nice try," he growls, grabbing me around the waist and swinging me over his shoulder.

I have severe regrets as he walks toward the barn, my full stomach pressing into his shoulder, but as I watch the round globes of his ass move back and forth, I have to admit that the view is spectacular.

66

———

Jack grins like an idiot as he hands me a helmet, making me nervous. Did I make the wrong decision? I should have played it safe and told him I wanted to do the tour in the truck. I pull the helmet over my head, wincing as I think about what my hair will look like this evening.

"Come on, get in," Jack says, chuckling when he sees my hesitation. "I'll go easy on you."

"I never said I wanted you to go easy on me," I say. "In fact, I'm pretty sure I said the exact opposite."

"Aye, that you did," he rumbles, a twinkle in his eye. He checks to ensure I'm safely inside before closing the door and double-checking that it's secure. He walks around to the other side and climbs in, his head almost touching the roll bar above us, his hands making the steering wheel look like a toy car. My gaze follows the veins from his fingers over the back of his hand and up his forearms. I clear my throat and shift in my seat, squeaking when he grips my knee, sliding his hand up to the top of my thigh and squeezing. My knees open on their own as his hand travels higher, and I slam them closed, but not before his pinkie brushes against me, lighting me up.

"Ready?" he asks, chuckling.

"Always," I murmur, checking that my seatbelt is locked in place. Jack presses the pedal to the floor, and we peel away from the barn, mud and rock flying out behind us as we skid out. He whips the wheel around to straighten us out, and then we're flying over the field, my butt flying out of my seat with every bump.

"Is this made to take this kind of abuse?" I ask, my teeth knocking together, my knuckles white as I hang on for dear life.

"It can take way more than these little bumps," he laughs, his attention snagging on my breasts, jiggling like Jell-O under my sweater. "I think we're going to have to do this more often," he says, winking, his lips twisting as he tries to hold back his smile.

"I'm wearing a sports bra if there's a next time," I say, grimacing as I cup my hands over my boobs and hold them in place.

"Why don't I do that for you? You can steer," he suggests, wiggling his eyebrows. And that's when it happens. He's concentrating on my tits and doesn't see the giant mud puddle in front of us. He tries to avoid it at the last minute, but it's too late, the muddy water drenching us from head to toe.

"Fuck, I'm sorry," he says, stricken, pulling to a stop. I look over at him, the streaks of mud on his cheek, down his shirt and pants.

"Again," I laugh, wiping mud from under his eye. All I can think about is how we'll clean this mud off later. Hopefully, it will involve us being naked. Together.

The farm tour turns into three hours of mudding. It's the most fun I've had in years – maybe ever. The second Jack notices me shivering, he turns back toward the barn. Then he's by my side, pulling off my helmet and drawing me into a gritty, muddy kiss.

"Thank you," I whisper, wrapping my arms around his neck and giving him a tight hug.

"For what?" he asks, taking my hand and pulling me toward the castle.

"For the tour," I say, smiling up at him. "I had a lot of fun." He looks down at me, a light blush staining his cheeks. God, I want to see him blush like that in the bedroom.

"My pleasure, mo chridhe. We better get washed up before the chef comes," he says, attempting to brush the mud off his clothes before we step inside.

"I forgot to bring a change of clothes," I groan, mentally cursing myself.

"No worries, I have a robe you can use," Jack says, leading me down the hallway.

"You want me to wear a robe while we cook dinner?"

"I will if you will," he says, a dare in his eyes.

I imagine him in a robe. Easy access to all that warm skin and muscle. Easy access to *everything*.

"Deal."

Jack opens a carved wooden door, and a gust of steam billows out, enveloping us. The entire room is covered in marble, including the sunken pool in the middle of the floor.

"Holy shit," I breathe, looking around in awe. "What is this place?" I ask, looking back at Jack, the flickering light from the wall sconces bathing him in a golden glow.

"Isla and I think it used to be the bathing chamber for the lady of the house," Jack says, encouraging me inside with a hand on the small of my back. "Once upon a time it was filled by a hot spring, but that dried up years ago. My parents had it plumbed when I was little. We would come in here, spread out a picnic on the side, and swim and splash while we ate."

He shakes himself out of the memory, shrugging off his flannel and letting it puddle on the floor. Grabbing the hem of his t-shirt, he pulls it over his head in one swift motion.

I can't move. Can't even breathe.

The humidity beads on his skin, tiny droplets caressing the ridges of his muscles before they disappear into the waistband of his pants. I bend and catch one with my tongue, licking up over his ribs and chest, swirling my tongue around his nipple. I straighten, pulling off my sweater and dropping it on top of his clothes. His eyes are molten lava, an inferno of tension burning between us. I hook my fingers in the waistband of his joggers and push them down over his ass so they fall to the floor.

"Much better," I breathe, closing the distance between us. I pull him against me, his cock hard against my stomach. He pushes a strand of hair out of my face and tilts my chin, pressing a kiss to my lips. His callouses scrape my skin as he smooths his hands down my arms, over my waist, fumbling with the button of my jeans before helping me take them off. We shed our underwear, and then we're yelling as we plunge into the pool together.

Jack backs me against the ledge, his hands tangling in my hair as he angles my head and plunders my mouth. When we're both out of breath, he kisses my neck, licking and biting down to my clavicle. He cups my breast rolling my nipple between his fingers, a groan from deep in his throat lodging in my core like a poker, stoking the fire impossibly higher.

I hoist myself onto the ledge, and it becomes clear that this room was not made with only women in mind – Jack's cock is exactly level with my pussy.

"Fuck," Jack whispers, his gaze pausing between my open legs before traveling up my body. "Charlotte," he says, his voice rough, "Lay on your stomach with your legs in the water. I want to eat you out without worrying about you being uncomfortable."

How could I refuse when he asked so nicely? I flip over, letting my legs dangle in the water, resting my cheek on my folded arms, the tile cold under my hands. He slides his palms over the flare of my hips to my ass, kneading my cheeks, pulling them apart. He walks to the side of the pool and lathers soap in his hands, comes back and begins washing me, carefully avoiding the sensitive bits. The slap of water between my legs makes me jump.

"What are you doing?" I ask, him looking back at him.

"Washing my dinner," he rasps. I choke back a laugh, but it quickly becomes a moan as he kneels behind me, his hands spreading me apart, his tongue rolling against my clit. He stops when I start bucking against his mouth, dragging his tongue up through my folds, then higher, circling my asshole. I jerk in surprise, not sure how I feel about it, but then he pushes two fingers into me, massaging my g-spot, his thumb circling my clit.

Oh fuck.

I ride his hand, his tongue dipping in and out of me as I move. How can something feel so wrong and so fucking good at the same time? I bite the base of my thumb to keep in a scream and push my ass toward him even more. I pull my legs up, my knees splayed on the ledge, opening myself and giving him everything. He groans against me, the sound vibrating against my skin.

"Charlotte, if I get my cock in you, I think I might die," he pants, pressing his forehead against the base of my spine, his breath hot and heavy on my skin.

"Then do it," I say, encouraging him. He stands up and lifts me by the waist, turning me around to face him.

"I don't want to yet," he says, his jaw clenched. He looks down at my pussy, and I look down at his cock, focusing on the two inches separating us. "Fuck," he groans, "I have to feel you." He takes his cock in his hand, stroking it several times and then meets my gaze. "Just the tip," he says, his voice ragged. "Only the tip, do you understand?" I bite my lip, nodding. He drags the head of his cock over me, positioning himself at my entrance and holding himself there.

"You're so fucking wet," he groans, sliding his thumbs over where the lips of my pussy stretch around his cock. I angle my hips, but he pulls away, making me promise not to do it again before he comes back.

We're both looking at how his cock is nestled between my lips, our breathing unsteady, barely able to form a coherent thought. He flexes his hips until a fraction of the tip is inside me. I whimper, desperately wanting to wrap my legs around him and pull him toward me, forcing him to slam in deep.

Jack pushes in a little more, clenching his jaw as I squeeze around him. One more tiny push and the head of his cock slips in completely, coming to rest against my g-spot.

An alarm clock sounds, the noise muffled by our pile of clothes.

"Fuck. Fifteen minutes until dinner."

67

"Fuck," Jack mutters, his jaw flexing as the alarm bounces off the walls around us. His eyes are locked between my legs, his hands trembling on my hips as he struggles for control. My gaze travels down his torso, over the length of his cock, to my engorged pussy lips hugging his shaft. I whimper, desperate for him to bury himself inside me. His gaze meets mine, regret written all over his face.

"Jack, no," I beg. He groans, his expression pained as he slowly withdraws. My body follows him, my hip sliding along the stone to keep him in me for as long as possible.

"Charlotte, I don't want to keep the chef waiting."

"I know," I whimper.

He studies my face. "You're close?"

I nod, protesting as he pulls out, barely keeping myself in check.

"Lay down, he says gruffly, helping me lower myself against the cold marble. He grabs my thighs and pulls me toward him so my ass is on the pool's edge. He stands there, looking between my thighs, his hands shaking as he drags his thumbs up my pussy, meeting at the top of my vulva, trapping my clit between his thumbs. My moans echo around us, melding with the sound of the alarm.

"I love the way you move when I touch you," Jack groans, watching my body as I respond to his touch. He brushes his thumb over my clit and I jerk against him.

I'm so close.

"Fuck," he growls, finally giving in. He bends down and presses his open mouth against me, his tongue dipping inside before sliding up to circle my clit. Over and over again until my fingers tangle in his hair and I'm begging him for more. He looks up at me as he slowly drags his teeth over that aching bundle of nerves, a wicked gleam in his eyes. I lose my grip on reality as he seals his lips around my clit, sucking me into his mouth. I scream as he pushes in two fingers, curling them against my g-spot.

"Jack, that makes me feel like I have to pee," I say urgently, trying to twist away from him.

"You won't," Jack growls, holding me in place. "Cum for me, Charlotte." He pulses his tongue over me, and the current drags me under, the pressure building to impossible heights. He feels me tense and pulses the suction, pushing harder against my g-spot. My back bows off the floor as my orgasm rips through me, waves of pleasure pulsating through my body. I clamp my legs around his head, holding him there, riding his face and fingers until the sensation is too much and I try to push him away.

"I'm not stopping until you cum all over my face, Charlotte. I want to drown in you." He brings his other hand up, one finger sliding through my moisture and then circling my asshole. He pushes against that tight ring of muscle, slowly pushing up to his first knuckle.

"You're so fucking tight, Charlotte," he grunts, pulling out and pushing it a little more. He groans as he sucks me back into his mouth, the vibrations catapulting me over the edge. I scream his name as he pushes all the way in, his other hand working at my g-spot. I dig my heels into his shoulders, tears leaking from my eyes as my world splinters. He wrings every last drop of pleasure out of me until I lie boneless on the cold marble floor.

"Fucking hell," Jack rasps, splashing water over his face. "I don't think I have ever wanted to fuck somebody as much as I want to fuck you right now," he says roughly, grasping my neck and pulling me into a heated kiss. He pushes himself up on the ledge and climbs out of the water, holding his hands down to help me up.

True to his word, Jack produces two fluffy robes for us to wear to dinner. We pad down the hallway, our feet bare and hair dripping.

We walk into the kitchen to find Greer behind the counter, prepping food. "Greer! I didn't know it would be you!" I say, giving her a tight hug. "If Jack had told me that, I wouldn't have kept you waiting."

"Then I'm glad I didn't tell you," Jack chuckles, winking at Greer.

"It's good to see you again, Charlie," Greer says, sweeping my wet hair behind my back, "You look... refreshed?" The corner of her mouth pulls up as she returns to the food.

"What's on the menu for tonight?" I ask.

"Three courses of fondue," she explains, "Cheese, meat, and chocolate. Jack mentioned something about teaching you both how to make it. I have everything ready to go if you want to learn."

"I would love that!" I say, excited. "I tried a couple of years ago, but it didn't turn out well – it was a big gloopy greasy mess." I cringe, thinking of the fifty dollars' worth of cheese I had to throw in the trash.

"Perfect. Why don't I do a quick rundown of all three? Everything is prepped and the instructions are super simple. That way I can leave you to eat your dinner together without interruption." She winks at me, then wiggles her eyebrows to drive the point home.

"That would be great. Thank you, Greer," Jack says, chuckling, drawing me around the counter so that the three of us are on the same side. Greer takes about twenty minutes to explain the steps to us, the ingredients for all three fondues laid out in different spots on the counter so that we can't screw it up. When she's finished, she hugs us both and tells us to text or call with any questions.

After she leaves, Jack pulls out a hot plate and sets it on the kitchen table. We bring over the ingredients for the cheese fondue and go step-by-step through the instructions Greer left. Jack adds the last ingredient and I stir it, my mouth watering at the creamy, perfect cheesiness.

"So," Jack says, dipping a piece of bread in the pot, "have you thought about what you want to do now that you're staying?" He holds the morsel to my lips. I take it from him and think about the question seriously while I chew.

"The only thing I've been able to come up with is to continue doing my genealogy charts." I dip a slice of apple in the cheese and blow on it before popping it into my mouth. "I don't want to go into landscaping again, and that's the only other thing I have experience with."

"Can I make a suggestion?" Jack asks, apprehension in his words.

"Of course."

"I've been thinking for a while now that I'd like to open the castle up to tourists. The farm doesn't make enough to keep the castle afloat, and I've been pulling out of savings for years. Savings I was hoping would be there for future generations. I don't have a head for that kind of thing, but I think you'd be perfect."

My mind starts spinning, thinking of everything I would need to do to get the castle ready, everything that needs to be done to market it. "Are you thinking of having guest rooms?" I ask. "Do you have any social media accounts yet? Does anyone even know the castle is here? Any website or ad accounts?" I think back to the time I worked at getting Rob's business off the ground and how much I loved the challenge of it.

"No, to everything you just said," Jack says, looking at me like I'm speaking a different language. "You don't need to give me an answer tonight, but I want you to think about it. If you decide not to, I'll have to hire somebody anyway."

"I'll think about it, I promise," I say, his vulnerability striking a chord. Doesn't he know I'd do anything for him?

"So, are we going to talk about this?" Jack asks, grabbing my hand and thumbing the ring Lach gave me the other night.

"Lach didn't tell you?" I ask, surprised.

"No. The three of us agreed that we wanted the proposals to be private. I knew he was going to do it, and I saw the ring, I just didn't know how or when."

"What about Cam?" I ask, the worry about him feeling left out creeping back. Jack only pretends to zip his lips closed. Fuck. I'd have to find a second to sneak a look at my phone and see if Isla found anything.

"How do you feel about the proposal?" Jack asks, threading his fingers through mine. "You didn't seem too keen before, so I wasn't sure how it would go – especially when Lach told me he was asking you so soon."

Does that mean Jack's not asking soon? A jolt of disappointment races through me, but I push it down deep. "It was a complete surprise, but honestly, I think what surprised me more was how much my feelings had changed. I still don't want you guys to support me, and I still want to be independent, but I don't want to do it alone."

"Good," Jack says, his face betraying the emotion behind that simple word.

"Do you mind if I check my phone quick?" I ask, "Isla was supposed to text me and I completely forgot about it till now."

"Of course. Why don't you check while I'm getting the next course ready?" he says, standing up and starting to clear the dishes.

I pad to the front hall and grab my phone off the console table, unlocking it to find ten texts from Isla. Fuck. My heart is lodged in my throat as I unlock my phone, but I relax a little when I realize they're from only a few minutes ago. She sent pictures of five different rings. I scan through them quickly, my gaze snagging on a ring that looks hundreds of years old. It's a gold signet ring, the engraving almost completely worn down, but it gives it an air of mystery instead of looking worn. Isla had written a little blurb under it: *they're telling me this is from the 16th century – found here in the Outer Hebrides.* I fire off a text telling her it's perfect, then leave the phone on the table. When I return to the kitchen, I lean against the doorframe and watch Jack add ingredients to the pot. He has his hair pulled back, his sleeves pushed to his elbows as he pours the broth. The tie on his robe has loosened, giving me a glimpse of his hard chest.

"Jack," I breathe, my body coming alive for him.

"Don't look at me like that, Charlotte," he says, his voice low and husky.

"Like what?"

"Like you want to push me down on the table and devour me."

"Yes, please," I rasp, walking toward him. He grabs my wrists, trapping me between his chest and the counter.

"You need your energy for tonight, mo chridhe. We eat first. Then I'll blow your fucking mind."

68

Jack washes the dishes while I chop the chocolate for the third course, the tension between us palpable. I scrape the chocolate into the pot and pour in the cream according to the directions, then take it over to the burner on the table. Greer left us with all sorts of goodies to dip in the fondue – marshmallows, brownies, cookies, and a handful of gorgeous strawberries. I would be excited to dig in any other day, but tonight, I can only think about how it'll feel when he's finally inside me.

Jack turns off the water, wipes his hands on a towel, and walks back to the table, his cock bobbing against the robe with each step. My heartbeat takes up residence between my legs, and I shift in my seat, agitated.

"Like what you see?" he chuckles, lifting my chin with his fingers until I'm looking him in the eyes. He sits beside me, drawing me close. I twist my body, throwing one leg over him so I'm straddling his thighs.

"Yes," I murmur, opening his robe and sliding my hand down his shaft. He grunts, pushing his hips against me.

"Fuck, Charlotte," he groans, capturing my wrist with one hand and dipping a strawberry in chocolate with the other. He lets it cool for a moment before holding it to my mouth. I bite down, our gazes locked as I lick the chocolate from my lips. "I don't know how much longer I can wait," he breathes, running his thumb over my bottom lip.

"Then don't wait. Fuck me now."

"God, you're a bad influence," he groans, sliding out from under me and standing, taking the fondue with him to the counter. He grabs a small dish from the cupboard, sets it on the counter, and pours the chocolate into it.

"What are you doing?" I ask, popping a marshmallow into my mouth.

"What I've wanted to do since the first time I touched your tits," he says, setting the dish on the table and pulling me out of the booth.

"Yeah?" I look up at him, at his blown-out pupils, and I know I'm done for. Lifting me by my waist, he sets me on the edge of the table. He unties my robe, groaning as it falls open. Pushing me down gently, he stretches his body over me, pulling my wrists above my head and holding them with one hand.

"I've been thinking about doing this for weeks," he rasps, holding the fondue over me, watching as it drizzles over the tip of my breast. He dips down, swirling his tongue over my nipple before pulling it into his mouth.

"Jack," I beg, "Please."

He ignores me, giving the same attention to my other breast until he pulls a sob from my throat, my body a fast-burning fuse. I'm so close. I pull a hand free and slide it over my stomach and between my legs, cradling my clit between my fingers. Jack pulls back, his eyes dark, pushing my knees open so he can watch. I dip a finger inside myself and bring it back up to circle my clit. His gaze follows my movements, his chest heaving with each breath, his bottom lip caught between his teeth.

"Enough," he growls, circling my wrist with his fingers and bringing my hand up to his mouth, licking me clean. "It's time for your surprise."

I groan. "I don't want a surprise. I want you. Inside me. Now."

"You'll want it, trust me," he insists, pulling me into an upright position and then scooping me up, one arm under my legs and the other behind my back.

"Where are we going?" I ask after he turns down a third hallway, electricity slowly giving way to candlelight as we walk further away from the kitchen. He stops, setting me gently on my feet. I look around at the art hanging around us, noticing the large open space on one of the walls that I'm pretty sure wasn't there the last time I was here.

"I'm confused—" I say, but then I see a massive piece of black canvas spread out over the floor, tubes of metallic paint lined up along the top edge. "What is this?" I ask, looking over at him. My eyes dip down, my attention snagging on his fully erect cock peeking out of the robe. My mouth waters as I think about what he would do if I dropped to my knees right here.

"I found a company that makes water-based, body-safe paints," he says, pulling me out of my thoughts. "If you're open to it, I thought our first time could be on this canvas."

"And then hang it?" I ask, looking up at the bare wall.

Jack nods, a gleam in his eyes. "We would be the only ones that know what it really is."

"This is genius! Can I paint you first?" I ask, my body thrumming with excitement.

"Do your worst," he chuckles, slowly untying the belt of his robe and letting it pool on the parquet floor.

Fuck. Me. The candlelight flickers over his skin, burnished gold melding into deep shadow.

I force myself to take a deep breath, shrug the robe off my shoulders and squeeze a tube of gold paint onto my palm, rubbing my hands together to warm it up. I walk toward him slowly, my heart hammering in my ears. He watches me, a dangerous gleam in his eyes, then pulls me against him, his cock hard against my stomach. I swipe my thumbs beneath his eyes, leaving two streaks of gold across his cheeks, then I smear the paint everywhere the light touches – the sides of his pecs, each muscle in his abdomen, and finally, the V pointing me toward what I really want. I forget the paint as he pulls me up on my toes, crushing his lips against mine. His hands tangle in my hair as he draws my head back and plunders my mouth, fucking me with his tongue. He releases me with a groan, looking like a golden god as he picks up a tube of deep blue paint and empties it into his palm.

"God, Charlotte. You're so fucking beautiful," he groans, sliding his hand over my breast and down my side.

I grab some silver paint, painting two lines on either side of his spine, planning to smear the rest over his backside, but he snatches the tube from me, squeezes it into his palm, and spreads it over my other breast. He tries to pull me to him, but I dance away, snatching a magenta tube, and squirting the bulk of the contents into my hand. Jack catches me by the wrists, scrapes his hand over mine, and smears the paint over my torso. He jerks me against his body, adjusting his cock to nestle between my legs. I push up on the tiptoes to give him better access, and he pulls my legs around him, his hands supporting my weight. I grind my hips against him, moaning as his cock slides over me.

"Goddamnit, Charlotte," he groans, flexing his hips.

"There's not enough paint yet," I say breathlessly, using his shoulders to pull myself up along his shaft and then sliding back down slowly, the friction on my clit almost doing me in. Jack balances me with one arm, leans down to grab several tubes of paint in his hand, twists the caps off with his teeth, and squeezes them over the canvas without looking.

"Good?" he asks

"Good enough." I move my hips until his cock is nudging my entrance, his jaw tensing as he barely holds himself back. He drops to his knees on the canvas, his arms supporting my back as he lowers me to the floor. The paint is cold against my skin, drawing my nipples into sharp points. His hands slip against me as he cradles my face, nipping at my bottom lip and pulling me into a searing kiss.

Our moans echo around the room as he moves down my body, kissing and licking me where my bare skin is still showing. I protest when he slides his hands under my hips, lifting me, but my words become unintelligible when he fits his mouth between my legs, licking me in long strokes. I try to tell him I want his cock, not his mouth, but I can't get the words to come out. He pulls away when he feels me tense, sits back on his heels, and stares down at me, his chest heaving.

"I don't think I can take much more, Charlotte," he rasps, sliding his clean hand over his cock. "Are you ready?"

"I've been ready since the first day I met you."

He leans over me, elbows on either side of my head, our breaths mingling as he positions his cock between my legs. He flexes his hips, pushing so that he's sliding along my inner labia, dragging the length of his cock over my clit. I buck against him, begging him to fuck me.

"Open your eyes, Charlotte."

69

"Open your eyes, Charlotte," Jack says, his deep brogue skittering over my skin. I open my eyes, the scorching heat in his gaze burning me alive.

"There you are," he breathes. Every muscle in his body tenses as he flexes his hips, pushing the head of his cock against me, nudging at my entrance. My back bows off the canvas, my body strung so tight that I can barely breathe. He bears down and slides into me completely, a garbled moan tearing from my throat as he bottoms out, filling me completely.

"You're so fucking tight," he chokes out, holding still, giving me time to adjust. He pulls out and slams back in, pushing me higher on the canvas with every thrust. I scramble for purchase, quickly giving up and pushing against his shoulders until he's sitting on his haunches. He ignores my pleas to be lifted and widens his knees, fingers digging into my hips as he slides me forward, impaling me on his shaft. His gaze shifts from where we're joined to my breasts, bouncing with each hard thrust.

"Turn over," he says roughly, "I want to know your tits were all over this canvas every time I look at it." I slip in the paint as I attempt to push myself up, so he grabs me by the waist, flipping me over like I barely weigh anything. "Fuck, Charlotte," he groans, kneading the globes of my ass cheeks, spreading me wide. I can feel the heat of his gaze on my pussy as he slowly brings me to him, the head of his cock pushing past my lips before sliding home. He stretches his body over mine, trapping my wrists above my head, driving into me with strong, sure strokes.

"You were fucking made for me," he growls, his breaths labored against my ear. I whimper as he slows his pace to a torturous crawl, the head of his cock hitting my g-spot with every thrust. He pulls out suddenly, stands up and reaches down for me, hauling me up against his chest. I grip his waist with my thighs, position his cock against me and take him deep. His breath stutters, and he looks up at the ceiling, swallowing hard.

"I have to get this paint off so I can fuck you properly," he growls, walking us out of the room and down the hallway.

"Won't someone see us?" I ask, swiveling my head.

"There's no one here tonight except us," Jack says. "Cam is staying at Lach's tonight."

The image of them fucking enters my head immediately, my pussy convulsing around Jack's cock.

"You're thinking about them fucking, aren't you?" Jack asks, setting me on a windowsill without regard for the paint covering my body. His fingers dig into my hips as he rams into me, our gazes locked between my legs. "Does thinking about them turn you on?" He palms my breast, rolling my nipple between his fingers.

"I can't help it," I groan, "There's this picture that forms in my mind..." I clench around him and Jack curses, sinking into me again.

"What turns *you* on?" I ask him, readjusting my grip on his shoulders as he picks me up, continuing down the hallway.

"All of us coming together, coming at the same time," he says without pause, his eyes dark.

"All three holes?" I ask, an image quickly forming in my head.

"No," he says gruffly. He doesn't elaborate.

"Then how?"

Jack moans in my ear as he shoulders open a door. "I don't know if I can tell you while I'm in you," he grinds out, his jaw clenching.

"Tell me when we get where we're going then," I say, trying to look behind me as Jack shoulders through a door and sets me down carefully, his cock sliding along my clit as he pulls out. He clamps his arm around my waist when my knees threaten to give out, chuckling into my hair. Once I'm steady, he flips on a light, and I gasp as the room comes into focus.

"Is this your bathroom?" I breathe, my eyes wide, not sure where to look first. It's as if we're in the middle of the jungle, standing in a room carved from boulders. Two sinks are carved out of a granite slab along one wall, plants filling the gap between matching mirrors. After that, the room splits off, flagstone pathways taking you to what I can only assume would be the toilet and shower.

"Amazing, isn't it? Lorna needed something to put in her design portfolio, and this is what she came up with."

"If this were mine, I would never leave," I sigh. "Now will you tell me what turns you on?" I ask, looking up at him.

He slides his hand over my hips, pulling me tightly against his body. "There is one thing I haven't been able to get out of my head since you said you wanted to be with all three of us," he says, capturing my gaze with his. "I'll be on my back, you'll be on top of me, facing the ceiling."

I clear my throat. "What hole?" I ask, my voice hoarse and my mouth dry. Jack slides his fingers along the crease of my ass until he feels the puckered skin, massaging it. I arch my back, pushing against his hand, every nerve in my body screaming for him to be inside me.

"I'll lube you up and tease you until you're begging for me, then I'll push against you here," he says, pushing his finger against me, "until you open up for me and let me in." I relax my body, and his finger slips in, his hips flexing against me as he struggles for control. He positions his cock at the V of my legs, sliding between them easily, pulsing the head of his cock over my clit.

"Fuck," I whimper.

"Lach will kneel between your legs and fuck your pussy," he

breaths, sliding his hand up to cup my breast, pinching my nipple. "Cam will position himself in front of Lach." He bends, putting his mouth against my ear. "Do you think you can handle two cocks in that tight pussy, Sassenach?" He pulls his hips back, leaving room for his other hand as he sinks two thick fingers inside me, his palm grinding against my clit. I moan, rocking against his hands, the image he created in my mind so fucking hot I can barely breathe.

"Is that even possible?" I rasp, dropping my forehead against his shoulder as he slowly wrenches my world apart.

"We'll find out Saturday, won't we?" I shiver as his breath fans over my neck. He gently pulls his fingers out, making sure I'm steady before walking to the shower and turning it on.

"You look like you belong in an art museum," he says, his voice hoarse as his gaze lazily slides over my breasts, down my stomach, stopping at the apex of my thighs.

"And you," I say, walking toward him slowly, my eyes locked on his cock, "Look good enough to eat." I wet a washcloth, wiping the paint off his cock before I grasp him with a firm hand, sliding my fingers over him until the the head of his cock glistens. I drop to my knees, looking up at him through my eyelashes.

"Don't," he protests weakly, his jaw clenching.

"Are you sure?" I sweep my tongue over the head, breathing in his heady scent.

"No, I'm not fucking sure," he groans, looking down at me. He cups my chin, running his thumb over my bottom lip before hooking it on my teeth and pulling my mouth open. He presses his cock past my lips, his moan crackling over my skin and lodging between my legs. I slide my hands over his ass and pull him toward me, taking him deep. Holding him tight, I swallow around his cock, feeling like the most powerful woman alive as his body trembles under my hands. He moans as I pull my head back, my cheeks hollowed around him. He pushes his hands into my hair, his fingers flexing against my scalp as he wrestles for control.

Hooded eyes watch me work, his lower lip caught in his teeth. I whimper around him, reaching between my legs to ease the ache. He curses, wrapping my hair around his hand, slamming into my mouth, pulling me back, and slamming in again.

"Fuck. Come here," he says roughly, hauling me up to my feet and pulling me through a different door into a dark bedroom. He picks me up and throws me onto the bed.

"On your back with your head hanging over," he commands, sliding his hand over his cock.

"I'll ruin your bedding!" I protest, hopping off the bed and looking to make sure I hadn't gotten paint anywhere.

"I don't fucking care about the bedding," Jack growls, "Get on the bed. Now."

His command sends heat flooding through me, desire dripping down my legs. Jumping to get on the bed, I spin myself around, laying down with my head hanging over the edge. His words from that day on the terrace come back to me. I told him I wanted this side of him, and now he's finally ready to give it to me.

"If you need me to stop, tap the back of my leg three times, understand?"

"I understand," I murmur, reaching for him and pulling his cock against my lips. He pushes in, sinking deeper than anyone ever has, my throat constricting around him as I struggle against my gag reflex. He pulls out, giving me a second to breathe, palming my tits and pinching my nipples, groaning as I pass my tongue over his frenulum. He looks down at me, running the head of his cock back and forth over my lips before sliding back in, his hand cupping my throat.

"Fuck," he grunts, squeezing my throat as his cock passes under his hand. I concentrate on breathing through my nose as he thrusts again, tears leaking from the corners of my eyes. I desperately want to sneak my hand up the back of his thigh to massage his prostate, giving him the best orgasm of his goddamn life, but I don't know if he's open to that, and I'm not exactly in the position to ask.

He slides his hand over my stomach, pausing to rub my clit before hooking two fingers in my pussy, pushing against my g-spot, the heel of his hand anchored on my clit. I moan around him, and his hips stutter, the vibration tipping him closer to the edge. I slowly run my hand up the back of his thigh, pausing at the crease of his leg to give him time to protest. He pushes back against my hand before thrusting into me again. The next time he pulls back, I push my thumb against his perineum, covering my pointer finger in my saliva before sliding it up between his cheeks. I trace my finger over the ring of muscle, massaging it as he pushes his ass back toward my hand with a low groan. I feel him relax, and press my finger against his sphincter, not letting up until I've breached the muscle and can feel his prostate under my fingertip.

"Fuck," he groans as I massage him, his hands moving to grip the bed on either side of my head, his entire body spasming. He loses control, bottoming out in my throat, then pushing back against my finger. Slamming in one more time, I feel his cock pulse and I press deeper, applying steady pressure to his prostate.

He whimpers above me, his hips jerking, and I swallow around him, drinking him down like he's giving me the nectar of the gods. I press harder, and his back bows, a broken moan ripping from his lips as I wring out every last drop.

"Holy fuck," he says, his voice trembling as he pulls away from me, hauling me into his arms and cradling my face. "I didn't fucking want to do that," he whispers, tracing my cheek with his finger.

"Yes, you did, and that's okay," I assure him, "I wanted you to do it. I enjoyed it."

"Enjoyed it?" he asks, wiping mascara from under my eyes, "I'll fucking give you something to enjoy, mo chridhe."

Before I can process his words, I'm straddling his face, his mouth buried between my legs. He licks, sucks, and bites, ripping an orgasm from me in record time. I ride him until the last tremors stop, and collapse next to him on the bed, cradled in his arms.

"You actually like when I fuck your face, don't you?" he asks, something different – darker – in his gaze.

"Was I wet?" I ask, cocking my eyebrow. He already knows the answer to that question.

"So fucking wet," he rasps, his lips warm against my temple.

"My body can't lie, Jack."

He props himself up on his elbow, his gaze hot and heavy, fire simmering in its depths. "I'll be going to hell for the things I want to do to your body, Charlotte," he murmurs, pushing a lock of hair behind my ear,

"At least we'll be there together," I smirk, "Come on, let's take that shower you promised me."

70

The carved surface of the bathroom door bites into my back as Jack presses me against it, his hands sliding over my hips as he lowers his mouth to mine. He explores my lips lazily, nipping and sucking at my bottom lip before pushing into my mouth, our tastes melding together like a fine wine.

"I'll never get enough, Charlotte," he murmurs.

"You're willing to give this up?" I blurt, my heart hammering in my throat.

"What do you mean?"

"This. Us. Just the two of us," I whisper, my voice cracking.

His eyes narrow, studying me. "That's what we all decided on, Charlotte."

"I know. But now I'm asking you if you're okay with giving this up. Answer me truthfully."

He pushes away from me, his jaw clenched. I stand my ground, holding his gaze. He blows out a long breath, running his hands through his hair, his muscles rippling.

"No, I don't fucking want to give this up," he growls.

"Then why are we? Why are we making rules that our hearts don't agree with? On top of forcing the four of us to always be in the same place at the same time, it also means Cam and Lach can't ever have sex alone again. How does that make any sense?" I ask, throwing up my hands.

"I just don't want Cam, Lach, and I to be torn apart again," he says, pulling me close, his lips in my hair.

"I don't want that either. There are better ways to do this, Jack. Where all of us will be satisfied and happy."

"Let's talk about it this weekend," he murmurs, reaching behind me and twisting the doorknob. He stops me from falling into the bathroom, hauling me against his body, his cock hard against my stomach.

"Do you have a bionic cock?" I ask, pushing it down with my finger and watching as it bobs back up.

"I told you, I don't think I'll ever get enough," he says, backing me against the wall, the giant boulder cool and smooth against my skin. Sliding his hand down the outside of my thigh, he pulls my leg up to wrap around his waist, sinking into me in one firm thrust.

"Fuck," I groan, dropping my head against the rock and rolling my hips against him.

"Do you think you're ready for the butt plug?" he asks, pulling out and sliding back in with a grunt. "I need you ready for Saturday."

"Yes," I breathe, the picture he painted in my mind earlier coming back in full force.

"Good. Go down the short path on the right and through the door to the shower. I'll meet you there in a second." He pulls out slowly, pulsing the head of his cock on my clit before releasing me and walking back into the bedroom, his muscular ass teasing me with each step.

I walk down the path he indicated, confused as to why there's a wooden door leading to the shower. I turn the handle and push the door open, freezing mid-step. There's a shower sticking out of the ground directly in front of me, glass walls on every side, tall plants giving a sense of privacy. Gravel covers the ground, large flagstones forming a path. I walk to the shower in a daze, feeling like I'm in a dream. The piping for the shower runs up a rough wooden beam, a simple handle allowing the water to travel up to the shower head. I turn it on, waiting until steam billows around me before stepping under the scalding water. I lean back into the spray, the water cascading over me and disappearing into the gravel below my feet. There is no warning except a low groan before Jack captures me in his arms, lifting me, impaling me. I clutch his shoulders as he manhandles me, his grip on my ass tight as he moves me over his cock.

"Plug or dildo?" he murmurs against my ear, his finger sliding down my crack.

"You choose," I gasp, arching against him as he pushes a finger into me, grinding his pubic bone over my clit.

"Good girl," he growls, the baritone in his voice vibrating over my skin.

He lowers me to my feet, his cock leaving me slowly, dragging over my clit. I whimper, rocking against his head as he pulls away. He angles the shower head and turns me around, pressing down on my back until I'm bent over, perpendicular to the floor.

"Hold on to the post," he commands, sliding his hands down my legs and pushing my feet wider.

"Fuck," he grinds out, sliding his hands over my ass, "you're so goddamn gorgeous." He kneels behind me, pressing his face against me and licking from my clit to my ass. I arch, pushing my ass up unashamedly as he eats me out. He doesn't stop until I'm rocking against his face and sobbing his name. Stepping away for a second, he comes back, one hand gripping my hip as he slides into me from behind.

"I wish you could see how your pussy stretches around me," he groans, pulling out and slamming back in. "Is that position comfortable?"

"It won't be for long," I say honestly, pushing back to meet his next thrust.

He pulls me back up and hands me a curved, triangle-shaped,

silicone-covered object. "Figure this out while I go grab something else." I take it from him, turning it over in my hands. I step under the shower spray to warm back up and press the button on the back, heat pooling in my stomach as it vibrates against my palm. I hold it between my legs, loving how perfectly it fits against me. My head drops back as the vibe does its work, my hips rocking against it. Jack's chuckle races down my spine, and I jerk my hand away, heat flooding my cheeks. He reaches around me and turns off the shower, and I step to the side as he hooks a black contraption to a ring in the post near the shower head.

"I bought this for this weekend, but I think it might prove more useful tonight," he says as he straightens the straps.

"Is that a swing?" I ask, trying to figure out what straps go where. There's a wide, solid bar at the top, loops, and bands hanging off it.

"Your knees go here," he says, holding one loop steady as I tentatively put my knee in. He holds the second one, encouraging me to use him for balance as I fit my other knee into it. The bar above me keeps the loops in place, spreading me wide open. "Lean forward," Jack says roughly, fitting a wider band of material under my torso. I slowly put my weight against it, clutching the vibe with one hand and a strap with the other.

"Oh fuck," Jack breathes, stepping back slightly to look at me suspended in front of him. He steps between my legs and grips my hips, angling me up before bending down to drag his tongue over me. Tapping his cock against my clit, he takes a second to position himself before slamming into me, the swing giving him the leverage to go deep. My pussy clenches around him, and I cry out in frustration as he pulls all the way out.

"How do you want it?" he asks, sliding something cold against my asshole. "Do you want me filling you when I fuck your ass with this?" I flinch as he squirts lube onto my asshole, sliding it over me with his finger before easily pushing past the ring of muscle. "Fuck, you're ready, aren't you?" he groans, massaging and stretching me with his finger.

"Yes," I moan, pushing back against his hand. He goes deeper as he slides his cock into me again, bottoming out and holding me there as I clench around him.

"This is slightly bigger than me," he murmurs, sliding cold silicone against my skin, "It should prep you enough so that we don't have to be worried about being gentle Saturday."

Fuck.

"I want you to use the vibe to help you relax."

I turn on the vibe and reach between my legs, but instead of putting it on my clit I press it against Jack's balls, moving it over his perineum.

"Fucking hell, Charlotte," he hisses, his hips spasming. My giggle turns into a low groan as he spreads lube over me and presses the dildo against my back entrance. I move the vibe to my clit, forcing my body into submission as he slides the tip of the dildo into me, working it slowly back and forth. I want it so bad that I don't think I'd care if he pushed it all the way in right now. I just want to be filled and fucked until I don't know my name.

"Little bit more," Jack rasps, his cock flexing inside me as he works the dildo in another inch. I swivel my hips against him, pushing my ass up to take more, keeping the vibe steady on my clit.

"God, I wish that were my cock," he groans, keeping the dildo in place as he slams into me.

"It can be." I push up again, taking all of it in until only the base is left on the outside.

I whimper. So fucking full.

"Don't you dare come. Not yet," he groans, ramming his cock in deep, "Your pussy is mine tonight. Your ass will be mine on Saturday." He slows down, gently pulling the dildo out and pushing it back in as he slides his cock into my pussy.

"We still don't know if they'll both fit." My whisper becomes a moan as he swivels his hips against me, pushing his cock deeper.

"Don't move," he says, leaving the dildo in me as he pulls out his cock and walks back toward the bedroom. He returns with a box in his hands, a grin pulling at his lips. "I was going to give this to you later, but now seems like the perfect time." He holds his hand out for the vibe, exchanging it for the box. There is something really fucking hot about doing such a mundane task with a dildo shoved up my ass – completely decadent and sinful. I dig my fingernails into the top and pry it open, then turn it upside down over my hand, gasping as the most life-like dildo I have ever seen falls into my hand. A ribbon is tied around its velvety base, and tied in the ribbon is a ring. I look up at Jack to find him on one knee, a goofy grin on his face.

"Is this your cock?" I ask, looking between him and the dildo.

"Yes, It was supposed to be symbolic, but now all I really care about is using it on you. Marry me, Charlotte." He tugs at the ribbon, and the ring falls into my hand.

"You're proposing to me with a dildo in my ass?"

"I'm proposing to you before I fuck your brains out and make you forget about every man that's existed before me," he corrects, picking up the ring from my palm. "I'll spend every day for the rest of my life making you the happiest woman alive, Charlotte."

"You already do that without trying," I whisper, holding my hand out to him. He slips the ring on my finger, pushing it flush to Lach's. It's fashioned to look like two hands, the fingers forming the prongs, wrapped around a gorgeous salt and pepper diamond. "Yes," I say, holding his gaze, "Yes. I'll marry you, fuck you, anything you want, Jack. A thousand times, yes."

"Thank fuck." He takes the dildo from me, his lips crashing against mine before getting into position behind me. He slides the dildo over my clit, then along my vulva until it's nudging at my entrance. "I wish you could see how swollen you are, like a ripe, juicy peach just waiting to be eaten." He squats down and sucks my clit into his mouth as he pushes in the dildo. I buck against his lips, my world narrowing. "Not yet," he breathes against me, giving me one last lick before standing and pulling both dildos out, then pushing them back in at a snail's pace.

"Are you ready?" he says hoarsely, handing me back the vibrator.

"God, yes," I pant.

He pushes both dildos in all the way, coating his cock in lube before positioning it above the dildo in my pussy, and then flexes his hips until the tip is inside me.

"Does that feel okay?" he asks, grunting as I squeeze around him.

My entire life condenses to that very moment, to the fullness, to his fingers digging into my hips, to the vibe against my clit. He holds himself there, fucking my ass with the dildo, getting me used to the feeling before pushing his cock in another inch. He repeats those steps until he's bottomed out, my world about to fracture into a million pieces.

"They'll fit," he says roughly, pulling out and thrusting in again, pushing everything inside me as far as they'll go.

"Jack," I sob, so close to coming I can't get out any other words. He pulls the dildo from my pussy, grips my hips with both hands, and swings me toward him, slamming into me with a fierce curse.

"Now, Charlotte," he commands, swinging me forward and then back onto his cock, ramming into me repeatedly, my entire body going limp as he fucks me. I feel his hips spasm as he loses control, and I get sucked into his orbit, an orgasm ripping from my body, his cock pulsing so deep inside me I can feel him against my soul.

"More," I whimper as he pulls out, my body still strung tight, and even I can't tell if it's not enough or if it's too much.

"Fuck, Charlotte," he pants, breathing hard. He helps me get out of the swing and turns me around so the straps support my back and thighs. "I'm still hard. Me or the dildo?"

"The answer to that question will always be you," I say blearily, watching as he positions himself and pulls me onto him. "Vibrator?" he asks.

"I don't need it," I say, our gazes locked as he steps closer to me, grinding his pelvis against mine. The gold in his eyes darkens as the first tremors start.

"Not yet," he murmurs, changing his mind and picking me up out of the swing, laying me down on a bench near the wall. He keeps eye contact as he fills me, pressing his pubic bone against my clit as he moves his body over me. My nails scrape down his back, my entire body tensing as I angle my hips, meeting him thrust for thrust. "Fuck,

Charlotte," he whispers brokenly, his body shuddering over me as I clench around him.

"Oh God," I whimper, my eyelids fluttering as the tide rises with me in its clutches.

"Open your eyes," Jack whispers. He cradles my face in his hands, our gazes locked, riding the wave together until we come crashing back to earth in brutal ecstasy.

71

I stand under the steaming shower spray, Jack's moans still echoing in my ears. He has his arm wrapped around my torso, supporting my weight as he reaches for the shampoo.

"Can you stand by yourself?" he asks, a ghost of a smile teasing his lips, the tenderness in his gaze nearly buckling my knees. My finger-nails dig into his forearm as I transfer my weight to my feet, locking my knees to keep my trembling muscles in check.

"Good girl," he murmurs, his praise bringing a flush to my skin. He pushes his fingers into my hair, massaging my scalp and then gently running the soap into the ends of my hair. Tilting my head back, he carefully rinses out the shampoo, keeping the water away from my eyes. He picks up a bar of soap, the smell of lemon verbena enveloping us as he rubs it between his palms and then over my body, the gentle sweep of his hands over my breasts, down my stomach, and between my legs, stoking the fire in my core. I move my hips against him, his answering chuckle sliding down my spine, making me shiver. He tips my chin up, his gaze putting me in a chokehold.

"You're fucking incredible, Charlotte," he rasps, pressing his lips to mine, the roughness of his beard re-igniting my nerve endings. I cradle his face between my hands, pouring my entire soul into this kiss. He walks us under the spray, his lips still moving against mine as he washes the soap from my body before turning the water off. Pulling away with a groan, he grabs a towel from the stack by the door, wraps it around me, and lifts me into his arms, carrying me through the bathroom to the bedroom. The springs in the mattress creak as he climbs onto the bed, pulling the towel away before pulling me flush against his body and covering us with a fluffy duvet.

"Do you think I'm ready?" I murmur sleepily, turning in his arms, unable to bear one more second without the warmth of his gaze.

"I *know* you're ready," he whispers, a smile pulling at his lips as he fans my hair out over the pillow. "I've never seen anything so magnificent. The way you move, Charlotte... just thinking about it makes me hard."

I hum my approval, running my hand over his stomach, not stopping until my fingers wrap around his cock. I stifle a yawn as I slide my hand over his hard length, my insides quivering. He circles my wrist with his fingers, pulling my hand away before I get in a second stroke.

"Get some sleep, Charlie. We have a big day tomorrow, you need your rest."

"Tomorrow?" I ask, wrinkling my brow in confusion.

"It's almost three in the morning, Sassenach," he grumbles, pulling me closer, tangling his legs with mine, and tucking my head into the space between his shoulder and neck. The last thing I remember is the heat of his skin and the way his breath tickles as he whispers he loves me.

I WAKE LITTLE BY LITTLE, awareness slowly taking hold of my senses. The feel of warm skin under my cheek. Steady breaths dancing through my hair. The heady scent of sex and lemon verbena making my heart pound in my chest, incessant throbbing taking residence between my legs.

I crack my eyes open, greeted by the large expanse of Jack's well-muscled chest. Sometime during the night, I had thrown one of my legs over his hips, trapping his cock under my thigh, dangerously close to my core. I stifle a groan as he twitches, his fingers flexing, digging into my hip as he pushes his pelvis against me in his sleep. Fuck. I angle my hips, pressing my clit against his hip bone. Before I even realize he's awake, he hauls me on top of him and thrusts into me with a groan. My eyes roll to the back of my head as I adjust to his size, circling my hips until it feels like he's filling every part of me.

"Good morning, Sassenach," he says roughly, his eyelids fluttering open, his gaze sweeping hungrily over my body. His fingertips press into my hips, angling my pelvis so my clit grinds against his pubic bone with every thrust. I brace my hands on his chest, a strangled moan falls from my lips as an orgasm violently rips through me, Jack's answering groan coming from deep in his throat as he loses himself in my body.

I collapse on top of him, our breaths mingling as we slowly return to earth.

"I'm going to carve a statue of you, mo chridhe. And then I'm going to put a little plaque at the bottom," Jack says, his lips moving against my hair, his cock still pulsing inside me.

"And what will that plaque say?" I ask, sliding my tongue over the pulse in his neck.

"Charlotte. The Patron Saint of Hard Cocks," he chuckles, framing my face with his hands and pulling my mouth to his.

"Will you pray to me?" I ask, smiling against his lips.

"Oh, I'll do more than pray to you," he growls, rolling me underneath him and thrusting into me. He looks down at me, a look in his eyes that I can't place.

"What?" I whisper, losing myself in his gaze, his hair curtaining us from the outside world.

"You're right," he sighs, kissing me before pulling out and climbing out of bed.

"About what?" I ask, propping myself up with my elbow.

"It isn't even that I don't want to give this up. *I can't.*" He pushes his hands through his hair, secures it on top of his head, and then holds his hands out to me. I swing my legs over the side of the bed, but instead of helping me jump down, he pushes my thighs apart and steps between them, cradling my body to his, his lips pressed just below my ear. "It wouldn't be a life worth living if I didn't have mornings like this to look forward to, Charlotte."

Thank fuck. I squeeze him tight, reluctantly loosening my grip as he pulls back to look at me. "Let's get through this weekend and then we'll all sit down and hash it out." He pulls at my left arm until I release him and brings my hand up to his chest, his lips pulling into a smile when he sees his ring on my finger. "It suits you," he murmurs. "Cam didn't propose to you?" he asks, his brows drawing together when he realizes there are only two rings on my finger.

"No," I say, clamping my lips together before I tell him about Cam's ring.

Jack doesn't say anything else, only wraps me in a fresh robe and leads the way to the kitchen. He insists I relax as he fries eggs and bacon, serving it on one plate with two forks. He cuts off a bite and holds it to my lips, watching me intently as I lick yolk from the corner of my mouth.

"I thought it would be nice for all of us to eat dinner together tonight," he says, clearing his throat before scooping up a bite for himself.

"I'd like that," I murmur, looking forward to the four of us being together again.

"I'll drive you home so you can pack, then we can all meet up around five to start cooking dinner. Then early to bed."

"You're a bossy SOB sometimes," I laugh, a thrill racing down my spine when his eyes darken.

"Trust me, Charlotte, you'll be begging for sleep by the time the three of us finish with you."

"I fucking hope so," I rasp, my body thrumming with anticipation.

72

I'm in the process of pulling a sweater over my head when I hear a knock at the door. Isla doesn't wait for me to answer before she explodes through the door, a waterfall of copper hair flowing down her back in loose waves.

"I can't stay," she says, giving me a quick hug. "I just wanted to drop the ring off and wish you luck before you leave." Isla sets a small ring box on the coffee table and pulls me into a tight hug. "I hope tomorrow is everything you want it to be," she says, shoving a bag into my hand while giving me an exaggerated wink. "See you in a couple of days!" she calls as she heads out the door.

"Thank you!" I yell at her back as she jogs up the path. I shove my shoulder against the door to get it closed and peek in the bag. I whistle as I pull out the tiniest piece of lingerie I have ever seen. That will be interesting to try to wrangle myself into. I set the bag on the table and pick up the ring box, doing a little jig when I see how perfect it is. I slip it on my thumb for safekeeping and check my phone, only to realize that I'm running late for dinner.

Lach is waiting for me at the top of the path, his hair ruffling in the wind. "How was your night?" he asks as he catches me in his arms, spinning me around before pressing his lips tenderly to mine.

"Perfect," I say, my lips pulling into a grin despite myself.

"Good," he murmurs, deepening the kiss, his tongue tangling against mine. He fists my hair in one hand, pulling my head to the side to give him access to my neck. He licks and bites his way to my collarbone, cupping my breast in his palm and rolling my nipple between his fingers. The ring of a cell phone startles us, and Lach pulls it out of his pocket with a guilty grin.

He doesn't say hello, just, "We'll be there in a second," before hanging up and pulling my body back to his.

"Can I ask you something?" I say when he breaks away from me with a groan.

"Anything," he smiles, helping me into the car and then squatting, so we're eye to eye.

I twist Cam's ring nervously around my thumb, my heart in my throat. "Do you think I'm ridiculous even to consider proposing to Cam?"

A goofy grin stretches his cheeks. "No, I don't think it's ridiculous at all."

"It's just that you and Jack have already proposed and I don't want him to feel like a third wheel. I want him to know without a doubt that he belongs with us. And then I worry that I'm stealing his chance to propose—"

"He'll love it, Charlie," Lach says, pressing a finger to my lips.

"You're sure?"

"Positive. We better get to dinner before Jack comes looking for us," he says, softening his eyeroll with a wink.

Lach and I walk around the back of the castle and enter directly through the kitchen, the smell of roasting meat and fresh bread hitting us in the face the second we open the door. My stomach growls loudly, earning me a dirty look from Jack – a silent admonishment for not eating lunch. Before I can explain myself, I look over to see Cam stalking toward me, his gaze stripping me bare. The heat in his eyes has me walking backward until I'm pressed against the door with nowhere else to go. He braces one arm on the doorframe and pulls me flush against his body with the other, capturing my lips with his.

"I missed you," he breathes, pulling my lower lip into his mouth before deepening the kiss.

"Why don't you two take a walk and catch up?" Jack says, winking at me. "Lach and I will finish dinner. It should be ready in about half an hour."

"Are you sure?" I ask, but Cam pulls me out the door, and Jack's reply is cut off as the door snicks closed.

"They'll be fine," he assures me, a smile pulling at his lips as his gaze sweeps over me. "Come on. We only have half an hour, and I want to show you something." He keeps his fingers linked with mine as we walk into the orchard, weaving through the trees before entering a wooded area, pine needles softening our steps. Sunlight streams through the branches, bugs and birds flitting over our heads as Cam pulls me in deeper. He stops suddenly, tugging a scarf from his pocket.

"Close your eyes," he says, his cheeks ruddy and his eyes sparkling.

"Did you have this planned?" I ask as I close my eyes. "Or do you keep blindfolds in your pocket just in case the need arises?"

"When doesn't the need arise?" I can hear the smile in his voice, and the corners of my mouth curl in response. "Hold on to my shoulders," he instructs, placing my hands where he wants them before walking forward slowly. He stops after a dozen steps and turns, his minty breath warm against my face.

"Cam?"

"Sorry. You're just so fucking beautiful, and I honestly have a hard time believing that we're even doing this right now."

"Doing what?" I ask, sliding my hand over his chest, feeling his heart pounding under my palm. There's a soft rustling as he steps away from me. "Cam?"

"Take the blindfold off, Charlie."

My heart is in my throat as I slide it off and open my eyes. We're in an old chapel, stone walls crumbling around us as the forest reclaims it. Old stained-glass windows cast rainbows over the ground, fighting with the dappled green light shining through the leaves. I drop my gaze to find Cam kneeling in front of me, his eyes bright.

"Charlie, in the beginning, I convinced myself we could never work. And then I left and found myself waking up every morning eager to see you, only to have my heart torn from my chest all over again. Then I returned and found you in the one place I had never even dared to hope you would be. And now I'm proposing to you, ready to place a third ring on your finger and make this official.

"Wait a damn minute," I protest, dropping to my knees in front of him, cradling his face between my hands. "I was lost after you left. I felt guilty for meeting Lach and Jack and even guiltier when I was with them and couldn't stop thinking about you. Wondering how you were. What you were doing. Never in my wildest dreams did I think things would work out like this. I am so grateful for you, Cam." A tremulous smile wavers on his lips as he wipes the tears from under my eyes.

"Charlie—"

"Let me finish," I say, cutting him off, "I know this isn't how our relationship started and I sure as hell know that you weren't planning on putting a third engagement ring on my finger, but fate is a fickle beast, and I'm going to ask anyway. Marry me, Cameron?" I pull the ring off my thumb and hold it out to him, my fingers shaking.

"Fuck, Charlie," he chokes out, wiping his eyes before pulling a ring box out of his pocket. He flips open the top, and there, nested in black velvet, is a sparkling sapphire ring. "This is a sapphire that was found here on Harris back in the 80's," he says, swallowing hard. "I wanted to give you something that will always remind you of what we've created on this tiny island. Will you be my wife, Charlie?" I nod, tears streaming down my cheeks as he takes the ring out of the box and slides it onto my finger, the band dainty enough to be a perfect complement to the other two.

"Don't make me ask again," I say, laughing as I grab his hand and wait for his answer.

"Yes, I will marry you, Charlie." His eyes shine as he watches me slide the ring onto his finger. "The adventures we'll have..." he rasps, emotion cutting off the rest of his words.

"Starting with tomorrow night?" I tease, pulling him to his feet and wrapping my arms around him. He tilts my chin up and presses his lips against mine hungrily, walking me back until my back is pressed against the stone wall, his cock hard against my stomach. He's moaning into my lips, his hand sliding over my breast when the first text comes through. He ignores it, pulling me closer and rocking his hips against mine. I'm in the process of unbuckling his belt when the second text comes through.

"Goddamnit," he mutters, "I already know it's one of the guys telling us dinner is almost ready."

"Not yet," I breathe, my forehead pressed to his chest as I pull his belt away. I make quick work of his button and zipper, pulling his boxers down so I can see the head of his cock. I'm sliding my hand along his length when his phone starts ringing. Betting on the distraction, I drop to my knees and swirl my tongue over his head just as he answers.

"Hell—fuck. Hello?" he manages, biting his lip to keep in a groan. "Yeah, we'll be right—" he moans as I take him all the way in, my lips against the taught skin of his abdomen as I hollow my cheeks. The phone drops into the dirt at his feet and his fingers tangle with my hair, his hips flexing, forcing me to take him even deeper. He pulls out with a grunt, grabs his phone, and walks away from me, fixing his clothes as he assures the guys that we'll be there in a couple of minutes.

I laugh when he matches me step for step as I walk toward him, turning and jogging away before I can corner him. "You're so much fucking trouble," he says, chuckling, "Save your energy for tomorrow. You're going to need it."

"Fine," I pout, settling for the feel of his hand in mine, wondering if Jack told him what he has planned for tomorrow or if he's keeping it a surprise. Just thinking about it sends a shiver of anticipation down my spine.

A cheer goes up the second we're in eyesight of the kitchen, Jack and Lach are waiting for us with four glasses and an expensive-looking bottle of champagne. I take the glass Jack hands me and raise it as Lach starts a toast.

"To the official start of the rest of our lives," he says, his gaze burning me alive.

"To being ravished by three of the hottest guys I've ever known." I smirk, clinking my glass against theirs and downing the champagne in one giant gulp.

73

I'm awakened by the smell of coffee and three very large, very hard bodies climbing into bed with me.

"Wake up, sleepy head." Lach's baritone slides over my body like electricity, making my nipples harden against my sleep shirt. I stretch my arms over my head, arching my back and pointing my toes to get the aches out of my body. All three of them groan. Lach's hand closes over my left breast as Cam's mouth descends on my right. Jack pulls the covers away from my legs and kneels between them, pushing my knees wide.

"Why aren't you wearing underwear, Charlotte?" His voice is rough, but his hands are rougher as he sweeps them up my thighs, stopping just shy of the throbbing ache at my core, kneading tender flesh, his thumbs sliding closer and closer until he's sliding them through the gathered moisture, trapping my clit between his thumbs. Is this how it's going to be? My brain is so overrun with stimuli that I can't think about anything but the pleasure they're giving me. I arch against him, a low growl vibrating over me right before he pulls me into his mouth.

"I hate to be the bearer of bad news," Cam says, breaking to tease my nipple with the tip of his tongue, "But if we don't hustle, we're going to miss the ferry."

Jack ignores him, his gaze locking with mine as he fills me with two fingers, massaging my g-spot while he eats me out. My head drops back as the first tremors start, and I feel Jack chuckle against me before he pulls out and rises to his knees. He stares down at me, his eyes making it very clear that this is just a taste of what's coming later.

"What the fuck, Jack." He easily dodges the pillow I throw at his head.

"I wanted to get you ready for tonight."

"I already *was* ready, in case you didn't notice."

"Oh, I noticed." His smile is wicked as he licks his fingers clean. Cam shoulders him out of the way and anchors himself between my legs, his eyes dark as he reaches down and pushes one long finger into me. I squeeze around him, rocking my hips against his hand.

"Please," I beg him.

He glances at his watch and pulls away from me, scrambling off the bed. "We don't have time, Charlie."

"Do I have time for one little taste?" Lach asks, his gaze wavering between my pussy and the finger I was just fucking.

"Absolutely not. We will have all the time we want later. We need to get our little witch up and moving before we miss the ferry."

"Fine." Lach's eyes are on me as he takes Cam's hand in his, bringing *that* finger to his lips and sucking it into his mouth before slowly pulling it out. "That will have to tide me over."

"Fuck," Cam mutters, adjusting himself before grabbing my feet and swinging them over the edge of the bed.

"All three of you are awful," I grumble, stripping off my shirt and walking to the dresser to figure out what to wear. The silence is deafening as they watch me, the tension in the air so thick I can hardly breathe.

"We're going somewhere nice for lunch," Lach rasps, his gaze sliding over my body like silk. I glance at all three of them, realizing they're all dressed nicely – rumpled but nice. I find the sexiest thong I have, bending over obscenely as I pull it up. I dig down to the bottom of my drawer and pull out a light, gauzy skirt, a matching top, and a chunky sweater. I grab my bra and pull the straps over my shoulders, but Jack stops me before I can fasten it, his fingers warm on my back as he wrestles with the clasps. He slides his hands down my waist once he's finished, cupping my ass and squeezing.

"I'll make coffee while you finish getting ready." He slides a finger under the string of fabric between my ass cheeks and tugs gently, putting pressure on my clit. I angle my hips to give him access, but he only slaps my butt before heading to the kitchen.

"We have a dilemma that we decided was yours to solve." Lach watches as I pull the skirt over my hips.

"What sort of dilemma?" I pull on my top and then the sweater, praying to the weather gods that my legs won't freeze.

"We can take my car or one of the trucks. My car will be an incredibly tight squeeze, but it will be a breeze to park in the city. We'll have room to spread out in the truck, but it will be a huge headache to find parking every time we go somewhere."

"Your car." I slide my feet into sneakers. I can feel the guys having a silent conversation over my head.

"It'll be tight, and it's a long drive," he reminds me.

"I'd rather be uncomfortable on the ride there than ruin the weekend because we can't find parking." I look in the mirror as I twist my unruly hair into a knot and secure it with a clip, ensuring I have a hair tie around my wrist in case of emergency. I grab my backpack from the foot of the bed, sling it over my shoulder, and then follow my nose to the kitchen.

"That's all you're bringing?" Jack raises his eyebrow as he eyes my backpack, then returns his focus to the travel mugs he's filling.

"I wasn't under the impression I would need a ton of clothing this weekend."

"God, I fucking hope not. If I had my way, you wouldn't leave the bed for forty-eight hours."

"But he won't get his way because we decided on plans together, right Jack?" Lach slaps Jack on the back and takes a mug from the counter.

"Hey, other than getting the supplies I need, I'm perfectly fine with staying at the hotel the entire time," I say, taking a careful sip of my coffee.

Cam looks at me in horror. "I don't think you realize what you're saying. Do you know how many historical sites there are to see? The abbey, the writer's museum, the national gallery—" He ticks them off on his fingers, his eyes lighting up at the thought of showing me his favorite places.

"I get it," I laugh, "I'm good with whatever you guys have planned for me. I hope the majority of it involves all three of you inside me for long periods of time," I call over my shoulder as I head out the door.

Unfortunately, as it turns out, I don't have to sit on anyone's lap. The only thing we don't have room for is Lach's cooler filled with drinks and snacks. I opt for putting it where my feet would go instead of between Cam and me. I'm trying to decide the best way to sit when Cam pats his lap, motioning for me to drape my legs over him.

"Are you sure?"

"Honestly, I was hoping it would be your ass in my lap, not your feet." He unlaces my shoe, tucking them under Jack's seat before pressing his thumb into the arch of my foot and sliding it up toward my toes.

"Cam!" I try to scramble away from him, but he holds onto me, continuing the assault until I'm a boneless, moaning mess. As Lach turns into the ferry parking lot, Cam presses my foot against his hardened length.

"I think I have a problem, Charlie," he chuckles, thrusting against my foot before tugging my shoes back on my feet.

"Are you turned on by feet?"

"There isn't a single part of your body that doesn't turn me on," he says, looking at me through his eyelashes. "You know what my favorite part is?"

"What?"

"The freckle right..." he slides his hand up my leg, beneath my skirt, stopping just shy of where I want him "...here." He circles his finger over the freckle, his eyes darkening as my legs open for him automatically.

How will I get through this car ride when I can't manage to go ten minutes without wanting one of them to fuck me? This is going to be the longest five hours of my life.

74

———————

After waiting about twenty minutes to get on the ferry, we park where the attendant tells us to and abandon the car, beginning the hike up to the tiny café. Jack traps me halfway up, pressing me against the wall, his knee nudging between my legs.

"Does this remind you of anything?" he asks, running a calloused fingertip across my cheek, along my jaw, and over the sensitive skin of my throat.

"I remember you were standing there looking up at me," I say, meeting his gaze, the memory making my heart race. "And I remember losing you." I swallow the lump in my throat as the feelings rush back.

He tightens his fist around the neck of my sweater and pulls me roughly to his lips. I stretch up to meet him, pushing my hands into his hair and kissing him like I wanted to earlier this summer.

"And then you found me in the library. I'll never forget how you looked with that white dress floating around your ankles, your skin gilded by the fire. If Isla hadn't interrupted us that night..."

"What would you have done?"

"If you had been willing, I would have hiked that dress over your head and tasted the nectar of the gods."

"The two of you are causing quite the scene," Lach whisper-shouts, chuckling as he jogs down the stairs toward us. He turns my chin toward him and captures my lips with his own. Someone whistles at us, and I break free, pushing away from them to continue up to the main level.

"You're the one causing a scene," I hiss back at him, looking around us, but I only see one woman walking away. She looks back and gives me an exaggerated wink. God, I hope everyone we encounter is that accepting.

"So, how are you feeling about tonight?" Lach asks me once we've settled into the chairs overlooking the sea at the front of the boat.

I tick my emotions off on my fingers. "Nervous. Excited. Horny."

"Why are you nervous?"

"The thought of being surrounded by three huge men…"

"We would never do anything you don't explicitly agree to, Charlie."

"I know," I say, "I'm nervous in a good way. I've never done this before, and I don't know how it's all going to work. Or fit."

"You don't need to worry about that, Carebear. All you need to do is let us worship you."

"But I'll have to—"

"You don't have to do anything," he interrupts, "Our focus will be on you and your focus should be on coming as many times as possible. Now relax and enjoy the view," he says softly, burying his hand in the hair at my neck and running his fingers over my skin.

I don't know if I'll ever get used to being with three guys that don't have a selfish bone in their bodies, but it's going to be fun trying.

Before we know it, we're crowding back into the car and waiting for the cue to drive off the boat. As soon as we're on the road again, Cam pulls my feet back onto his lap, but this time he unties my shoes and takes them off, tucking them up underneath Jack's seat. Next, he peels off my socks, puts them in the seat pocket, and wastes no time sliding his hands over one foot and digging his thumb into the arch.

"Fuck," I groan, my back arching as he works his magic: a torturous mix of tickling and the best massage I've ever had. Half an hour later, his touch has softened into light caresses up and down the soles of both feet. He catches my attention with a wave of his hand, mouthing something I don't understand. I shake my head, shrugging an apology. He looks down at his lap, then back up at me with wide eyes. When I still don't understand what he's trying to tell me, he hauls my foot higher in his lap, pressing it against his *very* hard cock. *I have a problem!* He mouths again, exaggerating the syllables and I finally understand.

"I see that," I murmur quietly, the corners of my mouth pulling up into a grin.

"Charlie, will you grab me a bottle of water from the cooler, please?" Lach asks, glancing back at me in the rearview mirror.

"Yep!" The cooler is wedged tightly between the seats and I struggle with it before realizing I'm going to have to pull it up onto the seat to get it open. I scooch next to Cam, trying to make enough room for the cooler. He hooks an arm around my waist and pulls me into his lap. His cock is hard against my hip as I lean over to grab the cooler and he takes the opportunity to slide his hand between us, adjusting himself so he's nestled between my legs. I straighten, handing Lach his water, fighting back a whimper as my nerve endings roar back to life.

"Does anyone else want anything?" I ask, having to clear my throat to get the words out.

"I do," Cam breathes into my ear, his fingers pressing into my hips as he flexes against me.

Fuck. I rock my hips over him, my brain telling me this is wildly inappropriate while my body is screaming at me to keep going. He slides his hands under my skirt and over my thighs, pulling them wide, my skirt bunching around my waist.

"Water, please," Jack says, holding his hand behind him. As I lean over to grab another bottle, Cam hooks his finger into my underwear, pulling it away from my body. Before I hand Jack his water, Cam slides his hand underneath me so that his thumb impales me as I straighten, his pointer and middle finger coming up to cradle my clit. I freeze, clamping my mouth closed as my pussy desperately clenches around his finger.

"Fuck, Charlie," he groans, his forehead dropping to my shoulder.

I give in to the moment, grinding my pussy against his hand, my body desperate for release. My eyes flutter open, meeting Lach's gaze in the mirror before he adjusts it so he can watch Cam's hands on me. I moan as Cam licks a path up my neck, biting my earlobe. Jack shifts in his seat, turning to look back at us, and I hold my breath, not sure what his reaction will be.

"Put the cooler back down on the floor," he says roughly. I carefully lower it to the floor and he motions for Cam to move to the middle of the seats. Cam slides over and pushes me forward on his thighs, fumbling with his pants as Jack takes the opportunity to slide two fingers into me, massaging my clit with his thumb.

"The three of you are going to mess around while I'm driving?" Lach grumbles, his gaze moving between the mirror and the road.

"I promise I'll make it up to you later," I pant, a whimper when Jack pulls away quickly becoming a moan as Cam's cock nudges at my entrance, a small warning before he slams into me. I bite my lip, tasting blood, as I attempt to hold in a scream. Jack leans through the gap in the seats, using Cam's knee to support himself as he lowers his lips against me and sucks on my clit.

"Oh, fuck," I gasp, pushing my hips forward toward Jack, then slamming back onto Cam's cock, holding Lach's gaze in the mirror as my body tenses, my orgasm washing over me like a tsunami, hitting me with wave after wave as I struggle to take a breath. Jack palms my neck and pulls my lips to his as the last tremors fade, his taste melding with mine as our tongues clash.

"You're so fucking hot when you come," he growls, kissing me one more time before sliding back into his seat. Cam thrusts one more time and then pulls out, straightening his clothes.

"You don't want to get there?" I whisper, surprised.

"Not until later." He lifts me from his lap, twists in his seat, and then pulls me against his chest so we can stretch our legs comfortably. I yawn, and he chuckles, kissing the top of my head. "Sleep sweet, my little witch."

75

I wake up to Cam smoothing my hair away from my face, his touch soft and tender.

"We're here," he whispers, smiling down at me like I'm the center of the universe.

"Where is here?" I ask, pushing myself up so I can look out the windows.

"The Abbey," Lach answers, opening my door and pulling me into his arms. He grips my jaw and holds me in place, kissing me soundly before grabbing the cooler from the backseat and tossing me a blanket from the trunk.

"We're having a picnic?" I squeal, feeling like we're in a movie surrounded by tall, crumbling spires and ancient stones.

"Yes," he chuckles, watching me take in our surroundings.

"So that's why you had the cooler crammed full. I wondered why we needed so much for a five-hour road trip." The four of us walk through the shadows of the church, following Cam to what he assured us will be the perfect spot for a picnic.

It *is* perfect. A vast, lush expanse of lawn shielded from the wind allows plenty of room to spread out and a perfect view of the abbey. I shake out the blanket, and Jack takes the opposite corners, helping me spread it on the grass. Cam and Lach sit on one side, Jack and I on the other, the cooler between us. Lach immediately starts unpacking the food. He sets two large foil packets on the blanket and then pulls out a bowl of fruit salad. He carefully pulls away the foil to reveal a gigantic focaccia sandwich, already cut into pieces.

"You brought enough food for twenty people," Jack grumbles, although he doesn't seem too upset about it as he grabs two pieces, handing me one.

"We all need our energy for tonight," Lach says, a grin tugging at his lips as he waggles his eyebrows at me.

"We still have dinner, you know," Cam laughs, taking a massive bite of his sandwich.

"I know. I just couldn't let this opportunity go to waste."

"It's perfect," I tell him, pushing to my knees and leaning over the food to kiss him.

"Sit the fuck down," Jack growls at me, jerking my hips down until my ass is firmly planted on the blanket.

"What's wrong with you?" I swat at his hands until he pulls them back into his lap.

"If you do that again, with that pretty little ass peeking out of your skirt like that – begging me to fuck it – I swear to God, Charlotte. I'll push you down on this blanket and fuck you out in the open where everyone can see. Do you understand?"

Oh God. His words are a potent aphrodisiac, racing through my bloodstream like venom until I can only focus on the heartbeat between my legs.

I nod, my voice abandoning me when my heart jumps into my throat, forming a knot so big that I can barely breathe. I have to get this sweater off. I grab the hem and pull it over my head, taking big gulps of air once I feel like I'm not choking. Cam makes a strangled sound, his gaze locked on the way my nipples are pressing against the fabric of the tank top.

"Why didn't we go straight to the hotel again? This is torture," he whispers, licking his lips before dropping his gaze and adjusting himself.

"This is either going to be the best or worst eight hours of our lives," Lach says, laughing.

"Eight hours?" How the fuck am I going to last eight hours? I'm *this* close to taking Jack up on his offer.

Lach nods. "Our dinner reservation is at seven."

"We can't just go to the hotel after this?" I ask, nibbling at my sandwich.

"Because we're going to wine and dine you properly, Charlotte," Jack says. "There are three of us and only one of you – the least we can do is buy you a proper dinner before we fuck you."

"*Okay*," Lach interrupts, finally starting to look as ruffled as the rest of us, "Why don't we change up the conversation a bit before we all combust?" He turns to me. "Have you thought about the job Jack told you about?"

Last night, when I was lying in bed having trouble getting to sleep, I gave the job offer a lot of thought and finally decided. "I'll take it," I say, looking at Jack.

"Thank fuck," Jack mutters, sending a silent prayer to the sky.

"We were going to have to hire somebody," Lach says, explaining Jack's reaction, "And that probably meant having to house them, too, since there aren't many people that live on Harris – especially ones that specialize in marketing."

"I'm actually really excited to start. I have so many ideas. Have you guys made any sort of plan yet?"

"Nothing is set in stone yet," Jack answers, "Now that I have your answer, we can meet with Isla and brainstorm."

"You, too," Lach says to Cam, giving him a stern look.

"Me? But I don't have any stake in it."

"You fucking live there, Cameron," Lach grumbles, annoyance flashing over his features.

"Fine. I'll be there," Cam says, lifting his hands in surrender.

"Charlotte, where do you want to live?" Jack asks me, the intensity of his gaze warming my cheeks.

"Um—" I stammer, not realizing I was going to be put on the spot like this, "I guess I had assumed we'd live in the castle since you and Cam are already there."

"Is that what you want?"

"Yes, I would love to live there," I answer truthfully. "What about you?" I ask, looking at Lach.

"I'll be wherever you and Cam are. I'm not picky." He turns to Jack. "What about Isla?"

"I'll talk to her about it. Knowing her, she'll love having the house to herself."

"What about your work, Cam?" I ask him, worried he'll be giving up too much.

"I'll commute into Stornoway during the school year, like usual. The only thing that will change is that I decided to never fucking leave you again."

"Cam—"

"I'm serious, Charlie. You have no idea how miserable I was. I don't ever want to go through that again."

"She could visit you, you know," Lach says, chugging from a water bottle.

"What would we do, sleep in separate rooms?" He shakes his head, scowling.

"Speaking of that..." I twist my fingers in the hem of my tank top as I attempt to find the right words. "I think that rule needs to go," I blurt, "It'll get broken eventually and lead to hurt feelings and a lack of trust. Plus, I don't think we should begin our relationship with a rule that's doomed to fail." Jack nods beside me while I watch relief wash over Cam and Lach's faces. "I think we should sleep in the same bed when we're all together. When we're not all together, anything goes as long as we keep communication open."

"Thank fuck," Cam whispers, his eyes shining.

"Are we all agreed?" I ask, relief sinking into my bones, making me giddy.

"Agreed," they echo.

"That leads us to the only thing we haven't talked about yet," Lach says.

"What?"

"The wedding."

"I'm not even divorced yet," I remind him.

"Then let's talk about the divorce," Jack volleys back, his voice firm. "When is it happening?"

"The lawyer will contact me as soon as she gets a date from the court. I plan to head back to the States a couple of weeks before that to attempt mediation with Rob."

"Good. Let us know the date as soon as you know so we can block off those weeks," Jack says, shoving the last bite of the sandwich in his mouth.

"What do you mean?"

"We're going with you, Carebear," Lach answers for him.

"You're what?" I stammer, my blood rushing in my ears.

"Did you really think we would marry you without talking to your parents first?" Jack asks incredulously.

"All three of you want to meet my parents?" Holy shit. Why hadn't this ever occurred to me? Why hadn't I thought more about how this would look to the outside world?

"Plus, there is no way in hell we're going to make you face Rob alone," Lach adds.

"How am I supposed to prepare my parents for meeting the three of you? 'Hi, mom and dad, let me introduce you to the three guys that give me the most mind-blowing orgasms I've ever had, especially when they fill all my holes'?"

I scrub my hands over my face. I'm so fucked.

"You don't need to tell them anything, Charlotte," Jack says, squeezing my knee. "They'll figure it out pretty quickly, and once they see how much we love you, it won't be a big deal."

"But what if it *is* a big deal to them?"

"Then we'll be there to support you."

"Why don't we circle back to this on the drive home?" Lach says, sensing my impending meltdown. "Charlie having a panic attack isn't on the itinerary today."

"I'm okay," I assure him, taking deep, slow breaths, "I'm going to have to come to terms with it eventually."

"Yes, but eventually is not today." He pulls a bottle of wine from the cooler, twists off the tops, and pours a healthy amount into a plastic cup, handing it to me. "Drink up."

"I know how to turn this around," Jack says, the gravel in his voice bringing out goosebumps on my arms. "Let's play a game of hide-and-seek. You hide," he says, mesmerizing me with the intensity of his gaze, "I'll seek."

"But—" I motion to the blanket and the food that needs to be put away.

"No buts," Cam says, the corner of his mouth pulling up.

I push to my feet and glance at Jack, desire blooming in my core as the heat in his gaze burns my skin. He slides a calloused palm up my leg, squeezing my thigh, his finger brushing over my clit.

"Run."

76

My heartbeat roars in my ears as I tuck myself into a tiny alcove at one end of the abbey. It's open from both sides, but panic is setting in so I take the best spot I can find, facing the direction Jack should be coming from, and hope for the best. After about a minute, I see him prowling methodically through the abbey, his gaze roaming like a beast on the hunt. I shrink back, my ass practically hanging out of the other side of the opening, and desperately try to steady my breathing. Someone grabs me by the neck, jerking me against their hard body. I shriek as they move their hand to cover my mouth, the other wrapping around my waist and lifting my feet off the ground.

"It's only me, Charlie," Lach whispers when I struggle against his grip. He carries me outside and around the corner to the front of the abbey, ducking into a dark doorway before releasing me. "That was a fucking awful hiding spot," he chuckles, setting me on my feet and spinning me around to face him, pressing me against the stone wall with his body.

"Jack's looking for me," I protest.

"I found you first." He pushes a lock of hair behind my ear and trails his finger over my cheek, down my throat and between my breasts. "I've been wanting to do this all fucking day," he groans, sliding his hand over my breast and rolling my nipple between his fingers. I moan, arching against him.

"Watching Cam fuck you – watching you come – was torture," he whispers, his lips skating over my jaw. He reaches between us, adjusting himself so his shaft is pressing against my clit, then rocks against me slowly as he presses his lips to mine. Sliding his hand beneath my skirt, he grabs my ass, pulling me against him as he picks up his pace. He pushes his tongue past my lips, demanding more. He pulls back, breathing heavily, fingering the string on my thong just above where it disappears between my ass cheeks.

"There's almost no point in wearing this," he rasps, following the string down, moving it to the side as he pushes into me.

"Fuck," I groan, bucking against his hand.

"Do you think I can still taste him on you?" he asks before crouching in front of me, pulling aside the rest of my thong and fitting his mouth over my clit, making my knees buckle with one long pull.

"Lach, someone will see us," I gasp, grabbing a handful of his hair, trying to pull him away from me.

"Harder," he chuckles, the vibration of his voice coursing through me in waves. He pulses his tongue against me until my knees shake, and I grip his shoulder to stay upright. Standing up, he wedges his knee between my legs to support my body and looks at me from under hooded eyes. "I live for these moments, Charlie," he whispers, his voice like gravel. "You're so fucking beautiful when you're needy." He angles his thigh higher, rolling my clit against his muscled leg.

"Lach," I moan, "Please." I don't care about getting caught anymore – I never want this to stop.

He pulls the end of his belt away from his body, unbuckling it, his eyes on me. "You're sure?"

I answer him by unbuttoning his pants, sliding down his zipper, pushing my hand into his boxers, and pulling out his heavy length. His jaw clenches, his head dropping back, a low moan echoing off the stones around us. He stands up straight and pulls my thong to the side, fitting his cock between my thighs and sliding back and forth in the moisture gathered there.

I whimper, desperate for him to fill me. To fuck me. He pulls my leg up, hooking it over his hip, and thrusts home. Lach muffles my scream with the palm of his hand, his eyes wide. The sunlight in the doorway flickers then disappears as a shadow takes its place. My heart jumps to my throat and my body freezes, my brain screaming at me to move.

"There's my naughty girl." Jack's brogue skitters over my skin as he prowls toward us. Lach pulls out of me and turns around so his back is to the wall, then hooks a hand under my knee, hoisting it higher before burying himself inside me again with a muffled curse.

"Is this my prize for finding you?" Jack breathes, kneading my ass.

I moan, relaxing my muscles and leaning back against his chest, the feeling of being pressed between them almost too much for my body to handle.

"The answer is yes," I say to Jack when I hear him take a breath and start to say something. The zipper of his pants is the only response, and then he's spreading me wide, sliding his cock over my ass and between my legs. He reaches between Lach and I, trapping my clit between his fingers, rolling it back and forth. I angle my hips back to give him easier access, and he guides the head of his cock to my pussy, nudging at my entrance next to where Lach is fully sheathed inside of me. Jack circles my clit until I push my hips back toward him, silently begging him to fill me. He holds his cock firmly as he presses forward, my body stretching to accommodate him.

"Oh fuck," Lach breathes, his eyes rolling back as Jack presses in more, "So fucking tight."

Watching Lach fall apart stokes the fire, a gush of moisture making it easy for Jack to slide in fully.

I forget how to breathe as my body adjusts to them, Jack's fingers still working my clit, forcing my body to relax.

"You better get there fast," Lach rasps, "I don't know how long I can hold out, and I don't want to get there until tonight."

"Don't wait," I groan, squeezing around them.

Lach whimpers when the sunlight coming through the doorway disappears once more. I swivel my head to see Cameron standing there, his cock already in his hand.

Oh God.

He walks toward us, capturing my mouth with his and then turning to Lach, kissing him with unrestrained passion.

"Turn around," Cam says roughly.

"Someone will see," Lach protests, "We're already pushing it."

"Nobody is here – I checked," Cam reassures him. I spin on my toes as the guys shuffle to change position, their cocks never leaving me. I have a front-row seat as Cam jerks down the back of Lach's pants, breathing deeply as he squeezes and spreads his ass. Reaching around Lach, Cam runs his fingers along where the three of us are joined together, scooping up my arousal and spreading it over his cock. Adrenaline pumps through my body as I watch Cam concentrate as he positions himself. Lach's throat bobs, his head dropping back, his body arching as Cam pushes into him.

"Holy fuck," Lach chokes out, impaling himself on Cam's cock before thrusting into me. I whimper as all four of us climb higher, Jack and Lach alternating thrusts but never entirely pulling out. Cam thrusts as Lach pulls back, burying himself, pulling out as Lach fills me again.

I squeeze around them, trying to hold my orgasm off, never wanting this to end.

"Come for me, mo chridhe," Jack groans, catching my earlobe between his teeth. That's all it takes for my body to seize up, my pussy clenching around them. "That's it, good fucking girl," he growls, pushing me higher.

Cam reaches around Lach's arm and palms my breast, plucking my nipple, his gaze burning me alive as he watches me fall apart.

My body explodes into tiny iridescent pieces, floating on the wind, riding the currents until the only thing left is the blinding ecstasy pumping through my veins. They all press against me as my legs give out, sheltering me. They pull slowly out as the last tremors wrack my body, quickly zipping and buckling before gathering me in their arms, all four of us stumbling out into the sunlight to collapse on a blanket of velvety grass.

"I don't understand why you guys held off," I say, turning my face to the sun.

"I thought I taught you this lesson already," Lach says, rolling to his side to look at me, a grin pulling at his mouth.

"Edging?"

"Ding ding ding." He pushes himself up onto his elbow and captures my lips with his. When he collapses to the grass again, I snuggle into Jack's arm, reaching across Lach to grab Cam's hand.

"Have you guys ever done that before?" I ask, curiosity getting the best of me.

"That was the first time," Cam murmurs, squeezing my fingers.

"How was it?" I ask Lach, wondering what it would be like to be a guy, fucking and being fucked.

"Better than I could have ever imagined," he answers truthfully.

"My turn next time," Cam grumbles, making a face at Lach.

"I think we should check in at the hotel and get washed up before we get on with the rest of our day," Jack says, groaning as he pushes himself up, grabbing my hand and pulling me up with him. He crushes my body against his, his kiss hungry and demanding. He doesn't break the kiss as he leans down and scoops me up.

"I can walk," I protest, pushing against his shoulders.

"I know you can walk, Sassenach," he grumbles, his stride eating up the ground as we leave the other two behind. "You'll have three cocks filing you tonight. You need to rest."

Fuck.

77

A clerk stands just inside the hotel's front door and hands Lach the key to our room as we pass.

"Thank you, Fergus," he says, squeezing his shoulder.

My jaw drops as we walk through the lobby – soaring ceilings tower above us, everything dripping with gold and crystal. Gray-veined marble covers the floor, seamlessly flowing up mammoth columns.

"You guys went all out, didn't you?" I ask, my gaze snagging on the mother-of-pearl elevator buttons.

"That's the bloody point, isn't it, Carebear?" Lach says, giving me a lewd wink before pushing the button for the highest floor. Jack sets me down once we leave the elevator, my feet sinking into the plush coral-colored carpet. Lach opens the door to our room with a flourish, stepping back to allow me to go through first. Before I can even step forward, I hear a scuffle behind me, and then Cam's clean scent surrounds me as he tips me into his arms and carries me over the threshold.

"Welcome to our home for the next couple of nights, little witch," he says gruffly, his voice caressing my skin like cool silk. He sets me on my feet, winding his arms around my torso as I look around the room in awe. On the wall across from us, windows stretch floor to ceiling, a sweeping view of Edinburgh castle squeezing the breath from my lungs. I can only imagine how majestic it must look at twilight with the city's twinkling lights below. The largest bed I've ever seen is to our right – easily twice the size of a standard king bed. It's piled high with fluffy blankets and pillows.

Cam looks down at me, his eyes sparkling when he sees how badly I want to jump on it. "Just do it, Charlie," he chuckles.

I run and launch myself on the bed, twisting in mid-air and landing on my back. I almost jump out of my skin when I see myself staring down from the ceiling. "Why is there a mirror on the ceiling?" I ask suspiciously. "Between the bed and the mirror, one would think this room is used for orgies."

"I'm sure it's seen its fair share," Lach says, biting his lip to keep the smile from his lips.

"Either way, it's nice that they have a bed that will fit all of us," I smile, patting the bed so they'll join me. Lach and Cam sit next to me, shrugging out of their layers and pulling off their shoes. Jack doesn't move an inch, he just shoves his hands in his pockets and stares at me.

"Come on," I say, sitting up and patting the bed beside me.

"No."

I raise my eyebrow at him and hop off the bed, stalking toward him. I grab his hand and pull him toward the balcony doors, determined to find some privacy, so he'll tell me what's wrong. We step outside, and the second the door closes behind us, Jack's fingers hook in the waistband of my skirt, and he pulls me roughly against him. I brace my hands on his arms, his muscles rippling under my fingers.

"What's wrong?" I ask him, leaning back so I can look at him.

"What's wrong?" he scoffs, "What's wrong is I'm half a second away from bending you over the railing and fucking you until I don't know where I end and you begin," he says roughly. "I can't be near you without touching you, and I can't touch you without touching things I shouldn't be touching right now." He slides his palm over my ass and squeezes.

"Then let's skip dinner."

"I'm not ruining the rest of the day because I can't control myself, Charlotte."

"You won't be ruining anything. Unless you plan on eating dinner off my naked body while the entire restaurant watches, I would much rather stay in the room and be thoroughly fucked."

"Is that what you want? To be watched?" he asks quietly, spinning me around and sliding his hands down my arms, his hands covering mine as he places them on the railing. I look down at the people walking on the street below us, a thrill racing over my skin.

"Maybe?" I whisper.

"Should I push your skirt up, pull your panties to the side and fuck you right here?" I moan as he rolls his hips against me. "I love learning new things about you," he says roughly, his lips against my ear. "How about a bath and a quick nap instead?"

"Who said anything about a nap?" I protest as he leads me inside, stopping at a clawfoot tub set into an alcove. Jack doesn't answer, instead turning on the water and watching me through the billowing steam.

"Arms up," Cam says from behind me, kissing the skin between my neck and shoulder. He peels off my top and then unhooks my bra. Placing a finger at the top of my neck, he slowly runs it down my spine, his breath hitching. "This isn't a race, Charlie," he murmurs as he unzips my skirt.

"It's a marathon. If we all want to reach the end together – without injuries – we need to take it slow." He pushes my skirt off my hips and turns me around, the hunger in his gaze speaking to something feral deep inside me. I unbutton his shirt and slide my hands inside the fabric, desperate to feel his skin on mine. He drops to his knees in front of me, eases my underwear over my hips, and helps me step out of them. His jaw flexes as he looks up at me, struggling to control himself. He gives in and grabs my thighs, pulling me toward him. My body spasms as his tongue slide over my clit in one long, languid stroke.

"Fuck," I gasp, pushing my fingers into his hair.

"His mouth is magic, isn't it?" Lach whispers as he walks up behind me. He cups my breast and rolls my nipple between his fingers. Tracing a finger over my ass, he follows the curve to my pussy, pushing a finger inside me. I sag against Lach as my muscles give up under the punishing onslaught of their attention. When Cam feels my thighs start to spasm, he pulls away, a tortured look on his face.

"Please," I beg.

"Not until tonight," Cam says softly, watching Lach lift me into the bathtub. Cam sits at my head, coaxing me back until only my face is out of the water. He wets it thoroughly and then helps me sit up before pouring shampoo into his palm and massaging it into my scalp. Lach sinks to his knees to my left, and Jack sits on the edge of the tub and rubs my feet, all three of them pampering me like a goddess.

The attention makes me uncomfortable at first. My body knows how to handle sexual touch, but this? The intimacy is overwhelming. Sensual. I steady my breathing, forcing myself to relax and enjoy their ministrations. Jack pulls one of my legs out of the water and opens a tub of salt scrub, carefully scrubbing one leg before starting on the other. Lach massages my left arm first, then moves to the other side of the tub and massages my right arm, then presses his fingers into my chest muscles until my nipples beg for his touch. Cam leaves for a second and returns with a cup, filling it with fresh water and carefully pouring it over my hair. Once he finishes rinsing out the shampoo, he pulls the stopper out and drains the soapy water.

"We'll fill it again, don't worry," he laughs when he sees the look on my face as goosebumps pebble my skin. As the last of the water swirls down the drain, Cam motions to Lach to turn on the water. Lach's gaze snags on my puckered nipples as he reaches over, cranking one of the handles without looking.

"Fuck!" I shriek, arching away from the freezing water.

"That's the cold water, you idiot," Cam laughs, covering Lach's hand as he turns the water off. Cam cranks the hot water, smirking at Lach's inability to move his gaze from my body.

Jack stands suddenly, looking down at me with dark eyes. "You have never looked more like a selkie, mo chridhe." His throat bobs. "Legend says fishermen used to steal the selkie skins so their women couldn't disappear back into the ocean," he murmurs, his voice sliding over me like velvet.

"Would you do that?" I ask him, my body humming beneath his gaze.

"Do you want the pretty answer or the real answer?"

"Real," I say without hesitation, my heartbeat pounding in my ears.

"I would lock it up in a chest with a thousand chains and drop it into the deepest part of the ocean."

"What if I wanted to go home?"

"I would tell you where the chest is, and you would dive for it," he says, crossing his arms.

"And then what?"

"I would help you."

"But you'd drown."

"Anything for you." He flips the switch on the towel warmer hanging on the wall and stalks away from us without another word.

"Is he saying he'd rather die than lose me?" I ask, turning to Lach, my heart in my throat.

"I think we all would if I'm being completely honest," he shrugs. I tuck that knowledge away to examine later.

I hear the shower turn on and have a hard time keeping my mind off the mental image of Jack's large soapy hand sliding up and down that magic cock of his.

Cam pulls my hair outside the tub and gently dries it with the towel before combing it with his fingers.

"I didn't make it awkward by proposing to you, did I?" I ask, the question falling from my lips without my permission. He stands and moves to the side of the tub, his ring flashing in the light as he grips the side and eases back down on his knees.

"Not even the tiniest bit. When I returned to find you and found out I would have to share you, I wasn't sure I would be strong enough.

I couldn't rip you away from Lach and Jack to start over again – plus, I don't think you would have been happy.

"Are *you* happy?" I ask him, his words breaking my heart more than a little bit.

"There isn't a word to describe how I feel, Charlie. I'm more than happy. When the four of us are together, it's like coming home. I feel complete." He flicks water at me to break the tension and then yelps and jumps away as I send a wave of water back.

"Will one of you hand me a towel?" I ask, rivulets of water streaming down my body as I push to my feet, steam billowing from my body. Both of them exhale sharply, reaching for me, trapping me between them as they lean over the side of the tub. Lach grips my chin and pulls my mouth to his while Cam kisses my neck, his hands skating down my body. Jack chooses that moment to burst out of the bathroom, a white towel wrapped tightly around his waist that does absolutely nothing to hide his raging hard-on.

"Why don't you two go take a shower? I'll get Charlie dried off." He tugs a towel from the rack and stalks toward me, lust radiating from him in waves. Cam and Lach leave me with a kiss on the cheek, and then Jack wraps me in a towel and lifts me out of the bathtub. He walks to the bed and throws me down, the towel opening and presenting me to him like a goddamn present. His gaze travels down my body, stopping between my legs. I open for him, desperate for anything he'll give me. I'll never forget how he looks at me at this moment, his jaw flexing, nostrils flaring, the way his eyes darken, and that predatory grace and quietness that seems to settle over his shoulder like a mantle.

"You're playing a dangerous game, Charlotte," he rasps, palming my thighs and pushing them wider.

"I hope so," I breathe, slipping from his grip, turning over to my stomach, and pushing my ass in the air. He grips my cheeks, spreading them wide as he slides a finger down my crack, brushing the sensitive area around my asshole.

"Stop teasing me," he growls.

"Or what? Your control will snap, and you'll finally fuck my ass?"

He makes a strangled sound, his beard scratching against sensitive skin as he leans his forehead against my lower back.

"God, I'm not strong enough for this," he says, his voice raw.

"Go ask them," I beg, my body buzzing with need.

"If I start, I won't be able to stop. It'll ruin our dinner plans."

"*Go ask them*," I say again, the last word ending with a sob.

He walks toward the bathroom, and I hear him murmuring something, then the dulcet tones of Lach's voice, then Cam's. I look back at Jack as he digs a bottle of lube out of his bag, millions of butterflies going haywire in my stomach. He's so goddamn beautiful.

"Don't fucking move," he commands when he sees me start to turn over. He drops the lube on the bed and pulls my hips up roughly, kneading my cheeks. "You want me to sink my cock into that virgin ass and have the best goddamn orgasm of my life while I watch your pretty pink pussy stretching for them? Is that what you want?"

He doesn't wait for my answer before spreading me wide and licking from my clit to my asshole, making me scream.

78

Jack hooks an arm under my leg and flips me over on my back, hunger burning in his eyes.

"This is my final warning," he says, dragging his hands down my body and pushing my knees flat on the bed.

"Fuck me," I demand, arching my back as he sweeps his thumbs along the crease of my thighs.

"You're sure you want to miss out on a Michelin-star restaurant?"

"I'm not missing out on anything when I have all I could ever want to eat right here in this hotel room," I say, gasping as he traps my clit with his thumbs and rolls it between his fingers. He walks over to the side of the bed and grabs something from the nightstand drawer, tossing it to me.

"Pick what you want and we'll call down and have it brought up."

I glance at the menu, an icon on the lower right indicating a Michelin star. "You mean we could have ordered room service this entire time?" I groan. "We wasted so much time." I toss the menu back onto the bed. "Since you guys have obviously been here before, why don't you order?" Jack grumbles something under his breath and grabs the phone from the nightstand, punching in a number. I roll off the bed and drop to my knees in front of him just as someone picks up on the other end.

"Hello, I—" his throat bobs, his knuckles turning white as I fist his cock and swirl my tongue around the head. His muscles tense as he reins himself in, barely moving as he orders, his twitching abs the only sign that this affects him. Grabbing the back of his thighs, I pull him forward, opening my throat for him, swallowing him down until my lips press against the soft skin of his torso. The phone drops next to me on the floor when I hum around him, his other hand cradling my head as he fucks my mouth. I take a greedy breath when he pulls out, holding it as he pushes back in until he hits the back of my throat.

He runs his finger over my top lip, his gaze like molten lava. "Those lips are going to be the death of me," he rasps, flexing his hips and burying himself. He wipes under my eyes with the pad of his thumb, wiping away the tears and then licking them off. Pulling out, he hauls me to my feet and crushes his lips to mine. The kiss turns desperate quickly when he pulls my leg around his waist and thrusts into me, both of us stumbling back into the wall. I groan, digging my fingernails into his shoulders as I meet him thrust for thrust.

"I don't think I'll ever get enough," he says, his breath fanning over my ear, hiking my other leg up so he can go deeper. "It's like you were fucking made for me." He walks us to the bed, laying me down and slowly pulls out of me. He grabs my waist and flips me over smoothly, lifting my hips as high as they'll go.

"You're not allowed to come until I say so. Do you understand?"

"I understand," I rasp, my entire body thrumming with anticipation.

"Good girl." He drops to his knees behind me, spreading me wide before feathering his tongue over my clit. My entire body tenses when I feel his nose press way too close to somewhere it shouldn't be, but he fucks me with his tongue and then moves up my crack and I stop caring. I push back against him as he slides his tongue back and forth over that forbidden spot. It feels so wrong and so fucking right at the same time.

"Jack!" I squeal, trying to twist away from his grip as he pushes his tongue against the ring of muscle. I moan, my body shuddering as sensation overrides my embarrassment. He pushes in further and I bite the base of my thumb, arching my back. I desperately want to reach between my legs, but I know I'll explode the second I touch myself, so I keep my hands fisted in the comforter.

He stands up and grabs the bottle of lube, pouring some directly onto my ass. He anchors his fingers on my ass cheeks, using his thumbs to spread the lube, massaging me until I'm squirming and pushing back into his hands.

"Take a deep breath and relax your muscles," he says, slipping his thumb in as I breathe out. He slides his thumb around the rim, stretching me slowly. "Fuck," he groans, slipping his other thumb in and massaging the muscle around and around. His breathing turns ragged as he steps closer, pressing his cock against my thigh and rocking his hips back and forth.

"Jack—" I plead, not sure if I'm asking him to stop because I'm close or to keep going so I can get there.

"I know, me too." He presses on my lower back, forcing me to lower my hips. He fists his cock and slides it up and down my crack. "God," he moans, "Please tell me I can fuck your ass now," he begs, his voice raw.

"Yes." The word isn't even all the way out of my mouth before I hear the top of the lube bottle opening. He positions himself behind me, the head of his cock nudging my ass. "You're in control," he says to me. "I'll only push until the tip is in. When you're ready, you can rock back on me. I won't thrust until you tell me to, okay?"

"Okay," I whisper. "Please, Jack," I beg, arching my back.

"Touch yourself," he says roughly, gripping his cock as he presses it against that tight ring of muscle. I push myself up to get a hand underneath me as he flexes his hips forward, stretching me. I roll my clit under my fingers, rocking my hips forward and then back, slowly letting him in. He doesn't move, only holds my hips as my body opens for him.

"Just a little more and the head will be in." He flexes his hips, pushing until the widest part of his cock slips in, and I feel myself close around his shaft. I whimper, squeezing around him as I adjust to his size. A strangled groan rips from his throat, his hands spasming on my hips.

"Don't you dare do that again unless you're ready for me to fuck you," he wheezes, his cock flexing inside me. I whimper as I circle my fingers over my clit again, pushing my hips forward and back. Over and over until I'm fully seated on his cock. My entire world condenses to the feeling of him filling me. Nothing else matters. I rock my hips forward a couple of inches, rolling my clit under my fingers before pushing back, taking him all the way in again. I squeeze my muscles around him, sliding along the entire length of his shaft.

"God, Charlotte," he groans, his hands trembling. "Give me a second."

"You may as well get the first time over with," Lach chuckles from the bathroom doorway, the towel wrapped around his waist doing absolutely nothing to hide his fully erect cock. "You know you won't last more than five seconds."

"Fuck," Jack says through gritted teeth. "This is not how I imagined this would go."

"Is my ass going to be what finally breaks you?" I ask him, failing to keep the smile off my lips.

"You found my kryptonite," he murmurs, laughter in his voice.

I feel the bed dip and look over to see Lach lying down, his head on a pillow. "Come sit on my face, Carebear."

"But —"

"Go." Jack pulls out and slaps my ass to get me going. I crawl over to Lach and climb on top of him, shrieking when he pulls me down to seal his lips over my clit.

"Hold on to the headboard and push your hips back," Jack says, straddling Lach's torso behind me.

Oh, God.

I angle my hips, offering myself to him. "Fuck me, Jack," I say, giving him permission before he has to ask. He drags his cock over me, holding himself in position as he pushes into me slowly. As Jack bottoms out, Lach pulses his tongue over me, keeping my body relaxed.

I hear a moan and look back to see Cam standing at the end of the bed, his cock in his hand. Jack follows my gaze and pulls back from me.

"Change of plans," he says, helping me climb off Lach's face. "Do you think you're ready for all of us? If we don't let off some steam now, we won't last long enough to fuck you the way we want to later."

"God, yes."

Cam prowls toward me, puts a knee on the edge of the bed, and palms the base of my throat, pushing me back into the pillows as he stretches his body over mine. He teases my clit with the head of his cock before ramming into me, my back bowing as neglected nerve endings spark to life.

Lach tilts my chin toward him, biting my lower lip and drawing me into a kiss that tastes like sex. "Flip her on top," he murmurs to Cam. "Jack looks like he might die if he doesn't get his cock in her again." Cam rolls, pulling me with him, and I collapse to his chest as he thrusts back into me.

Jack gets into position behind me, gripping my hips, his hands shaking with need. "We'll start with two and then change positions once you're comfortable," he says, his voice low and husky. "Are you ready?"

I've never been more ready for anything in my entire life.

79

I press my cheek into Cam's shoulder as I rock my clit over his pubic bone. The bed dips as Jack climbs up behind me, rough hands sliding over my hips as he positions himself. A low, strangled sound tears from my throat as he slides the head of his cock over me, teasing me.

"Are you ready?" he asks, his deep brogue sliding over my skin like silk.

"Yes," I moan. He holds his cock firmly in one hand as I push back against him. A breath hisses from between his lips as he slides past the tight ring of muscle.

"Fuck," I gasp, struggling to breathe, my body misfiring, signals confused. The feeling of fullness is overwhelming. Jack gives me a second to adjust and then slides in slowly, bottoming out with a groan. I whimper as the need to come becomes all-consuming. I slide my body forward, grinding my clit against Cam, and then push back. Jack meets me with a solid thrust, his resulting moan sending goose-bumps skittering over my skin.

"God, I can feel your cock inside her," Cam rasps, his breath stuttering as Jack thrusts again. Cam grasps my hips, pulling my body tightly to his as he circles his hips underneath me. Running my fingers over his stubbled jaw, I press my lips to his, our tongues tangling.

"Come with me, little witch," Cam whispers, his hooded gaze trapping me and dragging me under. I whimper as they push into me simultaneously, the three of us finding a rhythm and climbing together. I look up and meet Lach's dark gaze as my body explodes. My body grips them tight, their hips stuttering against me as their worlds narrow to this one moment. We collapse into a heap of slick skin, sweat-soaked hair, and gasping breaths.

Jack pulls out carefully, lying down next to Cam, his chest heaving. Lach reaches for my waist, helping me roll off Cam. I land next to him, our stunned gazes meeting in the mirror overhead. We burst out laughing, grinning at each other like love-struck teenagers. Lach rolls off the bed and grabs my ankles, pulling me toward him, not warning me before dropping to his knees and eating me out like a starving man. My entire body flinches when he sucks on my clit, the feeling riding the thin edge between pleasure and pain.

"Lach, it's too much," I gasp. "I don't know if I can—"

"Oh, you're going to," he pants, pushing two fingers into me, crooking them up to massage my g-spot. He continues the onslaught as he stands, his dark gaze pinning me to the bed. A lock of hair falls over his forehead as he leans over me, brushing his lips over the tops of my breasts before pulling a nipple into his mouth. I writhe beneath him as my body starts to spasm around his fingers. He pulls out and guides his cock into place, his jaw flexing as he slams home. He rests his weight on his elbows on either side of my head, cradling my face.

"Come with me," he whispers, smoothing tangled hair away from my face. He circles his pelvis against mine, grinding against my clit, and then thrusts again, angling his hips so the head of his cock hits my g-spot. I get lost in the swirling blues and greens of his eyes as he expertly brings me to the precipice. He tilts my chin up, forcing me to look in the mirror. I watch the long lines of his back as he claims me, his muscles bunching as I slide my fingers over him. One more thrust and he's dragging me over the edge with him, both of us tumbling into the abyss. His body tenses, hips spasming, ass clenching as he spills into me. I dig my nails into his shoulders as my orgasm rips through me, my entire body seizing.

We lay there gasping for breath until a knock on the door has us scrambling up. Lach scoops me into his arms and carries me to the bathroom while Cam and Jack shrug into thick, fluffy robes.

"We'll let them deal with that while I get you cleaned up," Lach murmurs, using his elbow to turn on the shower. He sets me on my feet, lifting the lid of the toilet. "Pee," he demands, "I refuse to have the memory of this weekend ruined by a UTI." I obey without complaint, then let him lead me into the shower, my knees wobbling like a newborn deer's. He positions me under the stream of water, steam billowing between us, making this feel like a fever dream.

"How are you feeling?" he asks softly, pulling my body against his.

"Maybe ask me that after I drink a gallon of water and eat something," I say, chuckling.

"That good, eh?"

"All four of us next time, right?" I tip my head back to look up at him, his gaze pulling me in. I run my fingers over his cheek, connecting the freckles.

He nods. "I wanted to this time, but I would never forgive myself if I hurt you."

"You won't hurt me," I murmur, resting my cheek against his chest as the water pummels my back. I relax in his arms as he slides soapy hands over my body and gently splashes water between my legs. He turns the shower off and wraps me in a fluffy towel, using another to squeeze the water from my hair. We help each other into robes, and then I turn to the mirror, carefully detangling my hair with my fingers. I study Lach, and he looks back at me, the corner of his mouth pulling up.

"You look like you were just thoroughly fucked," he says roughly.

"And you look like a smug bastard," I shoot back, unable to keep the smile off my lips.

His eyes darken, and he grabs my wrist, spinning me toward him.

"I may be a bastard, but I'll never be smug when it comes to you," he says, pressing his lips to mine.

Cam pokes his head in the door, a tenderness softening his eyes. "The food is here when you two are ready," he says. He starts to leave but decides against it, embracing us instead, kissing me thoroughly before turning to Lach and drawing him into a passionate kiss. A thrill goes through me, and suddenly I'm desperate to know what it would be like for the three of us to make love. My pussy throbs painfully, and I break away from them, holding up my hands.

"My body thinks it's a good idea to fuck you both, but I need food, drink, and a nap before the next round," I say, waving an imaginary white flag. They laugh, taking one hand each and leading me to the balcony where dishes covered in silver domes await us. Jack is lounging in a wrought-iron chair, his hair mussed, half pulled back, the rest hanging around his face. He's wearing a robe like the rest of us, only his barely fits over his large frame. Muscular thighs snag my attention, and I swallow hard, resisting the urge to touch him. I sit on his lap so I can't look at his body, immediately realizing my mistake as he presses a hand against my stomach, spanning the space between my hipbones as he pulls me against him.

"I ordered a little of everything," he says, slipping his hand inside my robe, the heat of his fingers making my breath hitch. Lach piles a plate high and sets it in front of me before serving himself. Jack picks up a slice of steak and holds it to my lips, waiting for me to take a bite before finishing it. Both of us groan as the flavors explode over our tongues.

"Watch it," he murmurs in my ear. "If you make that sound again, I'll have to take you into the bedroom and figure out how to make you do it again."

"Maybe I only make that sound when I eat something I like," I murmur, licking my lips.

"Mmm. Is that so?" He tightens his grip, flexing his hips against me, his cock pressing into my back.

"Already?" I ask, raising an eyebrow at him, trying to play off the desire coursing through my body.

"Always," he answers, a wicked gleam in his eyes.

80

"Eating that much was a horrible idea," I groan, sinking into my chair.

"How can you not when it tastes so fucking good?" Lach asks, spooning up a bit of chocolate torte and holding it to my lips.

"Sex and full stomachs do not go together." My eyes roll back as the chocolate explodes over my tongue.

"They're about to if you don't stop making sounds like that," Jack grumbles, giving me a dirty look.

"Now would be a perfect time to tour the castle," Cam pipes in, pushing his glasses up his nose. His hair falls over his forehead as he talks, excitement shining in his eyes. "We can burn off the food while we take the tour and then come back and..." he trails off, his gaze softening.

"Fuck like animals?" Lach finishes for him, grinning. His robe has fallen open, revealing the light dusting of golden hair over his chest.

"Yes, that." Cam clears his throat, heat creeping up his cheeks. He licks his lower lip and pulls it into his mouth without realizing what he's doing. Lach and I stare at him, imagining all the dirty things that mouth can do, and we lunge simultaneously, taking turns kissing him.

My forehead collides with Lach's cheek. "Fucking hell!" he splutters, covering his cheek with his hand, his eyes wide. I try to keep in my laugh but snort instead, the three of us dissolving into a fit of giggles.

The sound of dishes being cleared brings us back to the present, and we all scramble to help Jack clear the table, sneaking morsels of food before we can relinquish them back to the serving cart.

"We bought a dress for you; it was supposed to be for dinner tonight," Lach says as Jack pushes the cart into the hallway.

"And I ruined it for you." My heart falls.

"Wear it now!" Cam suggests, his eyes lighting up.

"To the castle?"

They both nod. "We can go out for drinks afterward," Lach says.

"We'll all dress up." Jack shrugs off his robe, my jaw dropping as I watch him haul a suitcase onto the stand, thick muscles rippling with every movement. Cam pushes a large box into my hands, stealing my attention from Jack. I set it on the bed and pull the end of the black satin ribbon. Easing off the top, I open the tissue to reveal a sleek black dress with sweeping mesh panels.

"This is gorgeous," I breathe, lifting it from the box. I don't think I've ever owned such an elegant dress. It has long sleeves and a high neck, but I can tell by the placement of the panels that it will show a lot of skin. Jack comes up behind me and slides my robe down my shoulders, the callouses on his hands leaving a trail of goosebumps over my arms.

"This goes with it," he murmurs into my ear, handing me a small bag. I pull a lacy black thong, matching garter belt, and thigh-high stockings from the bag.

"No bra?"

"The dress doesn't allow for one," Lach grins. Jack pulls the robe away from my body, sweeping his hands over my skin before kneeling behind me and sliding the thong over my feet and up my legs. My nerve endings are throbbing by the time the fabric brushes between my legs. Rough hands slide from my ankles to my thighs, tugging the fabric out of the way before dragging his thumb through my folds. He leans forward and bites my ass before returning to his feet and fastening the garter belt around my waist.

"Sit," Cam murmurs, crouching to slide the stockings up my legs, fastening them to the garter. My gaze collides with Lach's as Cam steps away, the heat in his eyes unbearable. The corner of his mouth twitches as he pushes off the wall and stalks toward me.

"Turn over," he says roughly.

"What?" I look up at him through my eyelashes, my pulse pounding in my ears.

"Lay down and turn over." He helps me flip to my stomach and then lifts my hips. I draw my knees under my body and arch my back, pushing back and opening for him. "Holy fuck," he rasps, pulling at my thong and watching as it tugs between my legs. He palms my ass, squeezing and spreading, his groan lodging in my core. He slides his finger under the string of my thong and follows it down until he's nudging at my swollen clit. "Fuck, Charlie." He circles his finger over me, my entire body shuddering.

"I bet it would only take one lick to get you there," he says, pressing his face against me as he pulls the fabric to the side. I jerk under the feather-light touch of his tongue, desperately pushing myself back on his face. He pulls back, chuckling. "God, I love how responsive you are." He flips me onto my back, pushing his pelvis between my legs as he leans over me. His cock is pressing against the front of his pants, straining to be released. I wrap my legs around him, locking him against me, riding my clit over the head of his cock.

He laughs as he struggles to break free but is not fast enough. My muscles tense, and the only thing I can think about is how badly I want his cock buried inside me.

"Oh fuck, hang on," he says, seeing the desperation in my eyes. Pushing to his knees, he fumbles with the button on his pants. He pulls my thong to the side and plunges into me just as I start to come, my world exploding into a kaleidoscope of colors and sensations as he grinds against me, keeping firm pressure on my clit.

"Fuck," I breathe as the tremors fade, my body melting into the bed.

"I thought you said sex and full stomachs don't mix?" Lach chuckles, zipping back up and scooping me into his arms, carrying me to the bathroom.

"They never have before. It's different with the three of you. Like my body is primed and ready to go all the time."

"I know what you mean. I don't think there's been a single time I've been around you when I'm not hard as a fucking rock. It's going to be a problem if it continues."

"Why would it be a problem?"

"Because we're going to be working together, Carebear. I don't want to greet my clients with a hard-on."

"Fair enough," I laugh. I grab my makeup bag, thankful that I brought more than my usual Chapstick and mascara. Lach leaves me in the bathroom as he goes to get dressed, and I make quick work of my makeup. I slide the nude lip gloss over my lips, wondering who will be the first to rub it off. One last swipe of mascara completes my smoky eye, and I walk back into the bedroom to get dressed. I freeze as all three turn and look at me like they want to fuck my brains out. All three of them are in suits. Jack is wearing a deep caramel brown that accents the honey tones in his hair. Lach is in a deep olive green that matches his eyes, and Cam's suit is the color of the sky just after sunset. They're so goddamn beautiful.

"Get dressed," Jack growls, his gaze sweeping over my body as he fastens his cufflinks.

"Yes, sir!" I salute him as I walk to the bed, unzipping the dress and stepping into it. Cam comes up behind me, kissing my back before zipping up the dress. I turn toward him, smoothing the dress over my hips. The mesh reveals the bottom of my left breast and sweeps over my hip to expose the dimples in my back before dropping down the side of my thigh.

"How does it look?"

Cam groans, adjusting himself before answering me. "You're so fucking gorgeous, Charlie." He caresses my cheek, tilting my chin to meet his gaze. "I'm jealous of every man that has the honor of laying eyes on you tonight."

Jack grips my elbow and spins me toward him before I can respond to Cam. His whisky gaze rakes over me. "We better leave now, or you won't be leaving this room 'till morning, Charlotte."

"Oh, yeah?" My grin falters as something dangerous flashes over his face. He backs me up into the doorway, leaning over me, and plants a hand on the frame.

"I'll fuck you against this doorway until you're screaming so loud they can hear you in the lobby." He slides his hand over my hip and hikes my leg up, pushing his pelvis against mine. I groan as he rolls his hips, turning to putty in his hands.

"Enough," Lach says, reaching behind me and turning the doorknob, watching with a smirk as Jack and I stumble into the hallway. He hands me a pair of black strappy shoes with blinding red soles. "Come on. Let's go make every guy in Edinburgh jealous."

81

L ach helps me into the shoes, carefully buckling the straps around my ankles. He stands, threading his fingers through mine as we walk down the hall to the elevator.

"It should be illegal for your ass to look that good," he groans, his breath hot on my ear. "I want to press you against this wall and fuck you right here." A shiver races down my spine, my body responding to his words.

"Prove it."

He grabs my hand and presses it against the front of his pants, pushing his cock against my palm.

"Stand down, soldier," I laugh, giving him a light squeeze before stepping onto the elevator.

As we exit the lobby, a sleek black limousine pulls up in front of the hotel. There's a dangerous charge to the air once we climb in and the driver closes the door. Desire crackles between us, and I wonder if we'll even make it out of the car when we pull to a stop. My heels click on the stout drawbridge as we cross over the moat and enter through a portcullis. The castle is even more impressive up close. An impenetrable fortress perched on a long-dormant volcano.

Cam has an animated chat with the lady at the ticket desk and returns to us with a grin.

"We have full access," he says excitedly, his eyes sparkling.

Lach groans. "Cam—"

Cam holds his hands up. "I know! I'll only show you guys the best parts. Just enough to walk the food off."

"I can't even pretend to be annoyed when you're so fucking cute," Lach laughs. "Lead on, Dr. Cameron." I watch, fascinated, as Cam's eyes darken, a little shiver shaking his shoulders. He pulls himself together quickly and motions for us to follow him. I pay more attention to him than his words, falling more in love with every story he tells us. He takes off his jacket and rolls up his sleeves as we enter the Crown room, and I have to bite my lip to keep from groaning. I must make a sound because he looks up slowly, our gazes colliding and jolting my system.

"Are you doing okay?" he asks softly, pushing his hair off his forehead even though it falls right back into place.

"Yep!" I cross my legs to stem my body's response to him. He raises his eyebrow but doesn't push.

"This is The Stone of Destiny." He gestures toward a rectangular stone nestled in a swath of black velvet. "This stone was used for centuries during the inauguration of Scotland kings. Edward, the first of England, stole it in the late 13th century. He built his throne around it, and it was used during England's coronation ceremonies for hundreds of years. On Christmas day in 1950, four students stole the stone, and its whereabouts were unknown until it reappeared three months later, five hundred miles away at Arbroath Abbey.

"That sounds like a movie," I say, wondering if the students were courageous or maybe they just did it on a drunken lark.

"Are you ready for the last part of the tour?" Cam asks, his eyes sparkling with mischief. "We're going down into the vaults."

"The what?" My heartbeat picks up.

"There's an entire underground city to explore beneath our feet. The lady at the desk told me there's an event tonight. We can enter the vaults through a passage here in the castle."

"How many ghosts do you think we'll see?" Lach asks nonchalantly.

"Ghosts?" I echo.

"Goddamnit, Lach." Cam shoots him a dirty look. "It's not haunted," Cam says, trying to placate me.

"Then why is it known as the most haunted place in Scotland?" Lach asks, antagonizing us.

"It's not scary, Sassenach. Promise." Jack slides his hand over my lower back and hooks it around my waist.

"You've been down there before?" I ask, looking up into his face.

"We all have." He tucks a lock of hair behind my ear, tracing the shell of my ear with his fingertip.

"And why were you down there, Jack?" Lach asks, his eyes dancing.

Jack clears his throat, looking guilty. "A ghost tour."

"There will be a bunch of people down there tonight, Charlie. It won't be scary," Cam assures me, taking my hand and guiding me into the hallway.

"Fine," I mutter, slightly ashamed about my overreaction. Cam leads us down several flights of stairs, the last carved from stone, through a long hallway that ends in a door that looks like it hasn't been opened in five hundred years. He wrenches on the handle, the resulting groan of metal sending a shiver down my back.

"This is the last set of stairs," he says, turning on his phone's flashlight and illuminating rough rock steps. He takes my hand and helps me down the uneven treads.

"I thought you said this wasn't going to be scary," I whisper, looking around at the cobwebbed walls. I take a deep breath and look down the dark passageway, blowing the air out slowly to calm my nerves. It doesn't help.

"We'll be through this part and into the lighted area in less than a minute," Cam promises, pulling me along. Lach flanks my other side, sweeping his hand down my back. I squeak when he grabs my ass, but it quickly turns to a stifled moan as he hikes up my dress and runs his hand over my bare bottom.

He fingers the strap holding up my stockings, snapping it against my leg playfully. "I can't wait to feel those shoes digging into my ass later," he says roughly, skimming his hand up the back of my thigh and pushing a finger between my legs, sliding it over the fabric of my panties. My knees buckle, his laugh echoing around us as he hauls me against his body, turning to press me into the wall, kissing me senseless.

"What was that for?" I ask breathlessly once we continue walking, my body buzzing from his touch.

"The ultimate distraction technique," he says with a smile, gesturing for me to pass through the door Cameron had opened at the end of the hallway. We enter a large cavern glowing with thousands of lights. A long bar is set up on one side, a DJ booth on the other, and the rest of the space serves as a dance floor. I still feel claustrophobic, but this is much better than the dark tunnel.

Jack asks me what I want to drink, but I shake my head and pull all three of them to the dancefloor. The music is pumping through my blood, a feral, minimalist beat that calls to something deep inside me. I close my eyes and sway to the music, letting it seep into my bones until it's part of me. I wrap my hands around Cam's and Lach's necks as Jack circles my waist with his hands, drawing my body against his. The guys close in, lips on my neck, in my hair. Palms coasting over my waist, my ribs, fingers brushing my ribs, the sides of my breasts. Cam slides his hand over my ass, wedging a thigh between my legs as he pulls me against him.

"What spell did you cast tonight, little witch?" he murmurs, his mouth against my ear. I roll my hips against his thigh, my mouth falling open as desire grips me, its talons relentless until all I can think about is feeling their skin on mine. Jack grabs my waist and turns me toward him, pulling my arms up around his neck, sliding his hands from my wrists slowly, dragging them over the sides of my breasts before settling on my waist.

"You look like you're ready to rip your dress off over your head and pull us down to the floor," he chuckles, caressing my face and pulling at my lower lip.

"I would say that's a fairly accurate observation." My fingers graze over his neck, tracing his collarbone until he captures them and brings my hand down to his cock, pressing against me with a groan.

"I need your hands on me, Sassenach."

"I think we should find somewhere a little more private," I say into his ear, desire pumping through my body, rendering me incapable of rational thought. I motion for them to follow me through what I assume is the door to exit. A man stops us as we get to the door, his brow furrowed until he takes Lach's ID. He seems to startle a bit, looking between Lach and the ID, and then ushers us through. We enter into a softly lit cavern, the music here slow and sensuous. There's a woman at a tall desk just inside the door, and she stands, motioning us over.

"Are you observing or playing?" she asks, looking between the four of us as she waits for an answer.

"Observing?" I say when we all seem equally confused. She snaps four glowing magenta necklaces around our necks. We look at each other, bewildered. We walk further into the room, our eyes adjusting slowly, and then the four of us freeze in place, our eyes wide.

"This is a sex club!" Lach hisses, shock giving way to humor.

Oh, God. I look around me, the dim light making everything soft and out of focus. There's a sleek, modern bar to our left, a long booth against the far wall, various couches – most of them filled with couples – and a long line of windows embedded into the wall on our right, most of them dark. I walk toward one glowing softly from within, realizing what my eyes are seeing halfway there. There's a room beyond the glass, a large bed in its center. A man is splayed across it, his wrists and ankles tied to each corner. He's breathing hard, his cock standing at attention as a woman approaches him, a flogger in her hand. She's gorgeous. Long dark hair falls over her bare shoulders in loose waves. A black mask hides most of her face, forcing the focus to her blood-red lips. She smiles down at the man, slowly dragging the flogger down the side of his face.

"It's your call, Sassenach," Jack breathes into my ear. "Do you want to stay or go back to the hotel?" Strong hands grip my hips as he pulls me against his body, his cock pressing into my back.

I watch the woman climb gracefully onto the bed, her breasts spilling over her black corset. She stands over him, gliding the flogger over his chest. She snaps it on his nipple, and I jerk, my eyes wide as the man groans, arching his body. Jack pulls the hem of my dress up as we watch, hooking his fingers under my thong, sliding easily in the moisture gathered there.

"Fuck, Charlotte," he groans, circling my clit before pushing a finger into me. I moan as I watch the woman drop to her knees, the man's cock barely brushing her pussy. She cracks the flogger over his other nipple as she impales herself, her head dropping back in ecstasy.

Holy fuck.

"Stay," I rasp. "Definitely stay."

82

I turn away from the window, my body throbbing, leaving the guys there as I walk on shaky legs to the bar. I sink onto a bar stool, attempting to wrestle back control. There are several other couples here, all in varying states of undress. I look up to find Jack stalking toward me, danger radiating from him in waves. His hair is falling around his face, his eyes trained on me, burning with carnal desire. Rough hands push open my legs, my skirt riding high on my hips as he steps between them.

"You're in dangerous territory, Sassenach," he growls, his gaze dropping to where my breast is peeking through the mesh of my dress. He licks his thumb and drags it over my nipple, rolling it under the pad of his finger until I'm arching into his touch.

"Maybe I like danger," I rasp, wrapping my legs around him and pulling him tight to my body. He rucks my dress up further, sweeping his hands over my hips, holding me in place as he rolls his hips against mine. He groans and bends over me, his lips coasting over the sensitive skin of my neck. My gaze catches on a couple on the couch as they slowly sink into a horizontal position. He pushes up her shirt, palming her a generous breast and then sucking her dusky nipple into his mouth. Her back bows, lips falling open, her low moan like gasoline on the fire. My core clenches as I watch the man unbuckle his belt and pull out his cock while she fumbles with her underwear, tossing it aside. She looks at me as he positions himself, our eyes locking as he buries his cock inside her. Heat flares in my cheeks, and I want to look away, but instead, I watch as her eyes roll back, ecstasy taking over.

Fuck.

Jack drops to his knees, pulls my panties to the side, and looks up at me through dark lashes as he slides his tongue over me. Oh, God. His hair is silky against my fingers as I hold on for dear life. He rolls his flattened tongue against my clit before sucking it into his mouth. Stars explode behind my eyelids, my breaths coming in strangled pants.

"Miss?" Jack breaks away from my legs to spin me around, and I come face to face with the bartender. "Can I get you something to drink?"

"Whisky sour, please." Jack holds me still when I try to turn back to him, his hands sweeping over my backside, kneading my ass.

"You have no idea how fucking sexy you are," he says, his voice low and husky. He sweeps my hair over one shoulder and kisses my neck. His breath tickles, making me shiver. He pulls my dress higher until it's bunched around my waist, sliding his finger under my thong and pulling gently, the fabric tugging at my clit.

I look up at him, my heart in my throat, a whimper on my lips.

"Don't look at me like that," he begs, his eyes dark.

"Like what?" I whisper.

"Like you want me to spread you out on this bar and feast on your pussy until you scream." He snakes his hand around my waist, pushing his fingers between my legs, rolling my clit beneath his fingers. Any reservations I have about fucking in public disappear beneath his touch. He leans forward, his lips against my ear. "Like you wouldn't say no if I told you I want to fuck you in front of all these people." I rock against his fingers, leaning back on his chest as he destroys me.

"Maybe I wouldn't," I breathe, my body humming, desire consuming me. He grips my hips and pulls me to the back edge of the bar stool, tilting my hips forward until I'm forced to lean on the bar for support. He slides a hand underneath me from the back, pulling my thong aside, and drags his finger through the moisture gathered there before slowly pushing inside. My back bows as adrenaline courses through me. My eyes flutter open, and I see Cam and Lach sitting at the opposite end of the bar, dark eyes watching us.

"Can I fuck you, mo chridhe?" Jack asks roughly, his lips skating over my jaw.

"Yes," I gasp. The need to feel him fill me overrides everything. I look across the bar to find Lach's eyes still on me, his hand working out of sight in Cam's lap. Cam's jaw is clenched, his head tilted back. He opens his eyes suddenly, his gaze pinning me in place as Jack's cock nudges at my entrance. He slams home with one hard thrust. Oh fuck.

"Whisky sour?" The bartender sets the drink down in front of me with a wink. My smile feels more like a grimace as I thank him, my words getting caught in my throat as Jack flexes inside me. As the bartender walks away, I drop my head into my arm and Jack thrusts again. I bite the base of my thumb to keep in a moan, but Jack grabs a handful of hair and tugs my head up.

"I want to hear you, Charlotte." He thrusts again, grunting as he bottoms out, my answering moan tearing out of me as my pussy clenches around him.

"We should get a room," I hear Lach say from behind me, a desperate edge to his voice.

"Don't want to stop," I say, my words stilted as Jack pushes in again.

"Would you rather go back to the hotel?" Cam asks, sinking onto the stool next to me. He turns my head toward him, cupping my jaw and dragging his thumb over my bottom lip.

"No," I gasp as Lach palms my breast, rolling my nipple between his fingers. "Here." Fire consumes me, my vision losing focus as my body surrenders. I'm vaguely aware of Lach speaking with the bartender as Jack's slow, steady thrusts drive me mad.

I whimper as Jack pulls out, fixing my dress before Cam spins me around and lifts me into his arms.

"Are you ready for this, little witch?" he asks, his smile tender.

"I was made for this."

83

I feel like I'm in a dream as Cam carries me through the club, Lach's easy grin leading the way, Jack's dark gaze burning me alive as he follows closely behind. We walk to the end of the bank of windows, turning the corner to find a long hallway lit by red neon lights. Lach stops at the fourth door, sliding the card over the lock. It flashes red.

"Fuck," Jack mutters, grimacing as he adjusts himself.

Lach tries again. Nothing. "Give me a second, I'll get a new key."

"No." I practically jump from Cam's arms to stop Lach, pressing my palm against his chest. "It's a sign." I turn to face all three of them. "Will one of you call the car around? We're going back to the hotel and doing this properly."

Lach nods once and pulls his phone from the breast pocket of his jacket. "The car will be here in ten." He grabs my wrist, spinning me to face him and crowding me toward Cam. Long fingers sweep over my waist and settle on my hips as Cam draws me back, sandwiching me between their hard bodies. I reach out and grab Jack's belt and haul him to me. I need to feel all three of them like I need to feel the sun's warmth after a long winter. I crave them. The heat of Jack's hand sears the curve of my ass as he bends to kiss the sensitive skin between my shoulder and neck, his beard sending tiny sparks skittering over my skin. Lach watches me with dark eyes, his usual easy humor replaced by a look of longing so intense that it pierces my soul.

I grasp his chin and pull his mouth down to mine. His kiss is a desperate, all-consuming thing. His fingers tangle in my hair, drawing me down into the depths with him. Cam circles my nipples, tracing his fingers over me in a maddeningly slow spiral. I moan, pushing into his hands, demanding more. He rolls my nipples between his fingers, causing my nervous system to short-circuit. Breaking away from Lach, I let my head fall against Cam's shoulder. Jack jerks my dress up, kneading my ass before roughly pulling my hips toward him and sinking two fingers inside me. Lach pulls one of my legs up, opening me wider.

"Do you like it when the three of us take care of you, Carebear?" Lach murmurs against my ear, his hand cupping my throat. "I want to see what you look like when you come with three cocks inside you."

A groan bubbles up my throat as Cam lazily drags his hand down my stomach, taking his time before tugging my panties to the side, his fingers sliding easily over me, the lightest touch making me jump.

"Open your eyes," Lach demands, gripping my chin and forcing me to look at him. I get lost in the smokiness of his gaze, barely registering my movements as I scramble at the front of his pants. I pull him out, our groans melding together as I grip him tightly and pump my hand over him. Cam's chin rests on my shoulder, watching me. Watching Lach.

Cam grasps Lach's cock with his free hand, guiding him between my legs. He holds his pointer and middle finger on either side of my clit, creating a V for Lach to slide through. Lach's jaw flexes as he rocks his cock against me. I push back on Jack's hand as he thrust his fingers inside me and then slide forward over Lach's cock, every nerve ending in my body begging for release.

"I—" The buzzing of Lach's phone cuts me off.

"Fucking hell," Lach grinds out, pulsing the head of his cock over my clit as he pulls his phone out. "The car is here." He cups my face, biting at my lower lip before pushing his tongue into my mouth, taking everything I have to give and promising to give me even more. He breaks away with a groan, adjusting himself inside his pants and zipping back up. I bite my cheek to keep in a smile as I watch the other two tuck their cocks into their waistbands, wishing I could tease them.

Fuck it.

I turn to Cam, rucking up his shirt and kissing the smooth skin of his abdomen before unbuttoning his pants and tugging them down until I can swirl my tongue over him.

"Fuck," he stutters, his hips jerking as he grapples for control. I stand, kissing him soundly before turning to Jack. I flatten my hand against his chest, pushing him back against the wall, the flare of desire in his eyes almost making me forget what I am doing. I push his shirt up, leaving a trail of kisses over steely muscles, admiring the several inches of him sticking above his waistband before sucking him into my mouth, pulsing my tongue over his frenulum.

"Goddamnit, Charlotte," he groans, his hips reaching for me, his body demanding more. He winds my hair around his hand, pulling me up, his gaze freezing me in place. "You've ruined me," he rasps. "There isn't a second of the day that goes by that I don't think about the way your eyes roll back when I push my cock into you for the first time. Or the way you bite your lip just before you come. That fierce, protective look in your eyes when you feel we've been wronged. The light in your eyes when we're all together. The way you trust us completely." My breath hitches as he slides his hand from my hair to my neck, his thumb caressing the wild pulse at my throat. "I am forever yours, mo chridhe." He crushes his lips to mine, consuming me.

"I hate to break this up, but we need to get back to the hotel before we consummate this relationship on the floor of a sex club," Lach says, glancing at his phone.

Jack growl as he breaks the kiss, his hands trembling with restraint. He scoops me into his arms. "Please tell me one of you know how to get the fuck out of here," he demands. I whimper as he rolls my clit under the pad of his thumb, my body losing in the fight for control.

Lach and Cam lead the way, stopping to ask for directions before leading us up a set of stairs and out into the cool city air. I take deep breaths, attempting to bank the inferno taking over my body. The steady movement of Jack's thumb makes it impossible. I arch in his arms, desperate to feel him inside me.

"What do you want, Charlotte?" He slides his thumb down, circling my entrance.

"You can't give me what I want right now." My voice comes out low and husky, sex dripping from every word.

The color of Jack's eyes deepens, ensnaring me as he pushes inside me, stoking the flames.

"Fuck," I whimper, writhing in his arms. The car pulls up, and he sets me on my feet, holding my gaze as he licks me from his thumb. Lach links his fingers with mine, pulling me to the car and helping me in. If I had thought the car ride earlier was charged, this one is absolutely electric. Jack wastes no time kneeling between my legs and pushing my knees wide, sucking my clit into his mouth in one long pull.

Oh fuck.

His tongue is relentless as I buck against him, his hands holding me tight. He slides his hands under my ass to give himself better access, pulling me up to his mouth, his tongue plunging into me before moving even lower.

"Jack!" My brain tells me he shouldn't be doing this, but God, my body wants it.

"We're here," Lach murmurs. I scramble away from Jack, pulling my dress down just before the driver opens the door. I climb out on wobbly legs, my body humming. Cam slides his hand around my waist, supporting me as we walk to the elevators.

"Are you doing okay?" His smile is crooked, tenderness in his eyes as he looks down at me.

"I need to come," I say bluntly, cocking my eyebrow in a challenge I hope he'll accept. The elevator door opens, and he crowds me inside, pushing me against the back wall. He waits for the doors to close before capturing my mouth, rocking his cock against my clit. My moan echoes off the walls, surrounding us.

"Brace yourselves," Lach warns before hitting the emergency stop. "Cover the camera?" he asks Jack as he unbuckles his belt and pulls out his cock. I whimper, watching as he strokes himself, desperate to taste the pearly drop at the tip. I press my forehead against Cam's shoulder as I fumble with his belt buckle, desire making my fingers unsteady. I pull him out, hot and heavy in my palm. He groans, thrusting against me before sliding his hands over my thighs and hiking me up, impaling me in one smooth motion.

My cry turns to a silent scream as Lach grips my hip with one hand, guiding his cock with the other, sliding his shaft snugly against Cam's, stretching me. Lach gives me a couple of seconds to adjust and then thrusts deep.

Cam's whimper sets off a chain reaction in my body, all of my muscles tensing, squeezing around them. "So fucking tight," he gasps as they slide against each other, taking turns filling me. The three of us race to the finish, but instead of riding me to completion, the guys stop their thrusts as my orgasm starts, flexing their hips, filling me completely as I explode around them.

"Enough messing around," Jack says darkly, his eyes on me as he slams the emergency button back in, the elevator going up as I come down. The second Cam puts me back on my feet, Jack throws me over his shoulder and strides out of the elevator, a dangerous glint in his eyes.

"It's my fucking turn."

84

———————

I hit the bed with a soft thud, the comforter fluffing around me. I watch Jack in the mirror above me, broad shoulders heaving as he wrestles for control, his eyes shining with a predatory gleam. A breath strangles me as he sheds his jacket and rolls up his shirt-sleeves, the veins in his hands drawing my gaze as he loosens his tie. Fuck, this man does something to me. Every nerve ending in my body hums with anticipation; heat and electricity crackling between us like a summer thunderstorm.

"Touch me."

"Your wish is my command, mo chridhe." Jack's hands are gentle, circling my ankles and sweeping up my calves, his touch reverent. He opens my legs, kneeling between them, looking down at me like I hold the key to the universe.

"Arms up," Cam murmurs, leaning over me to unzip my dress. Jack slides his hands up my thighs, following the hem of my dress as Cam slowly peels it off over my head. They groan as my breasts release from the fabric, my nipples begging for attention. Jack stops Cam from pulling my dress off, leaving my arms trapped above my head.

"I like this," Jack rumbles, sliding his finger underneath my garter belt. "But this—" he tugs at my thong, the material pulling against my clit, making me squirm, "—has to fucking go." He rips the flimsy material and pulls it away from my body, tossing it to Lach, who has stationed himself at the head of the bed. He holds my gaze as he brings it up to his nose, his eyes darkening as he inhales, heat flooding between my legs in response.

"Eyes on me." I turn back to Jack, drinking in his whisky gaze. "Tell me what you need." The roughness of his voice wraps around my nipples like a silk thread, winding its way down my body to slip between my legs, stringing me tight. I swallow hard as he massages my thighs, his callouses scraping over sensitive skin, pushing my need to dizzying heights.

"Undress," I say, struggling to pull my arms out of the dress.

"Only if you stop trying to free yourself." He leans over me, his scent invading my senses, one hand trapping my wrists, the other moving to my hip, holding me still as his hard length presses against me. My entire world shrinks to this moment – the only thing I can think about is the way the head of his cock rolls over my clit with each slow thrust.

"I need you naked," I beg, my voice rough with desire. Jack rises to his knees, our gazes locked while he unbuttons his shirt, his fingers moving so slowly it takes everything in me not to rip the dress from my arms and tear it from his body. I can almost feel his wide expanse of smooth skin beneath my fingertips. Hard muscle trembling under my touch.

"Please," I rasp, consumed with the need to press my lips to his stomach, breathe him in, and show him how he makes me feel.

His hands pause on the last button. "Tell me, Charlotte," he says again.

"I need to touch you," I half sob. "Taste you. Become part of you."

Jack nods to Cam, and he pulls the dress from my arms. I push myself up, ripping the last button from his shirt as I hastily open it to reveal his abdomen. I press my lips against him, nibbling a line down to his waistband. I fumble clumsily with his belt, my fingers shaking with need. He takes over, unbuckling and unbuttoning quickly. I unzip his pants slowly, holding my breath as I pull his boxers down. His shaft is thick and smooth, veins riding under his skin like underground rivers, and I want to fucking drown. My fingers dig into his hip as I lick him from base to tip. He hisses, pushing on my chin with his thumb until my mouth opens and he can slide past my lips. I push myself forward, taking in all of him, choking until he jerks back with a curse.

"Not tonight, Charlotte. Tonight is about you."

"Good. Now get back here, and let me taste you."

"No," he growls, picking up his tie from the floor. Before I can protest, he wraps it around my thighs, expertly tying a knot. "Much better," he chuckles, meeting my indignant stare with sparkling eyes. Without warning, he picks me up by the waist and flips me over. I struggle in his grip, self-conscious of how far my ass is sticking up in the air. "Do I need to tie your hands behind your back, too?" Jack asks gruffly, holding me in place.

I freeze, my chest heaving, so fucking turned on I can barely breathe. I can't see Cam or Lach, but the heat of their gazes caressing my body.

Jack palms my ass, squeezing and spreading my cheeks, his breath caressing my skin. He runs his tongue up the inside of one cheek, barely grazing my asshole, and then down the other side. Dipping down to push into my pussy, making me gasp before repeating the motions. On the next pass, he swirls his tongue over my clit, giving it some attention before sliding back up. I press back against him as his tongue slides over my ass, desperately needing something I can't put into words. He groans, spreading me wider, feathering his tongue around and around before flattening it against me.

"Jack," I beg.

"Tell me what you fucking want, Charlotte," he demands. "The truth this time."

I bury my face in the bed, embarrassed.

I moan when he laps at me, squirming in his grip, pushing my ass back as far as I can to get him to do what I want. What I need.

"Tell me."

Fuck. I cover my face with my hands, my cheeks burning. "Fuck me, Jack."

"With what?" he grinds out, the roughness of his beard abrading sensitive skin as he bites one of my ass cheeks.

"Your tongue," I whisper, barely able to hear the words myself.

"Where?" He demands, leaving no room for shyness.

"My ass." The moment the words are out of my mouth, his tongue slides over me, pushing into me, his moan vibrating through my core. He swirls his tongue around the tight ring of muscle, encouraging me to relax before plunging in deeper.

Oh, God. Why does this feel so wrong and so fucking right? I whimper as he pulls out, only to end in a guttural cry as he stretches me again, his hand reaching around to my clit. He stops as soon as I start writhing against him, leaning over me, his lips hot against my ear.

"Are you ready, Charlotte?"

"Yes," I moan. He slips the tie from my legs and climbs onto the bed, sitting down with his back against the headboard. I approach him on my hands and knees, so focused on getting his cock in my mouth that I don't expect it when he flips me over.

"Easy," he murmurs, his hands tight on my thighs, suspending me over his cock. He flexes his hips, making his cock slip to the front of my body. My clit rides over his shaft as he moves me against him, teasing me until I can't take it anymore. I grab him in my fist and impale myself, my pussy squeezing around him.

My gaze locks with Cam's as he practically launches himself toward me, pushing my knees wide. He looks up at me through his eyelashes, his pupils blown wide.

"You have bewitched me body and soul," he murmurs, his lips moving over me, "and I love you, I love you, I love you." He slides his tongue over me before greedily fastening his mouth over my clit.

"Oh, God," I gasp, burying my fingers in his curls, hanging on for dear life. Jack lifts me from his cock, letting Cam take care of me while he spreads lube over himself. He waits until I'm rocking my hips against Cam's mouth before dragging me up his body, holding his cock steady as it nudges at my back entrance. Lach kneels on the bed, reaching around Cam to push two fingers inside me. My entire body tremors as Jack's cock slides into me like he was made for me. I arch against him, my heels pushing into the bed, a scream caught in my throat.

Lach pulls the pillows out from behind Jack until he's lying flat on the bed. I'm sprawled on top of him, his cock stretching my ass, enjoying his curses every time I squeeze him.

"You two better hurry," I pant, chuckling as Jack's fingers press into my hips when I lift up, letting him slide almost all the way out before sinking back down onto him.

Cam hops off the bed, eyes on me as he sheds his clothes. Desire hoods an impossibly blue gaze, his halo of curls mussed from my hands. My fallen angel. He climbs back up as Lach finishes undressing, pressing my knees wide with gentle hands, sliding his cock over my clit before pushing into me with a low moan.

"Stop fucking squeezing," Jack begs, trying to hold me still as I raise my hips to meet Cam's thrusts.

I can feel my heartbeat pulsing through every nerve ending as Lach climbs onto the bed. I've been waiting for this since the day he told me they shared. He guides Cam forward, positioning his legs outside of Jack's hips. Cam's face is directly over mine, his gaze a wildfire of cerulean blue, trapping me amidst the flames. I feel Lach slide the head of his cock over where Cam and I are joined, desire pooling warm and heavy in my stomach.

"Are you ready, Charlie?" he asks, meeting my gaze above Cam' shoulder. I nod, our eyes locking as he flexes his hips, the last link snapping into place as he slides home. Cam's eyes roll back, his lip held tight between his teeth.

Oh fuck. I can feel all three of them. Stretching me. Filling me. Completing me.

I whimper, slowly rolling my hips, giving myself time to push through the overwhelming feeling of fullness. Jack pushes his hand between Cam and I, sliding his fingertip over my clit with the lightest touch.

"More," I gasp, covering his hand with mine, guiding him as I rock against his fingers, their cocks shifting inside me as I move. Jack flexes his hips, bottoming out as Cam and a Lach take turns thrusting.

"You're doing so good, Charlotte," Jack groans against my ear, his deep brogue shoving me closer to the edge. "Now come for us."

I don't need to be told twice. All three of them push into me as the first tremors start, filling me impossibly full. Cam's curls brush my cheek as he pulls a nipple into his mouth, moaning as I arch into him. Stars explode behind my eyelids as I squeeze around their cocks, relishing their harsh groans as I pull them over the edge with me.

"I'm—" *coming* my mind whispers, my body splintering into a million tiny pieces, ecstasy tearing me limb from limb. They thrust as one and my body spasms around them, claiming them as mine, dragging them down into the depths where pain and pleasure become one. As we tip into the abyss, Jack palms my neck, turning my face to his, capturing my lips as the four of us plummet toward the unknown in a tangle of limbs and cacophony of stuttered breaths and muttered prayers.

85

———————

Jack carries me over to the tub, holding me against him as steam surrounds us. He uses his teeth to remove the bottle's stopper and empties the contents into the bath. I take it from him, turning it to read the label. *Cunny Recovery.*

"Stop it," I say, laughing.

"Lorna made it just for you. She said it would help with the soreness."

"Does she have experience with stuff like this?" I test the water with my toes and then gingerly step into the scalding water, sinking down with a hiss.

"You could say that," he murmurs, color rising in his cheeks.

"What does that mean? I want to know what Lorna does that makes you blush like that," I tease, watching with fascination as his color deepens even more.

"She studies the female orgasm."

My jaw drops. "Wait. I thought she made body care products for a living?"

Jack shakes his head, swirling his fingers over the water's surface. "That's just a hobby. She's been working on earning her doctorate for the last year."

"A doctorate on orgasms?"

He grunts in affirmation, amber eyes warming, drawing me in as he circles his thumb over my areola.

"Jack," I press, annoyed that he's not forthcoming.

He clears his throat. "Ah. Well. She's experimenting to determine if pleasure can be increased through instruction." I raise my eyebrow, waiting for him to continue. He blows out an exasperated breath. "She has a fancy system to measure the strength of an orgasm. She measures the study participants when they first sign on to the study to get a baseline and then..." He trails off, his throat bobbing.

"Then what, Jack?"

"She holds sessions to teach them how to increase their pleasure."

"How does she teach them?" The visions flashing in my mind have heat settling low in my stomach.

"With her hands. With toys."

"She does it *to* them?" My nipples tighten. "Fuck."

"Exactly." He motions for me to move forward and lowers himself behind me, pulling my back to his chest, cursing at the temperature of the water.

Lach crouches at the foot of the tub, his skin golden in the low light. "You did so fucking good, Carebear." He grins, his eyes sparkling, joy vibrating in every cell of his body. "I hope we lived up to your expectations."

"It was better than I ever could have imagined." I snuggle into Jack, letting my head rest against his shoulder. "Even if we had completely screwed up the first time, we have a lifetime to get it right."

"Yes, we do," Jack answers, nuzzling my neck. "I'll gladly spend my days finding new ways to make you come."

I turn in his arms, grabbing Lach's hand and pulling him to the other end of the tub. I straddle Jack, careful not to slosh water over the side. "And I'll find new ways to make you lose control," I murmur, lightly scraping my nails over his shoulders and chest, flicking my thumbs over his nipples.

"God, Charlotte," he groans, flexing into me, his head dropping to the tub's edge. I hold Lach's gaze as I drag my lips over Jack's nipple, teasing him until he's pushing up to meet my mouth.

"Don't fucking play," Jack rasps, his hand tightening in my hair. Swiping my tongue over him, I swirl it around before drawing him into my mouth. I roll my hips against the hardening length between us, gasping when my clit catches on the ridge of the head of his cock. His hands move to my waist, holding me still.

"You need time to recover, Charlotte," Jack says, tipping my chin up to look at him.

"Do you really think your cock pressed between us like this makes me want to do anything but fuck you again?" I rock against him, rising to my knees and angling my hips so he's nudging at my entrance.

I close my eyes, the vision of the four of fucking in this tub taking hold of me, strangling me until I can barely breathe from want.

"Cam, come here," I call, catching his gaze as he pushes up from the bed. Sculpted muscles shift and flex as he walks toward me, his cock at half mast, bobbing with every step. Based on previous experience, I had always thought I didn't like giving blowjobs, but fuck, I would give my left arm just to have him in my mouth right now.

"Are you guys up to a little experimentation?" I ask, standing up, water streaming down my body.

"You think we'll say no to that?" Lach chuckles, standing. I pull Jack to his feet and then grab his forearms, shuffling around until we've switched positions. "Lach, sit where Jack was." He doesn't say a word, he just steps into the tub and sinks into the water, his pupils blown wide, looking up at me. I move between his legs and start to lower myself, but he palms the back of my thighs, bringing my pussy to his mouth. My fingers dig into his shoulders as he slides his tongue over me, possessing me. He doesn't let up until my knees tremble, then slowly lowers me into the water, rising to meet my hips with a solid thrust.

"Fuck," I groan, riding him, pulling his face to my breast. He gently drags his teeth over my nipple before drawing me into his mouth. Jack positions himself behind me, cursing the size of the tub. I release Lach, leaning back and motioning for Cam to come closer.

"Can you straddle the tub between Lach and me?" I look up at him through my eyelashes as he approaches, desperate for his taste on my tongue.

"Are you trying to kill me?" he asks roughly, one hand gripping Lach's shoulder for support as he stretches his leg over the tub. He lowers himself, his thighs spanning the tub, his cock right in front of my face. "I won't be able to stay like this for—" His words end in a guttural groan as I grab his ass and slide him past my lips, not stopping until he touches the back of my throat. I can feel my heart beating in every cell of my body as I rock my hips against Lach and swallow around Cam.

Jack has given up maneuvering into a position where he can claim me, instead following my spine with his lips, tracing the curves of my body with his fingertips. When his hand slips down over my ass, I push back into him, encouraging him. Lach sinks into the water a little more, covering my hands with his, spreading Cam wide. Desire floods my senses as Lach dips his head to slide his tongue over Cam. Cam's whimper shoots straight to my core. He flexes his hips, sinking into me, then slides out as he pushes back onto Lach's tongue. I whimper around Cam's cock, and Jack answers with a growl, his hand sliding between my legs. I choke on Cam as Jack circles my clit, losing control of my body as pleasure consumes me.

"We need more room," Jack growls, biting my neck as he slides his hand between my ass cheeks, making my back bow. "I need to be inside you." He pushes a finger into me, his groan roaring through me like wildfire.

"Everyone out," Lach pants, hauling himself higher in the tub. "Grab your underwear and robes. We're going on a field trip."

Cam doesn't move, cradling my face, muscles straining as he thrusts one last time. "That mouth is going to be the death of me," he murmurs as he slides out, wiping under my eyes with his thumbs. He kisses my forehead and gingerly climbs off the tub, helping Lach and me out. I watch as Lach's gaze drops to Cam's cock, the tip of his tongue coming out to wet his bottom lip.

"I have to fucking taste you," Lach breathes, desperation edging his words. He crashes to his knees and drags his tongue along the bottom of Cam's cock. Jack slides a hand over my waist, pulling me against him, his hand roaming lower as Lach closes his lips over Cam. Jack's fingers delve into the curls between my legs as Cam grasps handfuls of Lach's hair, thrusting deep. I whimper, and Cam's shattered gaze meets mine, both of us falling apart. He thrusts again, and I know he's imagining sinking into my pussy like I'm imagining his mouth on me. I moan as Jack pushes one thick finger into me, my body convulsing around him. Lach pulls away from Cam, his hair mussed.

"Fuck. Sorry." He scrubs his hands over his face. "Underwear and robes."

Cam is frozen in time, his eyes on me, a stormy sea I would willingly drown in. He drops to his knees and crawls to me, lithe power rippling through his muscles. He kisses the tops of my feet, my ankles, my calves, licking a path up the inside of my thighs. Jack moves his hand to leave me open for Cam, pushing two fingers into me from the back.

"Is this what you want?" Cam asks softly, dragging his tongue over my clit. My body jerks against him, my knees wobbling. "Use me, little witch," his voice vibrates against my clit, and I lose control. I slide my hands into his hair, pulling him against me, riding his face like this is the last time I'll ever feel his tongue on me.

A robe smacking me straight in the face brings me back to reality. Lach returns my glare with a grin. "Trust me. It'll be worth it."

"It better fucking be," Jack growls, pulling his fingers out of me and tracing my lips with one fingertip before licking them clean.

None of us say a word until we're in the elevator, the sexual current so strong I can barely breathe. "Where are you taking us?" I finally ask, my nails digging into my palm as I restrain myself from hitting the emergency stop.

"The pool. I made a call while you and Jack were in the tub. We have it all to ourselves."

86

My hands are balled in the pockets of my robe, my nails leaving dark crescents in my palm, determined to get down to the ground floor without jumping all three of them. I breathe steadily, wrestling my body back into my control.

"You think you're in control?" Jack's deep baritone slides through me like whisky, settling deep and warm in my stomach.

"Yes," I grind out, raising my chin and glaring at him down the length of my nose.

"You haven't been in control since the day we met, Charlotte." He braces an elbow above me, trailing his other hand between my breasts and over my stomach, chuckling when my breath hitches. "Are you in control now?"

"Are you?" I tear open his robe, pull down his boxers, and have him sliding past my lips before he has time to think.

"Bloody hell," he hisses, wrapping a hand in my hair and pulling me to my feet, crushing his lips to mine. He pulls back, holding me tight, his pupils blown wide. "This weekend is about you, remember? I have the rest of my life to feel your throat squeeze around my cock as you struggle to take every inch. Tonight I want to suffocate between your thighs, drown in your orgasms." He slides his hand down my stomach, his finger sliding over my clit before pushing deep inside, dragging his fingertip over my g-spot. My knees buckle, his wicked chuckle making me shiver as he hauls me up and tosses me over his shoulder.

"God, Charlie," Lach groans, his hands rough as he pushes my robe up, kneading my inner thighs. He pulls my thong to the side and fits his mouth to my pussy, dragging his tongue over my clit before pushing in deep. I can't do anything but hang suspended while he eats me like I'm his last meal. Licking, sucking, and biting until I'm sobbing his name. The elevator dings, and Jack pushes Lach away, swinging me down so I'm cradled in his arms before the door opens. He carries me down a short hallway, through a door, and into the pool area. It's dark except for the ripples of light bathing everything in an ethereal glow.

Jack sets me on my feet, and Cam pushes my robe off my shoulders, depositing it with his own on a chair. He snags my hand, pulling me toward the edge of the pool.

"Does this remind you of anything?"

My heart is in my throat as I lift his glasses from his face, carefully setting them down so they won't get crushed, just like I did on that special day months ago. I meet his dark gaze, his blood calling to mine, desire twisting her tendrils around us until we can barely breathe.

"Only one of the best days of my life," I whisper. My words end in a shriek as he pulls me in. I push out of the water with a spluttering laugh that quickly dies on my lips. Cam's hair is slicked back, his skin pale as moonlight, the light from the pool reflecting in the depths of his midnight eyes. His gaze trails over me, settling on nipples straining against the fabric of my bra, desperate for his touch.

"Do you know what I couldn't stop thinking about that day?" he asks, his throat bobbing as he closes the distance between us.

"What?" The edge of the pool bites against my back as he closes in.

"How you would taste." Hooking a finger into my bra, he pulls the cup down, swirling his tongue over my nipple. "If we hadn't been interrupted, I would have lifted you onto that rock—" he lifts me, setting me down on the pool's edge. "— then I would have laid you back." He puts his hand behind my head and gently lowers me. "Then," he whispers, pulling my lip into his mouth, "I would've kissed my way down your body." I jerk under his touch as his lips graze the sensitive skin over my ribs. "I would have stripped you bare so I could look at you." He pulls my panties over my legs, pushing my knees wide, the heat in his gaze burning me alive.

"And then what?" I ask, my voice low and husky, edged in desperation.

"Then I would have dipped my tongue into you just a little bit, dragging it over your clit. He groans as my taste bursts over his tongue, sliding it through my folds before flattening it against my clit. I whimper, my back bowing.

He drags his teeth over my clit, chuckling against me as I wrap my legs around him, trapping him. He says something, his words mumbled. I let my knees fall open, my stomach clenching as his predatory gaze meets mine. "Have you ever squirted with a cock in you?" He repeats, a wicked gleam in his eyes.

I shake my head, my face heating.

"Do you want to?"

"Do you really think she'd say no to that?" Lach chuckles, popping out of the water next to Cam. "Say yes, Carebear."

"Yes. Absolutely, yes."

Jack lowers himself to the pool deck next to me, caressing my cheek. "Close your eyes, mo chridhe. Focus." He covers my eyes with his hand, plunging me into darkness.

Cam laps at me again, pushing a finger in deep, fucking me with it. I circle my hips, dropping my knees open, arching into his touch. He crooks his finger, rubbing my g-spot with firm pressure, moaning against my clit. Fingers replace Cam's mouth, and I hear a breath shudder out of him, imagining Lach's hand sliding over Cam's cock, firm fingers sliding over silky steel, encouraging that first drop of come to bead at the tip. A whimper slips between my lips as the pressure builds.

Cam notches the head of his cock at my entrance, pushing in slowly, his finger still dragging me to dizzying heights with every pass. He grunts as he bottoms out, fighting the animalistic urge to take me hard and fast. One more thrust and the pressure becomes unbearable.

"Oh, God." I groan, praying to the gods that I'm not about to pee all over them.

"You're doing so good, little witch," Cam rasps, holding me steady as he fucks me, easing off as I get close.

"I'm—" Cam puts more pressure against my g-spot, and I lose the ability to speak. A second later, his entire body shudders, his low moan ripping through me. "What just happened?" I ask, the tension in Cam's body not letting up.

"I'm fucking Cam with my finger," Lach says thickly, his hand clenching on my knee every time he pushes into Cam.

"Jack, I want to see them." I shake his hand off my face. I meet Lach's gaze. "Fuck him."

"Are you sure? I'm too close to hold back now."

"I'll take care of her when you two are finished," Jack says, stroking himself.

"Let *me* take care of you," I beg, an overwhelming need to please him grabbing me by the throat.

"Charlotte—"

"*Please*, Jack." I must sound broken because the stubbornness leaves his face, desperation taking its place.

"I don't even know how in this position," he says, his voice ragged.

"Grab the pillows from the chairs and put them under my shoulders and head," I instruct. He helps me lift my body and slides the pillows under, making sure I'm comfortable. "Now kneel with your knees on either side of my shoulders. Lach, you're good fucking Cameron?" I ask. "I want all of us to come together."

"Yeah, I'll manage," Lach winks, squeezing my leg before turning to Cam and pulling him into a heated kiss.

Fuck.

Jack squats next to me, dragging his thumb over my bottom lip. "Are you sure, Charlotte?"

I let my love for him burn bright as I meet his gaze. "Positive." I take a deep breath he settles over me, trying to steady myself. I feel the moment Lach slides into Cam, his body seizing, his grip almost punishing. I whimper in response, squeezing around Cam as he thrusts into me, squeezing harder as he slams back onto Lach's cock.

Unable to wait any longer, I grip Jack's cock, urging him forward. I swirl my tongue over his head, scraping my teeth over the ridge. I pull him further toward me, forcing him to lean forward and support himself with his hands. "Now fuck me."

He does. Oh my God, he does. He flexes his hips and sinks into me with a groan. I grip his ass, encouraging him to push deeper. I moan around his cock as Cam picks up speed, his finger pressing into my g-spot until I cry out, raising my hips to meet his thrusts. Jack pulls out and slams back in, pushing me back into the pillows, cutting off my air supply, and sharpening my senses until I'm teetering on a knife point. I gag, and he pulls back, apologizing.

"Don't fucking stop," I grind out, pulling him back to me and not stopping until he's in my throat, my muscles squeezing around him. I reach down, bucking against my fingers as I circle my clit. Lach bats my hand away, taking my spot. Jack starts to pull back again, and I use his momentum to push a dripping finger into him, pressing against his prostate. His hips flex violently, and finally – *finally* – he loses control. One more thrust and the building pressure becomes too much for my body to contain. It's like a bomb hits us. Desperate guttural groans, hips and hands scrambling to hold on to reality as we fracture into a million pieces. We tumble in a relentless tsunami of ecstasy until we don't know up from down, one body from another.

Jack pulls away first, murmuring apologies as he wipes at my ruined makeup. Lach is next, pulling out of Cam and sinking underneath the water. Cam doesn't move. He pulls me into a sitting position, his cock still anchored inside me. "I was wrong," he pants, pushing sweat-soaked hair from my face. "You were never a witch. You're a fucking goddess."

87

I wake up cocooned in warmth. Lach has me cradled against his body, his hand splayed over my stomach. Cam's curls tickle my cheek, warm puffs of air caressing my collarbone, his eyelashes fluttering as he dreams. I carefully extricate myself from their embraces, sliding off the end of the bed. They shift, the space between them disappearing. I can't help the smile that pulls at my lips. I shrug on a robe and pad to the balcony, peeking around the door. Jack's standing at the railing in only his boxers, his knuckles turning white with the force of his grip.

"Everything okay?" I ask softly from the doorway.

He looks back at me, his gaze raw. Jaw ticking, he turns away, not saying anything.

My heart drops. I duck under his arm, forcing him to look at me. "What's wrong, Jack?"

He stands up straight, pushing me against the railing, trapping me. "Tell me you'll never leave." He cradles my face between his hands. "Please, Charlotte." My heart breaks from the desperation in his voice.

I have all three of them.

Cam and Lach have each other.

Jack only has me.

My stomach sours thinking about how I would feel if I were in his position.

"I won't leave. I promise."

"Fuck," he says, the word coming out on a harsh exhale, his relief palpable. He crushes his lips to mine, tracing my mouth with his tongue, angling my head to take me deeper. Heat pools in my stomach, my entire body tingling.

"I never want this to end," he says against my lips, pulling back to look me in the eyes.

"It won't." I tug on his beard playfully. "I'm looking forward to the day we're old and wrinkled, chasing each other through the hallways on our motorized scooters."

His gaze softens. "You know that thing you said about climbing in my skin?"

I nod.

"I understand now. I want to be inside you, and not just my cock. It's the most bizarre feeling."

"Your cock is a good start," I tease, looking at him through my eyelashes.

"That's not happening. You need a break."

"What I need," I rasp, running my hand slowly over his chest, "Is for you to push me against the wall, wrap my legs around your waist, look me in the eyes, and fuck me like you meant every word you just said."

"But you need—"

"Don't tell me what I need." I slide my hand inside his boxers. He's so fucking hard that it makes my body ache. He shudders as I drag my nails over him, his hips flexing into my hand.

"Don't say I didn't warn you," he says roughly, sliding his hands over my ass, then down to my thighs, hoisting me into his arms and wrapping my legs around his waist. His cock is trapped between our bodies as he turns and walks to the wall. "Is this what you wanted?" he asks, pressing me into the wall, sliding his cock through the moisture between my legs. I moan my affirmation, my eyes fluttering closed as he pulses the head of his cock over my clit.

"Look at me," he growls, his voice rough, demanding.

His golden eyes hold me captive, both of us trembling as he notches his cock at my entrance. Slowly – so very slowly – he pushes into me. His jaw flexes as he restrains himself from slamming home. My gaze loses focus.

"Stay with me," he murmurs, sinking into me, groaning as he bottoms out. He positions himself so his pubic bone rides over my clit, destroying me with long, slow thrusts. "Come for me, Charlie."

I freeze. "You called me Charlie."

The corner of his mouth pulls up, color rising in his cheeks. "I didn't think you'd notice."

"Explain yourself."

"Now?"

I raise my eyebrow.

"When I started calling you Charlotte, I wanted more than friendship. I didn't want to be friend-zoned. But now – now I want to be your friend. Your lover. I want every part of you, and that includes Charlie." His lips ghost over mine. "I can keep calling you Charlotte if that's what you want."

"No," I say, rolling my hips against him, "Say it again." I squeeze around him.

"God, Charlie."

"Fuck," I whimper.

He captures my gaze and thrusts hard, catapulting me close to the edge. His hips stutter as I clench around him, and he tries to hold back, but I can see it in his eyes when he gives in. A low moan from inside stops us in our tracks, mere seconds from teetering over the precipice. A husky 'fuck me' has Jack pulling away from the wall and carrying me inside.

I'll never forget this moment. Lach is lying on his back, hands fisted in the sheets, his head back, the long line of his neck exposed. Cam's knees are on either side of Lach's hips, one hand pumping Lach's cock while he fucks him with long, steady strokes.

A strangled sound tears its way from my throat, and Cam looks up, grinning sheepishly. "We didn't want to interrupt, but now that you're here, your pussy is better than my hand."

Jack slowly lowers me, his cock sliding out of me and along my clit before I step away. I climb on the bed and start to straddle Lach, but Cam stops me with a hand on my thigh.

"Turn around so Jack has room." I obey, turning myself to face Cameron, slowly sinking onto Lach's cock. Jack grabs the lube from the nightstand and climbs up behind me, straddling Lach's chest. God, this is hot.

"Lach, are you okay down there?" I ask him, trying to look over my shoulder at him.

"It's fucking perfect down here," he grins, winking at me. He holds one finger up to Jack, "Give me some of that."

"For what?"

"If your ass is in my face, I may as well help you out a little. Or I could use my tongue..." He wiggles his eyebrows lewdly.

Jack's eyes widen, his mouth opening and closing, no words coming out.

"Oh, come on. A finger in the ass won't make you gay."

"Fucking hell. Fine. Finger only. No goddamn tongue, Lach."

"Yessir," he says, giving a mock salute, the lube nearly dripping in his eye.

I'm so turned on that my entire body is trembling. I hold Cam's gaze as Jack positions himself behind me. He has a firm grip on his cock as he pushes forward, stretching me gradually until I relax enough for him to slide in with a grunt.

"Your ass is so fucking perfect," he whispers, catching my earlobe in his teeth.

Cam pulls out of Lach, lowering himself between my thighs, licking from the base of Lach's cock to my clit, pulsing his tongue against me until I'm close. He moves lower, licking where Lach and I are joined and then sucking and biting Lach's scrotum until he's arching up, begging for more. I nearly combust as I watch him notch his cock between Lach's cheeks, slowly pushing in, their moans alone almost enough to make me come. Cam's eyes are wild when he looks back up, desire burning bright in their depths. He palms my throat and pulls me forward, crushing his lips against mine in a scorching kiss. I hear Lach murmur something and then Jack's groan. His head drops to my shoulder, his hips stuttering as he skates a trembling hand over my stomach. I come before he can even make it down to my clit.

88

All three of them see me wince as I swing my leg over Lach and slide off the bed.

"I fucking knew you needed a break," Jack growls, scooping me into his arms and striding toward the bathroom.

"Jack—"

"No. I'm taking care of you. Pee." He sets me on my feet by the toilet and turns away to start the shower. I lean forward to keep my urine off the tender bits, gingerly wiping afterward. Yes, I'm hurting, but it's the best kind of hurt that reminds me exactly what we've been doing for the last twenty-four hours. Jack pulls me into the shower, gently washing and conditioning my hair before soaping me up. He rinses down quickly, refusing my help. Then he's holding a towel out for me, sitting me on the toilet seat, and blow-drying my hair. Cam comes in halfway through, sitting at my feet and feeding me tiny bites of fruit and croissant.

Once my hair is dry, Cam carefully picks me up and walks me to the bed, telling me to stay put while he showers. Jack is pulling on his boxers when Lach barrels through the door, his arms laden with bags, balancing a tray with four cups of coffee.

"Where were *you*?" I ask, looking at him with surprise.

"On a mission to make today as comfortable as possible," he says, grinning as he hands me a coffee. He sets the others down and dumps the contents of the first bag out on the bed. A heap of light gray cloud-like material falls onto the bed. "One ultra-comfy lounge set," he says, wiggling his eyebrows as he holds up the pieces. "Plus underwear that won't ride up. He holds up a pair of boyshorts. "And lastly, a blanket." He pulls a gray-blue plaid blanket from the bag and tosses it to me. My hands sink into its softness, and I immediately cuddle into it.

"I was right," he says, sinking onto the bed beside me and caressing my cheek.

"Right about what?"

"That it would match your eyes," he says softly, pressing a chaste kiss to my forehead.

"Thank you, Lach," I whisper, emotion rising in my throat.

"I'll help you get dressed, and then we're heading out to find the art store."

I drop the blanket and towel and then hop off the bed, feeling significantly better after the shower. Lach holds the panties while I step into them, sliding them up my legs and over my ass without so much as a pat or pinch. Next is a comfortable bralette made of the same material as the lounge set. Then baggy sweatpants and an over-sized button-up that I decide to leave open.

"Bloody hell, Lach," Jack mutters, tearing his gaze away from me to glare at Lach.

"What?" He raises his hands in mock surrender.

"All that outfit makes me want to do is peel it off her in layers to see what's underneath." Jack's jaw ticks as the heat of his gaze caresses me from my head to my toes.

"You already know what's underneath," I counter

"And that right there is the fucking problem."

I bite my cheek to keep from smiling, pulling on my socks and shoes before stepping into the steamy bathroom to check my hair. I pretend to be fussing with it, but really I'm watching Cam dry off in the shower, jealous of the droplets of water droplet sliding down his torso.

"What's this?" I ask, stepping up to him and wrapping my hand around his cock. He groans, thrusting into my grip.

"I can't stop thinking about this morning."

"I can't either," I admit, stroking him.

"Absolutely not," Jack grumbles, pushing into the bathroom, his eyes flashing. "Nothing sexual for twenty-four hours. You have to heal, Charlotte."

"Twelve hours," I counter, my fingers crossed behind my back.

"I'll make you a deal. If the pain is completely gone in twelve hours, we'll have the raunchiest sex you've ever had. If you show signs of even the slightest twinge, we're waiting the full twenty-four hours."

"Deal." I hold out my hand for him to shake. He eyes Cam's cock, then my hand. I take it as a sign that it doesn't gross him out when his hand swallows mine in a firm shake.

I return to the room to find all three guys wearing color coordinated sweatsuits. Cam's is midnight blue – relaxed fit joggers and a zip-up hoodie. Jack's is a deep caramel, his pants almost indecent with how much they show off, a relaxed-fit pull-over hoodie rounding out the look. Lach is in gray-green – baggy joggers and an oversized hoodie. They look like models from a high-end brand.

"You guys can't wear that," I moan, peeking at them from between my fingers.

"Why not?" Lach asks, looking between them to find what's wrong. "I figured we could all use some comfy clothes after the last twenty-four hours. These seemed perfect."

"Perfect if you weren't planning on ever leaving the room, maybe."

"She thinks we're sexy. She wants to fuck us," Lach croons, doing a little dance.

"God," Jack groans, grabbing my hand and pulling me out the door.

The elevator ride is slightly more bearable with the tension on the back burner. Cam pulls up directions on his phone, and we walk through the streets of Edinburgh. Light touches, shy smiles, pregnant pauses, and sultry looks make it a day I'll never forget.

This city is so fucking beautiful. Weather-worn stone collides with bright swaths of color, centuries-old buildings still in use like it isn't a miracle they're still standing. I think I'm in love.

Cam motions to one of the storefronts, and my heart jumps. An array of colorful paints and art supplies is laid out in the shop window, begging me to buy them all. I can't help the excited squeal as I walk into the brightly lit space, rows and rows of every type of art supply imaginable at the tip of my fingertips.

"You guys may want to find another shop – I think I may be here a while."

"And miss that grin on your face? I don't think so." Lach kisses both corners of my mouth, making me smile even wider. This may be the best day of my life.

I walk the rows slowly, starting at the front of the store and working my way to the back. I pick up the colors of paint I need, a new calligraphy pen, some colored inks, and new brushes, putting them all into the basket Jack is carrying for me. As I round the last row, I realize the store is much bigger than I initially thought. A row of windows divides us from an expansive studio space, canvases set up on easels around the room. A sign on the door reads *Welcome to The Studio. Paint to your heart's content. Pay by the canvas at the front of the store.* It concludes with a list of canvas sizes and prices.

"This is like the paint-your-own pottery places!" I grin, pulling open the door and ushering the guys into the empty room.

"The what?" Jack grunts, looking entirely out of place.

"Never mind. Can we paint?" I ask, looking between them, batting my lashes and giving my best puppy dog eyes. I'm met with a chorus of protests.

"Just for a little bit?" I plead, prepared to fall onto my knees and beg if I have to.

"God. How are we supposed to say no when you give us those eyes, Sassenach?" Jack sinks into the seat at the closest canvas, setting the basket at his feet. The other two take their places and look at me expectantly. The silence is deafening.

"What are we supposed to paint?" Cam asks, twiddling a paintbrush in his hand nervously.

"Would it be easier if I sketch something first?" I ask, hating that he seems anxious.

"God, yes," Jack bursts out, the other two chorusing him.

I keep my smile to myself as I rifle through the available supplies, sighing with relief when I find a stick of charcoal. I walk to Cam first, sitting in his lap with my charcoal poised over the canvas.

"What'll it be?"

"The fairy pools."

"Mmmm. Good choice," I murmur, taking a second to think about the composition before I start to draw. I sketch the landscape like we're looking down at it from above, the highest point beginning at the left side of the canvas and ending with Cam's truck parked in the bottom right corner. I stand back, making sure it looks okay, then come back and draw little movement lines at the corners of the vehicle, unable to hold back my snort when Cam gasps with mock outrage.

"You're next," I say, still chuckling as I move to Lach's lap.

"I know what I'm going to paint, but I wanted you to sit in my lap before I told you that." He grins, pressing his lips to my cheek. I huff and stand, walking over to Jack. He pulls me into his lap, wrapping his arms around my waist.

"The stones, Sassenach."

"Which ones? By the castle or when we went on the picnic?" My cheeks heat just thinking about that day.

"The ones by the castle. I want to look at it and remember the night I found you again."

"You mean you don't want to paint when I realized I found *you*? I probably looked like a startled pufferfish," I laugh, starting to sketch.

"You were the most beautiful thing I've ever seen, mo chridhe. You came in smelling like the summer air, your hair tousled, still in your pajamas—madder than a goddamned badger. If Isla hadn't been ther —" He stops, his hands tightening around me.

"What would you have done if she wasn't there?" I ask, biting my lip.

"I would have asked you for permission and then sat you on the counter and fucked you until you knew you were mine and I was yours."

Fuck. "Things probably would have turned out a little differently if that had happened," I murmur, adding the final touches to the sketch. I drew the castle terrace to the right and the stones in the background. A large expanse of grass stretches before them, littered with tiny hairpins, one of my slippers, and Jack's lion mask.

"I think you have confidence in an ability that doesn't exist, Charlotte," he says, his brows drawing together as he studies the canvas.

"Just paint in blobs of color. It's easier than blending and looks surprisingly good when hanging on a wall."

"If you say so," he mutters, pulling my shirt over my shoulder and kissing my bare skin before releasing me.

I stand in front of my canvas, knowing precisely what I want to paint but not sure if I have the courage. Fuck it. I swap the canvas on my easel for a larger one and then start my sketch. This will be rudimentary at best since we have time restraints, but I can always add the finishing touches later. It takes me a few minutes to get a rough sketch down, and then I head to the supply wall, grab a paint pallet and squeeze on the colors I need.

I start to walk behind the guys to see their progress but quickly alter my course when they cry foul. I walk the long way around, settle myself into my chair, and get to work. First, I cover everything with a sepia wash, giving the canvas the golden tones I need, and then I start laying down the paint little by little. I'm not even close to finishing when the guys' shuffling and fidgeting pulls me out of the zone.

"The three of you sound like a herd of elephants. All of you are finished?" They nod as one. "Can I see now?" They nod again, and I walk to Cam, standing behind him to put a little distance between me and his painting. The canvas is covered in a multitude of greens, crystal blue waterfalls ending in frothy white, delicate purple heather dotting the hillside.

"Look." He points to the car, and I see a tiny hand pressed against the foggy window. I choke back a laugh. "Now that day is memorialized forever," he grins, lifting my hand to his lips.

Lach motions for me to skip him and move on to Jack. Jack's painting is a little more rudimentary, but there is no mistaking the feeling behind his brushstrokes. It makes me wonder what we'll do against that rock during the next party. I lick my lips, trying to keep the huskiness out of my voice when I tell him how amazing it is.

"Thank you, Charlotte."

"Lach, are you ready to show me?" He nods, color blooming in his cheeks. I keep my eyes on the ground until I'm standing directly behind him, slowly lifting my gaze. "Fuck," I breathe, my core clenching. The insides of my thighs frame the sides of the canvas, the slope of my belly in the center. My back is arched, pebbled nipples atop the soft peaks of my breasts. It's his view when he's eating me out. "Holy shit, Lach. How?"

"Art classes through high school and university. Drawing and painting always came easy. I guess some of it stuck with me."

"We're hanging that in the fucking gallery," Jack says, clapping Lach on the back.

"Let's see yours." Lach pushes away from his canvas, leading the way over to mine.

"Before you guys look at it, just know that I still have to add a ton of detail." I look at my painting, seeing all the imperfections, where the color isn't quite right, where there's not enough highlight or shadow.

"Holy fucking hell," Lach rasps. "You're a goddamn genius with a paintbrush."

His words wash through me, pride swelling in my heart. I look at the canvas and try to see it through their eyes. I painted my favorite moment from this morning. Cam and I are locked into a kiss, one of his hands wrapped around my neck and the other gripping Lach's thigh. His muscles are bunched, his ass flexed as he fucks Lach. Jack's head is against my shoulder, his hand snaking over my stomach, only the tip of his cock inside me as he pushes back onto Lach's thumb. Lach looks devastated, his head thrown back in a world-shattering orgasm.

"I would love to live a day as a guy just to know how it would feel to fuck someone while being fucked," I muse, looking away from the painting before the throbbing between my legs starts.

"There are toys for that," Lach says, adjusting himself.

I raise my eyebrow. "To make me a guy?"

"No, but it'll give you a dick to fuck someone with."

"But I won't feel that."

"My sweet innocent lamb. I know where we're going next."

"Where?"

"We're going to see Ann Summers."

"Who's she?" I ask, Cam's smirk making me suspicious.

"Oh, just wait, Carebear. You'll love her."

89

With repeated assurances from the store clerk that nobody will see our paintings, we head out in search of Ann Summers. I assume from the previous conversation that she has something to do with sex. A therapist, maybe? When I ask Lach for more information, he smiles and tells me I'll see when we arrive. I push the mystery to the back of my mind, instead focusing on the displays in the windows of the shops we're walking past. I resist the urge to browse until we reach a tiny bookshop with crystals burned into its wooden sign. Bells ring as we pull open the door and walk into the dim interior. Sun shines through the windows, dust motes lazily dancing through the rays. I take a deep breath. This has to be what heaven smells like.

I browse for about twenty minutes, picking out several books and bringing them to the resister. The woman takes the books from me, eyeing me and the guys, a mischievous twinkle in her eyes. She's beautiful. Her deep tawny skin glows against the purple of her head-scarf. Layers of ethereal clothing float around her as she moves, jewelry tinkling as she works.

"Girl, I don't even need to do a reading to know you're the luckiest bitch alive." She laughs and grabs my hand, flipping it over. Her fingertips tickle as she traces the lines over my palm, her full lips pulling into a smile. "You must have done something right in the last life. Enjoy it." She drops my hand, and I shove it in my pocket, still feeling the tingle of her touch. "You have something important in the near future." It's not a question.

I nod. "Several somethings."

"I wish you the best of luck." She hands me the bag, bowing her head slightly before turning and disappearing behind a curtain.

"That was a little strange," I murmur once we're back outside.

"What books did you get?" Lach asks, steering us across the street.

"One on interior design, one on gardening in Scotland, and the third is on the history of the Outer Hebrides."

"Taking your future job seriously, I see," Jack teases, his eyes soft.

"Speaking of that, we haven't talked about salary. I have a list of things I'll need to buy, and it would be nice to know my budget."

"There are *a lot* of things we haven't talked about," he grumbles.

I ignore him and pull him into an ice cream shop, hoping the change of scenery will make him forget his train of thought.

"What's your favorite flavor?" Jack asks, studying the cooler in front of us.

"Wait!" Lach butts in, "Let's guess. The person that wins gets to introduce Charlie to Ann."

"Bloody hell," Jack mutters, giving Lach a dirty look. He looks me up and down, then back at the ice cream. "Strawberry."

"Cam?" Lach says, saving his guess for last.

"Hm. Butter pecan." He looks at me for approval, but I don't give anything away.

"I'm guessing the flavors here are different from the flavors in the States, so I'm going to guess which one you're going to order. Is that fair?" Lach asks, looking around at all of us.

I'm starting to think Ann must be far more important than I realized if he's putting this much thought into such a simple thing. Both guys nod, giving him the go-ahead.

He squints at the tags, reading them through before guessing. "The coffee toffee fudge brownie chunk."

"Ding ding ding!" I throw my arms around him and kiss the upturned corner of his mouth.

"Wait a damn minute," Cam says, sliding his arms around us. "How did you know that?"

Lach shakes his head. "Lucky guess."

"Nothing is luck with you," Jack objects, "I know you analyzed this just as much as you do everything else. How'd you guess?"

"She likes being filled with lots of—"

Cam coughs, drowning out Lach's words.

"So, I figured she'd like her ice cream filled with lots of stuff, too."

Motherfucker. "Did you just boil my daddy issues down to a flavor of ice cream?" I ask, swatting him on the arm.

"Who said you have daddy issues?"

"Nobody. I kind of just assumed based on stereotypes, I guess."

"ADHD issues, maybe."

All of us look at him like he's on drugs.

He shrugs. "Three of us are just enough to drown out the chaos in your head, aren't we?" He asks, tapping my temple with the tip of his finger.

Realization slowly dawns on me. I've never been able to focus on sex, but I always thought it was because Rob was so selfish in bed. My thoughts are cut off by the man behind the counter asking us for our order.

The cones are dripping before we even make it out of the store. We collapse onto the nearest bench, frantically licking before it runs down onto our hands.

"This isn't fucking helping anything." I watch the long strokes of their tongues, desperately wishing my pussy was getting the same attention.

"Wish it was you?" A smile pulls at Jack's lips and I have to look away as he drags his tongue around the cone.

"I thought you would be planning the wedding by now," he says out of the blue, licking a drop of ice cream from his thumb.

I freeze, taken aback by the abrupt change of subject.

"I guess I don't understand how it will work when I can legally only marry one of you."

"Which you need to do in case something happens," Lach chimes in. "We want to make sure you're taken care of."

"And the other two?"

"We'll have a handfast ceremony, Sassenach. We don't need a priest to tell us our bond is sacred. Hell, we don't even need a ceremony, but I've been having visions of you in a wedding dress since the day we met, and I'm not fucking giving that up."

"Let's finish this conversation over dinner tonight, Ann's waiting for us," Lach says, rising to his feet.

My pulse jumps. I'm not enjoying the surprise aspect of this – I would much rather know what I'm getting myself into.

"Will you please at least give me a hint?" I plead.

Cam's attention snaps to me when he hears my anxiety laced words. "There's absolutely nothing to worry about, little witch. I promise."

"I guess I'll just have to trust you," I say with defeat, standing and licking off my fingers. "Let's go, then."

Despite Cam's assurance, I can't help how my heartbeat ramps up with every block. The three of them pull me to a stop in front of a store with a pink neon sign in the window. Ann Summers.

"It's a store? I thought it was a person this whole time! One of you could have told me that!"

"Sorry, Carebear. I didn't want you looking it up and ruining the surprise."

"What surprise?"

Jack pulls open the mirrored door, and I glance inside, my jaw dropping.

"You brought me to a sex store?"

"Only the best sex store in the UK. Have you ever been to one?" Lach asks.

I step backward out of the door. The sheer number of colorful packages hanging on the walls is overwhelming, let alone the handful of people browsing. "Never."

"No, you don't." He grabs my hand and laces our fingers together, pulling me back through the doorway. "We've been using toys our entire relationship. It's time you picked out some of your own."

"But people will see us," I whisper, my cheeks burning.

"We won't ever see any of these people again," he assures me, tipping up my chin so I'm looking him in the eye. "Plus, everyone is shopping for the same thing. I guarantee you there will be no weird looks or judgments from anyone here."

"It's okay, Charlie. Even *I've* shopped here before." Cam gives me a reassuring smile, sliding his hands up my arms to my shoulders, digging his fingers into my tense muscles.

"Okay," I whisper, trusting them. "What exactly are we looking for?"

"Whatever your heart desires." Lach leads me over to the wall on our left. Dildos, nipple clamps, cock rings, vibrators, anal beads, fleshlights. It's all so fucking overwhelming.

"How do I know what I desire when I don't know what half of this stuff is or whether I'd like it or not?" I ask, looking between them, praying to the gods that one of them will take mercy on me and pick something they know I'd like.

"I know what I want," Jack says gruffly, pulling a pair of leather handcuffs from the wall.

"If you get to use those, then I get to use this," I smirk, picking up a matching flogger with small strips of leather at the end.

"Mmm, you can use that on me anytime," Lach purrs, sliding his hand up and down the shaft like he's jerking himself off.

"Lach!" I hiss, glancing around to make sure nobody is looking at us.

"They're way more concerned about the throbbing inside their pants right now to care about what we're doing, Charlie."

Cam walks a few feet away and surprises me by snagging a set of hot pink anal beads from the wall. "I cannot wait to see your face when I take these out of you as you're coming," he rasps, biting his lip.

"Only if I get to do the same to you," I tease, my jaw dropping open when I hear his husky 'yes, please.'

"I have a lot to learn, don't I?" I ignore the pulse that has taken up residence between my legs.

"So fucking much," Jack answers, his gaze burning me alive.

"Do these feel good?" I ask, pointing to a fleshlight and then pulling it down to get a closer look.

"Not as good as your throat." He palms my neck, squeezing gently.

I take two giant steps away from him. "You have got to stop that."

"Or what?"

"I'm not sure, but I'm thinking we'll find out if I can come without being touched."

His gaze dips to the apex of my thighs and I clench them together, desperate for relief.

"What about this?" Cam asks, holding up a tiny bright blue contraption. "These little legs help it stay in place over your clit so hands can be used for other things."

I take it from him, turning the box over to read the description. *Secure and comfortable fit even in adventurous positions.* I'm not positive, but I think the sex we have would be considered pretty adventurous.

"Sounds like a winner." We grab a few more things; a pretty jeweled butt plug, a candle that melts into massage oil, and an industrial-sized bottle of lube before Lach stops us in front of what he's been waiting to show me.

"What you said earlier – about wishing you could have Cam and I's experience? This is how you do it." He slides a package off a hook and hands it to me. A medium-sized dildo is attached to an egg-shaped protrusion. "This part—" he points to the egg, "—goes inside you. There's a vibe inside it and also in this little piece connecting it to the dildo, so you'd have vibration on your g-spot and your clit."

My pussy clenches.

"And you would let me...?" I don't finish, too embarrassed to say the words.

"Fuck, yes." Lach groans.

"How could we say no to that?" Cam asks. "I can already see your tits jiggling with every thrust." He glances at his watch. "How many hours has it been?"

"Not enough," Jack growls, drawing me away from them.

"Do we have everything we need?" He takes the package from me, studying it with a raised eyebrow.

"I think so. Can we find some food after we leave here?" I'm famished." My stomach growls on cue and the guys usher me to the counter so we can pay.

90

I take several gulps of my beer the second the waitress sets it in front of me. I know what's coming and need liquid fortification to get through it.

"That bad, eh?" Jack raises his eyebrow, the corner of his mouth pulling up.

"What's bad?" Cam looks around the table at us, completely oblivious.

"Let's just get it over with. We can start with the wedding and then discuss the trip to the States." The words tumble from my mouth, running together.

"Ready." Lach holds up his phone, showing that he has the notes app open, grinning like a fool.

"Why don't we start with our expectations for the wedding," I suggest. "Cam, you first."

He looks like a deer caught in headlights but quickly recovers. "The only thing I want is the four of us to say vows and have a handfast ceremony. I don't care who we invite, where it is, or what we wear. We could be naked for all I care."

"One point for naked vows." I pretend to add a mark to an imaginary tally on my palm. "Lach?"

"Definitely naked. Preferably near a bed." I roll my eyes at him. He reaches across the table and grabs my hand. "To be completely truthful, the details don't matter to me either." His thumb sweeps over my wrist, making my pulse flutter.

"It's going to be hard to plan something when nobody has an opinion."

"Oh, don't worry about that. If I know Jack, he's had this planned out since the day he met you."

I turn to Jack and raise my eyebrows, waiting. "Well?"

"It should be on the back lawn overlooking the loch. There's enough room for us to invite family and friends." He rubs his hands over his face, his cheeks flushing. "I keep having a dream where I see you walking down the aisle, petals under your feet, a crown of flowers on your head, your gown floating around you." He swallows hard.

My heart swells in my chest. "That's what we'll do then. The next question is when?"

They answer in unison: *Autumn. Fall. October.*

"A little over a year from now?" I ask, surprised they want to wait that long.

"Fuck, no," Jack says vehemently. "This October."

I balk. "That's barely three months away. I'm not even divorced yet!"

"Which brings us to the elephant in the room," Lach says grimly. "When's the court date?"

"Two weeks from now."

"Bloody hell, Charlie! When were you planning on telling us?"

"After this weekend?" I rub my palm over my sternum, trying to dissipate the anxiety lodged in my chest.

"What's wrong?" Jack asks, picking up on my mood. He sweeps my hair away from my face, caressing my cheek with the back of his finger.

"I'm worried Rob will be a complete asshole in court. I'm worried I'm going to flub it up with my parents. I don't know how to be truthful about us. They'll flip when they find out I'm with all three of you."

"What if we don't tell them? We can let them figure it out on their own, and then the ball will be in their court."

"Do you think that'll work?"

"If you're not explicitly telling them, you're not opening up yourself for immediate discussion. They'll have time to think about it before they say anything." He licks his lips. "Yeah, they could still get angry, but I think the chance of that happening will be less. Plus, they'll get to know us first."

"You say that like it's a good thing," Lach mutters, nervously shoving his hand through his hair.

"So, what – we all traipse into my parents' house and pretend to be friends?"

"Do you have a better idea?" Cam asks, looking at me like he hopes I have an ace in the hole.

I bite my lip, thinking of how to make this a little more palatable to my parents. "I can go a few days ahead of you guys and tell them you're coming on holiday and to help me move."

"You're sure you want to tell them you're moving before we're there?" Cam asks, worry in his eyes.

I take my time to think about it before answering. "I'm sure. Knowing them, they would think I'm being forced somehow. They need to know it's a decision I made alone, and that I'd still be moving even if the three of you weren't in the picture."

"You would?" He pushes his glasses up his nose, looking at me in surprise.

I nod. "This place is in my blood now. I can't imagine going back to living in my parents' pool house. No job. No future. None of you." I look up at them, my pulse quickening. I glance at my phone. Four hours to go until the twelve-hour mark. Fuck.

We pause our conversation as the waitress sets bowls of piping hot stew before us. It's quiet for several minutes as we dig in and drain our beers. I look at my phone again. Three hours and fifty minutes left.

"Any ideas what we can do for the next four hours?" I ask.

"What's in four hours?" Cam looks up at me in a way that reminds me of this morning, and desire blooms through my body. "Oh." He smirks, biting his bottom lip. Goddamnit.

"Yeah, what's in four hours?" Lach teases, enjoying the heat creeping up my cheeks.

"I'm serious," I grumble.

"A pub crawl on our way to an escape room," Jack says, downing the last of his beer.

"You're fucking brilliant!" Lach gives Jack a mock bow, a grin plastered on his face.

Two hours later, we're in the fourth pub, and I've lost count of how many beers we've consumed. Much to the guys' delight, this pub has several pool tables, and they're currently fighting over who gets to teach me how to play. I have to break it up after the conversation has circled around for the third time.

"You can all teach me," I interrupt. "Guess a number from one to one hundred. Whoever is closest without going over can go first." They whisper their guesses in my ear.

"Lach, you win."

"I fucking knew it," he laughs.

"Please tell me the number wasn't sixty-nine," Jack mutters, rolling his eyes.

I just shrug, letting my grin do all the talking. I patiently wait as Lach picks out two cue sticks, absently twisting my hair around my finger, doing my best to look completely clueless. He shows me how to rack the balls and then guides me to the opposite end of the table. Wrapping my right hand around the base of the cue, he leans me over the table, positioning my other hand on the opposite end of the stick. His breath skates over my neck, making me shiver. He presses his body against me, demonstrating how to slide the cue and keep it steady.

"This is a dangerous position, Carebear," he murmurs, pressing me forward against the table until I can feel his cock nudging against my backside. I whimper, biting my lip as I desperately try to rein myself in. Taking a deep breath, I follow his guidance, purposely making a sloppy hit and watching several balls scatter. Jack slides the cue away from us, crowding Lach out.

"In a normal game, you would claim which balls you want," he explains.

"All of them?"

He barks out a laugh, his eyes crinkling. "You have to pick, mo chridhe. Stripes or solids?" I study the balls and then point to the solids. He acknowledges my choice and hands me my cue, walking around the table to grab the other one. "Do you want this to be a regular game? Or just practice?"

"May as well make it a regular game."

He nods. "I'll take my turn, and then I can help you if you need it." He makes his shot, the sharp crack startling me as it slams into the pocket. "Now you try." I position myself, my hands nowhere near where Lach showed me on the last hit. "Can I help?" he asks, looking tortured. I nod, biting my cheek to keep in my smile. He walks up behind me, dwarfing me as he puts his hands over mine, sliding them to the correct position. I lean back against him, breathing him in. "I'm thinking we need a pool table at the castle," he murmurs as we bend over the table.

"Why is that?" I ask, feigning ignorance, but my voice comes out husky, revealing what's on my mind.

He pulls the cue from my hands, dropping it on the table before spinning me around. "So I can fuck you on it." I go boneless as his thigh notches between my legs. He slides his hand up my back, supporting me as he bends us over the table. "Please tell me you're not still hurting," he whispers, sliding his nose against mine, our lips a hairsbreadth apart.

"The pain has been gone since before we got ice cream." I smile at the relief in his eyes, pulling him into a kiss. I jerk when a ball crashes into the pocket next to my shoulder.

Cam raises his eyebrows at us. "Are we going to play sometime tonight?" He keeps a straight face, but I don't miss the slight crinkle of his eyes or the smoothing of his forehead.

"Don't be a party pooper," I tease, extricating myself from Jack. I rack the balls and slide them into position. "One quick game, and then we should probably head to the escape room."

"Why have you been pretending you can't play?" Cam whispers, picking out his cue as I chalk the end of mine.

"How do you know I'm pretending?"

"It's my job to notice obscure details, Charlie. Like the fact that you just racked those balls like a pro, and now you're chalking your stick without anyone telling you to do it."

Oops. "Don't rat me out," I hiss, handing him the chalk.

"I'm on Charlie's team," he calls out, giving me an exaggerated wink.

I swig the rest of my beer, my belly pleasantly warm. The light in here is dim, making everything hazy and muted. The guys look like models as they pick out their cues, their sweatsuits hugging areas of their bodies in a way that makes it impossible not to look.

A little less than two hours left.

"Who wants to break?" Lach asks.

"I will," I offer sweetly, sidling up to the table. I pause, sliding my hand up and down the cue, aiming for as much distraction as possible.

"Fucking hell, Charlotte. Take the damn shot." Jack covers my hand with his, squeezing it around the shaft. I shoo him away and bend over the table, lining up my shot, letting it rip, and pocketing two balls.

I glance over at Lach, biting my lip to keep in my grin. His mouth is hanging open like a fish, his eyebrows almost up to his hairline. Jack raises one eyebrow, the muscle in his jaw twitching. He's already figured me out.

"Solids," I say blithely, walking around the table to line up my next shot. Three balls later, I'm out of options, so I do my best to block their best chance at a shot.

"This is either beginner's luck or you pulled a fast one on us," Lach mutters as he walks in front of me, studying the table.

"I guess you'll never know." I smirk, biting my lip.

"Fess up," Jack grumbles, wincing when Lach misses his shot.

"I got sick of spending hours in bars watching Rob play, so I taught myself, and the rest is history."

"If I ever see that guy—"

"You're going to tell him how good I am in bed," I finish for him, unable to get all the words out before snorting with laughter.

"Hello, gentleman." A woman in tight jeans and a crop top saunters up, her gaze flitting between the guys. She either doesn't see me or is completely ignoring me. "Can I play?"

"No, thank you," Jack says, motioning for Cam to take his turn.

"Maybe a drink then?" she asks, turning the sultriness in her voice up to ten.

"No, thank you," Cam and Lach say in unison, eyes on the table.

"Not even one little—"

"We're taken," Jack says, cutting her off. He wraps his arm around my waist and pulls me against his side.

She turns toward Cam and Lach. Before she can make her offer to them, they walk over to me, Lach slinging an arm over my shoulder and Cam linking his fingers through mine.

"We're *all* taken," Lach says firmly, his baritone vibrating through me.

She pouts for a second, spins on her heel, and stalks back toward the bar.

A laugh bubbles up, and I don't stop it.

"You liked that, didn't you?" Lach chuckles.

"Do you know how many times I've imagined that exact scenario? I'm glad it finally happened so I can stop worrying about it."

"And what happens when a guy comes up next time asking if you want to play a game with him?" he asks, a smile pulling at the corner of his mouth.

"I ask him to join my harem, of course." Lach's guffaw sends me into a fit of laughter – bent over, holding my stomach, tears leaking from my eyes. When I can finally breathe, I take several deep breaths and wipe under my eyes, trying to collect myself.

"Your turn Charlotte," Jack says, "Why don't you finish it off so we can leave?"

"You have that much confidence in me?" I ask, eyeing the table.

"Always." He says it with complete certainty, making my heart thump painfully in my chest.

"Do you want to make another deal?"

"What is it?" he asks gruffly, his jaw set, ready to refuse me.

"If I can sink every ball without a miss, we return to the hotel now."

He looks at the twelve balls left on the table. "Deal. But if you don't, we wait the full twenty-four hours for you to heal."

Fuck. This was a mistake. "Fine," I grind out, chalking up my cue and mapping out a plan of attack. The chance of this working in my favor is practically nil. I pick off the outliers first, cleaning up the table so I have a clear shot at the balls clustered in the center. I aim for the solid orange ball first, watching with my fingers crossed as it ricochets in a corner and sinks home into a side pocket. Four to go. I miss the shot with the blue-striped ball, but the gods must be looking out for me because it knocks the red one in. A light tap is all that's needed to get the blue-striped ball into the pocket this time.

Now only the eight ball is left, tucked into an edge, making for a nearly impossible shot. All three guys are holding their breath as I walk around the table, looking at every possible angle. I have two crappy choices. Either I forfeit now, or I work with the only angle I have, which means shooting with the cue behind my back and risking losing *and* looking ridiculous. I go for the only real choice, my cheeks heating, knowing I'm about to look like an absolute d-bag.

"Don't fucking laugh," I warn them, swinging the cue behind me and backing up to the table. I hold my breath as I line up the shot, pray to any gods that might be listening, and then tap the ball. I feel my soul leaving my body as it inches along the edge of the table and teeters on the edge of the pocket. Jack loses patience and slaps the ball into the pocket, grabs my hand, and pulls me out of the bar.

"I hope you're fucking ready, Sassenach. I'm bringing out the ropes tonight."

91

My entire body is buzzing, ultra-aware of the Ann Summers bag swinging from Lach's fingertips, of the warmth of Jack's hand against the bare skin of my back, the slow sweep of Cam's thumb over the inside of my wrist. My breathing becomes ragged, my heart in my throat as we enter the hotel lobby.

"You okay?" Lach tips up my chin, studying my face.

"Just a little nervous," I admit.

"We don't have to—"

I press my finger against his lips. "I want to."

He nods once, accepting the truth in my answer. "Maybe a massage before we start will help you relax."

"Yes, please," I smile, standing on my tiptoes and pressing my lips to his.

We pile into the elevator with another couple, the tension unbearably thick by the time we get to our floor. Jack sees the tremble in my steps and scoops me into his arms, grinning.

"A little turned on, are we?" He laughs softly, carrying me into the room and setting me down on the bed. "Breathe, mo chridhe. In. Out.

In. Out." I follow his guidance, taking deep, slow breaths until my heart doesn't feel like it will explode anymore.

"Jack," Cam calls, "Lach says to give Charlie a massage. We're going to take a quick shower." The bathroom door snicks closed before he's finished talking.

"I wonder why they're in a hurry?" Jack chuckles, sitting down next to me.

"Would you let me do that?" I blurt, mortification taking hold the second the words are out of my mouth.

"Let you do what?" he asks carefully, standing to pull off his sweatshirt. My mouth goes dry as I look up at him, at the way the light caresses his golden skin, highlighting every peak and valley. I clear my throat, forcing myself to look him in the eyes.

"Fuck you."

His throat jerks as he swallows. "I'll try anything once," he says, the huskiness of his voice doing funny things between my legs.

"Anything?" I raise my eyebrow, surprised by his answer. He sits down again, and I climb onto his lap, straddling him.

"Maybe." He shrugs. "This morning changed my perspective. I'm going to need time to examine that. But right now, what I want to do is see if I can make you come without touching your pussy." He pushes my sweatshirt off my shoulders, letting it drop to the floor. Callouses scrape over sensitive skin as he slides his hands up my torso and under my bra, lifting it over my head. I arch into his touch as he palms my breasts, his low groan raising goosebumps. I drop my hips, nestling his hardness at the apex of my thighs. He grips my hips, sliding me against him until he's nudging at my opening.

"These sweatpants are way too fucking thick," I pant, rolling my hips. His grip tightens, holding me still.

"If you don't stop, I'm going to rip those sweatpants off and fuck you until your pussy is strangling my cock," he says roughly, his muscles rippling as he pulls himself under control. He tosses me onto the bed without warning, taking hold of the ankles of my sweatpants and pulling them off in one hard tug. "Up," he murmurs, sliding my panties down when I raise my hips. "Stay," he says, his hands warm on my waist as he turns me over.

Jack's POV

I can hardly bear to leave her there for two seconds while I look for the goddamn shopping bag. Her gaze burns my back, flames of naked desire singeing my skin. I spot the bag and snatch it up, pulling out the butt plug and the candle. Matches. Fuck. I rummage around in the nightstand drawers, then the desk, and finally find some in the console table drawer.

I walk back to the bed, my gaze sweeping up the curve of her calves to the softness of her thighs. I clench my fists to keep from spreading her wide and burying my cock in her heat. She turns to look at me, her gaze hungry. "You have to stop looking at me like that," I growl, my cock throbbing painfully. She smiles but doesn't argue, laying her head back down.

Good fucking girl.

I drop the plug on the bed and pull off my sweatpants before lighting the candle, not wanting to ruin them with the oil. As soon as there's a puddle around the wick, I climb onto the bed, straddling her upper thighs.

"Ready?"

She nods, the muscles in her back tightening. I tip the candle slowly, letting just a couple of drops fall. "Does that feel okay?"

"Yes," she whispers, her back arching as I pour a line down her spine.

I set the candle on the nightstand and smooth the oil over her back, pressing my thumbs into the muscles that worked so hard for us this morning. I slowly move to her lower back, her skin soft and supple under my hands. I know she's desperate when she starts pushing her ass up every time my hands dip low. I slide off the bed and spread her legs until I have a clear view of her pussy. My hands tremble as I pour more oil into my palm, my pulse roaring in my ears. She whimpers as I kneel on the bed between her legs, her pussy clenching on air. One thrust and I'd be buried inside her, and we'd be on our way to paradise. I grunt as I resist the urge, smearing the oil over the globes of her ass cheeks, her flesh molding to my hands. I slide my thumbs along her crack, and she pushes her ass into the air, exposing herself to me. A bead of moisture drips down her lips, and before I can stop myself, I catch it with my tongue. Her body shudders, her hands fisting in the sheets.

"I thought you said you weren't going to touch my pussy," she mumbles.

Shit. "One more time, then I won't do it again," I say gruffly, cursing myself for making up stupid rules. I run my thumbs on either side of her pussy, bringing them together at the front, her clit trapped between them.

"Jack," she begs, her muscles contracting as I roll her between my fingers. I'm true to my word and move my hands back to her ass, feathering the pad of my thumb over her, gently bearing down until she's pushing back onto my finger.

"I want to hear how much you like it," I rasp, waiting for her to dislodge her teeth from her hand before circling the rim with the tip of my finger. Her moan is a lightning bolt straight to my dick, precum leaking onto my thigh as she swallows my finger one knuckle at a time. Fuck.

"More," she mumbles.

This woman is my kryptonite. I can't function when all I can think about is how to make her moan louder and come harder. The way her throat constricts around me when she's trying not to gag. The sweet musk buried between her legs. The way she squeezes me so hard I think she'll break my cock, and how I'm perfectly fine with that. Those blue eyes, the color of the loch on a summer day, sparkling up at me while the sun turns her hair to burnished copper. The way she loves me without reservation. I would die for her a million times over.

"Jack, I need you inside me." She looks back at me, desperation in her eyes, her lip caught in her teeth as she impales herself on my finger.

"I'm supposed to be getting you there without that, remember?"

"You said without touching my pussy. You said nothing about your cock or my ass."

Fuck. Me. "Fair enough. We can try for the elusive anal orgasm."

"That's a thing?"

I hop off the bed and grab the lube, not willing to risk anal play with just the oil. "The clitoris extends internally behind the front wall of the vagina. Anal sex can stimulate a spot that is hard to reach other ways."

"It's called the a-spot. Similar to the prostate on guys," Lach explains, catching our conversation as he comes out of the bathroom, Cam right behind him, both of their cocks at half-mast. I don't offer them the chance to take over because I know what they have coming later, and I'm jealous as fuck. "Go on," Lach says, pulling on his robe, "We'll wait." I sigh in relief as they go out on the balcony, still feeling awkward about navigating this when we're all together.

I kneel between Charlotte's legs, spreading her cheeks wide and swirling my tongue over her.

"Fuck," she sobs, her body trembling. I lap at her, holding her still as I push past the tight ring of muscle and fuck her with my tongue. "More, Jack." I give her one last swirl of my tongue before sinking my teeth into her ass cheek, a sudden desperate urge to leave my mark on her.

"Please," she begs, looking back at me, her makeup smudged under her eyes, strands of hair stuck to her cheek. So goddamn beautiful.

"Butt plug first," I say, squirting lube on it.

"I don't need that. I need you."

"Indulge me." I wait for her nod of acceptance before pulling her to the edge of the bed, letting her legs dangle off. "This will be the best position to hit that spot. Are you comfortable?"

"For the love of God, Jack." Her eyes flash with annoyance, her hand sneaking down, headed toward her clit.

"Don't you fucking dare." I take her threat seriously and nudge the plug against her, a smile pulling at my lips as her hand moves back up and fists in the sheets. I push the tip in, watching with pride as she relaxes and breathes deeply. I pulse it against her, watching as she swallows it a little more each time. "Almost there." I push until the widest part of the plug disappears inside her, only the purple jewel left on the outside. I pull it out slowly and slide my tongue over her, swirling it around until I feel her muscles relax, and she's pushing back onto my face.

"Charlotte, I hope to God you're ready." I slide my hand over my cock, biting back a groan.

"Fuck me, Jack."

I don't need to be told again. I squirt a generous amount of lube on my fingers, spreading it over her and my cock. "I'll have to go deep to hit that spot," I rasp, sliding my cock back and forth over her entrance.

"Anything," she groans, arching her back.

I grip my shaft with one hand, spreading her with the other, nearly coming undone as the tip sinks in. So fucking tight. I grit my teeth, pulsing back and forth, watching as the ridge along the head of my cock stretches her. Fuck. My entire body shudders as I struggle for control. "Don't fucking squeeze," I tell her, my knees nearly giving out as she clenches around me.

"Do you know what happens to naughty girls?" I growl, pulling out of her before I make a fool of myself.

She looks over her shoulder at me, a wicked smile pulling at her lips. "Spank me, daddy."

I notch myself at her entrance and slap her ass, her gasp of surprise turning into a low, keening moan as I bury my cock inside her. She clenches around me, sliding herself up and down my shaft. Motherfucker.

"Charlie." Her name is a prayer on my lips – a plea. I wrap my fingers around her waist and hold her still, angling my hips as I thrust to hit that spot deep inside.

"Oh, God," she breathes, every muscle in her body strung tight as I thrust again. I pull out, grab the bottle of lube and apply it liberally, determined not to hurt her.

"Jack." Lach is leaning against the doorframe, watching me, an emotion behind his eyes I can't read.

"Yes?" My throat feels tight.

"Do you want me to..." He makes a motion with his finger that makes my cheeks burn.

"You said you'd try anything once," Charlotte mumbles into the covers.

"This would make twice," I remind her, turning back to Lach.

"And did you like it?" He sinks his teeth into his bottom lip, his eyes darkening as he waits for my answer. Did I like it? I think back to this morning, to the best orgasm I've had in my entire life.

I clear my throat. "Yes," I admit, the word coming out low and husky.

"Do you want me to do it again?" His words hold no expectation, no judgment. I bite back the indignant response that's waiting on the tip of my tongue, instead digging deep to get to the raw truth.

"Yes."

He nods once, holds his hand out for the lube, and then motions for me to continue with Charlotte. Every nerve in my body tingles with awareness as I fist my cock and slowly sink into her. Two thrusts and she's begging me not to stop. I slow down, taking my time to get the angle just right, pushing hard and deep. I feel Lach's presence before his hand touches my hip, anchoring himself.

"Ready?" he murmurs, his breath teasing the hairs on my neck. I can't get my throat to work, so I only nod. I brace myself, all of my muscles tensed. "That's not going to work, Jack. Lay on top of her." I brace my arms on either side of Charlotte's head and test the angle, thrusting hard and deep.

"Oh fuck," Charlotte mewls, squirming under me. Lach's fingers press into my hip, giving me a warning before sliding his finger down my crack. My hips stutter, my body confused. I thrust into Charlotte, and as I pull back, Lach presses the pad of his finger against me, circling me, teasing me. This is different than this morning. This morning seemed almost clinical. This... this is raw, unadulterated sex. I whimper and thrust again, two of Lach's fingers sliding against me as I pull out. I push back into him more, and his hand slides further down. I can feel him hesitate, but I arch my back, and that's all the invitation he needs to cup my balls.

Holy fuck. I don't give myself time to think about what I'm doing. I thrust into Charlotte again, Lach massaging my balls, his other hand coming up to circle my asshole. I lean my forehead against the back of Charlotte's head, breathing hard. "I don't think I can hold on much longer."

"Fuck me hard, Jack. I'm close."

Our skin slaps together with the next thrust, and as I pull back, Lach keeps his finger still, allowing me to take as much of him as I'm comfortable with. I pulse my hips, pushing into Charlotte and then back onto Lach's finger.

"You like that?" Lach murmurs, his hand leaving my balls to grip my hip, pushing me down into Charlotte and holding me still while he presses two fingers against me. The sound that comes out of my mouth is indecent and embarrassing, but I don't fucking care when it feels this good. I flex my hips against Charlotte, pushing as deep as I can. This time Lach doesn't wait for me to pull back; he's already there, two fingers massaging my prostate while I'm balls deep in our lover. Charlotte moans, biting my hand to muffle her scream, pulling me with her over the edge, plunging headfirst into the unknown.

92

LACH'S POV

The chill of the marble vanity seeps into my bones, the stone biting into my hips as I look at the stranger in the mirror. Who the fuck is the person looking back at me, and why is he risking his relationship with his best friend?

'I want him to feel good' is the first thought that crosses my mind, but that's only a fraction of the truth. It's the way his throat bobs, the surrender in his eyes, the rippling muscles, the groan when I push in, knowing that *I'm* the one making him feel like that.

Fucking hell.

Cam knocks and pokes his head in the bathroom, slipping through the door and closing it behind him when he sees the look on my face.

"What's wrong?" He tilts up my chin, his thumb caressing my jaw.

"I—" I swallow hard. "I helped Jack again."

Cam blinks, his midnight eyes almost black in the dim light. "And how do you feel about that?" he asks finally.

"How do *you* feel about it?" I ask, shoving my hands through my hair. "Why does it feel like I'm cheating on you?"

"Lach. All of our dicks touch every time we sleep with her. It's not a big deal."

I shake my head. "This was different. This morning was out of convenience. Curiosity maybe. Tonight was lust."

"Or love," Cam says softly.

"I would have fucked him if he asked," I say, ignoring that four-letter word.

"You mean you would have made love to him."

"Goddamn it, Cam. Don't."

"He might not see it, but I do."

"See what?" I look up at him, my heart pounding in my ears.

"You've been in love with him since that day when we were at uni." A statement, not a question.

"What am I going to do?" I whisper, dread wrapping its bony fingers around my throat.

He shrugs. "You either tell him and see how it plays out, or you go back to how it was before today."

I feel sick. I press my forehead against the marble, breathing hard. "What about you?" I ask, turning to look up at him.

"What about me?"

"Won't it be weird for you?"

He pulls me away from the counter and wraps his arms around me, tucking my head against my shoulder. "I am so goddamn thankful for you and Charlie. I love Jack like a brother, but it won't ever turn into more. I'm proud of you for acknowledging your feelings, and I'll be here for you if you need me. I want you to be happy, Lach."

"You guys are up," Jack says gruffly, pushing into the bathroom, stormy golden eyes making brief contact with mine before sliding to my lips. He stops behind me, holding my gaze in the mirror, muscles flexing as he pulls his hair back. Cam squeezes my arm in encouragement and leaves the bathroom, closing the door behind him.

"What was that?"

"What was what?" I raise my chin, challenging him, my heart beating a thousand miles a minute.

"Cut the bullshit, Lach."

"Did you like it?" I ask, trying to sound flippant but failing miserably.

He growls, ripping open my robe, his gaze in the mirror falling to my cock. "You sure as fuck do."

I nod, resisting the urge to pull the robe from his hands and fold it over myself.

"Do you want to fuck me?"

Why did he have to ask me the one question don't know how to answer? What if I say yes and it ends all of this? What if I say no and it never even starts?

"Tell me the truth, Lach."

I hold his gaze in the mirror, my heart crumbling into a thousand pieces. "Yes," I whisper, my voice breaking, a single tear streaking down my cheek.

His hands clench at his sides, knuckles turning white. "I don't want this—"

My shoulders sag under the weight of his words. I jerk away from the counter, barely holding myself together. I have to get out of here. I pull the door open several inches, but he slams it closed, cornering me.

"You didn't let me finish, goddamnit."

"I don't want to hear it, Jack."

His nostrils flare, the lines bracketing his mouth deepening as his eyes search mine. "Too fucking bad." His voice is rough, scraping over my skin like calloused palms, settling low and heavy in my core. He grabs my chin, forcing me to keep eye contact. "How do you know this won't ruin our friendship?"

"I don't."

"Yet you're willing to risk it. Why?" There's a desperate, wild edge to his voice.

"Because I'll regret it for the rest of my life if I don't."

"And what about Cam?"

"I think he's wondering what took us so long. He brought up that day back in—"

"I told you not to mention that again," he says sharply, cutting me off.

"Does that matter now? I just fucked you with my finger, which, last time I checked, is a little more gay than an innocent kiss."

"That kiss wasn't fucking innocent, and you know it," he growls.

"I guess I don't remember correctly. Remind me." I keep my words light, giving him an easy out. He doesn't take it.

Jack crushes his body to mine, his cock hard against my hip, our chiseled edges and sharp angles fitting together like the last two pieces of a puzzle. He pauses, his gaze dropping as he pulls at my lower lip with his thumb, his breath hitching. I swirl my tongue over his finger, his pupils blowing out as I sink down on his thumb, scraping my teeth over him as he pulls away. I rock my hips against him, the answering groan a siren's song dragging me down into the depths. He angles his head, our lips a hairsbreadth from touching. Our tongues meet in a slow sensual sweep.

"Goddamnit, Lach." He cradles my face in his hand, the hooded lion eyes that haunt my dreams ripping the breath from my lungs. "You're sure?" he rasps, "I don't think we'll be able to forget about it this time."

"I never fucking forgot, Jack." His lips crash against mine before the last word is out of my mouth, his tongue sliding against the seam of my lips, pushing in to tangle with mine. Not a second later, I hear the bed banging against the wall, Charlie's moans floating under the door and wrapping around my dick.

Jack pulls away, a rueful smile tugging at his lips. "Let's go take care of our girl."

93

―――――

Cam comes out of the bathroom with a smile on his face, holding a finger over his lips as he gently closes the door.

"What's going on?" I whisper, pushing myself into a sitting position as he climbs on the bed.

"They have some heavy shit they need to figure out. It's been a long time coming."

"I kind of figured that after today. They have history, don't they?"

He winds a strand of my hair around his finger. "Only one kiss, as far as I know. Though Jack would deny that it meant anything."

"And Lach?"

He shrugs. "Love? Lust? Something in between? I'm not sure even he knows. He's sensitive to visual stimulation and incredibly sexual, which is great for all of us if they can figure it out."

"That doesn't bother you?"

"I could ask you the same question about me or Lach. I've never believed in the prescribed notion that we only have one soulmate. People come into our lives for different reasons. Some are lovers, some are platonic, but all of them grow and shape and mold our lives to be better."

My brain is rearranging itself as I think about his words, the foundations of my idea of love crumbling, only to be rebuilt stronger by Cam's words.

I shake my head, stunned by his emotional maturity. "If I had realized that years ago, I would have done a lot of things differently."

"But then you may not be here now, little witch. Everything happens for a reason." He leans against the headboard and pulls me into his arms, smoothing his hand over my hair, tracing my eyebrows with the tip of his finger.

"Tell me about this kiss." An image of Jack and Lach embracing forms in my mind, my belly clenching in response, heat climbing up my cheeks as my nipples pebble.

Cam cups my breast, flicking his thumb over the peak. "It turns you on, doesn't it?"

"Maybe," I hedge, folding my arms over my breasts.

"The kiss wasn't a big thing. They were both drunk and cozied up on the couch together. We were watching a movie, and it just happened."

"This was before you and Lach...?"

He nods. "I had feelings for Lach at that point but hadn't told him yet."

"And then what?"

"Jack told us never to mention it again. And we didn't. Until today."

I feel disoriented – like I'm looking at my life through a mirror – everything is in reverse, but still the same. "This is a mind fuck," I say bluntly.

"Tell me about it," he says, chuckling.

"Will this change anything?" I muse, trying to think of scenarios that would upset me but coming up blank.

"In my opinion? No. They already act like a married couple. This just adds another dimension when we're fucking."

"Sharing Lach doesn't bother you?"

He huffs out a laugh. "I've *always* shared him with Jack. His happiness benefits all of us. I'm not a jealous person, Charlie."

I relax against him, my head fitting perfectly in the space between his neck and shoulder. Our proximity has him hardening against my back, but he doesn't acknowledge it, keeping the focus on our conversation.

"What about me and Jack?" The question hangs in the air, my heart in my throat as I wait for his answer.

"I wish you could have known him before he met you, Charlie. He gave up on everything but the farm. I barely recognized him. You did something we couldn't do – you brought him back to life."

I blow out a long breath and close my eyes, centering myself. I can't find it in me to be upset or disappointed. I love all three of them with every fiber of my being and know they feel the same way about me. What more could I possibly need? Cam cups my cheek, and I open my eyes, twisting in his arms so I can see his face.

"I'm so proud of you." His voice is rough, filled with emotion. "We don't fucking deserve you, but we're going to spend every second of our lives trying to make it up to you." He tips up my chin, pressing his mouth to mine. I want to tell him they have nothing to make up for, but he holds me close, deepening the kiss.

"We need to tell them to get the hell out here, but I'm not leaving you alone in this bed," he murmurs against my lips, sliding his palm over my breast with a groan.

"Bang the headboard against the wall. That'll get them out here fast."

His lips curl against mine, his low chuckle raising goosebumps on my arms. He breaks our kiss to grab the headboard and shoves it against the wall rhythmically. I moan loudly, stifling a giggle with my hand when Cam's jaw drops, forgetting the headboard completely. One more moan, and Jack and Lach are fumbling with the door, tripping over each other to be the first one out.

"Now that you're both out here, we need to have a family meeting before continuing our evening." I untangle myself from Cam, pulling the sheets over my chest.

"Which one of you wants to go first?" Cam asks, looking between Lach and Jack.

"We kissed," Jack says, holding my gaze, emotion swirling in his eyes.

"And?"

"And I've never been more confused in my entire life." He glances at Lach, heat creeping up his cheeks.

"So, where do things go from here?" Cam asks, "Where does that leave all of us?"

"Can I be honest here?" Lach asks, his gaze flitting between all of us. "Jack is my best friend. That's not going to change. Is it?" He looks at Jack, vulnerability shadowing his expression.

"Never," Jack reassures him.

Some of the tension leaves Lach shoulders. "I'm attracted to all of you. I can't help it. When we're all together in bed, my brain flips a switch, and there is absolutely no discrimination. I will gladly fuck all of you and have all of you fuck me." He runs a hand aggressively through his hair. "I don't know if it's love or lust, but whatever it is, I don't want it to change what we have together." He turns to me. "It's your call, Charlie."

"Mine?"

He chuckles at my surprise. "You still don't get it, do you? We aren't anything without you."

Fuck, if that wasn't the exact thing I needed to hear right now. "I want you both to do what feels right to you, but communication needs to stay open between all of us." They both murmur their agreement. "Good. Now can we please fuck?"

Cam's POV

Jack is on the balcony, Lach's in the bathroom washing the toys, and I'm lying between Charlie's legs, breathing her in. She trembles as I lick and bite my way up the inside of her thigh, stopping just shy of where I want to bury my tongue. She mewls in protest as I switch to her other leg, gently scraping my stubble over sensitive skin, bringing her to the edge. I lay my cheek on her thigh, lightly blowing over her pussy, watching as the moisture drips from her. Catching it with my thumbs, I glide them up her labia, groaning as she arches into my hands, her clit begging for mercy. I slide my tongue along her slit, her taste exploding inside my mouth. My cock throbs painfully, desperate for attention. I lock eyes with her as I drag my tongue over her clit, pulsing there as her nails scrape my scalp, pulling me closer.

Lach drops the toys on the bed beside us, watching me eat her out, his hand riding over his cock in a steady rhythm. I push myself onto my knees, grabbing the toys and holding them where she can see them.

"Strapless strap-on or anal beads?"

"Both?"

My balls tighten. "That's my girl." I side off the bed, grab her ankles and jerk her toward me, getting perverse satisfaction in the way it makes her tits jiggle. My cock nudges between her legs as I bend over her, swirling my tongue over her nipples, sucking them hard and deep. She locks her heels behind me, pulling me closer, rocking herself against my shaft.

"Cam." My name is poetry on her lips, the desperation in her voice calling to something deep within me. I grab the strap-on, dragging it over her, sliding it back and forth over her clit.

She shakes her head, pushing my hand away. "I need you first."

"I'm already too close," I rasp, fisting my cock and dragging it through her folds. "You're so goddamned beautiful. I can't help it."

"I don't want control. I want you to fuck me and make me forget everything but the way your cock feels inside me."

I stand no chance. The way her hair halos her face, hints of copper creating a perfect backdrop for those luminescent sapphire eyes. My end. My beginning. I'm fucking wrecked. I slam into her, warmth wrapping around me, ripping a moan from deep in my chest. I curse as she clamps down, my hands trembling as I fight for restraint.

"Charlie, I'm too close to do this. You said you wanted to know what it was like to fuck and be fucked, and I'd still like to experience that with you tonight."

She has trouble focusing on me, her chest heaving, her entire body shaking. "I do want that. But I want you in my mouth first."

"Charlie—" She doesn't give me time to protest, sliding to the floor like a boneless jellyfish and pulling me to her, not stopping until the head of my cock presses into the back of her throat. She leans her head back against the bed, her nostrils flaring as she focuses on her breathing. I don't move, worried I'll hurt her, scared she'll be disappointed if I don't. She looks up at me, scrunching her eyebrows in anger.

"Uck ee!" she mumbles around my shaft, digging her nails into my ass and pulling me closer. I give in, pushing her head deep into the bed with every thrust. She swallows, her throat constricting around me.

"Fucking hell, Charlie." I cup her face, holding her still as I take everything she wants to give me, my hips driving into her despite my brain telling me to stop. She urges me on, massaging my balls, then my perineum. I pull away from her before she can do more damage, hands on my knees as I struggle to catch my breath.

"You're going to be the death of me," I pant, hauling her onto the bed and pulling her legs over my shoulders. I coat the silicone beads in lube, pushing them in one at a time. Her hands are fisted in the sheets by the time I slide the last one in, her back arched entirely off the bed.

I grab the strap-on and coat the part that goes inside her with lube, sliding it over her clit several times before pushing it into her. It fits snugly, the vibrator directly over her clit, just waiting to be turned on. She looks down at herself with wide eyes, the dildo rising perpendicular to her body, as close to having a real cock as she'll ever get.

"Do you want me to turn it on?"

"Not yet," she groans, rolling her hips, struggling to rein herself in. I pull her to her feet, fist the dildo, and pull her against me, our bodies flush as I ravage her mouth. She wraps her arms around my neck, mewling as I rock the silicone against her, alternating the pressure between her clit and her g-spot. I glance over at Lach, motioning for him to lie down, watching his cock bob with each step, a bead of desire running down his tip. I can't manage to drag my eyes away from him as he lies down, keeping his ass at the edge of the bed to make it easier on Charlie. He pulls his knees to his chest, legs spread wide, his chest rising and falling rapidly.

"Ready?" I ask both Lach and Charlie.

"You first," she whispers, her gaze moving between my cock and Lach's ass, her cheeks stained scarlet.

"Is that okay with you?" I ask Lach, my hands on his knees, the tip of my cock a hairsbreadth from brushing against him.

"Fuck yes," he groans, watching me as I spread lube over my cock, then dribble some down his crack. I lean over him, catching the bead of precum on my tongue, and turn to Charlie, pulling her face to mine, sharing him with her. She whimpers into my mouth, clutching my shoulder like I'm the only thing tethering her to this earth. Lach's abdomen flexes as I turn back to him, his cock twitching in desperation. I wrap my hand around my shaft, closing the distance, all three of us holding our breath as I push against him, barely breaching the muscle before stopping to let him adjust. He arches his back, eager for all of me, but I hold back, determined to give Charlie the show I know she wants. I flex my hips, and the head of my cock disappears inside of him. I pull out, pulsing, the ridge stretching him, pulling at sensitive nerve endings. Charlie's nails dig into my arm, the pain ripping away what little control I had, and I bury myself deep. That ring of muscle becomes a noose around my shaft, stealing my breath with every squeeze, every thrust.

I pull out, and Charlie takes my place, looking down at the quivering mess of a man lying on the bed before her. She's squirting lube on the dildo as I return from the bathroom, spreading it with shaking fingers, swirling the excess around Lach's asshole. He jumps at her touch, a long, low moan tearing its way from his lungs, more precum dripping down his cock. She hums in appreciation as she licks him clean, taking him all the way in, her cheeks hollowing as she backs off, releasing him with a pop. She bites her lip, her brow furrowed in concentration as she fists the dildo and nudges it between his cheeks, sliding it over him until he's begging for mercy.

"Don't you fucking dare be gentle," he begs, the demand falling from his lips like a prayer, the moan that follows raising the hairs on my arms. She flexes her muscles, sinking into him, her hips stuttering as she pulls back, causing the part nestled inside her to push against her g-spot.

"Oh, God." She plunges back in, pulsing her hips.

"Harder," he begs, his entire body straining toward her, his expression torn between pain and ecstasy. His hands are fisted in the sheets, refusing to touch his cock, edging himself.

"Cam?" Her voice has a desperate edge to it, big blue eyes looking up at me, pleading for something she can't put into words.

"You're sure?" She nods, leaning against Lach, arching her back, and pushing her ass toward me. I lube up a finger and swirl it around the silicone buried inside her. "Can I leave them in when I fuck you?"

Her nod is all the confirmation I need. I push my finger in slowly, my knees nearly buckling when she squeezes around me. So fucking tight, I reach around her and press the button to turn on the vibrator, her choked gasp spurring me on. I spread her cheeks, lubing her with my precum, and notch myself at her entrance, waiting for the backward swing of her hips to sink into her softness. I moan as her body constricts around me, the beads sliding along the underside of my cock, the combination nearly doing me in. I bury myself deep, pushing her tight against Lach, the three of us locked together.

I fist her hand around Lach's shaft, closing my hand over hers, guiding her. We all watch, mesmerized, as the head of his cock disappears inside our hands. We squeeze on the way back down, his moan like a gunshot propelling us toward the finish line. I give Charlie space, sliding almost all the way out of her as she sinks into Lach, greedily gobbling me back up as she pushes her hips back and pulls out of him.

"Cam—" her voice breaks, and I know I'm done for. I push into her, hard and deep, forcing her to do the same to Lach. His hand replaces mine, sliding Charlie's fist over his shaft at a punishing pace. I hook my finger into the handle of the beads, pulling them out slowly, Charlie's low, breathless curse shooting straight to my balls.

One hard thrust and the three of us are catapulted over the edge, our bodies writhing together in uncoordinated chaos, half-formed words of desperation dying in our throats as we're dragged into the depths of carnal bliss.

94

───────

My insides feel hollow as we pull into the driveway of the Manor house, and Lach puts the car in park. None of us move.

"This is a fucking problem, isn't it?" Jack says, rubbing his hands over his face and growling in frustration. "I don't want to leave you here. I can't bear to watch you walk down to that cottage alone, mo chridhe."

"I'm glad we're all the same level of fucked," I say honestly.

"Come home with me." Jack twists in his seat to look at me. "All of you," he clarifies when Lach makes a sound of protest. "I'll have to custom order a bed, but in the meantime, we can move Cam's bed into my room."

I blink rapidly, tears threatening to betray my emotions. "You'd do that?" I search his face for any sign that this isn't what he wants, but his expression is clear and open, no signs of disappointment or hesitation.

"I would move heaven and earth if it meant I could wake up to your face every morning."

Fuck. "What do you guys think?" I ask, looking between Lach and Cam.

"You don't need to ask me twice," Cam says. "Wherever you are is where I want to be. If you want to be with all of us, and Jack's willing to share his room, then I'm there."

"Same," Lach agrees. "That will leave Isla alone in the house, though."

"She's been talking about renting out the rooms for years," Jack says. "Maybe this will give her the reason to do it finally."

"Wait. Why does she want to rent the rooms out?" I ask, trying to understand why she would add anything to her already chaotic schedule.

"She has to stay busy twenty-four seven. Now that the gym is exactly how she wants it, she'll be looking for her next project."

"Does she ever slow down?"

"Not since she was old enough to start helping me on the farm. One of these days, she'll meet someone that will force her to take time off."

"Until then, maybe I can convince her to take some days off with me. We could go on a hike or down to the beach." Lord knows I could use the exercise – I need to increase my stamina to keep up with the guys.

"Don't forget wedding planning," Lach says, his voice soft, trying not to startle me. My heart jumps to my throat. I've successfully avoided the stress of thinking about it, but that can't last forever.

"I've never planned anything before, let alone a wedding."

"And that's exactly where Isla will come to the rescue," Lach laughs.

"We haven't even asked her. Maybe she's too busy and she'll say no," I protest.

"You know that's not true." Jack raises an eyebrow at me. "Plus, she's the one that plans all of the castle events. She's had years of practice. A small wedding will be easy."

"What other events do you have besides the masquerade party?"

"We have a themed party every solstice and equinox, a costume party on Halloween, a Christmas ball, and an Easter brunch with an egg hunt," Lach says, listing them off on his fingers.

"Are we going to keep sitting here talking about things we could discuss in a much more comfortable setting, or are we going to grab our shit and move in together?" Cam asks, the tilt of his mouth softening the impatience in his words as he gets out of the car.

"I'll go with Lach. Jack, you go with Charlie." He turns to me and helps me out of the car. "You may as well get everything you have. We'll take the truck back home, so there will be plenty of room."

Home.

Is this how people usually feel when they think of home? Peace. Warmth. Happiness. Safety. Feelings I haven't felt in a really, really long time. I look up at Cam, the tenderness in his eyes washing over me like cool rain after a hot summer day, wiping away the remnants of doubt and anxiety planted inside me all those years ago.

"We're going home," he whispers, reading me like an open book. He smooths his thumb over my cheekbone and presses his lips to mine, lingering in the beauty of this moment. His hand is warm on my back as he leads me around the car, handing me off to Jack as he heads inside to help Lach grab the essentials.

"You can be honest with me, you know," Jack says once we're alone, head down, pushing at the pebbles under our feet with the toe of his boot.

"What do you mean?"

"About yesterday." He still doesn't look up, but I can see the blush creeping up his neck and into his cheeks.

"I was honest," I say simply, not wanting to feed his insecurity by saying the wrong thing.

"But—"

"There are no buts, Jack. There are no stipulations when it comes to my love for you. We can weather any storm as long as we stay committed to open communication."

"Is this a storm then?" He asks, finally meeting my gaze.

"Not even close." I smile, reaching up to push a strand of hair away from his face. "You know those days when it's sunny and cloudy simultaneously? It's sprinkling, but you don't even notice because there's the brightest double rainbow you've ever seen stretched across the sky above you?"

He nods, his lips trembling with emotion.

"That's what this is."

"I love you so fucking much," he whispers, wrapping me in a hug and burying his face in the crook of my neck. "Promise me you'll tell me if it starts looking stormy," he says, his voice muffled.

"I promise."

He kisses my neck and sets me back on the ground. "Let's get your stuff and go home, Sassenach."

There's that feeling again. I can't keep the grin off my face as I pull him down the path, knowing I'll remember this day for the rest of my life.

It only takes us ten minutes to gather all of my belongings. I leave Arty's commission for last, carefully rolling it and sliding it into a protective tube.

"I have a special place for this," Jack says, taking the tube from me.

"Really? I was wondering where I was going to put it. I didn't want to take up the kitchen table."

He sets the tube on the couch and walks toward me, the expression on his face changing to something dark and delicious. "Should we give the cottage a proper goodbye?" I step back, bumping into the wall, my breath wooshing from my lungs as he closes in, towering over me.

"What would that entail?"

"Your moans echoing off the walls as you get yourself off one last time with this." He pulls my vibrator from his back pocket.

"Why do you have that?" I try to snatch it away from him, my cheeks on fire.

"I found it in the nightstand when I was packing everything up. Show me, Charlotte. Please."

"Jack—"

"Don't tell me you don't want to. Your pupils dilated the second I pulled it out of my pocket. Is your clit begging for it, Charlie?" He pulls my wrists over my head, pinning me against the wall. "Is your pussy wet and ready?" I moan as he rolls his hips, the hardness of his cock pressing between my legs, torturing me.

"Are you soaking wet just thinking about me watching while you fuck yourself?" He lowers his lips to my neck, his free hand skating over my stomach, making me shiver. Fingers slipping past my waistband, he brushes over my curls before sliding his finger along my slit, sinking into me with a groan. I bite my lip to silence my sob as I drop my weight onto his hand, rocking against the heel of his palm while his fingers destroy me. He pulls away as my movements become more desperate, licking me off his fingers before carrying me to the bedroom. I rip my shirt off over my head the second he releases me, then drop my pants, impatiently pulling my feet out before scrambling onto the bed. I lean against the mound of pillows along the headboard, and he tosses me the vibe, walking backward several steps until he's pressed against the wall.

"Do you want to see what watching you does to me, Charlotte?"

"God, yes." I open my legs wide, exposing myself to him as he pulls down his pants, his cock springing free. I instinctively rock my hips, imagining how it would feel if he slammed into me. The silicone is cool against my skin as I slide the head of the vibe down my slit and back up, circling it over my clit, my hips mirroring the motions. Jack's hands are fisted by his sides, nostrils flared, jaw ticking as he watches me pulse it against my entrance.

"You want this tight pussy, don't you?" I flex my hips, holding the vibe still as I sink onto it, groaning as the pink bunny ears nudge at my clit. Jack's cock jumps, aching to be touched, sucked, fucked. "Do you want to slam into me over and over until my pussy strangles you as I come on your cock?" I get perverse satisfaction as his body takes control, his hips thrusting into the air. I turn the vibe on, gasping as I push it in further, rocking it over my clit, my pussy clenching around it. Jack's eyes are hooded as he watches me, harsh breaths filling the room, precum dripping down the tip of his cock. "And then you would work your way into my ass, watching as the head of your cock stretches me." I'm panting now, fucking myself good, rocking my hips to meet every thrust.

"You've got it all wrong," he growls, leaning over the bed to grab my ankles, his fingers biting into my skin. "Leave it in," he commands, dragging me to the edge and flipping me over. He turns the vibe off and slides a finger in next to the vibrator, stretching me. When he's satisfied that I can take him, he palms my ass cheeks and lifts my hips. "I want to feel your pussy stretch around me as I fuck you while your vibrator is still inside you." He watches as the head of his cock stretches me, pulsing at my entrance before sinking into me with a rough groan. "Then I'm going to play with your asshole and watch you squirm while your brain tells you that you shouldn't like it, but your body begs for it." He slides his thumb between my legs to get it wet and then circles it against me, pushing on that stubborn ring of muscle until it gives and lets him in. An inhuman sound comes out of me as I arch my back, desperate to take him deeper. "And then I'm going to turn the vibrator on and fuck you hard and fast, just how you like it. He reaches underneath me, pressing the button on the vibe until it's on high, and then anchors his hand at the base of my neck. "Are you ready?"

"Yes, sir."

"Good girl," he breathes, pulling back until only the head of his cock is inside me. "Such a good fucking dirty girl." Everything goes black as he slams into me, his hand holding me down, using me for leverage, pulling me back onto his cock as he drives forward. "This is what you do to me, Charlie. You drive me fucking wild. Now come on my cock and show me how good I make you feel." My body obeys him, spasming around his shaft in absolute fucking ecstasy as he takes me hard and fast, pushing our bodies to the brink, his roar of release joining my desperate cries as we say goodbye to the cottage together.

95

———

My heart is in my throat as we turn into the castle drive. I roll down my window and carefully sit on the door-frame, giving me a clear view of the landscape as we slowly roll by. I can't help the grin that pulls at the corners of my mouth. I look back at Lach's car and laugh when I see the glower on Jack's face. I'm sure he's worried that I'll fall to my death while Cam's driving five miles an hour. I hold on a little tighter, anyway. I close my eyes and tip my head back, and take a deep breath through my nose. This is what home smells like. Earthy. Salty. Slightly sweet from the heather blooming all around us. A lump forms in my throat as the castle comes into view.

"Welcome home, Charlie." Cam's palm is warm on my thigh, his light squeeze letting me know he's feeling the same way. I slide back into my seat as we come to a stop, the realization that this is my life hitting me like a ton of bricks. Jack opens my door, helps me up, and reads me like an open book.

"Overwhelmed?" he chuckles, turning me to face him, fitting his hips between my legs. His hands are gentle as he cups my face, fingers pushing into my hair, massaging my scalp. "If this is too much, too fast, you just have to say the word Charlotte. I let my feelings get ahead of me earlier and shouldn't have sprung this on you like that. I just couldn't imagine sleeping without you in the same bed after this weekend."

"It's not too much," I promise, reaching up and tugging on his beard. He pulls me into a hug, and I feel like I can breathe again.

"Ready, Sassenach?" I nod against his shoulder, and he whisks me up, carrying me in his arms as he strides toward the house.

"Jack. I can walk."

"You're moving into my house, Charlotte. I'm carrying you over the threshold." A delicious thrill slides through me at the possessiveness in his voice. I push my fingers into his hair, scraping my nails over the sensitive skin at the nape of his neck. His groan brings out goosebumps on my arms.

"Goddamnit, Charlotte. Do that again, and I'll pin you against the truck, spread you open and fuck you right here."

"Yes, please."

"Will I find my cum still dripping down your thighs?" he asks, his voice a growl in my ear.

"Will you lick me clean like a good boy?"

He stops dead in his tracks, nostrils flared, eyes wild. "Cam's right. You're a fucking witch. I need to go check on the farm, but all I want to do is fuck that dirty mouth of yours."

"Go take care of the farm," I say, caressing his cheek with the back of my finger. "I'll be your sacrificial lamb when you get home."

"Say that again," he says roughly, carrying me up the stairs and through the door.

"I'll be—"

"No, the other part." He sets me down, holding my gaze.

"Home."

"I'll never get tired of hearing you say that." He cups my cheek, tracing my lower lip with his thumb. "Are you craving anything? I'll grab something to cook for dinner before I come home."

"Surprise me."

. . .

BY THE TIME we wrestle Cam's bed into Jack's room and get it set up, the guys have stripped off their shirts, and I can't stop staring at the beads of sweat dripping down their bodies.

"Anyone want to go for a swim?" Lach asks, his hair sticking up in spikes as he runs his fingers through it.

"Yes!" Cam and I echo each other. We watch as Lach drops his pants, his boxers not doing much to hide what's underneath.

"Last one there has to blow me later!" Lach yells as he opens the door to the terrace and bolts across it and down the stairs. I leave my clothes in a puddle on the ground, running after Lach in my bra and underwear, pretending not to notice Cam moving like a sloth. By the time I get to the water's edge, Lach's powerful stroke has carried him halfway across the lake with no signs of stopping. Cam stops next to me, linking his pinkie with mine. We watch as Lach turns and starts swimming back toward us, his muscles gilded by the evening sun.

"He's so fucking beautiful," Cam murmurs, licking his lips as Lach reaches shallower water and stands up, the water lapping around his chest. I hold my breath as he walks toward us, my core spasming as his hips come into view, his cock jutting up against his stomach, the head peeking out of his waistband.

Fuck.

"Are you two going to keep staring, or are you going to join me?"

"I owe you a blow job," Cam says, his voice husky.

"You were last on purpose," I protest.

"Was not." His gaze hasn't left Lach's cock.

"He—"

"Both of you strip and get on your knees." We obey immediately as he stalks toward us, peeling his boxers off, his cock springing free inches from our faces.

"Since you can't agree, you can take turns."

Cam leans forward, burying his face against Lach and inhaling his scent before sliding his tongue around the head of his cock. Lach's groan sends a bolt of heat rushing through me, desire settling low and heavy. He runs his tongue underneath Lach's shaft, nibbling on his frenulum, sucking the sensitive skin into his mouth.

"Enough. Open." He hooks a finger into Cam's mouth and pulls his lips apart, nudging his cock past them, sinking deep with a growl, holding Cam's head still as he flexes his hips to push deeper. Cam's eyes are streaming as he struggles for control.

"Fuck, you take me so good," Lach rasps, his gaze locking with Cam's, his muscle rippling as he takes everything Cam will give him. "Charlie, be a good girl and suck him off. I want to know what his throat feels like when he's about to come."

Oh, God. Lach widens his stance, and I crawl between his legs, my breath catching at the beauty of Cam's body. He's sitting on his haunches, muscled legs spread wide, his cock sticking up proudly, precum already dripping. I slide my hand over him, using his precum as lube, twisting my palm over his shaft, swirling my thumb over his head. He groans around Lach's cock, his ab muscles flexing as he thrusts against my palm. I anchor my hands on his thighs and drop low, licking him clean before taking him in my mouth and sinking until my lips brush his skin. He makes a desperate sound, flexing into me, gagging as Lach pushes into his throat.

"Breathe through your nose," Lach commands. Cam's gasp of breath is muffled by Lach's cock, the sounds coming from them making desire leak down my thighs. I cup Cam's balls, massaging them, sliding a finger to his perineum. He strains toward me, the head of his cock hitting the back of my throat as he desperately tries to maneuver my finger to his ass. I reach between my legs to coat my finger and then slide it between Cam's ass cheeks. His whimper has me clenching on air. Cam tenses beneath my lips, and I'm suddenly pulled away, Lach's hand strong on my hip as he flattens me against his body, burying his other hand between my legs.

"What's this, Carebear?" He holds his fingers in front of my face, a mix of Jack's cum and my desire coating them. "I can smell him," he breathes, pushing his fingers into my mouth. Fuck. "Lie down," he says roughly, following me down until he's kneeling between my spread legs, his gaze locked on my pussy. "God," he moans. "Bear down, Charlie."

I obey, my heartbeat erratic, bearing down, pushing out what's left of Jack.

"Good girl. You're so fucking beautiful." He watches the cum drip from me, scooping it up with his tongue, his eyes rolling back as the taste explodes over his tongue. He pulls me to my feet, his hand circling my neck, my back against his chest. He pushes his shaft between my legs, fucking my thighs, the head of his cock catching on my clit with every pass.

Cam looks up at us, naked desire in his eyes, his hand working over his cock as he watches Lach drive me mad.

"Go on," Lach says roughly, his breath hot on my ear.

Cam leans forward, feathering his tongue over me, then over Lach as he thrusts forward. Lach pulls back a little, allowing Cam to fit his mouth over my clit. His long pull nearly brings me to my knees. I bury my fingers in his curls, moaning as Lach's next thrust has him nudging at my entrance.

"Please," I rasp, my body strung tighter than a bow.

"Tell me what you want."

"Fuck me, goddamnit," I sob, pressing my ass against him.

He slams into me, filling me until I feel like I may burst, stars flashing in front of my eyes. My body bows between them as we find our rhythm, a mad dash to the top.

"Ouch!" Lach's fingers clamp on my nipple as he pulls out of me, his chest heaving. "What the fuck, Lach?" I hold my hands over my breasts, shielding them from further attacks.

"I don't want you to get there yet. Do you think I'd let the first fuck in our new home happen that fast? I'm going to draw this out all night, Charlie."

"You realize I have two hands that are perfectly adept at meeting my needs, right?" I'm annoyed. And fucking horny. I bolt toward the water, diving in and swimming as fast as possible to the floating platform. I pull myself onto it, flopping onto my back, struggling to catch my breath. Cam explodes out of the loch, water sluicing down his body as he pushes himself up. He's on top of me before I can blink, one knee pushing my legs wide, sinking into me with one hard thrust.

"Fuckkk." His groan burns through me like pure grain alcohol, wildfire roaring through my veins. He cradles my head and rolls us over, giving me control. Lach climbs out of the water and sinks to his knees behind me, cold water dripping down my back as he pushes his cock along my crack.

"Do you know how many times I've fucked myself while thinking about how it will feel to have your ass strangle my cock until I can't breathe?" Lach cups my tits and rolls my nipples between his fingers, making me squirm.

"Stop talking about it and do it," I pant, planting my palms on the wooden planks, arching my back, and opening myself to him.

"I'll need to borrow some of this," he says, sliding his thumbs along Cam's shaft and spreading the moisture over my ass. An ungodly sound escapes from my throat as he pushes his thumbs in and stretches me.

"I need a little more." He notches his cock at my pussy, pushing slowly, the head of his cock sliding along Cam's shaft as he pushes in. He bottoms out in one smooth thrust, their twin groans driving me fucking crazy. I clench around them, rolling my hips, refusing to give them time to rein themselves in. Lach pulls almost all the way out then slams back in, smashing me against Cam's chest as he pushes his tongue into Cam's mouth. I whimper between them, so fucking close I could scream.

"Hold on, baby." Lach pulls out and notches himself at my back entrance, his breathing ragged. I look over my shoulder to let him know I'm ready, but he's looking down, sliding his hands over my cheeks, squeezing them together to hug his cock, every muscle in his body trembling with restraint. Cam turns my head back toward him, tipping my chin up, holding my gaze as Lach grips my hips and works the tip of his cock inside me.

"Does our dirty girl like being filled?" Cam's words are smooth and sultry, arrows of lust straight to my core.

"More," I beg, whimpering as the widest part of Lach's cock breaches the muscle.

"You take us so fucking well," Lach groans, giving me time to adjust before sinking into me with a long shuddering breath. "Fuck, Charlie, you feel too fucking good." Cam's eyelids flutter as Lach bottoms out, his head tipping back in ecstasy.

"I can feel him in you," Cam says, his eyes closed as Lach works his hips back and forth. "Every time he thrusts, I can feel the head of his cock riding up my shaft." He moans as Lach pulses his cock deep inside me, Cam's fingers spasming on my hips, drawing me forward and then pushing me back onto Lach. "Lean forward and tilt your hips," he instructs, maneuvering me so my clit rolls over his pubic bone with every thrust. My body shudders when we get the right angle, instinct taking over. I rock my hips forward, the friction of them sliding out of me almost as good as when I push back, and they slam back in, filling me until I wonder how I ever lived without this.

"Now," Cam mouths, clearly not on board with the edging. I clench around them, picking up my pace, my body shaking in anticipation.

"Charlie—" My name dies on Lach's lips, turning into a growl as I arch my back and slam back onto his cock. I can tell the moment he gives in, his hand sliding up the length of my back to grip my shoulder, his other has a punishing, desperate hold on my hip. We move together like we were made for this, a synchronized wave of desire – a tsunami demolishing everything except the push and pull of their cocks, their whispered curses and broken moans. I whimper as the first spasm starts, and Cam holds me down on his cock as Lach pushes in deep, pulsing his hips against me as I fall apart. They hold their positions until there are only aftershocks left, and then Lach pulls back and slams home one more time, Cam's groan all he needs to push them both over the edge. Cam closes his eyes and bites his lip as the pressure mounts, his whole body bowing as he drags me back and forth over his cock. His entire body shudders, and then his eyes are open, drawing me in, pulling me with him as the three of us descend into the depths of hedonistic bliss.

96

"When you said you booked our flights, I thought you would do it like a normal person," I grumble, studying the jet on the tarmac, wondering how something so small can get us across an entire ocean.

"First, the flights were sold out. Second, do you really think I would give up the chance for us to join the mile-high club?" Lach asks, his lips pulling up into a smirk.

"You think I'm doing *that* on *there*? I'm going to be terrified for my life the entire trip. The last thing I'll be thinking about is sex."

"We'll see about that." The baritone of Jack's voice slides over my skin as he steps up to my side, linking his fingers with mine.

"If we go down, then we go down together," Cam sings softly under his breath, his fingers tapping a staccato on his thigh as he joins us. He pulls several books from the satchel over his shoulder, half-naked couples on all the covers. "I'm nervous too, little witch. I brought these for distraction," he says, turning to me.

I snort. "God, you're the best. Good smut is always the best distraction." I take his hand, and we walk to the plane together, the four of us walking to the plane together.

"There's a bedroom through the door in the back," Lach says, motioning to the back of the plane. "The door to the right is the bathroom. The kitchen is behind me, fully stocked. We can access it before we taxi and then at cruising altitude."

"You'd make a great flight attendant." I laugh.

"I'll be your attendant anytime, Carebear." He wiggles his eyebrows lewdly, making me laugh. I jump as the pilot's voice blares over the speakers. *Five minutes until we taxi to the runway. Please find your seats and fasten your seatbelts.*

"In that case, I would love a drink. Something with alcohol, please." I can feel the anxiety creeping up my throat, coating my tongue.

"You got it. Get comfortable. I'll bring it to you."

Jack finishes stowing our luggage and leads me to the couch, crouching down in front of me to fasten the belt around my hips.

"Breathe, Sassenach." I have no idea how his hands got on my shoulders, but he's gripping me tight, a line of worry between his brows. "Cam, let's see one of those books." He settles beside me, buckling his seatbelt before cracking open the book, his brogue caressing every syllable.

I can't believe I'm going through with this. I should call the whole thing off. Return the money. Find some crappy job instead of going to graduate school. Meet a local guy, get pregnant... Fucking breathe, Lainey. *I can do this. One night. A weekend if it goes well, he said in his last email. He even said we didn't have to have sex if I wasn't comfortable with it, but what guy spends a hundred thousand on someone's virginity if they don't want to have sex with them?*

"Miss?" I jerk my face out of my hands and meet the Uber driver's gaze in the rearview mirror. "We're here."

I look out the window at the brick facade, craning my neck to look up at the top of the building. Five floors. This fucker is loaded. My heart is in my throat as I mentally flip through my possible decisions and their outcomes, but the decision is made for me when the front door swings open, a golden hallway luring me in. I can do this. I will do this. I grab my overnight bag and step out of the car, fixing my skirt and wrapping my cardigan tight around my torso before heading toward the steps.

"Her cardigan?" I echo, trying to focus on the story instead of how we're taxiing across the tarmac toward the runway. "Why would she wear a cardigan when someone just paid her a ton of money for her virginity?"

"What would *you* wear?" Lach asks, swiveling his chair so he's facing Jack and me.

"I would never have the guts to do that in the first place, but if I did, probably a trench coat with lingerie under it."

He hums appreciatively, the sound low and sexy. "Perhaps some role-play is in order when we get back?" He raises an eyebrow, dragging his gaze over my body, pausing to watch my nipples react to his words. I'm thrown against Jack as the plane speeds up, my fingers digging into his legs like talons. He continues reading.

I jog up the steps, not giving myself time to change my mind. I expect someone to be inside the door, but nobody's there. I close the door softly, setting my bag down on the elegant black and white tile. The house looks like the owner is in the process of moving in, boxes stacked along the empty walls.

"Hello?"

"In here."

I follow the voice across the foyer and down a stark hallway, looking through the doorway to the right. There's a man with his back to me at the largest stove I've ever seen, an apron tied around his waist, boxer briefs his only article of clothing. He has grill plates over the flames, carefully turning two steaks to get the perfect grill marks. I clear my throat, but he is either ignoring me or the sizzle from the steaks and the industrial fan over the stove are making too much noise.

"Hello!" I try again, a little too loud this time.

He jumps, but doesn't turn right away, taking time to compose himself. He sets the tongs down before turning to face me. My heart stops.

"Eli? What are you doing here?" His lips twitch, but he doesn't say anything, waiting for my brain to catch up. "YOU bid on me?"

"Why the hell did you do that Lainey? What if some pervert had won and kidnapped you or worse?" His jaw ticks as he tries to keep his temper under control.

"I needed the money, Eli. I'm sure you figured that one out. All of the bidders were vetted. I would have been safe."

"Why didn't you tell me? I could have helped."

"I don't want a handout, Eli."

"But you'll sell your virginity? Do you know how fucking pissed off that made me? I almost came in person just to drag you off that goddamned stage. The thought of some guy you've never met taking your... fuck, Lainey."

"I'm not doing this. I won't debate with one of the richest guys in New York about why I sold my virginity so I can go to graduate school. It's my body, Eli. I get to do what I want with it." I spin on my heel and walk back down the hallway, slinging my bag over my shoulder. I'm pulling open the door when his palm flattens against the wood, holding it closed.

"Don't leave. At least eat dinner first."

I turn, our faces only inches apart, so close I can count the brown flecks in his green irises. *"What do you want from me?"*

"Nothing," he says, lines bracketing his mouth, a tortured look in his eyes.

"Is that the truth, Eli Parker?" My heartbeat ticks up as his gaze dips to my mouth. Eli. My brother's best friend. The guy I've had a crush on for my entire life.

"You want the truth?" He places his other hand on the door, boxing me in. *"The truth is I couldn't stand the thought of someone else being your first. You deserve a man that will give you the world, Lainey girl. One that will get you there before he does every goddamned time. One that will show you what making love should be like so you don't settle for less."*

My entire body ignites, his words sweeping over my skin like wildfire. *"And who will do that for me, Eli?"*

"Me, Lainey. Please." He drops to his knees in front of me. This six-foot-four giant of a man that created his own company at eighteen and sold it for millions at twenty, this man that could have any girl he wants, is on his knees in front of me, asking to be my first.

"What about Michael?" My brother will not be happy about this. I can't even count the number of times he's told me to leave Eli alone.

"Let me worry about Michael." He takes my hands in his, sweeping his thumbs over the delicate skin of my wrists. "Let me give you this, Lainey."

Am I insane for considering his proposal? Haven't I always dreamed of my first time being with him? "Okay," I whisper, swallowing hard.

"Is that a yes?" His hands move to my waist, his fingers sweeping over the small of my back.

"Yes."

He growls, moisture flooding between my legs in response. He pulls me to him, his nose just above my pubic bone, and inhales.

"Do you know how long I've wanted this?" he rasps, his voice muffled against my skirt.

The seatbelt light goes off, and I loosen my grip on Jack's leg. "Better?" he asks, dipping his head to look at me, his hair tickling my cheek. "Better," I nod.

"Don't fucking stop now!" Lach protests. "If I had known there were books like this, I would have started reading novels a long time ago."

"Your turn," Jack says, handing the book off to Cam and pulling me against his side. Cam clears his throat and continues.

I blow out a shaky breath as Eli's fingers bunch in my skirt. I've imagined him taking my virginity too many times to count, but never would I have dreamed it would start with him on his knees begging me for it. He presses a kiss to my stomach and stands, grabbing my hand and pulling me back toward the kitchen.

"Dinner first, then we're not stopping until Monday morning."

Holy fuck. "The whole weekend? That's a little cocky to assume, isn't it?"

"I'll need every minute, Lainey. I've been dreaming of this for years."

"You can stop the act," I say, rolling my eyes. "You want my virginity, I get it. I need the money. Win-win."

"If that's how you feel, we can eat dinner, gossip until we fall asleep and you can leave in the morning. I didn't bid on you to sleep with you, Lainey. I bid on you so some other creep couldn't."

"Dinner, talking, and sleep? And then I get my money?" Why am I being a stubborn bitch about this when I've wanted to sleep with him for

years? Probably because I want him to WANT to sleep with me, not just because he doesn't want someone else taking my virginity. It makes him seem like an asshole, now that I'm thinking about it.

He nods. "I only have one bed at the moment, but I swear to God I won't touch you unless you ask me to."

"Deal." His hand envelops mine as we shake on it, callouses scraping over my skin, making me wonder what it would feel like if he touched me between my legs.

Cam looks up, his cheeks flushed. "Do you want me to skip forward a little?"

"Maybe skim it and tell us the important parts?" I suggest, knowing exactly where this book is about to go and wanting to get there as quickly as possible.

"Good idea." He runs his finger down the middle of the page, scanning it impossibly fast. "He doesn't have a table yet, so they eat in bed. He made steak, baked potatoes, and salad. Best she's ever had. Ah. Here we go."

I'm not sure if it's the fact that we're sitting on a bed, and therefore sex is the only thing on my mind, or if it's the fact that he's hot as hell, but all I want to do is push him down and impale myself.

"Now what?" I ask when the conversation lulls, leaning back against the headboard and patting my full belly.

"Why don't you find something you want to watch while I take a quick shower? My time management today was sub-par. Believe it or not, I wasn't planning on greeting you in an apron and boxers." He tosses me the remote and disappears into the bathroom, not bothering to close the door all the way.

I turn the TV on, flipping through the channels, trying to ignore that Eli Parker is naked in the shower less than twenty feet away from me. Soaping up his body. His hand sliding over his – God, I can't do this. I climb off the bed and tiptoe to the bathroom, nearly stumbling when I hear him moan my name. I peek around the edge of the door, and my knees go weak. I can see his side profile, his head tilted back as steam billows around him, his hand working over his very large, very erect cock. I may be a virgin, but I'm not a prude. The guy is hung. He says my name again, worshipping the syllables, and my gaze flies up to his face. He's looking me dead in the eyes.

"Fuck, Eli!" My hand slams to my chest, my heart trying to beat its way out of its bony prison.

"Do you want to join me, Lainey? Or do you just want to watch?"

I bite my lip, my gaze slipping back down his body, watching as he fucks his hand. His next moan is desperate, his hips picking up speed, his eyes never leaving mine. I clench my thighs together, the throbbing is almost unbearable.

"Last chance, Lainey girl." His voice is rough with desire, his words kicking me into action. I'm not going to deny myself pleasure any longer. I've wanted this forever, and I'm going to take what he's offering me with a fucking smile on my face.

"Wait," I beg, leaving my clothes in a heap on the floor, stepping into the shower still wearing my bra and underwear. Before he can stop me, I drop to my knees and run my tongue along his length, sweeping the drop of precum from the tip of his cock with my tongue, moaning as his taste permeates my senses.

"Lainey, that's not what I meant by having you join me," he says, holding my head still between his hands. I slide my hand over his shaft, holding my tongue out to catch him when his hips jerk involuntarily. "Fuck," he groans, pushing the head of his cock past my lips, watching as the ridge catches on them. He pulls back again, his hands trembling in my hair. "Lainey. Tonight is about you losing your virginity the right way, not me finally getting to live out my fantasies."

I stand, his words stealing the breath from my lungs. "What do you mean by fantasies?"

He cradles my face, the honesty in his eyes pulling at my soul. "I've wanted you for as long as I can remember, Lainey. Not just your body, either."

I push up on my toes and crush my lips to his, our bodies crashing together, rough hands trying to pull me even closer. He takes control immediately, turning and pressing my back to the glass, positioning his cock between my legs before sliding his palm up my torso to cup my breast.

Jack unbuckles me and pulls me into his lap, his cock hard against my back, one hand skimming up my side and cupping my breast.

"Are we doing a live-action version of the book?" I laugh, arching into his touch.

"Great idea, Carebear." Lach pulls me up, pressing me against the wall, adjusting himself so his cock is riding over my clit before capturing my lips with his. He cups my breast in his palm, weighing it in his hand before rolling my nipple between his thumb and forefinger.

He breaks the kiss, breathing hard, "What comes next, Cam?"

"What comes next is moving this to the fucking bedroom where we have room to play." Jack's voice has a dangerous edge as he pulls Lach away from me, scooping me into his arms and motioning for the other two to follow.

97

———————

Cam is already in the bedroom waiting. He tosses the book onto the bed, tackling me the second Jack sets me down. His hands sweep down my back as he crowds me against the wall, cupping my ass and pulling me tight against him.

"Lach, your turn to read," he says a second before crushing his lips to mine. He sweeps his tongue over my lips and I open for him, running my fingers over his stubbled jaw as I angle my head to deepen the kiss. Lach clears his throat and begins reading.

He explores my mouth with his tongue. Tentative at first, then rough and desperate, as if trying to make up for lost years. The glass is cold on my back as he presses me against it, his cock rolling over my clit as he rocks his hips. I lift my leg and hook it over his hip, an open invitation for him to fuck me.

"Not yet, Lainey. I have so many things I want to do before I feel your pussy squeezing around my cock. I've wanted this for so long. I won't be able to stop once we get that far, so I'm going to draw this out as long as possible." He drops to his knees, peeling my underwear off my legs and helping me step out of them. "Let me taste you," he begs, looking up at me with bedroom eyes, his pupils blown wide with desire.

Cam drops to the floor in front of me, his cheeks flushed, dark curls framing the stars in his midnight eyes. He hooks his fingers into my leggings and drags them down slowly, his gaze never leaving my face, desperate to see the desire blooming there.

"What say you, little witch?" he rasps, swallowing hard. "Will you let me bury my tongue between your legs? Allow me to drown in your essence?" He inhales, his eyes fluttering closed. I have never felt more powerful than in this moment. This gorgeous, kind, brilliant man is on his knees for me. *For me.* Fuck.

"Yes," I breathe, needy and desperate for his touch. The throbbing between my legs becomes unbearable as he teases me, licking the crease of my thigh, nibbling at my lips, sliding his thumb in the moisture gathered there.

"Cam," I moan, tilting my hips toward him, my hands flat on the wall. "Please."

"Not yet," he whispers, waiting for Lach to keep reading.

I nearly cry out in frustration as Eli stands up, putting too much distance between his mouth and my clit. He pulls my bra over my head, too impatient to unhook it, dropping it to the floor as he steps back, his dark gaze swallowing me whole. I lift my chin, fighting my insecurities.

"Like what you see?" I slide my hands up to cup my breasts, tweaking the tips.

"Do you know how many times I've wondered what color your nipples are?" he asks. "They're the same color as the lips that haunt my dreams." His thumb tugs at my bottom lip, and I catch it between my teeth, sucking him into my mouth.

"What kind of dreams are you having that involve my lips?"

"Usually they're stretched around my cock while you're giving me the best head I've ever had... which is funny since you're a virgin."

"I'm a virgin, not a prude, Eli." I grab his cock and slide my hand down his shaft in a twisting motion, smirking when his abdomen twitches in response. "I've learned a lot of things over the years," I say, making my words sound like a promise. "Let me show you." I flip us around before he can protest, leaning forward and flicking my tongue over his nipple.

"I already told you this night is about getting you there as many times as possible," he protests.

"I'll get there just from sucking you off, trust me."

His jaw drops, lips moving, but no words come out.

"Let me show you," I say again, dropping to my knees, looking up at him in a way I know will be impossible to refuse.

"You have thirty seconds, Lainey girl."

I try to switch positions with Cam, but he shoves his thigh between my legs, pinning me to the wall. He peels off my shirt, then my bra, cupping my breasts with his hands, flicking his thumb over my nipples. He shuffles back so he can draw my nipple into his mouth, and I take advantage of the moment, spinning him around and pressing him to the wall.

"My turn." I give him a wicked smile as I drop to my knees, eager for him. I unzip his pants and pull them to his knees, doing the same with his boxers. My core clenches as his cock springs free, the drop of precum on the tip beckoning me.

"Lube?" I ask, holding my hand out in Jack's general direction. He pulls it out of his pocket and squirts some into my hand.

"You're keeping the lube in your pocket now?" I ask, biting my lip to hold in a laugh.

"We never know when you'll want us to stuff you full, Sassenach. Would you rather we tell you no, or would you like us to be prepared?"

God, this man. He's fucking perfect. "You're next," I promise, turning back to Cam and spreading the lube over him before gripping him hard, twisting my hand as I slide it down his shaft.

"Fuckkkk," he groans, his fingers digging into my shoulders, his hips stuttering.

"Lach, keep reading."

I revel in my control over him. In the way his hips move forward to meet my hand, in the desperate grip he has on my shoulders. I push his shaft against his stomach, licking from base to tip, feathering my tongue over his frenulum. I let him fall back down, sucking him into my mouth, bringing my hand up to cup his balls, lightly squeezing as I bury him in my throat. I hum my approval as he threads his fingers through my hair, holding on for dear life.

"Lainey, Goddamnit." His eyes are dark as he looks down at me, burning this moment into his memory. I shift, tucking my heel underneath me, rocking back and forth as I fuck him with my mouth.

I'm trembling with desire when I finally lick the drop of precum from the tip of Cam's cock, my eyes rolling back as raw sex explodes over my senses. Lach is next to me a second later, lowering himself to the floor and manhandling me until I'm straddling his face.

"This wasn't in the book," I chastise, my protest cut short as he runs his tongue along my slit.

"Forget the damn book," he mumbles against me, "I need this like I need air to breathe." He punctuates the passion of his words by pulling me tight against his face and sealing his lips around my clit. Stars burst across my vision, white-hot balls of flame setting my world aflame. I hook my hands around Cam's thighs and pull him closer, gripping the base of his shaft and running my tongue around the head of his cock. Jack starts reading, his brogue rolling over me, waves of desire driving me higher as I act out what he's saying.

Cam groans as I lick him, following the ridge before sliding my tongue back and forth over the sensitive skin where the shaft meets the head. I lean forward, taking him all the way in, sealing my lips around him and hollowing my cheeks as I pull back. Jack stops reading, tossing the book aside to unzip his pants and pull himself out. I let Cam's cock pop out of my mouth and crawl over to Jack, gagging myself on his length before pushing him back onto the bed. I climb up his body, holding him in place as I impale myself on his cock, desperate for relief. His fingers press into my hips, tilting me forward and pressing me down so my clit is riding over his pubic bone. His lips move over my neck, but I can't hear his words. I push myself up, letting myself get lost in his whisky eyes.

"What did you say?" I push a strand of hair off his forehead, tracing my finger down to his beard, rolling my hips as I pull at his lower lip with my thumb.

"I said it feels good to be home. He pushes my hips back until his cock slides out of me, my clit stopping it from springing back up to his stomach. "I'd follow you around this godforsaken world just to listen to the sound of your voice, Charlotte. If you tell me you want to live in the pits of hell, I'd be there putting out a 'welcome home' door-mat. You'll always be home to me, Sassenach." He licks his lips, his throat bobbing as he cups my breast, squeezing lightly. "Home." His callouses are rough as he sweeps his palm over my stomach, holding it there. "Home." He slides me back up his cock, my clit dragging along the top of his shaft. He notches himself at my entrance, slamming into me with a broken groan. "Home, mo chridhe." I melt against him, fitting my lips to his, putting everything I'm feeling into that kiss. "I think it's time to let them join us," Jack says, the desire in his eyes taking on a wild edge. I look over my shoulder at Lach as he climbs up behind me, his eyes dark.

"How do you want to do this, Charlie?"

I shiver as Lach sweeps his hands over my ass cheeks, spreading me wide, his hum of approval shooting straight to my core.

"I don't care. Just get in me," I beg, pushing back into his hands. He slides his shaft along where I'm stretched around Jack, coating himself.

"Jack, will you share with me?" Lach asks, the head of his cock nudging at my entrance.

"Let me turn around," I say, my voice sounding desperate to my ears.

Jack lifts me in the air, flipping me around to face Lach. I impale myself again, my entire body clenching in anticipation as Lach shuffles closer. He grips himself in one hand, sliding the head of his cock up the underside of Jack's shaft. A whimper catches in my throat as Lach tips my chin up to meet his gaze, a maelstrom of emotion in its depths.

"You want to watch?" He runs his tongue over my bottom lip before pulling me closer and drawing me into a searing kiss. He pushes my chin down, and I watch as he swirls his thumb around the base of Jack's cock and slides that thumb between his ass cheeks. The groan that rips out of Jack's throat is a sound I could listen to forever. Lach pushes the head of his cock against us, my slick folds stretching for him.

"Cam, come over here." I hold my hand out for him, needing to feel complete. "I don't care where, I just want you to get there with us."

"Fuck that," Jack grumbles, motioning for Cam to straddle him. Cam climbs into place, lubing himself up before fisting his cock and nudging it between my cheeks.

"Is this okay?" he whispers, his breath tickling my neck.

"It's perfect." I push back onto him, my breath hitching as he fills me, riding the edge between pleasure and pain. I pull his hand to my front, guiding his fingers to my clit. Lach drapes my arms around his neck, driving my hips up and down, three cocks filling me with every thrust. My world goes quiet – their hands on my body, their groans, the way their cocks fill me – become the only things that matter. My body clenches around them, holding them tight, strangling them with desire, greedy for completion.

"Now." Jack's voice is harsh. Demanding. Lach cups my breasts, pinching my nipples as I slam down onto them, and I lose control as the beginning of my orgasm catches me in her vice grip. I go limp, clinging to Lach as they fuck me, our bodies moving against each other in uncoordinated ecstasy. I lean back against Cam as we come down from the high, their cocks twitching every time an aftershock ripples through me.

"Welcome to the mile high club," Lach says, pressing a kiss to my cheek, a tender smile pulling at his lips.

Welcome, indeed.

98

My heart is in my throat as familiar landmarks fly by the window. The guys are safely ensconced at a nearby bar, awaiting my instructions. I have ninety minutes to report back before they come to my rescue. Ninety minutes to tell my parents I'm moving an ocean away from them. To tell them three guys came to help me through this transition. And then one week to make them see that they're more than friends – that each one of them complements a part of me that was waiting for them my entire life. That they belong to me, and I to them.

My palms are sweaty as the driver turns into the driveway, my fingers slipping on the handle as I push open the door. I stand on shaky legs. I can do this. I pull out the long tube with Arty's commission plus my one ratty suitcase, looking worse for wear after the last three months.

Before I can start around the side of the house, determined to set my bags down and collect myself before I see them, my mom flings open the front door and runs down the steps, wrapping me in a tight hug.

"Welcome home, Charlie! We missed you so much!"

The word 'home' startles me. Home is a little rocky island surrounded by cerulean seas. Home is a feisty redhead that loves to gossip. Home is a cozy bedroom in a fairytale castle on the shores of a loch. Home is the three men waiting to rescue me.

"Thanks, Mom. I missed you, too."

"I got you an interview at the museum tomorrow! I hope you have something nice to wear."

"What do you mean you 'got me an interview?'"

"You know my friend Jana? Her son – who's single, by the way – is the director. Jana took me over there the other day. I showed him a picture of you; I wish you could have seen his eyes light up! He offered an interview before I could even ask!"

I recoil from her arms, taking a step back. "Mom. No."

"Honey, you need a job. You don't have any sort of career experience to speak of. You have a lot of time to make up for."

"I built Rob's entire business, Mom."

She waves her hand in dismissal. "That's *his* business, Charlotte. Look what you have to show for it."

"Well, hopefully, I'll have half of it by next week."

"Oh, honey, surely you don't plan to do that?"

"Do what? Take what's rightfully mine?" I clench my jaw, stopping myself from saying something I'll regret.

"That poor man is working like a dog to keep that business running."

"That *poor* man? He's working like a dog because I'm not there to do it for him. Don't forget he's the one that cheated on me, Mother. With Bethany, no less."

"Well, that doesn't matter anymore, does it?"

"What do you mean?"

"They broke up a couple of weeks ago," she gloats, liking that she knows something before me.

My chest tightens. "How do you even know that?"

"He comes over every Sunday for dinner."

"Are you fucking serious?"

"Watch your language, young lady. Go sleep off your awful attitude. I'll drive you to the interview in the morning."

"I'm not going to the interview." I stand my ground, my heart in my throat.

"Yes, you are. Don't be rude."

"I'm not being rude. You're the one that scheduled the interview. Doesn't it give you the ick that he wants to interview me based on my looks?"

"The interview is at ten a.m., Charlotte."

"I already have a job, Mother." And there it is. The cat's out of the bag.

She huffs. "Why didn't you just say that to begin with?"

I shoulder my backpack, needing to put some distance between us.

"What job, Charlotte?" she presses, her fingers digging into my elbow to stop me from leaving.

I don't face her, trying to decide if I want to get into his right now.

"Are you lying to me to get out of the interview?" Her voice pitches higher with every word until she's screeching at me.

Fuck it. "It's in Scotland, Mom. I came back to deliver Arty's family tree, get the divorce over with and apply for my visa." I can't help the panicked giggle that escapes my throat at her fish-out-of-water look.

"Doing what?" she says finally. "You have no experience in anything that matters. Who would hire you?"

And there it is. "Jana's pervy son would have hired me for my non-existent skills." She's always been like this. Refusing to acknowledge the fact that I ran two successful businesses and that someone may think those skills are valuable.

"You're making a mistake, Charlotte. Who will be there to save you when you fall? Or will we be paying for your plane ticket to get you back home? Coming to the rescue like we always do?"

"You came to my rescue one time. Once. And it's because the guy you pushed me to marry before I was ready cheated on me with my best friend." I pull out my phone and send the guys my locations with an SOS message.

"Don't you dare blame that on me." She stops talking, crossing her arms over her chest and glaring daggers at me, when my dad comes out and then pulls me in for a hug.

"Daddy, I missed you." I breathe in his cologne, the scent bringing me back to my childhood.

"She got a job in Scotland," my mom says, a bite to her tone.

"What!" He holds me by the shoulders, beaming. "Congratulations, Charlie! What will you be doing?"

"Marketing for an estate on the Isle of Harris. They're in the beginning stages of opening it up to the public."

"That sounds like a dream. I'm so proud of you, sweetie."

I cringe as I hear a car pull up behind me, the guys' voices audible before they even open the door. When I texted them, I thought I would already be in the pool house, safely away from my mother. My stomach drops.

"Mom, Dad—" I don't get a chance to make introductions before the guys are by my side, extending their hands, introducing themselves.

"We're here to help Charlotte move," Jack says in response to their puzzled expressions.

"How do you know Charlotte?" my mom asks, her gaze taking in my flushed cheeks and how they're standing around me protectively.

"Jack is the owner of the estate," I explain quickly before one of them can jump in.

"Your future employer came to help you move?" my dad asks, his eyebrows almost touching his hairline.

"All four of us became *very* good friends over the last three months, Mr. Haines," Cam says, disarming them with his smile. "Charlie even helped me out at my parents' bookstore for a couple of weekends over the summer."

My mom clamps her mouth shut, looking suspiciously between me and the guys. I know what she's thinking, and I choose my peace, their presence giving me courage.

"I'd like to ask if they can stay in the pool house. They'll sleep in the bunk room. We'll be out of your hair as soon as court is over." I hold my breath, dreading the answer.

"You want them to sleep in the pool house with you? That's incredibly inappropriate, Charlotte. Do you know how that will look?" my mom asks, her face a disarming shade of scarlet.

"That she has some great friends that care enough about her to come to help her through her divorce?" Jack asks, his brogue making her flush. "Or did you mean something else?" He raises an eyebrow, waiting for her answer.

"I like you," my dad says, patting Jack on the shoulder. "Of course, they can stay in the pool house, sweetheart. You can all sleep in the same bed for all I care." He winks at me, not realizing the truth behind what he's saying. Heat creeps into my cheeks.

"Michael! Don't give her any ideas! You know how she is."

Lach steps forward, his hands balled at his sides. "How is she, Mrs. Haines? I'm dying to know."

She scowls, refusing to answer his question.

"You're implying she enjoys herself in the bedroom, but wasn't Rob the only person she's been with until this summer?"

"Until this summer?" she echoes, looking at me wide-eyed.

Lach's laugh teeters on maniacal as he turns away from her. "Lead the way, Carebear."

Once we're safely in the pool house, I close the door behind us and sag against it, letting my head drop back against the glass. Why did I come back?

"You never told us she was like that," Lach says, pulling me into a hug, his lips warm against my neck.

"She's a product of her parents. How can I be mad when that's all she knows?"

"That's not an excuse, Charlie."

I shrug. "She's not always that bad. I think she's worried about me. And maybe a little jealous."

"A little?" Jack snorts, shaking his head.

"It's always better when we have a little distance between us. And in a week or two, there will be a lot of distance."

"I'm proud of you, little witch." Cam snakes his arm around my back, hugging me into his side. Jack joins us, wrapping his arms around all three of us.

"Now we just have to tell them we're getting married. No biggie." My laugh sounds more like a sob. "I think I need a nap before we take the family tree to Arty. Anyone want to join me?"

99

———

The tube housing the family tree is clenched tightly in my hands as we wait for Arty to answer the door. I'm not nervous until we pull into his driveway, my heart jumping to my throat when I hear the bolt turning. This is it. I'm handing off the most important commission of my life.

"Arthur MacLeod! How are you old man?" Jack exclaims, stepping forward and pulling Arty into a hug, a warm smile tugging at his lips.

What the hell is happening? "You two know each other?" I ask, looking between them.

"Nice to see you again, Arthur," Lach says, grasping his hand.

"So this is where you disappeared to," Cam says, hugging him tight. "There's not a dig I go on that I don't wish you were there to give your advice."

"Hold up. You all know each other?" My head is spinning. Arty's eyes twinkle, lines creasing his face as he grins at me. "Did you send me there knowing I'd meet them? Did you guys know about this?" I ask, suspicious of how this is starting to feel like a setup.

"They didn't know, Charlie," Arty chuckles. "I had no way of knowing if you'd meet one of them, but I hoped you would." He looks at us, his eyes dancing. "It seems like you found all three. That's my Charlie, always shooting for the moon."

My laugh sounds more like a sob as I fold him into my arms, squeezing him as hard as I dare. "Thank you, Arty. For everything." He waves away my thanks away, taking the tube from me and heading inside.

"I called last night and special ordered the frame. The shop will call you when it's in, all you need to do is take it there, and they'll do all the hard work," I say, following him into the house.

He makes a beeline for the dining room, his steps a little more unsteady than when I left three months ago. He holds the tube out for me to pry off the top and then gently eases the heavy parchment from its home, his touch reverent.

"The moment of truth," he whispers as he carefully unrolls it.

The room is silent except for Lach's breathless *Holy Fuck* as three months of my life unrolls on that shiny mahogany table. My heart lodges in my throat, strangling me as the silence becomes deafening.

"Somebody say something," I beg, pressing my hand over my heart to ease the tension.

"It's the most beautiful thing I've ever seen, Charlie." Arty wipes under his eyes with a gnarled knuckle, leaning closer to the parchment. "You added their stories," he says, tracing the writing under one of the vignettes.

"Now their stories will never be lost again," I smile, wrapping my arm around his shoulders.

"You have no idea how much this means to me, Charlie."

"I feel the same way," I sniff, looking down at his watery eyes with so much affection that my heart could burst.

"What are your plans now?" he asks, rolling the parchment back up and carefully sliding it into the tube.

"She's going home with us, Arty," Jack says, unable to hide his pride in his voice.

"Do I smell a wedding in the future?"

"We'll have a handfast ceremony in October," Lach says, a grin spreading over his face.

"Are you still looking for an officiant?"

"You would marry us?" I ask, blinking back tears.

"I'll need to brush up on my handfasting knots, but I wouldn't miss it for the world." He ushers us toward the door. "I have a date coming for dinner, so I'm going to be rude and ask you to leave. Send me an invitation, and I'll be there."

I wrap my arms around his neck and give him a peck on his cheek. "Not a word to my mother, Arty. She doesn't know yet."

"I would love to be a fly on the wall for that conversation," he laughs. "Good luck, Charlie." He pats my cheek and then releases me, waving goodbye as we drive away.

I feel like a million-pound weight lifts from my shoulders. Now to get through the divorce and tell my parents about the wedding. I blow out a controlled breath. I can do this.

"That was a work of art, Charlie. Truly." Cam's voice is soft, filled with awe.

"Draw me like one of your French girls," Lach whispers, turning to bat his eyelashes at me.

"I hate to interrupt whatever that was, but I need to know where we're going," Jack says from the driver's seat.

"Are you guys up for checking out the local bar? I'm not ready to go back to the house and risk bumping into my mom." They all agree enthusiastically, and I give Jack the directions, snuggling into Cam's side. It's so strange coming back here when I've changed so much, but everything has stayed exactly the same. I'm looking forward to getting through the next week, going home, and starting a new life with these three incredible men.

I balk when we turn into the parking lot of the bar. It's way busier than I was expecting it to be on a weeknight. The chance of running into someone I know is exponentially higher, but instead of apprehension, a reckless thrill races down my spine.

We order our drinks at the bar before heading to the pool tables. I decide not to ruin the fun and instead I let the guys battle it out with the understanding that I'm playing the winner. I sink into a plush chair along the wall, enjoying their banter, shadows enveloping me.

Enjoying the view. They're down to only a few balls and empty pint glasses when I spy a familiar face walking toward us. Painted on jeans. Blood-red lips. Tits pushed up as high as they'll go. Fucking Bethany. I sink deeper into my chair, hiding my face in the shadows.

"Hello, boys," she purrs, winding a strand of dark hair around her finger.

Jack lines up his next shot and motions with his head toward his empty glass. "I'll have another beer, please."

Cam and Lach push the empty glasses toward her, rattling off their drink orders. They turn back toward the pool table, dismissing her, cheering loudly when Jack misses his shot. She looks down at the glasses in her hands, then at their backs, trying to decide what to do. Finally, she sighs and spins on her heel, taking the glasses to the bar.

I stifle a giggle with my hand, waiting to see how this will play out.

She comes back loaded with their drinks and sets them on a table, sidling up to Jack. He glances at her, his brow furrowing before understanding dawns on his face. Pulling his wallet from his back pocket, he shoves a couple of bills into her hand and murmurs his thanks. Her face turns red, and she backs up a couple of steps until she's standing right in front of me, rethinking her strategy. My heart slams against my chest when Jack roars in victory, the last ball sinking into the pocket with a dull thud.

"It's you and me, baby," he croons, looking at me, the warmth in his whisky eyes doing funny things to my stomach. "If I win, I get to tie you up and lick you within an inch of your life." Cam and Lach protest, not liking being left out of the fun. "And then these two knuckleheads can see if they can make you come again. Deal?" He walks toward me, hand outstretched, not even seeing Bethany.

"Deal." Bethany reaches to take Jack's hand, but he jerks it back, struggling to mask the distaste sliding over his features.

"We don't need any more drinks right now."

"I'm not a waitress," she huffs, hands on her hips.

"Did you think I was talking to you?" he asks, incredulity dripping from his words.

"Well, who else would you have been talking to?"

"Hey, Bethany." My voice comes out smooth as silk, the exact opposite of how I feel on the inside. She spins toward me, staggering back several steps before regaining her composure.

"Charlie." Complex emotions shift across her face.

I stand, linking my arms around Jack's neck. "I'll take you up on that offer. What do I get if I win?"

"Whatever you fucking want," he growls, kissing my neck.

Bethany scowls and turns toward Cam and Lach, plastering on a fake smile. "Do you guys want to find somewhere a little quieter?"

"Bethany, are you still hoping to get some of what Jack offered?" Lach asks, his smile not reaching his eyes.

"I'd like that," she says, her voice cracking with lust.

"Good. You can watch us get Charlie off more times than you can count. Maybe it'll make up for her having to see Robbie stick his tiny dick in you."

Heat crawls up her cheeks. "He does not have a tiny dick," she lies through her teeth, her voice pure venom.

I snort. "Bethany, all three of them are going home with me. Go find someone else to stab in the back."

"I didn't—"

"Shoo." Cam waves her away like the nuisance she is.

Lach and Cam crowd around me, pushing me and Jack into the pool table, hard bodies plastered to mine. Lach tips my chin toward him, caressing my cheek. "I can't wait to fucking destroy you tonight."

Bethany makes a loud sound of disgust, stamping her foot. "Charlie, you're—"

I stick my arm out from between their bodies, flipping her the bird until she stalks away.

"Can I be you when I grow up?" Cam asks, chuckling as he presses his lips to mine. "That was amazing to watch, little witch."

"I couldn't have done it without the three of you backing me up. Hopefully that's the end of it. Now what's this about a wager?" Jack repeats his terms, his cock hardening with every word out of his mouth. "And if I win, I get to do whatever I want?"

"You won't win."

I don't win.

At the end of my turn, we're down to one ball left on the table. Jack makes quick work of it, picking me up and striding out of the bar before I can process what happened.

"In a hurry for something?" I ask, clinging to his neck.

"I have a black rope dying to bite into your ankles, mo chridhe. I'm going to spread you open and make you come so hard you forget how to breathe." He sets me on my feet by the car, bending over me to fit his lips against mine.

"See! I told you!" I break away from Jack to see Bethany dragging Rob toward us, her fingers digging into his arm.

"Get your hands off my wife!" Rob looks... awful.

Cam and Lach move to block him, their hands in their pockets.

"What are you," Rob asks, "her fucking bodyguards?"

I squeeze Jack's arm as I step out from behind him, squaring my shoulders.

"What do you want, Rob?"

"Stop messing around and come home."

"Home?" I swallow a laugh, wondering how he could be so goddamn clueless.

"She's coming home with us," Jack says, standing at his full height, towering over us, a Celtic god ready to fuck someone up.

"This isn't a fucking joke," Rob says, snapping his fingers at me like a dog. "Come on, Charlie, let's go."

Lach steps forward, his finger pressing to Rob's chest. "The only joke here is you, little man. You lost the best thing that ever happened to you."

"I'm not talking to you, asshole. Let me talk to my wife." He tries to skirt around Lach, but Cam blocks him, rage simmering in his eyes. "Are you going to let them treat me like this?" Rob asks me, his eyes bulging.

The guys hover around me protectively as a crowd starts forming around us.

Rob looks between us, realization dawning. "Bethany was telling the truth, wasn't she? You're fucking all three of them. You goddamn slut. How could you do this to me?" He stops pacing directly in front of Cam, hands flexing. "I'm going to tell everyone, Charlie. You and your stretched-out cunt will never be able to step foot in this town again."

Cam moves so fast that I don't see the punch, only Rob crumpling to the ground and Cam shaking out the pain in his hand. "Get in the car. We're getting as far away from this godforsaken place as possible."

100

———

My heart thunders in my chest as we speed past my hometown, streetlights illuminating random snippets of a place I'd be happy never to see again.

"How did you stand being around those people for your entire life, Charlie?" Empathy laces Cam's words, his brows drawn together, face stark in the moonlight streaming through the windshield.

"I never knew it could be different, I say softly, taking a deep breath, forcing my body to release the adrenaline. "Where are we going?"

"Lach is figuring that out. We can take the next few days to relax, then return for the trial and to pack up your stuff. That way, we're spending the least amount of time there as possible."

"That sounds perfect," I say, trying to ignore Rob's words ringing through my head.

"They never deserved you." Jack's voice is rough, his hand snaking through the seats to squeeze my arm.

"I know," I half laugh, half sob. "I wish I had realized earlier. I wasted so much of my life thinking I was the problem. That I was the one lacking something. That I deserved everything meted out to me. Karma and all that."

"Yeah, well, look where karma brought you, Carebear. I promise you'll never be mistreated again."

His words are a balm to my soul. "Thank you, guys. For everything. I don't know what I would have done if—"

"There is no if." Cam looks over at me, his eyes black in the dim light of the car. "We're here, and we're not leaving."

"We have a few options," Lach says, smoothly turning the conversation away from what could have been to the present. "We're within driving distance of New York City, Boston, and most major cities in the northeast. There are also some rentals in more remote areas."

"Remote sounds nice." Me and the guys. Nature. Nothing else. Just what I need after the disaster of the last twelve hours.

"There's a treehouse, an earth ship..." he trails off as he scrolls through the app, his brow creased in concentration. "There's a cute little cabin in the Finger Lakes. It's not anything special, but it's private and cozy. Perfect to unwind." He turns the phone, showing me and Jack. I can't deny that it looks idyllic. A tiny log cabin nestled among towering pines, the scene mirrored in a glass lake.

"Looks pretty damn perfect to me," I say, knowing that no matter where we end up, spending two uninterrupted days with my men will be unforgettable.

"It has a boat!" Lach blurts, excitement making his voice rise.

"Sold," I say quickly, scenes of my time with Lach on his yacht flooding my mind.

A couple of hours later, we're pulling into the dirt driveway of the cabin, the sounds of the nighttime forest deafening when Cam cuts the engine.

"I don't think I'll ever get over how many trees there are here," Jack marvels, unfolding himself from the car and gazing at the shadowed pine trees overhead. "When we get back home, I want to plant forests. Get the estate back to what it would have looked like when my ancestors chose to make it their home."

Lach punches a code into the door, the heavy wooden plank swinging open noiselessly. He fumbles for a light switch, the room flooding with light.

"This is beautiful," I gasp, looking at the ceiling soaring above us and the thick wooden beams crisscrossing the space.

"Wait until the morning. If it's anything like the pictures, the outside will be a million times better than in." Lach smiles, pressing a kiss to my forehead. "Why don't you get settled and decompress? I'm going to go find a store and grab some essentials."

"I'll go with," Cam says, pressing his lips to mine before following Lach outside. Jack waits until the crunch of gravel under fades away and then draws me into his arms, tucking my head beneath his chin.

"I wish you had told me, Charlotte."

I squeeze my arms around his neck, my lips moving against his throat. "I'm being sincere when I say I don't think about any of it when I'm with the three of you. You force me to be present, which is the greatest gift you could give me."

He wraps my hair around his fingers and tugs, pulling my head back so he can look me in the eyes. "You're the best thing that's ever happened to me, Sassenach. I won't ever let you forget that."

His lips coasting over mine ignite an insatiable need that burns hot and fast. He pulls my bottom lip into his mouth, greedy for my moan as I open for him, our tongues warring for dominance. Rough callouses scrape over my back as he pushes his hands under my shirt, his thumbs sliding over the sides of my breasts, making me squirm.

"I've been thinking about doing this all day," he groans, pulling me closer, fitting his body against mine like a missing puzzle piece. I'll never understand how each of them feels so right. Being in Jack's arms makes me feel safe; the Robs and Bethanys of the world can't touch me when he's around. I surrender to him, exposing my neck to his lips, clutching his shoulders for dear life. He scoops me into his arms and walks into the bedroom, tossing me on the bed and stripping off my pants with one smooth motion.

"I'll be right back," he murmurs, pressing a kiss to the inside of my thighs before turning and striding out of the bedroom. Thirty seconds later, he's back with a length of rope in his hands.

My laugh is choked with desire. "Where did you find that?"

"I was incredibly hopeful when I packed. I've been thinking of doing this for weeks, and I didn't want to miss out if the chance presented itself." His eyes darken, his gaze tracing my body, desire darkening the color in his cheeks. He unbuttons his shirt slowly, sliding it over his shoulders before working at his belt.

I watch him. His thick, nimble fingers. His whisky eyes. The way he keeps looking at me like he's making sure I'm real. I would do anything for this man.

"Let me be in control, Charlotte."

Fuck.

"Just until they get back, then you can do whatever you want to me," he amends, hopeful.

"Whatever I want?" I bite my lip, thinking of the possibilities. I nod my agreement, but he stares me down, waiting for me to say it. "Yes, sir," I whisper, heat pooling between my legs.

"Pick a safe word." Judging by his voice, I would think this wasn't affecting him, save for the way his throat bobs, the slight tremor in his fingers, the way his pants tent in front of him.

"Kelly Clarkson," I say, sticking with the same word I told Jack when he first asked me.

He goes still, trying to figure out if he heard me correctly before doubling over in laughter. "God, I fucking love you," he wheezes. "Kelly Clarkson it is." He climbs up on the bed, the smile slowly melting from his lips as he hooks his fingers into the sides of my underwear and peels them down my legs, then unhooks my bra, sliding it off my arms carefully.

"Can I tie you up?" he asks, his gaze locked on my lips, his pupils blown wide.

"Are you supposed to ask me questions when you're in control?" I ask, biting my lip to hold in a smile.

"I still need your consent, mo chridhe. Once I have that, all bets are off."

"Yes, I give you consent to tie me up, lick me, fuck me, use me."

He launches himself on the bed, tackling me, framing my face between huge hands, plundering my mouth, taking everything I have to give. He reaches toward the end of the bed and grabs the rope, looping it around my wrists before securing it to the headboard. More rope loops around each ankle, and he spreads my legs wide, securely tying me to the end posts. The pulse between my thighs is almost unbearable as I wait for him to make a move.

"Close your eyes," he commands, kneeling beside my head to tie his t-shirt around my eyes.

Oh, God.

My senses heighten the second the blindfold is on. The sound of his pants hitting the floor, his feet on the carpet as he walks to the end of the bed, the slight inhale as he looks at me spread wide for him.

"Do I have permission to send a picture to Cam and Lach?" he asks, his voice husky.

"Yes," I say immediately, ready to agree to anything that will get them back here faster. Wanting nothing more than to be surrounded by them. Filled by them.

"That's the last thing I'm asking permission for," he warns, his hands trailing over my calves, thumbs digging into the arches of my feet. Then, finally, the brush of his beard on the inside of my knee, callouses sweeping up my thighs, lips so close to giving me relief that I sob as I strain against the bindings.

"Tell me what you want." His brogue skitters over my skin like lightning, making it hard to breathe.

"Your tongue," I pant.

His thumbs frame my pussy, sliding up the crease of my thighs, making me squirm.

"Where?" he presses, the pads of his thumbs massaging me on either side of my clit.

"Jack, please," I sob, struggling against the ropes, desperate for his touch, my brain short-circuiting. Rough hands cup my breasts, pinching my nipples hard, his low hum of approval lodging deep in my core. He slides his nose along mine, his hair tickling my face. "Where?" he asks again, his lips brushing mine.

"Between my legs." I cry out as he draws a nipple into his mouth, pain warring with pleasure.

"There are lots of things between your legs, Sassenach." He slides his middle finger down my slit and between my cheeks, circling my asshole. I moan, every nerve ending hypersensitive, my body needy for anything he'll give me.

"Here?" His breath skates over my stomach as his finger works over me, pressing against me until my body yields to him. Stars bloom behind my eyelids, breath trapped in my lungs. "Or maybe here?" He sinks his thumb into my pussy, a desperate, guttural moan leaving my lips as my brain and body fight for control. He peppers my stomach with kisses as he works his magic, driving me wild but not letting me tumble over the edge. "Or here?" His lips vibrate against me as he fastens them over my clit, sucking me into his mouth like he's been starved for years. He pulls back just as quickly, tears springing to my eyes at the loss of his touch. "Where, Charlotte?" he asks again, his voice coming from across the room.

"Everywhere, Jack. Please."

"Good girl," he praises, the bed dipping beside my head. I'm going to untie your hands but keep them above your head. Understand?"

"Yes, sir." Once both wrists are free, he moves between my legs, the heat of his hands burning me alive. He grabs my hips and pulls me to the end of the bed, my knees spreading impossibly wide.

"Are you comfortable?"

"Just fuck me, Jack. Please." I feel vulnerable like this, but when I listen to the hitch in his breath, the tremor in his voice, it makes me feel like the most powerful goddamn woman on earth. I hear the lube, and then silicone is sliding down my slit, pressing into me, filling me. I lift my hips off the bed to take it in further, and he pushes in deep, rocking the rabbit ears against my clit.

Fuck. I'm so close. He coats my ass with lube and pushes his cock into me with a groan, not stopping until his hips are nestled between my thighs where they belong.

"Ready?" he asks, his voice thick with desire. He turns the vibrator on, alternating thrusts.

"Keep it in," I beg, my hands fisting in the sheets as I stretch to accommodate him and the vibe. One more thrust, and I'm barely holding on, ready to hurl myself over the edge. The bang of the front door hitting the wall startles both of us. Lach and Cam bolt into the room, lunging to pull us apart. I pull up my blindfold, curious to see how this plays out.

"Somebody has been a naughty boy," Lach purrs, wrestling Jack until his hands are trapped, tying them together with a rope.

"Charlie, you get to decide what happens to naughty boys," Cam says, untying me.

Fuck. Yes.

101

"What do naughty boys deserve, hm, Charlotte?" The timbre of Jack's voice slides down my spine like liquid fire, somehow still in control of my body despite being tied up. His teeth sink into his lower lip, and I barely hold myself back from dropping to the floor in front of him right then. The guys have forced him against the door, pulling the rope over the top and tying it to the doorknob, trapping him with his arms over his head, making it hard to look away from his bulging biceps. His chiseled abs. His goddamned perfect cock.

"*Dirty* boys get special treatment." I drag my fingertips down his torso, digging my nails into his abdomen, his muscles rippling in response. "Lach, grab something to clean him off with, please." I'm not wasting the opportunity to give him head while he's tied up. I turn to Cam and help him take off his clothes, then push him down on the bed, impaling myself.

"Fuck, Charlie." His back arches off the bed, his fingers digging into my hips as I squeeze around his shaft. He throws his head back, the long lines of his neck exposed, his skin marble in the dim light. I lean down and swirl my tongue over the hollow of his throat, moaning when he sinks his hand into my hair, pulling my mouth to his. Warm lips devour me, his tongue pushing into my mouth, then retreating, encouraging me to follow. God, I could kiss this man forever.

"Charlie."

I look over my shoulder to see Lach holding a bar of soap, a towel, and a bowl of water. I can't help the grin that stretches my cheeks. Throwing my leg over Cam, I turn around, holding his cock steady as I sink down onto him, fully seating myself so I can watch the show.

"I want you to wash him so I can give him a blow job." My voice is husky, my heart in my throat. Lach's eyes widen, looking down at the soap in his hand before meeting Jack's gaze, the color in his cheeks deepening. Jack's nostrils flare, his jaw clenching. I hold my breath, waiting for him to refuse, but he doesn't. It's almost like he's been stretched thin waiting for this moment, and now that it's finally here, he can breathe again.

"Is this okay?" Lach's voice is so low I can barely hear him. Jack gives him one tight nod, looking up at the ceiling, his lips moving silently. Lach swallows hard, setting the bowl down, getting his hands wet before rubbing the bar of soap between them. He adds more water, creating a decent lather before facing Jack. Behind me, Cam pushes to his elbows, dragging us both backward until he's propped against the headboard, pulling my body back against him, careful to stay inside me.

"Clever girl," he whispers into my ear, sliding his hands up my body to cup my breasts. "I wasn't sure how they would ever get to this point when they're both too scared to make a move." Time seems to move in slow motion as Lach extends one soapy finger, running it from tip to base along the underside of Jack's cock. Jack's head falls back against the door, swallowing hard, his shaft jumping as Lach takes hold. Heat rushes through me as Lach's grip tightens, pushing his hand forward, his gaze glued to Jack's face, ready to stop the second Jack tells him to stop. He doesn't.

"Fuck." Jack's voice is hoarse, his gaze dropping to watch Lach's hand work his shaft.

I rock my hips against Cam, my entire body throbbing with need.

He reaches around, slowly rolling my clit under his fingers, bringing me to the edge before backing off. I lean forward, my hands gripping his calves for support, and sit back on his cock, bouncing my ass up and down, fucking him fast and hard. I look back up, watching the head of Jack's cock disappear inside Lach's hand and then push back out, precum leaking from the tip. Jack meets my gaze, raising an eyebrow like he's daring me to do something.

"Lach?" I don't need to say the words, he already knows exactly what I'm asking. He rinses Jack off and then helps me off the bed, watching Cam's cock slide out of me.

"I thought this would become a little more normal the more we did it, but fuck if this isn't all-consuming," Lach rasps, his hand tightening on my hip. "I wish I had four cocks so I could fuck all three of you at the same time."

"What's the fourth one for?" Cam asks, a smile pulling at his lips.

"So he can fuck himself while he's fucking us," I answer, barely holding in a giggle.

Cam doubles over in laughter, taking his glasses off to wipe tears from under his eyes.

"I'm right, aren't I?" I ask, gazing up at Lach, tracing the freckles on his cheek with my fingertip.

"You know me so well," he chuckles, pressing a kiss to my temple. "Go get your man." He smacks me on the ass, propelling me toward Jack.

My steps falter as I take in Jack's endless expanse of smooth skin. He's so fucking beautiful.

"Come here," he says roughly.

I don't need to be told twice. I slide my arms around his torso, pushing up on my toes to press a kiss to his chin. His beard tickles my nose as I press my lips to his jaw, moving down to his throat, nibbling at his collarbone, a rough groan urging me on. My lips coast over his chest, and I flick my tongue over his nipple before licking a line from his sternum down the midline of his abs. I drop to my knees, his cock sliding over my jaw as I kiss and bite down his happy trail, driving him mad.

"Charlie, please," he begs, his hair falling into his face as he looks down at me, golden eyes snatching the breath from my lungs.

"Let me worship you," I plead, sweeping my hands up his thighs, tracing the outline of his muscles with my tongue, savoring how his body reacts to my touch. When I reach the top of his thighs, I cradle his balls in my hand, bringing them to my mouth, sucking on him until precum is dripping from the tip. I wait for it to slide all the way down and catch it with my tongue, licking him like an ice cream cone, sliding my tongue along his slit to catch it all. His taste explodes over my senses, obliterating the last remaining thread of restraint I was holding on to. My fingertips dig into his hips as I take him in, pushing forward until he touches my throat. I breathe through my nose, sliding my tongue forward to take him even deeper. He's frozen in place, his muscles trembling from holding back. I hum my disapproval, looking up at him with narrowed eyes as I swallow around him.

"Fuck!" he roars, pulling at the ropes until they stretch enough to slide over the edge of the door, giving him enough slack to slip them from his wrists. His hands are buried in my hair before I can register what happened, his fingers gentle as he holds my head still and fucks my face. His whole body tenses, and he pulls back, stepping away from me.

"You're way too fucking good at that, Sassenach. You bruise my ego every time."

"I can show you how, if you'd like?" I arch an eyebrow at him, biting my lip.

"Maybe another time. Right now, I only want to feel you squirming as I eat you out."

"Do you know what else naughty boys get?" I ask as he backs me toward the bed, my heart rising in my throat, wondering how quickly he'll shut me down.

"What's that, mo chridhe?"

"A good ass fucking. With a dildo," I amend, making sure he knows I'm not pushing him toward something he may not be ready for.

"Mmmm," he groans, pushing me down on the bed, pulling my ankles up to my shoulders, and slamming into me. "You like sucking my cock, don't you?" he asks, watching as he pumps his cock in and out of me, sliding his thumb in the moisture gathered there and bringing it up to my clit.

I arch into his touch, every nerve ending vibrating with need. "Will you let me fuck you?" I ask, not letting him ignore me. He stops thrusting, looking down at me with dark eyes.

"I would let you do anything to me, Sassenach."

"I want you to want it, though," I protest, thinking he's saying yes because that's what I want.

"The thought of you fucking me scares the crap out of me and turns me *all the way* on. I want it. As long as your hands are on me, I want anything you're offering. But first—" He drops to his knees and sucks my clit into his mouth, alternating pressure as he pushes a finger into me. Fuck. I buck against his face, seconds from coming. He releases me just as suddenly and pulls me to my feet. "Go get it. I'll be here ready for you to rock my fucking world."

Oh, God. Is this really happening? I run out to the front room and dig through my bag, holding the dildo up in triumph when I finally find it. I quickly wash it in the kitchen sink and then head back to the bedroom, pausing in the doorway to marvel at these men I call mine. I don't think I'll ever get used to this. Jack's gaze is on me, apprehension and lust warring for dominance in his eyes. I glance over at Lach and Cam, but they're in their own world, making out like they haven't seen each other in months.

"We don't—" I start to say, but Jack cuts me off.

"I already told you I want to. Stop doubting me." His words are softened by the gentle sweep of his fingers over my cheek as he pushes a lock of hair behind my ear. "Let me?" he asks, taking the dildo from me, palming the part that goes inside me to warm it up. Rough callouses scrape my hip as he nudges me toward the bed, his eyes dark. "Get on your knees."

102

My heart is thudding in my ears as I crawl onto the bed, every beat flooding my body with intense desire. I arch my back, sticking my ass out so Jack can insert the dildo. Before I can react, there's the light scratch of his beard, and then his tongue is circling my asshole, making every muscle in my body clench.

"Jack—" I protest, my words cut off when I bite the fleshy part at the base of my thumb to keep from moaning.

"Do you want me to stop?" He raises one dark eyebrow. My cheeks heat. "You don't like it?" I bury my face in my hands, embarrassment taking over. "Do you like it, Charlotte?" he asks again, his lips against my ear.

I nod, mortification flooding my system.

"Sexual acts between consenting adults shouldn't be embarrassing, mo chridhe," he says softly, pulling my hair back from my face.

"I just feel like it's wrong."

"How can it be wrong when it feels so right?" His chuckle slides down my spine, lodging between my legs, making it hard to breathe. "Empty your mind and try to relax. Focus on what you're feeling, not on what you're thinking. We'll give it one more go. If you want me to stop, just tell me."

"Okay," I whisper, taking in several deep, calming breaths. His hands slide down to my waist, callouses scraping over my skin in the most delicious way. His lips are soft on the nape of my neck, his teeth hard as he nips the slope of my shoulder, his tongue soft and wet as he licks his way down my spine. Rough hands press me flat to the bed, pushing my knees wide, cold air sweeping between my legs. I blow out a long breath, forcing myself to stop thinking about what he might be seeing and focusing on the way his hands grip my ass, his thumbs so close to my pussy, it makes me want to scream. He lowers himself to his knees, kissing my inner thighs before sliding his tongue back and forth over my clit. I tilt my hips, giving him easier access. He rewards me by sucking me into his mouth, pulsing his tongue, taking me right to the edge.

"God, Charlie," he moans, his lips vibrating against my clit. The warm drag of his tongue through my folds has me trembling, my fingers twisting into the sheets. He thrusts inside, pulling out to tease my perineum, then diving back in. When I'm squirming against him, he pushes a finger into me, then two, massaging my g-spot as his tongue ventures higher. The only thing on my mind when he finally pushes his tongue against that ring of muscle is coming. The first swipe of his tongue has my core clenching, the second has me tumbling over the edge of conscious thought and into absolute mayhem. I push back toward him, and he goes harder, lapping, fucking, driving me hard, not letting up until the aftershocks are over.

"I may have misinterpreted the way your body responded, but I think you liked it," Jack says, a smirk on his face as he rolls me over, my limbs as boneless as a jellyfish. He grabs the dildo from the bed, holding it up. "Ready?"

"Always." I open my knees, my eyes tracing the contours of his face as he slides the silicone between my legs, circling my pussy before pushing it in. I gasp, my back arching as it presses in places that are still too sensitive.

"Too soon?"

"No, just give me a second." I turn my head to look up at the head of the bed, this angle giving me a very intimate view of Cam and Lach. Cam is on top, his hands framing Lach's face, their lips locked together. Lach has a firm grip on Cam's ass, pulling him down tight. I want to paint them – the fluid lines of their bodies, layering light and shadows until I've captured their quiet desperation. Jack massages my thighs, sliding his thumbs closer and closer to my pussy with every pass until I'm straining for his touch.

"Ready?" he asks, holding his hand out to help me off the bed.

"Are you?" I counter, my stomach fluttering as I step away from the bed.

He chuckles. "I'm ready for everything you want to give me, mo chridhe."

He's not lying. He's hard as steel in my hand, twitching as I run my thumb over his head. I push him back on the bed and he bends his legs, planting his feet flat. I climb up and nestle my hips between his thick thighs, loving how they squeeze around me.

"Should we see who can last longer?" Lach asks, his gaze ping-ponging between all of us.

"What does the winner get?" Jack asks, folding his arms behind his head, his biceps giving me butterflies in my stomach.

"I'll cook dinner for whoever wins," I offer, realizing how lame that sounds once the words are already out of my mouth.

"*You?* Cook dinner?" Lach asks, his eyebrows raised.

"I haven't seen you cook anything more than a piece of toast the entire time I've known you," Jack says, a smile pulling at his lips.

"Same," Cam agrees. "Very intriguing." The three of them exchange glances, a silent transfer of information I have no hope of figuring out.

"It's a deal then," I say, trying not to be too offended that they think I'm incapable of following a recipe. "What if I win?"

"You have your pick of rooms to turn into your art studio," Jack says, not even having to think about it.

"Seriously?"

"Do your worst, Sassenach."

Cam untangles himself from Lach, motioning for him to lie next to Jack. Cam squirts lube on his cock before handing it over to me. I'm already throbbing–there's no fucking chance I'll be able to last much longer. I squeeze some lube onto my finger, giving my body a reprieve for the time being.

My breath catches as I get a front-row seat to Cam sinking into Lach with one sure stroke. The ripple of their muscles as they adjust to the sensations, their moans as he begins to move. I'm so fucked. I squeeze my hand around the base of Jack's cock, sliding my lubed-up finger between his cheeks to tease him. His abs flex, his whole body tensing, then he takes a deep breath, his gaze holding mine as he forces his body to relax. My finger slips in to the first knuckle and I put pressure on the muscle, stretching him before sliding in further and massaging his prostate.

"Jesus," he groans, thrusting into my hand, desperate. I pour lube into my hand, spreading it on the dildo and over his cock with gentle strokes. I nudge the dildo between his cheeks, bearing down with my hips with light pressure until he's opening for me, ready for more.

"You're doing so well," I say, my voice husky. I watch as the head of the dildo disappears inside of him, giving him time to adjust by stroking him from base to tip. When he's thrusting into my hand again, I put steady pressure against him, the dildo sinking all the way in.

"Fuck, Charlie," he pants, his chest heaving, eyes barely open.

"Too much?"

"Never enough." He reaches down and turns on the vibe, then covers my hand with his, both of us jerking him off, allowing me to concentrate on fucking him the way he deserves. Cam's hips slap against Lach's thighs with every thrust, the sound like the crack of a whip urging me on. The vibe's insistent attack on my clit combined with the push and pull against my g-spot makes my extremities feel fuzzy, and my vision blurs around the edges. Fuck. I lean forward, planting my free hand on the bed, leaving space for our hands between us.

"I—"

"I know." He cups my face, his gaze locking with mine, and my world explodes. Before I realize what's happening, Jack pulls away, discarding the toy as he hooks his leg under mine, fliping us over, and buries his cock deep. One thrust and he's coming with me, his hands tight on my hips, pulling me tight to him. Our lips crash together before the aftershocks wear off, wild desperation turning into tenderness.

"Come here," I murmur to Lach once I've come back to earth, laughing when he scrambles out from under Cam. Jack disentangles himself, and Lach takes his place, spreading my legs wide, his nostrils flaring. He runs his finger through me, gathering Jack's cum and pushing it back inside before dragging his cock down my slit and sliding home with a relieved groan.

I can't manage to tear my gaze away from Lach's face as Cam moves into position behind him. I clench around Lach, a visceral response to his eyes rolling back as Cam fills him. Lach's broken groan is wildfire in my veins, igniting everything in its path. I whimper, my body making the climb whether I'm ready or not.

"Hold the fuck up," Jack grumbles, launching himself against the headboard and pulling me on top of him, my back pressed to his chest. He slides into my pussy before Lach can shuffle over, getting his cock slick before positioning himself between my cheeks. Lach takes his place between my thighs, fisting his shaft, sliding the head of his cock through my folds before they both push into me simultaneously.

Holy fucking God.

Cam reaches around Lach, sliding his thumb over my clit as he slowly sinks into Lach's ass. Jack grabs my knees, opening them wide and using them as leverage to bounce me up and down on both of their dicks. I have no hope with how their muscles flex around me – in me, their hands all over me, all over each other, two cock filling me so full the line blurs between pleasure and pain. I want it all. With one last violent thrust, we shatter into a million pieces, floating in the ether until consciousness slowly rears her sleepy head.

"I swear I heard bagpipes playing when I was coming," Lach groans, rolling off of me.

"You're full of shit," Cam says, laughing.

"More like full of cum," Lach yawns, winking at me. "Who won?"

"Charlotte came first," Jack says, ratting me out. "I was second. So I think that means you and Cam tied for first."

"Can't wait for that dinner," Cam murmurs, holding his hand out to me and helping me off the bed. "Family shower, and then we're all going to get the best sleep of our lives."

Family. I like the sound of that.

103

———————

I wake up to the smell of bacon tickling my nose, dust motes dancing in the sunlight streaming through the windows. My cheek is warm pillowed against Cam's dark curls, Lach's arm draped over us both. I can hear Jack pouring coffee in the kitchen, humming under his breath. I wish I could stay here like this forever. Jack comes into the room holding two steaming cups of coffee, his hair pulled into a messy knot, his smile making my stomach flutter.

"Would you like to join me for coffee, Sassenach?"

I nod, carefully disentangling myself and sliding off the bed. I pull on underwear and a tank top before padding out to meet him. I stop in the doorway, overwhelmed by the beauty. The lake is glass under the fingers of mist dissipating into the brightness of the morning. Sunlight bathes Jack in an ethereal glow, limning his profile with gold as he turns toward me. I swallow hard, my breath catching as his whisky eyes rake over me.

I take one step forward, then another, wrapping my hands around the mug he hands me, leaning into his touch as he cradles my face in his palm.

"What kind of creature are you?" he whispers, studying me. "A siren born of misty mornings, luring unsuspecting men to their fate?"

His thumb tugs at my bottom lip. "A selkie that shed her auburn coat among the crashing waves, venturing to land to find her lover?"

"Or a Charlotte that was discarded by her old life, grew a pair, and went on an adventure, finding more than she ever thought possible."

"They're all fools not to see how fucking amazing you are," he says, tilting my chin so I'm looking him in the eyes.

"I know," I murmur, and for once, I mean it. I smile, pushing to my tiptoes and pressing my lips to his. We pull two chairs together and sit facing the water, sipping our coffee.

I hear Lach and Cam stirring after several minutes, both coming out laden with plates of food.

"You did all this?" I ask Jack, my mouth watering at the spread on the plate Lach hands me. Bacon, eggs, hashbrowns, cinnamon rolls, and a glass of orange juice to wash everything down.

"Jet lag," he shrugs, "I'll probably get used to it the day we leave."

"So, what are you cooking us tonight, Carebear?" Lach asks, shoveling a forkful of eggs into his mouth.

"Tonight?" My voice breaks, the word coming out more like a squeak.

"Unless you have other plans?" He knows exactly what he's doing with his lopsided grin, boyish freckles popping in the sun, eyes twinkling.

"Fine. But I'm dessert."

"Fucking deal."

"I can be your sous chef," Cam says, licking frosting from his fingers, his wink making my heart melt into a puddle of goo.

"Once you know what you want to make, give me a list, and I'll make a grocery store run," Jack says, reaching out for my empty plate.

NONE of us can bear to go back inside after breakfast. Lach is hunched over his laptop, his hair spiky from running his hands through it so many times. The echo of Jack chopping wood reverberates off the trees around us, and I'm almost tempted to find him except for the warmth of Cam's torso on my back as we scroll recipes on Pinterest together.

"What do you like to cook?" he asks after a few minutes, his lips against my ear.

"I don't *like* to cook anything," I say honestly.

"Okay... what *can* you cook?"

"Everything."

"You're a cocky little witch, aren't you?" he chuckles, catching the shell of my ear in his teeth.

"Not cocky. Just good at following directions."

"That's a dangerous bit of information." He slides his hand down my arm, taking my phone from my hands and setting it down on the deck.

"Oh yeah?"

"Number one: don't make a sound." He cups my breasts, rolling my nipples between his thumb and forefinger. I clamp my mouth closed, swallowing my moan.

"Number two: open your legs," he whispers, glancing over at Lach to make sure he's still engrossed in his work. I let my knees fall open, relaxing against him.

"Number three," he groans, sliding his hand over my stomach and inside my panties, "Show me what you *really* like." He slides his middle finger down my slit, bringing it back up to tease my clit. I arch my back, pushing my hips toward his hand. He switches to two fingers, circling them over me until I'm bucking against his hand.

"You're so fucking responsive," he breathes, his voice low and husky. "It makes me want to spend every minute of every day in bed with you until I find what makes you squirm, what makes you scream my name, what makes you cum with a single touch." He switches positions, trapping my clit between his pointer and ring finger, his middle finger riding over the top as he slides his hand back and forth.

"Fuck, Cam." I strain against him as he drags his hand back, an orgasm ripping through me without warning.

"There it is. Good girl," he groans, keeping his hand between my legs until the aftershocks fade, then brings his fingers so his mouth, licking them clean.

Lach's shadow falls over us, blocking out the sun.

"Number one," he rasps, his eyes dark. "Turn around."

I obey, my heart in my throat.

"Number two: take out Cam's cock."

Cam swallows hard, his gaze following my hands as I pull down the front of his boxers and set him free.

"Number three," Lach groans, desire dripping from every word. "Taste him."

I swipe away the drop of precum with my tongue, one taste not nearly enough.

"Cup his balls," Lach commands, giving up on pretenses. "Good, now massage them, pulling down gently." I do as I'm told, and Cam becomes putty in my hands, his eyelids fluttering closed with a muffled curse. Lach kneels on the chair behind me, pulling my underwear to the center to expose my ass cheeks. His low groan has me arching my back and pushing back into his hands. "Slide your tongue back and forth over his frenulum while you massage him."

The realization that Lach is telling me what Cam likes from experience has moisture flooding my panties. This is so fucking hot. I press the flat of my tongue to the sensitive skin on the bottom of Cam's cock, pulsing it there. My entire body shakes when Lach bites my ass, a warning before he sucks my clit into his mouth through my underwear, flicking his tongue over me.

"Now fuck him with your mouth," he says, straightening, pulling my hair back as he watches me swallow Cam's cock.

"God, Charlie, you're too fucking good at that," Cam gasps, gripping the sides of the chair, his knuckles white.

"You're such a good girl," Lach praises, gripping my waist to anchor me before pressing his hips against me, my underwear preventing him from slamming home.

"All the way, love. Show him what that mouth can do. Don't hold back."

I whimper around Cam's cock as Lach pulls my underwear to the side and sinks his finger into my pussy. I moan, Cam's hips flexing in response, his cock pushing into my throat, making me gag. Lach stands up, walks to the head of the chair, and slowly lowers it until Cam is flat. Then he returns to me, pulling my ankles so I'm lying flat on my stomach, straddling one of Cam's thighs.

"What—?" Whatever I was going to ask turns into a moan as he spanks my ass; then he's jerking my underwear to the side, notching his cock at my entrance, and sliding home.

"I don't like hearing you gag, Charlie. Hold him steady." I look over my shoulder at him in confusion, only for his meaning to dawn on me when I see he's in the perfect position to suck Cam off.

"I—" Cam starts to protest, but Lach swallows him down, taking him deeper every time he thrusts into me. The rhythmic press of his hips has my clit sliding along Cam's leg, the friction building quickly. I palm Cam's balls, my fingertips positioned just above them, pulling gently in time with Lach's thrusts. Cam's broken groan rips the ground out from under us. Cam's balls tighten in my hand, emptying into Lach's eager mouth while Lach's cum fills me up. Lach sits back on his heels, pulling me up, his hand rough on my jaw as he crushes his mouth to mine, Cam's cum sliding off his tongue and onto mine.

Holy fucking God.

He breaks away with a gasp, his nostrils flaring. He slides his thumb between my thighs, pulling it back slick with cum, then coats my lips, pushing into my mouth. I lick him clean, my body throbbing. "Now go find Jack and see what he wants to do about my cum dripping down your thighs."

104

I pad across the deck and down the steps, careful not to snag my toes on the planks. Jack's facing the water, back to me, the axe across his shoulders with his arms slung over it. His pants are slung low on his hips, his torso glistening. He has no right to look so fucking good.

"Hey," I whisper, trying not to startle him.

"Hey, you." He turns toward me, setting the axe against a tree. His gaze slides from my lips to my nipples, then down to the apex of my thighs, his eyebrow cocking. "Have you been a naughty girl?" He grips my waist and lifts me onto an old stump, his palms scraping over the delicate skin of my shoulders as he pulls me against him and buries his face in my neck. I wind my arms around him, squeezing him tight, breathing him in.

"I like you like this," he mumbles, his lips moving against my skin.

"Like what?"

"Freshly fucked. Soft. Carefree."

"I like me like this too," I chuckle, nipping at his earlobe.

"Whose cum is dripping down your thighs, Charlotte?" His voice is rough, every word coated in desire.

"Lach's," I whisper, gasping as he drags his hands down my body.

"I want to see." He lifts me off the stump with one arm, pulling his t-shirt from his pocket and laying it over the rough wood before my ass makes contact. He drops to the ground in front of me, hands rough as he pushes my knees wide. "Fuck," he growls, his jaw ticking. The button on his pants is undone before I can blink, and he's pulling out his thick cock. He slides his fingers up my thighs and then wipes them on his cock, hips flexing as he fucks himself.

God, that's hot. I whimper, my pussy throbbing.

He wrenches my panties apart, his eyes darkening when he sees his best friend's cum coating me.

"Fuck, Charlotte," he groans. I shiver as he dips his tongue into me, his eyes fluttering closed at the first taste. "The taste of both of you together is the best fucking thing I've ever had in my mouth," he rasps, his breath stuttering. He licks me clean, sucking my clit into his mouth in one hard pull before sitting back on his heels, breathing hard. "Not yet," he says in answer to my mewl of protest. "I have something to show you." He pulls his pants up, holding a hand out to me and helping me to my feet.

"Look what I found." A wood-fired jacuzzi tub and a small cylindrical sauna sit tucked into a stand of pines. The chimney of the jacuzzi is already chugging out smoke, a small pile of wood standing at the ready next to it. I practically melt off the stump in anticipation, my muscles desperate for relief after last night. And this morning. And the last three months, if I'm being honest.

Jack helps me with my tank top, and I peel off his pants and boxers.

"Charlie!" Cam's melodic voice floats down to us in the breeze. "Text me the recipe and we'll run to the store for the ingredients!"

"Okay! Give me one second!" I call back up. "Can I borrow your phone?" I ask, turning back to Jack.

"Get in. We'll pick something out together." He helps me up the steps and into the steaming water, sinking in behind me with a groan. "Fuck this is nice. I know what I'm buying the second we're back home."

I settle between his legs, staring up at the trees towering above us. Perfect solitude with the perfect man. I'm in heaven.

"What's your favorite thing to cook?" he asks, lightly massaging my shoulders.

"What's your favorite thing to eat?" I counter, groaning when he focuses in on a knot. "If I'm cooking, I want to make sure it's worth the effort."

"You're my favorite thing to eat, Sassenach."

A spike of desire streaks down my spine as his words come to life in my mind. The scratch of his beard on my thighs, his tongue sliding through my folds—

"Concentrate, mo chridhe," he chuckles, sweeping my hair over one shoulder and pressing a kiss to my neck.

"What's your favorite thing to eat other than my pussy?" I ask, looking over my shoulder at him.

"You're not going to like the answer to that, either," he says, giving my ass a squeeze.

"Jack!"

He laughs, drawing me closer, forcing me to relax into him. I don't need encouragement.

"A good stew with fresh bread is probably my favorite thing," he says, finally giving a serious answer.

"What about Cam and Lach?"

"Neither of them would turn that down."

"Will you hand me your phone? I'll look up a recipe."

"You don't need a recipe, Charlotte. If you'll let me, I'll teach you how my mom used to make it. How she taught me to make it."

"But I'm supposed to cook for you guys."

"Nothing in the bet said we couldn't cook together. We did come together, so technically, we both lost."

"True. Thank you, Jack." I turn around, leaning against the opposite side of the jacuzzi to look at him.

"For what?" he asks, looking up from his phone, his fingers pausing while listing ingredients.

"Everything." That's the honest answer. This man has changed everything about me in the span of three months. The way I view the world. The way I view myself.

He fires off the text and throws his phone over his shoulder, grabbing my calves and wrapping my legs around his waist. Warm water drips down the side of my face as he pushes a strand of hair behind my ear, his eyes glowing gold in the morning light.

"It's me that should be thanking you, lass." He tips my chin up, holding my gaze.

"I didn't do anything," I protest.

"You did *everything*. You grounded us. Gave us purpose. Something to work for. A reason to keep going. Keep breathing. A reason to live. I didn't think I'd ever have that again."

Fuck.

He wipes my tears away with his thumbs, lowering his lips to mine in a tender kiss.

"Fucking hell," he laughs, clearing his throat. "Time to change the topic. Can I ask you a question?"

"Always."

"I asked you a while ago what your plans for the future looked like. What about now?"

My smile trembles, emotions running high. "I see tourism at the castle thriving to the point that the entire estate is self-sustainable. I see us all learning how to live and work together and doing a damn good job of it. I see us going to the best fertility doctor the UK has to offer so we can have some babies running around those halls."

"Don't go *too* fast," he laughs, his eyes sparkling, "We have years to make up for before we have little ones to take care of."

"Well, that can be the ten-year plan," I concede, smiling. "How about you?"

"My ten-year plan is keeping you happy."

"Oh, come on," I pout, wanting a real answer.

"You gave my life meaning, Charlotte. Do you think I'm going to fuck that up?"

"But what about your dreams and goals? You can't give that up because of me."

"Then I guess I'm pretty lucky they align with yours, aren't I? My lifetime goal has always been for the estate to pay for itself so that I'm not passing on a burden. You and I working together to accomplish that? It's better than I could have ever dreamed of." He curls a strand of my hair around his fingers, his gaze holding mine. "The sex is good – scratch that, it's fucking great. The best sex I've had in my entire life. But if something were to happen, I *need* you to know that sex is just the cherry on top, Charlotte."

"And what about Lach?"

"It's complicated, Sassenach. He's still my best friend outside of the bedroom, and I don't want that to change. But when we're all together, and I'm watching him fuck you..." he trails off, scrubbing his hands over his face. "It's like all bets are off. There is something feral in me that craves giving pleasure. I want to make him come harder than he ever has before. Tell me you understand."

"I understand." And I do. I've done things with them that I never thought I would do in the bedroom. I surge forward, the water sloshing over the side of the tub, and trap his face between my hands, kissing him hard, letting him know I accept him exactly the way he is. He opens for me, one hand tangling in the hair at the nape of my neck, the other pressed between my shoulder blades, holding me close. I jerk in his arms, startled by the cold splash of a raindrop hitting my nose.

"Should we go inside?" I ask, looking up at the ominous clouds rolling in.

"We're already wet, Charlotte. And if you think I'm going to give up a chance to make love to you in a jacuzzi in the rain, you better think again" He pulls my face back to his, plundering my mouth, his cock hard between us. I flex my hips against him, dragging my clit up and down his shaft. I use his shoulders for leverage, pulling myself up until his cock is notched at my entrance. He holds my gaze as he grips my hips, pulling me down while thrusting up at the same time, filling me hard and deep.

"You're so fucking tight," he groans, holding me still. Lightning flashes overhead, thunder rolling across the lake several seconds later. The rain is pelting us now, steam rising from the ground around us.

"It's now or never." I rock my hips against him, breaking his hold. He slides his hand down my back and over my ass, his middle finger nudging between my cheeks. I arch my back, pushing into his touch, moaning as he sinks his finger into me, gripping my ass with the rest of his hand and pulling me up and down his cock. His hair brushes my cheeks as he dips down, catching my nipple in his mouth. I ride him in earnest then, electricity crackling over our skin, my nails raking his back as I scramble for purchase against wet skin.

"Come for me, Charlie." He catches my lower lip between his teeth, taking me under with a searing kiss. He grips my hip with his free hand, forcing my pelvis to tilt, changing the angle of his cock until he can feel my clit dragging along his shaft with every thrust. We explode together, fragments of stars dancing behind our lids as lightning tears the world apart around us.

105

Jack wraps me in his shirt and bolts through the pelting rain up the stairs and into the cabin. By the time we're finished showering, Lach and Cam are banging through the cabin's front door loaded with bags, including several from the liquor store. Lach finds me in the bedroom, pulling me down to sit beside him on the bed.

"Was what we did on the deck earlier okay?" he asks, a crease of worry between his brows. "I feel like I should've stayed with you, but I knew you would want to go down to Jack, and—" I put my head on his arm, pressing my finger to his lips.

"Lach, I'm fine. More than fine."

"You're sure?" he asks, tipping my chin up and searching my eyes.

"I'm sure." I bite my lip to keep my grin tamed, wondering how long it will take them to realize I won't break.

"It was pretty hot, wasn't it?" he asks, cocking an eyebrow. I laugh, framing his face with my hands and pressing my lips to his.

"What will you and Cam do while Jack and I cook?" I ask, pulling on thick socks to keep my feet warm on the kitchen tile.

"I have some emails to catch up on, and Cam was mumbling incoherently about a poem most of the time at the grocery store, so I'm guessing he'll be working on that." He shrugs.

"A poem? Does he usually write poetry?"

"Not that I know of, but he likes to write, so I wouldn't put it past him. He gets a little *extra* when he's in that headspace, though. Just to give you a heads up."

"What does that mean?"

"You'll see."

Color me intrigued. "Would you like a cocktail while you finish working," I ask, feeling very fifties housewife-ish and loving it.

"Yes, darling," he drawls in a posh English accent.

"Negroni. Sbagliato. With Prosecco in it?" I ask, butchering the accent. He snorts, his eyes sparkling.

"God, I love you. A drink would be great, Carebear. Thank you." He presses a kiss to the corner of my mouth, and I turn, catching his lips with mine, deepening the kiss.

"Thank you, Lach."

"For what?" he murmurs, folding me into his arms.

"For knowing me better than I know myself. For believing in me when I couldn't."

"That was all you, baby."

"But it wasn't. I wouldn't be with any of you if you didn't help me see what was staring me in the face the whole time. If you hadn't encouraged me to go with my gut, I would be back living in the pool house and going on that horrible interview my mom set up." I shiver in disgust.

"I doubt that, Charlie. Maybe that's who you were when you were younger, but not anymore." A call comes in that he has to take, and he kisses me quickly before picking up his laptop and heading outside.

I make my way to the kitchen to find Jack unpacking the last of the groceries, joggers slung low on his hips, hiding absolutely nothing.

"How am I supposed to learn anything when you look like that?" I ask, raking my nails down his abdomen and watching his muscles quiver.

"And how am *I* supposed to teach you anything when the counter is the perfect height for fucking you?" He grips my waist and hoists me onto the butcher block, my legs reflexively wrapping around him, pulling him closer.

"I *bet* you could teach me a thing or two," I say, my voice husky, leaning forward and flicking my tongue over his nipple. My stomach chooses that very inopportune moment to growl. Loudly.

"I bet I can," he murmurs... "But we need food first." He pushes away from me with a groan and starts organizing the ingredients. While he's doing that, I work on making Lach a drink.

"Not a negroni, but hopefully an old-fashioned will do?" I ask as I step out onto the deck, setting one of the glasses on the side table for Cam.

"Thank you, beautiful." He takes it from me, then pulls me down into his lap, setting his laptop to the side. "I hope you know how much I love you, Charlie. I'm so thankful for your presence in my life," he mumbles, his lips buried in my hair.

"Is everything okay?" I ask, twisting in his arms to look at him.

"No," he says truthfully, his eyes sad. "I'm organizing a trip for a couple who just returned from their honeymoon two weeks ago. She went to the doctor a few days ago and was told she has two months left to live. Life is so fucking unfair."

I wipe the tears from his cheeks, wrapping my arms around his neck. My heart breaks for him. I never thought about the emotional toll the trips must take on him.

"What you're doing is amazing," I whisper, tilting his chin so his gaze meets mine. "I'm so fucking proud of you. Is there anything I can do to help share the burden?"

"Having someone to talk to about it is more help than you know, Charlie." His smile is watery. "Get back to the kitchen. Cam is coming out in a second, so I'll have company."

"Okay. I love you."

"I love you too, Charlie Bear."

"Yes!" I pump my fist. "New nickname unlocked!" I grin and head back inside to the sound of his laughter, my heart a little lighter, having made him laugh.

Jack's putting the finishing touches on two cocktails when I walk back into the kitchen. It feels like the air has been sucked out of the room when he looks up at me, whisky eyes making me tipsy with one glance. I bite my lip, unable to stop my gaze from sliding down his body. God help me.

"Don't look at me like that, Sassenach." He hands me my drink, a dangerous glint in his eyes.

"I can't fucking help it." I take a sip, looking at him over the rim, trying to tamp down the lust surging through my system. I know exactly what I need to do to balance the scales. I strip off my sweatshirt and leggings, leaving on my knee-high socks, thong, and cropped t-shirt.

"Why, Charlotte?" he asks, his words choked.

"Now it's fair. We'll both be equally distracted."

"Supper will be inedible."

"There are other things to eat," I remind him, wiggling my eyebrows.

"Bloody hell." He pushes his hand through his hair, his gaze raking over me. "Get over here."

I walk around the counter, stand at his side and wait for instructions, blowing out a long breath.

We quickly get into a rhythm as he shows me how to make his grandmother's no-knead bread, leaving the dough to rise at the opposite end of the counter. Next is the stew, which needs to cook for a few hours.

"Do you want to tackle the veggies together?" He asks, holding a knife out to me, handle first, his fingers pinching the blade.

"Sure." He sets a cutting board down in front of me. "I'll do the onions," I offer.

"Charlie. Are you sure? I don't want you to chop a finger off."

I snatch the onion from his hands, slice off the ends, peel away the outer layer, and have it diced in under twenty seconds.

His jaw drops. "Is this like what you pulled at the bar when we were playing pool? You pretending not to know how to cook, but you actually went to culinary school?" he asks, his eyes narrowing.

"Is it my fault you assumed I don't know how to cook?" I ask, planting my hands on my hips.

"Charlie, I've never seen you cook a single thing the entire time I've known you."

"That doesn't mean I don't know how. I just don't find it fun or relaxing like so many people seem to. Although, I'm starting to see its appeal," I say, looking at the outline of his cock pointedly.

"Duly noted." He slides the rest of the onions and garlic my way, taking the carrots, potatoes, and celery for himself.

"Now we brown the meat," he says, turning on the heat under a heavy cast iron pot. I watch him while he works – the way he moves, the concentration etched on his face, his easy smiles – and fall for him all over again.

Once the meat is brown and the veggies caramelized, we dump in tomatoes and beef broth and lower the heat. Jack sets a timer so we know when to get the bread in the oven, and then we finally have the opportunity to join Cam and Lach on the deck. I reach for my drink, but Jack grabs me first, swinging me onto the counter.

"Do you think I'm going to let you leave this kitchen without taking advantage of these countertops?" he rasps, running his hand under my shirt and cupping my breast.

"I thought you said we needed to eat first?" I tease, moaning as he nips at my ear.

"I did. And I mean it. We're not having another fuck fest until we have food in our stomachs. Kissing? Sure." He bites my nipple through my shirt, and I arch into him, my body thrumming. "Heavy petting? Yes, please," he continues, pushing me back on my elbows as he kisses his way down my stomach.

"So what are the rules?" I ask, breathing hard.

"No coming."

I open my legs wider as he presses a kiss between my legs, my clit begging for attention.

"Are you guys almost done?" Lach calls, a panicked ring to his voice.

"Rain check," Jack murmurs, pulling my underwear aside and sliding his tongue over my clit before straightening.

"You'll pay for that!" I hiss, hopping off the counter, grabbing my drink, and stomping outside.

I stop dead in my tracks when I see Cam. He looks like he's been trying to pull his hair out for the last thirty minutes – curls disheveled, eyes wild.

"Everything okay out here?" I ask, keeping my voice soft.

"Cam has had a poem knocking around in his head all day—" Lach begins, but Cam cuts him off.

"But now that I'm sitting down to write it, it won't come out." He looks rather desperate, and I have to bite my lip to keep from smiling. He's so goddamn cute.

"Can I hear what you have so far?" I ask, wincing when he drops his head into his hands.

"I'll read you what I have, but then I'm putting it away for tonight." He scrubs his hands over his face, unfolds a crumpled piece of paper, clears his throat, and begins reading.

My heart cannot contain
these deep-rooted feelings
that flood the banks
of what used to be stone,
then turned into mud,
and now into bone.
A skeleton forged
in the furnace of love,
strong enough to withstand
the harshest conditions,
yet soft enough to quake
with the touch of her hand,
and turn to dust
with the gentlest kiss.
Only to be made whole again

when those three words leave her lips.

"God, I love your brain." I sit down facing him on the lounger, flinging my arms around his neck. "Please never change," I whisper, inhaling his scent, memorizing this moment.

He buries his face in my hair, holding me tight. "I won't, little witch. I promise."

106

JACK'S POV

I can't stop staring at her. The way the breeze off the lake makes the silky auburn strands of her hair get stuck in her eyelashes. The way her graceful fingers sweep the waves away from her face and tuck them behind the delicate pink shell of her ear. The way her teeth sink into her bottom lip when she catches me staring. The sparkle in her eyes as she's describing her dream art studio. I glance over at Lach, trying to hold back a smile as he asks her more questions so we can give her exactly what she wants.

He and Cam share a lounger, fingers intertwined, Lach's chin resting on Cam's dark curls. When I see them together and the glow of happiness surrounding them, I feel a profound sense of contentment, like everything is finally right with the world. I turn my gaze inward, trying to puzzle out my emotions surrounding Lach. He's the only man I've ever been attracted to, and I don't think that will ever change. I've been sheltering that piece of myself for years, thinking it would shrivel with time, but our friendship only nurtured it and made it stronger.

This desire to dissect and label our relationship comes from societal pressure. I've always bucked the system and don't plan to stop now. We can see where things go with no end destination in mind.

We've been friends through situations a lot more difficult to navigate than this, though admittedly, this is uncharted territory, and I'm determined to become an expert corporeal cartographer.

The alarm on my phone goes off, and Charlie jumps up, taking my hand and pulling me into the kitchen.

"What do we do now?" she asks, bringing the bread dough to the island. I position her between my body and the counter, slinging flour over the granite before turning out the dough.

"We need to knead the dough a few times and then shape it," I say, hooking my thumbs into the sides of her underwear. "Sprinkle some flour over the top and smooth it over the surface, I instruct," pressing my lips to her hair as she follows my instructions. "Now, give it a little tap." I bite my lip, waiting to see what she does.

"Good dough," she says, mimicking my brogue. She slaps it and promptly dissolves into laughter as we watch it jiggle. "That's strangely satisfying, isn't it?" She looks up at me, the heat in my gaze bringing out the color in her cheeks.

"Now we shape it," I rasp, unable to ignore the way her scent wraps around me. I cover her hands with mine, showing her how to roll the dough into shape, bringing in the edges to form a perfectly round loaf. I swallow my groan as I step away from her to line a Dutch oven with parchment paper. "The loaf needs to proof for about twenty minutes before we put it in the oven," I say, placing the pot on the opposite side of the stove as the stew for some residual heat. I turn back toward her, catching her checking out my ass, except now her gaze is on my very erect cock. She licks her lips, pupils dilating.

"And what do we do while we wait?" Her voice is husky, practically dripping with desire.

I wipe the counter off and wash my hands, the heat of her gaze roaring over my skin like wildfire. "We test my theory about the counters being the perfect height." I spread a clean hand towel on the counter and lift her up, her legs wrapping around me and pulling me close. Her face feels so delicate and soft under my hands as I draw her mouth to mine, nibbling on her lower lip. She groans, sweeping her tongue over my lips before pushing into my mouth, taking what she needs. I fit my hips between her thighs, rocking against her. The sound of her moaning my name nearly ends me.

"Jack," she pants, pulling back. "I need you in me. Now."

She doesn't need to tell me twice. I slide her panties down her legs, pushing her thighs wide so I can see how wet she is for me. Fuck. I palm my cock, dragging the tip along her slit, pulsing at her clit. She gasps, her tits swaying with each trembling breath. I push her shirt up with my free hand, palming her, tracing her areola with my thumb before flicking it over her nipple. Her reaction has my balls drawing up, my core clenching with need. Foreheads pressed together, air mingling, we watch as I notch myself at her entrance. I stay like that for a few seconds, the anticipation of her wet heat clenching around me almost too much to handle.

"God, Jack. Please," Charlie groans, the desperation in her voice like gasoline on a fire.

"I'm no god, Charlie."

"It sure as fuck feels like it when you're in me." My moan drowns out her words as I slam into her, her pussy squeezing around me, transporting me to another dimension.

"You feel so goddamn good." I seat myself to the hilt, slide my hand around her neck, pull her mouth to mine, our tongues lashing out in a battle of wills. Two more thrusts and we're riding on the edge of life and death. My balls throb painfully as I pull out and drop my head against her shoulder, breathing hard. "Not yet, mo chridhe. Not yet."

DINNER TURNED OUT PERFECTLY. Eating it around a bonfire with my favorite people made it even better.

"Who wants to play a game?" Lach asks once we're finished, flames reflecting off his features as he looks around the fire at us.

"What kind of game?" I ask, suspicious of the smirk twisting those full lips.

"One that will take our minds off tomorrow."

"I'm game," Charlie says, grinning, sitting forward in her seat. You would never know by looking at her that tomorrow is one of the most important days of her life.

"I'm in," Cam seconds, a spark in his eyes.

"Fine," I say, raising my eyebrow as I wait for him to explain the game.

"I have four sticks in my hand. Three long, one short. Whoever draws the short stick gets to tell the rest of us what to do for the rest of the night."

"Yes!" Charlie jumps up, eager to be the first to try her chances. She pulls a stick from his closed fist and quickly realizes she has no idea if it's long or short.

"Come on, somebody else go!" She bounces on the balls of her feet, adrenaline clearly kicking in. I reach over and pull a stick from Lach's hand. It's the same length as Charlie's. Nerves batter my stomach, anticipation snatching the breath from my lungs.

"Cam, it's you or me," Lach says, holding out his hand.

Cam pulls the stick from Lach's fist at a snail's pace. Short. I blow out a controlled breath, the rush of disappointment surprising me.

"There it is," Lach says softly, looking up at Cam with complete trust. "What's first?"

"I want all of you to strip. I'll be right back," Cam says, pulling out his phone and playing music. He sets it on the arm of his chair, then turns on his heel and jogs up the steps to the cabin.

Charlie grabs the hem of her shirt, peels it off, and tosses it to the side, quickly followed by her thong. The moisture between her thighs reflects the firelight as she removes her socks. Her gaze goes to Lach, and mine follows. The veins in his hands catch my eye as he unbuttons his shirt. I swallow hard as he shrugs it off, letting it fall to his chair.

For the first time in a long time, I let myself look. His nipples pebble in response to the cool evening air, his impeccable muscles lit to perfection by the rippling light. The sound of his zipper has air catching in my throat, my hands fisting at my sides as his pants drop to his feet. He hooks his thumb in the waistband of his boxers, pulling them down slowly, my hand going to my cock automatically when he exposes the base of his shaft. I run my palm over myself through my pants, barely breathing as his waistband catches on the head of his cock before he springs out, thick and heavy. I can feel Charlie's gaze on me, and I know without even looking at her that this is turning her on.

"Your turn," Lach says, his voice rough with desire. I hold his gaze as I reach up and gather my hair, watching his eyes darken as I tie it back. I stretch the waist of my joggers, letting them dip even lower in the front, my cock straining at the fabric. I slide them down slowly, stopping just before the head is exposed.

"Jack—" Lach says, his voice cracking.

"—Please," Charlie finishes, the word barely more than a whimper.

Fuck. I push my joggers down all the way, fisting my cock, the tip already glistening.

We all turn as we hear Cam banging down the stairs, a lounger hanging awkwardly from one arm, and a pile of blankets held tight in the other, the lube sticking out of his pocket. He drags two chairs away from the fire, laying blankets on the ground, saving one to drape over the lounger. He strips in record time, his pale skin rosy in the light of the fire.

"If anyone is uncomfortable at any time, we all stop. Okay?" he says, looking between us, waiting for our verbal affirmations. "Charlie, come here." He beckons for her, and she obeys immediately. "We'll let them watch for a minute, and then it's their turn." He sits in the lounger, spreading his legs so Charlie can sit between them. Lach and I watch as he slides his hands over her waist, cupping her breasts before flicking his thumbs over her nipples. My cock twitches in my hand as she responds to his touch, arching her back, her body begging for more. Goosebumps race over her skin as his hands slide over the dip in her waist to her thighs, pulling them wide. He whispers something in her ear, and she moans, covering his hand with hers and sliding it between her legs.

Lach and I groan in tandem as Cam sinks his middle finger inside her, getting it wet before bringing it back up to tease her clit. He whispers into her ear again, and she nods, her gaze bouncing between me and Lach.

"Jack—" Cam begins his first command.

"Wait," Lach interrupts, breathless. His body crashes into mine before I register what's happening. I slide my hands over his muscled back as our lips meet, angling my head, teeth and tongues clashing. He pulls back just as suddenly, his hands cradling my face. "You can say no if you want to."

"I don't want to," I whisper, admitting it to both of us for the first time.

"Jack, stand behind Lach and jerk him off the way you would if it was your own cock. Show him what you like," Cam instructs, his breath hitching as Charlie works her hand over him.

My heartbeat fills my ears, blood rushing as my heart goes into overdrive. I walk behind Lach, glancing over at Charlie to make sure she's okay with this, but in my heart, I know that's what Cam whispered to her, making sure she was on board before he uttered a word to us. Her eyes are hooded, gaze molten, barely hanging on as Cam slowly fucks her with his fingers. She raises an eyebrow, and I know she's challenging me to give in, to let the feelings simmering under the surface finally see the light of day.

I can barely breathe as I shuffle closer, my cock nudging at Lach's cheeks as I reach around him, hesitating several seconds, my mind racing.

"Don't fucking tease me, Jack." The desperation in his voice has me pressing closer, positioning my fist a hairsbreadth from his cock. He flexes his hips, groaning as the head of his cock pushes past the ridges of my fingers.

"Those callouses are going to be my undoing," he says shakily. I band my arm around his waist, hauling him closer, my cock nestled tight between his cheeks as I drag my hand down his shaft, squeezing at the base. I make another pass, using his precum as lube. I push my hips forward, sliding along his crack, not even ashamed at the broken moans falling from my lips. Charlie's whimper has Lach's stomach clenching under my fingers, muscles rippling as he struggles for control.

"Stop," Cam demands, not letting Lach get any closer to coming. "Switch places."

I don't want to release him, but I do anyway, my chest heaving as I try to catch my breath. I shiver as he grips my hips and pulls me to his body, his cock pressing against me intimately. The first slide of his hand over my aching shaft rips a trembling moan from deep in my chest. His grip is strong and sure, his thumb sweeping over the head of my cock to catch the precum leaking with each pull and push of his hand.

"You're fucking close, aren't you?" he murmurs, his breath hot on my ear, hips flexing against me.

"Stop," Cam commands. "Jack, on your knees."

Oh, God.

"Lach, tell him how you like to be sucked off. Jack, follow his instructions."

Fuck. I turn to face Lach, my anxiety burning off like fog on a lake, the sun a burning hot ball of need lodged deep inside me. Lach's hand trembles as he reaches down and runs the pad of his thumb over my bottom lip.

"You can say no at any time," he reminds me, terror and need warring for dominance over his features.

"I won't." He hisses as I catch his thumb in my teeth and bite down. He jerks his hand away and grips my chin, forcing me to meet his gaze.

"Taste me."

I breathe him in, memorizing this moment – Charlie's soft moans as Cam slides his fingers over her, Cam's dark gaze filled with love as he watches Lach come apart, Lach's hazel eyes locked with mine as he sinks his fingers into my hair as I lean forward to catch a drop of precum. His taste explodes over my tongue, a shiver of desire shaking me to my core.

"Feather your tongue on the underside," Lach rasps, breathing hard.

I flatten my tongue and drag it over that sensitive spot, pulsing it there until his fingers are clenching my head, and he's struggling to keep himself from sinking past my lips.

"Fuck, Jack," Lach moans, his eyes never leaving mine.

"Tell him what you want him to do," Cam says, his voice husky with need.

"Grip the base and suck the tip," Lach blurts, his voice strangled as he wrestles for control.

I wrap my hand around him, watching his face as his cock pushes past my lips. I hollow my cheeks, sucking him in deep, needing to see him fall apart. But he doesn't, he holds onto his control like it's his last lifeline.

"Goddamnit, Lach," I say, my lips moving against him. "Fuck this virgin mouth like a good boy."

His control snaps, his fingers digging into my head as he thrusts past my lips.

"Again," I say around him.

He thrusts once, twice, and then he's seated to the hilt, taking everything I've always been too scared to give him. Charlie cries out, and I groan around Lach's cock, the vibrations making his hips stutter.

"Switch," Cam says, his voice hoarse.

I stand, my breath rushing from my lungs as Lach hits his knees in front of me, those gorgeous blue-green, freckled eyes looking up at me, begging me to fuck his mouth. I glance at Charlie, sweat glistening on her body as Cam brings her to the edge over and over. Her lips curve up as she nods, encouraging me to take that last step. I look back down at Lach, swiping the precum from my cock with my thumb and coating his lips. He licks them clean, moaning my name, his hand working over his cock.

"Jack." Charlie's rasp has my gaze colliding with hers as Lach's hands latch onto my ass, pulling me forward until my cock sinks past his lips.

Lach's tongue sweeps over me, his lips suctioning around me like a goddamn vacuum. I clench my jaw, desperately trying to stay in control. She holds my gaze as we climb the mountain together, her body writhing against Cam's as I fuck Lach's face until I'm sure we're too far gone to go back.

"Stop." Cam's voice freezes us in our tracks, all four of us toeing the edge of no return. "I'm handing over the reins to Charlie," he says, struggling to catch his breath.

"Finally! On the blanket, boys. This is going to be a night you'll never forget."

107

LACH'S POV

My knees feel like jelly as I push to my feet, Jack's taste permeating my senses. I'll never forget the sound he made as I took him into my mouth, the way his hands trembled in my hair, the desperate surrender to this roaring inferno that's been building for almost twenty years. I lock eyes with Cam. He's grinning like a fool, his fingers buried deep in Charlie's pussy. She's looking at Jack and I, need burning bright in those hooded baby blues. She's so fucking beautiful that I can barely breathe. Even the firelight can't resist caressing her skin. I sit on the end of the lounger, intending to wait for her to tell us what to do, but the sounds she's making have me sinking between her thighs, nipping at her velvety skin, breathing her in. She flexes her hips toward my mouth, and Cam moves his hand, allowing me to suck on her clit. Her back bows, thighs clamping around my head. I duck out of her hold before she gets too close, pulling away.

"You're in charge, Charlie. Tell us what to do."

"All I want is for us to fuck until I forget about tomorrow. Can we do that? Please?"

"If that's what you need, that's what we'll do, Carebear." I pick her up, cradling her in my arms, waiting for further instructions.

"Cam, lay down on the blankets." He obeys, his cock throwing a gigantic shadow that makes us all laugh. Charlie wiggles out of my arms, stepping over Cam's hips and looking down at him as she slowly lowers herself, letting the anticipation build.

Watching Cam's eyes roll back in his head as Charlie sinks down onto his cock nearly does me in. I keep my eyes north of where her pussy is stretched around the base of his shaft, thinking of anything other than what's happening right now. I only make it thirty seconds before sliding my thumb around the base of Cam's cock, then dragging it up to circle her asshole.

"Lach, please," she begs, her entire body trembling as her control slips. So goddamn fucking hot.

"If you're close, I can take over for a second," Jack murmurs from over my shoulder. I glance down at his cock, standing proud against his stomach, precum dripping down the tip. My hand moves without my permission, swiping the drop with one finger and popping it into my mouth before I register what I'm doing.

"Fuck, Lach," Jack breathes, his cock twitching. I move out of the way, shuffling behind him as he takes my place. He squirts a generous amount of lube at the base of her spine, watching as it slowly drips down her crack. He slides the head of his cock up and down, spreading the lube, then notches himself and fills her with one smooth thrust. Charlie's moan has goosebumps racing over my skin, my balls spasming, riding the edge of pleasure and pain.

"Fuck, Charlie," he groans, his voice like worn sandpaper, rough around the edges with a smooth finish.

Jack rides her hard, the muscles of his ass clenching with each thrust, fingers digging into the blanket on either side of her as he keeps his weight from crushing them.

"Lach, are you able to reach her clit?"

"I think so." Instead of going in from the side, I reach around his waist, pressing against him as I slide my hand between Charlie's and Cam's bodies. She presses her hips down, riding over my hand. I move even closer, my cock nestling between his cheeks, my breath stuttering as he pushes back against me. Molten-hot desire races through my veins, the fingers of my free hands digging into his hip as I flex against him. He groans and bends over Charlie's body, giving me free rein. There's no way I'll be able to last when I could come just looking at him. I squeeze lube on my cock and nudge between his cheeks. Positioning my fingers on either side of Charlie's clit, I slowly slide my hand back and forth, riding my cock up and down Jack's crack at the same time. Charlie's entire body spasms, squeezing around them, their chorus of moans echoing around us in a hedonistic melody.

"Lach." Jack looks back at me, a million emotions written on his face. "Please."

"Please, what? Tell me what you want, Jack." I have to hear the words, see his lips moving, begging. I don't want to wake up in the morning and wonder if he really wanted it or if it was only me.

"Fuck me, Lach. Please."

My gaze flickers to Cam, then down to the grin he's not even trying to hide. I don't need to ask him to know he's completely on board. "Charlie?"

She looks over her shoulder at me, cheeks flushed, hair falling around her face, the most beautiful creature I've ever seen. My Aphrodite. "If you don't fuck him right this second, I'll make you watch us while we get there without you. I swear to God, Lach."

"Don't threaten me with a good time, Charlie." I fist my cock, sliding it back and forth over Jack's asshole. My stomach clenches with anticipation, "Jack, are you—" He doesn't let me finish.

"I'm sure. Fuck. Me. Now."

I blow out a trembling breath, my control slipping through my fingers like silk. Cam pulls my hand away from Charlie, taking over so both hands are free. Jack's skin is smooth under my fingertips as I trace the slope of his shoulders, around his chest, over his ribs. Muscles tremble under my touch as I drag my hands south, memorizing the feel of his skin under my hands.

"Lach."

God, the way he says my name – that desperate edge. Like I'm the one thing he never knew he needed but now can't live without. My hands shake as I slide them over his hips, caressing the dimples in his lower back before squeezing his cheeks and spreading them wide. His moan is gasoline on fire, my restraint going up in flames. I hold my cock steady as I press against him, giving him time to adjust. All three of them freeze as Jack takes a deep breath, forcing his muscles to relax. That ring of muscle is so fucking tight it strangles the head of my cock as I push forward. Jack's entire body shudders, squeezing around me like a fucking vice.

"Jack—" My voice breaks as my world shatters, rearranging itself into something new.

"Stop holding back," he growls, pushing his hips back until I'm bottomed out, his curse muffled in Charlie's shoulder. He thrusts into Charlie, my cock sliding almost all the way out before I snap. I fuck him hard, my fingers digging into his shoulders as I pull his body back to meet my thrusts. Charlie's moans build until she's crying out, begging for release.

"Now." The command in Cam's voice is impossible to deny. I intertwine my fingers with Charlie's, pulling her hand to Jack's hip as Cam grips the back of my thigh, linking us all together. Jack sinks into Charlie, and I sink into him, holding him pinned between us, fucking him with short hard thrusts. Charlie falls first, her hand squeezing mine as her body gives in. Cam's broken groan has my balls drawing up, but it's Jack's moan of surrender that tips me over the edge, his muscles clenching around my cock as he starts to come. I angle my hips, thrusting once, twice. My climax rips an ungodly sound from my throat as I pound into him, filling him, wringing out every last bit of pleasure his body will give me.

"I'm taking back my control privileges," Cam says, his voice hoarse. "Jack, go inside with Charlie and help her wash up. I have a date with Lach."

Fuck. I pull away from Jack, rolling onto my back on the blanket, watching Jack lift Charlie off of Cam, swinging her into his arms.

"Don't do anything I wouldn't do," she says groggily, tossing us an exaggerated wink that ends in a yawn as Jack carries her up the stairs.

"Everything okay?" I ask Cam as soon as I hear the door close behind them. I look at him as he sits up, his cock still rock hard. "You didn't—?"

He crawls toward me, his eyes dark, a soft sheen of sweat glowing over his entire body. Elegant fingers grip my legs and push my knees toward my shoulders. He looks at me, his gaze hungry. "Spit or lube?"

Oh fuck. My cock twitches, roaring back to life.

"Spit," I rasp. My heart pounds in my chest as he looks down, curls falling over his forehead as he spits on me. His teeth sink into his bottom lip as he notches his cock, pushing into me with one long stroke. I groan as I stretch to take him, my body struggling to adjust. He feels so fucking good.

"Is this how it's going to be?" I pant, my body bowing as he fists my cock, his grip strong and sure, exactly how I like it.

"What do you mean?"

"Are you going to have to re-claim your territory every time all of us fuck?"

"Is that what you think this is?"

"I did until just now," I say, mentally wincing as I second-guess myself.

"This is so you don't lay awake while the rest of us sleep, wondering if everything is okay between us. It's my reassurance to you that I still want you. Still love you. Still need you."

Cam has always had a way of knowing the deepest, darkest depths of my soul. He sees past the smoke and mirrors, tearing down my defenses, always aware of exactly what I need. I pull his face down to mine, nibbling on his bottom lip.

"I love you so fucking much," I whisper, my voice breaking. Pressing me into the ground, he cradles my face as he fucks me with his tongue, riding me hard. He's in complete control, my body answering his demand for more. He presses his face into my shoulder, reaching between our bodies to wrap his hand around my shaft.

"Come with me," Cam groans. His breath trembles against my neck as his hips slap the back of my thighs. I grab his ass, pulling him closer as he fills me, ragged breaths filling my ears as ecstasy wraps her fingers around my throat and squeezes. Stars burst behind my eyelids, a moan ripping from my throat as we fall apart in each other's arms.

"Fuck, Cam," I pant as he slips out of me and rolls onto his back, chest heaving. He turns to face me, moonlight reflecting in his eyes, one corner of his mouth pulling up.

"When you wake up tonight with those doubts in the back of your mind, my cum leaking out of your ass will remind you that nothing has changed." He stands up, looking down at me, firelight gilding the lithe lines of his body. I take the hand he holds out to me, letting him help me up. The stroke of his thumb over my cheek is tender, the love in his gaze so fucking pure and sweet, it makes me want to protect him from everything wrong in this world. I swallow hard, blinking away the onslaught of emotion.

"Come on," he whispers, giving me a watery smile. "Let's go get washed up."

108

The shower spray pummels my face, water pouring into my mouth as I stand there, grinning like an idiot. I never thought it could be like this. I'm totally, completely, undeniably in love *and* having the hottest, most mind-blowing sex of my life.

That sound Jack made. God. My body tingles, my nipples puckering as I re-live the moment.

"Charlotte." Jack's voice rolls over me like a thunderstorm, electricity crackling between us. I turn, wiping the water from my face, my heart jumping to my throat when I open my eyes. He's leaning against the shower opening, one arm above his head, his whisky gaze caressing every dip, every swell.

"Jack." I mimic his brogue, biting my lip to keep my smile under control. He steps forward and tugs my lip free, sweeping the pad of his thumb over the offending teeth marks. The corner of his mouth pulls up when my breathing hitches.

"Same, mo chridhe." He backs me to the wall, pressing his thigh between my legs, trapping me. "In the beginning, I thought this insatiable need would dull with time. That it would become more comfortable. Familiar, even." He touches his fingers to the place just over my heart, then slides them up my throat, tilting my chin so my gaze locks with his. He searches my eyes, something wild and desperate in their depths reaching out to me. "So tell me why it's only getting stronger? I can't be near you without needing you, Charlotte. Your strength. Your opinion. Your love. Your body."

"Go on," I murmur, memorizing every word that falls from his lips.

"Tell me why I've had a permanent hard-on since the day we met." He leans forward, his cock pressing into my hip, like his cum isn't already dripping out of me. "Tell me why I can't fucking get enough." His lips are gentle at first, then all-consuming, his tongue demanding entrance, fucking my mouth until I'm boneless and out of breath. "I need you to know that if I had to choose, I would choose you," he rasps, cradling my face between his hands.

"You're not going to have to choose, Jack." I sweep a strand of hair behind his ear, trying to decipher the emotions flitting across his face. "The four of us are tied together in a knot so complicated, we'll never unravel."

He searches my face, desperate to make sure I'm being truthful, doubt and hope warring for dominance in his eyes.

"Jack, If you're worried about what happened tonight, it didn't change anything. The two of you were already a couple in every way except physically. It just makes being in bed together that much hotter."

"You're being completely honest?"

"Always."

"Fuck, Charlie." He pulls my leg around his waist and thrusts into me without warning, pinning me to the wall, his chest heaving. I moan as the head of his cock pushes past my g-spot, then gasp as he bottoms out, filling me. I rock my hips against him, rolling my clit back and forth over his pubic bone. "Tell me you love me."

"I love you," I gasp as he sweeps his hand over my ass, his middle finger sliding in easily.

"Again."

"I love you, Jack." He crushes his lips to mine, fucking me hard and fast, claiming me with his cock, his finger, his tongue.

He groans my name, his lips still touching mine, his eyes staring into my soul. "Be a good girl and come for me." My body obeys, clenching around him as he pounds into me, reality suspending as we fall apart in each other's arms.

I want to stay in this lavender haze forever. Bodies pressed together, water streaming down around us, sweet nothings on our lips.

"I love you, Charlotte," Jack says, pressing his forehead to mine, his hands anchored on either side of my face.

"I know." I smile up at him, my heart so full I swear it could burst.

JACK and I pad to the kitchen in our robes, leaving the bathroom free for Cam and Lach. I root around in the fridge while Jack puts milk on the stove for hot cocoa. By the time the guys join us, there's a charcuterie board and mugs of hot chocolate waiting. We sit down at the table, looking around at each other, waiting for someone to say something.

"That was fucking hot," Cam says, hiding his grin in his mug.

"Agreed." I lift my mug in a toast, then take a sip, moaning as the first chocolatey sip kisses my taste buds. I watch with interest as Lach lifts his eyes from his hands, glancing at Jack. This is the first time I've ever seen him with that shadow of doubt in his eyes.

"It was perfect," Jack says roughly, holding Lach's gaze. Lach's entire body relaxes, the doubt replaced by something that lights his eyes from within.

"Easily in the top four," Lach says, grabbing a handful of grapes from the platter.

"Top four?" Jack asks, eyebrow cocked, a warning in his eyes.

"First time with Cam, first time with Charlie, first time all together, and then tonight."

"I need to hear about how you and Cam first got together," I say, snatching a grape from his fingers.

"That's a story for another time," Lach's chuckle turns to all-out laughter when he sees the panic in Cam's eyes.

"Don't you dare," Cam warns.

"Not fair!" I protest, looking between them.

"All you need is some good tequila, Carebear. It works like—" he stops short when a piece of cheese smacks him square in the forehead. The look of shock on his face has us cracking up, but the laughter quickly turns to a chorus of yawns when I can't hold mine back. I'm exhausted.

"Come on," Lach says, standing up. "Time for bed."

"CHARLIE, TIME TO WAKE UP," Cam whispers, caressing my cheek with the back of his finger. I squint up at him, smiling sleepily, stretching my arms above my head and pointing my toes. Then reality crashes down on me like a thousand gallons of cold water. It's court day. "Lach made breakfast. We'll eat first, drive back into town, get you changed, and head to the trial."

I sit up, scrubbing my hands over my face. I want to disappear.

"Don't overthink it, Charlie."

I huff out an incredulous laugh, adrenaline already coursing through my system.

"Hey," he puts a finger under my chin, tilting my face to his. "This is your day to get what he owes you for the past five years. The overtime hours, the blood, sweat, and tears you poured into that business. This is your time to shine, Charlie."

I know he's right, but fuck if I don't still feel guilty about it. The guys feed and caffeinate me, and then we're in the car, headed toward my worst nightmare. Lach plugs my phone into the aux, blasting my favorite playlist the whole way back.

"Lorna told me your lawyer is the best in the state," Jack says, helping me with the buttons on my shirt. "Just sit back and let her work her magic, Sassenach."

"Don't say anything unless she tells you to," Lach reminds me, helping me into my blazer. "If Rob tries to antagonize you, ignore him." I shiver as he pulls my hair free and turns me around. "It'll be over before you know it, and you'll never have to see that bastard again."

I nearly hyperventilate in the car on the way to the courthouse. The only thing keeping me sane is the gentle, rhythmic sweep of Cam's thumb over the back of my hand. I suck in a deep breath as Lach pulls to the curb and jumps out to open my door.

"This is the first day of the rest of your life, Charlie. Take it by the fucking balls." He squeezes my shoulders, holding back from kissing me like we had agreed upon. I face the courthouse and stiffen my spine. I can fucking do this.

My heels click on the concrete as I walk toward the stairs. I look back at the guys once, knowing they'll follow once I'm inside. They're so goddamn gorgeous in their suits. They'll stick out like a sore thumb, but I can't find it in me to care anymore. They're mine. I should be able to scream it from the rooftops if I want to. Why do I give a shit what anyone thinks?

The metal banister is cold against my fingers as I climb the stairs. The thrum of my heartbeat in my ears counts down my steps until I'm sliding into the seat next to my lawyer. After emailing back and forth with her for months, I want to hug her, but I'm not sure if that's appropriate, so I just sit in my chair and smile at her like an idiot.

"Breathe, Charlotte. We have this, no question."

I bite my lip and nod, taking several deep breaths, praying she's right. I can feel the guys' presence the second they enter the room, the hairs on the back of my neck standing up with awareness. They slide in behind me, a silent, solid wall of support.

"Lauren, this is Jack, Lach, and Cam," I introduce her reluctantly, directly responding to her raised eyebrows and narrowed gaze. I hate feeling like I'm in trouble. She twists in her seat, looking between them.

"I don't want to hear a single word from any of you until we're outside the courthouse. Understand?"

"Nice to meet you, too, Lauren," Lach murmurs, winking, then pretending to lock his lips and throw away the key. The door on the far side of the room bangs open a second later, startling all of us.

"Let me talk to her!" Rob shouts, trying to break free from a man that must be his lawyer.

"No. Sit down." The man pushes Rob into his seat, straightening his suit jacket. "Stay."

"I'm not a fucking dog," Rob mutters darkly, his gaze swinging around the room wildly.

"Then stop acting like one." His lawyer sits next to him, blocking his view of our table.

There's some shuffling and muffled whispers behind me, and then my dad squeezes my arm and murmurs words of support. I whisper my thanks and kiss him on the cheek, watching him walk over to where my mom sits several rows back. She doesn't look at me.

Thanks to Lauren's expertise, everything goes off without a hitch. All the nights I spent in the cottage looking up bank statements, old bills and tax information were worth it. Rob has nothing prepared, and the judge doesn't take kindly to him, awarding me half of all marital assets within twenty minutes of stepping foot in the courtroom. I drop my head in my hands when he bangs the gavel, relief bringing tears to my eyes. It's over.

"You couldn't resist showing how much of a whore you are, could you?" Rob calls out, his face red. "Do your parents know you're sleeping with all of them?" Security grabs his arm and walks him down the aisle, but he has enough time to look at my parents directly. "How does it feel to know you raised a fucking whore?" He looks back at me as he's jerked out the door, rage pouring from him. "You'll pay for this, you fucking slut."

I look at my parents and see it on their faces that they're connecting the dots, recognizing the truth in his words.

"Whatever's going on in your head, stop," Jack murmurs, his voice low. "Lauren, I know you said not to, but she's hurting, and I need to get her out of here. Thank you for going to battle for her. We can't thank you enough."

"So it is true? You're with all three of them?" Lauren asks me, curiosity burning in her eyes.

Heat flares in my cheeks, mortification sinking in. I nod, too tired to pretend otherwise.

"Good for you, Charlotte. Get it, girl." She winks at me, packs her briefcase, and kisses me on the cheek. "Have a good life. I hope I never see you again."

"Charlie!" My mother's screech has me ducking down, nausea rolling in my stomach as years of verbal thrashings flash through my mind. Jack doesn't give her a chance to get close. He swings me into his arms, pushing past my mother, ignoring her demands to put me down.

"If you want to talk to her, you'll have ten minutes while we're packing her things," I hear Lach tell my mom, her indignant scoff making a wildly inappropriate giggle rise in my throat. Then we're out in the open air, speeding toward Cam, who's waiting at the curb with the car. I tense as Rob sees us and starts walking our way, ignoring the pleas of his lawyer.

"Just you wait, Charlie," he seethes, his voice getting louder with every word. "Everyone in this town will know what a cheating sl—" He crumples to the ground as Lach taps the back of his knee with the side of his shoe as he walks past. Lach looks down at him, hands balled into fists at his side.

"If her name ever passes your lips again, I will hunt you down and fucking ruin you, do you understand me?" He shoves Rob's shoulder with his foot, forcing him to lose his balance and fall back onto his hands. "I said, do you fucking understand me?" Lach seethes, enunciating every word.

"Yes! Okay? I understand." Rob holds his hands up in surrender, staying on the ground as Jack rushes me toward safety.

The car is dead silent as we pull away from the courthouse. I drop my head into my hands, my shoulders shaking uncontrollably.

"Charlotte?" Jack's hand is warm and heavy on my shoulder. I look up, tears streaming down my face. "Are you laughing?" he asks incredulously, his eyebrows nearly disappearing into his hair.

I snort, wiping at my eyes. "Did you see the way Rob looked up at

Lach? Like he was two seconds away from saying 'Yes, Daddy.'" Laughter grips me again, stealing my breath.

I sober up quickly as we pull in front of my parent's house. My mom is waiting for me on the front porch, arms crossed, a scowl on her face. This is going to suck.

109

My heart jumps to my throat and decides to stay there as I step out of the car and slowly start walking toward my mother. Her arms are folded over her chest, the muscle in her jaw clenching as I approach.

"Is this what you wanted? To make me a laughing stock? To drag my name through the mud? I always knew you didn't care about me, but I didn't realize how much until today."

I sigh, a dull pain stabbing behind my right eye. "Not everything is about you, Mom."

"It is when your husband yells in front of the entire town that you're sleeping with three men. What am I supposed to say when they start asking questions?"

"Ex-husband," I whisper, massaging my temples. "You can start by telling them the truth."

Her face goes even redder. "You want me to tell my friends you're *fucking* three guys?"

"At the same time. Yes." The corner of my mouth tilts up when her eye starts twitching. "Or you can tell them I moved to Scotland to be with the men I love. Men that respect and cherish me. Men that love me."

"And what? Huh? Live in some hovel while you pimp yourself out to market some grimy, run-down castle?"

I rear back like she slapped me. "You have no idea how far from the truth you are."

"Enlighten me."

I struggle internally before finally deciding to tell her, at the very least so she doesn't think badly about the guys.

"Jack is a *baron,* Mother. We'll all be living in his in-tact, gorgeous waterfront castle. Cam has his doctorate and works as a professor and researcher of archeology at a university one island over. Lach, well, let's just say Lach made some very good choices and isn't struggling. So, no, I won't be living in a hovel while all three of them rail me. I'll be helping make the castle sustainable for future generations."

"Future generations you can't have?" She sneers, looking down at my stomach like she can see the failure of my uterus from the outside.

"Fuck you." The words are out before I can stop them, and If I'm honest, I don't regret them one bit.

Suddenly, the front door swings open, and my dad peers out, tossing me a wink before grabbing my mom's elbow and hauling her inside the house.

"Give us one second, Charlie."

I nod, barely able to breathe with the adrenaline coursing through my system.

"Charlie, do you have boxes somewhere?" Lach asks, poking his head from around the side of the house.

"They're in the hall closet along with the tape. I never got rid of them because I hoped I'd be moving out of there quickly."

"And you were right, Carebear. Do you want me to stay with you while you talk to them?"

"No," I whisper, shaking my head. "I need to do this one on my own."

"Okay, you know where we are if you need us." He grasps my neck and pulls me toward him, kissing my forehead.

I blow out a long breath as he disappears around the side of the house. I can get through this. I *will* get through this.

"Congratulations, sweetie." My dad exits the house, closing the door firmly behind him.

"Thank you, Dad." I walk into his arms, melting into his embrace.

"I'm so proud of you, Charlie. I hope you know that. It took guts to stand up to that sorry excuse of a man." He holds me at arm's length, studying my face. "I'm going to miss you so much."

"About what Rob said," I begin, needing to explain.

"What Rob said is none of my business," he interrupts.

"I need you to know. I need Mom to know. I know it's unconventional, but I love them, Dad."

"Convention is for cowards. You've made a beautiful life with people who appreciate and love you. What more could a father want?"

"What about Mom?" I ask, my voice cracking.

"Give her time, Charlie. She'll come around."

"And if she doesn't?"

"Then she's missing out on the best thing that ever happened to us. And I may need you to make up a guest room for me."

I half laugh, half sob, hugging him tight around the neck.

"Go find your men and start your new life, Charlie. You deserve every single bit of it. I'll see you at the wedding." His gaze roams over my face like he's trying to memorize every feature, then he kisses my cheek and disappears inside.

Holy hell. I turn around, looking up at the sky in wonder. The two things I've been dreading for months are finally over.

"Charlotte?" Jack's gruff breaks me out of my euphoric reverie.

"Yes, Jack?"

"Where's the rest of your stuff? We found some art supplies, a few books, and winter clothes, but that's it."

"That's all I have."

"Is any of the furniture yours?"

"Nope."

"Nothing in a storage unit?"

I shake my head.

"Thank God. Let's get the fuck out of here."

"Where are we going?" I ask after they dump a couple of boxes in the trunk, our suitcases stacked between Cam and me in the back seat.

"Home," Lach says, meeting my gaze in the rearview mirror.

"You were able to schedule the flight that quickly?"

Jack laughs. "He's had the plane on stand-by the entire day, Sassenach."

The whole day? That must have cost a fortune. "We're really going home? Right now?" I wipe away tears of relief with the back of my hands.

"Right now, little witch."

My nervous energy turns to exhaustion the second we're in the air. I blink up sleepily at Jack as he lifts me into his arms and carries me back to the bed, getting under the covers with me, my head pillowed on his bicep. The next time I open my eyes, we're on the ground, and the guys are busy carrying all my worldly possessions to the waiting car. I stop at the top of the stairs, the wild Scottish wind whipping my hair around my face. It feels like it's been two days since the trial, but the sun is only beginning to set on this first day of the rest of my life. I grin at Cam as he jogs up the stairs, his blue eyes sparkling behind those dark-rimmed glasses. My heart fills to bursting as he folds me into his body, the embrace like something out of a movie.

"Ready to go home?" he asks, framing my face with his hands, neither of us able to keep the smiles from our lips.

"Yes," I breathe, blinking rapidly.

The sun sinks below the horizon as we pull into the driveway of the house, the sky streaked with orange and pink as the gravel crunches under our tires.

"Welcome home, mo chridhe. For good this time," Jack says as we pull to a stop, the castle lit up like a Christmas tree. It's the most beautiful thing I've ever seen.

Lach opens my door, extending his hand to help me out of the car.

"We have a surprise for you, Carebear. Would you like to see it now or in the morning?"

"Now!" I bounce up and down on my toes, excitement coursing through my system. The guys guide me around the side of the castle, along the loch, and up into the orchard.

"Close your eyes, little witch." Cameron ties a t-shirt over my eyes and takes my hand, drawing me out of the orchard and into the forest. I trip over a root, but strong arms sweep me up, whiskey and leather permeating my senses. A handful of steps later, Jack sets me down, removing the blindfold, his hands gripping my waist.

My heart thuds in my chest as I crack open my eyelids. Strings of fairy lights weave through the trees, warmth illuminating the run-down stone cottage I fondly remember. Except it's not run-down anymore. Glass has been fitted to the borders of the crumbling rock, extending the walls another story, making what looks like a giant greenhouse glowing from within.

"What is this?" I whisper, looking between them.

"Go inside," Lach says roughly, a smile pulling at his lips. I slip around the side of the building and push through a heavy wooden door. I stop dead in my tracks, tears streaming down my face. Over-flowing shelves fill one entire wall – neatly stacked canvases in every possible size, all kinds and colors of paints and brushes. A stack of easels leans against the opposite wall, the center of the room left open except for a gorgeous tufted leather couch. I look up at the soaring glass ceilings, dying to see the daylight streaming through, my fingers itching to pick up a paintbrush.

"When did you find the time to do this?" I ask, choking on a sob as I turn in a full circle.

"We worked on it before we left, but Isla's the one that pulled it all together so we could surprise you," Jack murmurs, coming up behind me. Lach and Cam stand to either side, looking around like they can't believe what they're looking at either.

"It's perfect," I whisper. "More than perfect. How can I ever thank you guys enough?"

"By painting us and hanging it on the wall so you don't forget we exist while you're holed up in here," Cam says, chuckling.

"I don't think it's possible to forget about you guys, but I would love to paint you." Lach starts unbuttoning his shirt, those perfect pecs making my heart jump. "Now?" I breathe, my gaze following his fingers down, down, down.

"Now." Lach folds his shirt and sets it on a shelf, doing the same with his pants. I gulp at the firm roundness of his ass, boxer briefs clinging to his skin and hiding absolutely nothing. Cam and Jack follow suit, and in under thirty seconds, I have the three hottest men I have ever seen standing in front of me, waiting for instructions. Fuck. I cross my legs casually, trying to stem the heartbeat that has taken residence between them, but Jack notices. I almost choke when his nostrils flare, his gaze locked to the V of my thighs like he can see through my clothes.

My artist's brain takes over quickly, and I know exactly how I want them. "Jack, you sit in the middle of the couch, lean back and drape your arms over the back. Lach, you sit on his left, your back in the corner, your legs angled toward Jack." I watch as they get into position. "Cam, you do the same things as Lach but on the opposite side. Good." I step back a couple of steps, studying them. "Both of you extend your outer legs, pointing them toward Jack," I instruct, pointing to Cam and Lach. "Perfect. Now reach toward each other with one arm – like in the Creation of Adam painting." With that reference, their posture changes to take on the fluidity of the painting. My heart jumps to my throat, their beauty hitting me in the gut. I swallow hard and clear my throat. "Let me snap a picture so you don't have to stay like that." I pull out my phone and take several pictures. I'm studying the photos, ensuring I've captured all the important details when I see the bulge in Jack's boxers. Fuck. I look up from the phone to find all three of them walking toward me, gazes dark, lust written clearly over their features.

"Let us celebrate you tonight, Charlotte." Jack reaches out, the rough sweep of his thumb over the back of my hand making my nipples pucker.

"We can help you forget all the shitty things that happened today," Lach says, cupping my face tenderly.

"Let us make this the best first day of the rest of your life, Charlie." Cam turns my chin toward him, nipping at my bottom lip.

How the hell can I resist them? I walk over to the light switch and turn it off, the soft glow from the fairy lights illuminating their features. I strip as I walk back to them, leaving my clothes in a puddle on the floor.

"Welcome home, Sassenach." Jack flattens his body to mine, our lips tangling in a heated, desperate dance.

Welcome home, indeed.

110

My bra slips through my fingers, joining the puddle of clothes at my feet. I don't move, my heart so filled with love that I can barely breathe. Soft golden light filters through the trees soaring above us, the high glass ceiling almost invisible. It reminds me of that day that Jack chased me out here, the vines and I both tumbling over crumbling stones. I look at them, at this place they've made for me, and I can't quite believe it. Jack reads every emotion on my face like he's been doing it his entire life. I don't need to say anything for him to know exactly what I'm feeling.

His lips meet mine with a need so fierce it brings tears to my eyes. "Don't think, Sassenach, just feel," he says roughly, his lips moving against mine, strong fingers cupping my face. I empty my mind, focusing on how his callouses tug at my skin as he slides his hand back to cup the base of my skull. He angles my head, deepening the kiss, giving me more than I would ever ask for. Lightning streaks over my skin as I pull him to me, our bodies fitting together like puzzle pieces. My breath strangles me as his hands sweep down my back and over my ass. He grips the back of my thighs and lifts me without breaking our kiss, my legs automatically wrapping around his waist.

He walks several steps, loosens his hold, and I slip from his arms onto the couch.

"Tonight is about you, Charlotte." Jack kneels at my feet, pulling them into his lap and pressing his thumbs into my arches until my eyes flutter closed, and I groan with pleasure. The couch dips on both sides as the guys join us, Lach on my left and Cam on my right. Having all three of them focused on me is overwhelming in the best way.

"The history nerd in me is geeking out over the fact that we're going to have sex in a chapel," Cam murmurs before bending toward me, his lips skating over my cheek.

"A chapel?" I ask, glancing around, tiny details I didn't notice before jumping out at me. The arched windows, the raised area that must have been the dais.

"Mmm," Lach groans, the sound slithering over my skin, leaving goosebumps in its wake. "Dirty. I like it." He nips at my bottom lip, hooded eyes stealing my attention.

"Our forbidden fruit," Jack rumbles, pulling my hips to the edge of the couch and pulling my knees wide. "So fucking sweet." He drags his lips up the inside of my thigh, and I shiver as his beard creates the most delicious friction. He stops shy of where I need his mouth, looking up at me as he drags his finger along my slit, then sinks it into his mouth, his eyes rolling back. He grips my neck and draws me to him, pushing his tongue into my mouth, our flavors melding together. Fuck. His hair is silky between my fingers as he kisses his way down my body. Cam and Lach move in, Lach tracing around my nipple with the lightest touch as Cam tilts my chin toward him, his gaze filled with so much emotion I nearly choke on it.

"I love you, Charlie." His touch is gentle as he closes the distance between us. Our lips spark as they touch, igniting a fire in my veins that will never be quenched. Soft curls crush beneath my hands as I pull him closer. I echo his moan as Jack traces his finger over my outer lips, the pressure so light that it has me arching my back, chasing his touch. Lach finally stops circling my nipple and drags his thumb over it, cupping my breast like it's a treasure he'll never give up.

"You're so fucking beautiful." I break the kiss, and Lach's hazel gaze locks with mine, holding me prisoner as he lowers his mouth to my nipple, swirling his tongue over me before sucking hard, a lightning bolt of desire hitting me squarely between my legs.

"More," I gasp, pushing my hips off the couch, desperate for relief. As Cam concentrates on my other breast, Jack commands my attention, hooded lion eyes tracking me like I'm his next meal. He drags his thumbs over my outer lips again, eliciting a choked, gasping sob.

"Jack." My voice breaks as his fingers move closer together, callouses riding over hypersensitive nerve endings. He switches direction before touching my clit, dragging his thumbs lower and lower until he's pushing them into me. I whimper, my body undulating beneath them as they worship me. Cold air caresses my breast as Lach moves his hand, skimming my stomach before sliding two fingers in a V over my vulva, narrowly avoiding my clit.

"Please," I beg. Cam swallows my groan as Lach presses down, rocking his hand back and forth before trapping my clit between his fingers and repeating the motion. I sink into a pool of molten lava, stars exploding behind my eyelids as I wrestle to keep my body under control.

"Charlie. " Jack's voice rips me out of my head and into the present, whisky eyes making me tipsy as he lowers his face between my legs. He moves Lach's hand back to my breast and then licks me right up the center, flattening his tongue against my clit. God. My thighs clamp over his ears, trapping him in place. He growls and pulls me closer, prying my knees open and pushing them wide until he has everything on display, like a king preparing to feast. He watches me with that predator's gaze as he bites my ass, slipping his tongue along my crack to circle my back entrance before focusing on my clit.

"This isn't working," Lach says suddenly, frustrated by his lack of access. He picks me up and hauls me outside, waiting for the guys to spread out an armful of blankets before laying me down. Jack is the first to join me on the ground, reaching and hauling me against his side, not stopping until my body is draped over his.

"Ride me, Charlie. I need to be inside you." I straddle his hips, holding his gaze as I lower myself onto his cock until he fills me completely. "Fuck," he breathes, his nostrils flaring, control slipping. He may have been desperate to be inside me, but *I'm* desperate for all of them. Right now.

"Can we try something?" I ask, my cheeks heating, unsure of myself.

"You don't have to ask that. Ever. The answer will always be yes," Lach smirks, eyes twinkling.

I stand up and move away from Jack. "Lach, lay down on your back and get as close to Jack as possible. I want your balls touching."

"Yes, ma'am." He salutes me and then steps close to Jack, sinking onto his ass and getting himself into place.

"Lach, put your left leg over Jack's leg. Good. Now the opposite on the other side." I watch as they follow my instructions, realizing this will be trickier than I thought.

"What is going through that dirty mind of yours, little witch?" Cam asks, raising one dark eyebrow.

"You'll see." I instruct the guys to get even closer, not happy until their cocks are only an inch apart. I step over them, facing Jack, sinking to my knees and spreading them wide to span their legs. Jack grabs my hips, Lach my ass, and I wrap my hand around their shafts, keeping the head of their cocks together as I lower myself onto them.

Fuck. A shiver wracks my body, pleasure coursing through me as they hit all the spots one cock will never reach. I breathe deeply, forcing myself to relax until they're buried inside me, their groans like a soundtrack to a filthy dream.

"Don't fucking move. Either of you," Lach pants, his hands kneading my ass cheeks as he struggles for control. I grin and squeeze around them, the pained look flashing over Jack's face telling me he likes this – a lot.

"Okay, Cam. Pick a hole. Mouth, ass, or pussy?"

"Three at once?" he asks, desire flashing in his dark blue eyes.

"This is a horrible idea," Jack grumbles, involuntarily squeezing his fingers as I adjust my position, leaning forward to give Cam access.

"It's the best idea I've ever had. I wasn't even sure it would work." I trail off as Cam lowers to his knees behind me, running his hands down my back and over the swell of my hips

"You're sure?" He slides his cock along the sides of my pussy, coating himself in my arousal, then adding some lube for good measure.

"I'm sure." His hand is warm against my lower back as he presses me down, his breath hitching when he sees them impaling me. "God, I wish you could see this, Charlie. Those pretty pink lips stretching wide for them." He hums under his breath, an erotic sound that has me pushing my ass back toward him, my nipples dragging over Jack's chest.

"Cam, please." My words are coated with desire, dripping with need. Cam gets closer, holding his cock steady as he slides it against me, searching for a place to notch himself. He finds it where Lach and Cam's shafts are pressed together, both of them groaning as he pushes forward, the tip not even in when the cursing starts.

"Charlie, I won't last," Lach pants, his thigh tensing under mine as he struggles for control. "My cock is being fucking sandwiched by three of the hottest people I have ever seen. I don't think I can do this."

I laugh, and all three of them shout at me to stop, making me laugh harder, my body squeezing them without mercy. I wipe at my eyes, getting myself under control. "Only a couple strokes, and then he can pick another hole, okay?" I look back at Cam and wink, making him blush. "Keep going," I urge, arching my back for him.

He blows out a breath as he pushes in a little farther, all three of them swearing when the head of his cock finally enters me. Oh, God. A moan claws its way up my throat as I adjust to being filled by all three of them.

"Are you doing okay?" Cam asks, tugging on my hair, so I turn my face toward him.

"Do it again," I whisper, my body strung tight as a bow.

Jack's jaw clenches as Cam pulls back out and pulses the head of his cock against them, against the already stretched skin of my pussy, the ridge catching with every pulse of his hips until all of our breaths join together in a ragged chorus.

"Cam," Jack growls his name like a warning, eyes wild, neck corded. "Fuck her or we'll all come before we want to." Cam's reply is muffled, his mop of curls the only thing visible as he watches his cock slide along Lach's and Jack's, finally – *finally* – filling me.

It was always supposed to be like this, all of us as close as we can possibly be, the heads of their cocks nestled at the entrance of my womb. I swivel my hips experimentally, obsessed with how it feels, but at the same time, knowing there's no way we can all finish like this without something tearing.

Cam pulls out and pushes back in, his fingers clenching on my waist, holding me still as he flexes his hips. So fucking deep. I whimper, squeezing around them, desperately wanting to reach for my clit, but knowing this will be over the second I do.

"One more time," Cam whispers, turning my face toward him, watching me with hooded eyes as he draws himself out, pushes me down on their cocks and slams back in. Pleasure rips through me, nearly toppling me over the edge, but he pulls out just as quickly, waiting for my instructions. I rise to my knees, motioning for him to come around to my front.

"Charlie—" he protests.

"Don't you dare tell me this is all about me, and I don't need to suck your cock, Cam. I want to taste all of us on you."

"Bloody hell," he rasps, coming closer, wrapping his fist in my hair and tilting my head back so he can watch me. I don't waste any time. I pull him to me, licking him from base to tip before swallowing him down to the hilt, rocking my hips as I take all three of them in a different way. Jack's hand slides down my back, spanning my ass as he teases my backdoor before pushing his middle finger in. I gasp around Cam's cock, struggling to control my gag reflex as Jack uses his finger like a hook, pulling me up and down on their cocks.

"Fuck, Charlie," Cam hisses, pulling my head back until only the tip is in my mouth. I sweep my tongue over him, greedy for anything he'll give me. Loosening his grip, he pulls away from my mouth, crouching down and fitting his lips to mine. The kiss is messy – need and desperation tangling us together until we can't breathe.

"Charlie, this is torture," Lach says, his voice husky. I hold back a smile, loving that they can't move, that I'm completely in control.

"Ready, Cam?" I ask, gazing up at him as he stands, his perfect body bathed in golden light. He doesn't need to ask what I want. Positioning himself behind me again, he spits on his fingers, massaging me until I squirm, my entire body clenching in preparation. I freeze as Cam slides the head of his cock back and forth over me, teasing sensitive skin. He doesn't make a move until I'm pushing back on him, and then he's sinking into me, filling me until I don't think I can take anymore.

"Fuck," Jack grinds out, his body bowing beneath me as he struggles to hold back.

"Now," Lach rasps, the word melting into a moan as I clench around them. Cam pulls me against his body, my back plastered to his front. He rakes his nails over my stomach, then slides his hand further south, trapping my clit between his fingers. Cam jerks, his body tensing, then groans, pushing his ass back before slamming into me.

"A little warning would be good next time," he says, looking back at Lach.

"Surprise!" Lach laughs, low and sexy.

Electricity races over my skin as we get into a rhythm, and I swear I can hear it crackling between us as ecstasy takes hold of the reins, whipping us into a frenzy of unbridled lust. My muscles spasm around them as I scramble for control, not wanting this to end.

"Come for me, Charlie." Cameron's breath is hot on my ear, his hand moving to my throat, forcing me to submit. Waves of agonizing bliss rock through my body, Lach and Jack's hands pulling me down onto their cocks as I come. Cam thrusts, his hip stuttering before he gives in, and then they all fall like dominoes.

They come as one, cocks flexing and hips straining as their empty themselves into me.

Holy fucking shit.

I slump against Cam, my thighs burning. He bands his arms under my breasts, lifting me as Jack disentangles himself and makes a spot for me to lie down. As soon as I'm free from them, Lach is between my legs, massaging my thighs, his gaze burning hot.

"There's no way I have a round two in me," Cam says, looking between us. "I'm going back to the house to shower and scrounge up some food." I reach up to him, pulling him down for a kiss before slapping him on the ass, yelling after him how much I love him.

"You look so fucking good with our cum dripping out of you," Lach says finally, sliding his thumb through it, and pushing it back inside. Jack comes and stands over his shoulder, his eyes dark.

"Whatever the two of you want to do, just do it," I chuckle. In the blink of an eye, I'm sitting on Jack's face. Lach straddles Jack's torso and pushes me forward so I'm supporting myself with my hands.

"This is what we want," Jack growls against my pussy, dipping his tongue into me. Lach spreads my ass cheeks, sliding his thumb in Cam's cum before getting in the same position as me to eat out my ass. God, this is so dirty. I should hate it. Make him stop. But I only push back, wanting more, greedy for every swipe of their tongues. Lach groans behind me and shifts his body back. I look underneath my arm as he pushes forward, Jack's cock dragging along his, both of them still hard as a rock. I stay in that position, watching what their bodies are doing as they feast on me. A wave of need grips me as Lach pulses forward enough for Jack's cock to catch on his ass, and then it slips between his cheeks as he pushes back, sliding along his crack. Jack groans beneath me, the sound vibrating against my clit, stoking the fire higher. I scramble to turn around to face Lach, moaning as Jack pulls me back down, fitting his mouth over my clit.

Lach sits up straight, letting Jack slide his cock up and down, precum dripping onto Jack's abdomen. I grab the lube and hand it to Lach, trembling hands squirting it over his ass and Jack's cock. If I weren't so fucking turned on, I would have laughed at the mess he made. I can tell the exact moment the head of Jack's cock slides over Lach's back entrance – the held breath, the need, the hope. And then it happens. Jack's cock doesn't slide past this time, it catches on the rim, and time seems to stop. After a moment of hesitation, Jack angles his hips and thrusts up, impaling Lach, their broken moans melding together. I'm already coming as I lean forward, grinding on Jack's face as I take Lach's cock in my mouth. One more thrust, one more sweep of my tongue and Lach's cum is filling my throat, his ass strangling Jack's cock, both of them coming together. We collapse against each other, breathing hard, Lach's low chuckle chasing goose-bumps over my body.

I swing my leg over Jack's face, collapsing to the blanket, trying to catch my breath. I hear clapping and glance over to see Cam grinning as he picks up the phone he must have forgotten. He drops to his knees beside Lach, kissing him hard, then turns to Jack and claps him on the shoulder.

"I'm proud of both of you," he says, angelic eyes flitting between them. "Now, let's go to bed, so we can wake up and do this all over again – every day for the rest of our lives." He helps the guys up, wraps me in a blanket, and swings me into his arms, kissing me softly. "Let's go home, Charlie."

The End

EPILOGUE
OCTOBER

The sun-warmed balustrade is rough under my fingertips as I trace circles on its time-worn surface. Orange leaves glow in the sunlight as they swirl in the breeze coming off the loch. I sit down on the top step, pulling my bare feet close to my body. I could look out over this view forever, though admittedly, today it's looking a little different with all the people running around like little ants. True to her word, Isla has taken care of everything. She showed me a ton of pictures, had me pick my favorites, and then took it from there. I couldn't be more thankful to have her carry the burden of decision-making while I settle into my new life.

I squint into the morning light, shading my eyes. Isla is hauling stacks of chairs into the field, a guy from the rental company huffing and puffing behind her. She sees me as I stand to grab my shoes and gives me a stern look.

"Don't you dare," she shouts. "If you want to help, grab the baskets by the door and collect moss from the woods." I gape at her. "I'm serious, Charlie. I have everything else covered."

"Okay, okay!" I throw up my hands in surrender. "Just promise to tell me if you get into a bind and need help."

"Don't forget about your makeup and hair consultation—" she glances at her watch, "—in three and a half hours."

"I won't. Setting an alarm now." I pull my phone out of my pocket and set a second alarm in case I miss the one I set a week and a half ago. I run inside, shove my feet in my barn boots, and grab the two gigantic baskets by the door. The grass tickles the backs of my knees as I trudge through the orchard and into the thick canopy of the towering trees. Everything here is muted and other-worldly, and it has quickly become my favorite place on the estate. Isla didn't tell me where she's planning to have the ceremony, but I secretly hope it's right here. Under these old-growth trees that have seen generations of love and heartache pass beneath their boughs. Trees that belong to the man I will soon share a last name with. Legally marrying Jack was the easiest decision any of us have ever made. We all agreed that the estate would eventually need a new generation to care for its ancient walls, plow its fields, and tell its story. All four of us wrote each other into our wills, doing more to cement our importance to each other than a marriage license ever will.

"Charlie?"

I spin on my heel, my heart in my throat. "Arty!" I drop my baskets and run to him, hugging him tight before leading him to a tall stump to rest his legs. "What are you doing all the way out here?"

"Nice to see you, too, lass," he chuckles, his eyes sparkling.

"I didn't mean—"

"The Scottish air is good for me. My bones felt younger the second I stepped off the plane. I'm not quite sure why I ever left."

"Arty. If you love it so much, stay. There is plenty of room, and I would be overjoyed to see your smiling face every day."

"I couldn't possibly impose on newlyweds." He pats my hand and closes his eyes, taking a deep breath of the pine-scented air.

"It's not an imposition if you're invited." I crouch in front of him, taking both of his hands in mine. "Thank you for coming, Arty. It means the world to me that you'll be performing the ceremony for us."

"*Thank you*, Charlie. I haven't had this much excitement in years."

Isla takes time out of her hectic schedule for the test run of my hair and makeup. I let her take the reins, and the result is stunning. My lips are a dark nude, putting all the attention on my smokey copper eyes that make the blue of my irises pop. The stylist pulled my hair off my neck, letting soft curls fall around my face.

"You're fucking perfect." Isla grins, taking out her phone and snapping a few pictures. "Your job for the rest of the day is to have a couple of glasses of wine and *relax*. Got it? Dinner will be here at eight and then we'll go over last-minute details with everyone. Have you heard from your parents yet?"

I collapse onto the couch, staring up at the ceiling. "No. The last time I talked to my dad, he said he was coming with or without my mom. At this point, I don't even know if I want her there."

"You'll have an amazing day either way, Charlie." Isla grabs my phone, connects it with the speaker, and plays my favorite playlist. "Enjoy the peace and quiet while you can. I doubt you'll get much time to yourself during the honeymoon."

I sit up, my heart pounding. "What honeymoon?"

She zips her lips closed. "Don't worry, I already packed for you." She crouches down in front of me, squeezing my shoulders. "*Enjoy yourself*, Charlie." She kisses my cheek, her intoxicating perfume invading my senses.

"You always smell so good."

"I'd say you could borrow it, but I don't think Jack wants you smelling like his sister."

"Yeah, probably not," I laugh, taking the champagne flute she holds out for me. She fills the glass a quarter of the way, then takes it from me and hands me the bottle.

"Drink up, bitch." She clinks her glass against the bottle, downs it, and walks out the door.

I watch her head back outside, my heart full. What would I ever do without her? I'm almost positive I wouldn't be getting married tomorrow if it hadn't been for her pep talks and gentle nudges. I only hope that one day I'll be able to return the favor.

Arty meets me in the front hall at promptly five minutes until eight, dressed up in his Harris Tweed. We walk outside together, arm in arm. I lead him around the side of the house and down the path to the long table Isla has set up near the loch. Cafe lights, strung between tall poles, twinkling over the sparkling place settings, mismatched tapers dotting the center of the table, candlelight flickering over mounds of cascading flowers. There's a smaller table to the side, two tall candelabras lending their light to show off a dozen silver chafing dishes. Isla is peeking into them, fussing with the levels of the fire beneath.

"Isla, this is beautiful!" I wrap my arms around her, squeezing tight.

"I'm glad you think so, Charlie." She holds me at arm's length, tears welling in her eyes when she sees what I'm wearing. "The family tartan?" I look down at my gown, the blues and greens of the tartan muted in the dim light.

"I wanted something special. Arty got in touch with the people he knows here in town and they were able to steer me in the right direction. Did I get it right?" I twirl, the full skirt swishing around my feet.

"It's not just right, it's perfect." She looks behind me and grins, taking a step back.

"Charlotte."

My heart jumps to my throat as I turn toward Jack. An impeccably tailored suit covers his giant form, the rich brown bringing out the gold of his eyes.

"That's a dangerous game you're playing, mo chridhe. Seeing your body draped in my colors makes me want to steal you away and keep you for myself." He slides his fingers over my palm, pulling my hand to his mouth, warm lips grazing my knuckles.

"I like dangerous games," I murmur, shrieking when strong hands wrap around my waist and spin me around. The emotions flickering across Lach's face rip the breath from my lungs. His eyes darken, that full bottom lip trapped in his teeth as he rakes his eyes over me.

"Am I invited?" he asks, raising an eyebrow. "You look ravishing, Charlie. God damn." He spins me under his arm, the corners of his mouth pulling up when I giggle. "I don't know what I did in a previous life to deserve you, but what I do know is I'm not going to take a single second for granted."

"You can take me for granted anytime," Cam pipes in, approaching with an easy smile. He stops dead in his tracks as I spin toward him, his hand flying to his chest. "Charlie. Fuck." He caresses my cheek, and then his hand is sinking into my hair and he's pulling me close, warm lips fitting to mine like a missing puzzle piece. "In less than twenty-four hours until I'll be able to introduce you as my wife," he says, pulling back, grinning. "I didn't think this day would ever come, but here we are. I love you so much, Charlie."

The dinging of silver against crystal grabs our attention, and we all turn to look at Isla standing at the head of the now-filled table.

"Welcome, everyone! Thank you so much for joining us in the union of four of my favorite people on this planet. If you have any questions about your part in the wedding, please ask me tonight. Also, we are keeping the details a surprise for our grooms and bride, so please, no chitter-chatter if they're within earshot. Now, eat, drink, and be merry!"

"The only thing you need to know," Isla says in response to my look of panic over the lack of instruction, "is Lorna and I will come to your room at three tomorrow so we can all get ready together."

"Okay." I take a deep breath, letting the nerves roll off my shoulders. "Thank you, Isla. I truly don't know what I would do without you."

"It's the least I could do to get the guys off my back," she jokes, waving off my praise.

I wrap my arms around her neck. "I mean it, Isla. *Thank you.* For everything."

"Anything for you, Charlie."

"I promise I'll return the favor someday."

"I'm counting on it."

Isla didn't plan fancy food for dinner; instead, she asked what everyone's favorite food was and, as a result, made everyone feel like a treasured part of the evening. I know almost everyone at the table:

Arty, Cam's parents, Lorna and her kids, Greer and Pen. There are two people I don't know: a priest and the man sitting beside him, their hands linked together, resting on the tablecloth. After dinner is over, Jack leads me over to them.

"Charlotte, this is my long-time friend Father Calum."

"It's nice to meet you, Father."

"Call me Calum. The pleasure is all mine." He turns toward the man beside him, "This is my—" he stops, his jaw working for a second.

"—his partner, Tyler," the man finished for him, his eyes sparkling. Forgive him, this is the first time we've been out together.

"The infamous Tyler," Jack says, shaking his hand. "I've heard a lot about you."

"I bet you have." The corners of Tyler's mouth pull up.

"Calum will preside over our formal vows, Charlotte. I'm not usually one to follow tradition, but we need our marriage properly recorded by both church and government to cover all bases." He turns to his friend. "Thank you for coming out."

"I'm not going to turn down a free meal, Jack. Nor will I ever turn down an invitation to this beautiful estate. It's been too long."

"We'll remedy that after the honeymoon. I'm ready to get back to our weekly dinners."

"Really?" Isla appears out of thin air, startling all of us. "We can start them up again?" She whips out her phone and presses record before Jack answers.

"Yes, Isla. We'll talk about it after the honeymoon."

"I'm going to hold you to that," she says, pointing at her phone, a stubborn tilt to her chin. She turns to me. "Charlie, I've come to steal you away. You need your beauty sleep."

"Isla, no. Please let me help clean up."

"Nope, the guys have it covered tonight. I'm coming up with you to check my email and go to sleep myself. I'm exhausted."

Jack takes me to Cam and Loch to say goodnight, then walks me up to the terrace, stopping on the bottom stair.

"Any signs of your feet getting cold, Sassenach?" he asks, studying my face.

"My feet are hot. So hot they're—" he pulls me in for a relieved kiss before I can finish. "—on fire," I murmur, my lips moving against his.

"Thank God, because I don't think I'd be able to give you up now, mo chridhe."

"Never gonna give you up," I sing softly.

"Did you just Rickroll me the evening before our wedding?" he asks, incredulous.

I laugh, his beard rough beneath my lips as I kiss his cheek. "Good night, Jack."

"Sleep sweet, mo chridhe."

I CRACK OPEN MY EYES, watching dust motes slow dance in the beam of sunlight streaming through the gap in the curtains. I was expecting some anxiety – panic even – not this effusive joy pumping through my body or the overwhelming sense of peace that has me grinning and kicking my feet. I get to marry three of my best friends today. Men that love me for who I am, not what I can do for them. It's the best fucking feeling in the world.

I check my phone to find a barrage of missed texts. Isla sent an itinerary: hair and makeup at two-thirty, get dressed at five, wedding at five-thirty. All the guys sent good morning texts and instructions to look outside the bedroom door.

I pull on my robe and pad to the door, peeking out into the hall-way. A pile of jewel-toned boxes sits in front of the door, a cream-colored envelope propped up against them. I gather everything into my arms and dump it on the bed, tearing open the card first.

Charlotte/Charlie/Carebear,

Open the red one first and the teal one last. We cannot wait to see you walking down that aisle toward us. We've been waiting our entire lives for you.

All our love,

Jack, Cam & Lach

Despite their instructions, I eye the teal box, my fingers itching to rip the paper off. I pick it up, turning it over in my hands. DON'T EVEN THINK ABOUT IT is written in thick black marker on the underside. I drop it like it burns me, stifling a giggle with my hand. I slide my finger under the bright red paper on the first present, carefully unwrapping an ebony velvet box. I open it carefully, revealing a delicate bracelet made from interconnecting links. A slip of paper reads *A little something to memorialize the moments we want to live on forever.* I set the box on the bed and unwrap the next one. Nestled inside are two tiny charms – a bar stool and a painter's palette. A piece of paper flutters to the ground, I pick it up and read *The moment I knew I was never going to be able to forget you and how I made sure you'd never forget me.* I chuckle. Our first time could have been missionary position in my bed, and I still never would have been able to forget him.

I clip them both to the bracelet and open the next box, snatching up the slip of paper before it can fall. *The moment Milo and I knew you were something special, and the moment we gave it all up for each other.* He chose a charm that looks exactly like Milo when he barreled into me that first day, and a tiny shack with the door hanging off its hinges. I blink back tears as emotion threatens to overwhelm me.

There are two boxes left before the teal box. I choose the one the same size as the previous two and open it to find an iridescent drop of water made from glass and a miniature book. *It's nearly impossible to choose only two moments. The tiny drop reminds me of when we walked out of the bookstore that first night. The way the sun shone through the sea spray and turned our world into something magical. The book is for so many memories — the weekend you helped me with inventory and we skipped out to go to the fairy glen, the night before I left when we made love surrounded by the classics, and finally, all the lonely nights I spent writing in the margins of Pride and Prejudice, desperate for you to understand the depth of my feelings.* I wipe the tears dripping down my cheeks as I clip on the charms. I'll treasure this for the rest of my life. The second to last box has a card tucked alongside it.

We each chose a memory of all of us together to commemorate. We'll let you guess who chose what. Tucked into the velvet are three charms. I carefully pick up the first, my mouth falling open as the details come into focus. It's a clawfoot bathtub like the one in the hotel in Edinburgh. The second charm is a picnic basket – it immediately reminds me of the day we spent at the abbey. The last charm takes my breath away. It's an exact replica of the castle: every tower and every turret are memorialized in shining gold.

My vision is blurry as I clasp them to the bracelet and fasten it around my wrist, lovingly running my fingers over each memory. Their gift couldn't have possibly been more perfect. I pick up the teal present, shaking it and trying to discern the rattle. There's a velvet pouch inside the box – this one is a beautiful shade of turquoise. I dump the contents into my hand, and my heart stops. It's a key fob. I clench it in my fist and run out of the bedroom, racing down the hallway and into the foyer, and burst through the front doorway. And there, in all her blinding glory, is a beautiful turquoise Jeep sparkling in the October sun. I snatch up the sheet of paper tucked into the windshield wiper.

Charlie,

I saw how you looked at every Jeep we passed when we were back in the States. I figured it would be the perfect vehicle to get around the farm and islands. I can't wait to see you in the driver's seat with your hair whipping around in the wind. We all paid for it, but I picked it out. Just needed to make sure you knew that ;)

Yours Forever,

Lach

I back up a few steps, taking in the tires that reach my hips, and the black accents that make her look like a bad bitch. I open the driver's door and launch myself inside, not able to wait to take her for a spin. It takes me a couple of minutes to get used to the feel of the tires, but by the time I'm turning onto the farm road, I'm golden. All the windows down, crisp air in my lungs, my hair blinding me, I race over the uneven graveled surface. I feel so free. Free from Rob. Free from my mom. Free from the judgment of a small-minded town. Free from a job I hate. Free to run toward everything I want. Suddenly this evening feels so far away. I want to see the guys now. I want to be wrapped in their arms, whisper sweet nothings in their ears. I turn around and drive back to the castle, resisting the urge to turn onto the main road and drive until I find them. Isla is standing on the front steps when I put the Jeep in park, her hand pressed over her heart.

"Is everything okay?" I ask her, hopping out.

"I swear to God, Charlie. If you ever scare me like that again—" She doesn't finish, just pulls me into a tight hug, tucking her chin between my shoulder and neck.

"Wait. You didn't think I was running, did you?"

"I didn't know what to think."

"I'll never run away from you or the guys, Isla. You're stuck with me whether you like it or not."

"Good. Lach did a good job, didn't he?" she asks, her gaze caressing the lines of Jeep. "I have to admit that I'm a bit jealous."

"I'll make you a deal. You can drive her anytime you want, as long as I get to drive the Mustang."

She snorts, then coughs, her eyes watering. "I'll think about it. You know that Mustang is my baby. Come inside and eat lunch with me while we have the chance. Lorna will be here in an hour, and then it will be absolute mayhem until the ceremony."

"Ready?" Isla asks a few hours later, tears threatening to carve a watery track through her freshly done makeup. She looks so beautiful wrapped in burnt-umber velvet, the dress fastened at her left hip with a kilt pin.

"Ready," I whisper, my heart in my throat. She turns me to face the full-length mirror. I take one look and squeeze my eyes closed, breathing long, shuddering breaths in and out. I slowly open them again, hardly able to believe the reflection in the mirror is me. "You're both fucking magicians."

"We *are* pretty amazing, but this is all you, Charlie," Lorna says softly, smiling.

It's only my second time wearing this dress. It was the first one I tried on, and both Isla and Lorna were insistent that it was 'the one.'

It fits like a glove and is the most beautiful gown I have ever seen, let alone worn. The neckline sits just off my shoulders, the sleeves puffing slightly at the shoulders and tapering to a snug fit at my wrists. Boning in the bodice sucks me in tight and puts the girls on display. The full skirt, made from the same blue-gray material, should be the perfect color to match the kilts I'm almost positive the guys will be wearing. Lorna spent the last two weeks adding embroidery to the contrasting center panel. I run my fingers over the stitching, marveling at the details.

"I hope you like it," Lorna says shyly, eyes shining, porcelain skin glowing against the deep russet brown of her dress.

"Like it?" I breathe, stepping closer to the mirror to see her work better. "You are incredibly talented, Lorna. When you said you would add embellishments, I thought you meant flowers or crystals. I never imagined this."

She had embroidered the story of our love into my wedding dress. A stack of books, a croissant, and the pub sign from Portree decorate the bottom of the dress. A little further up is a masquerade mask, the ferry, the cottage, and a piece of toast with one bite out of it on a plate with crumbs surrounding it. The cab, the abbey, and hotel are all there. Lorna has lovingly stitched every important piece of our story into the fabric, autumn leaves, acorns, and flowers tie everything together into a beautiful masterpiece.

I look closer at the castle stitched over my breastbone, down at the charm on my wrist, then at Lorna. "Did you—?"

"Guilty as charged," she says, winking. "The guys commissioned me to carve wax figures of the charms so they could have them molded and poured." She lifts my wrist, gently prodding at the charms. "They turned out beautifully."

"Thank you both." I sniffle, blinking back tears.

"Don't you dare start crying," Isla threatens, patting tissue at the corners of my eyes. She stuffs a couple of clean ones into the bodice of my dress. "Better safe than sorry," she chuckles, fussing with my curls before cupping my face and meeting my gaze. "You've made our whole family so incredibly happy, Charlie. Now it's our turn to attempt to pay you back. Enjoy yourself tonight, okay? Soak it in. Make memories."

Lorna hands us champagne glasses and holds hers up in the air, holding my gaze. "To the first day of the rest of your life."

We walk out onto the terrace, and they help me down the stairs, fluffing out my dress once we reach the grass. Lorna hands me a stunning bouquet of autumnal colors with hints of blue. The three of us link arms as we walk through the orchard, a deep sense of sisterhood tugging at my heartstrings. As we approach the forest, I can hear the dulcet tones of "The Skye Boat Song" greeting us. My heart flutters as the mounds of hydrangeas lining the aisle come into view, beams of sun shining down over pews tucked between the trees. I close my eyes and take a deep breath, then another, trying to calm my racing heart. When I open them again, my parents are walking toward me, a huge grin plastered on my dad's face, tears running down my mother's.

"Charlie. I'm so sorry." My mom holds out her hands but drops them when I don't come any closer. "I started going to therapy. I promise I'm going to do better. Be better."

"I'm glad you came, Mom." I smile at her and then turn toward my dad.

"Charlie. My baby girl. I don't think I have ever seen you this radiant. I am so damn *proud* of you."

"Thanks, Dad." I squeeze him tight, blinking hard to keep back the tears.

"Are you ready?" He links his arm with mine, ready to lead me down the aisle.

"I've never been more ready for anything in my life."

I CAN'T BELIEVE this is real life. Tiny fairy lights strung high in the trees fight off the twilight, lanterns illuminating the cascading hydrangeas spilling along the edges of the aisle. Only a couple more steps and I'll be able to see the guys standing there, waiting for me. Holy shit. I gulp lungfuls of air, trying to calm my nerves.

"Hey," Isla frames my face with her hands, locking eyes with me. "You've got this. Three men are standing at the end of that aisle that have been waiting their entire lives for you. You could be wearing a potato sack and they wouldn't care."

I know what she's saying is true, but my heart still feels like it's trying to gallop out of my chest. Lorna grabs my hand, squeezing it before heading down the aisle. Isla takes one last look at me and grins. "I'm so excited to call you my sister." She turns and sashays down the aisle, smiling and whispering greetings the entire way.

The music fades as the notes from a solitary bagpipe drift through the trees, bringing tears to my eyes.

"That's our cue, Charlie." My dad draws me to the head of the aisle, goosebumps racing over my body as strings accompany the bagpipe for a full rendition of "Red is the Rose." As we step past the trees blocking our view, everything comes into focus at once. A soaring arch at the end of the aisle is dripping with billowing hydrangeas. Moss and lichen tucked around the blooms make it look like it's been there for centuries. Arty is standing underneath it, wearing his best Harris Tweed suit, cheeks creased with a wide grin. I take a deep breath before swinging my gaze to the right, blinking back tears. Nothing could have prepared me. They're standing side by side, dressed in the MacLeod tartan, matching jackets hugging their frames. But all I can see is how they're looking at me, the tears in their eyes, the looks of disbelief passing between us, like none of us can quite believe this is really happening.

Lach staggers back a step. "Fuck, Charlie," he mouths, his gaze raking over me. Cam slowly shakes his head, his throat bobbing as he wrestles for control. Tears streak down Jack's cheeks, lower lip trembling, hands flexing at his sides like everything would be right in the world if he could just touch me.

My heart is in my throat as we reach the end of the aisle. Standing beside Isla, I kiss my dad on the cheek, and he joins my mother in a pew. Jack's luminous golden gaze traps me like a fly to honey. I can't look away as emotion devours us, the realization that our hopes and dreams are coming true finally hitting. Lach is standing at his shoulder, the joy pouring from him palpable. He reaches back, enfolding Cam's hand in his own as Cam clears his throat, his lips twisting as he struggles to contain everything he's feeling.

"I would like to welcome everyone to the handfasting ceremony for Charlotte, Cameron, Lachlan, and Jack," Arty begins, his voice ringing loud and clear. "I am honored to know all of them well and am thrilled that they found each other and asked me to perform their ceremony. Through this symbolic act of hand binding, they express their dedication to each other. The intertwining of their hands symbolizes the everlasting ties that will keep them united in matrimony." He holds up a cord that Isla and I wove together of ribbons we gathered from shops all over the island. "This cord serves as a continual symbol, a reminder of the unbreakable connections they establish today and the solemn promises they exchange."

He draws us around him, Jack across from me, Cam to my right, and Lach next to him, placing our right hands together. He begins weaving the cord around our hands and wrists. "As this knot is tied, so are your lives bound. All the dreams of love and happiness you have wished for are woven into this cord, infused into its very fibers. May this first binding serve as a firm foundation for your marriage, providing strength in times of struggle and a constant source of light during the darkest of nights." He squeezes our hands as he comes to the end of the ribbon. "Now it's time for the vows. Who would like to go first?"

"I'll go first if that's all right?" Jack fumbles around with his free hand, pulling a sheet of paper from his breast pocket. "As we stand under these ancient canopies, autumn leaves crumbling beneath our feet, I can't help but be reminded of you." He looks up from the paper, holding my gaze as he continues. "The sky is the exact color of your eyes when I told you I love you for the first time. The blush of the rowan tree reminds me of your freshly kissed lips. The gentle breeze against the nape of my neck is like the tender caress of your fingertips. Our love feels as old as the roots stretching through the dirt beneath our feet, as strong as the trunks reaching toward the warmth of the sun, like I find myself reaching for your hand day after day. You brought me back to life, mo chridhe." He pauses, his gaze encompassing all of us. "I am forever in debt to the force of nature that brought the four of us together, and I promise I will spend every day of our lives proving I'm worthy of this love."

Cam nods at Lach to go next. Lach sniffs, clearing his throat before beginning. "I'm not a wordsmith, so this will be simple and straightforward," he says, hazel eyes stealing the breath from my lungs. "I'm in awe of you, Charlie – of your bravery, your courageousness, the depth of your love. You've inspired me to be a better man since the day I met you, and I will spend the rest of my life attempting to deserve even a fraction of the love you give us." He looks around the circle, "I promise never to take what we have for granted." I give him a tremulous smile and then look at Cam.

The tumult of Cam's midnight gaze drags me under, drowning me in the depths of emotion radiating from him. He angles himself, our shoulders touching, his face only inches from mine.

"My nights belong to you, little witch," he begins, the rasp of his voice barely above a whisper, making the moment intimate, precious. "My days, too, of course, but God, nothing will ever compare to the gentle puff of your breath on my cheek while you sleep, the soft murmured words when it's only the two of us awake, or the way our legs tangle because we can never seem to get close enough." He cups the back of my head with his free hand, his thumb sweeping over my jaw. "You're my end and my beginning, the music to my words, my supernova. I'm nothing if you're not by my side, Charlie. Thank you for choosing me. For choosing us. For loving us for exactly who we are, nothing more, nothing less. I promise I will be here for you – for all of you—" he looks around, his gaze encompassing all of us, "—until my time on earth runs out."

I take an unsteady breath, not sure how I can possibly do my vows justice after they've poured out their hearts and souls so eloquently.

I steel myself so my voice comes out steady and true. "If I had known the pain I felt all those months ago would lead me to this – to the three of you – I wouldn't have wasted a single tear. My only regret is not jumping in head-first from the moment we met. I didn't understand at first, but I've come to realize I don't *need* to understand, I just need to accept your love. Jack, thank you for being my rock, the light-house that guided me to safe shores. Lach, thank you for being my ultimate hype man. For believing in me before I could believe in myself. For your unfailing belief that I would figure it out eventually. Cam, my poet, thank you for your quiet words and unfailing love. For your unquestioning faith that we could somehow make this work. And will you look at us now." A tear runs down my cheek when I meet his gaze, the poignancy of it all crashing into me like a tsunami. "I will never have the right words to tell the three of you how happy and fulfilled you make me, so I'll just have to spend the rest of my life showing you."

Arty begins winding a second cord – this one ancient, handed down through generations – around our joined hands. "Just as your hands are tied in unity, so too are your hearts, minds, and souls inter-twined. Bound by love, trust, and companionship, these knots symbolize a lasting connection. May the bonds of this handfasting strengthen with every hurdle you overcome and success you achieve. May your love shine as a guiding light, inspiring all who cross your path."

"As a representation of your everlasting love and unwavering commitment, please exchange rings."

I turn to Cam, pulling one of four identical rings from the bodice of my dress. "With this ring, I give you my heart and my forever." I push the ring onto his finger and kiss him on the cheek, my heart swelling as he turns to Lach.

"This ring signifies my eternal commitment and love for you." He slides the ring onto Lach's finger, both of them exchanging a grin before Lach turns to Jack.

"With this ring, I pledge my unwavering devotion and a lifetime of happiness together." Lach pushes the ring onto Jack's thick finger and then squeezes his hand, slapping him on the shoulder.

I'm holding my breath as Jack turns to me, the final vow officially closing our circle of love.

"As I slide this ring onto your finger, I seal a promise transcending time and space. Through the highs and lows, I vow to be your rock, companion, and greatest advocate. This ring symbolizes not just our commitment to each other, but our shared dreams, our shared joys, and our shared future."

Our hands stay joined together as Father Callum takes Arty's place. "Jack, repeat after me." I hold Jack's gaze, his words washing over me.

"I, Jack, take you, Charlotte, to be my wife, to have and to hold from this day forward, for better, for worse, for richer, for poorer, in sickness and in health, to love and to cherish, till death do us part. This is my solemn vow."

"Charlotte, repeat after me."

"I Charlotte, take you, Jack, to be my husband, to have and to hold from this day forward, for better, for worse, for richer, for poorer, in sickness and in health, to love and to cherish, till death do us part. This is my solemn vow."

Arty switches places with Father Callum. "I now pronounce you —" Arty stops abruptly, all of us realizing at the same time that we didn't discuss this part. "—husbands and wife," he finishes, shrugging his shoulders, his eyes sparkling. He takes his time undoing the cords, a smirk pulling at his lips. "Kiss if you must," he grumbles, giving us an exaggerated wink. All three of them are on me before I can blink, kissing me until my toes curl in my shoes.

"That'll have to do. For now," Jack murmurs, all of us breathing hard, dying to disappear into the woods for some privacy. We turn as one, gripping each other's hands, raising them in the air, celebrating a love that should have been impossible. Cheers go up as we race down the aisle arm in arm.

Orange streaks across the sky as the photographer takes his pictures, nothing posed, only candids of us in our post-nuptial haze. We let the music guide us to the reception, where we find that Isla has outdone herself, yet again. The studio is lit up from within by hundreds of candles, white tablecloths, crystal, and hydrangeas giving an ethereal feel to the space. A parquet dance floor is set up outside under the cafe lights strung through the trees. It feels like we've been transported to a court in some faraway fairy land.

"What do you think?" Isla asks, slipping between the guys to wrap her arm around my waist.

"Isla, you've truly outdone yourself. I owe you big time."

"We can talk about that when you get back. The boss just told me he's getting ready to retire and the bar is mine once he does. I'm going to need help giving it a facelift."

"What? Isla, that's so exciting!"

"Shh, you're going to jinx it. I'm not going to tell anyone else until the paperwork is signed." She swirls out in front of me, her dress swishing around her ankles, a huge smile on her face. "Ready to dance?"

Our first dance isn't traditional – how can it be when there are four of us? Instead, we choose to have all the guests join us on the dance floor as "At Last" floats in the air around us, and we all croon along. Wrapped in their arms, I know I've finally found the home I've been searching for.

"So, who's going to give me a hint about the honeymoon? When do we leave? Where are we going?"

Jack's chuckle slides over my skin like silk. "God, I can't fucking wait."

Lach checks his watch. "We leave in ninety minutes. We're going somewhere private and warm."

"That's all I get?"

"Oh, that's not all you're going to get," Cam whispers, his gaze raking over me like I'm not wearing a stitch of clothing.

Jack pulls me close, his lips against my ear. "We're going somewhere we don't have to wear clothes—"

"—and you can scream as loud as you want when you come, and nobody will hear you," Cam finishes.

"And it has a playroom," Lach says nonchalantly, his poker face failing to hide the need burning in his eyes.

"A what, now?" I whisper, my jaw on the floor.

"Otherwise known as a sex dungeon. It's exactly what you think it is, mo chridhe. Get ready for the best seven nights of your life." Jack spins me around and presses me against a nearby tree, pushing his thigh between my legs as his lips devour mine.

Seven Nights. Three guys. One sex dungeon.

This is going to be the hottest honeymoon ever.

Do you want to keep reading? Charlie's honeymoon and so much more available Ream! https://reamstories.com/daphneleigh

ISLA

Keep reading for a preview of Isla's story! Available November 26th in ebook and paperback. Audiobook coming soon!

    https://a.co/d/9y39WT0

Want to read Penelope's story while I'm writing it? Come join us on Ream!

    https://link.Authordaphneleigh.com/Exclusive

1

I slide off the bed like a boneless jellyfish, desperate not to wake the snoring fucker who fell asleep with his cock still inside me. *Before* he got me there. Asshole.

All I need is a good dicking down every two weeks, and I'm golden, but that's nearly impossible when I depend on tourists to visit this tiny remote island I call my home. And then finding one that knows their way around a woman's body? Not likely.

I gather my clothes and tiptoe straight through the front door of his Airbnb, the brisk April breeze nipping at my ass as I pull on my jeans, sweatshirt, and jacket. What a fucking waste of a good cock. I take one last look at the door, hoping he'll stick his head out, make up some excuse about his sub-par performance, and drag me back inside to change my mind. He doesn't. I gather my hair over my shoulder, braiding it quickly before jamming my helmet over my head. I swing my leg over the bike, stomping on the kick start and revving the engine. I get lost in thought as I take the winding streets back to my house, the full moon casting an ethereal silver glow over the landscape.

If I'm honest with myself, I no longer have the emotional fortitude for this. Becoming a celibate cat lady seems like a far better option.

My stash of toys can keep me happy without dealing with the headache of men. I have too much on my plate anyway. Between my sister-in-law, Charlie, almost ready to give birth, helping my brother with the castle, and rehabbing the bar, I'm lucky to make it home at the end of the day with the energy to wash my face. Thank the gods Charlie's guys like to cook–I would have starved to death by now.

I can taste a hint of summer in the air as I take a deep, calming breath. I tell myself everything will settle down soon. Charlie and the guys will finally find a crew to work on the castle, and I'll book an appointment with the lawyer so James can sign the pub over to me— something I've been putting off for far too long. The dark, hulking shape of the house looms over me as I pull into the driveway. I cut the engine and sigh into the silence. It's too quiet now that Lach and Charlie moved in with Jack. I promise myself that I'll move my stuff to the cottage behind the house first thing tomorrow and list the house online as a holiday rental.

After a good night's sleep—thanks to my battery-operated boyfriend—I roll out of bed, gulp down a protein shake, and spend the day moving into the cottage. I have no idea why I waited so long. I've always loved it. A huge picture window looks out over the sea, an office, a tiny bedroom, and an even tinier kitchen. Perfect for a single gal. All I need now is a cat.

AFTER SPENDING the day moving my belongings and cleaning the house, I work a full shift at the pub.

I fucking hate this place.

No. That's a goddamned lie.

I love it so much that sometimes I can't stand it–like a lover that hangs around so long that you start to feel claustrophobic. I look up at the thick wood beams, scrubbed clean from years of smoke by Charlie and me. James had looked at us like we were crazy, but I could tell he was impressed with the final results.

Tonight, the bar is overflowing with regulars. So regular, I don't even need to think about what they want to eat or drink. I know their wives and their kids, their vices and idiosyncrasies. I also know exactly which ones will bitch and moan when I kick them out promptly at eleven. I lock the door behind them, take the till back to the office, and bag the money to take to the bank in the morning.

"Night, James!" I call as I head toward the back door, wincing as my boots stick to the floor. I'll have to come in extra early to mop tomorrow. "James?" I backtrack toward the bar. Every other night, he's there like clockwork, babying the scarred wood that's provided a good life for him and his family–but it's empty tonight. A low groan has me throwing my shit on the bar and launching myself over it. James is slumped in the corner, drool stringing from the side of his mouth to his shoulder. I curse as I snatch my phone from my back pocket and call an ambulance. I set it on the bar, hitting the speaker button before crouching on the floor. I grab his jacket and pull him onto his side. My legs fold under me as I sit, gently resting his head on my lap. I murmur softly to him as I run my fingers over his thinning gray hair. His breaths are shallow, each one ending in a horrible wheeze.

"James, stay with me. Please stay with me." Why the fuck are they taking so long to get here? I press a hand to my mouth, holding back a sob. He can't die. He's the only father figure I've had since I was barely a teenager. My parents had taken care of me financially before they died, but James gave me the unconditional love that was missing. My siblings had been there for me but were older and had their own lives to worry about. James had swooped in and provided a safe space and a comforting shoulder. I didn't need the money, but I started working for him as soon as I was of legal age just to help him out. He never stopped needing help, so I stayed.

I jump when a stretcher bangs through the kitchen door next to the bar. I stand up, shoving my jacket under James' head before standing, wiping at my cheeks with my sweater. The paramedics ask me a million questions I can't answer. "Just please fucking hurry," I whisper, my heart breaking with each rattling breath. I follow them out, locking the door before I climb into the ambulance.

"Miss, are you family?" a man asks, reaching toward me.

"I'm not fucking leaving him," I spit, swatting his hand away. The man holds both hands up and backs away. "Is he going to be okay?" I ask the woman taking his vitals, my gaze glued to James' face, willing his eyes to open. Desperate to see those sparkling blue eyes one more time.

"I'm not sure," the woman says honestly, fitting an oxygen mask over his face. "I think he may have had a heart attack. His vitals aren't looking good. They'll try to stabilize him at the hospital and then run some tests." I can feel her looking at me, but I can't bear to look at her face and see the truth.

They wheel him away the second we get to the hospital. I wait in the hallway, pacing back and forth for what seems like hours. I've seen this scene too many times in a million different movies, and it never ends well. I slump into a chair and drop my face into my hands. I have to keep myself together. No matter what happens, I'll have to be at the bar tomorrow or the day after. People in our community rely on it—whether it's to drown the sorrows of the past or for a hot dinner and company.

"Miss?"

I look up into the face of a doctor barely older than me.

"Please tell me he's okay," I rasp, blinking back tears.

The doctor shakes his head. "I'm sorry. We tried to stabilize him, but his heart just couldn't keep going."

I wipe away my tears with the back of my hand, forcing myself to take a deep breath.

"Are you the next of kin?"

I shake my head. "His son lives in London."

"Do you have someone that can come pick you up?"

I nod, sniffling. "Yes, I'll call my brother. Thank you for trying." I give him a watery smile and walk away, the sob I've been holding in constricting my chest until it hurts. I text Jay quickly and then burst through the doors, taking deep gulps of the night air.

Then I scream.

I scream for James and the reconciliation he'll never have with his son. I scream for me, for the hole in my chest he used to fill. I scream for the pub and the uncertainty surrounding it now that he's gone. Jack pulls up on his motorcycle, sweeping me into his arms and hugging me tight, my sobs muffled against his chest.

"You're staying at the castle tonight," he says gruffly, leaving no room for argument. Not that I would have argued anyway. I want to be surrounded by people I love. Lord knows I'll need their help to figure everything out come morning.

I STUMBLE up the steps to the castle's front door a few minutes later, falling into Charlie's soft embrace. She squeezes me and kisses my forehead.

"I'm so sorry, Isla. He was a great man." I can only nod, not trusting the tremble in my lip. "Come on, I'll make you something to drink." She pulls me by my hand as she waddles toward the kitchen. "Liquor or cocoa?"

I laugh weakly, dragging in a ragged breath. "Cocoa would be nice."

"Sit." She pushes me into a chair at the table.

Lach and Cam come into the kitchen together, Jack a few steps behind them. Cam squats down next to me, pulling my hand into his. He and Lach were Jack's roommates back in college, and over the years, they've become like brothers to me. Charlie was the one that brought them all back together again. Now she wears three stacked engagement rings and one wedding band on her left hand. I've never seen them happier.

"What can I do?" Cam asked, his fingers squeezing around mine.

"Just being here helps. I don't want to be alone."

"You got it, Bug."

I wrinkle my nose at the nickname, pretending to hate it even though I've grown to love it. Not that I would ever tell any of them that.

Lach sits on my other side and pushes his phone into my hand, a video queued up.

"What's this?" I ask, thankful for the distraction.

"Charlie started making promotional videos for the castle. They're brilliant."

Charlie pauses in the middle of stirring the pot of milk, her eyes sparkling at the praise. "I opened a couple of social media accounts. I'm just experimenting right now."

"Did you find a crew yet?" I ask them.

"Not yet. Everyone's booked up for months. Right now, I think we're just going to do tours," Lach says, sitting next to me.

I raise my eyebrow, looking at Jack, "You're okay with that?" Before meeting Charlie, he treasured privacy the most, so this is a complete surprise.

"I'm more than okay with it. Starting slow is better than not starting at all. I've been hemorrhaging money for years to keep the castle up."

I wince slightly, feeling bad that the castle had fallen into Jack's responsibility by default. I was too young, and our sister Laurel had no interest.

I WATCH THE VIDEO, grinning from the first second to the last. Charlie had made the guys take off their shirts and do a mini-tour. It's possibly the best thing I've ever seen. I wipe tears from my eyes for the tenth time that day, but they're happy tears this time.

"Cocoa is ready!" As the guys grab mugs, Charlie brings the pot and ladle to the table, setting it on the scarred surface.

"What will happen to the pub?" Jack asks, wiping the cocoa from his mustache.

"James told me a million times he would leave it to me, but I don't think he ever actually made it legal." I sigh, wishing I had pushed him to make a will. "It'll go to his son, I guess."

"What will his son do with it? He's some city bigwig, right?"

I nod. "He lives in London. If I could guess, he'll sell it to the highest bidder."

"That's in our favor, then," Jack says.

"True, but I'm not going to overpay for it when the money goes to the person who never once came to visit his only living relative. Fuck him."

Charlie chokes on her cocoa, eyes watering as Lach slaps her on her back. "Just make sure you call him soon, Isla. If he's that cold, he may try to sell it right away."

"That's going to be a fun phone call." I grimace.

"I can call for you," Lach offers.

"No, I need to do it." I yawn, exhaustion settling over me.

"Finish up," Charlie says, gathering empty mugs. "I'll sleep with you tonight."

"Thank you. All of you." I smile at them, failing to smother another yawn.

"G'night, Bug," Lach says, ruffling my hair.

"Night," I murmur, squeezing Cam's hand as he passes.

Jack pulls me into a quick hug. "Let me know if you need anything. Love you."

"Love you, too."

Charlie pulls me out of the chair and down the hall to the guest bedroom. I flop on the bed, descending into sleep almost immediately. I barely feel her untying my boots or easing my jacket off. She had shown up out of the blue a year ago and became the bond that glued our family together. She's my ride-or-die. My best friend. I snuggle into her side and fall into a deep, dreamless sleep.

2

———————

The silence is suffocating as I hoist myself into a seat at the empty bar. I closed the pub yesterday in honor of James, but we're open as usual tonight, and I need to be on my A-game. I know that's what he'd want. I fiddle with my phone, trying to drum up the courage to call James' son. I never let guys intimidate me, but this is different. I thought I would spend my entire life in this pub. It's my home. Now that everything hangs in the balance, I can't stop thinking about what'll happen if he doesn't accept my offer.

I slam my fist on the bar. Fuck this. I punch in his number and hold the phone to my ear. Taking a deep breath, I count to ten before releasing it.

"Thank you for calling Andersen Law Firm. How may I direct your call?" a sweet voice asks on the other end of the connection.

"Mr. Andersen, please."

"May I tell him who's calling?"

"Isla MacLeod."

"Please hold, Ms. MacLeod."

My heart ratchets up a notch as the hold music nearly ruptures my eardrum. *Fucking breathe, Isla.*

"Andersen."

I jump at his curt voice but quickly recover, pulling myself together. "Mr. Andersen, this is Isla MacLeod. Before I begin, I want to offer my condolences for your father's death. He was a great man."

He grunts.

I clear my throat, plowing ahead with my spiel. "I've been working for your father for years. We had a verbal agreement that I would take over the pub. I'm not sure if he talked to you about it. Or me." I know full well he didn't. He never picked up when James called him.

"He didn't."

"I'd like to make an offer."

"How much?"

Fuck, this guy didn't mess around. "I looked at similar businesses in surrounding towns, and seventy-five thousand pounds seems more than fair."

He grunts again. "I'll have a real estate lawyer look into it and get back to you."

"I'm open to negotiation," I say, unwilling to risk him selling it to someone else. He ignores me.

"Is the pub closed down now?"

"I was planning on opening it today and keeping it open through the sale–if that's amenable to you."

"As long as you're aware that you can't keep the money just because you're running the pub in the interim. All proceeds will be transferred into my father's estate."

"That's perfectly fine as long as we agree that you'll get back to me on my offer."

"Good. Anything else?"

"When are you planning on having your father's funeral? There are a lot of us here that would like to attend and pay our respects."

"I'm flying his body to London. His burial will be here."

"Oh." My heart breaks. James would hate that.

"If there's nothing else, I need to end our call."

"That's all, thank you." He hangs up before I can give him my information, so I call back and give it to his secretary.

Goddammit. I should have flown to London to talk to him face to face, where I could see his body language and get him to agree to the sale in person. I sigh, jerking my hands through the knots in my hair. There's no time for a pity party when I have so much work to do. With James gone, I'm the only one here besides the kitchen staff–who are now getting paid out of my pocket. Which means I'm the only one working front of house. It's a bloody nightmare.

Days pass by in a blur. I collapse into my bed at 1 a.m. every morning and head back to work at 10 a.m. to prepare the pub for lunch. As soon as I get word on the sale, I'll hire help, but until I have the signed contract in my hands, I'm not spending a single cent more than I need to. So, for now, it's just little old me. And little old me is fucking exhausted.

I STILL HAVEN'T HEARD from James' son two weeks into this hell. I've called and left messages with his secretary three times, but beyond going to London myself, I'm not sure what more I can do. If I haven't heard from him in two more days, I'm going to close the pub and make the drive down. I'm getting desperate.

A NOTIFICATION STARTLES me awake at four the following morning, telling me the house has just rented for the next three months. It's a fucking headache, but there's no way I can resist the influx of much-needed cash. I receive a monthly stipend from a trust fund my parents set up before their deaths, but I'm stretching that thin by paying the kitchen staff. Now I have to spend my entire Sunday–my only day off–cleaning a gigantic house for a stranger. Far from the day of rest I had been dreaming about all week.

The Manor House is technically the groundskeeper's house for Amhuinnsuidh Castle. Jack took over the maintenance of the castle when our parents died. I lived with him until I turned eighteen, when I realized I didn't want him breathing down my neck every time I brought a guy home. Lachlan joined me in the manor house a year later when he returned to help Jack with the estate. It was nice having him around—especially his cooking.

I'M SERIOUSLY REGRETTING my decision to rent out the house by the time I finish scrubbing the fifth and final bathroom. It's nearing nine o'clock when I wheel out the last of my odds and ends in an old, beaten-up suitcase. I pick my way down the treacherous path to the cottage with only the light of the moon to guide me. By the time I reach the door, it feels like my shoulder has been ripped from its socket. I jerk up on the door handle and jam my hip into the wooden planks, huffing in frustration. No matter how many times I've tried to fix it, the door insists on being a stubborn asshole. I have to throw my entire body against it before it finally opens. I leave my suitcase in the entry, set my alarm on the way to the bedroom, and throw myself onto the bed, passing out the second my head hits the pillow.

I JERK awake to my alarm blaring under my ear, my cheek sliding over a cold puddle of drool as I slide my hand around the bed, trying to find my phone.

"I'm bloody awake," I mumble, stabbing the off button. The cold morning air sends a shiver down my back as I throw my legs over the side of the bed and sit up. I haven't woken up this early on a Monday in ages. The only saving grace is that I'm headed to the café to pick out some pastries for the new tenant. I'll also be grabbing the largest coffee they offer. Maybe two. I stumble to the bathroom and step into a scalding shower. After scrubbing myself from head to toe, I dry off and pad into the bedroom, grimacing at the state of the clothes over-flowing the drawers of the tiny dresser. I pull out the least wrinkled tank top and a pair of jeans. A leather jacket over the top hides most of the creases, and my boots complete the whole 'leave me alone, I'm a bad bitch' vibe I have going on. I stop by the bathroom once more to brush some mascara over my lashes and attempt to wrangle my hair into a braid. I snag my keys from the table by the door and walk up the path toward the garage. My fingertips are freezing as I key in the code to the garage door and watch my pride and joy come into view.

Years ago, Jack had imported a motorcycle. I jumped on the opportunity and upped it to a shipping container, importing the twin of Jack's bike and the car I've wanted since middle school. Her sleek lines give me goosebumps every single time. Nothing compares to the '67 GT500, my very own Eleanor. I sink into the seat and start her up, the sound of the engine roaring through my veins. I open the throttle as wide as I can for the two miles to the café. I pull into the parking lot slowly, trying my best not to disturb any of the customers. *I love how the car sounds, but that doesn't mean everyone wants to hear it at seven o'clock in the morning.*

This café is my favorite place in the entire world. It sits on the edge of a cliff, a gorgeous beach with turquoise blue water off in the distance. Besides the scenery, their food is fantastic. I come here almost daily, primarily because I can barely cook an egg, let alone an entire meal.

"You're up early, Isla," Jan says, greeting me with rosy cheeks and a huge smile.

"Right? It's a miracle," I laugh. "Someone's renting the Manor House, and I wanted some pastries to give them. Do you care to make me up a box?"

"Of course! Would you like anything to eat for yourself?"

"What kind of question is that?"

"Your usual, then? Morning bun and extra-large iced coffee to go?"

"Yes, please." I run my card through and thank her as she hands me a box, a bag, and my coffee.

"Give me the scoop as soon as you can, okay?" she whispers conspiratorially.

"You got it!" I whisper back, winking at her before I shoulder through the door and walk out into the brisk air. Jan is single, too. But unlike me, her biological clock is ticking. Loudly. It's been sad watching her wait for the right man to walk through the door year in and year out. I wouldn't be surprised if she takes matters into her own hands soon. Lord knows she has enough people in the community willing to help her care for a baby.

I place the box carefully in the car and sit at one a picnic table with a gorgeous view of the sea while devouring my morning bun and sipping on my coffee. I save the middle for last, licking the cinnamon sugar from my fingers before tossing my trash in the bin and heading home. I open the throttle, the wind whipping my hair free from its braid, enjoying my last moments of freedom before I have to worry about a tenant.

I notice three things as the house comes into view. The first is that the renter must be early because there's a car in the driveway. The second is the group of burly men standing on the front stoop, all staring at my car, their mouths hanging open. The third thing has my tires squealing to a stop in the driveway. I know them.

Glasses Guy, Henry, and Grumpy McGrumperson are standing in front of my house. The same three guys I *almost* considered entertaining last summer before I decided it would be way, *way* too much trouble. I fling open my car door, boots crunching in the gravel as I step out. I stare at them, hardly able to believe my eyes.

"Isla?" Henry asks, his voice cracking, eyes wide.

"The three of you rented my house? If I had known it was you, I wouldn't have spent the entire day yesterday spit-shining the fucking floors." I grab the box of pastries from the car and stalk toward them.

"This is *your* house?" Grumpy asks, incredulous.

"Yes, this is *my* house." I smirk. "But don't worry, you three will have it all to yourself. You can walk around naked and flex your muscles at each other all you want. I'll be staying in the cottage back there." I point with my chin.

"I got these for you." I shove the pastries into Grumpy's arms since he's the closest. "What are you guys doing here anyway?" I eye Henry. "Coming back to your favorite place for another holiday?"

Henry clears his throat. "Not quite a holiday. We bought the pub. The one where you work."

The blood drains from my face. "You what?" I whisper, needing to hear it again.

"We bought the pub," Grumpy repeats, annoyed.

"*I'm* buying the pub." My heart's in my throat, making it hard to breathe. I blink hard as tears start to sting the back of my eyes. I *will not* cry in front of them.

"*You?*" Grumpy laughs.

"Yes, me, you motherfucker. I talked with the owner's son. James and I had a verbal agreement for months."

Glasses Guy takes a step toward me. "He didn't tell us he had another offer. If we had known..." He trails off.

"I call bullshit." Grumpy snatches a croissant out of the box and tears into it.

"Is the fact that I've worked the front of house *alone* for the last two weeks bullshit? Maybe me paying the kitchen staff out of my own pocket is bullshit. OR MAYBE ME WORKING THERE SINCE I WAS SIXTEEN, POURING MY BODY AND SOUL INTO THAT PUB IS BULLSHIT!" I yell in his face. I knock the croissant out of his mouth and stomp on it.

None of the guys say anything.

"Sell it to me," I say finally, looking between them, holding their gazes until they look away.

"Never." Grumpy folds his arms over his chest.

I don't trust myself, so I throw the house keys at his head and return to my car, spraying gravel as I peel out of the driveway.

I SPEND the rest of the day on the tractor, readying the ground for my annual sunflower field between the Manor House and the castle. My mom used to plant one yearly, and I've kept it going in her memory. I usually would have already sown the seed, but with the chaos at the bar, I had let the rest of my life slip.

The sun is heading toward the horizon when I see Grumpy walking across my freshly plowed rows. Motherfucker. I turn the tractor off, climb down, and lean against the tire as I watch his shiny boots get swallowed up by the freshly turned dirt.

"Isla–"

"I don't want to talk to you."

"Will you just fucking listen?"

I sigh, tearing my eyes away from his full lips and picking at a rock stuck in the tire. "First, I don't even know your name. Second, why would I listen when you've been such an ornery asshole?"

He growls at me. "Theo. Nice to meet you. I'm sorry, okay? I know I was a jerk back there. At least let me explain."

"Explain why you're an asshole? Or why you think you can come in here with your daddy's money and buy up a piece of my town?" I die a little inside the second the words leave my lips. Why did I say that when I directly benefit from generational wealth? Fuck me.

"Stop." His countenance darkens. "You know nothing about me."

I sigh. "Fine. Tell me all about you, Theo the Asshole. Just help me while you do it."

He nods and follows me to the edge of the field. I push a bag of seeds into his arms and scoop out a handful, dropping them a few inches apart as we walk down the row.

"First of all," he says, his voice gruff, "every single penny my brothers and I have was earned by us."

"Got it," I say, grabbing another handful of seeds.

"Second, we're here because my brothers need a distraction. The last time they acted like themselves was when we were here in Harris. The day I saw the advertisement for the pub, I thought it was fate. If I had known you were planning to buy it, I wouldn't have pursued it."

"Now you know. You can sell it to me," I point out.

"I'm getting to that," he bites out, keeping a tight rein on his annoyance. "Like I said, we need a distraction–"

"From what?" I interrupt.

"Our parents were murdered a little less than a year ago."

"Oh my god." *Oh my god.* And here I am, acting like a total bitch.

"My brothers went downhill really quickly after it happened. The construction business we ran together started to struggle, so I decided to do something drastic to get us out of our funk. I drained our savings to buy the pub. They need this, Isla." The evening sun highlights the planes of his face, turning his dark brown eyes into caramel.

"I understand. I'm sorry I went off the deep end like that."

"Don't apologize. It must have been quite a shock."

I laugh, "You could say that." I grab another handful of seeds and turn away, but he shifts the bag to his hip and touches my wrist. I freeze.

"I have something to ask you."

I only raise an eyebrow at him, desperately trying to ignore how my skin is buzzing where his fingertips press into my flesh.

"Will you help us at the pub?" He squeezes me before dropping his hand. "We'll pay you, of course."

"I have a better idea."

"Let's hear it."

"I'll help you at the pub–for free–but you and your brothers have to help me renovate a building. Contractors are few and far between at the moment." I start on the next row.

"What building?"

"I'll show you tomorrow. I want to get this row done before the sun sets."

"It's a deal," he says, his lips curling into the smallest of smiles.

"Really? Even without seeing the building?"

"I don't know why, but I trust you. Even if you did try to bust my face open with a set of keys and ripped a croissant out of my mouth."

"I'd say I'm sorry, but I'm not." I shrug, biting my lip to keep myself from smiling back at him.

"No worries." He's silent for a few moments as I finish the row. "What are you planting?"

I drop the last seed in and stand up, smiling. "Sunflowers."

3

---

heo's POV

My heart stutters as Isla turns that mega-watt smile on me. Her hair glows like molten lava in the evening light, her skin golden, sun-kissed freckles beckoning me. My body's response to her annoys me to no end. She is the feistiest slip of a woman I've ever met. Watching her bend over repeatedly in those tiny little jean shorts and muck boots is not what I had envisioned when I stalked over here a few hours ago.

After that red-eye, I tell myself that I want to drink a beer, fill my belly, and go to sleep, but that's a gigantic goddamned lie, and I know it. The only thing I can think about is getting her to smile at me like that again. This move was supposed to be simple. Easy. A fucking walk in the park, for Christ's sake.

"Hey, Grumpy McGrumperson, are you coming?"

"What did you just call me?" She laughs, green eyes sparkling as she swings onto the tractor.

She pats the wheel well next to her. "Come on up. I'll park her in the barn and drive you back home."

I don't want to be that close to her. She's the exact kind of trouble I don't need right now. Or ever. I tell myself the only reason I'm taking her up on her offer is because it's almost dark, but I'm lying to myself. I grab hold and climb up, perching beside her like a goddamned parrot. She gazes up at me out of the corner of her eye, a grin pulling at the corner of those full lips.

"Drive," I snap, quickly turning my head away so she can't see the smile I can't seem to hold back. Isla puts the tractor in gear, her hand so tiny on the shifter it's almost startling. It can't be safe for her to be out here alone like this. "Where's the barn?" I ask, noticing that we're driving away from the house.

"On the other side of the castle grounds."

"The other side? Does that mean the field is part of the grounds?"

She nods. "The Manor House, too."

"Wait a damn minute." My mind races as I scramble to put the pieces together. "You own the castle, too?"

"Not just me—my brother, sister, and I each own a third."

"Then why the hell are you staying in that run-down shack? It looks like it could tumble off the cliff's edge at any moment."

Her shoulders stiffen. "It is *not* run down."

"Fine, why are you staying in the minuscule cottage instead of the castle?"

"Because my brother is a damn busybody, that's why. You're starting to remind me of him–sticking your nose places it doesn't belong."

I raise my hands in mock surrender. "Apologies. I didn't realize it was a sore subject."

She glares at me, her eyes dark in the dusky light. She pulls the tractor into the pitch-black barn like she's been doing it since childhood. Hell, maybe she has. God knows she's full of surprises. I jump to the ground, reaching my hand up to help her down, but she jumps off the other side and waits for me by the door instead.

"Come on," she says roughly, grabbing her jacket from a hay bale.

I follow her to her car, folding myself into the passenger seat with some difficulty. I look over at her as she gets in, amazed at how twilight has transformed her. Instead of a spicy ray of light, the night has turned her into a darkling sprite, complete with mahogany hair, leather, and the attitude of a honey badger. I hate to admit it–even to myself–but I'm enamored. I can't wait to see what she's like when it rains. When it snows. At sunrise. Hell, I'm starting to think every day of every season will never be enough.

Those thoughts fly out of my head as she peels away from the barn, her hair billowing around her head as she shifts through the gears. Gravity presses me back into my seat, and I hang on for dear life. Thirty seconds later, she cranks the wheel, and we skid to a stop in the Manor House driveway, perpendicular to the road. She carefully backs into the garage and turns off the car, hopping out before I can say anything. I slowly unclench my fists, my knuckles aching. She's pulling her hair into a messy bun as I join her in the driveway, my knees trembling.

A glimmer of skin shows between her top and her shorts, and before I can stop myself, I'm toe-to-toe with her, breathing in the smell of her shampoo. She looks up at me, a doe in headlights. I jam my hands in my pockets to keep from wrapping them around her waist. Her tongue darts out to moisten her lips. Fuck me. I want to grab a handful of her hair and pull her mouth to mine. Find out what she tastes like.

"Fuck," I say under my breath, trying to rein myself in. Her pupils blow out at that one word, and I nearly lose control. I kiss her cheek, inhaling her as I slide my lips over her skin. "Goodnight, Sunflower," I whisper against her ear before turning around and heading to the house. I don't let myself look back.

I CLOSE the door behind me and sag against it. This was a mistake. Images flash on the back of my eyelids. The teasing smirk as I rode beside her on the tractor. The hard-ass that shrugged on her leather jacket and got behind the wheel of a vintage muscle car. The joy on her face as she whipped into the driveway and scared the ever-loving shit out of me. The surprise when I stepped close. The lust when I whispered that one word. Every expression, every laugh is burned into my mind forever. God, this is so fucking bad.

I stalk into the kitchen to find Henry at the stove and Dylan on his laptop. "We need to talk."

"What the hell took you so long?" Henry asks, slamming a spatula on the counter.

"It's a long story."

"Did you find out why she was so upset?" Dylan asks, worry lining his face.

Shit. "Not exactly."

"What the fuck, Theo? That's the whole reason you went. I knew Henry or I should have gone instead."

Henry turns toward me, anger hardening his mouth. "If you didn't find out why she was so upset, what exactly did you talk to her about?"

"I told her about us. Why we're here–"

Dylan cuts me off, "So you told her all about us and didn't think to ask her what the pub means to her? What we're *stealing* from her?"

Fuck. "We're not stealing anything. I'm sorry I'm not as good at this stuff as both of you." I rub the back of my neck, guilt creeping in. "We did come to a compromise, though."

"One she's happy with?" Henry asks, raising an eyebrow in disbelief.

"I think so. Isla will help us at the pub while we get everything figured out, and we'll help her renovate a building. She's had trouble finding contractors, so it works out for all of us."

The guys perk up, and I'm almost positive it's because they'll get to spend more time with her. It pisses me off. "I know I can't tell either of you what to do, but you shouldn't get involved with her. Remember what happened last time."

Dylan's only response is to slam his laptop shut and head upstairs. Henry motions for me to sit at the table and then places a skillet with a delicious-looking frittata in the middle. He grabs two plates and portions it out. "Asking us not to get involved with her is asking a lot, Theo. Dylan is already infatuated with her. I haven't been able to stop thinking about her since that night at the pub months ago. Maybe coming here was a horrible idea."

"Maybe so, but there's no going back now."

Henry sits across from me, raking his hand through his hair. "I know what happened with Katie has stuck with you, but it's in the past for us. We're all adults. We can handle ourselves." He shoves a bite of food into his mouth, his gaze on his plate.

"Fucking hell. You're both completely whipped, aren't you?"

Henry studies me, smirking. "She got under your skin tonight, didn't she?"

"You don't even understand," I groan, grabbing a beer from the fridge and taking a long drag.

"Then tell me."

I shake my head. I'm not ready to share. "Maybe tomorrow," I mumble, taking my plate to the sink. "Thanks for the food. See you in the morning." I take the stairs two at a time, not daring to look back at him. Scared of what he'll see in my eyes. I vow that I'll stay away from her as much as possible. Katie is still a barely healed scar across my heart, and there's no way I'll let another woman rip the three of us apart again.

I have difficulty falling asleep that night, but when I finally do, I dream of fiery hair and a freckled nose.

4

I wake exhausted, head foggy, muscles sore. I grab a towel, shove my feet in my sneakers, and head out the door like I do every morning. My attention is glued to the path as I carefully pick my way around the rocks, careful not to twist an ankle as I make my way to the beach. I don't see Henry until he's jogging across the sand toward me. His torso is gloriously bare, thick muscles shifting with every step, his skin burnished by the morning light.

"Morning, Isla." The baritone of his voice slides over me like whiskey, lodging deep in my core.

He stops several feet away, blue eyes sparkling, a shy smile pulling at his lips, dark hair falling in gentle waves over his forehead. I squeeze my hands into tight fists, resisting the urge to reach out and run my fingers through it.

"Morning," I mumble, realizing I didn't look in the mirror before leaving the house. I wipe underneath my eyes, hoping yesterday's mascara hasn't turned me into a raccoon.

"You came down here for a swim?" he asks, eyeing my towel. I nod. "It has to be freezing." He shivers at the thought, goosebumps racing over his skin.

"It is," I say, looking away from him so my eyes don't wander places they shouldn't.

"Why, then?"

"Try it every morning for a week. You'll never go back, trust me."

"Deal," he says, grinning.

"Wait–" That is *not* what I meant. I sigh and follow him toward the water. I should have kept my stupid mouth shut.

I drop my sweats in a heap on the sand, hesitating for a second.

"What are you waiting for?" Henry calls, testing the water with his toes.

I grimace. "I usually swim naked. I didn't bring a change of clothes, and it'll be freezing walking back up with wet clothes on."

Henry steps away from the water, turns his back on me, and drops his shorts to the sand. He looks over his shoulder, grinning from ear to ear. "Your turn. I won't look till you're all the way in the water." He keeps his back to me as he walks into the waves. I can't tear my eyes away as the rounded globes of his backside disappear below the surface. I swallow hard. Holy fuck. I drop my bra and underwear and jog into the water, dropping down once I reach my waist, so the water covers my breasts.

"You can turn around now." Henry turns toward me, powerful muscles bunching from the cold. I laugh as his teeth start chattering.

"Shut up," he chuckles, splashing me. "How are you not freezing?"

"I come from tough stock. My mom always said we're the type made for surviving long winters, not running."

"You sure about that? You look pretty damn fit to me."

I laugh. "Thanks to the hours I spend at the gym every day."

"Gym, huh?"

"Yeah, you don't look like you'd be familiar...they usually have weights you lift to build muscle," I say, somehow managing to keep a straight face.

He rolls his eyes at me. "There's a gym near here? I searched online yesterday but couldn't find anything close."

"It's a private gym only open to our community, so it's not listed. You and your brothers are welcome to work out anytime."

"If you'll tell me where it is, I'll check it out this morning," he says, dipping down so he's at eye level with me. "How much is it?"

"It's free. I'll take you there if you'd like. I'm going anyway."

"What do you mean free?"

"My brother, brothers-in-law, and I opened it years ago. We've expanded it over time to accommodate everyone. It's a way to give back to the community that has done so much for us."

He dunks his head under, blowing water from his lips as he comes back up. His eyelashes clump together, highlighting the depths of his ocean-blue eyes. "I have to admit that I'm envious of your way of life here. Time moves slower than it does in the States. Everyone is so incredibly kind. Back home, it seems like everyone is too busy struggling to survive to care about their neighbors."

"That can't be a healthy way to live." I can't imagine my life without the community that has supported me since I was a baby.

"It's not," he says, his teeth chattering.

"Fuck, you must be freezing!" My gaze hangs on his purple-tinged lips for a second too long. I pull my hair over my shoulders and stand. It plasters to my skin, shielding my breasts. Henry stays low in the water, his eyes hooded. "You ready to go?" I ask him, my heart pounding in my chest.

"I'll stay in if it means I get to spend more time with you."

I laugh, ignoring the butterflies fluttering in my stomach. "You'll freeze to death."

"It would be worth it, Isla." He pushes his hair out of his face, droplets cascading over his nose and cheeks. "I always wondered how sailors could be lured to their deaths by a siren's call. I understand it now." He pushes up, water lapping at the V of his abdominal muscles. Heat pools in my belly. He takes a step toward me and reaches out, running the back of his fingers over my cheek. His thumb sweeps down over my chin, catching on my bottom lip, pulling slightly. My knees buckle, and he catches me easily, one arm behind my back, drawing me onto my tiptoes, my nipples pebbling against his chest. I barely breathe, not sure if I want to break the spell or if I want to climb him like a motherfucking tree. He holds my gaze for a few more seconds before shaking his head like he's trying to wake up from a dream. His whole body trembles as he releases me, whether from desire or cold, I'll probably never know. He raises one eyebrow and then turns his back, waiting for me to leave the water and get dressed.

I try, but I can't get my feet to move anywhere but closer to him. I suck in a ragged breath, and he looks over his shoulder at me, his gaze dropping to my lips before bouncing back up. "Isla, I need you to go get dressed. This tension is testing my limits. You're supposed to hate me, remember?"

"You're really fucking hard to hate." My heart pounds in my chest as I press my hand to his shoulder, muscles rippling under my touch. Turning him toward me, I sweep my fingers over his throat, watching in fascination as his Adam's apple bobs. I run my hand over the ridge of his pecs, biting my lip when he jerks as I pass over his nipple.

"Isla," he growls, catching my hand in his before I can continue my exploration. A full-body shiver goes through him, and I notice he's clenching his jaw so his teeth don't chatter.

"God, I'm sorry. You're freezing. Come on." I pull his hand and walk toward the beach. "I won't look if you don't look."

"What if I want to look?" he asks, keeping his eyes on my face as we step out of the water.

I laugh. "Do you want *me* to look at *you* right now? You were just in freezing cold water."

He grimaces. "Good point. Don't you dare look at me." He runs toward his clothes, leaving me laughing in the arctic wind.

As much as I want to, I don't look until he gives the okay. I really shouldn't have encouraged him to swim. He only had his shorts and T-shirt, which are now stuck to his wet skin. He looks colder than he did before we got out of the water.

"Come on," I call, jogging toward the path. I make sure he's following me, worried about the blue tinge to his skin. When we get to the cottage, I grab his hand and lead him inside. "You're not getting out of my sight until I'm sure you're not going to die of hypothermia."

"I'm fine," he scuffs, a violent shiver wracking his body.

God, he looks big in here. His head almost hits the ceiling. I blow out a breath, trying to focus. I motion for him to follow me into the bathroom, cranking the shower handle and turning toward him. He dwarfs me in the tiny space, making me feel small. Delicate. Feminine. I drag my gaze up along the column of his throat, taking in the strong lines of his jaw, the dimple in his chin. We stare at each other, steam billowing between us, making it seem like a dream.

I turn to leave, but he grabs my hand and pulls me toward him. I stop myself from careening into him with a hand on his chest. "I will not have you dying of hypothermia because of a morning skinny dip. Get in the shower, Henry."

"Yes, ma'am," he whispers, his voice husky. Sexy. Sensual. I slam the bathroom door as I leave and head straight back outside, desperately needing the cold air to blow away the needy bitch that had taken over my body.

I almost trip over Dylan's feet as I rush out the door. "E-Everything okay?" He stammers, looking into the cottage like something will burst through the doorway and attack us.

"Fine," I bite out, fanning my shirt away from my body.

He points to the laptop cradled in his arms. "I thought we could go over numbers sometime today and maybe even procedure if you have the time."

"What time is it?" I ask, completely turned upside down. This morning could have been thirty minutes or eight hours.

Dylan pulls his phone from his pocket. "Almost 9:30."

Fuck. I normally finish up at the gym right about now. "Meet me at the pub in an hour?"

"Do you want to drive together?"

"Are you going to stay the whole night?" I ask, realizing I have no clue how this arrangement will work now that I'm not the one taking the bar over.

"Are *you*?"

I sigh. "I guess we probably have a lot more to talk about than numbers and procedure, don't we?" Henry chooses that very inopportune moment to appear in the doorway, a *very* small towel the only thing covering him. My gaze dips below the hem of his towel, taking in the perfection of his thighs. Fucking hell. I clear my throat. "This is NOT what it looks like," I tell Dylan, taking a step away from Henry.

"Of course not," Dylan says, pressing his lips into a hard line. I panic, thinking he's disappointed, but then I see the wink he throws Henry. What the hell?

"I'll meet you up at the house in an hour," I tell Dylan, watching him walk up the path until he's almost at the house before I spin around to give Henry a verbal lashing.

"I thought we were going to the gym," Henry asks before I can start my lecture. He's holding the towel loosely, and I'm having a tough time not focusing on how it dips–

"Isla?"

My gaze snaps up to his, and I clear my throat. "Can I get a rain check?"

"Sure. Speaking of the pub, what's the slowest time of the day?"

"Around three, usually."

"Perfect. I have a meeting at the visa office in an hour, but if I get done early, maybe the four of us can hammer out this agreement today. I want to make sure we're all happy with it."

"Fine. Now please go get dressed."

"Anything for you, my prickly pear." He turns and saunters into the cottage. I watch slack-jawed as his muscles shift with every step, and fuck if I don't want to trace them with my fingertips. With my tongue. With my teeth. This summer is going to kill me.

5

I shoo Henry out of the cottage the second he's dressed, not trusting myself with him for a moment longer. My body is in overdrive. These are three men I shouldn't be able to stand to be around. I should hate them, just like Henry said. But now I have a total infatuation with Henry. And I was *disappointed* when I thought Dylan was upset over Henry being naked in the cottage. Why should I even care what Dylan thinks? I barely know the man! And then there was last night. Planting the sunflowers with Theo was—well, it wasn't awful. I still don't like him, but I can't stop thinking about him. I give myself a pep talk in the mirror as I'm getting ready, reminding myself that these men *stole* the pub right out from under me and then refused to sell it back to me. Theo's explanation niggles at the back of my brain, but I ignore it. I need to stay emotionally detached. I need to become the Ice Bitch of Harris.

Smirking, I pull my hair into a ridiculously messy bun—I should be embarrassed, honestly. I wiggle into ripped black jeans, an old ripped band tee, and my jacket, running back to the bathroom at the last second to fasten my biggest pair of gold hoops to my ears. I sit on the couch and lace up my trusty boots. This pair has been with me for three years, but I've been wearing the same style for ages. They're my safety blanket. All I need to do is look down at them to feel like a bad bitch. Although anyone who knows me knows that if my shoes matched my personality, I'd be wearing Dorothy's red sparkly slippers. I snort at the thought. I debate between my car or the motorcycle on the way up to the house, but I don't think I have the guts to make Dylan sit behind me on the bike. Arms around my middle. Chin on my shoulder. Thighs–I pull myself out of my daydream when I see Dylan waiting for me by the garage.

I thought he was kind of dorky that first night in the pub, but that first impression was horribly wrong. He's dressed in all black, slim jeans and bomber jacket, making him look like he just stepped out of a cologne commercial. He's wearing his glasses, but whatever the opposite of nerdy is, they're that.

"Hey," he greets me softly, a huge smile on his face.

"We're twinsies," I laugh.

"I like it." His gaze sweeps down my body and back up, catching on my lips.

Sweet baby Jesus. I'm in so much trouble.

"Everything okay?" he asks, studying my face.

"Yeah, just having an existential crisis."

"Do you do that often?"

"Pretty much daily," I chuckle.

"We should start a club. The Existential Islanders."

I snort. "I'll have jackets made."

He grins. "I like you." There is no ulterior motive behind the words—just honesty.

"I think I like you, too." I key in the garage code. "Don't tell anyone. I have to keep up my bad girl image."

He pretends to lock his lips and then throws me the imaginary key. I motion for him to get in the car as I sink into the driver's seat. I turn her on, and Dylan's eyes roll back, his head dropping against the headrest. I shift in my seat, my visceral reaction to him burning through my body, turning my cheeks scarlet.

He looks at me, his glasses slightly askew, those big brown eyes wide open. "Holy shit, Isla."

"Right?" I grin and pull out of the garage, taking a left out of the driveway. I hold back on the gas, not sure if I can handle finding out if he likes a wild ride. If he does–Lord help me.

"You're not going to open her up?" he asks, confusion on his face. "Theo told me he thought he was going to die last night."

I laugh. "Do you have a death wish?"

He shrugs. "I think I'd be okay dying in this car."

"Yeah?" *Fuck me.* I don't dare look over at him. If I see the look that I *know* is on his face, I'm done for. Instead, I turn on the radio and stomp on the gas pedal, shifting through gears seconds apart. Dylan rolls his window down and sticks his arm out, riding the air current. The wind roars through the car, pulling my hair from its elastic. I blow past the pub, feeling too free to deal with what's waiting for me there. I sneak a look at Dylan and find him staring at me with a look I can't place. He blushes, throws his head back, and croons along with the song, using the dashboard as makeshift drums. I join in, singing at the top of my lungs. When we come to the roundabout, I do the responsible thing and head back toward the pub. I wish I could keep driving like this forever. Music up, good company, the sound of the engine drowning out the noise in my head. I pull into the parking lot and turn off the car. We both stare out the windshield in dead silence before bursting into laughter.

"God, I haven't had fun like that in so long," he wheezes, wiping tears from his eyes.

"That's kinda lame," I joke. "It was just a car ride."

"No, it wasn't. It was a ride in *this* car with *you.*"

The grin slips from his face, and suddenly, the high-fashion model version of Dylan is looking back at me, oozing sex appeal. Heat roars through my veins, my fingers itching to slide off his glasses and pull his face to mine. I push the urge down and hop out of the car, slamming the door behind me. I look at Dylan before going inside. He's still sitting in the car with a slightly dazed look on his face. I raise my eyebrow at him when his gaze meets mine. He gives me a shit-eating grin and unfolds himself from his seat, pausing with a hand on the door, looking at me looking at him. He's fucking gorgeous. He closes the door gently, his eyes locked with mine.

"Say it."

"Say what?" I ask.

"What you're thinking. Life would be much easier if everyone were honest with each other."

He's right, it would be. But that's also terrifying. I clear my throat. "I was just thinking about how good you look in my car."

"Yeah?" The corner of his mouth tilts up.

"Yeah." My breath stutters as he stops in front of me, the toes of his shoes touching the toes of my boots. I crane my neck to look up at him, my heart in my throat. He dips his face closer, his thumb brushing my cheek.

"You have freckles in your eyes," he whispers in wonder.

"Are you two going to stand there forever, or are we going to get to work?" Theo asks roughly, poking his head outside, grumpy as ever.

Dylan blows out a loud sigh, pushing his glasses up his nose. "I guess we better get started." He holds the door open for me to pass.

The second my foot crosses the threshold, I'm struck by how different it feels inside. The hope I always carried with me, knowing that it would one day be mine, has disappeared. It's not a good feeling. Dylan sets his bag on the bar and pulls out his laptop. I round the bar and pour two glasses of water, making sure there's lots of ice. I watch as he pulls up the spreadsheets I sent him last night. We spend the next hour in accounting hell. Once we hash out all the numbers and I walk him through payroll, he closes his laptop and pulls out a notebook.

"What about marketing?"

I laugh. "What marketing?"

His eyebrows shoot up. "Really? So that's a completely untapped market. I know you must have some ideas–anything you're willing to share?"

I think for a second. "I've been wanting to go check out some of the pubs in Edinburgh. Not to copy," I clarify, "but to get inspiration."

"Great idea. Maybe you and I can go next weekend? I'm sure Henry and Theo could keep it running for one night."

"Can they, though?" I wince, thinking of everything that could go wrong.

"I'm sure it won't be as seamless as when you're here, but they're capable. We all took a bartending class before we came out, and lord knows we all know how to pour beer. Surely the two of them can keep up with you."

The dirtiest thoughts come to mind the second his sentence registers. My cheeks flame, and I gulp down my water, immediately choking on it. Dylan hits my back, trying to help. I look at him to tell him I'm okay, but there must be something in my expression. He sucks in a strangled breath. "I did *not* mean it like that."

Coughing turns to laughter. I wipe at the tears leaking from my eyes. I shrug an apology.

"You have a fucking filthy mind, don't you?"

"Guilty as charged," I admit. Why am I like this?

"Ready to talk about how this whole thing is going to work?"

I nod, shucking off my jacket and draping it over the barstool to my left. "I've been mulling it over, and I think we need to have two people here and two at the job site. Obviously, I'll be here every day, so maybe the three of you can rotate? That way, each of you learns how to run the pub from open to close, inside and out. Then the other two can work with my brother on the renovations. What do you think?"

"That seems fair. I'll tell the guys tonight and let you know if they have any issues with the arrangement." He pulls an envelope out of his bag and slides it over the bar to me.

"What's this?" There's a check inside for almost ten thousand dollars.

"The wages you're owed plus paying you back for the kitchen staff."

My heart softens the tiniest bit. "You don't need to do this. That was my decision."

He scoffs. "It was your decision when you thought the pub was yours. We owe you that money, Isla. It's only fair." He squares his body, facing me head-on. His teeth press into his bottom lip, making my heart jump. "I don't want us starting off with bad blood." He reaches out with one finger, brushing it over my knee in the lightest of touches. "You're sure we're good?"

"I can't promise I won't miss the dream I had for this place, but yes, you and I are good."

"And Henry? Theo?"

"Henry and I are good. Theo? That's to be determined."

"Understandable." He glances at his watch. "Ready to teach me some stuff?"

Before I can answer, Theo pushes through the door from the back, three plates in his arms, a kitchen towel slung over his shoulder. "Thought I'd experiment a little," he mumbles, setting the plates in front of Dylan and me. He puts his plate on my left, moving my jacket out of the way before sitting down. I wonder if he's met Greer yet or if she knows he's using her kitchen. I can't wait to see how that goes down.

"What's this?" I ask, breathing deep, my mouth watering.

"I found a recipe online for cottage pie. I tweaked it the tiniest bit to elevate the flavor." He looks at me, his eyes searching mine, "I'm not trying to change things. Just improve on what's already here. I want you to understand that."

I'm stunned. Is it possible this man is empathetic? "Thank you," I whisper. He nods, stretching his mouth into what I think is supposed to be a smile but looks more like a grimace.

ACKNOWLEDGMENTS

I have to close-out this story by thanking my husband. In the rollercoaster of life, he's been the one waving the biggest foam finger, cheering me on through every twist and turn. While I dove into the world of words, he stood on the sidelines, giving me unwavering support and endless encouragement.

This book isn't just a story; it's a testament to the love story he and I have written together. His encouragement has been the wind beneath my words, the force that turns doubt into determination and hesitation into a resounding "yes."

Here's to my biggest fan, confidant, and the one who turns every ordinary day into an extraordinary adventure. He's not just my lover; he's the plot twist that makes life unforgettable.

ABOUT THE AUTHOR

Tucked away in the misty Smoky Mountains with her husband, three kids, and a menagerie of furry companions (three dogs and two cats who think they run the household), Daphne weaves stories that make readers blush, gasp, and fall helplessly in love.

Known for her wickedly spicy romances and vivid imagination, she's been crafting tales since she first learned to hold a pen. When she's not steaming up the pages with her latest novel, you'll find her curled up in her favorite reading nook, devouring books like they're chocolate.

Her mountain sanctuary provides the perfect backdrop for dreaming up deliciously scandalous stories that push boundaries and set kindles aflame. Fair warning: her books are known to cause sleepless nights, excessive swooning, and an insatiable appetite for more.

linktr.ee/daphneleighauthor